WASTELAND

OF FLINT

WASTELAND
OF FLINT

THOMAS
HARLAN

A TOM DOHERTY ASSOCIATES BOOK

NEW YORK

WASTELAND OF FLINT

Copyright © 2003 by Thomas Harlan

Edited by Beth Meacham

A Tor Book
Published by Tom Doherty Associates, LLC
175 Fifth Avenue
New York, NY 10010

www.tor.com

Tor® is a registered trademark of Tom Doherty Associates, LLC.

Library of Congress Cataloging-in-Publication Data

Harlan, Thomas.
    Wasteland of flint / Thomas Harlan.—1st ed.
        p. cm.
    "A Tom Doherty Associates book."
    ISBN 0-765-30192-X (acid-free paper)
    1. Antiquities—Collection and preservation—Fiction. 2. Life on other planets—
Fiction. 3. Space colonies—Fiction. 4. Mexico—Fiction. I. Title.

PS3558.A624244 W3 2001
813'.54—dc21

                                                                    2002040944

First Edition: April 2003   3 1984 00205 0100

Printed in the United States of America

0   9   8   7   6   5   4   3   2   1

Without the inspiration of James H. Schmitz, H. Beam Piper,
and Leigh Brackett, there would be no book.

Without the excellent advice of Russ Galen,
it wouldn't be nearly as interesting.

Thank you!

A NOTE CONCERNING MEASUREMENTS

Though her later victories rendered the full terms of the Lisbon Accords moot, the México Empire abides by the common set of weights and measures set forth by the Accords in A.D. 1724. As a result, distances are in kilometers, weights in kilograms and so on.

RANKS OF THE IMPERIAL MÉXICA MILITARY

NISEI TERM	FLEET RANK	MARINE/ ARMY RANK	MÉXICA TERM
Thai-sho	Admiral	General	Cuauhnochteuctli (EAGLE PRICKLY-PEAR LORD)
Chu-sho	Vice Admiral	Lieutenant-General	
Sho-sho	Rear Admiral	Major-General	Tlacoccalcatl (COMMANDING GENERAL)
Thai-sa	Captain	Colonel	Tlacateccatl (GENERAL)
Chu-sa	Commander		Cuauhtlahtoh (CHIEF)
Sho-sa	Lieutenant Commander	Major	
Thai-i	Lieutenant	Captain	Cuahyahcatl (GREAT CAPTAIN)
Chu-i	Sub-Lieutenant	Lieutenant	
Sho-i	Ensign	Sub-Lieutenant	
Sho-i Ko-hosei	Midshipman		
Gunso		Master Sergeant	Cuauhhuehueh (EAGLE ELDER)
Joto-Heiso	Chief Boatswain		
Gocho		Sergeant	Tequihuah (VETERAN WARRIOR)
Itto-Heiso	Chief Boatswain's mate		
Heicho		Corporal	Yaotequihuah (LEADER OF YOUTHS)
Nitto-Heiso	Boatswain's mate		
Ittohei		Senior Private	Tiachcuah (OLDER BROTHER)
Itto-Shihei	Spacer		
Nitohei		Private	Telpolcatl (YOUTH)

In the beginning was the First Sun,
4-Water was its sign;
It was called the Sun of Water.
For water covered the world,
Leaving nothing but dragonflies above
and fishy men below.

The Second Sun was born,
4-Jaguar was its sign;
This was called the Sun of the Jaguars.
In this Sun the heavens collapsed,
So that the Sun could not move in its course.
The world darkened, and when all was dark
Then the people were devoured.

The Giants perished, giving life to the Third Sun.
4-Rain was its sign;
It was called the Sun of Rain.
For this Sun rained fire from bleeding eyes
And the people were consumed.

From the torrent of burning stones,
The Fourth Sun was born.
4-Wind was its sign, and it was called the Sun of Wind.
In this Sun, all which stood on the earth was carried
Away by terrible winds.
The people were turned into monkeys,
and scattered from their cities into the forest.

Now, by sacrifice of the divine liquid, the Fifth Sun was born.
Its sign was 4-Motion.
As the Sun moved, following a course,
The ancients called it the Sun of Motion.
In the time of this Sun, there were
Great earthquakes and famine,

No maize grew, and the gods of the field
Turned their eyes from the people.
And all the people grew thin, and perished.

The Lord of Heaven cut the heart from his living son,
And so was born the Sixth Sun, which sustains
The universe with infinite light.
Its sign was 4-Flint.
Those who watch the sky say this Sun
Will end in annihilation, when the flint-knife
Severs the birthcord of the Sun, plunging all
Into darkness, where the people will
Be cut to pieces and scattered.

This is the time of the Sixth Sun. . . .

WASTELAND
OF FLINT

THE GREAT EASTERN BASIN, EPHESUS III, IN THE HITTITE SECTOR

The *Gagarin* sped out of the east, engines running hot, heavy night air hissing under thirty-meter wings. Though the sky behind the little ultralight was still pitch-black, the dawn wind was already beginning to rise, stirring the air. It was very cold, worse for the wind whipping through the airframe. Russovsky's goggles were rimmed with frost and her suit's rebreather left a white smear of CO_2 ice across a cargo bag stowed behind the seat. Kilometers of sand blurred past beneath the *Gagarin*. Ahead, hidden in night but standing out sharply on her vid-eye, the Escarpment shut off the horizon. Tiny green glyphs bobbed at the corner of her vision as a micro-radar taped to the forward wing surface measured and remeasured the height of the cliffs. The mechanism was resetting every second, unable to resolve the summit.

Down on the deck, where a vast soda-pipe field slept among night-shrouded dunes, a haze of fine dust was beginning to lift, stirred by the wind's invisible fingers. The *Gagarin* droned on, long silver wings glowing softly in the darkness, engines chuckling as they burned hydrogen and spat out fine trailing corkscrews of ice crystal. Russovsky's vid-eye flashed, alerting her to a break in the horizon. An annotation flipped up, showing a snatch of recorded video—flinty cliffs in harsh white sunlight. Blinking in annoyance, her face grim, Russovsky banished the note. She drifted the stick left and the *Gagarin* heeled over. The ultralight banked, sweeping over a knife blade of red sand rising three hundred meters from the nominal bottom of the basin. As *Gagarin* rose over the dune, she goosed the engines, wary of treacherous winds coiling close to the mountains.

Now she could feel the enormous mass of the Escarpment, looming darkness against a sky riotous with stars. The mountain range rose up endlessly and ran left and right to the edge of sight. She could feel the ocean of air around the ultralight changing, the quiet stillness of deep night falling away, disturbed by currents, eddies and whirlpools tugging and pressing at the wings. The mouth of the Slot loomed up, a hundred meters wide, an abrupt fissure cut into the mountain. Sweat beaded on her neck and along her spine, but the moisture wicked away into the skinsuit so quickly Russovsky did not chill. The radar threw back a confused jumble of images, trying to resolve the jagged cliffs and boulders at the mouth of the Slot.

She blinked twice and the radar image folded up and away. She clucked her tongue once, then twice. Her goggles gleamed and light-amp faded back for a second. She flew blind, the *Gagarin* winging into the slot, her hands light on the stick, keeping the ultralight centered between the cliffs. Another tongue cluck. Along the tips of the wings, phosphors woke to life, throwing a diffuse, soft white light over the flinty walls rushing past.

The goggles adjusted automatically and Russovsky could see again. A rumpled floor of broken scree, cockeyed temple-sized boulders and blown sand whipped past below her boots. Walls hemmed her in to either side, kilometers high and relentless, all jagged surfaces and overhangs. The whine of the engines rose, reverberating in the thickening air. A low hissing sound began to grow behind her in the east.

The planet's air was thin, though a human could stand outside without a z-suit. She would need a compressor and a filter to breathe, but it was possible. Such thin air exacerbated the planetary weather, making the wind and sky a menace to man and machine alike. In some places, like against the world-girdling ring of the Escarpment, a storm roared at every dawn, as the rising sun heated the atmosphere and pressed it against an impassible barrier.

Slot canyons cut through the Escarpment, knife-blade thin in comparison to the bulk of the mountain range. Gusts darted down the Slot, and Russovsky felt the *Gagarin* twist and flex in the air. Her chrono said she had fifteen minutes before the sun actually peeked over the eastern horizon.

By then a gale would be howling in the canyon, spitting sand, rock, and gravel westward like a cannon at three or four hundred k. The craft bucked, riding up on an eddy, and Russovsky's fingers gentled the aircraft back, away from the looming cliff. The wingtip, still glowing white, danced away from an obsidian wall, almost brushing against the ancient stone.

Russovsky corrected with unconscious grace. Ahead, a slab jutted nearly a third of the way across the canyon. Its eastern face was worn smooth as glass, a sweeping ebon wall rising up from the rubble. Russovsky's left hand brushed over the pressure control. Hydrogen hissed through fuel tubes running over her head. The wings stiffened, pressure rising. Motors whined and both airfoils levered up into a v. *Gagarin* slowed dramatically.

The ultralight swept past the slab, wing lights reflecting in an inky mirror. Beyond the monolith, there was a curving bowl of sand and—the vid-eye flashed urgently. Russovsky glanced over and saw a sharp angle in the darkness, distinct against the irregular wall of the canyon. She dropped the wings back level, then airbraked as the ultralight started to gain speed and drifted the stick to her right. *Gagarin* slowed into a stall. Hissing softly through clenched teeth, Russovsky feathered the engines and let the wheels touch down. A bump, a queasy sliding moment and the *Gagarin* slid to a halt on hard-packed sand.

Russovsky unfolded herself from the chair, thumbing loose her restraints, each motion quick and assured. Her left leg started to cramp, but she went stiff-legged for a moment, moving jerkily, letting the muscle relax. Working swiftly, acutely conscious of grains of mica and sand pattering down out of the dark sky above her, she triggered one sand-anchor with a *tunk!*, then leaned back into the cockpit frame and threw a switch glyphed "fold." The wings trembled in response, then began to deflate, hydrogen hissing back into the reserve tank behind and under the seat. The p-cell battery in the main wing joint woke up with a *click* and the controls dimmed in preparation for system shutdown.

While *Gagarin* folded up, Russovsky dragged her pack down from above the H_2 tank and slung it onto her wiry shoulders. She was not a big woman—not and fly a *Midge*-class ultralight like the *Gagarin!*—but she had a lean strength and end-less endurance. The pack conformed to her back, belt straps sliding around her flat waist like warm hands. A sharp tug freed the winch from the forward centerline strut. Monofil line whined out of the spool as she backed toward the right-angled darkness in the cliff face.

In the fading light of the wing phosphors, the rock glowed a pasty green. The angle stood out clear and sharp. Half of a trapezoidal opening, faced with cut stone—a door—yawned in the side of the cliff. Russovsky nodded to herself, unsurprised. Ephesus had been a dead, shattered world for millennia, but *some-thing* had lived here once. Dust was blowing past now, clouding the air. Hurrying, she climbed up into the opening, then flicked a glowbean inside. Pale blue light spilled out like milk from a fallen pail. There was a chamber, a big one, with a canted floor and more sand. It seemed big enough for the ultralight.

Stepping carefully around the edge of the chamber, one hand on the smooth sloping wall, Russovsky slapped the winch-patch onto the wall opposite the door.

Outside, the *Gagarin* was beginning to rock from side to side as wind began to stir in the sandy bowl. Russovsky counted to five, then ran back to the door. At the side of the ultralight, she ratcheted the sand anchor back in, then stabbed the winch control. The little motor woke up with a tinny sound and began to reel in the monofil. Sliding on its landing skids, the *Gagarin* bumped up into the door. Russovsky paced behind the aircraft, then put her shoulder against the aft cargo door, pushing. Wind-blown sand began to hiss against her back. Breathing hard into her mask, she shoved the *Gagarin* into the chamber. On the smoother sand inside, the winch continued to whine until the nose of the aircraft touched the opposite wall.

Russovsky ducked in, her head turned away from the canyon. The wind was rising to a monstrous howl, and the lee of the jutting slab was filling with a swirling dance of dust, sand and fingertip-sized gravel. Working swiftly, she uncoiled a length of fil-tube from her belt, then tacked it along one side of the half-buried door. At the top of the tube was a thumb tab. Snapping the tab down and away, across her body with a sharp motion, Russovsky unfurled the filament screen and dragged the gelatinous material against the opposing jamb. Pressing firmly, she ran the thumb tab down the side of the door. The material sheened pearl for a moment, then stiffened. Dust and sand rattled against the polymer, skittering away from the charged filaments. Carefully, Russovsky used the thumb tab to seal off all the edges and corners. By the time she was done, the rattle of sand was a constant drumming.

Russovsky flicked another glowbean against the ceiling, where it spattered and stuck, making a spray of cold cobalt stars. Despite a sudden feeling of exhaustion, the woman moved around the ultralight, checking the exposed surfaces for cracks, wear or abrasions in the silvery composite. The dust on Ephesus had incredibly corrosive properties. At the starboard engine she paused, clicking her teeth together. Her goggles dialed up high into the ultraviolet, revealing the faint glow of pitting on the intake nacelle.

Shaking her head in disgust, Russovsky removed her helmet and the over-goggles, revealing high cheekbones and a seamed, weathered face. She was not young, and the hot sky of Ephesus had given her a steadily deepening tan. Clipping the helmet and goggles to the back of her belt, Russovsky adjusted her bugeyes—it was dangerous to leave the moist human eye exposed to the raw air of Ephesus—and took the big v-cam from a flat pouch on her left thigh.

"Recor . . . *cough!*" Russovsky cleared her throat, tasting bitter alkali. She unclipped the suit's drinking tube and took a swallow. Her fingers dug into a pocket on her z-suit and she popped a round, polished stone into her mouth. When her throat had cleared, she started again: "Recording inside a manufactured structure at the eastern end of slot canyon twelve."

She raised the v-cam and slowly panned around, pausing on the door. By now the sun would have risen in the east, but the canyon outside was still pitch-black. The wind was still rising, making the monofil membrane in the doorway shudder. Completing her slow turn, she walked away from the *Gagarin* to the edge of the light thrown by the glowbeans. The chamber ended in a slick, glassy wall. There was another trapezoidal door cut into the rock.

One-handed, she kept the v-cam up while she flicked a glowbean into the passage.

More blue light filled the space—a corridor with slanted walls, matching the angle of the door. It ended no more than a dozen meters away, abruptly, in rough, uneven extrusion. Frowning with concern—*how queerly even*—Russovsky advanced gingerly across a glassy, slick floor. The rock here, like that throughout the Escarpment, was Ephesus's particular trademark—a jumbled, compressed, mangled aggregate of sandstone, rhyolite, granite, and flint. She paused at the irregular wall, staring into another chamber opening off to her right.

"Ah . . . *krasivaya devushka!*" Russovsky's faded sapphire eyes crinkled up in a broad smile. Her fingers were trembling a little as she set the v-cam down on the sandy floor, letting the camera adjust itself level so it could record the wall in detail. Kneeling, she ran gloved fingers over the rumpled, irregular surface. There were whorls and lumps and patterns familiar in kind, if not in detail, to her experienced eyes. Here, a fluted shape, the outlines of stalklike legs, a curled shell. There, the echo of flat-pressed reeds and tiny nutlike cysts.

Limestone. The muddy floor of a primordial Ephesian ocean. The wall rose up at a queer angle, obviously trapped in the greater matrix of the mountain. Russovsky rose, picked up the v-cam and panned it around, showing the way the passage ended at the shale. A gray eyebrow rose, seeing a set of cylindrical objects scattered near the wall.

Russovsky bent down, examining one. They seemed to be stone, or crusted with ancient fossilized earth. There were three of them, regular in length and width. Sucking cautiously on the stone in her mouth, Russovsky backed away, still recording with the v-cam, and then walked carefully back to the ultralight. The smooth, almost mirror-smooth tunnel floor could have been cut with a plasma torch.

She was exhausted and hungry from the long night-flight. After choking down a threesquare bar Russovsky drank some more water and lay down on the sand under the *Gagarin*. The suit kept her body temperature within a survivable range and was far too much trouble to shed. The glowbeans were beginning to die, letting soft darkness steal back into the chamber. Russovsky tugged a folded woolen blanket from under the seat of the ultralight and tucked it under her head. Faded red, orange, and black stripes made a repeating series of pyramids on the blanket. The wool was scratchy on her cheek and the woman closed her eyes and fell asleep.

The storm beyond the door roared like a distant sea.

CTESIPHON STATION, THE EDGE OF IMPERIAL MÉXICA SPACE

"Porlumma . . . Flight sixty-two . . . *squawk!* . . . boarding for Porlumma . . ."

Gretchen Anderssen pushed through a heavy crowd, cursing her lack of height. The receiving bay of the station was hundreds of meters wide and at least sixty high, but the crowd of hot, sweaty, strange-smelling beings made her claustrophobic. The booming, distorted voice of a station controller announcing departing flights made the air tremble. Gretchen wiped her forehead, turning sideways to slide past two huge Kroomākh. Their scaly, pebbled skin smelled like juniper pine resin, but the sharp tang was not welcome, not in this heat.

The crowd began to thin, though when she stepped out of a milling group of Incan tourists, all in plaid and tartan and bonny caps with white carnations, she saw a power fence separating the landing bays and their high-vaulted tunnels from the exit doors. The whole huge mob of passengers was funneling down into six gates, each labeled by caste or nation. Gretchen stopped, standing in the middle of the grimy floor, and put down her bags. A migraine was beginning to tick behind her left eye. *Why is there always a line?*

Looking up, she frowned, seeing the first-class receiving bay above, half-visible through arching metal girders. There, in cool scented air, slidewalks were conveying parties of rich Imperials through station customs. Their glittering feather-capes flashed and shimmered with rainbow hues and shining jungle colors. Smiling dark-suited servants carried traveling bags, sleepy children, cold drinks for their masters. One of the nobles, glossy black hair trailing down below her waist, earrings flashing gold in the soft white light, looked down. Gretchen stared back at the México woman, then grimaced politely when the Imperial lady waved.

She looked down at her own hands, muscular, the left scarred by an accident with an ultrasonic cleaning tool on Old Mars, deeply tanned by too many hours exposed under alien suns. They were not smooth and soft. They were nicked and calloused and entirely inelegant. She had to work, with her hands, in poor conditions. She wondered, and not for the first time, what it would be like to be well-born, into one of the families of the Center. To be up there, above, in the cool air, gliding down a slidewalk, a beautiful feather-cape hanging from pale smooth shoulders, with jewels and gold around her neck.

Her grandparents' flight from the wars on Earth—on Anáhuac, as the México would say—had crushed any hope of social status—not only were they refugees from a defeated nation, but they had given up the properties they once held in Old Stockholm. On New Aberdeen, colony law prevented a newly emigrated family from owning land for at least six generations. Gretchen grimaced, thinking of how easy it would have been to get into university, or an Imperial *calmecac* school, if she could have claimed the landowner's right. *A burden to be borne in good grace,* whispered the voice of her mother. *If you work and study hard, you can still succeed.*

"Enough," Gretchen muttered and slung the duffel over her shoulder. It was almost as large as she was, but she was strong enough to carry the bag unaided—it was lighter than a hod of Ugaritic mud brick! The equipment case in her left hand was heavy too, but much easier to carry. She trudged across the broad floor, heading for the customs gate labeled MACEHUALLI. The line was longest there, with the "common" people queued up, much longer than the gates for nonhumans or landowners or those in military service. Suddenly anxious, she checked the inner pocket of her vest for the company papers and ID card. The thick heavy shape of the packet was comforting.

"Doctor Anderssen? Anderssen-tzin?"

Gretchen looked up, taking a firm grip on her bags. A thin, balding man with a short, neat beard was waving at her from the other side of the power fence. A flight jacket covered with patches covered narrow shoulders, and baggy combat pants hung on him like burlap sacks. He held up a hand-lettered sign marked with the Company's circle-and-moon glyph. Gretchen's eyebrows raised in surprise. The last message had not mentioned a guide or being met, just a kiosk number to pick up the ticket for the next leg of her journey. Ctesiphon station might be at the very edge of human space, but it was a convenient hub for travel along the frontier. Groaning to herself—leaving a line in the Empire was always a cause of dismay, since they never got shorter, only longer—she trudged over to the black warning stripe outlining the security fence.

"Yes?"

The man smiled, showing irregular smoke-stained teeth. "You're Doctor Gretchen Anderssen? The xenoarcheologist?"

"Yes," she allowed, not putting down the bags. "That's my name."

"Great! I'm Dave Parker, your new pilot. Come down to the Jaguar gate—they'll let you through."

"Why?" Gretchen began to walk, matching Parker's pace along the shimmering half-visible fence. "I don't have a military pass." Parker nodded, his head bent over a compressed tobacco stick. There was a hot spark and he took a drag.

"No," he said, blowing a fat ring of smoke, "but I do. Your mission's been upgraded, but we should talk about that later."

There was no line at the Jaguar gate, though there were two customs officers in pleated tunics and long white overcapes. Both men were copper-skinned, with slick dark hair. They were not México—Gretchen guessed they were from the old Shawnee lands. She bowed politely to both men, then waited quietly while Parker talked with them in low tones. There were no soldiers within sight, but Gretchen could feel a slow crawling sensation on her arms and neck. The gate was traditional, with heavy stonework and a huge, feathered Jaguar head jutting out of the apex. She was sure that if trouble occurred, the stone would answer with violence. The Imperials were very fond of traditional images that could move, speak, or strike.

"Come on," Parker beckoned from beyond the gate. The two Shawnee watched with cold, disinterested eyes as she shuffled through. The pilot stuck out a hand, which Gretchen shook. His grip was dry and firm. "Take a bag?"

"No. Thanks." Gretchen had her whole life packed up in the duffel, equipment case, and backpack. She wasn't going to give either bag over to some balding, smirky, fly-by-night Company pilot. She didn't trust her employers either. The Company might pay her to do the work she loved, but it had never gained her loyalty. Too many sites had been outright looted—ripped whole from the ground and packed up for shipment back to Anáhuac—for her to believe anything they said. "I've got it. Where are we going?"

"Downstation," Parker said, cutting away from the crowd of people coming out of the customs area. He kept inside the pattern marked with interlocking Jaguar heads on the metal floor. "Like I said, things have changed."

Five minutes later Gretchen was stuffed into a standing-room-only tube-car.

Parker was pressed into one side, his hand covering the back of her duffel so no one could cut it open, and two Catholic priests on the other. The monks smelled funny—dust and paper and incense—but Gretchen was used to the smell of ancient things. She was not used to the complete lack of space and air in the car or the incredible humidity. The insides of the plastic windows were already running with thin streams of water, even as the car rose up on the tracks. A queasy moment followed, and then everyone in the car leaned slightly as it accelerated into the long-axis tunnel of the station.

"The Company has offices here," Parker mumbled into her ear. Gretchen made a face as smoke tickled her nose. "The main man is named Per Rubio Gossi—he's Maltese."

"A Knight of the Order?" Gretchen refused to look at the pilot, though that meant she was staring down at three small dark-haired children, all alike, with their hair cut in sharp bangs. They stared back at her, eyes huge and dark in pale white faces. They were dressed in severe blue capes and tunics. Gretchen wondered where their mother was.

"No," Parker laughed. He made a deprecating gesture. His hands were thin and wiry like brown sticks, and they folded over, flat, almost like flippers, the fingers lying together seamlessly. "He's fat and not very energetic. He's the Company rep here—handles outfitting, transshipment, that sort of thing. Warehousing is his big gig. He has the mission plan, though. Have you seen it?"

"No." Gretchen stiffened, feeling the car shudder as it switched from high speed to low. They were approaching a station. "Do we get off here?"

"Not yet," Parker said, craning his head over the people crushed in between him and the door. "This is only the first stop—temples, the market, the upscale hotels. We're going to the end of the line. Another twenty minutes, probably."

Gretchen felt mildly ill, but persevered. Twenty or thirty people crowded out and, thankfully, only two women with shopping bags got on. The three little children were gone. Parker sat down, brushing wrappers and bits of sweet roll off the seat. Gretchen also sat, ignoring the stains. The tube-car had once been painted a light orange, with a roof covered with a stenciled image of the Great City, the true Center, glorious Tenochtitlán. Most of the mural had peeled away, leaving bare rusting metal. Graffiti, most of them *kanji*, covered every flat surface.

The car shimmied back up onto repulsion coils, then the outside—briefly visible with people hurrying back and forth, and neon, and huge v-screens showing a recorded *tlachcho* contest—was gone and there was darkness filled with streaked blurry lights. Gretchen checked the bags, leather jacket, the travel papers, everything she was wearing. Grimacing, she peeled a self-stick advert off her boot. It flickered to life at her touch. A naked woman, glossy black, writhed in her hand for a moment, surrounded by violently throbbing pink glyphs. She wadded up the paper and threw it away. Nothing seemed to be missing.

"Worked for the Company long?" Parker ventured, hands behind his head, watching her with half-lidded eyes. Gretchen supposed it was his "cool" pose. She shook her head.

"Three years, on Ugarit and Old Mars. Digging."

He nodded, making a wry half-smile. "I'm new, only six months. You said you didn't get the new mission plan?"

"No. Last I heard I was heading to Kolob Four to replace Dr. Fearing as xenoarch of the Singing Temple dig."

"Yeah. Well, you're not going there anymore. I was on another assignment, too, but they pulled me in to fly shuttle for you and your team."

"Team?" Gretchen's face screwed up like she'd taken a long gulp of bad coffee. "I don't have a team."

"You do now." Parker rubbed the side of his face. "You, me, Maggie Cat, and a gunner named Bandao. They're waiting at the office. You'll meet them in a minute."

The tube-car slid to a stop, then settled with a *clang* onto the station rails. Gretchen let Parker go first, then scuttled out of the car. The tube-stop was finished in more faux Tetzcoco-style murals, mostly destroyed by pasted advertisements and graffiti. Everyone on the tube-car walked very quickly, taking long shuffling steps, from the platform to a rank of escalators. Gretchen felt a little queasy, and her bags seemed lighter.

"We're in-core?"

"Yeah." Parker blew a smoke ring into the air. It began to twist into a helix as the escalators rattled and clanked up to the top level of the tube station. "Rents are cheaper here, right? Hard to keep your coffee in the cup, though."

At the top of the escalators there was a security gate and a kiosk selling grilled dogs, mézcal and tobacco sticks. There was a line, though Gretchen found it interesting there were no nonhumans to be seen. Most Imperial stations had a few Kroomākh or Hesht hulking about. The corridor outside was ill-lit and lined with small shops, showing signs in Norman or French or Imperial. Young men and women loitered around the entrance to a *pulque* counter, smoking and watching people pass by. Like the young everywhere, they were wearing brilliant capes, though here the feathers were polychrome plastic over workaday tunics and rigger's boots. *A bad neighborhood,* she thought, almost laughing aloud. Even in light g, trash collected in the corners and the walkway was covered with a moiré pattern of dried chicle. *And I feel safe.*

The stairs up to the Company offices passed by a narrow shop crowded with different kinds of v-screens and senso-gear. Every screen was ablaze with a booming discordance of newscasters and chant videos. The landing stank of ozone and rotted meat. Gretchen's nose wrinkled for a moment, but she'd worked in worse. On Ugarit the excavation of a city midden six hundred feet deep had killed four of her workers in a methane pocket explosion. *That was a truly foul smell.*

The pilot thumbed open the door lock. Pausing, Gretchen raised an amused hand to touch the long list of companies residing at this address. There were six, and the Company was listed fourth.

"Greetings!" A very stocky human, not fat, but very round in features, limbs and body, rose from a chair. There was a table, too, surrounded by cheap office chairs. "I am Gossi. You would be Doctor Anderssen."

"Yes," Gretchen said, putting her bags by the nearest chair. She inclined her head politely to the two other people in the room. Parker was already pouring himself a cup of coffee from an ancient-looking silver pot on a side table. "There has been a change of plans?"

The Maltese nodded, his round face beaming. His dark hair was close-cut and flat across a high forehead, making him look like a doll. "Please sit. I will introduce you."

Gretchen sat, nodding to the human sitting on her right. He was short and muscular, in a nondescript patterned shirt and slacks. He had thick wrists and short, curly hair. Her immediate impression was of . . . very little. A man who sat back and watched, revealing nothing of himself.

"This is Dai Bandao, your gunner," Gossi said, inclining his head toward the man. Bandao smiled faintly and nodded back. He did not offer his hand, as Parker had done. "And this is Magdalena, your communications tech."

Magdalena looked something like a compact, sleek jagarundi with forward-canted shoulders. She seemed to be female. Gretchen smiled, but did not show any teeth. The Hesht was curled up in the chair, fat tail lapped around bare paws.

"Hello," Gretchen said, putting her fingertips to her forehead. The Hesht responded with the same gesture, her fingers covered with tightly napped fur. Glittering claw tips peeked out of the soft black pelt. "I am Gretchen, daughter of Jean, daughter of Elizabeth."

"Well met," purred the Hesht. "I am *yyrroowwl-mrrrwerup.* You should call me Magdalena, as these males do."

Gretchen lowered her hands. The Hesht smiled by showing the tip of a pink tongue. Her claws slid out of their muscle sheaths, digging into the nostain fabric of the chair. A sequence of cuts was already visible, revealing torn foam padding.

"Well then," Gossi said smoothly, sitting down, "let us to business. A situation

involving valuable Company equipment has developed. I have been directed by
the home office to see these materials are recovered in an efficient matter."

The round man pressed both thumbs against the sealing strip of a courier
package. The packet unfolded, revealing a set of *v*-pads. "Here are briefing materials the Company has assembled for you. However, I will summarize."

Gossi smiled at all of them, a tight expression that did nothing to betray the
essential smooth roundness of his face. Gretchen suddenly wondered if the man
were human at all. There was a plastic quality to him—an android? Some species
requiring a humanoid environment suit? Were all Maltese this slick?

"Recently, the Company acquired a contract from the Imperial government to
explore and assess this planet, Ephesus Three." His hand brushed across a panel
inset in the tabletop. There was a slight hum and a holo image appeared in the air
before them. A dusky tan globe appeared, rotating slowly. There were large polar
ice caps and scattered whorls of cloud. There was a great deal of desert and low
mountain, interspersed with glittering salt pans. Gretchen nodded to herself—
thin atmosphere, brutal working conditions, no ozone layer; filters, day-suits and
goggles required if you stepped out of your shelter—then raised an eyebrow as the
image continued to rotate, bringing a mountain range into view.

"An Imperial scout probe surveyed the system six years ago and eventually the
data was processed and flagged for human review. This notable mountain range is
called the Escarpment. It girdles the planet, running north to south at an angle. As
you see, it has a sharper incline on the east than the west. Some of the peaks pierce
the atmospheric envelope. The Escarpment divides the world."

"It's not natural," Gretchen said, her mind beginning to shake off the travel
fatigue. Her migraine was coming back, too. She really needed to sleep or take a
real bath rather than go through a mission briefing. "Unless crustal tectonics are
completely awry on this world?"

Gossi continued to smile, nodding. "You are correct. It is not natural. Initial
analysis indicated a possibility the world had been *shaped*. An expedition was
approved, of course, to take a closer look at the situation."

"To muck about for First Sun artifacts, you mean." Parker slumped in the
chair next to Gretchen, hands cradling his cup. Steam drifted up in the moist air.
"Poke about looking for something portable, easy to carry, easy to sell—"

Gossi raised a hand. "A full *scientific* expedition was sent, with the *Temple*-
class support ship *Palenque* as transport and orbital base. All this has been officially approved and registered, Parker-*tzin*. The Company has never had a great
presence in this sector, and it was decided that—given the nature of the planet—a
substantial effort was warranted."

"What happened?" Gretchen felt her patience fray. An exploration ship like the *Palenque* carried a crew of fifteen and a full expedition would be at least twenty people. This grimy little office couldn't provide the support a real dig needed. The Company was rushing things, as usual. If the initial expedition found something interesting, then Gossi would suddenly have a whole operation here on the station to run. More money, more status, someone to serve coffee for him—he had to like that prospect. He might be able to get rid of all those other name plaques on the door. "Parker here says he was rerouted from another mission. My last posting order said I was going to Kolob. Now I'm not. . . . So, are they all dead?"

Gossi's round face crinkled up in disgust and Gretchen felt a spark of amusement. She was getting grumpy, which was not wise. "My pardon, Gossi-*tzin*, it's been a long day."

"Well." The Maltese visibly reboarded his train of thought, "Sixteen days ago a transmission was received from the *Palenque* with the usual weekly report. At that time, everything was fine. Unfortunately, we have not received any reports since then. When the second report failed to arrive, I informed the home office and efforts began to mount a relief effort."

Parker tilted his head to one side, thinking, then said: "How long does it take a courier drone to reach Ctesiphon from Ephesus? A week? You're saying they've been out of contact for as much as three weeks?"

"No . . ." Gossi tabbed through the briefing document, glancing sideways at Magdalena. "The *Palenque* is fitted with a new, experimental tachyon transmitter. It allows immediate communication between the station main relay and the ship. So, as I have said, sixteen days have passed since our last, ah, active communication."

The Hesht's ears flipped back and yellow eyes blinked as she came awake. "Why do you say *active*? Has there been some other message? A distress beacon?"

"Not as such . . ." Gossi seemed to struggle with the words. Gretchen leaned forward, interested. "I am told by the station technicians they have a *t*-lock on the *Palenque,* but the transmitter is not responding to requests for an open channel. I have been informed this means the transmitter is still nominally operating, but it is, ah, on standby."

"It's turned off? And the crew haven't noticed?" Parker made a face.

"Something else must have happened," Gretchen raised her voice slightly. "But the ship still has power or the transmitter is on a battery of some kind. . . . Can we turn on the transmitter from here? Send a wake-up command?"

Gossi spread his hands. "I am told . . . no."

Out of the corner of her eye, Gretchen saw Magdalena's whiskers twitch, but the Hesht said nothing.

Gretchen looked around at the others, then back at Gossi, eyes narrowed. "You have another ship to take us to the Ephesus system? I presume Magdalena knows how to fix the transmitter, and Parker can pilot the *Palenque* home if it's not entirely disabled. Bandao will shoot anything dangerous. Why am I going?"

"You're the senior Company field employee in the sector." Gossi's round smile had returned. He was comfortable with this avenue of discussion. "You are also the only person we could find, quickly, with experience in a biosphere like Ephesus's, due to your time on Old Mars."

Gretchen nodded slowly. The polar excavations had been her first posting. Tedious work in a very hostile environment, picking bits of an unidentified spacecraft out of permafrost. "What else are we bringing back? Something from the surface?"

"Perhaps nothing." Gossi tabbed the briefing packet again. The holo image of the planet expanded, then shrank, focusing in on a section of the southern hemisphere. Long shadows cut across a desolate plain. Some of them made what seemed, in the low resolution of the orbital scan, to be a double-circle. "One of the field reports from the scientists in the initial team says structures—manufactured structures—have been observed from orbit. I wonder—I fear—the team found something and brought it up to the ship for examination. It's an old story . . . everyone's heard it before, yes? A dangerous artifact, an accident, the crew so horribly slain. Another sixty-five million quills of Company money wiped out."

Gossi stopped, shaking his head in dismay, and there was a moment of silence. It *was* an old story. The Company suffered a very high rate of attrition—in personnel, in spacecraft, in equipment—which made the recovery of saleable material critical. To the Company, anyway. Graduate students were far cheaper and more plentiful than Nanhuaque-drive starships. Gretchen didn't think it was a good idea to trade her own life—of which she had only one at last report—for some broken indecipherable bit of ancient machinery. She looked around. Parker, Bandao and Magdalena were looking expectantly at her.

It was an odd moment. Gretchen thought later that time didn't stop, but it did *stretch*. She had never really been in charge before. Gangs of native workers in the pits on Ugarit didn't count . . . the dig director had been breathing down her neck the whole time. These three strangers wanted her to make a decision, to tell them what to do, to be the leader.

In that crisp moment, she saw blue smoke curling up past Parker's head, the glow of the holo-cast shining on his forehead; the points of Magdalena's teeth were showing, fine and white; Bandao was plucking at the sleeve of his plain cotton shirt, the subtle woven pattern almost obscuring the outline of a small flat pistol tucked into the back of his belt. A perfect full awareness filled her—this was *not* what she wanted to do—but it was what she was going to do. She looked down, breaking the moment.

Gossi coughed, batting his hand at Parker's smoke. Gretchen picked up her briefing pad and tabbed through the pages, a dizzying red-tan-blue-white glow flashing in her eyes.

"The *Palenque* requires a crew of at least six to operate safely." She looked up, raising an eyebrow at Gossi. "What kind of ship are we taking? Can we split her crew to cover both?"

The Maltese raised both hands, then flared them slightly. He smiled. Gretchen's nose crinkled up. "What kind of ship, Gossi-*tzin*? We do have a ship to take us there?"

"Oh yes! The Company does not have any ships in this sector, oh no. They are expensive, you know, and the Company is spread thin. . . . I have arranged for you to be taken to the Ephesus system and delivered to the *Palenque*. If she proves unfit to make transit back to the station, then you will be able to return with the . . . other ship. However, since the transmitter remains operating, if unreachable at this time, I expect the *Palenque* will be flyable and you can return in her."

"What ship?" Gretchen tabbed to the end of the briefing packet, watching budget figures and details of the original mission flip past. "A miner? Some tramp freighter working the Rim?"

"It is an Imperial ship." Gossi spread his hands even wider. "They were already going in that direction, you understand. It is . . . convenient."

"Imperial." Gretchen rubbed her nose, sharing an arch look with the others. Parker seemed amused, Bandao's face was even more expressionless than before, and Magdalena was puzzled. "No *Imperial* ship is going to truck some *macehualli* scientists—"

"Or pilots," Parker interjected in a soft voice.

"—to the back of beyond, much less help them recover a derelict—possibly contaminated—spacecraft."

"The captain of the *Cornuelle* has kindly agreed to investigate the matter, and to take you there, and render you what assistance he can." Gossi's expression changed and Gretchen saw, to her wonder, that he did own a real smile. The corners of his eyes tilted up and his tiny round teeth became visible between rubbery lips. She wondered, briefly, how the Company man had pulled off Imperial "assistance."

"The *Cornuelle*." Parker tapped the top of his briefing pad, clearing the active document. "That's not a Náhuatl name. What class of ship is she?"

"A warship." Gossi cleared his own pad and keyed in a locator code. The holo image above the table flickered, was replaced by the station transmission screen for a moment, and then resolved into a view from an outside cam, showing an arc of star-filled sky, dominated by the twin primaries of Ctesiphon A and B, then the sleek black shape of an Imperial starship. "This is your conveyance," he said, smug pride creeping into his voice. "The *Henry R. Cornuelle* is an *Astronomer*-class light cruiser commanded by the esteemed *Chu-sa* Mitsuharu Hadeishi. She has been assigned to the Hittite sector on anti-piracy patrol. I understand from her executive officer, Miss *Sho-sa* Koshō Susan, they will be able to spend several days in Ephesus orbit, assisting you in recovery operations."

He paused, running one finger along the side of his pad. The holo image rotated, showing an elongated wedge shape with three heavy drive fairings at the back of the ship. Like most Imperial combat craft, she was matte black and the work-lights of the station barely limned the vague shapes of rounded weapons emplacements and recessed sensor arrays. "There have been some rumors, lately, of illegal mining in this area. Of solitary ships attacked by raiders. This is lawless space, so close to alien enclaves—your pardon, Magdalena-*tzin*, I have only the utmost respect for your people."

"Fine." Gretchen looked at Parker, tilting her head in question. "Can you fly the *Palenque?*"

Parker nodded, running a hand back through thinning brown hair. "Sure. Six crew could run everything—shuttles, powerplant, environmental, flight control— but if all we do is a jump back to the station, Maggie and I can handle that." He looked down at his pad, brows furrowing. "This *Temple* class can run almost auto with a soft upgrade. Maggie, do you have this package in archive?"

The Hesht uncurled from her chair, light shifting on her glossy fur. A harness of leather hung around her shoulders and upper body, holding tools and storage pockets. Each wrist was circled by the gleaming mirror of a comm unit. A claw extended from a long finger and tapped the surface of the briefing pad. "This ship," she hissed in a grumbling voice, "has an older model brain, but it will take most of the newest control package. I might have it, or we can buy one here on-station."

Gretchen eyed Gossi. "Do we have any money for this?"

"Some." Gossi put on a poor face. "So much was invested in the original expedition—"

"How much?"

The Maltese looked away and Gretchen sat back in her chair. All the exhaustion of a long flight from the Jupiter Yards came crowding in. The migraine, which had been distracted while she started to work the problem of this recovery mission, woke up and began rustling around behind her left eye, throwing clouds of white sparks across her vision.

Without thinking, she thumbed her wristband, jetting a serotonin regulator into her bloodstream. It would hurt later, but she had to think clearly right now. All the bad things about being in charge started to come to mind.

"So . . . no money to speak of. How many days do we have to prepare?"

Gossi's face assumed the shining round mask again. "The *Cornuelle* is already on a schedule—you will load your equipment tomorrow, then boost for Ephesus the day after."

"Two days?" Gretchen tasted something sour. "Well then. We'll be busy employees, won't we?"

"Talk to me about the transmitter."

Space aboard an Imperial warship was at a minimum, so Gretchen was doing sit-ups hanging from a bar set into the ceiling. Working in the field was good exercise, but sitting in a three- by four-meter cabin for weeks on end during transit did nothing for her girlish figure. Magdalena was perched on her bunk, surrounded by data pads and printouts on quick-cycle sheets. The Hesht looked up, yellow eyes narrowed to slits over the top of amped-up sunglasses. The cat had an earbug as well, letting her hear the soft invisible voices of the processors riding in the pads. Gretchen had used field goggles before, with v-feeds and a sound interface, but they had been big, bulky units. Maggie's sunglasses were as sleek and dark as she was.

"It's an experimental unit, sister. A commercial version of the old military-grade Wayfarer ship-based transmitter. The Company is field testing it for Tera-Wave—according to the logs, it's a one-oh release. That means light encryption, no redundant power supplies or emitters, about a six to seven light-year range." Maggie made a chuckling sound like a hydrogen-powered chainsaw starting up. "Thirty or forty predefined channels—very primitive."

"But . . . *grunt* . . . not hand mirrors and smoke . . . *grunt* . . . from the mountaintop."

"No." Maggie clawed a pad and let some schematics drift past. "A little better than that. Each channel is identified by headers tacked onto the message packets, then thrown out in a single emitter stream. Sort of a faster-than-light telegraph. But it works and it's as cheap as you can build a tachyon unit. I've tested the connection myself by patching through Ctesiphon comm—they have a big industrial emitter and router—the unit on the *Palenque* does respond to a 'hello', but refused to open a conversation. I think the unit is actually in maintenance mode, on standby, waiting for the shipboard operator to reset the system." The Hesht paused, then held up a pad. Gretchen jerked her head and Maggie flipped the device upside down.

"That . . . *grunt* . . . still makes no sense to me. Plain Náhuatl, sister."

Maggie laughed again, rolling on her back and lolling her head off the edge of the bunk. Now she seemed upright to Gretchen, though her ears were pointing off at a strange angle. "The Wayfarer has a manual mode, where the operator can pick and choose which channels are live. This is also used for maintenance, where you don't have to shut down the whole system. Specific components can be turned on or off, even removed from the chassis. When I send a 'hello' across the t-link, the refused connection message comes back with an error code. Of course, the code isn't documented yet, not on a test system, but it matches the older military code for 'standby'."

"So . . . *grunt* . . . there was a problem, they turned it off. The problem got worse . . . *grunt* . . . no one came back to push the 'on' button."

"That's what the momma cat said."

Gretchen finished her count of two hundred and eight, then swung down off the bar. The *Cornuelle* was accelerating out from the station on normal-space drive, chewing up antimatter pellets and spitting plasma, which gave them one g inside the habitat areas of the ship. A bigger ship, a commercial liner or an Imperial battlewagon, would have g-decking everywhere. The *Cornuelle* was not a big ship. Gretchen stepped carefully over the duffels and equipment boxes strapped to the floor. The Marine *gunso* they had bumped back to hot-bunking with the rankers already had their cargo allotments aboard, so there was very little room for the Company people. A two meter–high polyfoam crate holding spare transmitter parts occupied the space where a little table and seats were usually pulled down.

She frowned at the clothing spread out on her bunk. Playing in the dirt, as her father would say, did not require dress-up clothes. Unfortunately, this was an Imperial ship of war, which meant chu-sa Hadeishi would have a dress evening mess. Gretchen sighed, turning over her "good" shirt. It had stains. Ruin bugs had eaten a hole in one sleeve.

"A citizen is humble, simply-dressed, respectful, pious. . . ." she mumbled to herself, fingers twitching her trousers straight.

Maggie laughed again, her tail twitching. "You're the kit who always has dirt on her nose and looks so surprised! Will this clan-lord Hadeshee nip your ears for a dirty pelt?"

"Yes. Miss *Sho-sa* Koshō has been very polite and accommodating, but we need the commander's good will. He is Nisei, too, which means he will be very proper and traditional. He may have guests—I can't embarrass him too much. Time for the ol' enzymatic cleaner."

Gretchen squeezed into the end of her bunk, found a clean cloth, then picked up her boots. They were good boots—her mother had had them fitted and built for her by hand, of realcow leather, with shock-soles and brass fittings—but the dust of Ugarit fouled everything it touched. She sighed, seeing the soles were beginning to separate from the uppers.

"No matter . . ." She shoved them to the back of the bunk. Aboard ship they went about in light disposable deck shoes designed to adhere to the walking surfaces when they were in zero-g. She spat on the shirt stain, then began to gently rub it between her fingers.

Two Imperial Marines in sharply creased black dress uniforms with crimson piping stiffened to attention as Gretchen approached a hatchway outlined in pale blue. Each Marine had his hands behind his back, but heavy flat pistols were slung on their belts and they had visors as sharp and sleek as Maggie's. The Navy rating escorting her bowed politely and thumbed a comm pad set into the bulkhead next to the hatch.

"Doctor Gretchen Anderssen, Commander," he announced in a stiffly formal voice.

The pad chimed and the hatch recessed with a slight *chuff* and then slid up into the bulkhead. Her mouth suddenly dry, Gretchen nodded to the young man, then stepped inside. The room was small, like everything on the *Cornuelle*, but managed to hold a low traditional table for six, dressed with crisp white linen and thin porcelain cups. A very short man, barely reaching Gretchen's shoulder, bowed in greeting from the head of the table. The five other officers—ranging from the petite executive officer, *Sho-sa* Koshō, down to a midshipman, or *sho'i ko-hosei*, with pale red hair—also bowed in place, their hands flat on the tatami mat floor. Their incline was slightly deeper than Hadeishi's. Gretchen kept her face composed, hands together in front of her, and managed a bow halfway between those that had greeted her.

"Welcome, Doctor Anderssen," Hadeishi said. Gretchen blinked in surprise—the Nisei's Norman was flawless. "Please, join us."

Gretchen slipped off her deck shoes before entering the room, turning the motion into a second bow.

The midshipman scooted a little to one side. Gretchen knelt, smiling politely at the boy. He couldn't have been more than sixteen. Like the other officers, he wore a perfectly white dress uniform, with the fire-snake emblem of the Imperial Navy worked in copper at his collar. Above his heart rode the sunburst symbol of the *Cornuelle* and a square glyph holding a running man.

The other officers remained still, heads lowered. The captain smiled down the table at Gretchen, and raised a thin porcelain teacup in polite greeting.

"Doctor Anderssen, welcome to the *Cornuelle*. I am Mitsuharu Hadeishi, her captain."

"*Konichiwa*, Mitsuharu-*san*. Thank you for making me so welcome."

"Your Japanese is excellent," Hadeishi said, smiling, eyes crinkling up. Gretchen felt an odd sense of dislocation. She had worked with many Nisei; at the university, on Old Mars, even on Ugarit. They were unfailingly polite but she had never encountered a Japanese man, particularly one her social superior, that had genuinely smiled at her.

"Thank you. Your Norman is perfect."

"No, please, I have a slight accent." Hadeishi set down his cup. "You have already met Lieutenant Koshō, my executive officer and pilot. This fellow next to her is Lieutenant Second Hayes, our weapons officer." Hayes nodded, somehow appearing deferential to Koshō, though the XO was a tiny woman, even slighter of build than the captain. Lieutenant Hayes was nearly six feet tall and powerfully built. Gretchen smiled politely.

"The young ensign is Smith-*tzin*, who runs communications, and this last is Lieutenant Second Isoroku, master of our engineers." Smith managed to nod politely and Isoroku, a bull-headed bald Nisei, had no reaction at all. Obscurely, Gretchen found this cold behavior comforting—his reaction was what she had expected, not the genial, almost cheerful tone expressed by the commander. Hadeishi stood and straightened his dress jacket. His uniform was very simple, expressing the best attributes of the Empire—humility, modest dress, quiet unassuming power—though his collar tabs were gold and the eagle glyph of an Imperial war commander sat next to the sunburst. An elderly man in a simple dark gray kimono appeared with a tiny green jade cup and a slim sake flask. Hadeishi bowed to him, took the cup and turned, facing his right.

There, on a bulkhead covered with inset wooden screens painted with mountains in cloud, were two portraits. They were not holo images, but traditional paintings on cream-colored rice paper, in a delicate ink-brush with faint washes of color. On the left, looking very young, was the Lord of the World, Ahuizotl, the sixth of that name, *huey tlatoani* of the México and all other peoples under the domain of the Empire. The artist had captured his pensive nature well, looking off to one side, slim hand pressed against his chest.

Hadeishi bowed deeply to the image of the Emperor, then raised the jade cup.

"So, meditate on this, eagles and jaguars," he began, his Náhuatl slow and measured, as flawless as his Norman. "Although you may be jade, although you may be gold, you too will journey to the fleshless land. We all must disappear, no one will remain."

The room became very still, each man and woman at the table looking down. The servant had disappeared. Gretchen saw the captain's face was composed and calm. She recognized the words, written nearly a thousand years before by a man who had opposed the policies of the Empire when it was still young. Her eyes drifted to one side, watching the faces of the other officers. The poetry of Nezahualcóyotl, the doomed prince of Tetzcoco, was banned throughout the Empire. The poet's philosophy did not express the ascetic martial spirit deemed fitting by the great powers of the México.

Hadeishi lowered the jade cup, pressing it against his lips, then raised it again, to the second portrait. This was a grumpy old man, his face pinched in a scowl, his hair bound up in the traditional samurai knot at the back of his head. He frowned, irritation alive in the smooth brushstrokes. He was Juntoku, the one hundred and thirty-sixth *Tenno no Nihon*, Emperor of Japan and all the Nisei people. Hadeishi smiled faintly, saying; "Mere green herbs they are, grown in the mountain soil; yet if I pluck them with grace, how joyful is the toil!"

Then he placed the jade cup into the hands of the little old man and turned to face the table again. The welcoming ritual complete, two ratings slipped out of the tiny galley behind the officer's mess and began serving the first course. Gretchen felt her stomach grumble, smelling sweet onions and broth. For a moment, she was frozen, watching everyone else pick up their spoons.

Then the captain somberly tasted the *miso* and nodded to the two cooks. They grinned and everyone was eating. Gretchen forgot about her worries for a moment, listening to the quiet cheerful banter among the officers and enjoying the excellent meal.

"You were worried by my poetry." Hadeishi was sitting in his office, a tiny cluttered room dominated by a wall of old books and a great deal of quick-cycle paper in stacks on an inset metal desk. He cradled a heavy Jomon-style sake cup in his hands. The liquor was hot, steaming up in the slightly chill air of the ship. Gretchen was sitting opposite him, in a real chair, still uncomfortable, holding a similar cup. She cradled it gently, having determined as the captain was pouring that it was an artifact and possibly two thousand years old. Her training urged her to pack it in shockfoam and label it, not sip smooth, old sake from the broad-mouthed bowl.

"Yes. Is it treason for you to speak those words?"

"No." Hadeishi shook his head, a grin hiding in his dark eyes. His hair was long and a little stringy, though he kept it tied back. Here, in this softly lit room, filled with the familiar odor of old books and ink, he seemed elfin with delicate features and sharp little mustache. "It is traditional, among the Nisei and Náhuatl both, to offer songs to the great. It is not disrespectful to offer a small portion of a masterpiece—particularly those composed by royalty. But I understand your situation. From your mouth, Nezahualcóyotl is treason. Where were you born?"

"On New Aberdeen," she said quietly, taking a small, careful sip.

"But you are not a Skawt? Surely not with a family name like Anderssen."

Gretchen shook her head. Her poor family situation had weighed against her in school, at university, in getting employment, even under the burning suns of Ugarit. As a child, her ancestry had been a fierce burden, but she had struggled, and survived, and she felt no need to hide or dissemble.

"No, we are Swedish. Refugees."

Hadeishi smiled over his cup, then put the bowl aside on the desk. "Your people fought well and accepted defeat honorably. It pains me you should suffer for this, but I suppose not everyone can be blessed like the Skawts, the Irish and the Nisei, with the favor of the Lord of Men. Someone, after all, needed to stand fast in the face of the Empire. Glory is impossible without a mighty opponent."

"I suppose." A little over a hundred years had passed since the México had crushed the last independent nations on Anáhuac. The Swedes and Russians, fighting on in the ruins of their great cities, had surrendered only when all else had fallen to the Jaguar and Eagle Legions. Many of the survivors had scattered to the trans-solar colonies, or even beyond the embrace of Sol. Gretchen's grandparents had managed to settle on New Aberdeen, one of the lusher, Earthlike planets the Empire had apportioned to those races of men who were "Third From the Center." Her grandparents and parents had never spoken of The War, but the colonial government's nationalistic propaganda had filled in the blanks. "That is past history."

"Perhaps." Hadeishi leaned forward, his face suddenly serious. "You are uncomfortable with me and my crew—we are not what you expected. You are even surprised I speak passable Norman."

"Yes." Gretchen set aside a stack of age-yellowed magazines and put down her cup. "I am surprised, though I have never been on an Imperial warship before. All of the Imperial officials I have ever met have been very forbidding men and women, ascetic and distant. I have never heard an official use any language save Náhuatl. Isn't that the recommended style?"

"In many places, yes. You've stumbled into an odd corner of the Empire with us, I fear. The Imperial Navy is a strange creature, one head on two distinct bodies. I know you have found your place in society restricted by your birth—our Navy suffers the same fate. Certain kinds of ship commands—really, anything large and impressive—are reserved for commanders and senior crew drawn from those 'close to the Center.' This leaves the smaller ships—destroyers, cruisers, light cruisers—to those 'further away'. And among those who are not of the Great Clans, you will find the Nisei are the most trusted." Hadeishi paused, thin mobile lips twisting ironically. "So we are repaid for trading horses and steel for food and shelter so long ago.

"If you were to go down into the ship's enlisted country," he continued, "you would find crewmen and women of many races, even some with hair the color of beaten gold, like yours. Nearly a quarter of light-ship crews are of macehualli descent. Despite the nepotism of the Imperial Clans, crew rosters must be filled and the navy is not picky about lineage and birth—for crewmen at least! Haven't you noticed everything is labeled in Norman? Our manuals, our computer systems, everything is in Norman. Every Imperial officer must be proficient if they are to speak with their crews." He paused. "Of course, they have reliable officers to guide them, like myself."

Gretchen stifled a laugh. She was suddenly aware there had been sake with dinner too, and most of the Jomon bowl was empty. The air seemed chillier than it had been.

"I am still surprised," she said, fingertips brushing the medband on her wrist. It could dispense more than serotonin regulators. A cool sensation followed, rushing up her arm. Objects in the room began to assume a preternatural clarity. "Are you judged so reliable you lack a political officer? Someone to help you guide these clanless, landless crewmen?"

She stopped, aware of the bitter tone in her words. Hadeishi raised an eyebrow, shaking his head gently. He put a thin finger to his lips in warning. "Careful, Doctor. In this world, we must keep in our places, at least with open words. My command staff and I have been together for six years—first on the destroyer *Ceatl* and now here. We are very comfortable together—a family. You've seen in the door of our house tonight, watching us laugh at dinner. Perhaps we should have been more circumspect."

He smiled gently, putting both forefingers to his temples. "Keep your true life here, inside, and you will be safe. Now listen, Doctor, for there are things I must tell you."

Gretchen straightened up, her mind now crystal clear. Something about Hadeishi had changed as well, the captain-ness of him coming forward. Now that she knew him a little better, she could see him change, his openness fading away, though he was still genial and polite.

"The sector admiral agreed to let you and your team ship with us to Ephesus because this benefits the Empire, not as a favor to your Company. The ruins on Ephesus Three, and the marks of shaping the planet bears, make it important to the Navy. Our own scientists have reviewed the data from the probe. At some time in the distant past, at least a million years ago, the world was violently transformed by the First Sun People. It may be an abandoned project—we have found those before—or may have been completed.

"Regardless of what happened to the *Palenque*, the investigation must continue. I have been entrusted with seeing you safely there and then making sure your work is a success. Whatever you need—transport shuttles, men, equipment, repair parts—I will provide."

Gretchen sighed, weariness hidden behind the booster. "I understand, Commander. If we find anything *interesting* we will turn it over to you." She pressed the palms of her hands to her eyes. "I've worked under military supervision before."

"I know." Hadeishi did not smile, but there was a trace of humor sparkling in his eyes. "On Old Mars—the Polaris excavation—under Director Huicton. You are young, Doctor, but you were chosen for this mission because of your experience and skill. Listen to me, I am here to *help* you, not to stumble around in your investigation, shooting people or being heavy-handed. I cannot imagine there is a great deal of trust between us, but I hope to gain yours."

"Why?" The side of Gretchen's mouth twisted and she had to quell the urge to chew on the inside of her lip. "You certainly don't need my trust. You can order me to do whatever you want. What you are trying to say, politely, is that we are *consultants* to the Navy."

Hadeishi nodded in agreement. "This is true. But this is not a military mission."

Gretchen's eyebrows raised in question. "I don't understand."

Hadeishi ran his finger around the top of his drinking bowl. He seemed pensive, uneasy. After a long moment he said, "This has become a matter of concern to the Smoking Mirror. We are both under the direct jurisdiction of an Imperial *nauallis*—a judge."

Swallowing, her throat tight and dry, Gretchen managed to speak. "Is this *brujo* aboard ship?"

Hadeishi nodded, his face a tight mask. "Yes, you will speak to him soon. His name is Huitziloxoctic."

Green Hummingbird, she thought. *A powerful name.*

Gretchen thumbed open the hatch to her quarters, and stopped in the doorway, finding Parker and Bandao sitting on the deck amid drifts of bits and pieces of metal, plastic flasks and wads of cloth. The pilot was in a T-shirt and ragged work pants lined with pockets. Bandao, as ever, was in sharply pressed slacks and a dress shirt. Maggie was still on her bunk; though she had squeezed down to make room for the equipment cases that had been sitting on the deck.

"Hello. Why are you cluttering up my floor?"

Parker looked up, pale brown eyes twinkling. "Sorry, boss, but we don't have any room in our cabin." His hands were spotted with light oil. Gretchen could smell it hanging in the air, a bitter thick tickling in her nose and throat. The pilot had an automatic pistol in his hand, mostly disassembled, with the gas venting mechanism sticking out.

"They weren't clean already?" One of her eyebrows inched up. She stepped inside, letting the hatch slide closed, then stepped over the two men and swung up into her bunk. "What makes you think a pistol will be useful on Ephesus?"

"A gun is always useful," Parker grinned, sliding the top of his automatic back together with a sharp *click*. He nodded at Bandao, "Isn't that so?"

Bandao nodded, his face as calm and composed as ever. A heavy cloth, almost a rug, lay over his knees holding a heavy round barrel and a dizzying array of smaller parts, as well as a stock formed of honeycombed plastic. His hands, which seemed small on a solid, muscular body, held a rag and a shining metal component. Unlike Parker's mess, the gunner had arranged his tools on a cloth in neat and orderly rows.

"Well," Gretchen smiled across at Magdalena. "If it makes you happy."

"How did the *yrrrchuu-owl*, go?" Maggie was lying on her back, a heavy flat comp on her furry stomach, a v-screen flipped up. "I mean, the hunting feast."

"It went." Gretchen rummaged in her bag, frowning at the mess her rack had already become. She glowered sideways at Maggie—her bunk was carefully ordered, with everything in place. *Damn cat.* "It was even pleasant. I had a talk with *chu-sa* Hadeishi afterward, in his office. He says that there is an Imperial *nauallis* on board."

Parker looked up, quizzical. Bandao continued to work on cleaning the assault rifle, but Gretchen thought the smooth, assured motion of his hands paused for a moment.

"A what?" Parker put down his pistol and scratched his chin, leaving a glistening smear of oil along the line of his jaw.

"An Imperial judge," Gretchen said, pulling a holocard out of her bag. The side of her mouth twisted unconsciously. She ran a fingernail along the back of the card, then jammed the holo against the bulkhead. It adhered to the painted metal, then flickered on. The image was set to 'still', extending its life from days to years. Three young children, a boy and two girls no more than six years old, were smiling up at the holocam. They were in a swimming pool, all blue water and glittering sunlight. In the high definition of the holocam the green tint of too many summer days spent in chlorinated water was very clear. "An agent of the Mirror. A spy. Both Hadeishi and I are under his jurisdiction. This is a government mission now, not the Company's."

Bandao looked up, forehead creased by a single frown line. Parker stared at Gretchen, grimacing. "The secret police? Sister's smile, this sucks!"

Gretchen nodded, turning away from the holocard. "Listen, we have to be careful with this. We still work for the Company and will be held responsible for getting back the *Palenque* and any material, objects, artifacts, data—everything the first expedition collected. Gossi's 'great deal' was forced on him by the Navy and he didn't have much choice about shipping us out with them. This judge will keep out of the way, but anything that we find he wants, he gets. Poof."

Parker shrugged. He didn't care. Bandao slid the barrel of the shipgun back into the firing block and locked it in place with a twist and a sharp *chink*. Like everything else he did, the motion was assured and without waste.

"Let's talk about the *Palenque*." Gretchen pinched the bridge of her nose. "The captain has offered us a Marine boarding team to secure her. However, an agent of the Company has to be the first on board, to reassert claim to the ship. Otherwise, it will be a derelict and the Navy will have possession. Now, the Company could get the ship back, eventually, but not without putting a case to the Naval court of adjudication. Parker—you have z-g experience, right?"

The pilot nodded, fingering one of the patches on his jacket. "You bet, boss. My suit is in storage, but I'll pull it out and checklist it tomorrow. Who else goes? Or is it just little ole me with the big mean Marines?"

Gretchen pointed at Bandao with her chin. "Mister Bandao, are you qualified in a suit? Can you use this cannon of yours in z-g?"

The gunner nodded, looking up. He had very pale blue eyes.

"Do you ever say anything?"

"Occasionally." Bandao snapped the stock and the body of the shipgun together. "Parker talks enough for both of us."

The officers' mess seemed colder as Gretchen entered and sat down. The lights were dimmed and the hatchway to the galley was closed. A man was sitting cross-legged on the mat at the head of the table, watching her. He seemed to be of medium height, lean and wiry, with a solid nut-brown face and deep-set eyes. Gretchen sat quietly, her face impassive. She felt on edge, but not nervous. The man was wearing a plain white shirt, cut to resemble a traditional mantle with long sleeves. His hands were hidden under the edge of the table.

After a long period of silence, he said, "Do you understand how dangerous you are?"

Gretchen blinked, then shook her head. "I don't follow your meaning."

The man continued to sit. The nearest ceiling light illuminated the crisp white cotton of his shirt, but not his face. "You are a scientist, a thinking being. Tell me why you are dangerous."

"I am not dangerous," Gretchen replied, her voice acquiring an edge. "I am a loyal citizen of the Empire, a dutiful employee, a careful scientist. My work may place me in physical danger, but I am not, of myself, dangerous. I have never hurt anyone."

The man continued to sit quietly, watching her. More time passed.

At last, nervous, Gretchen said, "Is this interview complete?"

The man shook his head, *no.*

"You have not given me enough information to form a hypothesis," she said, after another long pause. Then she stopped before saying anything more. She realized that he had provided her with three—no, four—data points. *Enough for a three-dimensional structure. . . .* Unconsciously, her head bent down a little, and she frowned, her lips pursing.

"You say that I am dangerous. I am a scientist. I think. If my work is successful, something unknown to our science becomes known. That would be something new. Newness is change, which may inflict pain, or suffering, or death. Do you think there is something on Ephesus I might find, where others have not? Something dangerous?"

The man leaned forward a little, and the overhead light caught in his eyes. They were a smoky, jadite green. "There is a man in your cabin. His name is David Parker. He carries a weapon. Is he dangerous?"

"I don't think so," Gretchen said, turning her head a little sideways, eyes narrowing. "I know him, he is a companion. He is not dangerous to me. But yes, I understand. He is, of himself, dangerous. He could kill or hurt another."

The man leaned backward, the smoky green light fading. "Is he very dangerous?"

Gretchen bristled at the new tone in the man's voice. Where before it had been calm and level, now it took on a patronizing tone, as if she were a small child having trouble with her maths. "No, not very. Not in a large context. He might kill one other, then be slain himself. The duration of his dangerousness is limited."

"Is yours?"

"Limited? It must be, for I am only one person. What could I do? I could be easily killed or imprisoned if I prove dangerous. Is that what you do? Do you watch for 'dangerous' persons and remove them from society? Is this what it means to be a judge?"

The man placed a small blue pyramid of what seemed to be leaded glass on the table. In the brief moment when his hand was visible, Gretchen saw that it was gnarled and twisted, muscular, a farmer's hand. Like her grandfather's hands, roughened and seamed by the elements. Fine puckered scars ran across the palm and the wrist. The stiff white shirt-cuff hid the forearm, but Gretchen was suddenly sure his whole body was marked in this same way, like etched glass.

"The *tlamatinime*, the wise men, have a sacred duty. It is to sustain the world." The man turned the pyramid a bit, so the light fell upon it squarely. "They are ceaselessly vigilant, watching over each of us while we go about our daily business. Do you see this book?"

Gretchen raised an eyebrow in surprise. The blue pyramid did not look like a book at all, though she supposed it might contain a holostore or memory lattice. "Yes."

The green-eyed man smiled faintly, holding up the pyramid. "It is very dangerous. A world might be destroyed by it. But it is not as dangerous as you are, right now."

Gretchen felt a chill steal over her. She could not see the man's other hand, and she suddenly imagined the scarred fingers holding a gun, a weapon, a small flat gray pistol with a round black muzzle. The gun, she was sure, was pointed at the pit of her stomach. It would fire a shock pellet, striking her flesh, ripping through her shirt, then bursting violently, shattering her pelvis, gouging a huge gaping red hole out of her back. She would die slowly, as blood leaked away from her brain and the wrinkled gray organ asphyxiated.

"Why am I dangerous?" Her voice sounded very faint.

The man put the blue pyramid away. "Telling you why would serve no purpose. It is enough, for you, for now, to know you *are* dangerous. In you, the life of every living human being is at risk." His gaze sharpened and Gretchen felt his scrutiny like a physical pressure against her face. "Are you are afraid of me?"

"Yes."

"That is good. Are you afraid of death?"

"Yes."

"Better."

Then he was silent. Gretchen waited, sitting, her palms damp with sweat. She wondered what the blue pyramid contained. *A dangerous book?* Books had always been friendly to her, offering her succor, sanctuary, and advantage. Friends who didn't mind if you only called once a year. *But it might contain plans for a weapon—a virus, a bomb, something truly deadly.* With that, she thought she understood his question. *What if I find something like that on Ephesus? Some First Sun weapon that could shatter a star, or burn a planet to a cinder?*

Green Hummingbird stood up, moving stiffly. Gretchen realized he was very old, far older than his voice suggested. He looked down at her, his face grim, then limped to the door. Without turning her head, Gretchen tried to see if the man really had a pistol. *Nothing.* The hatch *chuffed* open and the México went out into the passage. Gretchen let out a long, slow breath, feeling suddenly awake and relieved of a great weight which had lain upon her.

"We have orbital match in . . . three . . . two . . . one . . . Orbit match locked."

Sho-sa Koshō's cool voice echoed in Gretchen's earbug. She and Magdalena were crowded into the secondary weapons station on the command deck of the *Cornuelle,* sharing a combat chair. The flat black display in front of them was con-figured into three v-panes, one showing an orbital plot of the planet with the *Palenque* and the *Cornuelle* in their velocity dance, another the view from the war-ship's forward cameras and in the third a colorful, annotated image culled from the sensors on Parker's suit as he stood in an airlock.

"Main engines at zero thrust. Steering at zero thrust."

Around them, the officers of the *Cornuelle* began to go through a checklist in soft voices. Gretchen bit her lip, watching the image of the *Palenque.* The ship seemed intact, without visible hull damage or scoring. It was an ungainly monster in comparison to the rakish profile of the *Cornuelle.* The *Temple*-class were work-horse ships, with a big rotating habitat and lab ring sitting forward, squeezed around a command and sensor array platform. Behind the habitat ring was an enclosed shuttle dock assembly, surrounded by mushroom-shaped cargo modules, then a flare shield and the bulk of the engines. The Company logo, white on maroon, stood twenty meters high on the thruster fairings.

"Maggie, do you have anything on ship-to-ship comm?"

Maggie shook her head, long ears angled back. "Quiet as high grass, sister." Her claws made a *tic-tic-tic* sound as they worked the console. The view of the *Palenque* tightened, zooming in on an airlock beneath the command deck. The hatch was hexagon-shaped, with a clear window. Gretchen could see something through the opening.

"What's this?"

Maggie worked the panel and the image cropped, then zoomed again. There was a brief ripple across the v-screen as the console kicked in to interpolate the image. Gretchen leaned in a little, squinting through her com-glasses. There was an amber light shining above a control panel on the inner door of the lock. She tapped her finger on the v-screen. "Do we have a pattern match for this?"

"Yes," rumbled Magdalena in her I'm-working-on-it-already voice. A v-pane unfolded on the console display. It contained a schematic of the airlock control panel, with highlights indicating the meaning and use of each control, light and display. "There is interior pressure, but the airlock is in manual mode—no power for the automatic mechanism."

Gretchen nodded, pressing a fingertip against her cheekbone. "Parker, did you hear that?"

"You bet, boss." The pilot's v-feed shifted as he looked around the *Cornuelle*'s lock. There were two Marines with him and Bandao. Both civilians were wearing dark gray z-suits, with bright Company logos on their chests, white-lettered nametags on each shoulder and over the heart. Both Marines were nearly invisible in matte-black suits far slimmer than the Company rigs. Both had nametags, but they could not be read in the ambient light. Gretchen frowned, but Maggie was already working. Text materialized on the v-feed, showing FITZSIMMONS and DECKARD above the two Marines. "We'll have to crank the lock ourselves."

"One kilometer," Koshō announced. The *Cornuelle* was approaching on the last dying bit of her insertion velocity, coasting in not only to match orbital paths with the *Palenque,* but to come within eyeball distance of the abandoned ship. "Three minutes."

"Maggie, are there any other lights? Radio emissions? Any EM at all?" Gretchen leaned back in the chair. The shock-cushion adjusted, cradling her back. The Hesht tapped up an ambient light gradient over a ship schematic on her main control window. The derelict showed heat and light loss at the personnel airlocks and around the big shuttle bay doors.

"She's cold. Just waste heat from standby systems," Magdalena said, "but there seems to be atmosphere inside from end to end. The hull shielding is blocking everything else, but when Parker gets the telemetry relay in place, we'll know more. Still no response from the comm system or the tachyon relay." Her shoulders shrugged in a rolling ripple of muscle. "Station-keeping is still on line; she's not spinning or losing altitude."

"Two minutes," Koshō announced. "Correcting roll with braking thrust."

Gretchen felt a very faint shudder through the decking under her feet. The feed from Parker's suit suddenly showed the planet rolling past in the window of the airlock, huge and ruddy tan. Then the *Palenque* slid into view. Gretchen touched her cheek again.

"Parker, we're almost ready. Start your checklist."

"Copy that," the pilot replied and the feed-image bent toward Bandao. Each man would double-check his z-suit, his equipment, the telemetry relay, their weapons before the lock opened. The Marines were already checking each other's suits. All four men were wearing propulsion packs. Gretchen's request for a wire-tether fired from the *Cornuelle* to the derelict had been refused. Hadeishi had no intention of establishing a physical connection between his ship and the *Palenque*.

Gretchen turned, looking up across the control station behind her. Hadeishi was ensconced in a command chair, half enveloped in shock-foam and control consoles. Faint lights from his panel displays mottled his face and combat suit. Koshō sat slightly below him, on his left, and Hayes down and to the right. She and the Hesht were at a station in the third ring of the bridge, matching the position of the ensign, Smith, on the opposite side of the U-shaped deck. The Imperial commander raised his head slightly and smiled, meeting her eyes.

Hadeishi toggled on his voice channel. "Near space scan, Smith-*tzin?*"

"Clear, *Chu-sa*. Two trailing asteroids, six low-orbit Company peapod satellites, no other ships, shuttles or unidentified objects. No radio or t-wave transmissions except the telemetry from the satellites. Everything's quiet."

"Engines, Isoroku-*tzin?*"

"Hot, *kyo*, idling at zero thrust. Power plant is at twenty percent. Spin time to hyper is six zero minutes. Repeat, six zero minutes." The engineer's voice echoed in Gretchen's earbug, coming from the downship channel.

"Weapons, Mister Hayes?"

"Weapons are hot, Captain. One flash bird rigged and solution locked. Point defense system is online and tracking."

"One minute," Koshō said softly.

Hadeishi nodded to her. "Full stop."

Koshō ran her finger down a control bar on her console. There was another slight shudder. In Gretchen's displays, a counter indicating meters-to-target slowed and then stopped. "Six hundred meters," announced the pilot. "We have velocity match."

"Are you ready?" Hadeishi's voice was soft in Gretchen's ear and she started. A blinking glyph in the bottom right corner of her glasses indicated they were on a private channel.

"Ready," she said, swallowing. This was it. She changed back to the open channel. "Mister Parker, have you completed your checklist?"

"Copy that, boss. We are ready to take a walk."

Gretchen looked sideways at Magdalena. "Cameras ready? Suit telemetry online?"

The Hesht grinned, showing double rows of white teeth like tiny knives. "Cameras live. Recorders are rolling. Suit telemetry is clean. All bio readings are in the green." The cat flicked a claw at a newer, smaller window on the console. Gretchen saw it showed a string of beadlike lights circling the planet. The peapod survey satellites Hayes had picked up. *Excellent.*

"Mister Parker, you are free to take a walk."

Unconsciously, she bit her lip, eyes fixed on the v-feed of the *Cornuelle*'s airlock. One of the Marines, Fitzsimmons, punched a code into the airlock control panel. The hatch opened swiftly and raw sunlight flooded into the chamber, picking out every detail with brilliant clarity.

Deckard stepped out into the void. He was briefly silhouetted against the monstrous glowing disk of the planet. Bandao followed, white jets of vapor trailing behind him. Parker followed and Gretchen felt a moment of vertigo as he stepped out over an infinite distance. Then the suit cam focused on the distant, surprisingly tiny image of the *Palenque*.

"Five minute count to contact." Parker's voice was calm, even cheerful.

There was a faint *clank* as Parker's boots touched down on the metal skin of the exploration ship. Bandao landed a moment later, flanking the airlock, while the two Marines held back. From the viewpoint of the cameras on the two Company suits, Gretchen couldn't see either Marine, but she guessed they were covering the opening, weapons armed and ready.

"Checking lock diagnostics," Parker said, his voice still light and cheerful. The camera view stabilized on the entry pad. All of the keys were dark. The pilot's fingers tapped on them experimentally. There was no reaction.

"Some emergency power is offline," Magdalena commented, tail twitching. Parker echoed her a moment later. Bandao's camera shifted and a plate sealed with four spring bolts came into view.

"Stand by," the gunner said. "We'll try a manual entry."

Despite surface pitting and a faint layer of ice on the shadowed entry plate, Bandao's quick fingers released all four bolts, then set the magnetized cover aside to adhere to the skin of the *Palenque*, and swung the unlock bar over in a smooth motion.

Gretchen heard a slight hiss from Parker as the airlock recessed. Puffs of vapor squeezed out of the opening door as Bandao cranked the locking bar around and the hatch swung inward, revealing a dark cavity only barely illuminated by a single amber light.

"I am entering the ship," Parker said, only the faintest tremor in his voice. Gretchen blinked as the pilot's suit lamps swung to reveal the gleaming white and gray interior of the lock.

"No debris, no organic contaminates, no high-order radioactives," Magdalena said softly into a voice log, yellow eyes glued to the environmental sensors relaying from the z-suits of the men in the lock. The brass-colored snout of Bandao's ship-gun appeared at the edge of Parker's video feed, swung back and forth, quartering the compartment, then withdrew. "Parker is inside the lock."

Gretchen looked back at Hadeishi, still sitting in the command chair, watching quietly, his face illuminated by lights from his combat displays. He raised an eyebrow at Gretchen's formal expression. "*Chu-sa* Hadeishi, Mister Parker has boarded and taken possession of the exploration ship *Palenque*, Company registry . . ." She read off the official registration and identification of the *Temple*-class starship. "I would like to request the assistance of the Imperial Navy in recovery operations at this time." She bowed politely and the captain returned the motion.

"Lieutenant Koshō," Mitsuharu turned his head slightly. The executive officer was waiting with a politely interested expression. "Please render all aid and assistance to the Company representatives in securing their ship and restoring power and environmental controls."

"*Hai*, Captain." Koshō touched her cheekbone, and began speaking to the two Marines floating outside the airlock.

"You may proceed with your recovery operation, Doctor Anderssen." Hadeishi nodded politely to Gretchen. In the cameras, the two Marines entered the airlock as Parker and Bandao moved aside to let them handle the ship-side hatch. A second plate was removed, and the inner airlock opened slowly as Deckard operated the manual release bar.

Gretchen bent over the panel, watching a hallway slowly emerge into the light. Everything was very dark. She looked sideways at Magdalena. "Atmosphere?"

"Clear," the Hesht replied, though she was frowning.

"What is it?" Gretchen tapped open the ship frequency. "Parker, hold up."

The video feeds stilled, and Gretchen caught sight of two stubby black Marine shipgun barrels swinging up, pointing down the newly revealed passageway. Parker's camera shifted as he swung to cover the now-closed exterior hatch.

"There's . . ." Magdalena twitched her nose, claws tapping softly on the display. "Mister Parker," she growled, "is your suit envirosensor working properly? Does it show green?"

"Yes," Parker said a moment later. "Everyone's does."

Gretchen started to turn toward Lieutenant Koshō, but the little Nisei woman's fingers were dancing on her own panel, and Magdalena's array of v-panes and gauges suddenly doubled in number, showing the telemetry feed from all four z-suits. The Hesht frowned again, black lips curling back from white incisors.

"Ship air is very, very clean," she said a moment later in a slightly disbelieving voice. "I show barely any contaminants, no waste products, only a slightly oxygen-rich standard oxy-nitrogen atmosphere. Scattered traces of free carbon and hydrogen."

"Dioxide levels?" Gretchen leaned over, searching out the air mixture readout for herself.

Magdalena waved a paw in dismissal, making the rows of bracelets on her wrists tinkle. "Negligible. Couldn't grow a fern if you wanted to. It's like no one is aboard, and never has been."

"All right. Parker, you're free to advance. Head for the bridge with all due precaution."

"Ok . . ." The pilot edged out into the hallway, his helmet light swinging across mottled gray bulkheads and an irregular-looking floor. "This is funny . . ."

While the observers on the bridge of the *Cornuelle* held their breaths, Parker moved to the base of the closest wall and knelt down. His hand—a little bulky in the z-suit—brushed along the baseboard. Bare metal under his fingertips gleamed and shimmered in clear white light.

"Discolored," Bandao commented, "like it's been flash-heated."

"Yeah . . ." Parker's camera shifted again, and fine gray ash puffed up from the deck at his touch. "Boss, could there have been a fire?"

"Huh." Gretchen slumped back in her shockchair, biting her lower lip. "Then where's the carbon scoring, the fire-suppression foam residue?"

Neither Bandao nor Parker had an answer. After a moment's pause, they pressed on.

Gretchen watched in silence, her frown steadily lengthening, as the four men moved forward along the main access passageway. Hatches revealing half-seen rooms drifted by. Everywhere, power was out, the ship dark and silent. When they entered what the ship schematic described as a crew common area just forward of the main lab ring, she opened the suit channel again.

"Parker, turn slowly. I want to see the whole room."

The camera view panned, and Gretchen doubled the size of the v-pane and dialed up feed magnification. Parker's camera slid across tables, chairs, counter-tops, drink dispensers, refrigerator and synthesizer doors. "Stop. Stop right there. Parker, do you see the door of the refrigerator?"

"Sure. . . . What about it?" Parker's pistol could be seen on the bottom left of the screen, steady on the suspicious door. "Looks like a refrigerator door. Must be the snacks locker."

"Have you ever seen a ship fridge door that wasn't covered with stickers, leaflets, announcements, photos from home?"

Parker didn't answer for a moment, and his camera flicked back across the rest of the common area. "There's nothing here," he said, surprised. "It's like they cleaned up the place and left or . . . or there was a fire and it burned up everything."

"Made a very clean job of it then," Gretchen said in a dry voice.

"More than that, look at this," Bandao said, and his camera view drifted over to a food prep counter set into one bulkhead. Gretchen turned her attention to his display. There was a rack of chef's knives pinned to the surface on a heavy magnetic strip. She hissed in alarm.

The muzzle of Bandao's rifle touched the hilt of one of the knives. Where a heavy rubber or wooden grip should have enclosed the steel tang, there was nothing, only bare gleaming metal. "This was a set of Hotchkiss cooking knives from New France, on Anáhuac. These models have walnut handles and surgical-quality blades. Very expensive."

"Check the rest of the room," Gretchen said, feeling suddenly cold. "Check for anything organic, anything at all."

"Nothing here either," Parker said in a dead voice. He was standing on the bridge of the *Palenque,* one hand pushing the commander's chair back and forth. There was only a bare metal frame, lacking any plastic, leather or fiberfill. "Everything's just . . . gone. This is creepy."

Bandao's camera shifted, looking across the display panels of the command station. Like everything else, they were dark and mottled by heat. The gunner rapped the knuckles of his z-suit on the glassy plate. "Aren't these touch-panels plastic? What about the corridor walls, the doors—aren't they plastic of some kind? Why were they just melted a little, and not destroyed completely?"

Gretchen and Magdalena looked up. They had been poring over the shipyard diagrams and materials lists used in the construction documents on file for the *Palenque.* Gretchen rubbed her face. The maze of ship documents was giving her a headache. "I—"

"Command panels are made with an electrically active composite, which is not a long chain polymer, Mister Bandao." Lieutenant Koshō's cool, correct voice intruded on the circuit. "The range of materials removed from the ship is rather distinct."

Gretchen's glasses flickered and Hadeishi's private channel glyph was winking again.

"Yes?" she said, turning away from Magdalena. She was starting to feel sick.

"We think the ship was attacked by a 'cleaner' agent of some kind." Mitsuharu's voice was very calm and steadying. "Only certain molecules and sets of longer-chain compounds were affected. Particularly, those which form organic life. Paper, glue, bedsheets . . . all those things were swept up in the general criteria."

"A weapon." Gretchen felt a band of tension release from her chest. Vague fears crystallized and she felt relieved. *See,* she thought, *the universe is filled with reason.* "Something from the planet?"

"Perhaps." Hadeishi sounded thoughtful. "There have been reports of illegal activity in this region, but no *human* miners would have access to this kind of a nanoweapon. You should continue searching the ship. Perhaps something survived in one of the lab habitats."

"Of course," Gretchen turned back to Magdalena. The Hesht was talking Bandao and Parker through the removal of an access panel under the command display. "Maggie?"

"Just a moment. Yes, Mister Parker, use some muscle. You won't break anything. There! Now look inside."

Parker hesitated, heart rate spiking on the monitor, and his pistol and a detached lamp went first. In the dark cavity, ranks of crystalline system modules sat quietly, without showing any sign of activity.

"Still no power," Maggie grumbled to herself. "*Yausheer* Bandao, please take out a v-pad, if you have one. I will send a detailed ship schematic to you. I want you to go down to engineering and start checking the power-runs out from the batteries and fusion plant."

Parker muttered something obscene and crawled out of the access panel. Bandao said nothing. Both men kicked down the long central access passageway, gliding expertly from stanchion to stanchion, their suit lamps flaring on the white panels and dark openings onto surrounding decks.

"Koshō-*san?*" Gretchen looked across the dim, softly glowing command deck of the *Cornuelle*. "Could your Marines search the rest of the ship?"

"*Hai,*" the exec answered. "I will send another pair across to secure the bridge while Deckard and Fitzsimmons search deck by deck."

Parker grunted, putting his shoulder into a length of hexsteel pipe. The pipe extended the manual locking release on a massive pressure hatch marked with radiation warning symbols. Bandao had his helmet pressed against the metal surface, listening. The pipe squealed, the sound tinny and faint after echoing through the pilot's gloves and suit.

"Nothing," Bandao said over the open channel. "The bolts aren't backing out."

"Is there another way in?" Parker spoke to the air.

On the *Cornuelle*, Gretchen shook her head. Magdalena's entire control panel was covered with schematics showing the engineering space, the reactor cores and every crawl space, access tunnel and passage in the aft half of the *Palenque*. The Hesht's ears were twitching in frustration.

"No, Mister Parker," Gretchen said wearily, only half-listening to the men on the ship. "Lieutenant Isoroku says the reactor has gone through an emergency shutdown procedure. That hatch is the only access, and the manual lock mechanism *should work*."

"Sorry chief, there's no joy here." Parker worked the pipe free from the locking bar, and then slammed the length of metal into the hatch in frustration. There was another tinny echo. The pilot swore again, and this time he did not bother to keep his voice down. "We'll have to burn through *this door* to get to the other side. How thick is the damned thing?"

Gretchen listened to the other channel for a moment, chewing on her lip. "Too thick, Mister Parker. It's supposed to restrain the core in case of a failure."

"What do we do, then?" Bandao stood up, the pilot's lamp throwing a huge shadow behind him. "Run the ship from the batteries? We can't get at them either. Everything's through *this door*."

Gretchen sat up straight in her chair, a vague thought trying to worm free of her tired brain. "Maggie, show me the electrical connections for the hatch mechanism."

The Hesht nodded sharply and a *tap-tap* of her foreclaw zoomed a section of the schematic into full view. Gretchen hunched over the panel, fingertips brushing over the band at her wrist. A tickling feeling of clarity welled up, banishing her fatigue. She punched the schematic onto the v-channel shared by the team on the *Palenque* and the watchers on the *Cornuelle*. "Isoroku-san, do you see the display on your three?"

A muttered acknowledgement echoed over the *Cornuelle*-side channel from Engineering. The *thai-i* was down in his engine room, watching a duplicate of the video feeds in front of Gretchen. "I do. Yes, I believe such an approach would succeed. *Sho-sa* Koshō?"

"I agree," the exec said. She had her own echo of the schematics. Koshō turned to look inquiringly at the captain. Mitsuharu frowned.

"Hayes-*tzin*, threat status?" The commander was very slowly stroking his beard.

"No change, Hadeishi-*san*." The armaments officer made a sketchy bow from his position on the bridge.

"Two ratings and a work carrel," Hadeishi said, nodding to his exec. "They'll need the cargo space for the power cell."

Gretchen turned back to her panel and toggled to Parker and Bandao's channel. "Parker, an engineering crew from the *Cornuelle* will be joining you shortly with a portable fuel-cell unit." She glanced down at the diagrams. Maggie's long, claw-tipped finger slid under her arm, indicating a section of corridor. "You can speed things up, I think, if you move—ah, about five meters back down the corridor—there will be an access plate—ah, from your current vantage, overhead—marked with an engineering glyph. Remove the plate and you'll find a pair of power-runs which lead to the hatch motor—"

"Understood," Parker cut in, already moving with his length of pipe. He kicked away from the blast door and tumbled gently to fetch up near the panel. "I see it—"

Beep beep beep!

"All units, hold position!" A raspy voice barked across the shipside channel, overriding Parker's comment. Gretchen flinched back from the panel as a series of warning glyphs flashed on her display. An audible tone silenced the quiet chatter on the bridge of the *Cornuelle*. "We've found someone."

"Who is this?" Gretchen hissed at Magdalena, waving her hand at the display board. The Hesht bared her teeth in response, almost spitting, but white claws flashed and the video feeds of all the men aboard the *Palenque* leapt into view on the panel.

"This is Sergeant Fitzsimmons, Anderssen-*tzin*." The Marine's Skawts accent was very dry and controlled. On the medical feed, his heartbeat had ticked up a little, but his respiration was holding steady. "V-channel six."

"I have it," Gretchen snapped, then she froze, grasping the image being projected from the Marine's suit camera. In comparison to the quality of the video thrown by the Company suits, Fitzsimmon's transmission was as sharp as a 3v broadcast at home. "What—"

"Three bodies, ma'am," the Marine said, gliding forward, his boots making a *shhhhh-thup* sound on the deck as he moved. The muzzle of his shipgun was not pointed at the sprawled gray-and-tan shapes on the open decking in front of him, but on the dark recesses of some enormous open space. At the very edge of his camera's field of view, Gretchen caught sight of the second Marine also making a slow advance, gun at the ready. "They're wearing Company tags."

"Where are they?" Gretchen muted her throat mike, whispering to Magdalena.

"The main shuttle bay, sister." Maggie zoomed both Marine camera feeds and jacked up the ambient light amplification.

A huge space sprang into view, curving walls looming overhead and the heavy, blunt-nosed shape of a shuttle filling the darkness to the right, a pale light gleaming in the cockpit windows. Directly ahead of the two Marines, three crumpled shapes in z-suits were sprawled on the decking only a meter or two from some kind of an access hatch. Gretchen felt a creeping chill at the loose, floppy limbs of the suited bodies.

"Maggie, what is behind that hatch?" Gretchen was whispering again.

"The starboard power, data and environmental venting lines." The Hesht was distracted, staring at her displays. "Wait one, wait one . . ."

Gretchen ignored her, watching in sick fascination as Fitzsimmons advanced on the bodies, the glare of his suit light throwing them in sharp relief against the corrugated decking. The Marine paused, gun high, and gave the side of one of the helmets a soft kick with his boot. There was no sound, but the glassine helmet rolled over, revealing emptiness. The suit tag read PÂTECATL.

"The chief engineer," Magdalena said after a moment. "Pâtecatl, Susan Alexandra. Company employee, six years. Master's chief certification and engineer aboard the *Palenque* for three years."

"Sergeant, check all the suit seals." Hadeishi's voice was very calm and even over the channel. "*Sho-sa* Koshō, please halt the movement of the engineering team toward the *Palenque*."

Fitzsimmons's gloved fingertips slid back the metal plate covering the environmental controls on the empty z-suit. A row of faint green lights appeared. "Suit integrity intact, sir."

Gretchen sat back in her seat, a tiny bead of blood oozing from her lip. *Damn.*

"Check the other two," Hadeishi said in a conversational tone. "Deckard, advance to the power panel door and open the accessway. Isoroku-*san*, please observe *heicho* Deckard's suit camera."

A distant *Hai!* echoed in the silence on the bridge.

Fitzsimmons stood up, his camera view swinging to check the rest of the boat bay. Though his shipgun was still at high port, Gretchen thought the man had ceased to worry about something leaping out of the darkness at him.

"Captain Hadeishi . . ." She started to say, but the commander met her eye and shook his head slightly.

"The *Palenque* is now under level-two quarantine, Anderssen-*tzin*." He said quietly. "Something consumed the men inside those z-suits after they had a sealed environment. We must presume everyone aboard is in the same danger—indeed, they may already be exposed—and we cannot risk the *Cornuelle* as well."

"How long—" Gretchen was almost immediately interrupted by Magdalena sinking a claw into her shoulder, and Isoroku's voice grumbling over the engineering channel.

"Hadeishi-*san*, look at the feed from Deckard's suit." The engineer's voice sounded both depressed and filled with righteous anger. "Sloppy civilian contractors . . ." He muttered.

Deckard's v-feed showed the inside of the utility run, a circular space filled with the heavy blue shapes of air and water returns, the darker reddish channels of data feeds and the charred black traces of power conduit.

"What happened to this stuff?" Deckard snorted, poking at the ruin inside the utility tunnel with the tip of his rifle. "It's all burned up!"

"Stay alert, *Heicho*." Fitzsimmons's voice was very sharp on the comm, and the sergeant was almost immediately in the accessway, shining his lamp up and down the shaft. "Back up and cover the boat bay. *Thai-i* Isoroku, are you getting a good feed from my camera?"

The sergeant panned his lamps slowly over the tangled mess, letting the engineer get a good look.

On the bridge of the *Cornuelle*, the captain leaned on the arm of his chair, watching Isoroku's face twist in thought on the v-feed from engineering. "Well?"

The engineer scowled into the pickup. His bald head was shining with a faint, fine sheen of sweat. "Poor materials, Captain." A thick finger stabbed at a screen out of the field of view. "We'll need a sample, but I'll say now the material used to insulate and EM-screen the power conduits was substandard—using some kind of organic in the composite. Something the weapon attacked and stripped away." Isoroku shrugged his heavy shoulders. "The conduit temperature spiked from all the waste heat, and then the superconductors failed and power went out."

"Did conduit failure shut down the fusion plant?" Hadeishi was smoothing his beard again.

"Unlikely, *kyo*." The engineer looked off-screen. "All three of those suits have engineering cert badges on them. Perhaps the attack started on the starboard side, power started to fail unexpectedly and they started a reactor shutdown, then moved to see what was happening."

Hadeishi nodded to himself, sighing. "And fell dead on the way, consumed."

"Captain?" Gretchen had risen up in her seat, tucking one leg under. "We've found something interesting."

"Yes?"

"There are higher levels of waste products in the hangar bay," Magdalena said, her throaty voice rolling and rumbling. "Complex carbon chains, waste gases, long chain organics. The sensors on the Marines' suits are starting to pick them up. And . . ."

Hadeishi raised one eyebrow and leaned forward. "And what?"

Gretchen tapped a control on the display panel and a section of video doubled, then trebled in size. A window, glowing with light, and a shadow against a bulkhead were plain to see. "There's someone alive inside the shuttle."

"Clip on." *Gunso* Fitzsimmons tossed Deckard a monofil line tab. The corporal caught the metal hook deftly and snugged the line to his belt with the ease of long practice. Both Marines had dialed down the audio on their comm sets, so the argument on the bridge of the *Cornuelle* was reduced to a dull thunder in the background.

"Clipped," Deckard replied after testing the line. He slung the angular black shape of his shipgun over one shoulder, and adjusted his gloves, bringing magnetic surfaces around to the palms. Fitzsimmons removed the little winch from his belt and adhered the metal box to the doorframe of the power conduit accessway. "Anchored."

"Anchors away, then." Deckard grinned, white teeth visible through the faceplate of his suit. He kicked off from the wall and sailed across the boat bay. As he approached the nose of the shuttle, the Marine tucked in his feet and rolled. Now feet first, he slipped past the window and reached out with both hands. The gloves slipped along the pitted, rusted surface of the shuttle, then slid to a halt.

"Quietly now," Fitzsimmons breathed over the combat channel. "Show me what's inside." Deckard spidered up to the forward window of the shuttle and paused just out of sight of anyone inside. Tugging one of his shoulder cameras free, the marine eased the filament up to the edge of the window. The sergeant, watching the spyeye view on a tiny, postage-stamp sized popup inside his helmet, made a scooting motion with his hand. "Just a hair more . . ."

Then he could see inside the cluttered, dirty cockpit of the shuttle, and—through the pressure door into the main cabin—two people sitting on facing piles of bedding. As he watched, the man tossed a playing card onto a pile between himself and the woman. Moisture was dripping from the walls of the shuttle, and the sergeant made a face. *Mold? They're certainly alive. Not disintegrated at all. . . .*

Taking a breath, Fitzsimmons dialed up the volume on his comm.

". . . the ship is entirely safe," Gretchen said, again, her voice rising slightly. "We've had men aboard for two hours and no one has been affected, there are waste gases loose in the boat bay, and they have not been destroyed—"

Hadeishi, his patience fraying—though only the sergeant or one of the crew would have been able to tell—interrupted. "Doctor Anderssen, I will not put my men, or my ship, at risk. Until we know exactly what happened and why, I will not put another man or woman aboard the *Palenque*."

"Ah, sir? Hadeishi-*san?*" Fitzsimmons made a face in the privacy of his suit. Luckily, the cameras only pointed forward, not at his grinning mug. "*Chu-sa?*"

"Hai, *Gunso?*"

"There are at least two people alive inside the shuttle, sir. They've been there quite awhile. Shall I go aboard and see what they know?"

"No," Hadeishi said, a slight edge in his voice. "If the contaminant is still loose on the *Palenque*, you'll only place them in danger. Hook up your exterior comm to the shuttle's data port and talk to them that way."

One of the other channels carried a muffled voice, and Fitzsimmons realized Anderssen-*tzin*'s voice channel had been muted from the command deck.

"Aye, aye, sir." Fitzsimmons signaled to Deckard, then took two long, bounding steps to reach the shuttle's airlock. The corporal walked sideways down the hull to meet him, spooling up the monofil as he went. "Time for first contact, Corporal. Undog the comm port cover, would you?"

"We don't really know what happened. They just fell over, you know, and we couldn't raise anyone on the ship-to-ship comm channel."

Gretchen suppressed a sigh, staring at two grimy faces framed by the shuttle's v-cam. On her left, security team crewman Carlos Fuentes' bearded visage stared out at her with sick desperation. Beside him, nose screwed up in a grimace, her entire body turned away from Fuentes, crewwoman Delores Flores seemed equally despondent.

"Tell me what you saw," Gretchen said, again. "From the beginning."

"Well, ah . . ." Carlos groped for the proper words.

"Shut up, idiot," Delores said, pushing him out of the field of view. "I'll tell you, ma'am. We've been having problems with the shuttle engines since we arrived," the crewwoman began. "After five or six trips down to the base camp, they started showing warning lights in the afterburner and air intake ducts. Finally, shuttle two refused to power up groundside—claimed the engine would overheat. So we took number one down to base camp and pulled the entire engine assembly out of number two." She jerked her thumb over one shoulder. Something large and bulky, wrapped with shockfoam and cables, filled most of the cargo space on the shuttle.

"We brought up Doc Clarkson at the same time—he was in a big hurry! And Doctor McCue—she wasn't in such a hurry. They went upstairs, but we were working down here to prep this bastard to unload."

"Did anyone else ride up with you? Did you close the airlock after Clarkson and McCue left the shuttle?" Gretchen was chewing on the stub end of a pointing stylus.

"Always!" Delores nodded sharply, waving her hand off to one side. "Standard procedure. The bay doors are airtight, but the boat bay is considered an unsecured environment. You lock in and out of the bay, or the shuttles when they're aboard. And it was just those two. No one else wanted to ride up with them, not when they were in such a mood!"

"When did you notice something was wrong on the ship?"

"An alarm went off shipside," Delores said. "We heard the horn go off and I ran into the cockpit. Carlos—" The crewwoman's lip twisted slightly "—called the bridge. We heard some noise, some shouting for maybe thirty seconds, and then nothing." She pointed off toward the front of the shuttle. "Then the lock cycled and engineer Pâtecatl and two others ran into the bay. I called on the comm, and she said something was attacking the ship. Then she made sort of a choking noise, we saw a hot glow inside their helmets—and all three of them fell over."

"And then?" Gretchen frowned at the ragged plastic end of her stylus.

"They didn't move. We couldn't get anyone on the ship-to-ship channel." Delores shrugged. "The bay doors were closed, and we couldn't get them open by remote. We didn't dare go outside, not with three people dead in suits right in front of our eyes. With the shuttle parked inside the bay, we couldn't even raise groundside on the comm. So we've been waiting for weeks, hoping something would happen. Something good, I mean." She ventured a smile. "Can we get out of this tin can now and get a shower?"

"You can have a *bath* when we get you out," Gretchen promised with a smile. "But right now we have to figure out *how* to get you out of there safely. I'll call you back in a moment."

She shut down the channel, then turned to face Hadeishi. The captain and Lieutenant Koshō were talking, heads close together, at the exec's display board. "Captain Hadeishi?"

"Yes, Anderssen-*tzin*?" He seemed tense, and she knew he was bracing for another argument about the quarantine.

"I would like to transfer my crew and supplies—and the loan of a fuel cell, if you will—to the *Palenque*."

For a moment, Hadeishi said nothing, staring at her with narrowed eyes. At his side, the lieutenant allowed herself the ghost of a smile. Then the captain visibly shook himself and nodded.

"You're sure of your analysis? Sure enough to risk yourself and your team?"

"Yes," Gretchen said in a firm voice. *Oh lord, I hope so! But we can't just sit here for weeks. Every day burns away at our nonexistent budget and our tiny little bonuses.*

"Very well." Hadeishi glanced at his exec, who had stepped down to her own board, attention already focused on her lading schedules, thin rose-colored lips moving silently. "Koshō-*sana*, we will leave Sergeant Fitzsimmons and Corporal Deckard aboard as a, ah, loan to Anderssen-*tzin* and her group. For the moment. After the quarantine period has passed, we will want them back." The captain raised an eyebrow at Gretchen, who smiled in relief.

"Thank you," she said, making a heartfelt bow.

"Please don't damage my crewmen," Hadeishi responded on his private channel. "Good luck."

"There is one more thing. . . ." Gretchen felt her stomach clench, knowing she was probably overstepping the bounds of hospitality. "If you could loan us an engineer's mate, I think we could get the power plant on the *Palenque* working again."

Hadeishi frowned. Gretchen kept her face impassive. The captain looked sideways, listening. He frowned again and said something into his throat mike. While Anderssen watched, the captain argued momentarily with someone, then gave up.

"*Sho-sa* Isoroku will be joining you on the *Palenque*," Hadeishi said in a tight voice.

Gretchen must have shown some of her astonishment openly. "I see."

"He," Hadeishi continued in a colorless tone, "wishes to see the damage caused by this weapon for himself. I believe he desires to submit a technical paper to the Fleet Engineering College on Mars. You should get ready to move your equipment."

Gretchen nodded again, in thanks, then began gathering up the v-pads, writing styluses and other bric-a-brac which had accumulated around the secondary weapons station. Magdalena was still hunched over her board, watching the feeds from the various suit cameras.

"I'll see you downstairs," Gretchen said, thumping the Hesht on one furry shoulder.

"Ya-ha," Maggie answered absently. "Be there in a bit."

The main lock of the *Palenque* cycled and Gretchen stepped through into a dark, echoing passage. A string of fading glowbeans cast the main access corridor in twilight, each shining dot throwing a circle of solemn blue-green light. She looked down at the enviro readouts on her arm—everything shone a friendly green—and she stepped aside to let Lieutenant Isoroku drag the battery pack into the ship. Magdalena followed, swimming through the opening with a flotilla of duffels, gearboxes and tools floating around her.

"You going to the command deck?" Gretchen lifted her chin in question. The Hesht shook her head.

"No, down to Engineering first. If we can get the hatch to the control compartment open we'll restart the ship's main comp before we try to bring up the reactor core. What about you?"

"I'm going to wander around," Gretchen said, looking at the readouts on her arm again. "The lab ring, I think. Keep channel four open." She looked over to Isoroku. "Lieutenant, could you use someone familiar with the ship systems?"

"Hai . . ." he answered dubiously.

Gretchen clicked her teeth, changing comm channel. "Sergeant Fitzsimmons, could you tell Miss Flores to suit up and go to Engineering? Lieutenant Isoroku will be waiting for her." She paused, listening. "I don't believe the ship is infected anymore, Sergeant. You and Corporal Deckard are proof of that, at least in my eyes. We would all be dead by now if the weapon remained active on-board."

There was an affirmative grunt on the channel and Gretchen smiled at the lieutenant.

"Crewwoman Flores will be along presently. Good luck—I'd love to see some light and heat in here."

Gretchen followed the battery pack—guided by Isoroku with a clever little hand-held gas-jet unit—down two main decks, then swung out of the access shaft to let her boots adhere to the doorframe of a large, doublewide portal labeled XA LAB ONE. The pressure hatch was closed, and she swore silently to herself. *Of course it's closed. Everything is.*

Feeling foolish, she found the manual locking bar and—straining to keep her feet wedged against the bulkhead for leverage—managed to crank the hatch open enough to get her suit through. On the other side, she paused, staring at the opening. Her arms were sore, but part of her brain was making a frightened sound. *I might have to flee back this way. . . .*

"No," she said aloud, though her throat mike was muted. "No I won't."

Dialing her suit lamps to a more diffuse illumination, Gretchen pushed off gently and made her way forward through the ring. After a few minutes, she pulled herself up short, staring through a thick oval window into the next lab. The hatch was closed tight, the chamber dark, but the fragmentary light of her suit lamps picked out the shape of a clean-box with something bulky inside. Some kind of debris was scattered on the deck, and there was a subtle sense of disorder among the white and steel surfaces.

Someone working on something when the disaster overcame them?

"Damn." The hatch was sealed, the pressure seals closed. The chamber had no manual lock—indeed, a heat-distorted label declared the space beyond a "secured environment." Gretchen clicked her mike on. "Maggie? How long until we have power?"

There was no answer. Gretchen froze, listening to the warble of static and an intermittent, distant pinging sound. Suppressing a cold shiver of fear, she changed channel again. "Anderssen to the *Cornuelle*, come in please."

There was still no answer, but—obscurely—Gretchen was a little relieved. *Something's blocking my suit comm*, she thought. *Of course.*

Only slightly less apprehensive, she made her way back to the access shaft, pushing away from the handholds set into the ceiling and floor. Squeezing through the hatchway, she breathed a sigh of relief to hear channel four wake to life with Maggie and Delores chatting amiably while they worked.

"Magdalena? How long until we have power?"

The Hesht made a coughing sound—laughter—then said: "We haven't opened the door to Engineering yet, but we're close. One of the hatch motors burned out and Isoroku is replacing the mechanism. So I'd say another hour, at least."

"Thank you." Gretchen muted the channel, staring around at the cold darkness filling the ship. The main accessway seemed bottomless, even with a receding line of glowbeans shining in the dimness. Somehow the faint little pools of light only made the gloom seem more encompassing and complete. Disheartened, she sat down, swinging her boots over the shaft. "I guess I'll just wait, then."

After an endless minute, she pulled a v-pad from the cargo pocket of her suit and thumbed it awake. *Might as well get some work done*, she thought glumly. *So something got loose in the ship, something which must have propagated through the air, a gas or vapor—how else could it move so fast and be unseen? Air is easy to penetrate, permeates most everything. An aerosol of some kind . . .* She called up the ship schematics Magdalena had been using to follow the power and utility conduits. Her pad still held the modeling and time-regression software she'd used on Ugarit, which could understand the volume of the ship, the rooms and chambers, even the lack of organic artifacts.

Just like a site abandoned so long all the organics have decayed away, she thought after thirty minutes. *Hmm . . . that's a good lab exercise for first-years.*

Steadily brightening light broke her concentration, and she looked up to see the pilot scooting up the shaft toward her. A little embarrassed, she tucked the v-pad away. "How goes, Mister Parker?"

"Good," he answered, cheerful humor returned. "Engineering is open, and Isoroku's got his battery hooked up. Looks like the ship's fuel cells still have some juice, though Environmental was still working for awhile after the accident. Magdalena's starting up the comp from local power. I'm heading for the bridge to check the relays and get the main comm array running."

Gretchen smiled. "Good. What about main power?"

Parker waggled his hand ambivalently, inducing a slow spin. "No promises there. Isoroku wants to check every centimeter of the reactor to make sure nothing got eaten away by our little friend. Can't say I blame him."

"No, I suppose not." Gretchen rose, one hand clinging to a railing surrounding the hatchway. "If power comes back up, I'll want you to unlock the hatches in the lab habitat for me. Don't open them, though. I'll take care of that."

Parker nodded, then kicked off, flying up into the darkness, his helmet haloed by the flare of his lamps. Gretchen watched him go, feeling the darkness close around her again. Her suit was starting to smell, even with only a couple hours inside. *Just like on Ugarit. Maybe the showers will work,* she thought hopefully. Then she realized all the towels on board would have been disintegrated and she was depressed again.

The wall against Gretchen's back trembled and her eyes flew open. For a moment, she was disoriented—she'd fallen asleep listening to the hum of the fans in her suit—and saw only darkness sprinkled with faint lights above her. *I'm outside?*

Then she looked down the main shaft and saw a ring of lights flare on—a section of overheads a hundred feet away, near the ring hub into Engineering—then another and another. Gretchen stood up, grabbing hold of the nearest handhold, and the wave of lights washed over her. The deck continued to tremble, echoing the sound of a distant power plant turning over.

"Backup power is up in Engineering," Magdalena growled in her ear. "Some of the emergency lights are on. I'm starting the heat exchangers and air circulation."

Gretchen swung into the lab ring and crabbed down to the first tier of labs. Puzzled, she stared around—the lights were still out—then they flickered on, one by one, casting a steady daylight radiance. She blinked and her helmet polarized slightly. In the clear light, the stark emptiness of the work cubicles and rooms was even more striking.

All gone, everyone's work destroyed, she thought sadly, shuffling up the curve of the lab ring. *Anything they didn't note down on comp—lost forever.* She reached the sealed doorway to the clean room and looked inside. Here, most of the lights were still off, but two spots shone inside the containment chamber. A rust-red and ochre cylinder stood in a stainless steel cradle, anachronous and startling with irregular chips and flakes of stone amid the clean, smooth lines of the laboratory. Gretchen swallowed. The artifact—what else could it be?—was sectioned, cut clean in half as by a surgical beam. A metal-clad emitter ring hung poised above the cylinder, distended from an equipment pod. She guessed the cut was very narrow, perhaps only a millimeter across.

She started to sweat again, and the fans spun up in the suit, trying to keep her temperature constant. Reflexively, she looked down, checking the pressure seal on the door. With power returned, the panel showed three green lights and one red. She blinked.

The door seal failed. Oh god. Gretchen stepped back, and then stopped, gritting her teeth. *Too late now, too late weeks ago. Whatever was inside escaped, ate through the containment pod, through the door seals, right out into the ship.* She unclenched her hands and stared at the door. Adrenaline hissed in her blood, making her arms tremble.

After a long moment, she clicked her mike open. "Magdalena, are you busy right now?"

A growl answered, and a string of curses. Gretchen smiled, though the motion felt strange. "Yes, sister, I can wait. I'm in lab ring one. Take your time."

Gretchen sucked the last of a threesquare from her food tube and stood up as Magdalena and Bandao drifted down into the lab ring. The Hesht was still surrounded by a cloud of tools and cargo bags, but the gunner seemed to have accumulated some of the bulkier items.

"What's our status?" Gretchen asked, catching Maggie's paw and drawing her to a stop on the deck. Magdalena yawned in response, showing an ebon mouth filled with white teeth. Her fur was rumpled and one ear lay flat back against her head while the other was canted forward.

"All we have is *sssrst-ta*—tail feathers," the Hesht snarled. "Fuel cell power is up, main comp is up, the main reactor is still down, and we're lacking power in most of the ship." A gloved paw flexed and Gretchen noticed the Hesht's z-suit was fitted with a flexible metal mesh to accommodate extended claws. The fine mail glistened like fish scales. "Isoroku-*san* thinks this tangle-tailed weapon chewed up most of the power conduit runs. Some survived, so we have lights in the main core and some sections, but everything replaced three maintenance cycles ago is gone."

Gretchen wrinkled her nose. "Bad parts?"

Maggie nodded. "The repair logs show they swapped out most of the original conduit for new two years ago, as part of a systems upgrade. The new conduit was supposed to have a higher load tolerance, so they replaced all of the high-draw lines with this *yherech-kwlll*—pardon—inferior product. So the lights are on, some comp panels are up, but most of the hatches don't work, and the drives are offline, along with sensors, weapons, and the boat bay doors."

"Okay." Gretchen stared at the hatch into the clean room. "What about this one?"

Maggie shrugged. "The lights are on, try it."

Gretchen took a breath, nodded abruptly and stepped to the door. Then she stopped, unwilling to touch the controls. She felt Bandao and Maggie staring at her and became aware of the man's shipgun, raised and pointing past her at the door. A smile twitched her lips. *Instinct! Danger in the high grass! As if his gun will stop this thing, if it's still in there.* Her forefinger stabbed the button and the hatch trembled. A motor whirred—the sound audible even through her suit insulation—and the heavy steel recessed, then drew up into an overhead panel.

There were bits and pieces of metal and ceramic scattered on the deck. Gretchen recognized the metal inserts from the soles of a pair of dig boots much like her own. The deck surface was a dark, irregular metal, and she realized the usual nonskid coating had been destroyed. She padded across the deck, giving a wide berth to the tumbled parts of a belt, a pen, a scratched and dented v-pad. Her eye shied away from two irregular shining white pebbles. *Someone's teeth. I didn't need to see that,* she thought fiercely.

The comp panel running the isolation chamber had power, but had gone through an abrupt shutdown. Gretchen studied the glyphs for a moment, then tapped in RESTART and RESUME. Magdalena leaned in at her side, staring into the chamber.

"These are the seal status indicators?" The Hesht ran a metal-sheathed claw across a line of winking red glyphs. Gretchen nodded, watching the system start up. The panel seemed sluggish, and one pane displayed a constant list of init errors. Magdalena hissed. "Sloppy work. The entire seal is gone. Why don't they make them of solid metal or ceramic?"

Gretchen shrugged, concentrating on getting the panel operative again. "Company probably bought from the low bidder. Here we go . . ."

A v-feed opened on the panel, showing the interior of the isolation chamber and the rocky, corroded-looking cylinder. Gretchen slid a control down, and the image rewound with a flash, ending with a similar image, though now the cylinder was intact and the lighting slightly different.

"Replay," Gretchen muttered, finding the glyph for movement-returning-to-the-source and tapping the stylized warrior in a loincloth holding two reeds crowned with white fluff. ". . . with audio overlay." Another tap, and a timer began to run in one corner of the image.

For a moment there was no sound and Gretchen frowned. Magdalena laughed softly and her claw-tip danced across a series of controls. An excited male voice suddenly filled Gretchen's helmet comm.

"...on day six-flint-knife, in the month of Offering Flowers, an artifact described by image log seven-seven-two was recovered from the surface of Ephesus Three with some assistance from Miss Russovsky, a post-doc performing a routine geophysical survey of the planet. This is the first artifact we have found which is of an obvious and patently manufactured origin." There was a throaty, satisfied laugh, and Gretchen's nostrils flared. She decided she did not like the speaker, whoever he was. *Assistance? You mean this Russovsky found the damned thing and brought it to you like a good little student—or did you take it from her?*

"Initial analysis shows a metallic cylinder surrounded by a matrix of sedimentary rock. The encrusting mixture is of interest, indicating the cylinder lay in mud or clay. Preliminary isotopic decay readings suggest an age for the matrix of nearly three million years." The laugh came again, and this time there was a sense of relief in the voice. "This places the artifact well within the timeframe of known First Sun activities."

Gretchen felt the cold chill flood back into her stomach. *What a fool!*

"Doctor McCue has suggested that we isolate the artifact and send it back to the Company labs for more extensive examination, but I believe it is safer and more prudent for us to make an initial survey here, aboard the ship." The voice settled, becoming pedantic and measured.

"She suggests the object may be dangerous, but if so, would it not be wiser to examine the artifact here—far from inhabited space? Any violent event would then affect only this one ship, and of course, myself. A loss, to be sure, but far better than losing Mars or Novoya Rossiya!"

Gretchen shook her head in amazement at the man's ego. She could feel him thinking, even through the distance of the recording, and he was so, so eager to see what was inside the cylinder. Any real thought of caution or wariness was entirely disregarded.

"Luckily," the voice continued, "the limestone matrix does not interfere with most of our sensors here in the lab. I am going to try a low-power microwave scan first, just to see what the exterior really looks like. . . ."

A succession of images unfolded—the cylinder's crusted surface was mapped, showing each ridge and bump and crevice in the stone—then the cylinder itself, a smooth metal tube, closed seamlessly at each end. There were no markings or signs on the outside of the metal, or at least none shown by the initial scans.

"I am initiating a low power intrusive scan, to see if the surface is permeable to x-ray."

Gretchen forced herself not to flinch as an emitter ring descended and began a pass along the length of the cylinder. At her side, she felt Maggie stiffen, and Bandao mutter: "Idiot—what if it's a booby trap, or a bomb?"

The image of the cylinder on the v-pane did not react, and a second image replaced the first. A murky picture showing the outlines of the limestone matrix, a metallic shell—very thin—and then a cavity within.

"Odd," echoed the voice from the past. "Half of the tube is solid, half empty. Wait—perhaps the solid half is only very dense . . ."

The image zoomed, focusing in, and zoomed again, revealing a dense, interlocking system of membranes and fluted, intertwined protrusions.

"Looks like a lung," Bandao said, staring sideways at the display.

"Some kind of structure," the voice continued, "very, very dense. The separations between the *alveoli*-like structures are barely measurable. Yet they exist. Hmmm . . . an information storage structure? Could this be a book?"

Gretchen had to suppress a start; the hard, dry voice of Green Hummingbird was whispering in her memory. *A book? Or some other storage media?* The man's voice started to trend upward, filling with a rush of excitement.

"It must be a book," greed dripped into his voice. "Or a visual storage mechanism. Ah, what a prize that would be! But how is it accessed?" The image shifted to focus on the empty half of the cylinder. "And what is this space for? Why use only half of the container? Hmmm . . . perhaps the empty half is not exactly empty?"

A glyph appeared in one corner of the recording, showing the visual feed was switching to a different sensor. Gretchen squinted at the icon, but didn't recognize the symbol. "What's that?" she asked.

"Super-shortwave sensor," Bandao answered with a slight hesitation, face tense. "It interpolates to sub-x-ray definition for medical use—but he's a fool to use a high power probe on this thing."

". . . beginning scan," the recording announced. The image tightened, flashed blank, then focused again. The "empty" half of the tube was momentarily revealed as a murky soup of tiny spinning particles, then the image jerked, the tube split in half and there was a warning whoop of sound from the recording. Then everything went black and the panel beeped quietly, indicating the end of the image file.

"Well," Gretchen said after a moment. "I guess you should have been here, Mister Bandao."

The gunner shook his head, his face a tight mask. "I'm not disappointed to come late. If I had been here before, I would have put the bastard down."

With that, Bandao left, swinging angrily out of the lab and bounding off up the ring toward the main accessway. Gretchen watched him go, but said nothing, and did not call him back. Instead, she turned to Maggie and said: "Can you make this panel play back the last part frame by frame?"

The Hesht coughed in amusement, her claws dancing across the display controls.

Sighing with relief, Gretchen thumbed the release mechanisms for her helmet and heard a sharp *click* as they retracted. Fresh, chill air bathed her face. The ship would be cold for hours yet, until hot air streaming from the heaters permeated all compartments. Then it would be too hot until the environmentals adjusted themselves. She sat down—in something like real gravity—and tugged the helmet free from the z-suit. Parker, sitting across the table in the crew common area, slid a cup of fresh, hot coffee to her.

"There's some creamer, but no milk," he said.

"Thank you. Black is fine." The cup was very warm in her hands. Three sugar packets from a pocket of her z-suit disappeared into the oily black liquid. She took a long swallow, feeling warmth flood her chest. "Better," she said after finishing the cup. "Better. Are the Lieutenant and Flores still down in Engineering?"

Magdalena nodded, her attention focused on sucking pale red fluid and chunks of raw meat from a mealbag.

Gretchen studiously kept her eyes away from the Hesht dinner. "Mister Parker, do we have flight control and comm up?"

"Sort of," the pilot said, putting down his cup. "Attitude controls are mostly working, though there are still miles of conduit to replace for the main engines. Luckily, the fine control jets use compressed air and need only on/off signals to operate. They work fine—since they're mechanical. Navigation is up, and we *have* lost some planetary altitude, so when we do have engines live again I need to make an adjustment burn to put us back in the proper orbital. We have spin in this hab ring, but not the others. Main comp is up, so you have shipboard comm and info retrieval—if you can find a working display."

He turned toward Magdalena, who was squeezing the mealbag in one paw, making thick goo ooze into her open mouth. Parker jerked back toward Gretchen. "Ah . . . we've found the experimental transmitter, which is on its own fuel cell system, but I haven't messed with it. The cat can do that later, I guess. The main comm array is down until we rebuild power, but we're close enough to the *Cornuelle* that our suit radios still work."

"Unless you're in the labs," Gretchen commented, "which are shielded."

"What did you find down there?" Parker stole a glance at Bandao, who was sitting with his own cup in his hands, content to say nothing. The two Marines were equally quiet and unobtrusive, sitting back from the edge of the table. Out of his combat suit, Fitzsimmons was of medium height, very fit, with broad shoulders and curly blue-black hair. Deckard was thinner, with a lanky build and a ruddy complexion. Carlos, still looking miserable, sat beside Parker, slowly chewing on his thumb. "Did you find the . . . weapon?"

"Yes." Gretchen drained her cup and set it down on the spotlessly clean table-top. "One of the scientists working on the planet—a geologist named Russovsky—found some stone cylinders in one of the canyons on the big mountain range. She brought an artifact back to base camp and showed her find to Doctor McCue, the dig supervisor. I think—not from anything said in record, but hearing between the lines—the lead archaeologist, a man named Clarkson, then took the cylinder from McCue and returned to the ship."

Gretchen looked down at the table, finding a ring of coffee-colored condensation where her warm cup had stood on the cold metal. She squeaked her finger through the liquid, drawing a line down the middle of the circle.

"Clarkson tried to see what was inside the cylinder with a high-powered sensor. Half of the tube seemed to be empty—but it wasn't, not really. Half seemed to be filled with a tightly packed membrane, like the filaments lining a human lung. The lab's isotope decay analysis estimates the cylinder is almost three million years old." A sharp, short laugh escaped her. "Clarkson was pretty sure the device wasn't working anymore, or if it was, it was a kind of *book* or information storage device, like a 3v pack. Well, he was right, in a way."

Her finger slashed across the circle of moisture.

"His probe injected enough energy into the empty chamber to make a sort of gas of very, very small particles expand violently. A thin wall between the two chambers broke down and the gas flooded into the membranes within a fraction of a second. They mixed, violently, and the cylinder broke open."

"A binary round," grunted Fitzsimmons, his brown eyes gleaming in the darkness. "But not the usual sort of explosion, I suppose."

"No." Gretchen shook her head ruefully. "The gaslike particles, I think, were some kind of tiny nanomachines. They dissolved the membranes—destroyed them—but at the same time they learned a pattern from the arrangement of the filaments. In less than a second, they were *trained* and they acquired enough raw material to duplicate themselves. Pressure expanded . . ."

Three fingers stabbed into the circle and swirled the last fragments of moisture out into an unsightly blotch on the tabletop.

"The weapon was released from its container and into the atmosphere." Gretchen sighed. "Clarkson had failed to evacuate the examination chamber, which ordinarily would not have been a problem, but in this case the waste gases in the unit atmosphere were fuel for more nanomachines. I'm pretty sure the machines ignore plain atomic components—O and N and so on—but they chew up CO_2 for lunch, and any kind of long-chain molecule in their attack pattern for dinner. Pressure built in the chamber, and the eaters reached the pressure seals.

"If the Company had not purchased second rate containment pods," Gretchen continued, "the eaters would have been contained. Their programming did not happen to include the stainless steel forming most of the pod walls. Unfortunately, a flexible sealant forming the join between the instrument package and the main unit was composed of long-chain polymers which were on the 'menu.'

"They escaped into the power and data conduit above the containment unit. The sheathing of the power cables gave them more food, allowing them to reproduce at an exceptionally rapid rate. I would guess, from the cut-off time of the recording unit, that they dropped power in the lab ring within sixty seconds of escape, and had penetrated into the starboard side of the ship within two minutes. Less than ten meters away is the starboard power coupling beside the boat bay. As the wave front propagated, power collapsed, and the engineering team—who had no idea, I imagine, that Doctor Clarkson was even aboard—started an emergency shutdown of the grid.

"Within five minutes, everyone on the starboard side of the ship was dead. The engineers, who had suited up on the run, will have run right through the weapon cloud without even noticing anything. Then, by the time they reached the boat bay, the eaters would have reproduced inside their suits . . . and you saw the result."

"Wait a moment." Fitzsimmons leaned forward, his tanned forehead creased in thought. "What happened to the eaters after they filled the ship?"

"They ate themselves." Gretchen looked around for something to clean up the puddle, then grimaced. *No rags. There are no rags.* "The last of their programming broke them apart when there was nothing left to consume. All they left was a cloud of component elements."

"And what happened to that?" Fitzsimmons looked mildly disgusted.

Gretchen nodded toward the rear of the ship. "Most of it will have been circulated into the air purification system, which continued to run on backup power while it detected impurities in the air supply. But when the cloud was processed, there was nothing but pure air left, and the system shut down automatically. The rest will have collected here and there, as grainy white dust—"

Parker suddenly snorted, coughing and spraying coffee across the conference table. He made a horrible face as he turned to Gretchen. "You mean this isn't nondairy creamer?"

Her ears covered with a thick cap of New Aberdeen cashmere, z-suit helmet parked on the display panel, Gretchen leaned back in a chair reduced to metal strips in the lab ring control cube. Curving hallways lined with hatches stretched up to her left and right. Light from the lab holding the broken cylinder spilled out into the hall. It was still very cold—the heaters in the lab spaces had failed to turn on with the rest—and Gretchen's breath puffed white as she hummed to herself.

On the display—only half of which was working—v-panes were running, speeding through the day of the accident. A crewman wandered through one feed, eating pine nuts from a bag, then out of one frame and into another. Mostly she watched empty rooms and quiet machinery idling in standby. All of the scientists were down on the planet, working at the main camp. Gretchen sighed, bored, and speeded up the replay.

Almost immediately, blurred figures appeared and she dialed back ten minutes. "Finally!"

A tall, lean man with a neat beard and field jacket swung down from the hab access tube, landing heavily in the partial gravity. His hair was silvered, with a few streaks of black remaining, and he was wearing a heavy pair of sunglasses. A battered, grimy fieldpack, bulging with a heavy weight burdened narrow shoulders.

"Doctor Clarkson—coming home with his prize," Gretchen murmured, keenly interested, watching the man hurry into the number one isolation lab. A moment later, a woman entered the lab ring by the same tube. Her tied-back hair was long, orange-red and very curly. She was also dressed in field kit, with a pocket-covered vest, sunglasses perched on her forehead and linen pants tucked into her boots. "And our mathematician in residence, Doctor McCue."

Gretchen felt a pang, seeing such familiar-looking people. She'd never met either of them, though the faces matched the briefing materials provided by the Company. But they felt so much like her friends on Ugarit, or the other graduate students and professors at the university. *And now they're gone, rendered down for Parker's nondairy creamer.*

She ignored Clarkson in his lab, following McCue from camera to camera as the woman wound her way through the maze of cubicles and rooms. The mathematician was pushing a g-box in front of her, a dented steel case with a built-in anti-grav, controlled by a hand unit. On the far side of the lab ring from the main control station, she stopped in front of a heavy reinforced hatchway.

Gretchen sat up, puzzled. She'd walked through the whole ring . . . she hadn't noticed a *security* door. But McCue's image punched in a keycode and the heavy blast door swung up and away, revealing a specimen vault and a bit of a room filled with racks of bins and cargo crates stacked on the floor. Then the door closed, and she was left with a nice picture of the hatchway.

"Well. What does Doctor McCue have in her box, which was so valuable it went straight to the vault?"

She advanced the recording, flipping ahead ten minutes. No change. Then she blinked—a smoky haze swept down the corridor, flames leaping from empty air. The flooring blackened and warning lights began to flash. Lighting in the hallway flickered, then failed. Gretchen tasted bile, knowing what had to happen next.

The hatchway cycled up, and Doctor McCue stepped out, alarm clear in her round, freckled face. She started to call out, raising her left arm—the shining band of a comm winked in the remaining light. Gretchen bit her lip, teeth clenched tight. A cloud of gray coalesced out of the air and McCue staggered, throwing up her hand uselessly. Her clothing vanished in sudden flame, burning away with frightening speed, then her flesh sloughed away into nothing, and there was a flash of bone and red meat.

The gray-and-black cloud lingered for a moment, then dispersed in a drifting cloud of white dust and bits and pieces of metal scattered on the floor. The hatchway remained open for a moment, and Gretchen could see the edge of the g-box, then the door rumbled closed, cutting off the vault lights, plunging the hallway into darkness.

Video replay ended with a *ping* and a motion-ceasing glyph.

"That's a hard thing to watch," rumbled a voice at Gretchen's shoulder. Sergeant Fitzsimmons was standing beside her, his black Marine z-suit blending into the dimness of the room. He had a bundle in his hands. "Sorry to bother you, ma'am, but I thought you might need something for the cold." He grinned. "But that's a prettier hat than I had in my ruck. I like the . . . ah . . . reindeer?"

"Oh." Gretchen touched the thick, felty plush of the cap on her head. "My mum makes them for all the kids," she said, tugging at the brightly-colored, shapeless mass. "Thank you for the thought, Sergeant. But Ugarit had its own bad weather, and Mars was bitterly cold. I've plenty of warm things."

Gretchen managed a smile, thinking of trudging across the brittle, rocky permafrost to the Polaris site, stiff in a triply-insulated z-suit and respirator. The Marine had a gray-green service wool cap and a pair of gloves, also a foul olive color, in his hands. *Good enough for our slowly heating ship*, she thought with a hidden frown, *but not good enough to keep your hands and ears attached on Mars.*

"Good," he said, stuffing the cap and gloves into a cargo pouch on the front of his suit. "Do you need help getting that vault door open?"

Gretchen started to shake her head—she had a video of McCue's keycode—but then realized refusing the offer might be rude. *Might need a big, brawny Marine sometime.* She stood up, snugging the sherpa cap under her ears. "Thanks," she said, "I don't think there'll be any trouble, but you never know. . . ."

The vault door proved to be hidden behind a standard wall panel. Gretchen supposed the panel had slid down automatically during the power failure. Fitzsimmons's combat bar made a suitable lever to pop the panel free from the floor, and then he rolled it up with one hand. The vault hatch was closed, and Gretchen stepped in—lips pursed in concern—to find the keypad in ruins. All of the pressure surfaces had eroded away, leaving only a contact panel and some pitlike holes where wires, perhaps, had once run.

"This is just fine!" Gretchen rapped the panel without result.

"Ma'am, let me try," the Marine waited politely until Gretchen stepped away, then drew a v-pad from his belt, unfolded a set of waxy-looking stems from the back and—humming softly to himself—matched them up with the holes. After a moment the v-pad beeped and the schematic of a keypad appeared on its glassy face. "Try this," Fizsimmons said, suppressing a pleased grin.

Gretchen tapped in the code recorded by the surveillance cameras. The vault door made a *chuff* sound, then rolled silently away into the overhead. The vault room was entirely dark. "Very handy," she said, handing the device back to the sergeant.

"We try," he said in a particularly dry tone, flicking a glowbean against the far wall. "Sister bless, do they make such a mess all the time?"

Gretchen stepped into a crowded room, now lit by a pervasive blue glow. Doctor McCue's g-box was sitting on the deck amid a wild jumble of straw-shaped mineral core samples. She stepped carefully around the striated tubes—most had broken apart, leaving a wash of grit and sand on the floor—and picked up the controller for the g-box. It hummed to life, and the box lifted up and drifted to an empty section of deck.

"No," Gretchen said absently, "the core samples will have been in packing material and a cargo crate—they're just stiffened cellulose and a sealant—very tasty, I imagine." She keyed the box to open, and the top latch released with a *clank*. Kneeling, she lifted the lid and shone her hand lamp inside.

"Oh, now . . ." She let out a long, low whistle of surprise. "That is beautiful."

Warily, Fitzsimmons leaned over. Inside the box was a chunk of stone—perhaps half a meter long and ten centimeters thick—a deep sandy red streaked with cream, glowing in the light of Anderssen's lamp. Gretchen brushed a fine layer of sandstone dust away, revealing a handsbreadth-wide whorl. A tapered tail of ribbed shell curled around the impression of stalklike legs.

"See, Sergeant? The fruit of some ancient Ephesian sea, preserved by chance in sandy mud, along with our . . . friend."

Most of the fossil was buried in the stone, and lying alongside the ancient cephalopod was the unmistakable shape of a machined metal cylinder. Like the artifact in the isolation lab, the cylinder was crusted with limestone aggregate.

Gretchen bit her lip gently, tracing the outline of the device with a gloved finger. "Russovsky's geological survey found wonders."

Fitzsimmons stood up, his face pale. "Ma'am—I know you won't like to hear this—but we should jettison this thing right away. What if it goes off like the other one?"

Gretchen looked up, face pinched with distaste. In that moment, she suddenly knew exactly how Clarkson had felt, clutching the prize close to his chest, rushing to make the first analysis. *He would see what no one had seen in three million years— he alone would look upon mystery revealed and he alone would learn truth. . . .* But the open fear on the Marine's big, bluff face was too real to ignore. She looked back at the cylinder, at the marvelous piece of shale, at the delicate beauty of the shell and its ancient inhabitant, all trapped together by circumstance. *The most beautiful, most striking, most wonderful thing I've ever seen. How did McCue keep from taking this to her laboratory, subjecting it to her experiments? Russovsky had the very luck to find this. If the cylinder is a First Sun device . . . my god.*

"Ma'am?" Fitzsimmons touched her shoulder, gently, shaking her out of the reverie. His voice was soft and insistent. "Doctor Anderssen, we have to isolate this weapon. Right now."

"You're right," Gretchen stood up, shaking her head. She felt a little shaky. "Let's close up the g-box and put it in an airlock we're not using. That should hold the eaters if they escape, and we can vent the lock to space if necessary."

"Doc, listen to me." Fitz stood as well, towering over her. His dark brown eyes were filled with worry. "There's no way to know if this cylinder holds the same kind of nanomechs as the other one—this one could be an explosive, a nuke, an antimatter bomb, *anything.* Poking something like this, even with a really, really tiny stick, is bad, bad business. Procedure says put the whole box on a carryall and have the *Cornuelle* boost it into the sun."

"No, I don't think so!" Gretchen stepped between the Marine and the box. "This artifact is worth my entire career, Sergeant. Worse, it's worth an enormous amount of money for the Company *and* for the Company's primary contractor— which is the Imperial Navy." She stopped, searching his face. He looked back, so plainly worried for his own safety, for her life and the others on the ship, her anger drained away as quickly as it had flared.

"I'm sorry, Sergeant, I've no business shouting at you." Gretchen put her hand on his arm. "Like you, I'm under pretty strict orders—and my first order is to make sure things like this are brought back intact and well documented. So even if we talk to Captain Hadeishi, the answer is going to be the same—the cylinder stays and comes back to Imperial space with us."

Fitzsimmons's eyes narrowed, and one hand made an abortive movement to his comm pad, but then he nodded, taking a long look at the battered, rusted box on the floor. "Are you going to try and study it on the ship?"

"I . . ." Gretchen paused. *Why lie? He'll know, and you'll look like an idiot.* "Yes, I have to try. But—I'm not going to try anything invasive, or high energy, and I'm going to run passive scans on this thing for a day or two first."

Fitzsimmons gave her an arch look and she blushed. "Really, Sergeant. And we'll be sure to evac the airlock of any atmosphere. *I'll be careful!*"

"Sure, ma'am," he said, picking up the g-box controls. "Why don't you call Parker—or Bandao if our coffee-drinking man is still horking up his lunch—and have them get the number three airlock ready, while I angle our little friend here out of this place?"

"See? Safe and sound." Gretchen leaned against the wall of a cargo bay, watching the atmosphere gauge sink toward zero pressure. Fitz and Deckard were packing up a welding kit they'd found in one of the workshops. Inside the airlock, the chunk of shale and its ancient passengers were firmly secured in a hexacarbon cradle. The metal cage was oriented toward the outer lock door on a pair of rails. A scratch-built launching mechanism—half blasting putty and a comm-controlled detonator—rode underneath. A couple of metal-cased sensors Gretchen had scavenged from the lab ring were pinned up on the gleaming white walls of the airlock.

"You seem a little more relaxed," Fitzsimmons said, in an offhand way, as he coiled up a length of comm cable. He was trying not to smirk. "Now your precious baby is on the other side of the lock."

"Maybe," Gretchen said, nodding. "I—"

Her comm warbled, and Magdalena's voice filled the air around them. "Huntsister, the main comm array is working, and there's someone who wants to speak with you."

"Patch 'em through," Gretchen said, turning away from the two Marines. "Someone on the *Cornuelle?*"

"No," the Hesht said in a sly voice, "I managed to whisker the camp planetside. Everyone seems to be alive—but they're pissed and hungry and want to know if the showers are working."

Damn. Gretchen clicked her teeth, cursing herself for forgetting about the scientists stranded on the planet. "I'm a fine leader," she muttered. "We should have called them first thing. They must be half-mad with fear from being abandoned."

"I wouldn't say half covers the strength of their feeling," Maggie commented. "You want to take this call from the bridge?"

"Doctor Lennox, I'm sorry, but Doctor Clarkson," Gretchen repeated for the sixth time, "is dead. Everyone who was on the *Palenque,* save for crewman Fuentes and crewwoman Flores, is dead."

In the v-pane beside the captain's chair—now covered with an Imperial Marine field blanket—a thin, distressed-looking woman stared back at Gretchen, her face framed by the hood of a z-suit which had seen better days. Two men crowded behind her in some kind of shelter—Gretchen could make out the roof supports characteristic of an extruded building—and both of them seemed to have grasped the facts of the matter, to judge from their stunned expressions.

"I—I don't understand. He just went on the shuttle . . ." Lennox had faded blond hair and high cheekbones. Gretchen guessed she'd been very pretty when she was younger, but years spent in the glare of alien suns had not treated her kindly.

"Margaret," Gretchen leaned forward, catching the woman's eye. "I know it seems very sudden, but you've been out of contact with the *Palenque* for weeks—surely you thought something had gone awry aboard?"

"Yes . . ." Lennox swallowed and seemed to become aware of her surroundings again. "I just hoped . . . he was still alive."

"I'm sorry, but there *was* an accident and the crew, Doctor Clarkson and Doctor McCue, were all killed. Now—is everyone at base camp all right? Do you need medical assistance?"

"We're fine," rumbled one of the two men, a hulking, bearded face with a stout nose. "And very, very glad to hear from you, Doctor Anderssen. I am Vladimir Tukhachevsky—*dobre den!*"

"Good day to you, Doctor." Gretchen bobbed her head in greeting. "I know you all want to get a real shower and eat a different brand of ration bar, but there's going to be a delay before we can bring you back up to the ship."

"What do you mean? Is there still a problem?" The other man—a smaller, wirier fellow—pushed his face into the camera. "Don't you have a rescue ship?"

"Mister Smalls," Gretchen smiled amiably in greeting. "The Imperial Navy has been good enough to bring us here to help you, but accommodations are lacking on the *Cornuelle* for guests. There is also a problem with the shuttle engines, which has to be resolved. When there is a place to put you on the *Palenque*, and we can retrieve you safely, we will do so immediately."

What a fine manager I make, passed through the back of Gretchen's mind. *Next I'll be expressing my profound sympathies at their recent layoff.*

Tukhachevsky frowned, heavy black eyebrows beetling in concern. "What kind of accident, Doctor Anderssen? Has the *Palenque* been damaged?"

"She's . . . a little Spartan right now, Doctor." Gretchen—watching the faces of the three scientists on the planet—decided not to explain the events of the artifact and its activation. *Not today, at any rate.* "The accident that killed the crew also . . . destroyed most of the amenities onboard. Luckily, the *Cornuelle* has been able to supply us with new bedding, towels and food." *If you call Marine ration bars and olive-colored threesquares food.*

"In any case, we should have a shuttle ready to go in a day, perhaps two, so call in your field crews and get everyone ready to ship up."

Lennox nodded, turning away with a distant, frightened expression on her face. Smalls was already gone, leaving only the bearlike Tukhachevsky with a troubled look in his eyes.

"Doctor? Is something wrong?"

"Ah . . ." Vladimir twisted the ends of his mustache with a nervous motion. "Almost everyone is already in camp. Since the *Palenque* stopped responding to our hails, I fear morale has suffered. No one is even working in the excavation anymore. But one of us, I fear, is not here. She's gone, out wandering in the wasteland."

"Who?" Gretchen felt irritated, but at the same time she knew who it must be, even before Tukhachevsky said her name aloud. *Who else would I want to talk to? Who do we need to talk to?*

"Our own dear Russovsky," Vladimir said sadly, scratching a sore on the side of his nose. "She left in her *Midge* the same day Clarkson and McCue went up to the ship. We've heard nothing from her since, not so much as a word."

"Captain? The civilians have established contact with their ground team. Do you want the recording on your number two?" The midshipman looked up with a painfully earnest expression on his face, fingers poised over the main communications panel.

Hadeishi shook his head. "No, thank you, Smith-*tzin*. Just give me a realtime on my display if anything interesting happens." He gave the young officer a stern look. "Has *Sho-sa* Koshō set you to updating our navigational charts?"

"*Hai*, Captain!" Smith managed to come to attention in his shockchair, a talent Hadeishi remembered all too well himself. His first posting had been under a México captain with a very strict sense of propriety. "All spare passive sensor time is already tasked."

"Good. Carry on." Updating local navigational charts was dull—most of the time—but frighteningly essential to safe navigation and the rapid response of the Fleet to any threat. Hadeishi tapped up the boy's report and found the usual litany of planets, planetesimals, asteroids and stray cometary bodies. *Too early to find anything interesting. A pity.*

The bridge was quiet and busy, filled with the little sounds of men and women working at routine tasks made fresh by a new duty station for the ship and at least the prospect of danger. Hadeishi let the shockchair take more of his weight, eyes roving idly from station to station. The well of the threat board drew his attention at last, as it usually did, and he frowned. The red sphere of Ephesus swam in the center, slashed with the white of enormous storms, surrounded by a scattering of tiny lights—each one tagged with ship identification numbers, directions of movement, thrust and mass figures—and there was absolutely nothing going on.

Even the tense atmosphere aboard the *Palenque* had abated—no new horrors had been discovered, the alien devices were secured—and everyone aboard was busy restoring ship's systems. Hadeishi considered remanding the gun control orders which kept two forward beam weapons targeted on the civilian ship. But he did not. Quarantine restrictions were strict and he had no desire to generate more paperwork for himself.

The rest of the system was equally boring; even the Ephesian sun was quiet, without particular flare activity, or mottling or magnetic storms. Hadeishi swung his chair from side to side gently, eyeing a trail of motes drifting along in the upper atmosphere of the planet. He moved a control on his display and the far side of the planet rotated into view. Immediately he frowned, seeing the fuzzy mottled streaks characteristic of delayed or corrupt data.

"Mister Hayes?" The weapons officer became entirely alert, his massive frame tensing like a hunting dog preparing to leap to the chase. Hadeishi did not smile. "I don't like the lack of surveillance coverage for the far side of the planet. Please secure communications control of the civilian peapod satellites—how are they configured?"

"Meteorological and geophysics survey, *Chu-sa.*"

"Good, well leave them to their business, but establish a tap. I would also like two reconnaissance drones launched into polar orbits to give us a real-time eye on farside."

"*Hai!*" The weapons officer settled into his seat, face lit with enthusiasm. Once Hayes was looking away, Hadeishi did smile, a little. He was flirting with boredom as well, which meant he should start working on the weekly reports for sector command. *What a horror . . .*

Instead of setting himself to his dull profession duty, Hadeishi tapped up the surveillance and comm feeds from the civilian ship. *No 3v feed so far from home,* he thought, rather guiltily, *but you can always see what the neighbors are doing.*

"This doesn't look very experimental to me." Gretchen had both hands tucked into her armpits—her z-suit was dumped in the cabin she'd appropriated—and her mother's sherpa cap tugged down almost to her neck. She kicked the corner of the tachyon relay very gently, though even such a small motion drew a deep growl and hiss from underneath. "Shouldn't they repaint the case, or something?"

The relay occupied one corner of the forward cargo hold, sitting on a standard cargo palette bolted to the deck with standard retaining bolts. The device was shaped very much like a standard cargo container, save for military markings and the particular gold-gray-olive color scheme of Imperial Navy equipment. A rat's nest of cables ran out of the back of the relay and down through an open floor panel. A pair of bare, furry feet were visible under the edge of the container.

Gretchen sat on the edge of the palette, humming softly to herself. Clanking, more muttering and then a *chunk* sounded from under the relay. Magdalena emerged, her fur awry, and sat down next to the archaeologist.

"I think, hunt-sister," the Hesht said, slipping a stiff brush from one of the cargo bags tethered to the deck and beginning to settle her fur. "I think your human guardpack calls things 'experimental' when they want to sell them for more money than they're worth." Magdalena smiled, showing a large number of sharp white teeth. "But this thing works."

"It's back on main power?" Gretchen pointed with her chin at the tangle of cables. "And reset? Ready for business?"

The Hesht nodded, slicking back the fur along her neck and shoulders. "Recycling the system and acquisition of the sector relay emitter at Ctesiphon will take a few minutes, but then she'll be ready to send and receive." Maggie paused, glowering at Gretchen with one half-lidded eye. "You have messages to send? Greetings to your cubs? Your mate lying at home in the den?"

Gretchen nodded sheepishly. "And reports for Gossi and the Company."

"Them!" Magdalena made a sharp coughing sound. "They eat bark."

"I suppose." Gretchen couldn't hide a smile. "Listen, I need to ask you some questions about the main comm array—can you use it to pick up the transponder on a groundside vehicle?"

Maggie blinked slowly, showing two clear lenses fluttering across her yellow eyes. "You want to search for the missing hunter from the sky? For Russovsky?"

Gretchen nodded. "The scientists on the ground have no idea where Russovsky went on her survey. She left no flight plan. Lennox says . . . well, that's immaterial. Lennox doesn't like her. The others, though—particularly Tukhachevsky—are worried."

Maggie scratched the underside of her jaw. "Do we have to find her right now? Why not wait until she returns from hunting—there's only one watering hole, one den—she has to come back sometime."

Gretchen's expression turned dour. "I need to talk to her about the cylinders, and about McCue and Clarkson and what she did, and what they did, on the day of the accident."

Magdalena grunted, leaning back against the relay. "Huh. Now the pride's golden pelt is heavy on the shoulders, ya-ha?"

Gretchen made a face. A dull, queer churning started in her stomach at the thought. "My job, now. But really the Company doesn't care about all the poor people who died on this ship. They'll pay the wergeld to the families and a pension, if one is owed. But no more. What they want, and what I need to find, is the place Russovsky found those cylinders—and anything else that might be there."

Magdalena's ears flattened back, and her eyes narrowed to pale, golden slits. "Ya-ha, hunt-sister, they would indeed. Well, I know a little about the main array and a little about these dragonflies—the transponder has only a short range, but if we knew exactly where to look, we could open a direct comm channel to Russovsky's aircraft."

"If we knew where to look. Big planet down there." Gretchen felt disgruntled. "Can we search the surface visually? Slave some kind of camera to the comp and tell it to look for the outline of a *Midge* in flight?"

"Hrmph. Perhaps." Magdalena scrunched up her nose. "I'll see if we can do that."

"Good." Gretchen got up and pulled on a pair of mittens from her pocket. "How's Isoroku coming with the heaters?"

"Is it still cold?" Maggie's tongue poked out between her teeth, then coughed merrily at the human's disgusted expression. Her breath frosted in the air. "You should have a nice thick fur coat, like me."

"Fine," Gretchen grumbled. "I'll go play with my toys, then. You just find our missing scientist."

Hadeishi grinned, though he was entirely comfortable in his shipsuit, sitting on the climate-controlled bridge of a modern warship. *Anderssen-tzin hasn't lost her sense of humor yet. Still . . .* He remembered being constantly cold more than once himself. And wet. He tapped open a channel to his wayward engineer.

"*Hai?*" The old bull's voice was aggrieved and distant. Metallic clanking and spitting sounds nearly drowned out his voice. "Yes, Captain?"

"What's your environmental situation?" Hadeishi didn't bother to hide his amusement.

"Cold and dark," Isoroku grunted. "We have power, but most of the heaters and lights are still down because we have no power conduit in place."

"Do you need more help?"

There was a short silence. Then the engineer ventured to ask: "Is the quarantine lifted, Hadeishi-*san?*"

"No," Hadeishi replied, sighing in disgust. Regulations required another week of isolation for the *Palenque,* and then a week's medical review for any returning crew. Any engineer's mate he sent across to the civilian ship would be lost to him for two weeks, and he was already shorthanded with Isoroku gone. "No, it's not been lifted. How about supplies? Do we have conduit we can spare ourselves?"

"Yes." Now Isoroku's voice changed and became wary. "We're pulling spares out of cargo storage here—most of the expedition supplies still in storage survived the attack because they were sealed in cargo pods—there should be enough to serve."

Hadeishi understood the engineer's decision. *No fleet officer is going to spend his hard-won supplies on a civilian ship. And I shouldn't ask myself.*

"Carry on, then." Hadeishi tapped the channel closed. "Bah."

The number of reports in his message queue had not shrunk. Two more had popped in while he was malingering. "Enough, to work. Duty. Honor. Empire."

Somehow, when Gretchen reached the number three airlock, *Gunso* Fitzsimmons was there already, looking bulky in a military field jacket, gloves and a pathetic fur hat. She looked at the musty, moth-eaten chapeau on his head and refrained—by dint of biting her tongue—from making any comment. "Sergeant."

"Ma'am." Fitz nodded genially. "Come down to take a look at your prize?"

"Yes." She scowled at him, then squatted down in front of a portable display pane she had salvaged from the lab ring. Since most of the ship was still dead, she could steal cycles from main comp for her analysis. Ignoring the Marine, who had maneuvered around to watch her work, she plugged her handheld into the panel, then loaded the suite of xenoarch software she'd been using on Mars and Ugarit. The pad and the panel beeped in synchrony, then a set of v-panes expanded, showing her feeds from the sensors in the airlock and the security cameras.

"Careful," Fitzsimmons breathed, radiating nervousness like a dark cloud.

Gretchen glared at him out of the corner of her eye. He was clutching the failsafe for the lock ejection mechanism in both hands. "You should be careful," she snapped. "Nothing's happened . . . and if the lock won't hold back whatever comes out, you're not going to have time to push the button. An atomic or antimatter weapon will just vaporize us where we stand."

The sergeant gave her an equally fierce look. "I don't like the prospect of being disintegrated, or dissolved, or anything which involves the end of my personal self-awareness. So I'll just keep hold of this, okay?"

"Whatever." Gretchen turned away to hide her hands—which were trembling ever so slightly—from the Marine. "Let's see what we can see."

Inside the airlock, the passive sensors had been recording for almost a day and her volume analysis software had built a fine-grained map of the outside of the cylinder, the slab of limestone and every nook and cranny of the pitted surface. From this, the soft had extracted a map of the inner structure of the stone fragment and the cylinder. In both cases, large sections of the display were blank or an all-too-familiar fuzzy gray. "Not enough data to see inside, not yet."

Gretchen opened a log and started talking into her throat mike. Her awareness of Fitzsimmons faded away, replaced by a smaller, more tightly defined universe of stone surfaces and densities. "Previous sample—as shown in Clarkson's logs—activated when exposed to high-density sub-x-ray scan. Previous sample did not activate when subjected to microwave analysis. I am starting, therefore, with low-power ultrasonic and will advance slowly to microwave."

She tapped a series of quick commands and held her breath. There was no explosion, no ominous hum, only a flickering on the sensor command relays and then a new v-pane appeared, showing an echo-scan image building. After a few moments, the first scan completed.

"The sandstone is unremarkable," Gretchen said, resuming her narrative. "Though the embedded shell is really quite beautiful. A number of smaller cephalopods and annelids are also recognizable in the matrix. The cylinder does *not* express the same characteristics as the previous sample. This low-power survey is unable to penetrate the metallic casing, but there are markings incised into the surface of the device. I am going to enter the airlock, move the sensors manually, and then run another set of low-power scans."

Fitzsimmons coughed in alarm, but Gretchen didn't even hear him.

"I hope to build a more complete image by interpolating the scan results and taking, oh, four complete sets from different vantage points in the airlock. Luckily, the heavy shielding of the lock itself is blocking out a great deal of outside interference. In fact . . ." She paused, thinking. ". . . as we are in orbit, a gravitometric analysis may reveal a great deal about the object."

Gretchen stopped, stood up, stretched and noticed the Marine watching her, arms crossed, with a distracted expression on his face. "Are you all right?"

"What? Yes ma'am, I'm fine. Need a hand moving the sensors?"

"Sure." Her lips pursed. "Should we suit up to work in the lock?"

"Yeah." Fitz nodded. "A pain, but better than finding yourself outside without a jacket."

An hour later, Gretchen was sitting again, cross-legged, watching a second set of images build on her display. Fitzsimmons had given in to complete boredom and was sleeping with his head on a wadded-up blanket behind her. A small heater had appeared from somewhere and was baking Gretchen's righthand side, though her left was still very cold.

She dragged a fingertip, rotating the interpolated image of the cylinder.

"A densely-packed inscription covers the surface of the object. Each character is very small and quite complex. My IdeoStat says the least complicated ideogram is formed by seven strokes, the most complicated by nineteen. There is a noticeable distribution, though the average tends toward the complex, rather than the simple." She rubbed her eyes, feeling a peculiar, too-familiar twitching prick behind her left eye. "Adamski would argue this indicates a glyph-based language, like old Náhuatl or pre-Kanji Japanese—one without a phonetic alphabet. I can't make any kind of judgment yet, not without even the faintest idea of the creator race's vocal apparatus or lack thereof. I would say, however, the information density on the object surface is very high. There are thousands of distinct ideograms, thousands . . ."

In the display, the mapping software unwound the surface image of the cylinder into a long luminous strip covered with thousands of tiny characters. The dizzying arrangement of glyphs filled Gretchen with an odd disquiet. They seemed to dance and twist across the v-pane and she was uncomfortably aware of a sensation the characters were shifting places as she watched, rearranging themselves into an almost recognizable pattern. She blinked and rubbed her eyes.

"The density of the exterior . . ." she continued, looking away from the Ideo-Stat display. As a result, she did not see the system monitor showing the translator drawing a gradually increasing rate of comp cycles. ". . . is far exceeded by the possible content of the interior. Unlike Clarkson's sample, this one is entirely filled with a dense membrane structure. If my hypotheses about the first device are correct, then this one contains an enormous amount of information, coded on the fine surfaces of the membranes."

Thinking, she chewed slowly on her thumb. "I think this one *is* a book, or perhaps an entire library. Yet, as with most glyph-based languages, we may never decipher the contents, not without an intersecting language to point us toward a translation." She began to feel ill, as if the promise of the cylinder were burning a hole in her stomach. The tiny fragments left by the First Sun civilization inspired awe and lust in equal measure. A clear window into the distant past might be sitting only meters away.

"What a loss," she murmured. "I want to read this! Well, as long as it's not legal documents. *Lort!* It's probably property records, or warehouse inventories or recipes."

Green Hummingbird was in near darkness, lying on a narrow bed in his quarters. Pale green and blue lights played across his angular face. A swing-out display hung above him, showing feeds from the cameras on the *Palenque* and *Cornuelle*. Most of them were muted and dialed down to thumb-sized squares. One mirrored the contents of Anderssen's work panel. In the main v-pane, a cylinder engraved with thousands of tiny glyphs rotated slowly. Two more v-panes showed her working, blond hair slowly becoming a tangled mass, and the object itself, resting in a steel cradle in the airlock. The *tlamatinime* watched and listened, eyes unfocused, thoughts distant.

As the scan image of the writing on the cylinder unfolded in the feed, Hummingbird stirred to life, attention sharpening. One hand, gnarled and scarred, brushed across the display, keying a series of preset searches. The panel chirped pleasantly, then began processing. Immediately, the video feeds flickered to a stop and the entire device dimmed noticeably.

In the small, crowded office beside his private cabin, Hadeishi cursed as his display slowed to a crawl, then snapped back to its normal responsiveness. A stiff finger jabbed a comm channel open. "*Sho-sa* Koshō, are we under attack?"

"No, Captain," came a quiet, level reply. "By ship's clock Hummingbird-*tzin* was using twenty percent main comp capacity for six seconds."

Hadeishi suppressed a curse, then curiosity washed away his anger. "What is he doing with that level of capacity?"

"I do not know, Hadeishi-*san*, and would not venture to guess." Koshō's voice was very demure.

"Understood." Hadeishi cut the channel, forcing speculation from his mind. There were logistics and supply usage reports to review and sign. *Twenty percent? Is he modeling planetary weather or something?*

Hummingbird scowled, lean old face twisting into a tight mask. Bits and pieces of the glyphs incised into the cylinder were coming back a match with examples from his archive. He thought briefly of using the blue pyramid, but discarded the notion. *I urge caution on others,* he thought with a trace of humor, *so should I practice it myself.*

What did match was troubling. Some of the more complicated signs were very like a series of temple carvings observed by a deep-range probe in a dead system beyond New Malta. Others suggested the contents of tablets secured by a Mirror agent from the marketplaces of Ik-hu-huillane. Both sets of documents were restricted to the highest levels of the Mirror—Hummingbird did not even possess translations of them, only symbol-match heuristics—and a series of winking red-and-white banded glyphs appeared alongside the comparison results.

"You say they're dangerous," he muttered at the panel. "But *how?*"

He began to feel uneasy, watching the Anderssen woman work with her probes and sensors, slowly revealing more and more layers hidden inside the cylinder. The arrangements of the membranes inside the structure did seem to contain more data—a vast amount, far more than even the writing etched on the outer surface.

"Are they access instructions?" he wondered aloud, wishing the upper levels of the Mirror had seen fit to provide him with more information about dead Gulatith and whichever race had chipped the Ik-hu-huillane tablets from interstellar ice. "Could she decipher them, given time? Or is the device too old—broken by the wear of so many millennia. . . . She has the inclination, I see." Hummingbird was glad Anderssen had such limited software.

On his v-pane, the woman was cursing at her slow panel and tapping commands at a furious rate. Hummingbird shook his head slowly—curiosity was a powerful drug—one whose effects he had felt himself and he wondered if the soldier was right. *We could throw the cylinders into the sun. There they might be destroyed, or at least lost for another million years.*

"But then," he said to the dark room, "we would not *know*, would we? And we are curious monkeys . . . even I am pricked by curiosity."

The densely packed strip of symbols taunted him from the display. He could sense—even through the filters running in his panel, even with well-ordered detachment—a tantalizing meaning in the angular, alien shapes. Hummingbird felt an urge to turn the power of his display—of the *Cornuelle's* main comp—to their decipherment. *The pyramid might contain a linguistic key. My tools might—*

"I think not," he said aloud, and tapped off the v-feed from the *Palenque.*

"Delores . . . take a look at this." Parker dialed up the magnification on his work lenses, head cocked as he stared down the throat of shuttle number two's air intake. The heavy machinery had been—at last—removed from shuttle number one's cargo hold, the mold cleaned away and the entire assembly mounted on a diagnostic rack in the *Palenque's* engineering ring. The morning had been spent laboriously attaching power feeds and exhaust vents so the engine could be tested. The exploration ship did not have a proper maintenance bay, causing Parker and Isoroku to waste a great deal of time trying to get reliable diagnostic relays established between the Sunda Aerospace Yards *Komodo*-class shuttle and the Novoya Rossiya–built mechanicals on the *Palenque.*

Eventually, the pilot had given up trying to make the Javan and Swedish equipment play nicely and had settled for a visual inspection. A multispectrum lamp was clipped to the lip of the intake.

"What?" Delores, surly again for some reason—though she'd greeted both Parker and Isoroku with a big smile this morning when she came swinging out of the accessway—climbed up on the rack and worked her head and shoulders inside.

"Switch to UV-band on your lenses," Parker said, gently placing his fingertip on a curving section of the intake wall. The highly polished ceramic alloy gleamed like a mirror, reflecting his face as an enormous, distorted monster. "And hi-mag, about six hundred."

"Now I can't see anything but the surface of the composite." Delores didn't bother to keep mounting irritation out of her voice.

"Follow my arm, then just ahead of my finger."

Delores grunted, making a face. "You need to take a bath sometime. Your nails . . ." Then she whistled softly in alarm. "By the Sister—what *is* that?"

"Something alive," Parker said, watching a faint discoloration shimmer like a rainbow in the hi-mag view of his work lenses. He could see regular, symmetric structures in the discoloration—not the stolid honeycomb of the ceramic, but something delicate and far, far more complicated. "Something eating the hi-temp ceramic lining and making more . . . more metallic lichen."

"Oh, Sister!" Delores scrambled backward out of the intake. "It's the eaters!"

"No," Parker said, watching the tiny gleaming lights with a bemused expression on his narrow face. "No, it's not them . . . we'd be dissolved or turned inside out. This is different—this must have come from the planet. Is there any life down there?"

"No," Delores called from across the engineering bay. "Just rocks, sand and barren mountains. Nothing green, no trees, no water. Nothing."

The pilot wanted to scratch his nose, but couldn't, not in the close confines of the intake. On a hunch, he breathed on the discoloration, trying to focus the flow of moist gas with his lips. In the restricted universe of hi-mag, he saw the delicate tendrils wave in the wind, and the textures and colors brightened. He blinked, then squinted in disbelief. "I think they got bigger," he called excitedly to Delores.

The crewwoman was still on the other side of the bay. She had found a welding torch and was hefting the slender wand like a bat. "Well, don't do that again, whatever it was! Come on, let's tell the engineer or Anderssen-*tzin* about this."

"Hmmm . . . ok." Parker backed out of the intake and swung the UV lamp to mark the discoloration. Even from the vast remove of a meter, he could no longer make out the lichen. Sitting on the steps of a work ladder, he tapped open a channel.

"Doctor Anderssen? Parker. Can you join me and Delores down in Engineering bay four? Bring your hi-mag lenses, if you've got 'em handy."

Squeezed into the intake, with Parker, Delores, Isoroku and the ever-present Fitzsimmons crowding around outside, Gretchen stared dully at the glassy, curving surface. Now she felt too hot—the heaters were working in Engineering for some reason—and there were too many people around. "All right Parker, what am I looking at?"

"Right where I've got the UV spot shining," the pilot said, trying to wedge in beside her. "You can't miss them, not in hi-mag."

"I don't see anything," Gretchen said after a moment, "except some discoloration, like some kind of acid spilled on the ceramic." She turned her head, then made a face. The inside of Parker's nose was not the place to be looking with work lenses dialed high. Flipping up the goggles, she looked at him inquiringly.

"What?" Parker swung down his own lenses and hunched over the section of metal. Almost immediately he started cursing. "This is . . . they're all gone! There's nothing but some kind of mottled smear left." He sat up, cracked his head against the roof of the intake, then wormed his way back out with a snarl. "I saw them," Parker declared, stripping off his lenses. "They were *there*, all glowy and fanlike and . . . they were alive! Delores saw them too!"

Gretchen looked at the crewwoman and she nodded her head in agreement. "He's not crazy. Well, ok, he saw what he said he saw."

"Fine." Gretchen looked at Isoroku. "Then what happened to them? Vanishing in thirty minutes is too great a rate of change for me. Did they cause the engines to overheat?"

"Maybe," Parker mumbled, scrunching up the side of his mouth. He took a tabac out of his pocket, shucked the wrapper and lit the stick on his belt. Gretchen stepped back, out of a rising gray whorl. In low-grav the tobacco smoke made corkscrew patterns in the air. "They grew—I saw them grow—with more moisture, more air, more oxygen. No, more carbon dioxide. Maybe they eat CO_2, like a plant at home?"

"Would that cause an overheat?" Gretchen spread her hands questioningly.

"No . . ." Parker squinted into the intake, then at the fleet engineer. "But if they got inside, into the rest of the engine, they would make turbulence—the airflow surfaces wouldn't be smooth anymore—and they do seem to be eating away at the composite."

"Even in a Javan machine," the engineer rumbled, his Norman tinged with a thick accent, "there are close tolerances. We will have to examine the entire engine for contamination."

"Do it." Gretchen started to turn away, but then a thought struck her. "Wait—find another patch, if there is one. Record the . . . um . . . the infestation or planting or whatever. Then shine Parker's lamp on it for a half hour."

"Good idea." Isoroku's eyes glinted. "The simplest explanation."

"I killed them with the multispec?" Parker seemed incredulous. "But if they came from the planet . . . the atmosphere's thin—everything's bathed in UV! Why should it kill them?"

"Try it anyway," Gretchen replied, swinging up onto the ladder leading into the main accessway. "And let me know what happens." She disappeared up the shaft, followed moments later by Fitzsimmons.

Parker shared a glance with Delores, who shrugged and looked at him expectantly, and the Nisei, who had no discernible expression at all. The pilot hunched his shoulders and shuffled back to the engine, glaring at the machinery. "And I thought you were pretty," he grumbled as he flipped down his work lenses. "Shows what I know."

Gretchen woke from a dream of endlessly mutating gray-green ideograms to an irritating beeping sound. Groaning—the sound was her comm paging—she unzipped her sleepbag and peered out into darkness. The lights in the crew quarters were on some day-night cycle which eluded her—they certainly didn't match the schedule on the *Cornuelle*—and her mouth tasted bad, her eyes were grainy and the persistent throb of a headache flared as consciousness returned.

"Oh Sister, mother of God, bearer of the Holy Savior . . ." Gretchen fumbled for her medband and pressed the cool metal against the side of her neck. A sensor flickered, there was a warning *beep*, and a cool, delicious sensation flooded into her bloodstream. With sanity restored, she picked up the comm and saw the pilot's face—even rougher-looking than she imagined her own appeared—staring back. "Good morning, Mister Parker."

"Its afternoon," he replied in a dead-sounding, slurred voice. "Planetside, anyway. I'm finished with your shuttle engine."

"Good," Gretchen said, clipping the comm to her duffle. She eeled out of the sleepbag and braced herself against the floor. A netted sack held her clothes, and she began dragging out an undershirt, pants, her skinsuit. "What did you find?"

"This engine is completely infested with these . . . these *chapoltin* . . . these locusts! Well, they're not insects, but plants, I guess. Ones that like to eat hexacarbon and ceramic composite and drink CO_2 and produce O_2 and C and some more O and lots of little crystalline frond-thingies." He rubbed his face, leaving a long smear of oil across his forehead. "We're sack-bound, but the number two shuttle engine is cleaned up, disinfected with your friendly multispec lamp set on hi-UV and then . . ." Parker groaned. "We resurfaced everything back to tolerance, or replaced the sections eaten clean through. So—maybe tomorrow—we can fly shuttle one back to groundside base and put this engine back in the grounded shuttle."

The pilot glared owlishly at Gretchen, who was worming herself into a skintight shipsuit. When she was done, he continued. "Before you ask: Yes, we checked the other engine. It was infested too, but not so badly. Anyway, Isoroku cleaned up number one. So both will fly, eventually."

"What happens when we go groundside?" Gretchen asked, straightening her hair and pulling the heavy blond mane back into a ponytail. "They'll get infected again, right?"

Parker nodded, listlessly pushing another tabac into the corner of his mouth. "Yeah, and we'll clean up again, I guess."

"Okay," Gretchen said, her attention already turning to the puzzle of the cylinder. "One trip, then, to repair the other shuttle and load everyone up. Then it's back upstairs for the entire team. If we need to make an excursion groundside, we'll use the shuttles in rotation and not leave them on the planet for more than a day."

"Sure." Parker took a long drag on his tabac, then tapped off.

Gretchen stared at the comm, then shook her head. *Should I call Maggie about her status? No, later. I'll just take a look at the latest translation runs before breakfast.*

Feeling much better, she banged the door open, then kicked off in a long arcing jump toward the main accessway. Behind her, a minute telltale flashed on her doorway, and not so far away, a chime went off in a cabin occupied by the two Marines.

A black sleepbag stirred in the dimly lit room, then an arm reached out from the cocoon and thumped the other sleeping soldier.

"Fitz, your girlfriend's up." Deckard closed his eyes and fell back to sleep.

Fitzsimmons crawled out of his own sleepbag, rubbed a chin covered with fine black stubble and started getting dressed. *I hope she gets breakfast first,* he thought forlornly, *so I can at least get some coffee.* Even the bad coffee on this barge—or the reprocessed, recycled "black crude" from the navy threesquares— was better than nothing. He hooked one foot in a hanging strap, then slung on his combat vest and gun-rig before picking up a jacket to hide the weapons. "Huh," he laughed softly. "I've been with the navy too long—like anyone aboard would worry if I was carrying."

His combat bar strapped to the side of one boot, a heavy utility knife to the other. The waist rig held eight flechette-wire clips, and a holster with the pistol-styled shipgun. The rest of the chest rig held various tools, lamps and spyeyes. His hand hovered over the squat, short-barreled shape of his heavy shipgun, then he plucked it away from the wall and slung the automatic rifle behind his back. Nervous fingers—this whole situation made him nervous—checked the loads in the pistol and the rifle. Both weapons were topped, lit green and ready to cook.

Pretty useless, he thought, mouth tasting oily, *but what else do I have? Nothing to stop a nanomech cloud, or a pocket-sized shipkiller, or a virus or a biological. Not much at all but spit and my knife.*

"Thank you, *Sho-sa.*" Hummingbird tapped his comm closed and took a deep breath. Lieutenant Isoroku's respectfully polite call reported the *Palenque* main environmentals restored to operation, the last of the air filters cleaned out and power working on most decks. *Almost time to go across and see these things for myself.*

The *tlamatinime* turned to his surveillance display and panned through the feeds. After a moment, he switched back to the video from outside the number three airlock on the *Palenque.* The portable work panel Anderssen had been using for her translations and analysis sat idle, the area lights dimmed low.

"Not there?" Hummingbird made an amused clicking sound with his teeth. "But not sleeping, or eating." He flicked through the feeds from the Company ship and his brow furrowed. The archaeologist was nowhere to be seen. A stab of intense irritation twisted his lip, but then he calmed himself. Large sections of the *Palenque* were still without power, and many video feeds were dead or offline. She could be anywhere, doing anything, and be out of his sight. He glanced around the cabin, reminding himself of the many luxuries afforded by the navy ship.

"Everything works here," he said aloud, "on a well-maintained Imperial vessel. There? On a private ship which has only known the attentions of the pious and dutiful Isoroku for a few days? Scattered feathers, filth, fallen shells."

Hummingbird switched the view back to the number three airlock, where the cylinder still rested quietly in its steel cradle. He bent close, though a fingertip's motion on the panel would zoom the image to almost any level of detail he desired. Red sandstone and milky white streaks of sediment filled the view. "But how could she leave your mystery, even for a moment?"

Anderssen had been spending every waking moment with the artifact for the past two days. The still-idle exploration ship's main comp was almost entirely tasked to her translation jobs, much to the annoyance of everyone else working aboard. Hummingbird suddenly closed the feed, feeling his own curiosity stir.

"A cunning lure," he muttered, then turned away from the panel and knelt before a small shrine set into the wall of the cabin. Nothing so fancy as the main chapel down in the heart of the ship, but this was a space reserved for him and him alone. The Blessed Virgin stared down, jade eyes looking upon him with radiant compassion. Hummingbird made the sign of the cross, bowed to the Lady of Tepeyac, she surrounded by so many shining rays, she of the dark cloak strewn with stars, with a mantle of flowers and shining feathers, possessor of the beneficence of man. On a narrow ledge before the icon sat a cup filled with milky liquid and a scattering of dried, perfectly preserved rose petals.

Hummingbird began to sing, his hoarse voice rising in the cabin.

> *So it has been said by the Lord of the World,*
> *So it has been said by the Queen of Heaven:*
> *It is not true, it is not true*
> *We come to this earth to live.*
> *We come only to sleep, only to dream.*
> *Our body is a flower.*
> *As grass becomes green in the springtime,*
> *So our hearts will open, and give forth buds,*
> *And then they wither. So did our Lady of Flowers say.*

The sound echoed and died, and he felt a great comfort from the long-familiar ritual. Hummingbird bowed again, before the image of the merciful one, then raised the cup of *octli* to his lips. The smell of bitter alcohol stung his nose and he took the sacred liquid into his mouth, let the fermented sap of the god's fruit wash over his tongue, then passed the fluid, again, into the cup.

"So does temptation wash over me, held at bay by your grace, Queen of Heaven, lady whose belt is a serpent, whose faith lifts the heavens and presses the earth." He made the sign of the cross once more, and pressed his forehead to the floor before the Sister. "So it is above, so it is below."

He stood, his heart easy once more, and passed his hand across the display set into the wall. The comm woke to life, and a blinking glyph—a youth bearing two rabbits by the ears—winked azure. Hummingbird grunted, feeling the moment of isolation and serenity pass.

"Yes, Sho-sa Koshō? Has something happened?" The *tlamatinime* did not feel entirely at ease with the dark-eyed lieutenant or her ever-pleasant expression. Hummingbird thought he'd reached an equitable relationship with the captain, but this woman . . . her eyes were filled with secrets. *Is she also an agent of the Mirror? One set to watch me, as I watch the others? Or is her malice solely a matter of our races, our stations in life?*

"Honorable one," the executive officer said, bowing her head slightly. "The

Companymen have launched one of their shuttles—they are descending to the surface to repair the grounded shuttle at the observatory camp."

"Ah." Hummingbird was surprised. He had not expected the civilians to finish their repairs so quickly. "Are they going to retrieve the scientists on the ground as well?"

"I believe so," Koshō replied, a faint smile hiding behind her usual, stoic mask. "You left instructions to be informed. Shall I prepare a work carrel to take you and your luggage across?"

Hummingbird's face tightened—*I should not have mentioned my intent to Hadeishi*—and then he nodded in agreement. "Yes," he said, turning his most severe expression upon her. Koshō did not flinch, or look away, but maintained her pleasant, polite expression. "I will go across in twenty minutes."

The executive officer bowed again and tapped the channel closed. Hummingbird stared at the blank display for a moment, then his fingers stabbed at the panel, bringing up the surveillance view of the bridge. From this angle, he looked down upon Koshō's command station—an inset showed the ever-changing contents of her panel—and the soft lighting on the bridge gleamed in raven-dark hair. A long plait hung down her back, wound with copper, jade and pearl. The *tlamatinime* watched the woman intently, listening to the subdued chatter on the bridge, her conversation with a midshipman being dispatched to carry his bags, the orders to an engineering crew to bring a carrel around to the main airlock and prepare for a trip across the quarantine zone to the *Palenque*.

In all of this, she betrayed no knowledge of his observation, though Hummingbird could only assume she knew he was watching. After ten minutes he closed the feed—the lieutenant had studiously continued about her business—and began packing his bags. A suspicion was beginning to ferment in his agile old mind, though he did not believe any officer would be so reckless to endanger her career in this way.

She should be properly respectful, even a little afraid. Hummingbird wrenched his thoughts away from the Nisei woman and back to the delicate matter of packing the blue glass pyramid into a shockfoam carrying case. The object was very, very old. Even handling with thin gloves risked scarring or chipping the precious, eons-old surface.

Hummingbird breathed easier when the artifact was safely stowed.

The door chimed, and he turned to let the midshipman in.

An orange spark swelled in the sky, the thin, attenuated roar of airbreathing engines piercing gathering twilight. The number one shuttle swept over the base camp, wings glowing with the heat of reentry. Dust swirled up from the landing strip—no more than a long rectangle of glowlights and flattened earth. Against the blue-black heavens, the long coiling contrail burned golden with the last light of day. The Ephesian atmosphere was thin, and even with the copper disk of the sun still hanging at the horizon, a wash of stars filled the east.

The shuttle set down, engines thrust-vectored to airbrake. More dust billowed up, burning red with jet exhaust, and the aircraft bounced and shivered down a thousand meters of flattened desert. The runway was a crude outline at best, scratched from the dry soil. At the far end, engines idling down to a rumbling shriek, the shuttle turned and began rolling back to the camp.

From a forward window, Gretchen peered out at a sprawling compound of brown huts and tall metal poles strung with swinging glowlights. Under fitful spots of illumination, she saw beaten paths winding between the buildings, a handful of figures shrouded in z-suits trudging toward the landing strip and the bulky shapes of crawlers parked under metal sheds. Everything was brown and tan or hidden in shadow.

Just another camp on another world, far from home. She felt a keen disappointment. There was nothing grand here, only the same prefab huts and camp buildings. Another brown, desolate world filled with dust and chokingly thin air. Even the diamond brilliance of the night sky was familiar—she was no astronomer to pick out differences in the constellations—this place seemed no different than Mars or Ugarit or Zhendai.

The shuttle rattled to a halt and pressure lights came on. Cabin lights flared awake and Parker called back from the cockpit in a cheerful voice. "Please have your customs and immigration forms ready. Welcome to Ephesus Three. Please enjoy your stay."

Gretchen gathered up a heavy courier-style bag and checked the seals on her suit. Fitzsimmons had stitched her boot back together with some kind of adhesive goo and fishing line. *Which was very nice of him,* she thought wryly. *He'll be glad to have me out of his hair for a day.* Her goggles slipped into their long-accustomed grooves beside her nose and around her ears. Sealing the breather mask and checking the tubes and respirator were second nature—quickly and efficiently done—then she turned and checked the seals on Bandao's suit as well.

The gunner waited patiently, calm brown eyes watching the figures crossing the field toward them through the window. When she was done, he returned the favor and signed she was tight. Gretchen smiled in thanks and wove her way forward past Delores to the main hatch.

"Mister Parker, cycle the lock please."

The pilot nodded over his shoulder, flipped a series of switches and the inner door recessed with a dull clang. Two minutes later, Gretchen was standing on the landing strip, feeling a chill, cutting wind tug at her legs. She'd left a little of her face mask open and the smell of the planet flooded her nostrils.

Ephesus at twilight was sharp and cold, tart dust and crushed rock, the methane-stink of a recycler in the camp, a faint aroma of something metallic tickling the back of Gretchen's throat. She was glad she'd put on field pants and a shirt and jacket over the z-suit. The thermal heaters in her leg pads were already starting to run and her fingers were cold even with two layers of gloves.

Bandao rattled down the landing stairs and took up a position to the left and behind, while Parker and Delores went around to the cargo doors to start unloading the repaired engine. The gunner had a hand on the butt of his rifle—a stocky, evil-looking thing with a shining dark finish and a stubby, rubberized scope—and his attention moved in careful, measured sweeps, watching the distant, flat horizon and the buildings.

"Mister Parker," Gretchen called, her voice buzzing on the comm, nearly drowned by the keening wind. "Don't forget to put those seals in our engine intakes."

"Crap!" Both the pilot and Fuentes turned around and jogged back to the shuttle. Isoroku had machined up a set of shockfoam plugs to close the air intakes and—hopefully—keep the Ephesian spores out of the engines. They were unwieldy, and Gretchen watched in amusement as Parker staggered down the stairs with a pair of multispec worklamps around his neck, arms filled with the fat round shape of an intake plug.

"Doctor Anderssen?" A bluff, accented voice called through the darkness and Gretchen turned. Three shrouded figures approached, bent into the wind. She walked forward, hand raised.

"Doctor Lennox." Gretchen clasped the thin woman's hand firmly and nodded. "Smalls-*tzin*. Doctor Tukhachevsky."

"Welcome to Ephesus," the Rossiyan answered, dark eyes sparkling over the green snout of his respirator. Neither Lennox nor Smalls said anything. "Come, let's get to the main hall and you can meet the rest of the crew."

Everyone began walking back toward camp, save for Smalls, who paused—indecisively, it seemed to Gretchen—and stared at Fuentes and Parker working on sealing the engine intakes. Then the meteorologist shook his head and hurried to catch up with the rest of the group. Gretchen watched him as they followed the path through the buildings—even in the poor light of the hanging lamps she could see he was a little pale. *Hmm . . . can't be Parker, no one here knows him . . . must be Delores.*

The main hall was a two-story building framed with hexacarbon beams, the walls and roof formed by extruded slabs of local gravel and sand run through a reprocessor. Gretchen passed into the airlock in the middle of the group—a line of dust-streaked backs, shining respirator tanks, the local equipment pitted and gray. She paused at the outer door, fingertips brushing across the metal frame of the door. The hexacarbon was scored and dark, riddled with tiny pits, as if acid had splashed on the exposed surfaces.

Inside, she pulled back the cap of her skinsuit and tugged the respirator mask aside. She was in the building atrium—a close, crowded room filled with worksuits, boots, stained jackets and dirt—with Bandao close at hand. Smalls was already gone, leaving a tired-looking Lennox and a beaming Tukhachevsky behind.

"How is everyone doing?" Gretchen slipped her nose tube free and tucked it into the collar of her suit. "I guess you'll be glad to get upstairs and hit the showers."

"Yes, our water supplies have always been minimal. There's no local source of water, though we'd hoped . . ." Lennox sounded even more exhausted than her haggard face suggested. "I'm sorry, Doctor Anderssen, I'm very tired. Do you know when we'll be able to return to the ship?"

Gretchen spared a quick glance for Tukhachevsky, who was watching Lennox with concern, and Bandao, who was waiting patiently at the inner door of the atrium. She could see the acid glare of overhead lights and the tinny sound of someone's music box playing year-old tunes. The smell was entirely familiar and for an instant—setting aside the pale, worn face of the woman in front of her—she could have been standing in Dome Six at Polaris again.

"I think," Gretchen said gently, "we'll send you up to the ship tomorrow. Do you have your things together?"

"Oh." Lennox seemed to come awake, blinking. "No—I've been busy. I suppose I should—"

"Mister Bandao? Would you help Doctor Lennox pack her things up, and take them to the shuttle? Tell Mister Parker we'll be wanting to ferry up most of the crew tomorrow morning—early, I suppose, before the air gets too thin to fly."

Bandao nodded and shifted his rifle behind him, out of the way and out of sight.

"Doctor? Bandao-*tzin* will help you get ready and carry your things." Gretchen took Lennox by the hand and turned her around.

Bandao nodded politely and introduced himself. While he did, Gretchen motioned to Tukhachevsky and they stood aside near the main lock.

"Is everyone still in camp?" She asked, quietly. The Rossiyan nodded, fingering his beard. The sore beside his nose was beginning to suppurate—Gretchen recognized the sign of an ill-fitting respirator mask—and he smelled of alcohol. "Have you heard anything from Russovsky?"

"*Nyet*," he said dolefully. "Not so much as a peep. I don't know—she seemed preoccupied when she was here last—maybe the desolation is telling on her. This is a bleak world."

"Did she talk to you, when she was here? Did she talk to anyone—say where she'd been, where she was going?"

Tukhachevsky shook his head again, beard wagging slowly in counterpoint. "No, Doctor Anderssen. She landed while we sat at breakfast and immediately went to see McCue in the main lab. Then Clarkson . . ." The Rossiyan paused, nose twitching, and Gretchen could see him weighing dirty laundry in his mind. After a moment, he shook his head slightly and continued. "Doctor Clarkson went out to the main lab as well. An hour later—I would guess—I was packing a crawler to go reset the sensors at the edge of the White Plain and I saw Russovsky's *Midge* taking off." He scratched his beard. "A little odd, that. By then it was full sun, but she took off anyway and headed north."

"When did the shuttle leave?"

"Later," Tukhachevsky said, a slow grin peeking out from his beard. "I heard Clarkson on the comm, shouting at Blake—he's the head of the security team—to get a shuttle ready. But number two was already sidelined on the field with some mechanical problem. So they had to wait for a shuttle to come down from the ship to pick him up."

"Him and the damaged engine, right?" Gretchen tucked a wayward tendril of hair behind her ear. "Carlos flew the shuttle down to pick them up?"

Tukhachevsky nodded. "Yes, Flores had been down for several days, working on the grounded shuttle. By the time the other shuttle arrived, Clarkson was about wetting his pants." The Rossiyan grinned again. "He was in a rare state—almost happy, if such a dour man could ever be happy—and he was even civil to Molly."

"You saw them while they were waiting for the shuttle? Were they waiting together?"

"No! They couldn't abide being in the same room." Tukhachevsky waved a hand dismissively. "I didn't see—I'd already taken the crawler out—but Frenchy told me Doctor McCue decided to go aboard at the last moment. Clarkson was already aboard, the engine already stowed. They had to delay departure a couple minutes for her." The physicist shrugged.

So, Gretchen thought to herself, *Russovsky and McCue didn't show Clarkson the limestone fragment, only the free-standing cylinder. That was enough to get him off their backs . . . but why did McCue suddenly go aboard the shuttle? What made her hurry? Or was she just trying to keep Clarkson from seeing what she'd put in the cargo hold?*

The Company dossier on McCue implied she was a careful, thorough woman. A mathematician from the Arkham Institute on Anáhuac, the dig coordinator and chief bottlewasher. Meticulous, detail-oriented . . . not the kind of person to rush a sample somewhere, even one so precious. *Huh. But if things between her and Clarkson were as cold as everyone is hinting, maybe she wanted to make him look bad.*

"What happened then?" Gretchen returned her attention to the Rossiyan, who was looking mournful, his memories of the past stirred up. "Did you hear anything more from the ship, from Clarkson or McCue?"

"No." Tukhachevsky laughed hollowly. "Blake received a call from *Sho-sa* Cardenas, saying the shuttle had docked on the *Palenque*, then nothing. For weeks and weeks, nothing. We made a telescope—we could see the ship—but . . ."

"I'm sorry." Gretchen squeezed his shoulder. "I'm sorry about what happened, and sorry it took so long to get here."

"But you did come," Tukhachevsky sighed, and shook himself. A weight seemed to lift from his broad old shoulders and he stood up straighter. "Please, we can't stand here talking all night—come and meet everyone else and—please!—

have a drink, on me." His eyes twinkled. "You will find men and women's interests are reduced to their base constituents when faced with a slow, lingering death abandoned on an alien world, far from home, without hope of survival."

Gretchen made a show of sniffing the air. "I can tell," she said with a laugh. "It smells like a distillery in here! What are you making?"

"Vodka, of course. You can make vodka out of anything." Tukhachevsky pushed open the door to the common room and Gretchen stepped in. A dozen people rose to meet her, some young, some old, and a stained plastic cup was pressed into her hand, sloshing with jet fuel of some kind. The Rossiyan's meaty hand was on her shoulder, guiding her to a chair at the long table and Gretchen caught a swift montage of tired, haggard faces—men and women seamed by the elements, burned dark by the sun—and everyone was smiling, relief plain on their faces, babbling their names, questions, rude jokes.

"Hello," she said, when things had quieted down a little and she'd taken a suitably long drink of the "vodka" in the cup. "I'm Gretchen Anderssen, and I thought you'd like to know the water cyclers on the ship are working just fine."

Everyone smiled and the last of the heckling died down. Gretchen swung a heavy bag from her hip onto the tabletop. No one made any particular movement, but a sense of expectation pricked the air, like ozone spilling away from an oncoming thunderstorm.

"And our Magdalena has the t-relay working back to Imperial space, so there was some mail waiting for you."

Hhhhuhhh . . . The simultaneous exhalation of a dozen breaths stirred the air. Gretchen didn't look up—it would be rude to grin at these men and women, who'd thought they were lost at the edge of known space, with no way home—and concentrated instead on dumping the bundles of printed messages onto the table. She'd sorted them on the flight down and tied up each set with string. Some events, she knew, were venerable enough to become rituals. This was one. Mail call, particularly when a new crewmember arrived on site.

"Blake." She called out, holding up the first set of letters. A stocky man, his pockmarked face twisted halfway from a grim snarl to disbelieving joy, scraped back his chair and leaned over the table.

"Thanks," he muttered, sitting down, almost-trembling fingers picking at the twine. "Thanks."

Gretchen nodded, then looked down. She'd already removed all the letters for the dead crewmen, for Clarkson and McCue. Strangely, there hadn't been any letters in the inbound queue for Russovsky, though her company file said she had an entire clutch of cousins and sisters at home on Anáhuac. *Better have Maggie check on that*, she thought while she held up the next bundle. "Fuentes, Antonio?"

The sound of a power wrench whining against a reluctant bolt roused Gretchen the next morning. She blinked, seeing actual, real sunlight spilling down a dirty brown wall above her head, then poked her nose out from the sleepbag. A pungent smell of cooking oil, coffee, sweat and heated metal washed over her. "Ah," she grumbled, sitting up, "home at last."

Surprisingly—considering how late she'd remained awake, talking to Tukhachevsky and Sinclair and the others about the dig and the planet—she felt good. Actually rested. "Gravity is a wonderful thing," she said, baring her teeth for a little hand mirror she carried in her jacket. "And whatever they put in the vodka here *stains!* Now I look like a real babushka."

Taking a carefully hoarded bottle of water out of her bag, she washed her face and brushed her teeth. "Two cups," she muttered, measuring the fluid level in the translucent canteen by eye. "I used to be able to take a whole bath in two cups."

Water rationing had been very strict on Mars, even with thirty meters of permafrost under their feet. The Imperial Planetary Reclamation Board guarded the native ice jealously, and charged the dig crews for every liter they extracted. IPRB had a vision of a green Mars, and weren't going to let some profligate scientists spoil their grand dream. Ugarit, for all the stink and humidity and flies and constant, deafening noise, had plenty of water. Some of it was even potable by human standards, but Gretchen had fallen out of the habits she'd learned on Mars. New Aberdeen was a wet, green world—flush with stormy gray seas, heavy forests and chill, cleansing rain pouring from massive, white thunderheads. *Home seems so distant* . . . Then she put the thoughts away and concentrated on getting the right boot on the right foot.

As Fitzsimmons had promised, his repair still held. *A Marine of a thousand uses*, she thought amusedly, trying to dig her fingernail into the seam. She failed, finding the military-issue adhesive goo holding the uppers to the sole like bedrock. "Time for breakfast, and I smell coffee!"

Downstairs, Gretchen found herself sitting at a table near the single window in the common room, a plate of eggs, toast and something which smelled—but did not taste *at all*—like bacon in front of her. The cook, a short, round Frenchman named De'vaques, poured her a big mug of coffee to which she added a liberal amount of sugar and creamer. By some unspoken conspiracy, she found herself accompanied for a lengthy breakfast by Tukhachevsky and the xenobiologist Sinclair. Both men were in a formidably happy mood, and Gretchen tuned them out almost as quickly as they started propounding at length on the peculiar nature of the Ephesian microfauna.

Hot food—and not a heated threesquare or mealbag—commanded her full attention until the plate was bare and the cup empty. She looked up, wondering if the kitchen was flush enough with supplies to allow her a second cup, and caught sight of the meteorologist Smalls's face from across the room. He was a thin, sallow-faced man in the sharp, bright glare of morning, with sunken eyes and lank black hair. Watching him, his body half-hidden behind Tukhachevsky's rotund bulk, Gretchen thought she'd never seen anyone so sad before.

A particularly sharp peal of laughter drew the man's eyes, his head moving with a sharp jerk. Gretchen looked over and realized the common room had already separated out, like some chemical precipitating out of solution, with the scientists—herself included—at one table, while the "crew" sat at another. Delores, her oval face slightly flushed with amusement, was telling a particularly poor joke at the other table. Parker and Bandao were watching her with amusement, while the groundside security people—Blake and a comm tech named Steward—were groaning.

". . . so she said she'd rather date a cattle guard than a cowboy, so we left her sitting by the fence until she had the sense to walk home herself!"

Only Smalls was sitting alone, at the end of a table near the kitchen door. Gretchen realized he was watching Delores, as covertly as he dared, and she remembered how he'd moved toward her on the landing field the night before. *Poor kid,* she thought, remembering a crush she'd suffered through on Mars. Being in the field for a long expedition—and one like this, on the edge of human-controlled space, might last for years without relief—was always tricky. Being married didn't make any difference, not if your spouse was sixty light-years away. *Distance washes away all attachments, makes us forget the old world and see only the new.*

There was a pause in the flow of words from Tukhachevsky and Sinclair, and Gretchen realized they'd asked her something. She turned and raised a questioning eyebrow. "I'm sorry?"

"Would you like to see the main excavation site before we leave?" Sinclair repeated, hair in his eyes, ragged fingernails twisting a fresh tabac from papers. "It'll take all day to load the shuttles, and we won't want to take off until dark."

"I would," Gretchen said, standing up, coffee cup in hand. "About fifteen hundred? Good."

As it happened, Parker had already snorked up the last of the coffee, but Gretchen felt alive enough to face the day. Standing in the door of the kitchen, she found the crew clearing out—Parker and Delores for the landing strip and the shuttles, Blake and the others to start packing and loading. *Good,* she thought, *no one will really notice if I take a bit of a look around. All I need is a guide.*

"Mister Smalls?" The meteorologist looked up, startled, apparently unaware of her approach. "Do you have time to show me around the camp this morning? I'd appreciate it if you could."

In the full glare of midday sun, the camp seemed even more desolate than by night. The horizon stretched away to a dim white line, unbroken by the sight of mountains or hills in any direction. Gretchen blessed the field goggles she'd packed and the battered straw hat that had survived from her very first dig in the ruins of the ancient Il Dioptre observatory on Crete. Her suit was proof against heat and cold alike, but there was no sense in subjecting the temperature regulators to more stress than necessary. Smalls, for his part, had adopted a *djellaba*-like white cloak which covered him from head to toe, with wide-mouthed sleeves and a deep hood.

Brittle sand crunched underfoot as they walked, a fine crust breaking away with each step. The ground sparkled and glittered, as if diamonds had been scattered among the gravel and stones. Tan and a cream-white color dominated, though as the eye reached to the horizon, the deep, deep blue-black of the sky made the distant plain seem yellow.

"How's the weather?" she said at last. Smalls had said nothing after suiting up and leaving the main building. He seemed lost in thought. "The prevailing wind is from the east?"

There were no east-facing windows in the camp, and every building had a smooth, sloping berm of compressed earth and stone facing the rising sun. Even the sheds for the crawlers were reinforced, as if fortified against enemy bombardment, with deep airlocked doorways. More than one of the huts was half-buried by sand, with sloping ramps leading down to battered metal doors.

Smalls said nothing, continuing to stump along. They approached the main lab—a long, low structure with tiny windows surrounded by reinforcing stone. Everyone seemed to sleep in the main building, on the second floor. Gretchen shaded her eyes, looking west. Sunlight flared on the raised tails of the two shuttles, and she could see dust rising from a crawler maneuvering around the back of one. She supposed they were preparing to remount the engine in number two.

Still silent, Smalls keyed the airlock. There was a squeal of tracks clogged with grit, and Gretchen stepped inside, into blessed darkness. She watched the outer door grind closed, seeing the frame was almost entirely eaten away.

"How bad are the storms?" She ventured again, hoping for some kind of response. Smalls pressed a softly glowing plate on the wall and the inner door cycled, dust swirling away at their feet. Beyond a line of glowlights shimmered awake, illuminating a dirty, narrow hallway. Despite the lock, the floor was covered with sand.

"The storms?" Smalls seemed to wake at last, his eyes dark pits in the bad light. Something like a smile twitched on his lips. "They're beautiful. Gorgeous, really."

Gretchen said nothing, only unclasping her mask and taking a moment to taste the building air. She could smell solvents, hot plastic, electrical components and the sharp smell of an overheated printer.

"We'd been here a week," Smalls said, turning away and shuffling down the hallway. "And my satellites weren't all deployed yet, when the first big storm swept over us. Two of the sheds were torn to bits and scattered—Fuentes found one of the roofing panels a couple weeks later, sixty k from here. A crawler got knocked over and we nearly lost shuttle one."

"Sounds bad . . ." Gretchen started to say, but then stopped. Smalls was still talking, apparently unaware of her comment.

"The planet got all smashed up, back at minus three million, and there aren't lots of mountain ranges to speak of, not big plate-driven ones like on Anáhuac or Hesperides. Heat builds up on these big open plains and you get enormous swings in air pressure as the sun moves. There's no humidity to speak of, not with such low temperatures. All the water is locked in the ice caps. No lakes, no oceans— nothing to moderate air temperature."

Smalls unlocked a door, and Gretchen followed him into a room filled with v-pane monitors, computer equipment and racks and racks of data-lattice storage. A huge map of Ephesus glowed in a mosaic of nine displays, half the planet shining bright in the sunlight, and half plunged into complete darkness. The meteorologist waved a hand across the face of the world.

"We have dust storms a thousand kilometers wide, with winds in excess of a hundred sixty k on a slow, quiet day. There are invisible tornadoes, which form and vanish in the upper air. When they touch down, rocks, stones, boulders get lifted and flung for twenty to thirty k." His finger stabbed at the mosaic display, tracing a thin black line just emerging from the terminator.

"And there's the escarpment. A wall across half the world, nearly from pole to pole. The planetary atmosphere's so tight on Ephesus there are peaks which brush the envelope." Smalls turned and looked at Gretchen for the first time. She was leaning against one of the tables, watching him quietly, arms crossed. "The sun is like a big broom, pushing a lot of air in front of the midday hot-spot. There's a fat gradient at dawn and when the wall of moving pressure hits the escarpment, well . . ." He shrugged, showing more than a little perverse pride.

"You get vicious storms in the canyons," Gretchen supplied. "The briefing packet says they're in excess of four hundred fifty k at 'high tide.'"

"They are." Smalls searched among papers and bits of equipment on one of the tables. After a moment, he handed Gretchen a heavy chunk of slate the size of her hand. "The wind rising from the sun compresses against the mountains and the only release is through narrow slot canyons. I have video—in places the walls are like glass, rubbed to near optical quality by sand and grit from a hundred k away. Look at the other side."

Gretchen turned over the piece of slate. The reverse was glossy and black, like fine glass, with a dimple near the center. In the depression was a spherical metallic marble. She looked up in surprise. "What's this?"

"Some bit of nickel-iron—native stuff, there are fields of it in some places, just sitting on the surface—rolling around for a few centuries, getting nice and round. Then a particularly bad storm picked it up and whipped it into a canyon. By the time the cyclone winds had slapped the marble downrange and it hit a certain section of cliff just right—the marble punched right into the slate and stuck. When Russovsky found that, the grit had worn away the splinter lines and cracks, but you can still see them with a . . ." His voice trailed away.

Gretchen put down the shale. She looked at Smalls, who was staring at his displays.

"Do you want to tell me about Russovsky?" Gretchen swung one foot up and sat on the table. "Did she find a lot of interesting things out there, in the wasteland?"

"She did." Smalls scratched the side of his face. The respirator had worn a deep groove across his upper cheek. "I guess Tuk told you she hasn't come back."

Gretchen nodded, politely looking away from the meteorologist at the view of the world.

"Are we going to try and find her, bring her back with us?"

"Of course," Gretchen said in a sharp tone. Smalls almost flinched, and she smiled in apology. "She's one of the crew, right? I won't leave anyone behind."

"Okay." Smalls seemed to relax and sat down. "Did . . . did she bring something back, that day, the day we lost contact with the ship?" He stopped, watching Gretchen's face. "There was a lot of shouting in McCue's lab—it's down the hall—that morning. Then, well, you know—my satellites route through the ship's main array for retransmit from farside, so I was the first to notice something had happened." Smalls shrugged. "The real-time map went out all of a sudden. At first I thought there was a malfunction in my equipment somewhere—the dust eats into things, you know, and they stop working. But everything seemed fine down here. I tried to raise *Palenque* control on the comm, but there was no answer. I guess—"

"Everyone was dead by then," Gretchen said softly. "Russovsky found something in the desert and she brought it back to camp. Did you hear what they were saying, when they were shouting?"

"Yeah, I guess." Smalls looked away. "Clarkson and McCue were always at odds over everything." He managed a bitter laugh. "You'd think they had been lovers or something, but they weren't, not those two." Smalls tapped the crown of his nose. "They just couldn't agree. Clarkson was very Company, very gung-ho, very—ah—results oriented. McCue just wanted to take her time, check things out, take—you know—a few more measurements, a few more readings."

For the first time, Gretchen thought she saw something like fondness in the man's sallow, exhausted face.

"She'd help with your data, you know? She'd take a look at it and do some raw analysis to see if you were getting instrument errors, or interference or something? And it would come back so clean . . . everything would be just . . . solid. Reliable. That was McCue. She was reliable."

Gretchen waited a moment. "Was Russovsky reliable? She and McCue were—"

"They understood each other," Smalls said, nodding. "Russovsky is like one of the old-timers out of Olympus Station, or the outbackers—you ever been to Mars?"

"Yes," Gretchen said, understanding. "I spent two years at the Polaris site."

"Ah." Smalls tried to raise an eyebrow and look knowing, but mostly he looked foolish and Gretchen felt a sudden warmth for the man. *Poor kid,* she thought, thinking of Delores. *He's just a squeeb. Probably never had a real girlfriend his whole life before he came here.*

"So Russovsky," Gretchen interrupted, "liked the emptiness. She liked to go out alone, in her ultralight, and just wander, looking for things. Just . . . seeing what there was to see."

"Yeah!" Smalls scratched the back of his head ruefully. "She was kind of pissed when we first got there—I mean, she's the planetary geologist, right? But Ephesus was smashed like an egg back in First Sun times, the whole planetary mantle was broken into about a million pieces and then slammed back together again. *There's no geology left!* Just slowly settling rubble. Everything's a jumble—you can't even get a depth reading most places—and her instruments just kicked back garbage and plots looking like an Englishman puked six pints of bitters in the street."

"I see." Gretchen frowned. "So why the flights?"

"Well, that was another argument. See, Russovsky tried playing by the rules and duly reported all of this to Clarkson—and he said if she couldn't do *her* work, she could help someone else do something *useful.*" Smalls grinned, and Gretchen realized with a start he was younger than she was. Much younger. *How old is this kid? Twenty?*

"Now, that set McCue off like a rocket, but Russovsky kept her cool and said—and I quote—'I believe my data are in error, Doctor Clarkson. I will endeavor to rectify the situation.'—and then she just walked out of her office, loaded up the *Gagarin* and took off into the blue yonder."

Gretchen answered his smile with one of her own. "Good for her. How many times did she go out?"

Smalls pursed his lips, thinking. "About once a week, I guess. You can't carry too much on a *Midge*, but you can cover a lot of ground. So she must have been all over the place. She always tried to bring me or McCue something pretty—like that shale—or once she found these raw diamonds. She gave those to McCue, I think."

"Did you see what she brought back the last time?"

Smalls shook his head dolefully. "No. I was lying low! Clarkson was already in a mood about something, so when Russovsky came in and made a beeline for McCue's office with a big bundle in her arms, he was spoiling for a fight."

Gretchen nodded. "Why don't you show me her office?"

"Shuttle two to shuttle one, come in." Parker tapped his throat mike experimentally, watching the newly repaired shuttle's control panels light green section by section. Most of the cockpit was still dark, or winking amber. The long grounding had played havoc with the ship's systems. A cursory examination of the hull revealed deep pitting and large sections of discolored, infected metal. "Bandao, can you hear me? Delores, are you on this comm?"

"I hear you," the gunner's voice answered on a crystal-clear channel. "How does it look?"

"Good enough, maybe, sort of . . ." Parker wiggled one of the control panels and the black glassite suddenly flickered to life. "This boat's all eaten up by the damned spores."

"Will she fly?" Delores's sharp voice came online. "Do you have an engine readout yet?"

"I have diagnostics live from the engine," Parker replied dryly. The crewwoman was crouching in the aft engineering space, squeezed in beneath the housing, trying to match up relays and conduits in a maze of pipes and hoses. "And I think she'll fly—at least one-way—and everyone on board had better be suited up. Our little friends have been eating away for weeks."

"Cargo in the damaged ship, then? Passengers in this one?"

Parker nodded, attention distracted by another panel coming online. The wing and airfoil surfaces were showing only sixty to seventy percent response to a basic microcontrol flex test. "Yeah . . . why don't you prep for takeoff. We can load cargo with Delores, me and the security crew. Get all the civilians up to the *Palenque* and into their blessed showers."

"Understood," Bandao replied. Parker squinted out the triangular window. Across the landing field, he could see the gunner rattling down the stairs from number one. "Delores—I still don't have any readout from the fuel gauges. They hooked up yet?"

A grunting sound was her only response. Smiling to himself, the pilot began running through the basic systems checklist. After an hour, he looked up, lean face creased with puzzlement. A line of people was climbing the stairs into shuttle one. He tapped open his throat mike.

"Chief? Anderssen? We're going to send shuttle one upstairs. Did you want to go?"

There was no immediate response, so he checked his comm band to see if Anderssen was in range. Her proximity icon was glowing green, so Parker tried again. "Parker calling Anderssen—hello? Anyone home?"

This time the channel chirped open, and the archaeologist's voice came back, a little thready. "Yes, Parker? What did you say?"

The pilot repeated his question. As he did, Delores climbed down into the cockpit and slid into the copilot's seat. Her hair was streaked with oil, her face shining with sweat and her work gloves were dark with grime. She looked pissed, but Parker made a point of looking respectfully off into the distance, listening to Gretchen speaking on the comm.

"Don't worry about me," Gretchen said, breath rasping as she scrambled up the side of an excavation trench. She squinted for a second while the work goggles adjusted to keep the flare of the late afternoon sun from spearing her eyes. "I'm out at the Observatory excavation site with Sinclair and Smalls. I believe *they* do want to go upstairs today, so tell Bandao to delay liftoff until they get back to camp." She waved to the xenobiologist, who was standing under a shining metallic sunshade a hundred meters away. "We've got two crawlers out here, so I'll take the other one back."

She tramped across a work ladder laid down over the trench as a bridge and passed one of the obelisks forming the main part of the observatory. The stone spire cast a long finger of shadow across the rumpled ground—each obelisk was at least twenty meters high. Four rings of the stones circled the "nave," which nestled at the bottom of a kilometer-wide depression in the desert floor, about three k from the camp.

A network of fresh trenches slashed across the ring arrangement. The expedition had been digging exploratory excavations at ten-meter intervals, trying to find the foundations of the edifice. Gretchen could tell from the desultory sensor grid layout in the trenches they hadn't found what they were looking for. Sinclair had admitted, as they were bouncing up the dusty road from the camp, the "observatory" did not seem to be anything of the kind. The current thinking proposed some kind of naturally occurring phenomena. *Just some rocks.*

Gretchen walked quickly down the path between two trenches to the long rectangular sunshade. Sinclair and Smalls were sitting at a camp table, their goggles glittering mirrors. Cargo crates made more tables and work areas under the strip of shadow.

"They've called from camp," Gretchen said, doffing her hat under the awning. Her skin felt tight, already dehydrated by the parched air. "Shuttle one is ready to make a run back to the ship. You should go, I think, and I'll take the other crawler back."

Both men shared a glance, then Sinclair tilted his head in a sort of temporizing way. "One of us should stay—it's bad policy to go about solo—even so close to the camp."

"I understand," Gretchen said, taking no offense. "But I'll be staying overnight, which means one of *you* would have to give up a shower and the amenities of the *Palenque* for another night. Besides—Parker, Blake and Delores are staying groundside with me, and I'll have the crawler."

There was some more hemming and hawing, but Gretchen just waited for them to convince themselves, then waved as the Skoda Armadillo chuffed away down the road to the main camp. When they were mostly out of sight, she tapped her comm open.

"Mister Parker? Yes, you've got two more passengers coming into camp for your milk run. I'd appreciate it if Bandao-*tzin* waited for them."

There were some disgruntled noises and Gretchen had to smile as she adjusted her hat. Despite the crestfallen attitude of the dig team, she wanted to go over their excavation herself. It had been a while since she'd had a chance to do *her* work, and she wasn't going to pass up the opportunity. A failed dig was almost more interesting than a successful one.

"We'll *all* be going back to the ship tomorrow," she said into the comm as she stepped out into the blaze of sunlight. "No, no, we don't have to pack the whole camp. People should just take their personal baggage. Well, bedding would be a good idea. Lennox and I need to decide if we're going to continue operations here or not. But that can wait a couple of days."

Still listening to Parker and Delores bicker about the damage to shuttle two, she hiked back down into the bowl and began a long counterclockwise circuit around the excavation. People working tended to fall into patterns, and her moderately-experienced eye could see most of the dig crew here were right-handed. All of the paths tended to circle to the right, to pass around the right-hand—or western—side of the obelisks. So, keeping a close eye on the ground, she moved left, peering into the trenches, inspecting the gridding, generally being as nosy as possible.

The sun drifted with her, and the shadows in the excavation slowly lengthened. By the time she'd reached the far side of the bowl, the trenches were almost completely in the shade. A ladder let her climb down into one of the larger cuts and Gretchen paused, seeing something odd lying in a cross-trench from the main. She stepped closer, head dropping into blessed shade.

A cylinder.

She stopped abruptly, her boots skidding in loose gravel. Her heart was pounding. "Oh, Mother Mary! Wait a minute."

Gretchen padded forward and knelt down. A *pulque* can was lying in the trench, abandoned and forgotten by someone. *None of our crew would be so sloppy,* she hoped. *Must have been one of Blake's security people.* She started to pick up the litter, then paused, taking a closer look. *What is that?*

Crouching down, head almost on the ground, she adjusted her lenses to higher mag and gave the can—a *Mayauel* from the faded rabbit on the label—a careful inspection from one end to the other. Something odd had happened to the can. The bottom, in particular, seemed to have fused with the ground, or more accurately, the ground had grown up around the underside of the can. Under hi-mag, she saw thin shoots of a stonelike substance working their way up the aluminum surface.

"Well now, this is interesting." Gretchen took an optical probe from her vest and moved around to face the opening in the top of the can, now lying sideways. Gingerly, she adjusted the tiny wand and eased it up to the mouth hole. Closing one eye, she clicked the worklens control around to match the input from the wand. A moment later, a highly magnified, light-enhanced view of the can sprang into view on the inside of her right lens. Then, gently, she drifted the wand into the opening.

The inside of the can was almost entirely filled with a delicate web of stonelike filaments. In the faint, reflected sunlight she could see hundreds—or thousands— of tiny cilialike fronds and a denser, hexlike structure of mineralized accretions. After taking a good look, she sat up, working a kink out of her shoulder.

"Personal log on," she said, cueing her throat mike. "I've found a discarded pulque can in the observatory dig. Looks like it's been here a couple weeks. Close examination finds the Ephesian microbiota Sinclair and Tukhachevsky tried to explain to me this morning in evidence. Something very much like what Parker found in the shuttle engines is eating the can." Gretchen stood up, stretching. She hadn't been grubbing in the dirt in months either. Her knees were already complaining. "Pretty soon the whole can will be gone, and the result will look just like everything else here, a mineral layer like sand and rock over this . . . mineral life form."

She stared up at the slender finger of the nearest obelisk. The pale cream texture made a sharp contrast against the blue-black sky. "Lennox's team was disappointed," she said, "to find their 'observatory' made of nothing but rock and mineral deposits—not set down by the hand of the First Sun people. They've decided the whole structure is just a natural formation, a quirk of geology. I wonder. . . . I need to talk to Sinclair about his microbiota. There's something . . . something here almost makes sense. Log off."

Giving the *Mayauel* and its tiny colony a wide berth, Gretchen continued her circuit, eventually climbing out of the excavation as the sun was setting. Her suit recorded a brief moment of moderate temperature before shifting from cooling to heating. Night came swiftly out of the east, flooding across the desert plains. Without mountains or more than a high thin cloud to catch the last light of the sun, darkness was quickly upon her.

She switched on a lamp as she trudged up the slope to the crawler. In the starlight, everything seemed very quiet and still, frosted with silvery light. Her spot danced on the ground, a pale circle of yellow sliding over rocks, boulders, the tracks of the crawler. Gretchen paused, hands on the ladder leading up into the cabin. *What was that?*

The hum of the respirator masked most sounds and the wind had died with the passing of the sun. Gretchen turned off her lamp. Darkness folded around her again, then slowly lightened as her lenses adapted to the starlight. Everything seemed very still. She waited, listening.

Only the hum of the suit fans reached her ears. Annoyed, she shut down the respirator. There was a *click* and then nothing. Now she could hear her heart beating, a steady *thump-thump-thump*. Gretchen stepped away from the crawler, taking one step, two steps down toward the bowl. Her head cocked to one side, listening.

There was a sound. Something like the wind stirring sand and gravel, a faint *tik-tik-tik*. She slowly dropped into a squat on the trail, holding her breath. Now the sound was a little more distinct and she could hear—feel almost—a slow, pervasive susurration all around her. Gretchen breathed again, feeling faint. The respirator wasn't just for show, she reminded herself. Her thumb slid the control to ON, and the fans started up again, and her nose tube felt cold with the slow breeze of a suitable air mixture. Gretchen stood, the faint, delicate sound drowned out by the clamor of her breath and machines, but she was smiling.

Treading carefully on the fragile ground, she walked back to the crawler and climbed aboard.

Inside the cabin, her mask hooked to the vehicle's reserve air bottle, she sat for a long time, listening to the busy night and watching the stars slowly wheel overhead. Her comm was shut down, the crawler's engine cold. Gretchen thought, sitting there in the darkness, a rime of frost slowly congealing on her mask around the waste gas vent, she knew how Russovsky felt.

Am I an old-timer, then? The thought was very amusing. She was sure none of the outbackers on Mars would think so. She doubted if any of the dig scientists had stayed out past nightfall. *I should go in. Parker's probably mustering a search party by now.*

Sighing, she shook her arms, sending a cascade of CO_2 frost to the floor of the crawler, then switched on machine power and let the big tracked vehicle start its diagnostic. A heavy rumble trembled through the seat and soles of her boots. Her respirator whined on, and the suit began to percolate heat through her limbs. "Damn!" Stabbing pains cramped her arms and legs. "Too cold to sit here."

Ten minutes later, she threw the Armadillo into gear and rumbled off down the road, the yellow headlights of the big tank dancing across the rutted track, a slow heavy cloud of dust rising behind. In the darkness, swathes of minute, glittering lights flared for a moment as the cloud of water vapor settled onto the desert floor, then faded as the windfall of energy from the sky was consumed.

Hummingbird swung onto the bridge of the Company spacecraft and paused, one hand on the railing leading up to the captain's command station. There was no threat-well, no gleaming banks of combat monitors, no subdued lighting or perfect climate control. Instead, bights of ratty wire and conduit hung from open panels in the overhead, there was an acrid, burnt smell in the air, and a racket of chattering comm feeds hissed from the communications station. Most of the control panels were dark and the deck had an uneven, mottled quality.

Lieutenant Isoroku started to say something, but the *tlamatinime* shook his head slightly.

"I've seen a damaged ship before, *Sho-sa*," he said quietly. His interest fixed on a panoramic view of the planet below—a sharp dun-red crescent silhouetted against ebon night, with the peaks of the Escarpment beginning to glow in the morning sun. *Somewhere down there, Russovsky found a book and a weapon—not so unalike. And where there is one, there will be others. . . .*

Hummingbird pushed himself to the main comm panel, scarred fingers brushing over the controls. "How awake is main comp—"

"*Hsst!* Who are you, stranger?" A sharp, inhuman voice cut across the *tlamatinime*'s question. "Stand away from my station!"

Hummingbird turned and found the brawny shape of Isoroku blocking the movement of the Hesht female onto the bridge. The engineer's back was tense, though nothing in comparison to the slitted eyes and flattened ear-tufts of the alien. Enraged, the Hesht loomed over the human, her long arms poised to slam the engineer out of the way.

"I am Green Hummingbird," the México said, putting a warning hand on Isoroku's shoulder. His voice was very firm and he met Magdalena's eyes squarely. "I am an Imperial Officer from the *Cornuelle*. There is no cause for territorial dispute, *ss'shuma* Magdalena. Your pride hunts for mine, and I have need of your place-of-watching."

Magdalena bared her teeth, circling through the darkened, inactive navigator's station, glittering nails digging into the backs of the seats to propel herself along. "You may be queens-pride, old crow, but you are not welcome here! Look, if you must, but keep your dirty paws to yourself."

Hummingbird felt a flash of irritation—one he suppressed before the emotion could color his face or make him react—and gave Isoroku a little push. "My thanks, Isoroku-*san*. I will comm if I have need of anything."

The engineer, still watching Magdalena with a wary eye, made a sharp, properly polite bow and swam off down the access tube. The Hesht watched him go with undiluted, unfeigned hatred burning in her yellow eyes. The claws of her right hand slipped reflexively out of bony sheaths, then retracted. Hummingbird kicked away from the deck and drifted into her direct line of sight.

"*Sho-sa* Isoroku is *not* one of your hunting-pride," he said, catching her attention. "He takes food from the kill of Hadeishi, who drinks from *my* watering holes. Do you understand me, *ss'hi'a?*"

Magdalena bristled at the word, black lips curling away from gleaming white teeth. "I am not a child! Insult me again, monkey, and—"

"You will do what?" Hummingbird drifted closer, ignoring the bared claws. Startled at his boldness, Magdalena backed up. "You will lose your temper? Attack me, without the pack-leader's permission? Have your entire pride seized and imprisoned, this ship-den impounded by the Imperial Navy?"

The Hesht flinched as if struck, then her anger surged, a deep rumbling in the back of her throat. Hummingbird refused to move, refused to show any reaction at all. Magdalena stood poised and stiff for a moment, then suddenly gave ground. Her tail was twitching, both ears flat against the long angular skull. "What . . . what do you want?"

"A civil reception," Hummingbird said, testily. "Where is Anderssen-*tzin?* On the planet?"

"Yes," Magdalena hissed, twitching from head to toe. She swung gracefully over into the comm station seat, one leg bracing against the command panel. "She's just returned to the base camp."

"And the other scientists? Where are they?" Hummingbird took care to remain standing, so he could look down on the Hesht from at least a tiny height. The bitter smell of tension in the air was beginning to abate, but he did not wish to give up any advantage.

Magdalena pointed sullenly at a v-pane showing orbital tracks, the ring of satellites and various other objects in near-Ephesian space. "Bandao-*tzin* is carrying them in shuttle one; they will be docking here in an hour and fifty minutes. The other shuttle is still groundside."

"All of the scientists? What about the security team?" Hummingbird chanted the names of the men and women on the surface—a quick mnemonic to remind him of their names, faces, specialties—under his breath.

"Not all." Magdalena's eyes narrowed again, yellow-amber wedges reflecting the intermittent glow of the instrument panels. "Our stray sister is still lost and Gretchen is hunting planetside until tomorrow. Blake and Parker and Fuentes are with her."

"Russovsky." Hummingbird nodded, remembering, and then turned a sharp eye on the Hesht. "You've not made contact with her by comm? Her ultralight is fully equipped, by my memory."

"She does not answer. Radar scans have not found her. The planet is large—perhaps you should go look yourself." Magdalena yawned derisively, showing a forest of razor-sharp teeth. "I am looking, but our search is slowed by the damage suffered by the *Palenque*. Maybe your pride helps, if you want to catch this stray *kupil?* Hadeishi's ship has excellent eyes."

Hummingbird did not respond. He was watching the time-to-dock estimate for shuttle one and considering which path was swiftest to his goal. *Russovsky could lead us to her discovery site immediately,* he thought. *But these others will have seen, done things on the planet as well. They are often jealous creatures—they may have withheld knowledge from one another, even from their public logs and records.* He sighed, estimating the time he would need to interrogate each of the *macehualli* technicians. *Ah, but the tenacious Anderssen will want to find Russovsky for herself. Let us not duplicate our efforts.* Hummingbird looked up, catching the Hesht making an insulting face.

"I am lair-guest, for a time, *ss'shuma.*" He made a pointing motion with his nose. "I will not disturb your efforts to repair the ship. Good day." With that, he sprang easily into the mouth of the access tube and then swam down into the main passage. Behind him, there was a spitting hiss, but nothing so loud or obvious he needed to take notice.

Hummingbird shook his head, coming to light at the entryway to the hab ring. "A waste of time," he said to himself, eyeing the various cabin doors. Some of the locks were dimly lit with the closed hand of a privacy lock, others were entirely dark. *But I am impatient,* he realized, feeling the queer, nibbling attraction of the cylinder and its contents. *This is not good.*

He found an unused cabin and tapped on his comm. "Sergeant Fitzsimmons? Yes, this is Hummingbird. I have some things by the number one airlock. Can you bring them to . . ." He read out the cabin number, then set about testing the lights, shower, refresher. Most things seemed to be working. The common, everyday motions served to settle his nerves.

A particularly disturbing thought had occurred to him.

What, he mused, *if the planet itself is a lure? So obviously shaped, marked with the tread of the First Sun people . . . any spacefaring race would light here and be intrigued. Then—scattered about, perhaps the cylinders are only one such bait—some dangerous items, some helpful devices. These things have happened before. But is the trap here on Ephesus, or are we picking up marker dye to lead something homeward?*

By the time Fitzsimmons and Deckard arrived with his baggage—and he'd brought everything from the *Cornuelle* save the little shrine to the Lady of Tepeyac—Hummingbird had disassembled the in-cabin comm panel and was wiring the data conduit to take his portable comps.

"Master Hummingbird?" The sergeant paused in the doorway, surprised to find the wizened old man surrounded by a cloud of components and glassite panels. "Do you need help? I can call Iso—"

"No, thank you." Hummingbird looked up, measuring the two men with a critical eye. He was not displeased with what he saw. Even aboard this ship, the Marines were carrying their weapons and tools, within a moment's notice of combat readiness. "Put those things there, yes, against the wall."

Hummingbird watched them move, and was pleased to see they were entirely at home in the z-g environment of the ship. *Well trained,* he thought. *A fine pair of tools. They should not be wasted.*

"Tomorrow morning," the *tlamatinime* said, drawing their attention. "You'll go down to the planet in shuttle one. There is—if you had not heard—a scientist missing from the team. A woman named Russovsky. Find and secure this woman and return her—alive, unharmed—to the ship."

"Aye, sir." Fitzsimmons seemed startled, pleased and concerned all at once. "With civilian help, or without?"

"Make use of their pilots," Hummingbird said. "Anderssen will be eager to find her as well. By tomorrow night, I want *everyone* off the planet with a minimum of fuss."

The sergeant nodded sharply, then spun backward out of the door. Deckard followed, and both men shot away down the curving hallway of the hab ring. Hummingbird closed the door, then pressed the small round shape of a privacy bomb against the wall. The device shivered, then winked blue. The *tlamatinime* felt his skin crawl, but the sensation of being watched faded away.

"Curious, curious cats," he said softly, easing himself back into the cocoon of comp parts and conduit feeds. "Out of my house . . ."

"I'm a pap-sucking kitten, am I?" Magdalena's claw adjusted a filter control minutely. A jittery, scrambled image of the México *nauallis* flickered, jumped, then cleared. The comm panel on the bridge of the *Palenque* was alive with v-panes, showing dozens of feeds from all over the ship, from Fitzsimmons and Deckard's z-suits, even from Isoroku's navy workrig. The Hesht bared all her teeth, then lashed her tail twice before settling down into the shockchair. "A hunter *sees*, a kit *hides*. Now, what are you doing, little bird?"

As it happened, Hummingbird was still assembling his comps, though Magdalena found the specifics of his equipment very interesting. Still, he was likely to be busy for a few hours. The Hesht turned her attention to the two Marines. After watching them for a few moments, her attention wandered. Her own kind might have amused her for hours, but these slick, shiny pink things . . . her claw idled over a glyph, then tapped out a save-for-later. "Males getting ready for the hunt. Hrrrr . . . boring. But hunt-sister might like to see. Hmm dee hmm."

A task-glyph popped to the top of her work queue—one marked with Anderssen's rabbit-ear symbol. Magdalena sniffed disdainfully—*More housekeeping,* she thought, then tapped the message open with a shining white claw. A still of Gretchen's face appeared, nearly unrecognizable behind a broad hat, the respirator mask and work goggles. "Maggie, I've remembered something—Russovsky didn't have a single letter in her t-relay queue when I printed out the mail last night—can you check to see if she ever got anything from home? Seems strange. . . . Talk to you tomorrow."

"No mail?" Magdalena shifted in her chair and tapped up the message logs from ship's comm. In her experience, humans loved to talk more than anything—one of them actually keeping quiet did seem very odd. *Maybe she's sick or something. . . . Let's see.*

The t-relay had never gone down, though the massive power failure on the *Palenque* had knocked out the message queuing system interface with shipboard comm. Magdalena hadn't done more to restart the t-relay than restore normal power and re-init shipside systems. As a result, she hadn't needed to navigate the obtuse and entirely military interface for the relay logs before.

An hour passed in increasing, tail-chewing disgust before she managed to find the interface for viewing traffic statistics. Then she found an entire security module had been deactivated in the transfer to civilian control, which had disabled the usual logging features. Three hours later, the Hesht was carefully keeping her tail curled under the shockchair, and a section of light construction-grade metal paneling was floating in tiny pieces around her like a constellation of broken, blue-gray moons.

"There! Finally . . ." Magdalena scanned through the message queue storage facility. Her initial feeling of triumph faded quickly. The queue storage subsystem was encrypted and her commercial decrypt soft said the jumbled hash of characters and letters was a military code. Maggie reached out and dug her claws into the back of the command station behind her, tearing another section of paneling away. It felt good to feel something rend between her claws. "So . . . so how are readable messages coming through at all?"

She broke into the current t-relay queue and glanced over two of the messages. They were as readable and plain as any human letter could be. Brow furrowed, the little claw on her smallest finger tapping against her left incisor, Maggie began tracing the interface between the public messaging system and the relay. After thirty minutes, she was curled up into a tight ball, only the horizontal yellow gleam of her eyes visible over her arm. A constant stream of what seemed to be garbage—code, machine dumps, encrypted text—drifted past on her panel. Her usage of main comp had crept up into the sixteen percent range, billions of cycles diverted to a multitiered array of searches, all trying to winkle out the encrypt key protecting the storage system.

A chime sounded, waking Magdalena from a dream filled with tiny green birds fluttering around her head, each one singing in an annoying voice, flitting only millimeters from her grasping claws. She uncoiled, staring at the panel. A queue flag had popped up, bearing the ideogram code encapsulating Russovsky's comm ID. Magdalena frowned, then her claws skittered across the panel, diverting the message into unencrypted storage and starting a system trace to find where it had come from.

"Addressed to Ctesiphon Station?" Maggie shook her head, blinking, and stared again at the message routing header. The sizeable message—several gigabytes in length—was slated to go outbound on the r-relay at a very low priority. The Hesht frowned, looking over the routing instructions, which were much longer than the usual *Please send four quills for a new pelt brush.* "Dispatch only during dead-time? No . . . in sections, to a commbox on station, to be forwarded . . ."

Her tail started to lash again, very, very slowly. "What a clever monkey. She's hacked the t-relay!"

———————

Hummingbird's face lit with the soft glow of a display panel, weary old eyes glittering with the spark of glyphs flashing awake. Reassembling his surveillance systems had taken much longer than he expected—he'd considered calling Isoroku for help—but resisted the urge. There was really no reason to let the engineer see Mirror equipment in operation, not when the man was entirely competent and a boon to his ship. Dealing with an angry *Chu-sa* Hadeishi would only waste more time. So Hummingbird stretched in place, broke open a threesquare and swallowed the vile mixture. Four panels faced him—a control display between his knees—then three v-panes in a wing. To his left, an array of local camera feeds showed him the corridors and rooms of the ship, now suddenly crowded by the arrival of the scientists from the planet. To his right, a mirror of the planetary view maintained on the bridge shimmered in the display.

Despite his earlier decision to let Anderssen and her people find the missing scientist, a thought had occurred to Hummingbird while he was working. *Setting up a search will only take a moment,* he said, arguing with himself. *Then they can make the pickup themselves.*

In truth, the scientists were all taxing the water and power supply of the ship with a half-dozen simultaneous, extended showers. After that they'd want to stuff themselves with food—Hummingbird smiled, noting the shipboard mess was entirely barren, save for the same kind of threesquares the crew had been subjected to on the planet—and sleep. *So I have a few moments to spare.*

He tapped up a schematic of the coverage afforded by the meteorological satellites the expedition had deployed in a long string around the planetary equator. The weather surveillance system managed nearly pole to pole coverage. "Good," he said with a trace of smugness. "Now show me what kind of video feed . . ."

More images flashed past on his displays. The peapods maintained an historical archive, which Hummingbird pillaged, looking for a highview shot of the base camp the day Russovsky delivered her deadly cylinder. A second later, the system chirped apologetically—the satellite array did not contain information older than a week. "Odd . . ." Hummingbird tapped up specifics on the Texcoco ISA-built satellites. "Ah, too much data to store locally." He queried main comp to see if there was an off-array archive. Moments later, an answer came back: a partial archive was maintained in crystal storage at base camp, in the laboratory of Smalls, Victor A., doctoral candidate, Mars Academy of Sciences.

Hummingbird nodded, glad the young man had taken proper care to protect his work. Seconds later, the main comm array had thrown a whisker to the base-camp station, and Hummingbird's search was causing dozens of pale firefly lights to wink on in Smalls's crowded lab. An entire wall of c-storage rippled awake in response to the *tlamatinime*'s request.

On the ship, Hummingbird sat back, eyes closed, breathing steady, waiting.

"Gretchen? Are you awake?" Magdalena bit nervously at a length of metallic support strut, leaving dimpled marks along the black metal. "It's Magdalena, hunt-sister. Are you mating? Cleaning yourself? Answer, please!"

"I'm here," came the muffled reply. The vid showed nothing, only darkness. Impatient, Maggie dialed up the light amp and image interpolate on the channel. This revealed the matte surface of a sleepbag, which then split open to reveal the mussed, tousled head of a very sleepy Anderssen. "What happened?"

"I think . . . oh, a fine hunt! I think I've found *ss'shuma* Russovsky." Magdalena grinned tightly, careful to keep her teeth covered, but the pink tip of her tongue poked gleefully between her lips. "At least, I know where she was sixteen hours ago, when the sun came up."

"Okay." The image of Gretchen rubbed her eyes and a giant hand reached out to adjust the comm band so she could see Magdalena. "Tell me."

"I was trying to find Russovsky's mail—like you asked—and I couldn't. Very strange, but then a message processed through the *Palenque* main comm array—a message from Russovsky's *Midge*, from the groundside—and my watchers picked it up. Hunt-sister, the doctor didn't have any mail waiting for her because *she's been picking it up all this time!*"

Gretchen, wondering why her mouth tasted so foul, managed a "Huh?"

Maggie looked off-screen for a moment, her ears pricked up. "The *Midge* houses a comm array in the upper wing, a big, broad surface. A great transmitter and receiver. So Russovsky changed her messaging configuration here on the ship—I found where she broke into the system and tweaked some access settings—so her *Midge* could connect to the *Palenque* on a maintenance channel and transmit her messages. The burst I intercepted was big—because it's filled with video from the cameras on the ultralight—and she uploads every morning."

Gretchen blinked. "Wait—so she's keeping a record of where she flew during the day?"

"Better," Maggie grinned, and this time she didn't bother to hide her fangs. "She's transmitting all of her *data* from the geosensors on the *Midge*; each day she flies, she's mapping the planetary surface, taking gravity measurements, even spectroscope of exposed rock formations . . . everything she can pick up."

"Ah." Gretchen felt her mind begin to work, sleep-rusty gears ticking over. "But her data doesn't go through a known channel—and nothing that Clarkson would notice. So everything's stored in *Palenque* main comp?"

The Hesht's ears flicked and a queer, pleased gleam spilled into her eyes. "Not at all. The *Midge* sends the data here with a tail-twister of a routing header—notes on where the message should go, who it's intended for—to sit on the t-relay until main comm traffic is low. Then Russovsky's message wakes up and sends itself to Ctesiphon Station. She lets it break up into sections if need be, so if there's a lot of traffic, *her* entire message won't get through for a couple hours. But once at the big emitter on Ctesiphon, it gets forwarded all the way to the University of Aberdeen, on Anáhuac!"

"She's sending the data to herself, at home, in her lab." Gretchen made a face. Her tongue tasted strange. *I am never drinking Blake's "special" vodka again. Ever. No matter how much he begs.* "That's very clever. She's not paying for the transmission time, is she?"

Maggie laughed out loud, a rumbling, crackling cough. "The accounting system here, and on Ctesiphon, always allows a certain amount of synchronization traffic between relays. Each station has to identify itself and make sure messages are passing properly between them. Russovsky's data goes over in the checksum of the synchro packets, or attached to other messages. If anyone pays, it's the Company."

"Fine. Fine." Gretchen didn't really care about the technical details. "The comm array has to get a fix on her transmitter then, right?"

The Hesht nodded. "I have a fix, to the centimeter, of where she set down at sunrise today. She's flying tonight, I suppose, but when she transmits in the morning . . ."

"Tell Fitzsimmons and Bandao to gear up," Gretchen said, lying back down, the sleepbag helpfully curling up around her shoulders. "They need to be ready to drop shuttle one as soon as you've got a fix and pick her up. Bring her back to the ship. Parker and I will come up in the other shuttle as soon as we can."

Maggie nodded, but Gretchen was asleep and snoring softly before the channel flickered closed.

Hummingbird's eyes opened and he looked expectantly at his display. A moment later there was a chiming sound and a v-pane unfolded with the results of his search. Smalls had been capturing an enormous amount of data—the entire planetary surface in visual, plus air temperature and density scans—for weeks and weeks. Scanning such a volume, looking for the silhouette of an ultralight flying a low altitude, proved far more time consuming than the *tlamatinime* expected. Now he unfolded himself from a waiting posture and tapped the first of the search results.

A highview shot of a *Midge* sitting on the landing field at base camp appeared.

"No . . ." Hummingbird flipped through the rest of the results. None of them were useful, though each picture was—with clouds, dust and other interference scrubbed away—a fine picture of a *Midge*-class ultralight seen from above. "Strange. Why only base camp? Oh, I see . . ."

Smiling at his own naiveté, Hummingbird expanded his search criteria to include an aircraft in flight, one where the silhouette changed as the ultralight banked or turned, or the recorded image was only partial due to heavy clouds or sandstorms. The search started again and he began reciting a long memory chant to pass the time.

"Even if a man were poor, lowly," he sang, "even if his mother and his father were the poorest of the poor, his lineage is not considered. Only the matter of his life matters, the purity of his heart, his good and humane heart, his stout—"

Another chime interrupted, which made Hummingbird frown suspiciously. "That's too quick!"

He tapped up the image, expecting to find a sand dune or rocky flat. Instead, the glittering shape of an aircraft wing catching the sun was frozen in the satellite picture. Hummingbird blinked in surprise, then zoomed the image. And again. At first the image was blurry, barely the shadow of an angular shape against a field of shattered black lava, then the display panel kicked in and the view sharpened. The *tlamatinime* pursed his lips. He'd found an aircraft—but not Russovsky's ultralight—or one of the Javan Yards shuttles from the *Palenque*. Something else, something without Company markings.

"Show me the rest," he muttered, dialing forward. Far below, in Smalls's lab, one particular c-storage lattice woke to life, reeling off snapshots of the planetary surface taken weeks before. On Hummingbird's panel, a jerky series of images spun past. But the mysterious shuttle was already gone. He backed up, frame by frame, then realized with disgust that Smalls's satellites were only shooting an image every half hour—more than enough time to track a storm, but not swift enough to capture more than an instant of a shuttle's swift passage through the atmosphere.

"Where did you go?" Hummingbird began composing a more detailed search. At the same time he kicked the one image to the *Cornuelle*'s main comp for identification. Then he waited, pondering the grainy, low-def image on his v-pane. The ident came back moments later and Hummingbird nodded, unsurprised, at the identification.

"A *Valkyrie*," he read from main comp's concise, clipped summary. "Mining shuttle, one hundred fifty tons displacement, four engines, sub-light capable. Usually paired with a *Tyr*-class mobile refinery." A schematic of the spacecraft was attached—a huge assemblage of ore tanks, drives and shuttle bays. Hummingbird was not familiar with the class of ship—he rarely devoted his attention to navy

matters—but the manufacturer was well known to him from certain other business. His lip curled. "Ship design and construction by Norsktrad Heavy Industries,
Kiruna system. A Swedish ship . . ."

The destruction of the ancient Kingdom of Swedish-Russia on Anáhuac in
the previous century had not prevented tens of thousands of Swedes and Russians
from leaving the homeworld for the colonies. Indeed, strict Imperial control of
their home provinces had probably precipitated the exodus into the outer worlds.
Entire companies—some once no more than Swedish governmental departments—had moved offworld as well. Two cold, desolate worlds—yet still habitable—orbiting Kiruna Prime were the center of a thriving manufacturing and
shipbuilding industry.

No one, particularly not the Voice of the Mirror, could say the Kirunan companies engaged in treacherous acts. Such an event would have precipitated the
destruction of both the colonies and their orbital habitats. Despite this—despite a
scrupulous and timely payment of taxes and every outward sign of loyal service to
the Empire—far too many Kirunan-built spacecraft found their way into the
hands of pirates, rogue miners, Communards, and insurrectionists of all kinds.

"Hummingbird to the *Cornuelle*," he said, tapping open his comm. "I need to
speak with *Chu-sa* Hadeishi immediately."

THE CORNUELLE

Finally.

Hadeishi nodded sharply to Hummingbird's image and closed the channel. He swung his command chair to the threat-well at the center of the bridge, a speculative expression on his face. "*Sho-sa* Koshō, ship to alert status one. All hands to stations."

Immediately, even as the captain's words faded from the air, the exec's slim finger stabbed a double-size glyph on her control panel. A sharp hooting sound rang out through every pressurized space on the light cruiser and every comm flashed an attention signal. Koshō was unable to keep a fierce smile from her face, though the cultured, exact voice issuing from the comm was perfectly devoid of emotion. "All hands to battle stations. All hands to battle stations. Ship will lock down in one hundred eighty seconds. Gravity will be zero in one hundred seconds. All hands . . ."

Hadeishi felt suddenly awake, his vision clear, hearing acute, his hands filled with an immediate quick energy. His combat display had already split—keyed by the alert—into four sections, one showing the status of his ship, another the immediate space around the *Cornuelle*, another with a summary of all known threats—empty for the moment—and the fourth filled with palm-sized v-feeds from the various divisions. Everything was entirely familiar, save for Engineering, where a suddenly sweaty and perturbed-looking *Sho-i Ko-hosei* Yoyontzin had started in horror at the sound of the alarm horns.

"Mister Hayes," Hadeishi snapped, feeling a cold, invincible calm settle over him. "Status?"

"No threats," the weapons officer replied, his broad face showing no emotion at all. "*Palenque* orbit is stable, engines cold. One shuttle docked, the other groundside at base one. Recon drones and survey satellites show no motion, no hostiles. Passive scan is quiet. Shall I go active?"

"No, Hayes-*tzin*, not at this time. *Sho-sa* Koshō?"

The exec tucked a curling trail of raven-dark hair behind one ear. She was leaning on her panel, one hand knuckled against the glassite, an antique gold stopwatch in her free hand. She was counting silently. After the briefest moment, she raised her eyes to the captain and said "fifty-eight" while clicking the stopwatch. Hadeishi waited while the lieutenant tapped open the all-hands ship channel. "Ship in lockdown," she announced, and the captain felt a distant rumble through his chair as the hab rings spun to a stop and locked in place, then a hissing clang as the main bridge pressure hatches sealed. At the same moment, his shipsuit stiffened and a warning tone sounded beside his ear.

"Gravity zero," Koshō announced, securing the watch and taking hold of the edge of her display. "Engines hot."

"All systems tracking," Hayes announced at almost the same moment. "Beam nacelles are live, missile racks one through nine are cleared to load. Shall I load out?"

"Rack with flash loads by evens," Hadeishi replied in a crisp voice. "Timing, Mister Hayes, I want timing." He turned slightly to look at his exec again. "Time, *Sho-sa?*"

Koshō came to attention, though no one save a shipmate could have told the difference from one moment to the next. "All hands to station in ninety-six seconds, *Chu-sa*. Engines hot, systems secured in one hundred fifty seconds."

Hadeishi's chair vibrated again and he knew the missile racks were loading, magazine carrels rotating into place, the slender shapes of *Hayai Roku* sliding into their launch tubes.

"Admirable," the captain replied, looking to the communications station. "Emissions status, Mister Smith?"

"T-relay offline," the midshipman replied, cheeks flushed, the beat of his heart thudding in the artery at his neck. "Main array in passive. Comm array on the *Palenque* forced down, ship to ground forced down, emissions are at minimum. Shipskin neutral."

"Hayes-*tzin*? Backscatter from civilian sources? Visual confirmation?"

The weapons officer suppressed a start—he'd expected to report the even-numbered missile racks loaded and their launch status green—hands moving in a blur across his panel. Hadeishi watched keenly—the request to double-check the light cruiser's emissions status from local civilian sources was unexpected, though they were rarely in position to take direct control of civilian sensor apparatus—and counted the seconds until the *Thai-i* responded. Out of the corner of his eye, the captain watched Koshō counting as well, ancient watch magically back in her hand.

"Civilian sensors are blank," Hayes said, his voice a fraction rushed. "Visual confirm is . . . is positive. I have outline from *Palenque* navigational cam." A finger speared sideways and a new v-pane unfolded on Hadeishi's display. With interest, the captain examined the image. "Backscatter from satellites is null, backscatter from *Palenque* main array is . . . null."

"Interesting." Hadeishi folded his hands in his lap. The civilian ship mounted an entire array of exterior cameras to assist in docking at a station or other orbital facility. Apparently they also included moderately sophisticated pattern-matching soft, which had picked the outline of the *Cornuelle*—even at one hundred kilometers—out of the background starfield. The *Palenque* comp could not make a match for ship type or registry, but it knew *something* was within its programmed avoidance limits. "Maintain feed from the civilian ship, Hayes-*tzin. Sho-sa* Koshō, please adjust ship orientation by degrees."

Cocooned in his command chair, Hadeishi could not feel the massive bulk of the *Cornuelle* begin to move, though the video feed on the *Palenque* picked up the spark of her maneuvering engines as they began a topwise spin. The threat-well and most of the displays remained constant—only the one pickup showing the arc of Ephesus shifted, the planet turning slowly upside down.

"Five second burn." Koshō's face remained porcelain, her eyes calmly tracking the movement of the ship. "Burn halted."

Hadeishi watched the comp on the *Palenque* adjust, seeing the image—and the identifier—flicker in and out, adapting, adapting . . . then the lock vanished and the civilian software declared the "foreign ship" to have vanished. "There you are. . . . Reverse roll, Koshō-*san*."

The *Cornuelle* reappeared for a moment on the civilian display as momentum carried the cruiser back into a recognizable configuration. A second series of burns halted roll, then nudged her back, second by second, into an unidentifiable "hole" against the wall of night.

Hadeishi nodded. Koshō was already making a note in the log, while Hayes and Smith spoke softly into their throat mikes, adding their own commentary. The captain waited until they were done, then lifted his chin. "Admirably swift," he said. "Lieutenant Koshō, please make a note to schedule an exercise—at a later date—to determine the detection envelope of the civilian cameras. Then double-check with Fleet to see they have the same information. Mister Hayes, you may stand down your missile crews." He glanced over his display again. Everything remained quiet.

"Now there is the matter of this mysterious shuttle. I want a full report by end of watch, which we will discuss over dinner."

Koshō and the others nodded sharply and Hadeishi cancelled alert status himself. *No need to disturb the cooks,* he thought, *though perhaps I should—an alert during dinner would certainly put everyone to the test. . . .* "We will remain under emissions control, Lieutenant. Move the ship to a different orbit. No sense in being too predictable."

Even though no one seems to be here to see us. . . . But Hadeishi knew exactly how easy it would be to hide in the interplanetary dark, unmoving, unnoticed, nearly invisible.

"Hrrmmm . . ." Magdalena was curled up again, both long arms lapped over her knees, snout resting on plush, close-napped black fur. One of her displays showed the faint traces of the *Cornuelle* shifting orbit—the flare of the big maneuvering drives were impossible to disguise, particularly at this short range—and the other presented an image of the "mysterious" shuttle the little bird had found.

The Hesht was not pleased with the man's efficiency or the power of his comps. She had watched with entirely open avarice as the México had unpacked three copper-colored blocks—each one no more than a forepaw wide—from his baggage and set them up in a cluster with the cabin display. She could smell something secret and powerful about them, and her tail lashed slowly from side to side, fur itching with the desire to take hold of them for *just a moment.*

At the same time, she was entirely convinced tweaking the tail of this human would be bad luck, for her, for her adoptive pack and for her hunt-sister Gretchen. So she watched impatiently, busying herself with a thorough search of the young skywatcher male's planetary scan archive. Magdalena had convinced herself there was a great deal of information hidden in the c-storage racks down at the observatory base. *Many secrets,* she mused. *Waiting to be revealed to the light of day, like a heep burrow peeled back by a gentle claw.*

She checked the progress of her image scan. The number was far, far too low to satisfy her desire, so a claw dragged an override and the *Palenque* main comp began to devote nearly thirty percent capacity to her search.

Hadeishi sat back, letting his steward remove the small dinner bowls from the table. The momentary burst of activity this afternoon had broken an almost imperceptible weight of boredom, though now—with nothing new to engage his attention—he felt the deadening effect of routine stealing up on him again. This pricked his mind to something like angry motion, and he'd spent the period between end of watch and dinner devising a series of sudden training alerts, each one timed to come at the most inappropriate or difficult time.

Standing on station like this—waiting, with nothing in the offing—was particularly trying. Hadeishi prided himself on being a calm man—particularly in the face of tumult or crisis—but amid this stultifying sameness he found himself reaching for something, anything, to enliven the day. Today, particularly after sensing *Sho-sa* Koshō's quiet pride in the crew's reaction time to the alert, he was tempted to press her until her imperturbable calm broke.

That is entirely unworthy, he reminded himself. *Your boredom is not an excuse to torment a fellow officer.* Still, the prospect intrigued—Hadeishi was beginning to wonder if the lieutenant had ever truly lost her temper.

The steward set down small pale green plates, each one containing a single orange wedge. Hadeishi speared his with a single *hashi* and popped the sweet fruit into his mouth. Around the low table, his officers did the same—each in their own way—and then the stewards finished clearing the last of the dishes. Mugs of tea appeared, each steaming, filling the air with the turned-earth aroma of a high-grade *sencha.*

"Very well, then," he said, after a decent interval. "What have you found?"

Koshō bowed politely. Like the others, she was officially off-duty, so she tied back the sleeves of her kimono with a deft motion and turned her head toward the captain with a very proper air. Beside her, Hayes moved aside, leaving a section of otherwise blank wall unobstructed.

"As Hummingbird-*san* reported, a *Valkyrie*-class mining shuttle was observed in the northern hemisphere of Ephesus Three. The aircraft was banking over an extensive lava field at north sixty, west ninety-eight degrees." Koshō indicated the blank wall with a control stylus and a rectangular image appeared—an enhanced version of the shuttle in flight. "Due to space limitations on the peapods, Smalls-*tzin* had set them to record one image every half hour at moderate visual density. As a result, this snapshot of the shuttle is only a very small section of a very large image area. We do not have enough data to extract a ship name or identification number from the visible surfaces of the shuttle."

The lieutenant commander motioned with the wand again. "We have scanned the snapshots for two-hour periods on either side of the sighting, and there is no evidence of the shuttle in flight. Given the altitude and location of the mining shuttle, we believe it was descending from orbit and then landed before the next set of pictures could be taken."

"And was hidden," Hadeishi commented. "Within thirty minutes."

"We believe so," Koshō said, inclining her head. "The *Valkyrie*-class is usually attached to a *Tyr*-class mobile refinery." Another image appeared, this of a huge, ungainly and entirely ugly collection of massive spheres, exposed girders and bulbous fuel tanks all arranged around an extended hexagonal core. "A *Tyr* can carry as many as fifteen shuttles, each with a nominal operating range of about eight hundred million k, with an operational duration of twenty days. They are designed for light exploration, survey and ore sample recovery."

"I see. Any pirate or wildcatter would be entirely pleased to have one under his control. Was the shuttle's descent within line-of-sight of the *Palenque*?"

"No, Hadeishi-*san*. At the time of descent, the civilian ship was on the opposite side of the planet."

"Then our friends knew of the expedition ship and its detection envelope."

Koshō nodded, though the stylus raised to indicate a point. "The miners may *not* have been aware of the weather satellites. Peapods are small and innocuous, with a relatively tiny aspect. If the refinery ship was somewhere else in the system—in the asteroid belt, for example—the shuttle might have made a scouting trip in, unaware of being observed."

Hadeishi frowned. "How did they hide the shuttle, then? Their first trip should have included a great deal of loitering in atmosphere, looking for someplace suitable to set down. They would have shown up on subsequent satellite images."

"This is true, sir. But what if they already knew where to land?" Koshō's eyes narrowed the tiniest fraction. "What if someone had already found a place for them to set down, had left a beacon, one leading them to something of interest?"

Hadeishi's boredom—ephemeral as it was—dropped away like silk crumpling to a courtesan's tatami. "Doctor Russovsky."

"She is the most likely candidate," the lieutenant commander said, slowly. The Fleet had avoided a great deal of trouble by promulgating a policy assuming all citizens, regardless of national affiliation or descent, were innocent as lambs. Treachery and rebellion, of course, were instantly and brutally repressed. Making racial distinctions about reliability . . . Hadeishi was only too aware of his own failing in this regard. Even Anderssen's name set his teeth on edge. *A Russian . . . who could really trust a Russian?*

"On the other hand," Koshō continued in a careful tone, "the other scientists have also made expeditions into the hinterlands. Russovsky's use of an ultralight, however, has allowed her to range far and wide across the northern hemisphere."

"Did the *Valkyrie* make this flight before or after Russovsky returned to base camp with the cylinders?"

"Before," Koshō said, cueing up a timeline. "But only by a few days."

"So—she could have found the cylinders, informed her compatriots and then headed back to base with *some* samples, while leaving the rest for these 'miners' to secure."

The lieutenant commander nodded, dark eyes glittering in the light of the overheads. "Yes, *Chu-sa*, but the real question is: Did Russovsky realize what the cylinder would do, if it were disturbed?"

Hadeishi grunted and a sardonic smile creased his face. "You mean, *Sho-sa*, did she murder the crew of the *Palenque* to ensure no one noticed a shuttle lifting off with a hold full of First Sun artifacts? That is an excellent question."

A burning spot appeared on the eastern horizon; Toniatuh lifting a gleaming limb over the rim of the world, his light gilding the crowns of a great army of stone pinnacles. Wind-carved tufa—fantastically sculpted into corkscrew towers, hollow mushroom-shaped domes, translucent veils and jagged peaks—began to glow yellow-orange as the dawn reached out. Beneath the shining towers, deep ravines and canyons filled with dust and sand twisted through the wilderness. Down below the gimlet eye of the sun, remaining night shone with a quiet, subtle glow. Myriad sparks and gleams hid among the sand, sheltering beneath meters of fine-grained dust.

The sun continued to rise, the pressure of his gaze sending gusts racing through the canyons and moaning between scalloped reeflike towers. With the keening hiss of slowly heating air came a second sound—something foreign to the sere landscape—a humming drone echoing back and forth between cliff and precipice and spire. Light glinted from metal and the broad-winged shape of an ultralight appeared in the eastern sky. A contrail of vapor twisted away behind shining metal and plastic, the *Midge* sweeping gracefully past three turretlike pinnacles. The drone of the engine reverberated in the canyons below, but the slow life hiding in the sand heard nothing.

Day continued to broaden, his shining white coat rising to cover the east, driving the last shadows of night deeper and deeper into the ravines and crevices. The ultralight drifted among the towers, trending north and west, wings dipping as the pilot searched for a landing place. The thinning air was robbing the aircraft of lift, making the engine work harder and harder.

The ultralight banked sharply, the engine's droning pitch sliding up in scale, and the *Midge* circled. One of the great mushroom-shaped domes had cracked and splintered in some lost age, leaving a great bowl ringed with ragged shell-like walls. Sand and splintered tufa made an irregular plain within. The approach was short, the space confined, but the *Midge* drifted in to within a meter of the ground, then nosed up—into a stall—and bounced to the ground. A curtain of dust rose, then drifted away. The pitted, scored canopy opened and a weathered-looking woman rolled out to stand upright. She stretched, rolled her head from side to side, and set about securing the aircraft.

When the sand anchors were set, she climbed a slope of pebbly, red sand to a shallow overhang. A flat stone blackened by carbon scoring made a rest for her cooking kit and a smudged line around the edge of the opening guided her hand in tacking up a mirror-bright sunshade. Then she lay down and closed her eyes, head resting on a tattered woolen blanket.

Below her in the basin, the *Gagarin* chattered and chuckled to itself, then the mirrored surface of the upper wing flashed and onboard systems oriented themselves towards the sky, searching for an answering signal.

"We're not going to be able to set down," Fitzsimmons shouted, trying to make himself heard over the roar of four airbreathing turbines. He hung half out of the starboard side of the shuttle, one hand gripping a stanchion inside the cargo door. Wind howled around him, rushing up from the basin below, in a tornado of flying sand and dust. The *Gunso's* combat visor was down, protecting his face from the rain of sharp-edged rock. His free hand was on a descender, back heavy with gun-rig and equipment bags.

"There's no place else to land," Parker's voice chattered from his earbug. "Can you drop in?"

"Yes," Fitz leaned out, arm stiff. The ground below was obscured by the dust storm, but he'd jumped into worse. "Deckard—let's fly."

The shuttle adjusted, tilting, and Deckard crowded into the cargo door beside Fitz. Both men were kitted out in drop gear—full combat suits, a light loadout of weapons, ammunition and tools. Their descender lines spooled out and their combat visors painted the nearly-invisible wire a virulent green. Fitzsimmons waited for the shuttle's natural roll to top out, then stepped off, monofil zipping through the magnetic clamp-ons in his hand and attached to his belt.

He landed gently, jerking up a half-meter short of the ground and dropping cat-like onto the sand. Fitz detached from the line and tucked his hand clamp away in one quick, automatic motion. Deckard was down a second later and both men broke away from the landing point at a run. Fitzsimmons led with his Iztanuma PRK80 riotgun—no sense in packing the combat rifle or even the lighter shipgun, not for a pickup—and sprinted up the slope toward the overhang they'd spotted from the air. Deckard swung to the right, laboring in heavier, softer sand, but he kept up.

Above them, the shuttle's exhaust vents shifted and the aircraft slid sideways, clearing the bowl. The whirlwind of sand gusted down, dropping veils of dust across broken stone.

A moment later, Fitzsimmons brushed aside the shimmering metallic drape covering the overhang entrance and found an older, sandy-haired woman staring up at him with a quizzical expression. "Doctor Russovsky?"

She blinked as if waking from a deep sleep. Fitzsimmons was struck by her lack of surprise or reaction to his appearance—he knew he must seem strange in a dust-streaked combat suit, pointing what was obviously a weapon at her. He glanced around the shallow cave. Her gear was neatly stacked against a sloping wall, the makings of dinner laid out on a stone.

"Ma'am, you'll have to come with me," he said, trying to keep adrenaline-fueled harshness from his voice. "We're going back to the ship, to the *Palenque*." Fitz released the riotgun, letting the automatic sling wind the weapon back against his shoulder. He reached down and took the woman's hand. She stood up, still looking at him with the same curious expression.

"I have to finish my survey flight," she said in a serious, untroubled voice. "I've another two, three thousand k to cover on this leg."

Fitz jerked his head and the corporal sidled into the overhang, the muzzle of his riotgun centered on the woman's abdomen. "I've got her, Deck. Pack up the gear. It'll all fit into the *Midge*. Ma'am—you're needed on the ship—so we're going to go right now. The shuttle will pick us up."

Russovsky frowned, lean face furrowing into deep wrinkles around her mouth and nose. "I really don't have time to attend some meeting, young man. I have real work to do."

"I don't like meetings either, ma'am." Fitz guided her down the slope, one hand under her arm—he was surprised at the heavy, solid feeling of her suit and the muscle underneath. For all her frail appearance, he realized she'd have to be pretty tough to fly the gossamer shape of the ultralight halfway across the face of an alien, unknown world. "Hold on to me."

Gathering her against his chest, her boots atop his, Fitz strapped them together with a beltline, then plucked his descender clamp free. The shuttle drifted overhead again, raising another whirling storm of dust and gravel, but the Marine's combat visor picked out the spiraling line of monofil as a writhing lime snake. He snatched the line with the clamp, then secured the end tab to his harness.

"Lift," he shouted into his throat mike, and high above, Bandao leaned out of the cargo door, guiding the winch with one hand. Fitz felt the wire draw tight, clasped the woman to his chest, and then they were soaring aloft with a smooth, effortless motion. Dust and wind roared around them, then Bandao caught Fitzsimmons's shoulder and swung them both into the cargo hold of the shuttle.

Russovsky staggered heavily as Fitz let go, releasing the strap, but Bandao was right there—all quiet efficiency—to take her in hand. The sergeant looked down, seeing Deckard piling gear into the cockpit of the *Midge*. "I'm going back down," he shouted, hoping Parker could hear him. "We'll winch up the *Midge* and stow her in the bay."

"Will it fit?" Parker's voice was faint—even with the earbug—over the roar of the engines. "Those wings are pretty big . . . and hurry, I'm really burning fuel too fast up here."

"The wings retract," Fitz said, stepping off again and hissing down the descender. The sand storm in the bowl was getting worse—an inch-long chunk of obsidian glanced from the armor on his leg, leaving a shining scratch on the ablative mesh. "It'll fit. If we don't blow away . . ."

"This is strange." Magdalena frowned, the tightly-napped fur over her nose wrinkling up. "Grr'chen, look at her flight path here . . ."

Anderssen leaned over, one white elbow on the edge of the display panel. Despite the luxury of sleeping in gravity down on the planet, she was glad to be back in the climate-controlled, amazingly clean bridge of the ship. A quick shower between arrival on shuttle two and hurrying onto the bridge to watch the pickup had washed away a layer of planetary dust. She supposed weeks would pass before the usual level of oil, grime and skin flakes built up in the human-occupied sections of the *Palenque*. "What is it?"

Maggie zoomed in on a map of the northern hemisphere, with icons showing the Observatory base camp and other pertinent features. "This is the course Russovsky took upon leaving camp during the trip where she found the cylinders." A fire-bright line appeared on the map, swinging north and west from the base in a long jagged arc. The path wandered over barren plains, tumbled mountain ranges and seas of sand. Eventually the indicator circumnavigated the globe, jogged through the Escarpment and returned to base.

"And here's the path of her latest flight." This time a blue line leapt from the Observatory, heading north and west.

"They look the same." Gretchen was nonplussed.

"No," Magdalena said, zooming in the display to show the two lines as a burning purple trail. "They *are* the same. She's been flying the same course, landing at the same sites . . . for the last twenty days." The Hesht smoothed her whiskers and cocked her head to one side, looking at Anderssen. "So what do you suppose *that* means?"

Sitting in his cabin, door secured, surrounded by a steadily growing maze of comp boxes, display panels and conduits, Green Hummingbird's suspicious expression formed an uncanny likeness to Gretchen's on the bridge. The *tlamatinime* stared at the map, chin pressed against his knuckles. After a moment's thought, a deeper frown settled into his lean visage and he tapped open a comm channel.

"Sergeant Fitzsimmons? This is Hummingbird."

"What did you say, sir?" Fitz turned away from the ultralight, bending his head against the gale of wind and sand. His earbug hissed and sputtered with interference from the blaze of engines howling above and he could barely make out the sharp, commanding voice. "Aye, sir, I'll look in the cave."

Fitz waved Deckard to continue prepping the ultralight for extraction. The Marines had flushed the gas reservoirs in the wings and retracted them. Without their extent, the *Midge* made a compact rectangular shape. The tail assembly had proven difficult to maneuver in the wind, but they'd managed to dismount the dual fishtail and clamp it to the top of the main body. The corporal chased down a monofil line and hooked the cable onto a winch-ring atop the *Midge*.

"Deck, I'll be right back." Fitzsimmons jogged back up the hill, glad to be out of the immediate blast of wind. His combat suit was impervious to the flying gravel and sand, but he was worried about Ephesian dust seeping into his tools, weapons and even the suit itself. Isoroku had warned him about the unexpectedly corrosive nature of the local microfauna and Fitz didn't want to wake up with his shipsuit disintegrating into sand.

He ducked under the overhang and knelt, letting his camera pan across the rock shelter.

"What now?" He asked in a normal tone of voice. "The cooking stone? Aye, aye."

Fitz knelt by the blackened rock, gloved fingers brushing over the evidence of a heating unit and a meal. Hummingbird's voice was an intermittent whisper. The

Marine rubbed a forefinger across the black streaks and was surprised to see the glove come away almost clean.

"This is an old fire," Fitzsimmons commented. "Really old. But who was here before Russovsky landed last night?" He felt a queer chill tickle his spine and his right hand drifted to the butt of the automatic slung at his hip. "Is there someone else out here?"

THE PALENQUE

A pressure gauge mounted into the green, then steadied as standard atmosphere was established—at last—in the shuttle bay. Gretchen waited impatiently, one boot tapping against the heavy door. She could see shuttle one resting in its cradle in the bay, windows shining with cabin lights, the forward lock cycling through its own regulatory process. Her door opened first and Gretchen kicked off into a sharp, distinct smell of heated metal, ionized gasses and ozone.

Brushing a tangle of hair out of her eyes, Anderssen clung to the cargo netting around the landing bay while the shuttle lock opened, spitting red dust, to let Bandao help a tired, worn-looking woman in an old-style z-suit and tan-colored poncho across to the passenger airlock.

"Doctor Russovsky?" She put out her hand in greeting. "I'm Gretchen Anderssen, University of New Aberdeen. Very pleased to meet you."

The Russian gave her an odd, exasperated look, hands hanging at her sides. "I'm very busy," Russovsky said. "I have no time for your meetings and weekly updates. I'll turn in a proper report when I'm done with my survey."

Gretchen withdrew her hand and gave Bandao a surprised look. The gunner shook his head slightly and subvocalized on his throat mike. *She's been this way since we picked her up.*

Anderssen took a moment to look the geologist over. The older woman seemed physically fit. Her face was much as the Company holos had represented—weathered by too much sun and wind, marked by the calloused grooves of goggles and respirator mask, her hair turned to heavy straw—and her suit, though battered and worn, was obviously in good repair. Gretchen was surprised at the state of the woman's boots and the sand-colored poncho—given the effects of the Ephesian dust, they were in excellent shape.

Only her eyes belied a sturdy, no-nonsense appearance. Though as sharp and blue as the holos recorded, they stared coldly past Gretchen, past the wall of the ship, past everything in her immediate vicinity. Anderssen had a strange impression the woman was viciously angry, though nothing else in her demeanor or the line of her body suggested such a thing.

"Take her up to Medical, Magdalena's waiting," Gretchen said to Bandao. The gunner nodded silently and took Russovsky by the arm. The woman allowed herself to be led away.

"That was a stupid thing to do!"

The sound of Parker's voice sharp with anger, real anger, swung Gretchen's head around, eyebrows raised in surprise. She hadn't known the pilot for very long, but he seemed eternally calm. To her further surprise, she found Parker and Fitzsimmons glaring at each other in the shuttle airlock.

". . . hang around for hours while you dink about recovering some salvage!"

Fitzsimmons's face grew entirely still as Gretchen approached, the corner of one eye tightening. Parker wasn't bothering to restrain his temper, his voice ringing through the entire shuttle bay. *Heicho* Deckard was watching from the top of the stairs, his face split by a huge grin. Gretchen looked behind her and was relieved to see none of the scientists had wandered into the bay.

"We don't leave equipment behind," Fitzsimmons replied in an entirely emotionless voice.

"Well, that's great," Parker snapped, "but we don't have unlimited fuel, like the navy, or some armored shuttle that can eat stone and bounce right back up!"

"What happened?" Gretchen settled on *her* stoic management-is-displeased face and shouldered in between the two men, looking up at Parker. To her disgust, she realized though the pilot was only a few inches taller, Fitzsimmons was head and shoulders above her. Despite her disadvantage, both men backed off a little—not so much as she'd have liked—but enough to put them at arm's reach.

"Your Marine," Parker said in an acid voice, "decided we should recover the Doc's *Midge* from down a freakin' hole today. I spent far too long juggling our wingtips between cliffs. We barely got back to base and I was flying on fumes the whole way. I don't think that was a *good idea!*"

"Her ultralight?" Gretchen turned and stared up at Fitzsimmons. "Why? Do we need it?"

The sergeant gave her a look—a considering, not-quite-baleful, not-quite-outraged look. "Fleet does not leave working equipment behind, ma'am. We recovered Doctor Russovsky and her *Midge* without incident and in a timely fashion." His voice was very clipped and precise. "Ma'am."

"We didn't *need* the u-light," Parker had calmed down a little, but Gretchen could feel his body trembling and she realized the pilot was coming down from a massive adrenaline shock. "All we needed was the *doctor*, whom we had extracted in two minutes, no muss, no fuss! Not thirty-five minutes wallowing around on top of razor-sharp stone with canyons on either side! Not thirty-five minutes with the air heating thinner and *thinner* every second!"

"Mister Parker." Gretchen managed to chill her voice appreciably and caught the man's eyes with her own. A baleful stare usually reserved for naughty children worked equally well on the pilot, who abruptly closed his mouth. "The cameras and geological sensors on the u-light are Company property, as is the aircraft itself. It is incumbent upon us—as specifically stated in our contracts—to recover any misplaced, lost or stolen Company property with all due speed. Failure to do so will—in some cases—result in the cost of the equipment being deducted from employee salaries, as appropriate."

She paused, watching an expression of disgust spread across Parker's face. *How does that taste?* She thought. *Tastes bitter—realizing the Company cares more for the contents of a camera crystal or sensor pack than for a human life. Very bitter.* "But I'm glad you came back alive, Mister Parker, with Doctor Russovsky and our Marines. And I'm glad you didn't have to walk home."

Gretchen turned to the sergeant. "I'm glad no one was killed, *Gunso* Fitzsimmons, and I *am* glad you brought back Russovsky's *Midge*. Her cameras and sensors might explain a mystery that's cropped up this afternoon." She smiled a little, seeing a glint in the Marine's eye. "But please don't risk your life this way again—you see how much you've upset Mister Parker." Gretchen patted the pilot on the arm. "He cares, you know. He'd weep to see your broken body scattered across some lava flow or field of calcite ash."

Deckard broke up—a big horse laugh—but neither Parker nor Fitzsimmons did more than stare at Gretchen in disgusted amazement. She didn't wait to see if they renewed their argument—she wanted to be in Medical. Russovsky, and the answer to so many questions, was waiting.

In comparison to the acrid heated-metal and testosterone smell in the shuttle hangar, Medical was quiet, cool and a little dim. The soft overheads had lost their matching pastel wall coverings during the "accident" and the bare metal of the ship's skeleton drank up what little light fell from the panels. Russovsky was sitting on an examining table in the main surgical bay, her pale hair glowing in a shaft of heavy white light. Gretchen paused at the doorway of the nurses' station. The geologist seemed entirely and unnaturally still to her.

"Doctor Russovsky? Victoria Elenova? *Kak vui chuvstvyete?*" Gretchen tried another smile.

This time Russovsky turned to look at her, brow crinkling in puzzlement. For some reason, she seemed tired now, her formerly straight shoulders slumped, her skin a little ashen. *The light in here? Or is she starting to relax after so many weeks alone?* Gretchen knew how hard a homecoming could be.

After her first tour on Mars, she'd taken a commercial liner home to New Aberdeen. After sixteen months crawling around on the ice, the thought of her mother's farmstead—of seeing her children, the gray sky pregnant with rain—the thought of domesticity had been overwhelming. A hunger she couldn't quench until she was in her own bed upstairs, listening to real spruce limbs brush against the roof, all three of her children packed in around her like loaves in an oven, so many quilts on top of them all, she could barely breathe. Mars had been bitterly cold.

For two days, she'd been entirely happy—able to smile again, able to feel safe again. Able to walk under an open sky without a respirator mask, without a z-suit chafing against her skin . . . feeling little hands clutch tight in hers.

On the third day, she'd come down sick. The rest of her vacation was spent shivering in bed, overcome with a succession of illnesses—flu, a cold, a sore throat, pneumonia and a racking cough. For three hundred and twenty days she'd lived and worked under terrible conditions at Polaris, never suffering any kind of sickness. Not so much as a sniffle. Then everything had caught up with her at once.

"I need," the geologist said, staring fixedly at Gretchen, "to get back to work."

"Of course," Anderssen said, nodding. "There are just a few things . . . were there more of the cylinder-shaped objects where you found the piece of limestone you gave Doctor McCue? Or just the two?"

"If," Russovsky said, in an inflectionless voice, "Clarkson wants me to do something useful, then he should let me do my work. I need to get back in the air."

Gretchen forced herself to remain standing at the edge of the examining table. She looked over to the nurses' station and was greatly heartened to see Bandao and Magdalena watching her with uneasy expressions. "Maggie, can you fire up the diagnostics on this table? Thanks."

"*Gagarin* could use more fuel," Russovsky said, as if to herself. "I'll top him up before I leave."

Gretchen turned back to the geologist, watching her intently, as if the woman were a particularly fragile artifact dredged from the bottom of a deep trench. "Victoria? Do you know where you are?"

Russovsky looked up sharply, her eyes glittering. The strange anger Gretchen had seen in her eyes down in the hangar returned, and now the lean old face was tight with fury. "Here's your geld for the water, *Master Clarkson,* and I hope you've the talent to find a *return on your investment!*"

The woman's arm blurred up as if tossing something away. Anderssen tried to jerk herself back, but a cupped hand smashed her head to one side. Gretchen flew into the bulkhead with a crash, and then fell heavily to the deck. Russovsky stood abruptly, her face in shadow as she stepped out of the light over the table. "I'll top up," she said in a conversational voice, turning toward the door. "And be on my way."

"Stop!" Bandao was in the doorway, the flat metallic shape of his automatic gleaming in the dim light. "No farther."

Russovsky stared at him, puzzled, hands hanging limply at her side again.

Gretchen blinked, stunned, then tested her jaw. *Not broken!* "Maggie, what is it?"

There was a long moan of a *hrrrwwwt* from the Hesht. Magdalena looked up from the display surface of the nurse's station, ears napped against her skull, the short hairs on her shoulders and back raised in a stiff triangular ruff. "Not human," she growled, shaking her head in confusion. "Something else . . . like a . . . living crystal."

Bandao took two steps back, his thumb flipping some kind of switch on the side of his gun. There was an answering *beep!* "The thing in the sand Sinclair was talking about?"

"The microfauna?" Gretchen stood uneasily, swaying slightly. Her medband hissed cold at her wrist. The woman, or the thing which looked so much like a woman, did not react, remaining as still as a statue. "But why . . . and *how?* Maggie, does she have bones, blood vessels, internal organs?"

"Yess . . ." Magdalena hissed, her claws skittering across the unfamiliar medical display. "The shapes of things are there—but body temperature is even throughout—there are no fluids—no movement. It's nothing more than a cold copy."

Gretchen's lips parted, her entire attention focused on the marvelous creature poised on the far side of the table. "But she can walk, speak—she remembers bits and pieces of her life. . . . The duplication must be at almost a cellular level!"

"They ate her," Bandao said, his voice tight with fear. The automatic in his hands was steady as a stone itself, but the gunner's face had grown paler by degrees. "They caught her somewhere—maybe she was sleeping and they came at night—and they ate her up, cell by cell. Like she was fossilized all at once."

"Mister Bandao," Gretchen's voice echoed his fear with a harsh tone. Sweat beaded her face. "Lower the gun and get out of the doorway. Maggie, cycle the isolation door closed."

"Sister, you're still in there!" Despite her outcry, a single claw stabbed the emergency isolation glyph and Bandao had to skip back to avoid being caught in the swift rush of the glass-and-steel door. A dull *thump* signaled the room sealing. "What are you doing?"

"I was out at night, in the dig." Gretchen said, circling the immobile Russovsky and climbing onto the examining table. "The ground is alive, you know, filled with tiny life. . . . Sinclair has video of them reproducing, expanding, building their geometric hives. Am I infected?"

"What?" Magdalena stared through the heavy isolation glass. "What are you talking about?"

Bandao stepped to her side, quick brown eyes sweeping across the medical display. "I can't tell," he muttered. "It's been too long since I used one of these. . . . Wait, Magdalena, load up her medical record from Company files. Then we can compare." The gunner looked up, mouth tight. "What about the scientists from base camp?"

"Oh, crap!" Gretchen stiffened, then tapped her comm. "Parker, where are you? The bridge? No, I'm not mad at you anymore—listen to me! Seal the ship, we need pressure lock between each ring *right now!* Then get on the surveillance cam and find all the scientists we just brought up from the surface. Yes, all of them, even in the showers." Gretchen keyed another channel open with shaking fingers. "Fitzsimmons, Deckard—we've got a problem."

In his dim cocoon of glowing displays and quietly chuckling comps, Hummingbird reacted immediately to the events in the Medical bay. His fingers slashed across the main input panel. There was a questioning chirp. "Four Jaguar," he said in a relaxed, unaffected voice. "Four Jaguar."

Palenque main comp immediately locked out every panel and sub-comp on the entire ship. In some areas, like Engineering, a low hooting alarm went off, signaling a communications failure. At the same time, a direct channel to the *Cornuelle* unfolded on Hummingbird's main panel. Captain Hadeishi stared out in surprise, his private cabin silhouetted behind him, a cup of steaming tea held in one hand, a paperbound book in the other. His mouth moved, surprised, but Hummingbird heard nothing—the channel was only one-way at the moment.

A tiny image of an outraged Parker jumped in one corner of the secondary panel. Hummingbird ignored him as well, lips tight, his eyes fixed on the v-feed from Medical. A preset routine spun through the civilian ship—even as the two Marines herded a gaggle of frightened, outraged scientists into the hab ring—closing hatches and ventilation ducts, sealing airlocks, isolating each section of the ship with brisk, invisible efficiency. Another preset shifted nearly sixty percent of *Palenque* main comp to flinging the data flowing from the examining table in Medical into a broad-spectrum search against the databanks in both Hummingbird's *Smoke*-class comp and the navy system aboard the *Cornuelle*. If those sources failed—the blue pyramid, which was shining softly in a golden nest of whisker-thin wires, stood ready as well.

The *tlamatinime's* thumb was poised over a sturdy red glyph—this was Four Wind—the sign of the Second Sun which had been destroyed so long ago, when all living men were swept away by terrible winds and gales, leaving only monkeys as their descendants.

"We're matching . . ." Bandao muttered, face screwed up in concentration, his fingers gingerly moving the controls on the medical display. Maggie had a paw tight on his shoulder, the white arc of her claws digging into the padded armor hiding under his jacket. "What does *this* mean?"

Gretchen crossed her legs and took a deep breath, head in her hands. Russovsky had not moved. Whatever lived inside her, whatever motivated her to action, to sudden motion, seemed puzzled by the closed door. The distant hooting of alarms, and the way—apparently unnoticed by either Bandao or Maggie—the main door to Medical had sealed itself, apparently without orders, was of more concern. She tapped her comm quietly, but there was no answer. No channel opened, no soft green light indicating the shipside comm band was awake and taking messages.

Now what? Gretchen waved at Magdalena, drawing the Hesht's attention. She tapped her comm and made a face. Maggie checked, finding her comm dead as well. The Hesht fiddled with her settings and was rewarded with a blinking light of some kind. Moving very quietly and staying away from the Russovsky-copy's line of sight, Gretchen slipped from the table and moved to the observation window. Magdalena held out her comm, letting Anderssen see which channel she'd changed to. *Ah, a local suit-to-suit circuit.*

". . . hear me?" Maggie's soft voice echoed in Gretchen's earbug. Anderssen nodded, moving back to the far side of the examination table. "Dai says your readings are okay, but there's some kind of *khu-shist* energy pattern permeating the Russovsky and you have something like it in your boots."

Gretchen looked down. *Aw, crap.* The sides of her soles were discolored and shiny. *Bet that doesn't come out with spit and a cloth, either.*

"Okay," Gretchen subvoxed, "can you tell what's happened on the ship?"

"I don't know," Maggie hissed. "Something's locked us out of main comp."

Gretchen stared around in mounting panic. The chamber was sealed and now she realized the air vents had sealed up. An ozonelike odor tickled her nose and she backed away from the Russovsky-copy again. *What a day to decide not to wear my z-suit.* "Can you do anything in here with just that panel?"

She saw Bandao lean over and speak into Maggie's comm. "Control the examination table, the lights, do an emergency atmosphere dump—"

"I don't want that—hey!"

Russovsky moved, reaching the glassite door, one arm swinging back. Before Bandao or Gretchen could react, the copy smashed a fist into the clear material and there was a resounding *crash!* The glassite flexed, spiderwebbed with cracks and rebounded with a singing, clear note. The copy staggered back, staring at its fist in wonder. Gretchen hissed in surprise, seeing the knuckles crumbling away like sand, spilling shining blue particles to the floor.

"She's breaking down," Gretchen hissed into her comm. "She's been getting weaker the longer she's been aboard the ship. Bandao—what's her energy field reading?"

"Weaker, but still hot!" The gunner snatched up his automatic from the display.

The copy smashed into the door again, this time with both fists. Metal squealed, glassite splintered violently, sending tiny flakes whirring past Gretchen's head, and the entire door frame creaked. More blue sand scattered the floor and now deep rents split the copy's arms and shoulders.

"Is there radiation shielding?" Gretchen shouted into the comm, scrambling back away from the blue dust winking on the floor. Some of the particles flickered with an inner light. "Cut her off, cut her off!"

Bandao stabbed a series of glyphs on the panel. The copy wrenched at the side of the hatch, grainy fingers digging into the twisted frame. There was a sound of metal tearing, then a deep basso hum welled up, filling the entire room. Secondary panels slashed down from the overhead, cutting off the observation window. One panel, over the hatch, ground down against the buckling frame, then stopped with a whine. Gretchen switched on her hand lamp and was greeted with the sight of the copy turning toward her, shining bluish-gray sand spilling away from massive wounds on its hands, face and arms. Even the z-suit and the poncho were breaking down. The copy lurched blindly toward Gretchen.

"Lort!" She cursed, flinging the hand lamp away. The copy swung, tracking the spinning light, and lunged toward the flare of illumination. Gretchen dodged sideways, heard a crash as the copy slammed into a medical cart, then leapt to the deformed hatch. Bandao was on the other side, kicking at the twisted frame, trying to clear the jam.

Gretchen caught the door frame, then pulled hard, foot braced against the wall. The distended frame squealed, then popped back toward her. With a *thud*, the radiation shielding dropped, sealing the hatchway.

There was a sigh behind Gretchen and she jerked out of the doorway. Her boots skidded on gravel and sand, but she managed to catch herself. There was no sign of the copy, only disordered bluish dust everywhere. Even the color was fading, moment by moment, leaving only a dull gray residue on the floor.

"Uhhhh . . ." Gretchen slumped against the wall, dizzy, her heart racing. "Maggie?"

There was no answer from the comm. Even the blinking light of the local suit-to-suit circuit had gone out.

Hummingbird looked away from the jumbled image on his display panel. A tiny Anderssen had her head between her knees, back to the bulkhead of the medical bay. He tapped open the comm channel to the *Cornuelle*.

"What happened?" Hadeishi had put away his tea and his book, and leaned forward, dark hair—unbound and loose, as he was off duty—framing a thin, concerned face.

The *tlamatinime* rubbed his jaw, feeling the wrinkled seams of age under his fingertips. "Anderssen's ground team recovered the missing scientist today," he said, eyes drifting across his panel. Everything had come to a standstill on the *Palenque*, all of the compartments sealed, everyone isolated and confused. Only Fitzsimmons and Deckard remained on the loose, and they were in their quarters, hurriedly donning full combat gear. "But she was not what they expected."

"She was a cartel agent?" Hadeishi's brown eyes had gone hard and cold.

Hummingbird laughed softly. The so-efficient *Sho-sa* Koshō had made her views known to him, in her direct way. However, the woman had access to only a fraction of the information known to the *tlamatinime*. "No, she was not in the pay of Norsktrad Heavy Industries or some other *pochtecatl*." He stopped and raised a temporizing hand. "At least, not anymore. The—ah, how to put it?—the *shape* the ground team returned to the *Palenque* was not human. It was, instead, an entirely lifelike copy—at least to the human eye. They took the *shape* to Medical and tried to examine her and there was some trouble."

"Was anyone killed?" Hadeishi's jaw twitched slightly, which made Hummingbird wonder who the naval officer would worry about on the civilian ship. *Certainly not me, or his Marines.*

"No. Though the shape—some kind of mobile crystalline lattice—has been reduced to its essential components. The immediate danger is past."

Hadeishi nodded and his shoulder shifted a fraction. Hummingbird realized the Fleet officer had prepared his own response, much like the *tlamatinime*'s own. In the crucible of the moment, as the *shape* had tried to escape the medical bay, Hummingbird hadn't hesitated to initiate a destruct sequence for the civilian ship. Now the moment had passed, now *Chu-sa* Hadeishi had taken *his* hand away from a similar glyph, the *tlamatinime* was filled with a chill sense of relief at escaping annihilation.

"There is a possibility of infection," Hummingbird continued. "But I believe Anderssen and the Marines have matters in hand. If not, then we will have to sterilize this ship."

Hadeishi nodded, black eyebrows beetling together. "What about you? We can relocate you in five minutes notice—"

Hummingbird shook his head. "There are more pressing matters than my safety. First among them is the matter of the mining refinery ship. Is it still in the system?"

The captain sat for a long moment considering the matter. "Perhaps. Hayes and Koshō are reviewing the sensor logs, looking for a transit spike—so far they've found none. Our arrival may have caught them by surprise, in which case they are hiding somewhere in the system, waiting for us to leave. Or they may have left before we arrived. We have been making a detailed survey of the system—those logs could be examined for traces of their passage or presence."

"Do it." Hummingbird stared at the Nisei captain for a moment, wondering how much to tell him. *Hadeishi is well regarded, a loyal and able captain. He's done me good service in the past, but . . .* He shook his head slightly, deciding to fall back upon the traditions of the Mirror. *There is risk enough already, and the Chu-sa is reliable.* "This situation could become very dangerous, Hadeishi-san. Not only to those of us in this system, but to the Empire. I am going to take care of matters both here on the ship and below on the planet. I must rely on *you* to deal with this mining refinery ship. But you must do so *quietly.*"

Hadeishi started to speak, then stopped, eyes narrowing. Finally, he said, "By *quietly* you mean in such a way no one will notice, or know, the miner was here, or we were here, or even the civilian expedition."

The *tlamatinime* nodded. "Even so."

"Without," Hadeishi continued, slowly stroking his beard, "the use of atomics, or antimatter weapons, or even—I venture—anything which might leave a lasting and detectable residue in the system, much less that which might be observed from the surface of Ephesus Three."

"Yes."

The captain straightened in his chair, tugging his tunic straight. He met Hummingbird's eyes with the slightest smile—barely a crease at his eyes, no more than the faintest twitch of his lips. "So the Mirror commands," he said, making a bow in his seat, "so we obey."

A sharp bark of laughter escaped Hummingbird, and he nodded, making a wry smile. A cold thread of fear was trying to wrap around his neck, but he kept such phantoms away by a concentrated effort. He hoped the blue pyramid did not reveal something beyond his power to comprehend, though the bits and pieces of this puzzle were assuming a dreadful shape. "But quietly, *Chu-sa* Hadeishi, quietly."

"What about you? To find the whereabouts of this miner—or even to discover if the ship is still in the system—will take us out of orbit, well beyond easy reach if you need retrieval."

Hummingbird suppressed a further laugh, for he was long familiar with the ways of men, and with the Nisei in particular. The captain was not asking about *Hummingbird*, but about the men and women on the *Palenque*. He was asking about his Marines—would they live to return to the *Cornuelle*?—and even perhaps about Anderssen and the scientists. *Delicately phrased*, the México thought, *very . . . what is that word? Ah,* kotonakare-shugi—*the willful disregard of troublesome matters.*

"Anderssen," Hummingbird said, trading time—which he felt pressing—for politeness, "is taking her own steps, even now. She has a quick wit, in her light-haired way. If she fails, then I will do what must be done. I hope," he added, "to return *Thai-i* Isoroku, *Gunso* Fitzsimmons and *Heicho* Deckard to you at the earliest opportunity."

Hadeishi made a sharp bow in response and the *tlamatinime* knew the man was a little embarrassed to have his concern referred to openly. The thought made Hummingbird a little sad. The *Chu-sa* obviously cared for his crew, as a grandfather did for even the meanest member of his clan. *And I would trade all their lives for the Empire*, he thought. Vague memories of a time when *he* had maintained such romantic notions threatened to surface and he made a sharp effort to keep them from distracting him. *They are knights, as I am, in the service of a greater power. Like flowers, we are nothing but a fleeting moment of duty and service.*

"Is there anything you need, before we cut comm and boost out of orbit?" Hadeishi's attention was already far away, calculating angles and fuel usage and a dozen envelopes of detection. Hummingbird shook his head, then made a shallow bow of his own.

"The road is long, crags above, ravines below," the *tlamatinime* said, raising his hand in parting.

"But our feet are swift, our eyes eager to see the home hearth," Mitsuharu said, and closed the comm.

———

Hummingbird rubbed his face, wrinkled fingers bronze in the glow of the comp displays. Fleet and civilian records had no record of a mineral or crystalline life-form which so deftly replicated a living human being. Too, he was intrigued by the degradation of the copy as time passed. It seemed, to his eye at least, the creature drew its strength from the planet in some undefined way. Travel to the ship, and then isolation behind the radiation barrier, had robbed it of the ability to move and hold shape.

"But what made you?" He wondered aloud, replaying the arrival of Russovsky on the ship at half-speed. "The world below was destroyed so long ago—has such a complex organism had time to flower in this barrenness? Or are you something left over from before—a ghost out of a dead epoch?"

There was a cheerful chirp from one of his sub-panels. Hummingbird looked over, a sudden feeling of unease stealing upon him. The blue pyramid had seen fit to reveal one of its secrets to him. He pulled himself to the display—which sat apart from the others, and was only connected to his comps by a series of cutout buffers—and tapped a convoluted glyph showing a flayed man's face draped over the blackened head of a priest.

A v-pane unfolded and Hummingbird began to read, his dark face barely illu-minated by the soft lights playing across the glassite surface. In his eyes, a queer twisting flame burned, reflecting the images dancing before him in the depths of the pyramid.

"Urrrh!" The tip of a metal bar scraped under the ragged edge of the radiation shielding. Maggie twitched her fingers aside—barely avoiding a bad cut—and then squeaked her own makeshift lever into the narrow opening.

"Together," Gretchen shouted, hoping Magdalena and Bandao could hear her. Anderssen bore down with all her weight and the pleated metal groaned. An inch of bright lamplight was revealed and there was an answering grunt from the other side. "Again!"

They'd managed to lift the radiation barrier nearly a foot when the main lights suddenly flicked back on and the medical comp beeped to announce it had reconnected to the rest of the shipside network. Gretchen looked up, feeling the cold breeze of the air circulators on her sweat-streaked face.

"Oh, that feels good . . ." She stood up, wiping her brow, and stabbed a fore-finger at the hatch controls. She was rewarded with a screeching sound, and the broken panel ground up toward the overhead. The radiation panel hissed back as well and she ducked through the opening into the nurses' station. "You two all right?"

Maggie nodded, her face contorted as she queried main comp through the medical display. "We've only got local power and environment back. The main system is still restricted—someone's dropped a shipwide lockout on us."

"Who ordered that?" Gretchen examined a secondary panel controlling the medical bay environment. A thought had occurred to her and she wanted to just check one thing. . . .

"I can guess," Maggie snarled, exposing her incisors. "A cursed carrion bird watching us from the branches of a dead, rotting tree!"

"Who?" Gretchen found the control set she wanted and tapped out a series of commands. A pale violet light flickered on in the examining room. "A bird? Oh—you mean a *hummingbird*." She glanced up at the surveillance camera. "He's just making sure our guest doesn't get out. Dai—does the outer hatch work?"

The gunner shook his head. He'd been trying to get the lock to override for five minutes—all to no avail. The door out of Medical into the rest of the hab ring was sealed tight. "We're still trapped," he said, running his hand over the metallic surface. "High-ex rounds from this Luger might penetrate."

"Not inside the ship," Gretchen said in a sharp voice. Her whole attention was fixed on the examining room, where the slow pulsing violet glow seemed to etch every surface in sepia tone. "Well, now . . ."

THE CORNUELLE

Hadeishi overhanded onto the bridge, tunic straight, uniform jacket entirely neat. Koshō and Hayes were seated at the main navigation station, heads bent over the display. The Marine *heicho* standing watch near the hatchway coughed sharply, then straightened to attention. A difficult task in z-g, but he *was* an Imperial Marine.

Heicho Tonuac started to announce Hadeishi's presence, but the captain shook his head minutely as he slid nimbly into his shockchair. Koshō and Hayes looked up in surprise, catching sight of his entrance, and the exec immediately moved to her own station.

"*Sho-sa*, sound battle stations. Recall all work crews and prepare to take us out of orbit," Hadeishi said without preamble as he settled into his chair, powered motors whining to align the shockfoam with his back and legs. "Full emissions control, *Thai-i* Hayes. Release active control of the weather satellites and spin the hyperspace generators down to minimum. Tell Engineering I want as shallow a gravity dimple as possible."

The bridge was filled with immediate activity; men and women shifting to combat stations, low voices keying comm to the various ship's departments. There were no questions, only a swift response. Hadeishi felt a stab of pride. *A fine crew.*

Koshō keyed open the all-hands channel, her oval face only showing the faintest hint of exasperation at Hadeishi's abrupt announcement. "All hands, zero-g in five minutes. Acceleration in nine minutes. All hands stand to battle stations."

A warning tone sounded throughout the *Cornuelle* and every starman and Marine aboard rushed to secure whatever compartment they were in. Even through the mass of the ship, Hadeishi felt the rumble of the hab rings spinning down, and the more distant, muted thunder of the hyperspace drive wicking to a low flame. A schematic of the ship unfolded on his side panel, each compartment showing status, each airlock and transit point glowing in a soft outline. One by one the sections changed color as they sealed and locked.

"One minute to z-g," Koshō announced, finally sitting down and letting the arms of her shockchair fold around her. There was a flurry of movement and a tousled-headed midshipman Smith slid into his own station, fingers working busily to seal his jacket. Hayes looked back to the captain from his panel.

"Satellites are ready to release—shall I force orbital decay?"

Hadeishi nodded, his stylus sketching a trajectory on his main panel. "A lengthy descent, Mister Hayes. I want no debris to reach the ground. Work crews?"

"All aboard," Koshō replied, listening to the boat officer on her earbug. "Hyperdrive has spun down. Skin mesh is active, comm arrays withdrawn, active tracking cold. We are on passive detection only."

"Sublight engines at low power, Mister Hayes. Here is your plot." The captain flicked a glyph with his stylus and the motion plot appeared in the threat-well. Hadeishi felt a tug of disappointment—Ephesus Three had no moon, which would have made the *Cornuelle*'s escape path much shorter—and he'd been forced into a long ellipse to swing away from the planet. "Refine please—we must orient our engine flare away from the planet. Once we have moved out of the plane of the ecliptic we can go to higher power, but only if the body of the ship blocks line-of-sight to our thrust plume."

"One minute to boost." Koshō began to count seconds.

Hadeishi felt the engines come up as a faint, thready vibration in the panel under his hand. Acceleration tugged at his sleeve, but in the tight embrace of the shockchair he barely noticed.

The *Cornuelle* began to move, slowly and carefully, swinging away from the planet and the distant dot of the *Palenque*. From Hayes's reworked plot, Hadeishi saw they could shift to cruising speed in approximately sixteen hours. *A long slow pull*, he thought with a flash of irritation. *My thoroughbred forced to plod in the mud.*

"Time?" Mitsuharu looked to Koshō with interest. The exec flushed, one slim hand diving into the pocket of her duty jacket, then looked guiltily to the clocks on her command panel.

"Seven minutes," she said. Hadeishi thought he could see a faint blush on her cheeks.

"Excellent."

After thirty minutes of acceleration gentle enough to win *Thai-i* Hayes a pilot's berth on a Pochteca starliner, Hadeishi ordered the crew secured from battle stations and raised himself from the captain's chair. Feeling Koshō's eyes on him as intent as any targeting laser, the *chu-sa* turned to the Navigation and Weapons stations. "We will discuss finding the *Tyr* in thirty minutes, after the duty watch changes."

Hadeishi returned to his cabin, where the steward had cleaned up his abandoned tea and put away the usual litter of books and 3v readers which accumulated around the captain's desk and workstation. Ship's night had already come, the dinner hour passed and a fresh off-duty uniform was laid out for him. Hadeishi took a moment to strip down and shower. After his allotted six minutes, he combed out his hair—grimacing at the threads of white beginning to appear among the oily black—and tied back a heavy queue behind his head. Koshō might boast a longer fall of raven hair, but Hadeishi thought he could present himself at court, if the need arose.

Which, he thought ruefully, *is extremely unlikely.* He owned an admirable service record, but his "secret" personnel jacket—where a Fleet officer numbered one's patrons among the Imperial clans or in the Diet—was sadly lacking. There was a single letter, carefully preserved, expressing the gratitude of the Laird MacLaren for the timely intervention of the *Bara*-class destroyer *Toge* during a Megair raid on the MacLaren-owned mining world of New Devon. But Mitsuharu doubted the MacLaren household even remembered the incident at this late date.

When he returned to the bridge, Koshō and Hayes—who had obviously not had the luxury of a shower—were waiting on either side of the threat-well, the softly glowing holospace crowded with indicators, icons and velocity markers. Hadeishi paused in the entryway and spoke softly into his comm. "Kusaru-*san*, please bring three teas—very sweet—and two tubes of miso."

There was barely a grunt in answer from his steward, but Hadeishi knew the old man would see to the matter immediately.

"So," he said, bringing himself to a halt by grasping the rail girdling the threat-well. "How do we find this miner? Or has he left, even before we begin our search?"

A lesser being than the lieutenant commander would have given Hadeishi an open glare, he was sure, but the young *Sho-sa* contented herself with failing to bow before beginning to speak. "We know the *Tyr*-class refinery was here, Hadeishi-*san*, not only from the evidence of the shuttle photograph, but from the results of our navigational survey." Her stylus tap-tapped on the control display for the threat-well. A series of points winked in the holo, describing a long, rough arc.

"This is a compressed display of the Ephesian system," she said. "This gray section is the asteroid belt occupying the orbits between Three and the distant, irregular orbit of Four. We acquired the navigational scans made by both the original Imperial probe and by the *Palenque* upon arrival in the system. Luckily," and she allowed herself a wintry smile, "*Sho-sa* Cardenas was a careful man. Like yourself, he ordered his navigator and exec to conduct a systemwide navigation survey as soon as they arrived in Ephesus orbit."

Koshō made a sharp motion with her stylus and most of the objects in the well vanished.

"This is the condensed version of the *Palenque* scan. You see it is moderately detailed. Luckily for us, Navigator Gylfisson concentrated a fair amount of his long-range scan activity on the asteroid belt. I believe that he—like the presumptive miner—was looking for planetesimals bearing heavy ores, radioactives, rare metals and so on. We made the same kind of scan during our survey . . ." The stylus moved again, and a second layer of data appeared, showing a much thicker representation. ". . . with superior equipment. Hayes-*san* has been running orbital comparisons of the three sets of data, looking for disturbances and anomalies."

The stylus indicated the arc of winking points.

"Something has moved through this cloud of asteroids, altering spins, altering orbits, producing a faint—but identifiable—trail. We believe this was left by the *Tyr* as she worked through the belt. I also believe the refinery is still in the system."

Hadeishi raised an eyebrow. Koshō's eyes glittered, though she remained outwardly calm.

"We have gravity scans from the moment the *Palenque* entered the system up to the accident. During that time, we see no evidence of a hyperspace transit. Our trail of sensor fragments begins in the middle of a dense pocket in the asteroid belt. I suspect the *Tyr* was already here—and working—when the *Palenque* arrived. The trail continues up to the end of the *Palenque* data."

"And now?" Hadeishi had been watching Hayes's face grow longer and longer. "Wouldn't the miners have been monitoring the *Palenque*'s transmissions? Wouldn't they realize something had happened and jump out as soon as the coast was clear?"

"I don't think they did." Koshō glanced sideways at Hayes. "*Thai-i* Hayes does not agree, but . . . the *Valkyrie* was photographed only three days before the accident. At that moment, the time to transit between Ephesus Three and the presumptive location of the miner was almost twelve days. So at best the shuttle has to go meet the refinery, which leaves the asteroid cloud to rendezvous between the belt and Three. If the shuttle leaves Three the same day; if they just dropped in, grabbed whatever they were looking for and jetted out, then the minimum time to transit is eight days."

Koshō's wand sketched a box in the air, describing a fat volume of space between the red disc of Ephesus and the gray scattering of the belt.

"So at event plus five, they could have met—somewhere in this volume—and made gradient to hyperspace. Now—a *Tyr* masses in excess of three hundred million tons *empty* and I think she'd have taken on at least another hundred million tons of ore samples, or more, by this time. The departure spike from such a large mass leaves a lasting footprint—and I don't see one in this volume."

"Hayes-*san?*"

"*Chu-sa*, I'm not sure we'd see one in this system for more than a few days, no matter where the departure took place." The weapons officer scratched his eyebrow. "The planetary orbits in this system are all messed up and irregular, there are queer gravitational tides and eddies. Our own footprint is barely discernible *today* and we know our entry-point to the centimeter!"

Koshō made a dismissive motion with her stylus. "We're a fraction the mass of a *Tyr* and our hyperdrive is tuned to leave as little footprint as possible. Look—" A new set of data clouded the well. "There's no spike on any record; not ours, not the *Palenque*'s . . . and I believe our scans of the asteroid belt in the projected path of the *Tyr* show evidence of further disturbance. I think the refinery ship is still here. I think her captain is greedy and kept right on working after the accident on the *Palenque*. He badgered as soon as we entered the system, hoping we'd go away. Now he's stuck—ore holds are full of rich samples—and he doesn't want to dump mass. If he tries to make gradient to hyperspace, he'll have to light up like a temple tree and we'll see him."

Hadeishi raised a hand. Kusaru appeared silently with the tea and miso. Both of the junior officers took the light meal with grateful bows, though only Hayes drank from his z-g tight cup.

"I understand," Mitsuharu said. "Is there a swift way to tell if the refinery ship is still here?"

Koshō nodded sharply. "Yes." Her stylus stabbed at the last winking point. "We creep in here and check the area of disturbance—if he's slagged out a rock, we'll be able to get a reading on his drive exhaust and be able to tell how long ago he was working." A flicker of hungry pride flashed across her composed oval face. "To the hour and the minute."

Mitsuharu nodded, privately calculating their course and time to intercept. "Hayes-*san*, plot us a course and execute. But gently, very gently. We must creep away from the planet and approach this prey with equal caution."

THE PALENQUE

The main hatch into the Medical bay opened suddenly, sliding into the overhead with a soft *thump*. Gretchen looked up from where she was kneeling on the deck of the examining room, her work lenses dialed to hi-mag. She heard Bandao hiss and step back and a low growl from Magdalena. Flipping up her lenses, she found herself staring into the black snout of a shipgun, held in the hands of one of the Marines—she couldn't tell which one—in combat armor.

"Over against the wall," the Marine said, his voice a buzz through the suit. Bandao moved back, automatic held gingerly between his thumb and forefinger. The Marine crabbed into the room and was immediately followed by another, taller, man also in matte-black combat armor. "Just lay the gun down on the deck."

Gretchen rose, spreading her hands wide to show they were empty. A heated sense of outrage was warring with the urge to laugh aloud at the insectlike appearance of the soldiers, and she managed to remain composed. The two Marines surveyed the room, then relaxed fractionally.

"Clear," the taller one—Fitzsimmons, Gretchen guessed—said, his voice almost unrecognizable through the faceplate of his suit. Then she stiffened as his rifle swung toward her. From this vantage, the weapon seemed very large. "Doctor Anderssen, please leave the examining room and stand over here by Bandao-*tzin*."

Almost tiptoeing, she ducked through the damaged doorway and moved to join Bandao—who had adopted a very calm expression—and Magdalena, who was emitting a near-subsonic growl which raised the hackles on the back of Gretchen's neck. Worried, Anderssen took hold of the Hesht's paw to restrain her.

The lean, wrinkled shape of Hummingbird stepped into the room. His high forehead gleamed like polished mahogany in the overheads and his dark eyes swept across the three of them to settle on the debris in the medical bay.

Without speaking, the México judge went to the adjoining room and knelt to examine the deck. The Marines said nothing, one of them covering the *nauallis* with his rifle, the other keeping a strict eye on the three civilians. Gretchen itched to speak, but guessed this was not the time and place to annoy Imperial authority. *He could just ask politely. . . .*

Hummingbird moved around in the examining room and Gretchen couldn't really see what he was doing but there was a strange muttering sound, and the man seemed to go back and forth, sometimes turning this way and that, making a slow, convoluted circuit around the long table. At length he returned to the doorway and motioned for the nearest Marine to hand him a small black bag. Hummingbird took out a small electrostatic vacuum and a specimen container.

He returned to the room and resumed moving slowly around the table. Again, Gretchen thought she heard a peculiar sound, but it was so faint and the acoustics in the two rooms so poor, she couldn't make out what he might be saying. Neither Marine showed any reaction, and even Magdalena was starting to settle down.

Eventually, Hummingbird returned to the nurses' station and stowed a newly-heavy specimen container in the carryall. The bag closed with a heavy *click*.

"The dust is inactive," Hummingbird said, looking up, his eyes dark as flint. "What did you do?"

Gretchen took a half step forward and felt both Bandao and Magdalena tense behind her. "I think the organism started to die the moment Parker's shuttle left the Ephesian atmosphere. When the radiation shielding dropped, it just came . . . apart. But five minutes of high-UV flooding the chamber seems to have stopped all remaining molecular activity."

The México nodded, glancing at the control panel for the examining room. "Like the spores infesting the shuttle engines. You think they are a related species?"

Gretchen felt a certain familiar hollowness in her gut. *And now,* she thought, *the Imperial authorities will step in and a great deal of work—months of observations, countless crystals of data, maybe a man's entire career—will vanish like night dew.* "Sinclair-*tzin* has a theory—and as expedition microbiologist, he should—which points to a commonality across all Ephesian life."

"All current Ephesian life?" Hummingbird's tone grew sharp, as if he already knew her answer. "Since the destruction of the surface?"

Gretchen's eyes narrowed and she felt a subtle tension tighten in the old Méxica. *He's fishing*, she thought, *but for what?* Then she thought of the cephalopod fossil and the entombed cylinder. Too much had been happening for her to show Sinclair that bit of evidence. In any case, she was familiar enough with the types of organisms trapped in the ancient limestone to know there was no evolutionary descendent among the microbiota flourishing on the surface today. The violent arrival of the First Sun builders had separated the two epochs of Ephesian life as night from day. "All *current* life," she said. "Like the spores in the intakes or whatever organism gave fruit to this . . . copy of Russovsky."

"Yes . . ." Hummingbird seemed suddenly older, the brief flicker of interest and tension ebbing away. He visibly slumped. "Everything made new, green shoots rising from desolation. You did well to destroy what remained, no matter how inert it seemed."

Gretchen nodded, and fought to keep from looking down at her boots. *Got to get these into secure storage*, she thought guiltily, *and figure out some way to keep them alive for study.*

"I have sent the *Cornuelle* away," Hummingbird said, abruptly changing the subject. "As *Thai-i* Isoroku informs me this ship will be able to make gradient to hyperspace within the day." The *tlamatinime* looked to the two Marines. "Ship's records indicate there is an unused *Midge* in storage in cargo ring two. Please assist our engineer in readying the aircraft for operations on the surface."

Fitzsimmons cracked his visor and pulled off his helmet. Gretchen noticed the Marine's hair had become a tangled, dark mass and had to stifle an amused smile. "Yes, sir. How many days' fuel and food?"

"As much as will fit," Hummingbird said wryly. His composure had returned, the brief appearance of fatigue falling away. "You will also need to rig for a high-altitude aerial insertion—I believe the *Midge* class has the proper mounting brackets."

Fitzsimmons nodded sharply and motioned with his head for Deckard to leave the room. The other Marine backed out, lowering his shipgun, and Fitzsimmons followed. Hummingbird nodded to Gretchen and the others, and then picked up the bag.

"What are you doing?" Gretchen said in a disbelieving tone.

"That is my business," he said, giving her a sharp look. "But your project here is at an end. There will be no further flights to the planetary surface and Mister Parker should prepare this ship to make the jump back to Ctesiphon Station."

Parker, seated on the bridge of the *Palenque* in the pilot's chair, a mess of tabac butts, printouts of ship's systems and partially torn-apart comp panels strewn around him, stared at the México as if he'd sprouted a forest of eyestalks. "You can't possibly be serious."

"I am," Hummingbird said in an entirely reasonable voice. "These *Komodo*-class shuttles have flyout tracks in the cargo bay. Isoroku assures me he can mount a *Midge* on a breakaway pallet. These are technical matters—easily solved by sweat and concentrated effort—but *you* concern me."

"Damn right I'm a concern!" Parker fumbled a tabac out of his vest pocket and jammed it, unlit, into the corner of his mouth. "You'd better explain to me why I have to make an unpowered, ballistic skip approach to the upper atmosphere of Ephesus—without active instruments—and then let you bail out the back of the shuttle—with the cargo doors open in a six hundred-k slipstream."

The pilot squinted at the México, then lit his tabac with a sharp snap on the stubble underneath his chin. "Fitzsimmons there could shoot you just as dead, right now, without risking anyone's hide with such a reckless stunt."

Hummingbird looked consideringly at the Marine, who shook his head in answer to an unasked—but apparently understood—question. "Sir, our other pilot's Fuentes," the Marine said, "and he's not as steady on the stick as Parker. Neither Deckard nor I are qualified on a *Komodo* or anything like it. Ground crawlers, sure . . ."

The México turned back to the pilot, his eyes flitting across Gretchen—who was holding position with her hand on the back of the pilot's chair—without a pause. "Parker-*tzin*, circumstances have conspired to put you in a position of responsibility. I *need* you to fly that shuttle—in the manner described—and I *need* you to return safely to this ship, so it can jump out to Ctesiphon Station as quickly as possible." As he spoke, the *tlamatinime*'s voice hardened by degrees, making Parker sink deeper and deeper into his shockchair. "Given another alternative, I would relieve you of these tasks, but *you* are the tool to hand, and you *will* serve."

"But . . . no sensors? An unpowered drop into atmosphere? That's—"

"Necessary, Parker-*tzin*. It is necessary." Hummingbird looked around at Gretchen and Magdalena and Doctor Lennox—who was looking entirely pale and washed out, like a cotton sheet left to hang in the summer sun for far too many days. "This is within my authority," he said, raising his voice very slightly, drawing every eye to him as iron filings to a lodestone. "As *nauallis*, as judge, as the voice of the Empire in this godless place. We have blundered into uncompromising danger and we will be lucky indeed to escape without harm."

Gretchen heard a stone certainty in the man's words and felt a chill wash over her. *What does he know? Something about Russovsky's spooked him—and why not? Something duplicated a human being, down to memories and language. Did the same something send the eater cylinder aboard? Is the other cylinder a trap?*

In all the busy confusion since her return from the surface, she hadn't had a chance to resume her translation work on the embedded slab. Thinking of it now, of the secrets which must lie concealed within, she felt a painful hunger wake. *Those translation runs must have finished days ago! I'm so stupid—they could be waiting for me right now.*

"More than this," Hummingbird said coldly, interrupting Gretchen's train of thought. "I will not explain. You will obey without question or dispute. In this way, you may yet live. Now Parker-*tzin*—during the next day, while Isoroku completes his preparations for the flyby, you will move the *Palenque*, very quietly, out of orbit. Minimal burn on the main engines, and you will do so by orienting us away from the planet. Anything we do must be unremarked from the surface. We are going to take care to leave no trace of our visit here."

Gretchen stirred, drawing the México's attention. "Hummingbird-*tzin*, your pardon, but if *Palenque* leaves the system, and *Cornuelle* has already departed, how will *you* leave the planet? And what about the base camp at the observatory? There are hundreds of tons of equipment, supplies, vehicles there. What about the observation satellites?"

"Those things," Hummingbird said with a steely lightness in his voice, "will be taken care of. And in the meantime—no scans, no active sensors on the ship, no experiments, no communications traffic. Nothing."

Gretchen started to speak again, but the *nauallis* gave her a fierce look, dark eyes glittering.

"We are mice," he said sharply, "creeping in a field of maize. We must step gently, or the stalks will rustle."

The pitch of the vibration humming through the deck and walls shifted and Susan Koshō looked up from her v-panel, head cocked to one side. "We've reached safe distance," she said, turning her attention back to the schematics on her display. With their gravity signature pared down to the absolute minimum by shutting off the g-decking, the *Cornuelle* creaked and groaned with odd noises. The main hull had picked up little tics and squeaks over time. In the depths of ship's night, you could hear her speaking, if you were quiet.

Hayes nodded absently, chewing on a stylus, pale blue eyes sunken in dark hollows. Susan pushed a cup of tea toward him, letting the sealed container slide across the worktable in the senior officer's mess. "You should drink that—you need to eat."

"Yes, mother," he replied, still paging slowly through the schematic. He set the cup aside. "This thing is a monster. Look at the shielding . . . and these mining beam rigs look like a Mark Ninety-Six proton cannon refitted for a civilian power plant."

Susan nodded, then took a long sip from her own cup. The tea was very strong and thick with honey. She was certain the steward had added stimulants and some kind of vitamin supplement. *There's an undertaste,* she thought, stealing a glance at her medband. The thin, flesh-colored circlet around her wrist was quiescent, indicating a lack of toxins. *Of cinnamon.*

"Don't fool yourself," Susan said aloud, tapping a section of the *Tyr* blueprints on her panel. "The power plant for one of these has more in common with our drive than any civilian liner. See? This report from the Mirror says a *Tyr* has three reactors, each capable of output matching or exceeding our own. She has to, to move so much mass."

"Wonderful," Hayes grumbled, finally putting down the pad. He retrieved his tea, which had slid back along the table toward the rear bulkhead. Grimacing at the bitter/honey taste, he downed the whole thing in one gulp. "So let's consider—she's surrounded by ore carrels which—if they're full, *and* loaded properly—give her the equivalent of a hundred meters of low-grade armor plating. Not a reactive shield, no, but enough to shrug off most of our lighter penetrators and beam weapons. Then her core section is clad in enough radiation shielding for a battle cruiser and she mounts the most godawful huge cutting beam assemblies I've ever seen. These are nearly dreadnaught-strength mounts!"

Susan nodded, finding a page she recalled from the Seeking Eye—Fleet Intelligence—report. "Pursuant to the Treaty of Rostov," she read, "the *macehualli pochteca*—or industrial combines—have been required to turn all armaments and munitions factories, orbital yards, workshops and other means of naval production to nonmilitary use. This they have done." A brief, fierce smile flickered across Susan's face. "In the case of the *Tyr*-class mobile ore refinery, the core of the civilian ship is a stripped down *Kaiserschlacht*-class heavy cruiser. Some of the early refinery models, in fact, are physically built around decommissioned K-schlacht hulls."

"Sister bless!" Hayes tabbed to the same page. "They didn't leave the original sensor net and ECM intact, did they?"

Susan pursed her lips and pointed with her stylus at another section of the report. "Navigating in an asteroid belt, or an Oort cloud, is a tricky business. This *requires* the refinery to carry advanced avionics and sensor equipment. The targeting systems and main comp aren't supposed to be military grade, of course. Just civilian models."

Hayes leaned back against the bulkhead, his broad face looking tired and pudgy. "Easy enough to replace from the black market—if the originals were ever actually removed in the first place."

"Or to upgrade," Susan said quietly. "K-schlacht hulls are over a hundred years old. Even a modern civilian rig would be superior in head-to-head with the old Royal Navy gear. And these ships are straight out of the Norsktrad yard at Kiruna—which means they have the very latest comp and scan on board."

Hayes rubbed his face and made a groaning sound. Koshō wanted to laugh derisively, but she felt a certain sisterly affection for the senior lieutenant. He was quick on his board, and quite adept at handling dozens of incoming threats and targets in the thick of the action—but he hadn't quite the taste for the hunt a commanding officer really needed.

"So," she said, in a brisk voice, "how do we kill this thing?"

Hayes stared at her, then leaned his chin on clasped hands. "Right. Kill it . . . well, the firing aperture of those mining beams is restricted—they can't have full traverse with the ore carrels in the way—so there are blind spots if we can get a target lock and proper orientation."

"Good." Susan laid down her comp pad and fixed him with her full attention. "And?"

"And . . . they probably don't have any missile capacity, unless they're hiding some kind of pods in the carrels—which they could be! But that wouldn't pass muster anywhere they docked—and they *did* come here to mine, didn't they?" He seemed to perk up at the thought.

"Yes, they did." Susan rolled her stylus between middle finger and thumb. "The ship's power-to-mass ratio is also against them—they will have a hard time outmaneuvering us, and a harder time hiding from us if they do move."

"Yeah." Hayes made a face. "So we have to maneuver for position, get into one of their blinds and just hammer them, knock out engines, break through the armor. . . . Could be messy."

"No, we can't be messy," Susan said, flipping the stylus deftly in her hand so the sharp point pointed down at the table. "We must be exact—" she made a sharp stabbing motion with the writing tool "—and swift. One blow, thrust past all that armor will—"

"—not be necessary." Hadeishi's voice was soft from the hatchway. Susan stiffened, aware her hair was unbound, her uniform jacket untabbed at the neck, and she sat up straight. Hayes had also come to attention. The *chu-sa* stepped into the room, nodded to them both, and drew a tea from the automat. "You two should get some sleep. We will be busy later."

"What about the *Tyr?*" Hayes said, betraying a little confusion. "We have to be ready to deal with this brute when we—"

Hadeishi waved him to silence, settling into a chair at the end of the table, hands curling around the warm cup. "If we engage the refinery in any kind of shooting match, we've failed. I am under strict orders to secure the miner without the use of any kind of missile, beam weapon or weapon producing an electromagnetic signature."

He smiled gently at both of them—particularly at Hayes, who was staring gape-mouthed.

"What is the pinnacle of a warrior's skill?" Hadeishi turned to Susan, his mellow brown eyes capturing hers. She felt a chill shock, as if he'd splashed ice water on her face. But her mind was quick, and she remembered both the question and the traditional answer.

"To subdue the enemy without fighting." She frowned in distaste. "You're quoting from—"

Hadeishi raised an eyebrow and finished his tea. "That does not mean," he said quietly as he stood up, "it is not true. Good night."

Koshō watched the *chu-sa* leave and wondered how he'd gained access to a copy of the *Ping Fa*. She was a little disturbed. *I'm very sure all those books were destroyed.*

Pacing was almost impossible with the bridge of the *Palenque* in z-g, so Gretchen resorted to staring moodily at an image of the planet filling the main display. Parker and Magdalena were working under the main control board—grunting and cursing by turns as they rewove the power and data fibers snaking up from under the floor and into the control surfaces.

Anderssen had rarely felt such distaste for another human being. Even the thoughtless racism of her instructors at university had not inspired such a bleak mood. *I will find some way,* she thought, letting fantasies of outlandish torture devices blossom in her mind's eye, *to make him suffer. What an arrogant bastard!*

Gretchen had been annoyed when Hummingbird took the remains of Russovsky away into "Imperial Custody," though her reaction had been mild compared to Sinclair's. The xenobiologist had begged to examine the strange dust, but the Imperial judge had flatly refused. The rest of the scientists were confined to quarters, which greatly reduced the possible range of disputes. Gretchen had been a little smug—she could go where she wished—but all of her good humor had evaporated when she finally made her way down to airlock number three.

Which was empty. The steel cradle remained, but her good field comp, the jury-rigged sensor panel, the *cylinder* and its attendant limestone block were gone.

For once, when she turned around snarling, Fitzsimmons was nowhere to be found. But Gretchen still knew who'd stolen her artifact.

"What does he think is down there?" Gretchen rattled her feet noisily—now in stiff-bottomed shipshoes—against the railing separating the captain's station from the rest of the crew positions. "Leave *no trace of our visit?* It's just not possible."

Magdalena peered over the top of the navigation panel. Her yellow eyes were bare slits. "What a whiny kitten you are," she declared with a sharp *yrroowl* in her voice. "Either ask him yourself or be a good packmate and help pull cable."

Gretchen ignored her to stare sullenly at the planet. Most of her hair was twisted into a thick corn-tassel plait. She started to bite at the braid, head cocked to one side. "He must believe something's down there, something that can see us. . . ." She paused, thinking. "No—it can't see us *now*, but it *might* see us in the future? Something which will notice satellites, spacecraft . . . but why wouldn't his precious *something* find the observatory camp?"

Magdalena's tufted ears disappeared with a disapproving growl. Parker managed a subdued laugh, but his hands were filled with bundles of conduit. The power leads to the navigator's station were proving difficult to restore. The substandard cables had ended in metallic connectors, which were still embedded in the panel sockets. Sitting flush, without the usual cable run to grasp hold of, Parker was forced to remove them one at a time with a hand tool. He'd already wrecked one panel by shorting the connector with too much pressure.

"Maggie? How did Russovsky communicate with the *Palenque* when her ultralight was on farside?" Gretchen poked some of the buttons on the captain's panel and a variety of plotted routes, icons and little winking glyphs appeared across the live image of the planet. The routes of the geologist's flights vanished over the curve of the world, then looped back again. "Does she have some kind of a relay station?"

A low, ominous growl trailing away into a hissing snarl answered Gretchen's question. Magdalena crawled out of the utility space under the floor, her fur slick with sweat and snarled with bits of wire and the particular brand of sealant grease used by the Imperial Navy. The Hesht shot Anderssen a fierce, quelling look—an effort entirely lost on Gretchen, who was staring fixedly at the main v-pane.

"If I tell you, witless kit, will you be quiet?"

"Sure." Gretchen nodded, though even Magdalena could tell the human woman hadn't heard her. "Do you have a log of her transmissions? Could we find the relays that way? Does *he* have a copy? I mean—what if she dropped a three-square bar somewhere, would he have to clean that up?"

Magdalena swung herself over the comm station—her toolbags and tail drifting behind her—and dug a claw into the back of the captain's chair to anchor herself. Gretchen finally looked at her with something like full attention.

"I think the dust would take care of litter," Maggie said, voice rumbling deep in her throat. "The base at the observatory—that's a problem—or our mystery shuttle—there's another difficulty."

"Why?" Gretchen gave the Hesht a puzzled look, then she grinned. "Oh, do you think the miners will come back? That would spoil our crow's plan to leave no trace!"

Magdalena twitched her ears. "They don't have to come back. I've been running nonstop image searches on Smalls's weather archive." One long arm reached out and tapped a command on the panel. "The mining shuttle didn't leave like everyone expected."

The big view of Ephesus shimmered away and the v-pane displayed a high altitude shot of the planetary surface. Gretchen could recognize the edge of the northern permafrost, as well as the tapering wing of the Escarpment running down to smaller mountains and then—almost at the pole—to nothing but barren, rocky plains. "I don't see—"

"*Hsst!*" Maggie cuffed Gretchen's head, catching one ear with the back of her paw. "Ow!"

"Watch. Quietly. Learn." Maggie moved a control and the image narrowed, the point of view zooming down from orbit. Mountains, valleys, vast plains of glittering sand flashed past. Suddenly, Gretchen caught sight of a triangular shape flitting across a queer-looking stone plateau. The ground was chopped up into smaller triangles of shadow, making the speeding shuttle almost invisible.

The shuttle was gone from the next picture—a half hour had elapsed—but the pattern of the ground had subtly changed. Gretchen stiffened in her chair. "What was that? What are those lines?"

"Interesting, isn't it?" Maggie's tongue was showing. Gretchen frowned at her. "Look at this," the Hesht said, moving the control again.

Another high-angle shot, but later in the planetary day. The image had been enhanced, but a long blackened gouge was clear, cutting across a rippling line of dunes to an abrupt end. Gretchen squinted as Magdalena zoomed again. The track ended in a welter of shining metal, a mostly recognizable wing canted at a queer angle, the twisted body of a shuttle scored with carbon and the signs of a fierce conflagration.

"The *Valkyrie* didn't get home," Maggie said. "So our nosy crow has a bigger mess to clean up than he thinks."

"Jesu . . ." Gretchen zoomed again, though now the image was very grainy and large sections showed the gray rippling tone of comp interpolation. "They suck up too much dust?"

"Looks like they got hit." Parker had come up on the other side of the captain's chair. He made a sign against ill luck, face screwed up in a grimace. "That fire damage didn't happen on the crash, not in such a thin atmosphere. Something swatted them down. Maybe some kind of beam weapon."

Maggie's ears twitched again. "I found the crash site last night, after everyone had gone to sleep. Old crow has been searching too. But he's not as good with the comp as this *paaha*, for all his shining-coat equipment. Now, you want to see what happened?"

Parker and Gretchen gave the Hesht a disbelieving look. "How? Smalls's satellites only take pictures every half hour!"

"True enough," Magdalena said, a deep purr beginning in the back of her throat. "But they don't take their pictures all at the same time, and near the poles the fields of view overlap." A claw tapped on the panel and the view of the planet returned, this time with white rectangular grids superimposed. Near the poles, the rectangles overlaid each other in a flurry of lines. "All this lets us see *sideways* into the area of the crash. So I cobbled together video from the adjacent satellites and from those further around the curve that had a horizontal vantage of the crash site. Which lets us see . . ."

The claw went *tik-tik* on the panel and a jerky, crude, massively interpolated vid unspooled on the display.

The shuttle arrowed down out of the eastern sky, sweeping across the crisscrossed plateau. The flare of the twin engines was very clear in the vid. The *Valkyrie* began to bank, turning south and Gretchen felt her breath seize—the entire plateau seemed to ripple with motion, the crisscross lines shifting noticeably—and there was a sudden, shockingly bright flash. The entire plateau was blotted out by a burst of white light. When the light faded—after only a fraction of a second—the shuttle was wreathed in smoke. Flames jetted from a smashed engine in a bright, blossoming cloud. They wicked out only seconds later, but the shuttle was already spinning out of control.

The vid skipped and they caught only a glimpse of the aircraft as it slammed into the desert floor and skidded wildly across the dunes, spewing debris, chunks of airframe, and engine parts. Then the vid ended, and the vast red disc of Ephesus replaced the grainy images.

"You see?" Magdalena had her brush in her paw and was smoothing out the kinks and twists in her fur. "Sometimes the planet eats more than your boots."

Parker shook his head, then flicked away his spent tabac and immediately lit another. Gretchen sat quietly for a moment, studying the images on the panel. She ran though the video again, her face composed and concentrated. After a moment, she said, "Did you extract more vid of this plateau with the lines?"

"Ya-ha," Magdalena coughed. "The second v-feed in archive—yes, that's the one."

Another series of images flowed past, these taken from weather satellite number eight at a slight angle from the west. Dawn spilled over the eastern horizon and the pattern of lines became apparent, elongated and stretched out, making a cross-hatching pattern. Day progressed and the lines shortened, shifted pattern, essentially vanishing at midday. Then, as the sun sank into the west, lengthened again—this time to the east—and went through a similar set of convolutions.

Gretchen played the vid again, but this time she stopped the feed about an hour after the sun had risen, then zoomed and zoomed again. The comp interpolated busily, refining the image, and then a forest of tall pipelike structures were revealed covering the plateau.

"Scale?" Parker was at her shoulder again, a coil of tabac smoke tangling in her hair and tickling her nose.

"They're four to five meters tall," Gretchen said, brushing invisible smoky gnats away from her nose. "But look . . . they bend as the sun passes. Not too much; the mineralized sheathing must be stiff to let them grow so high, but enough to follow the sun. Like flowers."

"Pipeflowers." Parker grunted. "What made the flash? Did they?"

Gretchen nodded, hand over her mouth. "Sinclair will have to look at this, but all of the microfauna he's found so far have used a kind of electron cascade as their . . . their blood, I guess. They store and release energy—the fuel that gives them life—by shedding electrons and storing potentials in segregated structures. And these . . . stems . . . must trap sunlight in some kind of photocell to sustain themselves."

Parker scratched the side of his head. "They don't look dark, like a solar array."

"No." Gretchen felt a vague thought rear its head. Something she'd almost grasped before, when she was in the medical bay, or when she was examining the book cylinder. "No, the sun gives life, but too much is deadly. Too much UV, right?" Her fingers drummed on the display. "So they build up a mineralized sheath—like the little creatures I found growing in the pulque can."

Gretchen felt the puzzle shift in her mind, some pieces falling into place and revealing a new orientation and shape for other sets of data. She suddenly felt alive, as if her skin were humming and everything became perfectly clear.

"The pulque can is the key," she said, looking up at Parker. "Because it's *new* and yet the organism had nearly filled the can. Sinclair thinks the whole ecosystem works very slowly, but he's wrong—the species he's examining are only replicating so slowly because they have so little energy to work with. The *can* was perfect for them—it's a substance they can digest—and it was in the shade of the trench. So they can grow and be protected from the sun." Gretchen nodded. "Because all of these organisms—all of this effusion of Ephesian life—are terribly sensitive to ultraviolet radiation. You saw what happened down in the examining room—everything just died. Or in the shuttle intake with your multispec lamp."

"Okay," Parker said as he stubbed out his tabac. "Then how did all of this develop here? There's no ozone layer to speak of, no heavy atmosphere . . . the surface is a kill zone for the *chapultin*. How would they ever get a chance?"

Gretchen's expression changed and Parker thought she looked terribly sad.

"Because there were so many of them to begin with," she said in a hollow voice. "Unnumbered billions, covering the world in a terrible killing mist. They must have blotted out the sun, turned the sky dark with their numbers. But of course, there was no one to see them, not by then."

"Huh?" Parker's tabac hung on his lip, sending up a slow, coiling trail of smoke.

"They were the eaters," Gretchen said, grinding a palm heel against her eye. "The First Sun people came to this world and they scattered thousands of cylinders—just like those Russovsky found. The cylinders broke open and the *chapultin* poured out, relentless and unstoppable. And, in the end, when they were done, there was nothing but barren rock and stone and an empty world."

Parker drew back, an expression half of amazement and half of disgust on his face.

"Then the great machines descended from the sky and the whole mantle of the world was torn away and reshaped in a way which pleased the gods of the First Sun. Lennox thinks their project was interrupted, that they went away in haste and I think she's right. Because they left behind a ruin and some of their expendable tools were still alive. Some of the eaters lived, burrowing into the stone, hiding from the sun which turned the newly shattered surface into the harshest desert imaginable.

"Smalls is puzzled by the levels of oxygen and nitrogen in the current atmosphere. They're much higher than they should be—like there's a chlorophyll reaction working somewhere—and there's really very little CO_2." A wan smile tried to intrude on Gretchen's face, but failed. "The descendants of the *chapultin* fill the sand, the rock, every niche—just as life always seems to do—and they gobble up any CO_2 they might find, releasing plain carbon and oxygen. And they fear the sun, so they've evolved in this swift million years, laying down waste products to protect their crystalline bodies, a shell to block the killing UV."

Her hand opened, indicating the plateau of pipeflowers. "Some of them have evolved to get their energy from the sun, though even then in only a specialized way. They must . . . they must have thought the engine flare of the shuttle was a new sun—so bright, so close—but there was too much energy, too fast." Gretchen nodded to the pilot. "What's a beam weapon, but a directed stream of excited particles? That plateau is thirty miles wide, Parker, and there must be hundreds of thousands, maybe millions of pipeflowers. And every one of them probably suffered a catastrophic electron cascade all at once."

"Ugly." Parker said after thinking about it for a moment. "Very ugly. Old crow better be careful flying around down there. Could get his tailfeathers singed."

Gretchen smiled broadly at the thought of the Imperial judge plunging in a ball of fire to the desert floor. The mental image was clear and vivid and accompanied by a very satisfying crashing sound.

"*Hrrwht!*" Magdalena shook her head, ears angled back. "A *Midge* won't attract them—it's quiet and unobtrusive—barely leaves a vapor trail. Russovsky was lucky—or figured it all out for herself. She was a careful hunter—well, before they ate her up, she was." The Hesht sighed.

"Yes . . ." Gretchen suddenly looked thoughtful. She was thinking of Hummingbird and his mysterious errand. "Parker, how much fuel does a *Midge* carry? How high can one fly?"

"So," Anderssen announced in a very satisfied tone, "he's not coming back."

Parker stared around in alarm, making a cutting motion at his throat. "Sister save us! Boss, don't talk like that! He's plugged into every surveillance camera on the ship."

The pilot had been working up fuel loads and the speed and range of a *Midge* on the navigator's panel for an hour. None of his scenarios allowed an ultralight to rise to a sufficient altitude in the Ephesian atmosphere to let a shuttle on ballistic path to make a skyhook snatch.

"Maggie?" Gretchen swiveled her head toward the black-furred alien.

The Hesht shook her head, the overhead lights swirling across her work goggles, attention far away. "Crow and the Marines are loading supplies into the fresh *Midge* and doing a systems check. He's away from his surveillance equipment."

"See?" Gretchen grinned at the pilot. Parker made a face.

"Don't cost anything to be careful," he muttered. "Look—maybe he's expecting a pickup from the *Cornuelle*. A navy shuttle could pick him up anywhere. No law saying he has to be snatched out of the upper atmosphere on a skyhook."

"I suppose." Anderssen's face fell and her grumpy mood returned. In her heart, she knew there was no reason at all for the Imperial *nauallis* to choose the same way down and back. "So you think he wants this crazy high-altitude insertion *now* because the *Cornuelle* isn't available?"

"Sure." Parker settled back in the navigator's chair, his nervous tension draining away as Anderssen's voice became more reasonable. "Our shuttles aren't equipped with any kind of stealth tech, no antiradar alloys and composites . . . just commercial birds. So if he wants a quiet delivery, then this ballistic skip is an entirely reasonable way to go. Coming back? The *Cornuelle* sends down some freaky, high-grade military shuttle to snatch him up all ghostlike."

"Hmm. Only if the *Cornuelle* comes back soon enough. These suits and other equipment aren't going to last too long down there, not if he's wandering around in the mountains. He'll need to be extracted in no more than a week or two."

"What do you mean?" Parker stubbed out his tabac. "People have been working down at base camp for months."

"Yes, in pressurized buildings and using de-dusting equipment when they come in from the field." Gretchen waved her hand for emphasis. "Plus, the observatory site is in the middle of a bright, well-lit plain—almost flat, a desert even by Ephesian standards—so the population density of the microfauna is very low. I checked the airlocks and storm doors—they're eroding, not quickly, but you can see signs of wear. If the camp was someplace sheltered, in a canyon and in shade part of the day? There'd be nothing but a mineralized sheath left, or even an animate copy, like Russovsky."

Parker's shoulder twitched in reaction. "That's a nice thought."

"Ah-huh." Gretchen looked at Maggie questioningly. The Hesht was still staring into the distance. *Still a little time,* Anderssen thought. *And what am I going to do? My prize is snatched away, the expedition cashiered short of any kind of deliverable—there won't be a single bonus now, not without something the Company can sell.* The thought of not being able to afford a holiday ticket made her stomach turn over. Her thoughts shied away from the prospect of the expedition crew being charged for the lost machinery, tools, equipment and data at the base camp. "Parker, can you tell where the *Cornuelle* has gone? When it might come back?"

The pilot made a coughing sound—a conscious imitation of Magdalena's diesel generator laugh—and shook his head. "Sorry, boss. We lost the navy as soon as they went passive, shut down their hull lights and snuck off into the dark. Those light cruisers are built for snooping around, and the poor lot of matchsticks on this tub won't light them up even if we try."

Parker sighed, tapping a fresh tabac from a dingy plastic box he carried in the front pocket of his work vest. "As to a return date? I don't know. One of Maggie's tapes has Isoroku saying *karijozu* on his last comm call as they were preparing to leave. 'Good luck hunting.' So I'd guess they're looking for the refinery ship." He squinted at one of the dead navigation panels, thinking. "A search of the asteroid belt could take weeks, even months."

"I see." Gretchen's expression had grown still. She started to speak, but Magdalena suddenly twitched, making a sharp motion with one hand.

"They've finished," the Hesht said, ears twitching. "Back to work."

Grumbling, Parker hitched up his work belt and swung himself gracefully up and over the ring of command panels. "Mags, I think we need to jimmy up some kind of specialized clamp to back these dead connectors out. . . ."

Gretchen sat quietly, thinking, while the Hesht and the pilot worked in the tight space under the deck, cursing and sweating. After almost an hour, she leaned forward and keyed up the *Midge* fuel-loading model Parker had put together. Her eyes were oddly flat and expressionless as she tapped in a new scenario.

A sleepbag muffled the sound of snoring, but Gretchen's work goggles were dialed up into light-amp mode and she pushed away from the door frame of Parker's cabin without a pause. She caught the far wall and bumped softly to a halt. With her free hand, she ran the sharp edge of her thumbnail down the sealer strip and a flap fell away, revealing the pilot's sleeping face.

"Breakfast time," she whispered, pinching his earlobe. Parker's eyes flickered open and he blinked in the darkness. Straining against her own exhaustion, Gretchen laid a finger across his lips before he made too much noise. "Quietly, Parker-*tzin*, quietly. Get dressed and bring your tools."

The pilot swallowed a curse, fumbled for his work shades, then hissed in disbelief at the hour. "Where—"

"I'll show you," Gretchen said, closing her eyes for a moment. *I am so tired.*

Parker eeled out of his bag with admirable skill, then started to gather up his work vest, toolbelt and clothing. The fingertips of Gretchen's left hand crept to the medband on her right wrist, and then a blessedly cool sensation began to prick up her arm. *Ahhh . . . nothing like a jolt of eightgoodhours.*

Fifteen minutes later, Parker had a very sour look on his face as they followed a guideline into the rear cargo deck of the number one shuttle. The docking bay was dark, lit only by the faint glow of lights around the airlock. Gretchen drew herself to a halt at the loading master's station, one foot hooked into a step-up to hold her steady. The hold was filled from side to side by the inelegant shape of a cargo pallet squatting atop the shuttle's deployment rack.

"Stand clear," Gretchen said, keying the loading master's panel awake. Frowning, Parker stood aside, keeping feet, hands and head behind a wedge of cross-

hatched yellow lines on the deck. Anderssen ran her forefinger down a control ribbon, her thumb plastered against an override.

A deep hum filled the air and Parker jerked back from the cargo rails. The
enormous pallet slid forward smoothly, tiny winking lights marking the outline of
the pod. As the pilot watched in growing alarm, the pallet rumbled past him, then
out of the back of the shuttle.

"Wha . . ." Parker turned to Gretchen, but she was watching the pod with a
grim, fixed expression. "Please say Maggie has subverted the surveillance cam—"

"She has," Gretchen muttered, her fingers dancing on the panel. "And Bandao
is watching outside, just in case."

Parker felt the air tremble and looked back. A cargo lading arm descended
from the roof of the bay, entirely ominous in the darkness, only a suggestion of
movement, of long reaching steel claws. Two massive lading braces appeared out of
the gloom and slid into matching grooves on either side of the cargo pod. The pilot inched back—he'd seen more than one spaceport worker crushed between a
pod and the side of a shuttle or the maneuvering arms. The pallet clanked away
from the shuttle deck, then swung away into darkness.

"Here we go," Gretchen said in a strained, tight voice. "Better get behind me."

Parker slid past her, then flinched as a second pod—just as large as the first—
emerged from the darkness. His hand tightened on a hold-on bar. "That's not—"

"—on the loading track?" Gretchen's busy fingers had slowed. Now they
drifted gently across the control panel. "No. No, it's not."

The new pallet was held by a second pair of loading arms, and Parker knew—
as he felt a cold curl of sweat slithering down the back of his neck—the new pod
was approaching at a strange angle. He dialed up his work goggles and saw the lading arms from the adjoining number two shuttle cradle were holding the new pallet. "Sister! Boss . . . there's too much stress on that armature."

"It'll be fine," Gretchen whispered, featherlight fingertips inching the arms
towards the bay doors. "Just fine. There's just enough . . ."

Metal squealed against metal, and the entire shuttle trembled. Parker bit back
a shout of fear. Gretchen hissed, then stabbed a forefinger at a "backup" glyph. The
pod shivered, there was another grinding sound and the huge rectangular bulk
popped back. Parker was immediately into the gap, catching the upper edge of the
shuttle cargo door.

"There's no clearance," he said in a strangled voice. "You've torn a sixty centimeter strip right off the edge of the seal." The pilot's upper half was invisible
above the four-ton cargo door. "I don't know if it'll close properly now."

Gretchen blinked, then called up a schematic of the shuttle bay on the panel.
When she looked up, she was startled to see Parker staring at her. For a moment,

she'd forgotten he was there. "We have to get that second pod into this shuttle in no more than . . ." Gretchen's eyes slid sideways to her chrono, then back to fix on the pilot, ". . . two hours."

"What happens in two hours?"

"Hummingbird and his Marines will be down here," Anderssen said in a flat voice. "And they'll strap him into the *Midge* in that first pod." She tried to grin, failed, and went on. "You'll be with them, of course, as pilot. And *you* are going to adjust for carrying two pods rather than one in the shuttle cargo bay."

"What's in the new pod?" Parker asked in a suspicious tone.

"Me." Gretchen's face twisted into a tight simulacra of a smile. "And Russovsky's *Gagarin*."

"Oh, boss, now wait a minute! That's—"

"What we're going to do." A sharp hand movement cut him off. "Right now. Maggie's not going to be able to fool the surveillance system for much longer, not without leaving tracks all over the onboard environmental system logs."

Parker swallowed, wished he had a tabac, then wiped his mouth. "Okay. Okay. We've got to load up differently—having the number two arm reach across is all crazy. These shuttles are designed to load straight on, right from the back. So . . ." He stared at the schematic, then shook his head, long thin fingers stabbing tentatively at the display, ". . . we're gonna hope the *Palenque* doesn't suffer an inertial event in the next twenty-six minutes."

In the darkness of the bay, the number two arm shifted, servomotors whining, and rose up. At the same time, the number one arm slid aside, stabilized and detached from the pod. While Parker sweated below, both sets of arms retracted with a rattling scrape. Both cargo pallets hung suspended in z-g, unsupported and unsecured. The massive lading assemblies swung up and away, changing places in an ill-seen dance, then gently drifted forward to switch pods.

The pilot was sweating rivers, hoping he didn't bump one of the two-ton pods and send it careening across the shuttle bay. With infinite delicacy, the number one arm approached Hummingbird's pallet. The steel tongues caressed the locking grooves, and Parker held his breath, feeling each second drag endlessly as the lading arm's attractor field locked with the magnetic striping along the groove.

Gretchen leaned up against the wall, eyes closed, both arms wrapped around a hold-on. Her mind was whirling with frantic, useless details. Parker's constant stream of muttered commentary seemed to echo in a vast distance, supplemented by soft clangs and squeaks.

The number two cargo pod—gripped securely in the shuttle one lading arm—advanced into the black mouth of the shuttle hold. The rectangular shape clanked to the deck and a series of telltales lit, indicating an acceptable lock with the cargo deck. Shuttle-side motors kicked in with a whine and the pod slid smoothly to the back of the bay.

Fifteen minutes later, the number one pod completed the same maneuver and Parker shut down the cargo lading system with a heartfelt sigh. His watch said forty-five minutes remained before Hummingbird's wake-up. Very close. *Sister— maybe I'll get to sleep when both of them are off-ship!*

Gretchen looked up from the shockchair of the *Midge*, a tangle of blond hair framing her face. A cocoon of straps covered her, and the tiny cabin of the ultralight was crowded with supplies and packets of gear. The retracted wings of the aircraft were folded around and behind her in a hexacarbon cloak. Above her, Parker and Bandao crouched at the edge of an access panel in the top of the pod.

"Now Parker-*tzin*, you remember to come back for me in sixteen days. Watch for us—we'll be in just one *Midge* if this is going to work—and don't miss with the skyhook."

"I never—well, hardly ever—miss, boss." Parker's grin was half-hearted. "What if the *Cornuelle* shows up? Should I stay away?"

Gretchen shook her head. "I'm sure they'll come, but you be there, too. I don't like heights."

Bandao shook his head at their badinage, placid face as still and composed as ever. Gretchen caught his eyes with a wry look.

"You can't go in my place, Dai. You'll have to keep Parker out of trouble for me."

"Impossible." The little Welshman did not seem concerned. He handed her a heavy package wrapped in olive-drab canvas. "The Company is paying me to protect you, Doctor Anderssen. My contract requires I exercise due diligence. So here—you might need this."

Weighing the package in her hands elicited a metallic clank. "A weapon?"

Bandao shrugged, pale eyes showing no trace of humor. "A Sif-52 shockgun. Very simple to use. Breaks down into four components for ease of transport. Just jack the loading lever, then point and pull the trigger. The ammunition will work even in a low-oxygen atmosphere. There is a manual in the bag. And extra rounds."

"Thank you, Bandao-*tzin*." Gretchen smiled warmly at the neatly-dressed man as she tucked the canvas case beneath the seat. "Time to lock me up."

Parker and Bandao disappeared from view. A moment later, the hatch cycled shut, leaving her in darkness. Gretchen tried to settle her shoulders comfortably into the shockchair and failed, though she was terribly weary. *Maybe I'll sleep anyway.*

Hadeishi watched the navigation plot in the threat-well shift, and the light cruiser's glyph swept across an entirely featureless volume of Ephesian space. The *chu-sa* looked up and nodded to his exec, who was sitting at attention, hands resting lightly on the chromatic surface of her control panel.

"Main drives, if you please," Hadeishi said, leaning back a fraction in his chair. They were now at sufficient distance from the third planet to risk a larger signature. "And configure the hull for maximum scan."

Muted activity followed, but Hadeishi smiled faintly as he felt the ship shift and tremble as the main power plant spun up. A counter began to run on his main panel, showing the time until he could call on cruising speed, then on maximum combat acceleration.

Koshō turned her head slightly. "G-decking on?"

Hadeishi nodded. He was tired of living in z-g. *Tea should stay in a proper cup by itself.*

A second tremor flowed through the ship and the *chu-sa* felt his stomach twist, then settle into a reasonable orientation. The shockchair adjusted, letting his weight settle into the comfortable frame, and the faintest thread of uneasiness receded. *That's better.*

"Deploy main sensor array," Hadeishi said, watching the threat-well stir to new life. Countless fresh details were now added to the holo as the hull and the main arrays began to soak up the sea of radiation and information sleeting past the light cruiser. He pointed with his chin. "Situation in orbit over Three?"

Smith perked up, nervously straightening his duty jacket. "I can throw a whisker to the *Palenque*, sir."

Hadeishi pursed his lips, considering his options. "Any motion?"

"All quiet at this lag and EM level," Koshō replied, her panel flickering with dozens of sensor feeds. The captain nodded. Without an active scan of near-Ephesian space, they were unlikely to pick up anything which was not in violent, reflective motion.

"Smith-*tzin*, see if you can raise *Thai-i*, Isoroku—but quietly. Don't paint the whole ship trying to acquire a comm lock."

The young midshipman nodded, his face composed in concentration. Hadeishi watched his panel with interest—one section mirrored the communications officer's display—and was pleased to see the boy had maintained constant targeting coordinates for the main comm array on the archaeology ship as the *Cornuelle* had sped away. *Good thinking*, Hadeishi observed. *Now, how much drift and interference has occured?*

"I have a channel," Smith announced a moment later. He struggled manfully to hide his pride. "Engineer Isoroku is on voice-only comm, channel sixty-six."

Very properly done, Hadeishi thought, glancing at Koshō. The exec did not seem to be paying attention. Her eyes were on the threat-well and her sensor feeds. Hadeishi did believe for a moment the *sho-sa* had missed Smith's initiative and efficiency. "Well done, Smith-*tzin*. Good morning, Isoroku-*san*. How are things aboard the *Palenque* today?"

There was a delay. Smith's comm laser trudged to the distant orbital, then back again.

". . . shuttle one is away with *nauallis* Hummingbird aboard . . ."

Hadeishi listened with mounting concern as the engineer related the judge's method of arriving on the planetary surface without attracting undue attention. A cold feeling began to well up in his breast, listening to the engineer describe Hummingbird's preparations.

This is not good, he realized, mentally counting the days until the *Cornuelle* could return to the space around the third planet. "Isoroku-*san*, how are your repairs progressing?"

"Speedily," came after a moment's delay. "Shuttle one will return in sixteen hours. We should have main drives operating today. Navigational control systems are also being repaired. In two days we should be able to ease out of orbit."

"Those are your orders?" Hadeishi clasped his hands. "From the judge directly?"

"*Hai, chu-sa,*" replied the engineer. "He wants us out of the way as quickly as possible."

"I see." Hadeishi's eyes lingered on the burning red disk of the planet at the edge of the threat-well. "Then you should move ahead with all prudent speed. *Sho-sa* Koshō, can we tap local visual from the *Palenque?* I would like to see this for myself."

Lying in darkness, Gretchen squirmed a little from side to side. The shockfoam in the cockpit of the *Gagarin* was old and stiff. There was a properly shaped cavity for lean old Russovsky, but not for the shorter and rounder Anderssen. A harness pinned her to the seat, holding her tight against the inevitable moment when everything would happen with violent simultaneity. For the moment, however, nothing was happening. The cramped cockpit of the *Midge* was entirely dark, every system shut down, the power plant quiescent. Outside the pitted, scored canopy, the wings of the ultralight folded around her like a shroud, nestled inside a web of shock cable and a tightly packed parafoil. Even with light, she wouldn't see the corrugated walls of the surrounding pod. All she could feel was equipment pressing in around her.

Anderssen doubted the Marines riding shotgun with Parker would bother to scan the interior of the cargo bay, but she wasn't going to risk discovery by powering up the *Gagarin*. Her z-suit was already providing air, water, and waste recycling. There was absolutely nothing to do but sit and wait in the darkness. Even the shuttle itself was quiet, falling out of the *Palenque*'s distant orbit with engines cold, only a dust-gray wedge spiraling down into the gravity well of the planet.

In the darkness, Gretchen tried to sleep. She was terribly tired, her nerves trembling with too many injections of eightgoodhours. The medband had finally stalled, passing some threshold, and refused to give her another jolt. Even requests for a sleep aid had been ignored. Anderssen picked at the lump the metal band made under the rust-colored layer of her suit. *Stupid thing*, she thought bitterly, *I want to sleep now! Why won't you help me?*

Trying to relax was impossible. Her mind raced, thoughts rushing past in a constant, dizzying stream. Every moment of the mission crowded her mind's eye, each memory sharp and preternaturally distinct. The airlock of the *Palenque* opening, revealing darkness. Parker spitting. The tons of white dust they'd cleaned out of the environmental filters. Shuttle one descending to the base camp in a huge brick-red cloud. Fitzsimmons laughing at her, dark eyes twinkling under a cloud of unruly hair. The cylinder lying in a pool of intense white light.

My find, she thought, and her thoughts fixed upon the slab of limestone, the jagged edges and the rough, weathered surface. Every pit and crack seemed perfectly clear in her mind's eye. *My ticket.*

The Company did not pay her well. She was a junior scientist without a patron in the Company hierarchy. Her postings to Mars and Ugarit had gone reasonably well, but neither dig director had decided to keep her on after the initial assignment. So there'd been no re-up bonuses. Field scientists were expected to maintain their own gear and tools, though each expedition provided food, transport and most necessities. But Ugarit and Mars had eaten up her clothes, tools, comps . . . she was never going to get rich bouncing from site to site this way. She needed a patron, a permanent posting, some status. Something no clanless *macehualli* technician scientist was going to get.

In the darkness, Gretchen bit her lower lip, wishing she had something useful to do. *If it were just me,* she mused, her thoughts turning into a well-worn groove, *I'd be fine.*

Junior-grade xenoarchaeologists were supposed to be solitary, clanless, without ties to home, hearth and district. They were not supposed to have three children of *calpulli* age at home. Gretchen's right hand moved automatically, blunt fingertips reaching sideways to brush the surface of a 3v card wedged into the rightside navigation panel on the *Midge*. A faint, greenish glow answered her motion and Gretchen snatched her hand back. She didn't need to see the three shining faces looking up out of the swimming pool. Her memory was better, sharper than a dying 3v from a cheap camera. In her memory, they were right in front of her. . . .

Mommy! Mommy! We saw an otter! A real one, like in the old books. It was swimming!

Gretchen gasped, feeling a crushing weight press down on her chest. Heavy emotion welled up, tightening her throat. There was a little boy at home, and two little girls, who deserved better than working on a lumbering crew, or running drag lines on a fishing boat, while age stole their smiling eyes. But her salary didn't go very far—not far enough to get them into a *calmecac* school with the sons and daughters of the landholders, or the tutors they'd need to pass entrance exams for a *pochteca* academy. Her own hard-won education had cost the last of the credits her grandmother had so carefully hoarded during the war.

Now all they had was a marginal farm on the edge of cultivation, a big rambling wood and stone house hiding amid stands of realspruce and fir, a truck which ran more often than not and the flitter. *And me. We have me out here, at the edge of human space, sitting in a cargo pod with nothing but some hexacarbon around me and an ultralight that's spent too many hours in the air already . . . uuh!*

Gretchen felt the world lurch, the restraining harness biting into her shoulder. Her stomach dropped away and a thundering roar began to penetrate the heavy walls of the cargo pallet. *Here we go,* she gulped, feeling the *Midge* rock against the cargo rails. The air-landing pod groaned, the joints of the four walls squeaking in darkness. Fighting against rising nausea, she grabbed hold of the control stick and flipped a series of "dumb" switches to life. The fuel cells woke up with a whine. Power trickled through the *Gagarin*'s main systems and faint lights began to gleam on the control panels.

Comm woke up, tumbled across a dozen channels and then locked onto the sound of Parker's voice—gone icy cold and even, as if he were reading from a script. "Rate six hundred, rate five hundred seventy, rate . . ."

The scream of air across metal and ceramic drowned him out and Gretchen felt sweat spring out all over her body. She tried to reach the main wing controllers and failed, gloved fingertips failing to answer her mind's command. Cursing, she clenched her hand, mastered control of her arm and then—aiming carefully—mashed down a pair of control switches. A bleat of warning—lost in the shriek of reentry—answered her, but the locked-down wings began to stiffen. She'd need every second she could cheat from time and physics once the pallet blew out of the back of the shuttle.

"Five hundred," Parker's voice cut through the steadily rising howl. "Brace!"

Gretchen ground herself back into the shockfoam, legs stiff against the firewall beside the foot pedals. Her eyes screwed shut, though her forebrain knew it wouldn't make any difference. . . .

The *Komodo* slammed into the upper atmosphere, a sheet of flame licking at the edge of the triangular wings, bounced and then skittered across the sky, slewing from side to side. Inside her dark box, Anderssen was slammed into the shockfoam once, then twice, then she lost count. After an endless series of jarring motions, the comm channel bleated a warning and light flooded into the bay as the rear cargo door clamshelled open.

A heavy hand pressed on Gretchen's chest and her fingers cramped on the control stick. The pressure spiked, crushing breath from her lungs and then lifted as quickly as it had come. There were two sharp flashes outside the canopy and the walls of the cargo pod flew away into a suddenly bright abyss. Gretchen felt her gut clench and the curving horizon swung past.

An enormous expanse of ruddy desert filled her field of view, then the horizon swung up like a hammer and she saw the stars glittering in velvet. The roof of the pod blew away, then the remaining walls. Rushing air shrieked through the web of netting holding the *Midge* to the floor of the pallet. Gretchen choked, slammed by another massive jerk. The parafoil deployed above her, snapping out in a four hundred-k wind. A giant unseen claw snatched the pallet and the *Midge* skyward.

She grayed out, head smashed back into the shockfoam. The horizon jerked from side to side, then stabilized. The parafoil—hundred-meter wingspan barely dragging in the nearly nonexistent atmosphere—and the pod dropped precipitously toward the distant surface of the planet. Panting, Gretchen came around, groping for the stick. In about five seconds she knew . . .

BANG!

The last set of bolts blew out, flinging the metal floor of the pod away. Now Gretchen had her hands on the stick, both feet on the pedals and the *Gagarin's* onboard comp was awake. The aircraft plunged toward the vast desert below, but the parafoil was keening, catching a little air. *Gagarin's* sensors tested the air rushing past and saw the retaining harness had gone the way of the walls and floor. Accordingly, the wings stiffened and began to extend. By design, they unfolded from the core of the *Midge* outwards, each new section conforming to a rough lifting body. The *Gagarin's* plummeting descent slowed, air thickening under the parafoil with each passing kilometer.

Gretchen watched the control panel with wide eyes. The structural integrity indicators were going wild. Wind howled through the frame of the ultralight and she could see black, jagged mountains looming up below. Only moments before they had seemed so far away, now she could pick out peaks, ravines, tumbled fields of splintered boulders.

Caught in some unseen current of the upper air, the *Midge* swept across the mountains, wings deploying centimeter by centimeter. For a moment, with everything seemingly under control, Gretchen checked her navigation panel. The chipped, yellowed glassite showed her a swiftly moving terrain map. Two glowing green diamonds sped across stylized mountains and plains. The comp on Hummingbird's *Midge* was still responding to broadcast position requests. *Good,* she thought, *I haven't lost him. Not yet.*

Her own comp beeped imperiously, dragging Gretchen's attention back to the ultralight. Both wings were fully extended to catch the steadily thickening air and the comp-controlled lifting surfaces were desperately trying to account for the drag generated by the cables connecting the *Gagarin* to the parafoil.

"Time to fly," Gretchen said, flipping a switch beside her left hand. There was another, barely noticeable jerk as the support braces for the parafoil separated. Without the drag of the *Midge*'s weight, the curving wing sailed off into the blue-black heavens. The ultralight plunged, yawing from side to side before the control surfaces had time to adjust. Both wing engines ignited and Gretchen felt the stick shiver alive in her hand.

Whooo . . . The *Midge* arced away across the mountaintops. Anderssen's eyes gravitated to the tracking display. Hummingbird was spiraling down toward the surface eighty, ninety k away to the northeast. A moment later *Gagarin* banked onto a new course, a tiny pale fleck poised between the dark immensity of the Ephesian sky and the splintered wasteland below.

THE CORNUELLE

A jerky, timelagged image flowed across Hadeishi's panel. He could make out the top of an ultralight—seen from orbit at long range, interpolated first by the sensor suite on the *Palenque* and then by the military-grade system aboard the *Cornuelle*—flying under its own power. The captain allowed himself to be impressed with the Anderssen woman's audacity. He was entirely familiar with Hummingbird's skill as a pilot, but he hadn't expected the archaeologist to hurl herself into such vigorous pursuit.

"Deftly done," the captain mused. His earbug was filled with outraged chatter from the Marines on the *Komodo*-class shuttle. Fitzsimmons, in particular, was expressing himself at great length and without professional restraint. Hadeishi dialed down the channel before he overheard something which would require overt action on his part. The momentary delight he'd felt at Gretchen's survival was fading, replaced by a nagging sensation of looming trouble.

Not trouble today—both ultralights were under power, on course and far beyond his power by any measure—but trouble in the future. He frowned, eyes narrowing in thought, quick mind leaping ahead to the presumed reactions of higher authorities. *How to report this? And why is she following him?*

The scientist had a perfect right to use Company equipment, so there was neither theft nor malfeasance in her use of the shuttle or the ultralight. There were no local traffic control restrictions, so her near-orbital insertion and flight were entirely allowable. Unfortunately, Hadeishi was sure the *nauallis* had logged a directive to place the planet off-limits as well as ordering the civilians to depart. The captain doubted the *nauallis* would fail to notice another ultralight following him—his panel made Anderssen's course perfectly clear—and the old Náhuatl was bound to react explosively to her disrespect.

Does that matter? A quiet voice much like his father's intruded on his thoughts. *Will the judge return to the land of living men? If he does not raise his voice to trouble the mighty, no harm will come to her. If you say nothing, then nothing will have happened. If the planet takes them both, who will know she disobeyed his orders?*

Hadeishi felt rising discomfort at the prospect. Hummingbird's departure—with only a single aircraft and minimal supplies—was rash and Anderssen's pursuit rasher still. Uncomfortable at the thought of leaving them both to die, the *chu-sa* tapped up the archaeologist's service record. He skimmed through the educational certificates, notes from the Mirror about her political reliability, reports from her various supervisors. After a moment he grunted, lost in thought. *She is not without experience in such a place,* Hadeishi allowed. Anderssen, in fact, had logged more hours in z-suits, in hostile environments, than the judge had. *Hummingbird will be surprised.*

The thought filled Hadeishi with bleak amusement and his mood lifted. *That would be a fine tale to hear,* he chuckled to himself, *should either of them live to relate the particulars.*

"*Sho-sa* Koshō?" The exec looked up. The end of the duty watch was fast approaching and *Thai-i* Gemmu had joined her at the secondary command station, preparing for changeover. Susan's face had a familiar pinched expression. Gemmu—though he was a loyal and dutiful officer—did not quite match the exec's rigorous expectations.

"Sir?"

"Shut down the comm feed from the *Palenque* and dump all transmission logs—raw and processed—to my station."

Koshō stared at the captain for a long moment—even a fraction longer than was polite—then abruptly nodded her head, fingers moving on her panel. Hadeishi saw the transmission begin and tapped in his own series of commands, dispatching a horde of system *dorei* to scrub all records of the transmissions from the *Palenque*, the voice and video log of bridge chatter and any other accumulated telemetry from the *Cornuelle's* memory. This required more than one override and Hadeishi became acutely aware of Koshō's continuing and entirely impolite stare as he worked.

After a moment there was a soft chime in his earbug, indicating a private channel had been opened from the exec's station to his.

"Yes?" Hadeishi kept his tone light, as if nothing out of the ordinary were happening.

"*Kyo*—" Koshō stopped, unable to bring herself to voice a question. Hadeishi smiled inwardly. Aboard an Imperial warship—even more so than among the rival navies of Anáhuac in the centuries before unification—the commander held absolute and unmitigated power. A captain's orders simply were *not* questioned by his subordinates. Hadeishi was keenly aware of this tradition—constantly reinforced from the highest levels of the Fleet—often led to tyranny and abuse, but in this tight instant of time he was glad for the shield.

"Nothing, sir." Koshō shut down the channel. Hadeishi did not look at her, knowing the usually proper officer would be struggling to contain embarrassment and chagrin. Showing any awareness of her near-insubordination would only make matters worse.

Hadeishi's panel made a polite chiming sound, indicating the *dorei* had finished scrubbing the logs. The *chu-sa* felt a little uneasy for a moment, but then put the entire matter from his mind. Long experience with such unpleasant events allowed him to shut his own memories away into a quiet, discreet box.

"Duty watch reporting," Gemmu announced to the bridge. Hadeishi nodded, looking up at last. Koshō was already gone and the second watch officers were taking their stations.

"Thank you, Gemmu-*san*." Hadeishi said, shockchair unfolding as he stood up. "You have the bridge. Hold current course, thrust and emissions control level."

"*Hai, Chu-sa!*" The junior officer's response was crisp. "Have a good evening, sir."

Choppy wind gusted across a basin striped with long, low dunes. Veils of dust and
sand streamed toward the west, casting watery shadows on the floor of the valley.
Gretchen felt the *Midge* shake and rattle as she banked into a landing approach.
The engines whined as the ultralight angled into the wind. Through cloudy, pitted
glassite, Gretchen could just make out the long scar left by the shuttle crash. Most
of the skid—which had seemed so sharp and dark in Magdalena's video—was
gone, wiped away by blown sand. A few bits of scattered metal remained, glinting
in fading sunlight. The main bulk of the wreck was visible off to her left.

The *Midge* labored through the turn, coming into the wind, and her airspeed
sank like a stone. Gretchen blinked sweat out of her eyes, gritting her teeth as she
lined up for a landing. Ahead on the windswept plain, she could see the shining
gray shape of Hummingbird's ultralight and a dark speck beside the aircraft. *Yeah,*
a single thought burned, *I'm coming to visit, old crow.*

Gagarin wobbled down, battered by the gusty wind, and Gretchen tried to
keep her hand from clenching tight on the stick. Flight comp was burning cycles at
a ferocious rate, trying to keep the nose up, the wings aligned, and the overheated
engines from shutting down. The busy little processors didn't need her trying to
wingover into the deck and smash them all to tiny bits. A rumpled red quilt of

thumb-sized pea-sand rushed up. Gretchen felt nauseated, her eyes glued to the altimeter. Numbers spun down to single digits. She tweaked the stick forward, popping the nose up, and there was a screeching jolt as the tires hit the ground.

The *Midge* shuddered, bouncing twice, then three times. A gust caught the ultralight from the side, slewing the back wheel around. Gretchen corrected, nearly blinded by sudden sweat, her hand moving in molasses. Dust plumed behind the aircraft and she feathered the brakes. Terrible high-pitched squeals answered, but the ultralight jounced and quivered to a standstill. Anderssen exhaled, staring at the looming mass of torn and blackened metal filling her field of view.

A figure in a z-suit emerged from the shadow of the broken shuttle, wind snapping dun-colored robes tight against a stocky, compact body. Gretchen let both engines wind down and the *Gagarin* settled into loose sand. Her arm trembling, she reached down to unlatch the door. As she did, the *Midge* shook in a fresh gust of wind, lifted a meter, then slammed violently down again. Anderssen gasped, breath knocked from her lungs, and put differential power to the engines. Obediently, *Gagarin* spun in place, nosing back into the wind. Gretchen locked the brakes, then waited, fingers light on the stick.

Another gust rolled across the sand, rushed over the ultralight and the whole airframe shook, lifting off again. The *Midge* jounced back five, ten meters.

"Oh, Mother of God!" Gretchen cursed, feeling queasy. Bile bit at her throat. "We're too light!"

She shot a glance outside and saw the suited figure squatting in the minimal shade of the other aircraft, which was tied down in a pentagonal pattern with sand anchors.

"How the hell did he—" The *Midge* bounced again, caught in a fiercer blast. Sand rattled on the canopy and a string of warning lights flared on. Number two engine had just taken a shot of grit right into the intake. "Sister, help me!" *How did he land and have time to put out anchors with positive buoyancy? Wait—ah, idiot, idiot, idiot!*

Gretchen slapped the lifting surface controls. Two hydrogen pumps woke up with a gurgle and began to evacuate the wing tanks. As gas compressed into pressure tanks behind the seat, Anderssen turned on the motors to retract the wings. Despite her best efforts, the *Gagarin* continued to bounce backward, leaving her a hundred meters from the crash by the time the wings were locked back into storage position, and the *Midge* was no longer so excellently airworthy.

Grunting under the weight of two sand anchors, Gretchen clambered down out of the pilot's chair, her goggles on, suit zipped up, one end of a heavy tan and white *djellaba* across her face. The footing was poor on such heavy gravel, but she paid no mind. Her muscles remembered what to do, how to walk, how to lean just so into the gusting wind. She labored toward the wreck, twin monofil lines spool-ing out behind her.

The squatting figure under the other *Midge* did not stir, watching with interest as she drew even with him and fired both anchors into the sand. Five minutes later, the winch on the *Gagarin* was in operation and the ultralight approached at a walking pace, bouncing and hopping across the rough ground. Gretchen squatted herself, her back to the wind, the control for the winch cupped in one gloved hand.

Gretchen secured the last of the tie-downs and stood up, feeling her back creak. *No substitute for planetside exercise,* she thought with a groan. Both aircraft lay in the lee of the broken shuttle, cowering in a tiny space protected from the constant wind. Anderssen turned, hands busy rewrapping the heavy scarf around her face and shoulders to protect her breather mask and the relatively sensitive gaskets and equipment around her neck.

The suited figure stood as well, face hidden by goggles and mask. Gretchen could see the suit was a little worn, the shine of newness long gone, and there was a suitable array of tools strapped onto the man's body. She guessed he'd put in plenty of hours in hostile environments, but the drape of his *djellaba* and *kaffiyeh* was poor.

"Well," she said, clicking open the groundside channel, "thanks for helping me tie down."

"Were we on ship," the voice had a little buzz around the edges, as if his comm gear were already suffering from dust, "I would have you incarcerated, or shot, for disobeying a direct order."

"You might," Gretchen said, her voice brittle with fatigue and too much adrenaline, "but I'm not an Imperial officer. I'm a civilian. I even have a *permit* to be on this planet. I checked—you didn't have time to file the proper forms and paperwork to revoke our exploration rights."

"Amusing," Hummingbird replied and she could hear an edge of weariness in his voice. "But I will not argue the point. You were foolish to come down here. What did you hope to achieve by following me?"

"You," Gretchen said sharply, "have something of mine. I want it back."

Hummingbird turned fully toward her. "What do you mean?"

"The cylinder. You had Fitzsimmons and Deckard take the artifact from num-ber three airlock and stow it in your quarters. That object," her voice rose, "is Com-pany property and my personal salvage. I'll be expecting you to return it to the lawful owner—me!—upon our return to the *Palenque*."

There was a moment of silence, then the *nauallis* laughed softly, a breathy, echoing sound on the comm link. "You . . . you came down here to beard me about a chunk of shale?"

"Limestone," she replied. "Compressed limestone strata containing a verifiable First Sun artifact—a knowledge storage device, in fact—which—praise the Son—is duly and legally logged as the evidence and dig-claim of xenoarch Anderssen, Gretchen Elizabeth, company employee number 337G4. My property. Not yours. Not the Imperial government's."

"I see." Hummingbird rubbed one hand across the back of his head. "You have me—and this is rare, Anderssen-*tzin*—at a complete loss." His hand came back into view with a small, snub-nosed pistol which steadied in such a way as to provide Gretchen with a fine view of the muzzle. "But I believe you are suffering from a psychotic reaction due to the overuse of stimulants, excessive fatigue and the psychological effects of exposure to said First Sun artifact. Now—turn around and clasp your hands behind your head."

"I am not psychotic," Gretchen said, remaining entirely still. "I suggest you consider the fuel capacity of your aircraft, your stated mission, and put the clever little gun away."

Hummingbird's aim did not waver, which showed commendable strength to Gretchen's mind. She could barely stand, her arms and legs cramping from the physical stress of landing. "My mission," he said, after a moment, "is none of your concern. Indeed, your presence here makes an already precarious situation even less tenable."

"I don't agree," she said. "And I'm going to sit down."

The gun moved as she did and Gretchen sighed with relief to be squatting. Her arms were shaking inside the suit and the three-times-cursed medband was still locked out. *Stupid, stupid machine.*

"So," she said, cocking an eye at the eastern sky, which was noticeably darkening. "You haven't shot me yet, which I'd have expected from a flint-hard Imperial judge. I am a little surprised."

"If you expected to be shot, why did you follow?" Hummingbird squatted himself, the gun having already disappeared into some pocket or holster hidden on his suit. "I doubt the *Palenque*'s bigeye is sharp enough to pick us out down here. I could make your body and the aircraft disappear very quickly. No one would ever know."

"You would," Gretchen replied, finally picking out the gleam of his eyes through the polarized goggles. She laughed softly. "I knew you wouldn't shoot. I would wager you're even glad to see me . . . you don't have to admit that. I understand how it is."

"Why would that be?" The *nauallis*'s voice had a cold edge. "You don't even have any idea why I'm down here. You don't even know who I am."

"I know enough," Gretchen said, still watching the eastern horizon. In such a thin atmosphere, night advanced like a solid wall, the sky darkening swiftly to blue-black as the terminator approached. "You got spooked by my cylinder, by the Russovsky-copy. I think you got enough bits and pieces of the big puzzle to make a guess—yeah, maybe an *educated* guess—about what's going on down here. Suddenly the funny little archaeological expedition became a serious problem. So everyone has to clear out fast, leaving you behind to clean up the mess."

"The cylinder," the *nauallis* interjected, "will remain in Imperial custody and will be destroyed before the *Cornuelle* leaves this system."

"I don't think so," Gretchen replied tartly. "Not without fair compensation!"

"It is worthless," Hummingbird said, the edge returning to his voice. "Don't you see the device is a lure and a trap? I've seen such things before, left behind to ensnare the unwary. Such things cannot *ever* be allowed into Imperial space or even onto one of the Rim colonies."

Gretchen shook her head, the motion barely visible through the suit. "Your little blue pyramid tell you that? Does your *book* have a picture of my cylinder in it, with a warning label?"

"No," bit out the judge, "but such things have been encountered before."

"Have they?" Gretchen felt curiosity stir. *Down!* She reminded herself. *Stay on task.*

"Yes. The mining settlement on Aldemar Four was obliterated by an equivalent device—"

"You know," Gretchen said, rudely ignoring Hummingbird. "I really don't care about some miners who found something they shouldn't have. *This find is mine.* Logged, duly reported, even surveyed and examined. Now, you can destroy the object if you want, but given the high likelihood the cylinder is in fact a First Sun information storage device—your masters in the Ministry of Finance will be very, very unhappy with you for doing so."

Hummingbird's head drew back a fraction and Gretchen felt a sharp stab of delight.

"If you destroy my artifact," she said in a cutting voice, "then a court of adjudication will weigh in my favor when the Company sues the Imperial Navy for confiscating and destroying something worth *billions* of quills. Now, you're a judge—you know what the rules for theft and destruction of property are like."

There was a strangled hiss from the *nauallis*. "You'd quote the law to me?"

"I would," Gretchen said, stiffening and rising up slightly. "You *stole* from me. If you destroy the evidence of theft, then I'll be compensated as if the object had a 'fair market value'. Now, let's say I put a *proven* First Sun artifact up on the block in the *zocalo* of Tlateloco. How much do you think I'd get? Can you even count that high? How many centuries of servitude to me would it take to pay off such a debt?"

"It–it is a trap!" Hummingbird's control was fraying. "Useless and dangerous! Not a prize, not a *find*, not worth a single quill!"

"Not to me." Gretchen glared at the stupid man, though he couldn't see her expression through the mask. "That slab and that cylinder are worth everything to me."

"You'd risk your life, and the lives of others, for money?" There was a pitying tone in Hummingbird's voice. "You can't spend all those quills if you're dead."

For a moment, Gretchen said nothing. Then, in a cold voice, she said, "I risk my life every day, Hummingbird-*tzin*, for one hundred and nineteen quills. I live for months in a suit, eating my own waste, breathing my own toxins, grubbing in the dirt, for one hundred and nineteen quills. I break into tombs filled with explosive gasses; I watch my friends get killed by accidents with earthmoving equipment, or suit ruptures or sheer carelessness, or from drink or drugs or mindless brawls in some grimy hole-in-the-wall bar, all for one hundred and nineteen quills a day.

"How many quills are in my bank account?" She shook her head, feeling enormous, crushing weariness press down on her like a planet. "Maybe two, three hundred. Everything else goes home to my mother, who manages to keep shoes on my children's feet, food in their mouths, maybe some new soft for the home comp so they can learn. My son is going to be eight years old next year, oh mighty Judge, and unless I have nearly *thirty thousand* quills in my bank account, he won't be able to get into a *calmecac* school or a *pochteca* academy, which means he'll have to work lookout on a lumbering crew, watching for woodgaunts or frayvine—just so we can keep paying the rent on what little land we do have."

"That's nonsense," Hummingbird said, startled. "The *calpulli* schools are—"

"Free? Maybe on Anáhuac they are, maybe for the sons and daughters of landowners, surely for the nobility—and you *are* a noble, aren't you? But on New Aberdeen, there aren't those kinds of luxuries, not for landless tenants. Not for Swedish immigrants. Not for my children."

The judge said nothing, settling back on his heels. Gretchen felt the pressure in her chest ease a little and she put her head between her knees.

"How did you get an education?" The anger was gone from the *nauallis's* voice. Gretchen didn't look up.

"My grandmother's father was a Royal Navy commander in the Last War." Anderssen wanted to lie down and close her eyes, but managed to resist. "He was killed in action off Titan and his service pension passed to her. When my grand-parents fled Anáhuac during the Conquest, she put the pension money—which wasn't much, but something—in a Nisei bank. When I was old enough to enter a school and I needed tutors and up-to-date software and living expenses, she broke it out. Sixty years of interest can make a little pile fairly big—but all that was gone by the time I finished university."

There was a hissing sound again and Gretchen realized the *nauallis* had a habit of biting on the tip of his oxygen tube when he was thinking.

"The Imperial academies are free—" Hummingbird started to say.

"—if you can gain admittance. How many students do you think apply every year? There are millions of applicants, *millions*. I'm sure your relatives back on Anáhuac think the system is fair, but they're *landowners* and inside the Seven Clans. They're not exiles on a backwoods hellhole like Aberdeen, saddled with a crushing tax burden to subsidize the landed colonists and treated like dirt by the so-victorious planetary government."

Silence again. Gretchen saw night had advanced to the peaks lining the eastern edge of the basin. The wind—thankfully—seemed to be dying down.

"So you've come for money." Hummingbird sounded suspicious. "No you haven't! If you were really only interested in the cylinder and your 'fair' compensation, you'd be sitting up on the ship, filing suits in district court at Ctesiphon by t-relay!"

Gretchen nodded, her bleak mood lifting fractionally. "So true."

"Then why?"

She sighed, forcing herself to her feet. Her left leg was starting to fall asleep. "Because I want *you* to give me the cylinder back without all that legal fuss. And you desperately need my help and I can't say I've ever let someone carry a load too heavy for them without offering a hand." The angle of the *nauallis*'s head shifted questioningly. "You're not getting back upstairs without me and my *Midge*, Hummingbird-*tzin*, and unless you do you can't remand the cylinder into my possession without us all spending years mired in the Cihuacoatl's court of appeals."

"I see. I am sure *Chu-sa* Hadeishi would find your lack of confidence disheartening."

"Ah-huh." Gretchen walked, creaking a little, to the cargo stowage of the *Gagarin*. "You're aware of the altitude limits of these aircraft?"

"Yes," Hummingbird replied, following her. "But they don't matter. A shuttle from the *Cornuelle* will retrieve me from the observatory camp when they return from their hunt."

"How long will that take, do you suppose?" Gretchen popped the latches and began unloading a pressure tent and her cook kit. "A couple weeks? A month?"

"I'm a patient man," Hummingbird replied, taking the bundle from her. "I've waited longer for retrieval before."

Gretchen looked the *nauallis* up and down with a wry expression. "I'm sure you have a lot to think about. Do you know how long these z-suits will last down here? Down here with this dust eating away at them every minute of every hour? I don't suppose you talked to Sinclair before loading up your gear?"

"The xenobiologist? No . . ."

Gretchen fished around behind the seat of the ultralight and pulled out a bulky object which looked for all the world like an old-fashioned hair dryer. "Got one of these?"

Hummingbird shook his head. "What is it?"

"It's worth an extra six, seven days in this acid bath. This thing uses a magnetic field to strip the microfauna living in the dust from your suit—or other equipment—if they haven't managed to burrow in yet."

Hummingbird became entirely still and Gretchen's nose wrinkled up at an undefinable, but unmistakable impression of the *nauallis* listening. After a moment, he stirred, then knelt down and ran his fingers through the pea-sand underfoot.

"Try an ultraviolet band on your goggles," she suggested. "They'll shine momentarily when you disturb the surface."

Hummingbird straightened up, shaking dust from his gloves. "How many days do we have?"

"Safely? About two weeks. Pushing our luck and assuming the buildings at the observatory camp are still intact when we get there, maybe twenty days."

The judge stared up at the darkening sky. "And the *Cornuelle?*"

"You can call them if you'd like. I'm sure the honorable captain will give you an estimate of when he hopes to return."

Hummingbird said nothing.

"I thought so." Gretchen marked out a rectangle with her boot, then dumped the tent bundle at one end. "You're serious about removing the traces of our expedition, aren't you? Well, you're going to need me, my *Midge* and the extra supplies I brought if you want to succeed."

"Will I?" The judge sounded irritated. "You have no idea what I intend to do."

"Doesn't matter," she said, unsealing the bag. With long-experienced fingers she flipped the rolled mat out onto the sand. At the motion, the tent stiffened and snapped into a long, broad rectangle. "I'll do my best to keep you alive so you can do . . . whatever you're going to do. Then, when we're back at the observatory camp, I'll make sure we get picked up before our suits erode and we wind up like Doc Russovsky."

"I don't need your help," Hummingbird started to say.

"Hummingbird-*tzin*, you are being stone-headed." Gretchen tried to glower, but gave up. She was too tired. "You cannot remove all evidence of human presence here if you remain." She paused a beat. "You are human, aren't you?"

THE CORNUELLE

Deep in shipnight, Hadeishi surrendered to futility and opened his eyes. The cabin was dark, only furtively lit by the soft glow of a chrono panel beside his desk. In the dim green light, shelves of books and papers loomed enormous against the walls. Hadeishi threw back the coverlet and swung out of bed. Sleep had eluded him, weary mind filled with a constant stream of images—phantoms of the day's events, wild imaginings of what would come, a nightmare of being dragged before a court of inquiry—and he felt worse than when he'd gone to bed.

"A fine hell awaits Hummingbird and Anderssen for inflicting this upon me," Mitsuharu grumbled as he found a robe. Silk and velvet slid across wiry, muscled shoulders and he glared at the comp. *Late in third watch,* he saw. *Four o'clock.* "What a wretched hour to be awake."

His stomach grumbled, making the captain think of tea and hot soup. Breakfast was still hours away, but the act of waking had convinced his body it was time to eat. Shuffling his feet into a pair of shipshoes, Hadeishi tucked long, loose hair behind his ears and went out, kimono cinched tight. Shipsnight always felt cold, though environmental maintained a constant temperature at all times and the corridors were brightly illuminated.

He was not surprised, however, to find *Sho-sa* Koshō in the tiny rectangular space of the officer's informal mess. Hadeishi was amused to see the young woman was dressed informally—no jacket, the collar of her duty uniform unsealed, the sleeves of an oatmeal-colored shirt rolled back. The exec was removing a cup from the automat as he shuffled into the room.

"Hello, Susan," Mitsu nodded at her, feeling stubbled, unshaven and out of sorts. Koshō, for her part, looked entirely composed. "Are you up early or out late?"

"Late, *Chu-sa*," she replied, studiously avoiding looking directly at him. "Hayes has been running navigational scans of the asteroid belt. I was considering the data and time elapsed."

Mitsu grunted, punching up a cup of *bancha*-grade *yamacha*. He waited, hands in the pockets of his robe, while a cup descended from the machine and filled with hot, black liquid. Cradling the tea, he shuffled to the table where Susan was sitting. She raised an eyebrow as he approached, nostrils flaring at the sharp, distinct odor wafting from his cup.

"With respect, *Chu-sa*, how can you drink such a cheap, bitter grade of tea?" Koshō seemed to shrink away from the harsh smell. "It's barely cured at all!"

"This?" Mitsu swirled the liquid, watching grayish foam twist into a corkscrew pattern. "My father used to make this for us every morning when I was little, before we went to school. If I rise early, I can't drink anything else. There is one thing missing, though."

"Which is?" Susan put her own cup—filled with a delicate golden broth of steaming water, boiled rice and finely rolled leaves—aside with a grimace.

Hadeishi smiled fondly. "The smell of diesel and wet pavement. In Shinedo there's rain almost every night, or fog . . . that's what I remember best. Sharp black tea and the sound of my shoes in the mist as I walk to school, hearing the heavy trucks on the old highway, bringing goods into the market district."

Koshō's grimace eased a little, but her head tilted questioningly. "What is a *truck?*"

Mitsu hid a smile. His executive officer's family background was not included in her service record, but no one who had spent more than a day in her company would classify her as anything less than a daughter of the nobility. In comparison to his own relatively low birth, Hadeishi was sure a great social gulf existed between them. His own family at the feet of an invisible mountain, hers somewhere in the clouds. Outside of the Fleet, he doubted they would have met, or even been allowed in proximity to one another.

"A truck is like an aircar, but it runs on wheels, on the ground. They burn petroleum distillate for fuel, which is cheap and efficient, though there is a distinctive smell from the combustion process. Very noticeable on a damp, cold morning."

"Are they still used today?" Susan's tone implied such devices were remnants of some ancient, time-shrouded age of barbarism and chaos. "On Anáhuac?" Or relegated to the colonies, where men struggled to carve a life from howling wilderness, only a single step from hunting with knapped-flint spears and knives of sharpened bone.

Mitsu nodded, eyes crinkling with a smile over the lip of his cup. "I believe so. The markets of the lower city deal in bulk goods—agricultural products, raw materials, metal, ceramacrete, goods delivered in lots of thousands—in such circumstances the cost of freight is an important consideration. Shuttles, aircars, lifters—they are reserved for luxury items, not for bundles of steel pipe and casks of beer."

"I suppose." Susan's expression settled from a grimace to a tight mask. "Efficiency must be profit in such an enterprise."

"Yes," Mitsu said in an equitable voice. *I am surprised to hear the filthy, dishonorable word* profit *from your lips, lady Koshō.* Again he suppressed amusement at her reaction. Hadeishi knew he'd never had a better second officer. Koshō was tenacious and hardworking and faultlessly competent, but there was a constant nagging tension between them. A divide which could not be crossed, though they had served together for the better part of three years. For his part, Mitsu was convinced his subordinate was aware of the division between them, but he was equally sure she did not know exactly why. *Susan will think this is the isolation of command; my role as captain drawing such a distinct line between us.* Yet, Hadeishi was certain the true gulf lay in the abyss of their respective births and upbringing. Their futures would be different as well, and therein lay the seed of bitter separation.

In time—in two years, or four, as Fleet decided in its infinite wisdom—Susan Koshō would leave the *Cornuelle* and be posted to a larger ship—a sleek battle cruiser or a light carrier—as captain and commander. Mitsuharu Hadeishi, of such low birth, would remain aboard the little cruiser, perhaps for the rest of his career. In twenty years, should luck favor him, he might become a flotilla commander, responsible for screening some larger battle group. In twenty years, Koshō would be an admiral and her inflectionless voice would descend to him from on high, ordering his ship into the raging maw of battle.

Fate, he thought and found solace there. *But for now, my duty is to guide her, to make her better, by such means protecting myself and my crew on some later day.*

"What did you find in Hayes's data?" Mitsu took another sip from his cup.

"Well, sir," Susan settled back in her chair. The tension in her face and shoul-

ders eased, her thoughts turning away from the disreputable mysteries of trade and
back to the mission at hand. "Young Smith-*tzin* had been reviewing our navigational data and found something he did not understand. He brought the data to
me, expecting he'd made a mistake or an error." The exec's lips quirked into the
ghost of a smile. "He did not make a mistake."

Susan leaned over and tapped the nearest wall panel awake. The Imperial crest
appeared briefly, accompanied by the tinny blare of flutes and drums. She accessed
an astronomy module from among a dizzying array of choices. A black field
appeared, anchored by a dim yellow disc surrounded by gleaming motes.

"This is the Ephesian solar system." Koshō's well-manicured forefinger indicated a reddish disk. "The third planet. And here is the asteroid belt which hides
our 'wildcat' refinery ship. Hayes has been building a navigational map of the belt,
searching for anomalies or radiation spikes—anything that might help us pin-
point the enemy. He became concerned today when—after the first pass of the
map was complete—it seemed the belt was too small."

Hadeishi nodded slightly and motioned for her to continue. Susan tapped up
a new screen filled with figures and graphs.

"Our dutiful *sho-i ko-hosei* then undertook a review of the projected initial
system mass, local stellar formation density and the current distribution of planetesimals throughout the observed volume. He wondered if some quirk of orbital
mechanics had distributed the non-aggregated mass into two or three belts, rather
than just one." A glitter entered Koshō's eyes and her lips curled back from daz-
zlingly white teeth. "This was not the case. Indeed, the analysis of the system as a
whole shows the total mass to be slightly *higher* than expected for this type of sun
and this area of space."

"How much so?" Hadeishi had already formed a tentative conclusion. *An
obvious answer*, he thought, feeling cold again. Even the cup in his hands had suddenly lost its comforting warmth. *But . . .*

"There should not be a noticeable asteroid belt here at all. Yet there is. The system mass is higher than astronav projects." Susan's fingertip drifted over the dull
red disk of Ephesus III. All traces of humor had vanished. "This extra mass came
from somewhere. I have spent the last eight hours considering the source of this
unexpected belt. I believe the cloud of planetesimals we are racing toward consists
of the inner core and mantle of the third planet."

Hadeishi did not respond. He took another sip of cold tea. Koshō continued
to stare at the screen. Her fingertip moved over a control glyph and the disc of the
planet rushed closer, swelling to fill the display like a sullen red eye.

"We will know for sure when we enter the belt. Our sensors are sensitive
enough to determine the densities and types of stone, rock and minerals in the

asteroids. But I believe we will find materials which can only be produced in the molten core of a planet, or compressed aggregates drawn from the friction zones between the planetary crust and mantle."

She turned to face Hadeishi with a cold, tight expression. "The First Sun people destroyed the third planet and dumped the remains in an opportune, gravitationally stable orbit. Then," and Koshō took a deep breath, "they reconstructed the surface."

"But they did not finish the job," Hadeishi said quietly, placing his cup in the disposal at the end of the table. "The scientists in the 'cloud house' say they fled, leaving behind a ruin; a rushed, incomplete work."

"Perhaps." Susan tapped a new command on the wall panel. "Doctor Russovsky filed a report with her superior soon after arriving on Ephesus Three, declaring the planetary geology so mangled by the efforts of the ancients that her planned georesonance survey of the crust was impossible. My understanding of the politics within the exploration crew indicates Doctor Clarkson was only too happy to reassign Russovsky to another task."

Hadeishi frowned. "He did not review her preliminary findings?"

"No." Koshō's dry tone expressed both her opinion of the late Clarkson and the equally late Russovsky in a single word. "He did not. Doctor Smalls, however, is very meticulous and he saved all Russovsky's work, including the geosensing readings she continued to make *after* declaring the effort was impossible."

"I see." Hadeishi felt a twinge of disgust. *Academics! Hiding data from each other, falsifying results to obscure their conclusions, scrounging and grubbing for advantage . . . bah!* "What do the data reveal?"

"This." Susan keyed a different glyph. "Shipside comp worked up these density readings in the past three hours."

The image of the surface of the third planet disappeared and was replaced by a mottled plot of tiny points, some brighter, some dimmer. There was the familiar ripple of the comp interpolating results and a new image began to build, shaded and colored by depth, describing an ovoid shape surrounded by a jumbled, chaotic shell. Hadeishi watched the display build—then interp again—then build—then interp. Section by section, kilometer by kilometer.

"The world is hollow," he said at last as the panel chimed to indicate a completed task.

"Like a *barē* ball," Susan said in a subdued voice. "With something massive nestled inside. The geodetic sensors cannot penetrate the inner shell, but the mass readings are conclusive. At least part of it is hollow, or at the least very diffuse. I think—no, I *fear* it is a ship. A massive, unimaginably large ship. An entire hidden world. Something which can only be out of the time of the First Sun."

Hadeishi found himself unable to speak. An image impressed itself upon his waking mind: two tiny figures in z-suits struggling across the curve of an impossibly huge egg. Minute, miniscule in comparison to the surface of the . . . the *vessel* they were slowly toiling across. *Is something inside? Something alive? Something which might . . . notice us?* Part of his mind began to gibber in fear and he struggled to keep such thoughts from overwhelming his consciousness.

"I understand," he said at last, not to Koshō—though she nodded in acknowledgement—but to the memory of Hummingbird speaking tersely over a high-security comm channel.

You must go quietly, echoed the memory of the *tlamatinime*'s voice. *Quietly.*

Hadeishi smoothed down his beard and fixed the exec with a stare. "Have Smith or Hayes seen this? No? Good. Sequester this data—you and I will know, but no one else. In particular, mention nothing of your speculation that this is a *ship* to anyone. We do not know that. Not in truth."

Susan almost saluted in response, but nodded her head jerkily. Hadeshi's face was grim and his thoughts were already far away. *What is inside? Does Hummingbird know? He must. Why else fling himself into such a reckless attempt to wipe away our tracks?*

The sun broke free of the eastern mountains and a steady bright light illuminated the roof of Gretchen's pressure tent. Almost immediately, a hot radiance filled the tiny, cramped space. Stale air trapped inside began to heat, making the shelter entirely uncomfortable. The archaeologist groaned and rolled over, burying her head in an olive-drab blanket she'd stolen from Fitzsimmons's rucksack. The cloth was filled with the irritating, precious smell of his aftershave. She wished she were still on the ship, listening to him talk about nothing. *Sister of God,* she thought wearily, *why didn't you remind me to put up the sunshade?*

"Because last night was pitch black and thirty below outside, idiot." Gretchen mumbled aloud, then raised her head and groped for her goggles. With her eyes protected from the morning glare, she looked outside and began cursing. Immediately to her left, one buckled, scorched wing of the shuttle cast a long shadow across the sand. The *nauallis*'s pressure tent was well placed to keep cool until the sun had risen above the wreck. "I was tired," she declared to herself, feeling thwarted. "He just got lucky."

Thirty minutes later, half-bathed in her own sweat, Gretchen rolled out of the shelter, her suit, goggles, *djellaba* and *kaffiyeh* squared away. She shook out her shoulders, letting the recycler, rebreather apparatus and tool bag settle comfortably on her back and hips. With deft, assured motions she struck and cleaned the tent, then packed the material into a small bag. Chewing a paline-flavored threesquare, she knelt beside Hummingbird's tent and peered inside.

No nauallis, she thought, shaking her head. *He shouldn't leave his gear lying around like this. Or does he think I'll play porter for him and pick up the camp?* Gretchen snorted at the thought, then gathered up her gear and walked to the *Midge.* Another fifteen minutes passed in careful scrutiny of the landing gear, the wheels and the lower parts of the aircraft. Russovsky had obviously taken meticulous care of the ultralight. There were many signs of microfauna infection, but they had been cleaned and patched. Gretchen, for her part, took the time to clean all of the exposed surfaces with the magnetic sweeper. Then she surveyed the interior of the cabin with her goggles dialed up into ultra. *Seems clean,* she thought.

After stowing her baggage and prepping the ultralight for takeoff, Gretchen ran a test on the shipboard systems, including the cameras and the geosensing array Russovsky had added to the underside of the wings. Everything checked out. She amused herself for a few minutes with the cameras, zooming the viewfinders and seeing what kind of magnification they were capable of. They were of moderate quality, so she left them focused on the horizon in case something happened.

Gretchen climbed up into the wreck. The shuttle had been reduced to a skeleton of twisted metal and soot-blackened surfaces. A jumble of unidentifiable wreckage filled the interior, leaving no way to crawl inside. Every nook and cranny was filled with spidery stone filaments and tubelike extrusions. Anderssen grimaced at the mess, then climbed down and began to circle the debris, paying close attention to the hull surface.

Atmospheric shuttles were fitted with heat-ablative polyceramic sheathing. This one had been twisted and warped by the impact of the crash, stripping away long sections of the hex-shaped tiles, leaving them scattered across the sandy floor of the valley. Anderssen bent down and gingerly turned over one of the black hexagons. To her surprise, the underside of the composite was dusty but not eaten away or encrusted with the mineralization she'd come to associate with the microfauna.

"They don't eat everything," she mused, picking up the tile. Under a rubbing fingertip, the ceramic came away clean and shiny. Gretchen frowned before realizing the composite would be designed for minimal air resistance as well as its heat-shedding properties. "Huh. We could collect the whole set and make ourselves a house."

Emboldened by this discovery, she took out an excavation tool and wedged the metal tip between a pair of tiles still attached to the wreck. Both tiles popped off, revealing a honeycombed, stonelike crust beneath. Gretchen drew back, but even the unaided eye could see the delicate filaments so-suddenly exposed to the bare sun wither and corrode. "Sister! They're already eating away the hull."

Her comm woke with a buzz and Hummingbird's harsh voice filled her ears.

"They are. The first storm of any magnitude will tear the sheathing away, scattering the tiles, and then there will be only dead stone."

Gretchen turned, following the winking light of her directional finder and saw a tan and black shape climbing down the face of a long, low dune to her west. A line of footprints smudged the perfectly smooth face. "Where have you been?"

"Two men survived the crash, one injured, one not," the *nauallis* said, his breathing a little short with the effort of moving in sand. Gretchen could hear a background hiss of his rebreather and the hum of suit systems over the comm link. "They went toward those hills."

The distant figure raised an arm, pointing west.

"Did you find their bodies?" Gretchen continued to move along the edge of the wreck, turning bits of metal and plastic over with her tool. "Or any sign they were picked up?"

"They found a cave at the edge of the hills. A deep cave. They did not come out."

Anderssen clicked her teeth in amusement. "You mean you didn't find any more tracks."

"No." Hummingbird's voice was still thready. "The cave could have another exit, but I did not explore beyond the mouth. The floor was covered with minute bluish crystals—they were not disturbed beyond a certain point."

"Hmm." Gretchen had rounded the western side of the wreck and stood near the tents again, staring at the long scarlike furrow torn across the valley. "These crystals only grow in shadow?"

"Yes." The *nauallis* began to make better time, having descended the dune to the gravel-strewn floor of the valley. "But there is enough space for two men to find shelter. How swiftly do these structures grow?"

"A good question, old crow." Gretchen bent down and began to unstake the *nauallis*'s pressure tent. "If they have something to eat—and are protected from UV—you can watch them expand with the naked eye."

There was a sigh on the comm, followed by an intermittent hissing sound. "Then both men could have gone deeper into the cave and the crystals might have regrown, covering their tracks."

"I suppose." Gretchen made a face, examining the bottom of Hummingbird's tent. The reinforced floor was discolored and ragged. *So much for impact-resistant microfiber. This looks worse than mine does, but it's been sitting here longer. At least a half-hour longer! Better figure out some way to sterilize the ground when we camp.*

Ah, I know! She stirred the sand with her boot, watching sparkling motes appear among the reddish grains, then disappear. "We should make camp early each day," she said in an offhand voice.

"Very well." Hummingbird approached, striding easily across the hard-packed gravel. Gretchen looked him over and saw he'd managed to get his head scarf and cloak properly secured and draped. "What are you doing with my tent?"

"Seeing how badly it's been damaged," she said, dropping the rotting plastic back on the ground. "Do you have a spare?"

Hummingbird shook his head as he came up. At close range, his eyes were only smudged shadows within the cowl of his *kaffiyeh*. "What happened?"

"The sand is hungry. I guess it likes the taste of double-flex, single-porosity polymer." Gretchen stifled a sigh and tried not to glare at the Náhuatl. "We'll have to double-bunk in mine. We'll keep yours as a ground cover for as long as the fabric lasts."

The *nauallis* turned over the tent himself and Gretchen heard the hiss of an interrupted breathing tube again. "I see," Hummingbird said at last. "What about the aircraft?"

"What about any of our equipment?" she snapped in annoyance. "Everything we have is at risk. Are we leaving here today?"

The *nauallis* shook his head. "There are some things I have to do first."

"Get busy, then." Gretchen felt a stab of worry, staring at the *Midge* landing gear. All three wheels were resting in the sand. *Great, an inch of dust is dangerous. Well—if we land on solid rock, we should be safe. What are those wheels made of? I'd better find something to protect them with.*

The day passed and grew hotter. The *nauallis* wandered around the wreckage in an aimless fashion, apparently ignoring the fierce, white-hot glare of the sun. Gretchen kept to the thin sliver of shade under the corroded, decaying wing of the shuttle. Her suit was insulated and cooled, but the thin atmosphere of Ephesus offered only meager protection against the radiation flooding down from the system primary. She amused herself by peeling hexagonal tiles from the skin of the shuttle. Each hex was cut with alternating tongues and grooves, allowing a secure fit between the sections.

Gretchen looked up, her attention drawn by a faint muttering sound. She felt disoriented and realized the sun had changed position noticeably, twisting the shadows cast by the wreckage and the boulders to the west. The quality of the air seemed different—though there was no single factor she could bring to mind to account for the feeling.

The *nauallis* passed by, facing into the sun. Hummingbird seemed to be limping, dragging his feet. Further, he was hunched over and swinging his arms as if he were weighed down by a tremendous weight.

"Crow? Are you all right?" Anderssen rose from her pile of black hexagons. An adhesive from her tool belt seemed to adhere to the ceramic, allowing her to make a series of meter square pads from the material. The first assembly was buried in sand at the base of the shuttle wing. She planned on excavating the offering in a couple of hours to see if the microfauna liked the taste of the bonding agent. "Have you hurt your leg?"

There was no answer, only a faint hissing and chuckling sound on the comm link. Gretchen felt a queer, stomach-churning tension overtake her and jogged out into the sunlight. The *nauallis* had turned away, heading out along the line of the shuttle's impact. Despite his unsteady gait, Hummingbird made good time. Anderssen blinked in surprise—it seemed the Náhuatl had suddenly leapt ahead, receding before her eyes. She began to run.

The *nauallis* shambled along the line of the skid, a long rough gouge in the sand and stony soil. He seemed to waver, weaving his body, kneeling, almost crawling on the ground, moving as if a wind pushed him, but the air was still and cold. Gretchen felt the heat of the pale white disk of the sun burning on her arms, even through the layers of insulation and her cloak. The air pressure in her suit seemed to rise, making it difficult to breath, though the gauges showed nothing abnormal.

Hummingbird grew smaller again, as if he had traveled a great distance over the desolate plain, but he still had not passed the nearest boulder. Gretchen felt her pace slow, following the line of his tracks in the disorderly sand. Now she felt a heaviness in her own limbs, as if the suit had grown thicker, more cumbersome.

Gasping, Gretchen forced her feet to move, to step forward. There was an instant of resistance and then she began to run. She became aware of a peculiar sensation—her legs had become long and heavy, tipped with something sharp, something which dragged in the sand. Her body moved strangely and she weaved, realizing a swing weight followed her motion, acting as a counterweight to her loping stride. Terror rushed up in her throat, green bile biting at her tongue. The sky had darkened to brass, the sun shrunken to a single point of steady white light. Under her feet, the footprints left by Hummingbird were obscured, blown away by the wind and only her heavy, three-toed tread replaced them.

"What was that?" Gretchen found herself standing beside Hummingbird on the crest of a low, scythe-shaped dune. The hills were a dim line along the horizon. Her entire body was aching, starved for breath and she crumpled with agonizing slowness to her knees. Sweat clouded the inside of her goggles and pooled in the hollows of her cheekbones. "What happened?"

The masked face of the *nauallis* stared down at her. A steadily rising breeze tugged at the man's *kaffiyeh* and cloak. He did not seem winded by the run across the desert. "You should not have followed me. Now you will have to walk back."

Gretchen tried to rise, but found her attention entirely occupied with the effort of breathing. "I saw . . . I thought I saw something. There were tracks in the sand. . . . They weren't human footprints."

"Really?" Hummingbird turned away and began moving down the face of the dune with a sideways, half-walking, half-slipping motion. "Come. It will be dark soon."

Both arms trembling with fatigue, Gretchen managed to get to her feet. She blinked, trying to clear away the sweat stinging her eyes. After a moment, she lifted the goggles a fraction to wipe the moisture away with the corner of her *kaffiyeh*. Even the brief instant of exposure stung her face with freezing cold and the terribly dry Ephesian atmosphere wicked the sweat away. Settling the goggles into their long accustomed grooves beside her nose and along the crest of her cheekbones, Gretchen set off after the *nauallis*. She felt entirely unsettled and the obvious— unexpected—distance between this unremarkable ridge of sand and the distant, glinting wreck made her feel a little queasy.

"Wait for me," she growled into the comm. "There may be siftsand or hidden crevices!"

Hummingbird did not reply, continuing to walk steadily west.

Swallowing another curse, Anderssen stumbled to the bottom of the dune and then noticed—at last—the *beginning* of the crash skid in the swale between two lines of dunes. The little valley in front of her was scattered with a litter of hextiles and bits and pieces of decaying metal from the initial impact of the shuttle. "What the— How far did we run? Hummingbird!"

There was no answer and the *nauallis*'s shape disappeared over the next dune. Gretchen stumped after him, uneasily aware of her own exhaustion and the relentless advance of night.

Thin night wind keened through the wreck, swirling among slender towers of calcite and quartz. Gretchen lay in the pressure tent, her head toward the entrance; her breathing mask, goggles and respirator blessedly laid aside. Her nose was covered with medical cream. The moment's exposure out at the end of the impact scar had given her a nasty burn. Part of the door was clear, allowing her to make out the dark shape of the wing surrounded by the blaze of stars. Ephesus had no moon and the constellations seemed terribly bright in such an ebon sky.

She felt a little strange, lying in the darkness, listening to the tent's compressor hum to itself, the shoulder of her z-suit touching Hummingbird's. The tent had an insulated floor, the walls trapped three layers of atmosphere in an airtight sandwich, and a heating element glowed along the roof ridge yet she still felt cold. The only warm part of her entire body was the right shoulder, where she could feel Hummingbird's suit resting against hers.

Is this how he feels all the time? A single warm point in a cold, friendless universe?

Gretchen could feel her legs complaining, even through the haze of painkiller and muscle relaxant dispensed by the medband—all the gods bless that infuriating scrap of metal, which had decided to unlock itself an hour after she'd stumbled, nearly crawling, back into the camp—and trying to cramp up.

"What happened this afternoon?" Anderssen grimaced, hearing her voice as a tight, tinny squeak. "I heard these sounds. . . . I saw strange tracks in the sand. . . . What were you doing out there?"

For a moment, Hummingbird did not respond, though she could feel him shift in his sleepbag. The ruined tent made a good cushion beneath them and Gretchen had managed to find the strength to lay out blocks of hextile as a floor to protect them from the hungry sand. There was a hiss, a clicking sound, then another hiss of air.

"There was nothing to see." In the darkness, his voice sounded contemplative.

Gretchen swallowed a very rude curse and then forced herself to breathe steadily until she thought she could speak without shouting. "I saw you walking very strangely. I heard a sound like someone *singing* over the comm link. I went out to see what you were doing and . . . and I felt something strange in the air. The sun seemed . . . different. I started to feel odd, as if my body were very heavy. Then—suddenly—I'm three k away on top of a dune! How do you explain that?"

There was another silence. Hummingbird turned towards Gretchen. She could see starlight glinting in his eyes. "You can't have heard anything," he said in a musing, suspicious voice. "I had my comm turned off."

"What? That's impossible. *I heard you chanting!*"

"You're very tired, Anderssen-*tzin*. You should probably sleep now."

Hummingbird's fingers closed around Gretchen's wrist and her head rolled back. Though she tried to keep her eyes open, sleep rose up and swallowed her whole. Distantly, she heard a raspy voice singing:

"*Tla xi-huâl-huiân, in Temic-xōch . . . tla xihuâl . . .*"

Gretchen became aware of a faint clear light filling the tent and she opened her eyes, wondering if the *nauallis* had turned on a flashlight. Instead, she beheld the full vault of heaven, flush with glittering stars. They were tightly packed, a carpet of gleaming, colorful jewels, and their light fell upon her face with a cold, delicate touch. Wind ruffled her hair and for a moment—just a moment—Gretchen smelled realspruce and pine and the bitter, pungent tang of wood smoke.

I'm home, she thought, then sat up, heart thudding with fear, the sleepbag clutched to her chest.

The tent was gone. Hummingbird lay beside her, a dark indistinct shape wrapped in a dirty woolen blanket. She looked to her right and saw both *Midges* sitting on the sand, undisturbed, the smooth metallic shape of the shuttle rising behind them, metal skin intact, the windows glowing with the light of flight instruments.

Impossible. Gretchen abruptly looked to her left. *What was that? Something moved!*

A man, crouching on his hands and knees, was staring at her. He was blond, square-jawed, with short-cropped hair. Dark ink circled his biceps with interlocking genome trails. A shipsuit clung to taut muscle and a broad chest. A name tag gleamed on his shoulders and breast beside a star-shaped logo.

You can't be here, she tried to say. Then she realized he was not wearing a helmet. *Neither am I!*

She woke up in the tent, the air stifling and close, blood thundering in her ears. A dry, parched taste filled her mouth, as if she'd gone without water for days. In the darkness, Gretchen managed to find the tube of her water pouch by feel and slumped in relief to feel the brackish, metallic fluid sliding across her tongue.

Beside her, Hummingbird was snoring softly, deeply asleep.

A warning tone sounded through the bridge of the *Cornuelle*. "Proximity alert," the navigational system announced. "Object at two thousand meters and closing."

Hadeishi sat quietly, watching Koshō leaning over the helmsman's shoulder. Despite missing a night's sleep, she did not seem at all fatigued. The *chu-sa* would have been envious, save he'd had to pull more than one all-nighter as an exec himself. The long cuffs of a Fleet uniform easily disguised the presence of a medband.

"Drop thrust to one-tenth," Koshō said in a quiet, level voice. "Turn ship one-and-one-quarter to starboard. Hayes-*tzin*, lighten the sensitivity on those meteor sensors. We've nearly a k clearance between us and the nearest rock."

Both the helmsman and the weapons officer responded immediately and Hadeishi watched the threat-well reorient as the *Cornuelle* nosed forward through the scattered debris at the edge of the asteroid belt. The main band of the planetesimals lay ahead and above of the cruiser's current vector—a dense cloud of massive fragments—but here in the dispersed fringe, they'd found it necessary to place the ship in harm's way.

"Just a tap, now, just a tap," Koshō said, one eye on the navigation plot and one on a vector map on the helmsman's comp. "Five hundred meters forward . . . reverse at one eighth . . . there you go. There you go."

Hadeishi watched the meteor shield sensors waver—flashing amber and crimson—then steady to a sullen yellow as the cylindrical bulk of the light cruiser drifted to a stop beneath the enormous shape of a mountain-sized asteroid fragment. In comparison to some of the monsters deep in the belt, this one—identified only by a long spatial coordinate—was a tiny baby. Against the jagged, crumpled surface the *Cornuelle* was the tip of a toe, or a little finger. Mitsu glanced over at Hayes and saw the weapons officer was crouched over his panel, neck shining with sweat.

Where an Imperial battlewagon or heavy carrier might mount the recently developed Kaskeala *yaochimalli* battle shield as a defense, the *Cornuelle* was blessed only with a porcupine-skin of point defense beam weapons and honeycombed ablative armor. Hadeishi had no illusions as to the fate of his ship if the cruiser collided with a multibillion-ton asteroid at any appreciable velocity.

"Hayes-*tzin*, deploy Remote One." Koshō turned a cold stare upon the weapons officer, who swallowed, then stabbed a control on his panel. Hadeishi felt the *thump* of the pod ejecting from a forward missile tube through the decking under his feet. A v-pane unfolded on his main panel, showing an exterior camera tracking the flare of the pod's thrusters. The brilliant green diamond swept away into darkness, fading quickly to a shining mote.

"*Chu-sa*," the exec said formally, turning to face Hadeishi, "Remote One is away. I expect we will have visual confirmation of the excavation area within twenty minutes."

Hadeishi nodded in acknowledgement, leaning his chin against the back of his fist. "Deft maneuvering on the approach, *Sho-sa*. I hope your effort will not be wasted."

Koshō stiffened, sensing a rebuke in the captain's quiet words. "Sir, we have invested a great deal of effort in mapping possible perturbations in the navigational maps of the belt. This planetesimal has markedly altered course, mass, and albedo between our two sets of data. I believe it has been mined by the suspected wildcatter."

Raising an eyebrow, Hadeishi cut her off. "There are dozens of reasons this particular rock could have changed vector, *Sho-sa*. Mining is only one of them. But I agree we need direct confirmation of such activity . . . and this is the only way to get such data."

Slightly mollified, the exec nodded her head and returned to the helmsman's station. Hadeishi eyeballed the progress of the probe, which had come within a dozen meters of the asteroid surface and was beginning a winding circumnavigation of the enormous shape, scanning for fresh scarification, hot-spots or other signs of mining activity. Sighing, the captain turned back to reviewing the engineering department's weekly report on the state of the engines, fuel systems and the primary and secondary reactors.

Movement on the bridge—no more than one of the sensor techs stiffening in his shockchair—drew Hadeishi's attention away from authorizing a request to draw higher-than-projected amounts of conduit sealant from stores. Koshō was already beside the helm panel, hands clasped at the small of her back as she scrutinized the data feed from the remote probe.

"We have a positive," she announced after a moment. "Mirror this to main screen."

A starfield image flickered onto the curving screen dominating the "forward" wall of the bridge. In truth, the command deck was situated at the heart of the crew spaces in the forward section of the *Cornuelle*'s main body, hidden deep in the heart of the ship and surrounded by cargo holds and two belts of reinforced armor. If Hadeishi remembered the engineering schematics correctly, he was really facing a hold filled with crew rations and then the back end of the primary particle beam mount. However, as in the world of men, the illusion of a window served to distract the mind and direct thought into familiar, predictable paths.

The v-feed from Remote One showed a deep shadow cleft in the flank of the asteroid. The nearer edge, now drifting into view in a cone of brilliant white from the pod's lights, was razor sharp. The pool of illumination spread over the abrupt juncture, then vanished into a enormous cavity. Hadeishi could see the wall of the pit was glassy and smooth.

"Radiation readings are up, thermal signature is up. Exposed rock surfaces show the effects of extreme heat."

The *chu-sa* nodded to his exec. "The cutting beam mounted by a *Tyr*. Can you drag a time frame out of this data?"

"Processing now." Koshō's face had subtly changed and Hadeishi realized she was trying not to grin in triumph. "We'll know within ten minutes."

"Good." Hadeishi tapped a glyph to dispatch his reports and leaned forward in his seat. "During this time, have Remote One do a complete circuit of the pit and log the data for later analysis. Copy one set to legal and time-stamp and lock the archive." He fingered his beard idly, frowning in distaste at the thought. "I doubt the *Tyr* will allow itself to be brought in as a prize, but legal action may result. So—take care to make an authoritative record."

Koshō stared grimly at him for a long moment, puzzling Hadeishi. Then he remembered the events of the previous day and made an equivocal motion with one hand. Her expression did not change. "And plot us a course to the next 'disturbance'. Take us underway as soon as Remote One returns to the ship."

The *sho-sa* nodded and returned to her business, but Hadeishi could tell she was still displeased with him. *She is young*, he reminded himself, setting his memories of the incident aside again. *She remembers too many things.*

"Here is our present location," Koshō said, pointing out a blinking icon in the midst of the threat-well. A light green thread arced back from the winking mote to the orbit of the third planet. Hadeishi, Hayes and Smith stood around the railing. "The perturbation map we've built shows an irregular track through the main body of the belt in an anti-spinward direction."

A second thread appeared—this one a virulent red—entering the belt far behind their present location and spiraling forward through the diffuse mass. The red overran the green and continued for a good hand-span in the holodisplay. Koshō frowned at the indicator signaling the end of the track.

"We do not know how quickly the refinery ship is moving. In fact, as a *Tyr* can carry up to a dozen mining shuttles, this track may only be an aggregate path of the refinery and its satellite ships as they work through the field." Her hand brushed over the threat-well's control panel and the thread expanded into a heavy-bodied snake. "The possible locality of the refinery is somewhat larger."

Hadeishi looked to Hayes questioningly. "Can we cover a volume this large with our passive sensor envelope?"

The weapons officer shook his head dubiously. "Some of this volume will be scanned, but our usual range is degraded by all the debris. Hadeishi-*san*, we've picked up a lot of ambient radiation and particle decay in this area—definitely the exhaust of the big Royce-Energia XII sub-light engines mounted on a *Tyr*—so we can track them pretty closely if we follow right along their transit path, but—"

"We don't want to come at them so obviously," Hadeishi finished the sentence. "I do not intend to court danger, much less have my ship take a particle beam shot at close range, to catch these . . . these criminals. We will have to parallel their possible course from the edge of the volume, hoping to catch the refinery within our detection range." He paused, thinking.

"When I was growing up," Hadeishi continued in a musing tone, "the prefecture police often used smart-nosed dogs to hunt down thieves. What is the operational range of our ECM drones if we deploy them as sensor relays?"

Koshō and Hayes stared at him in surprise. "The outriders?"

"Yes," Hadeishi nodded, tapping up profiles of the devices in question. "These units are . . . yes, they are modular. We can program their sensor packs to search for this particle trail. Get with Isoroku and pull the chaff, jammer and spoofing racks from three of the drones and replace them with hydrogen cells to extend their time-on-station."

The weapons officer looked a little sick, but Koshō shook her head minutely and he subsided before openly questioning Hadeishi's command. "Sir—"

"I know." Hadeishi looked up from the panel. "We only have six drones and I'm asking you to cut the heart out of half our defensive network. However—with three drones reconfigured as sensor platforms we can rotate them on duty-station and extend our detection envelope across all, or nearly all, of your projected transit plot for the refinery. Our chances of being surprised by the *Tyr* will be greatly reduced." The captain tried a wintry smile, but neither the exec nor the weapons officer responded. "We *have* to be able to see them first or we've no chance of defeating this opponent."

Koshō looked like she'd bitten into a rotten quince, but nodded sharply. "*Hai, Chu-sa.* I will find engineer Yoyontzin and oversee the conversions myself."

Yoyontzin? Ah, I'd forgotten—Isoroku is still aboard the Palenque. Hadeishi considered changing the plan. *But Koshō has an excellent eye for modifying equipment and we've some time, picking our way through this maze, before we come into range of the enemy.*

"Very well, proceed. Keep me informed of your progress."

Both officers bowed and Hadeishi turned back to the plot, considering the difficulties of finding and subduing one ship—particularly one so well suited for this crowded, dangerous environment—in such an enormous volume. *I have become a policeman,* he thought, a little angry. *So low has my house fallen. . . .* Then an amusing thought occurred. *But this will be particularly bitter for our lady Koshō! A fine lot of* keisatsu *we are, chasing thieves in the night with our lanterns and rattan canes!*

Despite lingering pain in her shins, Gretchen was suited up before sunrise. The *nauallis* was still a snoring lump in the tent, which let her range unmolested around the camp while he was safely asleep. With the sky still dark and her goggles dialed into ultraviolet, Anderssen felt a little queasy to see shoals of softly-glowing lights crowding around the edges of the tent. Close examination showed the tent to be free of infection, though the groundpad made from Hummingbird's shelter was rapidly disintegrating. Other scattered pools of radiance marked places where one of them had dropped a wrapper from a threesquare or bits of metal from the shuttle were still being digested. Despite walking in a long, wide circle around the camp, she did not find any tracks.

"Hmm," Gretchen muttered, pacing along the base of the nearest dune. She was surprised to see how quickly the wind wiped away the marks of human presence. Hummingbird's trail to the west had already been reduced to a shallow series of dimples, barely distinguishable from the ripples ascending the face of the ridge. "I must have been dreaming."

Anderssen was loath to put her gloves into the sand where she'd buried the sheet of hextiles, but the goggles didn't show her the usual glimmer under the sand. Gritting her teeth, Gretchen dug in and found the edge of the hexsheet. A moment later, the pad was uncovered and—remarkably, she thought—it was intact. *So . . . Paxaxl Corporation Ceramobond doesn't taste good. That is excellent news.*

Dragging the sheet of hextile to the *Gagarin* and under the forward landing gear was hungry work, and Gretchen was perched up in the wreckage eating a three-square when Hummingbird finally emerged from the pressure tent. The sun was still behind the eastern mountains, but a hot pink line silhouetted the peaks. With such a thin atmosphere, there was little warning of sunrise. She toggled local comm awake.

"You want breakfast?" Gretchen made a great effort to be civil, though the sight of the Náhuatl brought to mind all of the odd business of the previous day. "There's hot chocolate in the pot."

The *nauallis* looked directly up at her, which surprised Gretchen. *I'm not exactly drawing attention to myself up here,* she thought, *no lights, sitting in shadow.* He nodded gravely and climbed up, hands and feet finding plenty of purchase on the crumbling metal.

A bronze mealheater sat between Gretchen's boots, steam condensing to frost around the lid. Hummingbird opened the cover and pinched out a tube of chocolate and a threesquare from slots surrounding the heating element. He squatted nearby, back to a tortured chunk of drive coil, and ate quickly. Gretchen watched him warily, sipping from her entirely cold chocolate. In temperatures like these, heat bled out of everything almost as quickly as it was generated.

"Yesterday," she said after a moment, "you said you'd found tracks left by the survivors of this crash, leading off into the western hills. I note—merely out of curiosity—*your* tracks have already been obliterated by the wind. It seems odd you could find a trail left by someone six weeks ago."

The *nauallis* did not answer, taking his time to chew down the rest of the bar. The chocolate followed and he tucked the foil wrappers away in a pocket of his overcloak. Gretchen finished hers as well. When he said nothing, she pursed her lips and tried a different approach.

"Are we departing this morning, or do you have more to do here?"

Hummingbird's head turned toward her, the faint gleam of sunrise reflecting murkily from his goggles. "I will need another day. Will the aircraft be safe?"

"Likely," Gretchen said, trying to catch any hint of an expression on his muffled, masked face. "If no big storm comes up. I can make more pads out of the hextiles—they'll protect the wheels and the tent floor. Do you need my assistance?"

"No." The *nauallis* shook his head vehemently. "You . . . you should ignore me. Pay no attention to anything you might hear or see." He paused and Gretchen gained the undeniable feeling he was debating with himself. "If you can, try not to think of me at all, think of something inconsequential, random, useless. Don't watch me or concentrate on my actions."

"I see." Gretchen licked her lips. They were always dry in this bitterly cold air. "Like yesterday. I started to follow you and . . . got caught up in whatever you were doing."

Hummingbird stood up, saying nothing, and climbed down from the wreck. Gretchen glared at his back, but he did not turn or look back.

"Pigheaded Aztec!" She sat sullenly for awhile, watching him closely out of spite. The *nauallis* wandered around the camp aimlessly, then took off into the desert. Though Gretchen kept the comm channel open, she heard nothing more of the odd noise. Eventually, Hummingbird disappeared around the far side of the shuttle. She thought about pestering him on the comm, but the sun was rising and there were things to do. Gretchen climbed down and began gathering up hextiles scattered around the crash site.

After a half hour, the sun was full in the eastern sky, painting everything in bleached-out colors. Anderssen used the sunshade from Hummingbird's tent to make an awning. Being out of the direct glare cut at least thirty degrees off the heat load borne by her suit. She squatted and began piecing new tilepads together. *This is boring*, Gretchen thought after an hour had passed. She looked up and scanned the horizon. There was no sign of the *nauallis*. *Where is he now? Probably getting into trouble.*

Restraining her curiosity, Gretchen finished assembling the last of the pads and dragged them over to the *Gagarin*. Getting the rear wheels onto the tilepads was sweaty work and when she was done, Anderssen parked herself in the shade of the awning. Her suit water tasted more brackish than usual, so she broke out a fresh bottle and topped off the reservoir before drinking the rest straight.

Hummingbird had not returned. Gretchen's comp showed noon had come and gone.

A little concerned, Anderssen climbed up onto the wreck again and found a perch near the twisted spine of the craft. From this new elevation, she searched the valley, hoping to catch sight of a tan-and-black figure doing . . . whatever. As it happened, Hummingbird was only a few hundred meters away, off at an angle from the crash scar and the wreck. He was hunched over, walking slowly across the gravelly soil, peering at the ground.

As she watched, he bent down and picked up something bright—a bit of metal, she thought—and weighed it in his hand. Gretchen expected the *nauallis* to throw the fragment away, but he did not. Instead, he continued to wander aimlessly. A little later, he turned suddenly, curving back on his previous path, and dropped the metal on the ground. Without pausing, Hummingbird continued his lazy, winding circuit.

Shaking her head, Anderssen climbed down from the wreck and resumed piecing hextiles together. Boring work, but at least there was some sense and purpose to the activity.

Hummingbird returned after dark, suddenly appearing at the edge of a circle of light cast by a lantern hung on the nose of the *Gagarin*. Both aircraft and the tent were now up on hextile pads. Anderssen ignored Hummingbird as he unwrapped his *kaffiyeh* and cloak. Another pad of tiles held the mealheater and a water bottle. She was working with her big comp, collating the data collected during the day by sensors on the *Midge* and her suit. Despite the *nauallis's* admonition, nothing had prevented the cameras on the ultralight from recording his activities.

"Did you finish?" Gretchen did not look up. An interesting pattern had revealed itself from the camera data. Biting her lip in concentration, she sketched in a transform with the stylus. The comp obediently began to interp the data, building a three-dimensional model.

"Yes." Hummingbird squatted across from her, his back against the front wheel of his ultralight. "We can leave in the morning."

"Are we going far?" Intrigued by the display building on the comp, she turned the device sideways to get a different perspective. "Which direction?"

Hummingbird pointed southwest with his chin. "The comm records on the *Palenque* show Russovsky used a relay transmitter on one of the Escarpment peaks to communicate with the ship when she was on farside. The peak is called Mons Prion on her maps. That is our next destination."

Gretchen nodded and put down the comp. "And once we're there, you'll make the transmitter disappear without a trace."

The *nauallis* unwrapped a threesquare and began to chew methodically.

"There you go with the stone face again," she sighed. "Do you really think I'll just follow your orders blindly? That I'll ignore what you're doing, or pretend it hasn't happened?"

Hummingbird stopped eating and Gretchen thought he was actually paying attention. She tried not to swallow nervously and plunged ahead.

"You didn't want me to pay attention to you today, so I kept out of your way. But the cameras on the ultralights recorded everything you did on this side of the wreck. You didn't seem to care about that . . . they made me a map of where you went. Would you like to see it?"

Gretchen tipped up the comp, showing him a three-dimensional representation of his path. The trail looked like a snake with a broken back, but one which entirely surrounded the wreck in a long oval. Moreover, the path seemed to cover the sandy ground without doubling back upon itself. "This search pattern, master Hummingbird, is a thing of beauty. I am truly impressed."

There was a grunt on the open comm channel and the *nauallis* looked away. Gretchen tucked the comp back into its bag with a pleased expression on her face.

"At the university, on my first dig, the pit foreman tried to teach all of us—all the first-term students—how to look for things on the ground. He gave us thirty minutes on a newly mown soccer field to find all the things he'd hidden. Seemed very silly to us—the grass was cut short, the field was almost perfectly flat—where could you hide anything? I managed to find a copy of Schulman's *Techniques of Radiocarbon Analysis* by tripping over the damned thing."

Gretchen smiled wryly and shrugged her shoulders. "The flatness of the field was an illusion—it wasn't entirely flat, there were little dimples or furrows in the grass—and we felt very, very stupid when he took us around and picked up all the things he'd laid out for us to find. More books, pencils, a belt, a hammer, a walking stick. A whole set of white plastic rulers he'd laid along the goal box lines. It's funny to think, now, how blind we were to things right in front of us."

Anderssen stretched. Her back was tight and sore from assembling sheets of tile all day.

"Most people don't think looking at the ground and searching for things is a skill. But it is." She pointed out into the darkness. "Today, you covered the debris field thrown out by the crash centimeter by centimeter. I really doubt you missed a single bit of metal or ceramic or wire. Did you?"

Hummingbird lifted a hand and made a "turning-over" motion. "I don't think so."

"Two questions come to mind, master Hummingbird." Gretchen felt as if she were approaching a flighty horse or a sleeping, irritable dog. "I can't make you answer them, but it would be helpful if I knew how to help you do this . . . thing."

The weight of the Náhuatl's gaze grew heavy and Anderssen started to sweat, feeling as if an exam had suddenly been placed in front of her.

"First, you didn't pick up every piece of debris out there—only some of them. How could you tell there were materials the microfauna couldn't digest? You weren't using a comp—in fact, do you even *have* a comp with you?"

Hummingbird grunted and there was a hiss as he bit idly at his breathing tube. "There is a comp in the *Midge*. A powerful one."

"But you didn't use a comp today." Gretchen didn't wait for an answer. "You put the bits and pieces of indigestible debris back down on the ground. Sometimes you just adjusted them a little where they lay." Her heart was beating faster now and a curl of sweat was trickling down the side of her neck. "If I . . . if I went out there tomorrow morning, with this map, would I be able to find those fragments? I wouldn't be able to, would I? They'd be . . . invisible. Indistinguishable from the rock and gravel and sand out there."

Another hiss, followed by an almost-sigh. "With your map, you might be able to find some of them. All of this must be done in haste, which always leads to mistakes."

Gretchen stared at the *nauallis*. He turned his attention to the threesquare wrapper and empty chocolate tube in his hands. Slowly, he folded them up into a tiny ball which he placed in a pocket of his *djellaba*. Finally, she shifted to keep her legs from going to sleep.

"Will you answer my questions?"

"There are more than two!" Hummingbird replied in a tart voice. "Will you be content to let me be? I agree—I *do* need your help to escape from this world. I am entirely human and do not wish to be marooned here or consumed by the little creatures in the sand. If you stay out of my way, all of this will go much faster."

"How could you tell which fragments needed to be hidden?" Gretchen leaned forward, her voice rising. "Can you *see* a difference? Do you have special lens setting on your goggles?"

"No." Hummingbird shook his head in amusement. "This is part of my training."

Gretchen grew still. "Can you teach me how to tell the difference?"

"I will not," the *nauallis* replied with a dismissive snort. "Though I'm sure you think your career would benefit from such knowledge."

Anderssen settled back on her haunches. "If I could do what you did today, we would have been finished sanitizing this site *yesterday* and already on our way to Mons Prion. Two can cover more ground than one." She cocked her head to one side, squinting at him. "What if you are hurt? Or injured in an accident? Who will finish the job then? I won't be able to. The evidence of man—of the Empire—will be left scattered all over this world. Ready to be found by whatever you fear will come hunting us."

"I cannot teach you what I know." Hummingbird's voice sounded irritated. "You are a woman and my skills are a man's knowledge. I do not know *how* to train you properly." He stood up. Gretchen rose as well, a slow steady anger curdling in her gut.

"That is a remarkably stupid thing to say. Why should my gender make a difference?"

"It does," Hummingbird said. "Men and women are . . . different. They *see* differently. There is . . . there is some danger if you interfere with my work. Danger which springs from *you*. I think, when we get to Prion, we should make camp a distance away, so I can dispose of the relay by myself."

Gretchen shook her head in amazement at his naiveté. *This must be religious . . . some artifact of cult practice from centuries ago. It has to be. I'm stuck on this planet with a mentally disturbed Imperial agent. How delightful.* "What about this shuttle? How are you going to make it disappear? The smaller pieces I can understand, but most of the hull isn't going to be eaten away. Can you hide the shuttle in plain sight?"

"No." Hummingbird looked up at the dark mass of the shuttle wing. "In truth, I don't want to entirely hide the wreck, just obscure its origin."

"How? By filing off all the serial numbers?" Gretchen asked incredulously.

Hummingbird laughed—a short, sharp bark—and adjusted his breathing mask. "No—that would be a tedious effort. The comp cores were destroyed in the crash and the spaceframe mangled. The rest is only metal and ceramic. By the time we leave this world, most of the wreck will be in even worse shape than it is now. If someone examines the remains, they will draw a different conclusion than you would expect." Gretchen could hear a grim smile in his voice. "They will find a different trail."

"Leading them where?" Anderssen tried not to sound suspicious, but failed.

"Far from Imperial space," Hummingbird said. "To a dead world with no relation to Anáhuac or humanity at all."

"What world?" Gretchen felt almost itchy with curiosity. "Why would a dead world send a shuttle here?"

"The homeworld of the Mokuil is dead *now*," the nauallis said quietly. "But once they were a powerful, star-faring race. Their ships visited many worlds, even some near this backwater. Here is the truth, Doctor Anderssen: We have little time here and we are in great danger. I am rushing to confuse those who will follow. I hope—and this may be a frail hope, yet it is all we have—they will find the clues I've left behind and they will be led away from human-controlled space. They will go coursing into the dead realm of the Mokuil and find . . . nothing."

Gretchen stood up, feeling a chill at the undiluted seriousness in the man's voice. "Did the Mokuil find a world like this one? A place where the First Sun people had trod?"

Hummingbird nodded. "We believe so." He raised a hand to forestall another question. "We do not know what they found. All we know is they were powerful and curious and then their civilization was destroyed, leaving only ash and ruin. The best we can do is hide quietly among their corpses, hoping to avoid notice."

He's completely insane, popped into Gretchen's mind. *I have a crazy religious zealot for a tentmate.* She snorted, suppressing a laugh. *This is almost as bad as my third-year roommate at the university.*

"Okay," she said aloud, suddenly losing her desire to badger him with more questions. "We'll be really careful, then."

Hummingbird did not respond, stowing his litter in the ultralight. Gretchen looked around the camp and made sure everything was tied down and put away. Putting her head in the cockpit of the *Gagarin,* she checked the latest feed from the weather satellites. Everything seemed clear for a few thousand k in every direction. The *nauallis* had crawled into the tent by the time she had turned off the lantern.

Anderssen stood for awhile in the darkness, looking at the sky. She wondered which tiny spark of light was Anáhuac and which—if any of them—was the Mokuil homeworld. Somehow, without pressing the *nauallis* or checking her comp, Gretchen was sure the vanished alien race was bipedal, running on long reptilian legs, with a heavy, three-toed foot.

Shaking her head, she turned off her comm and bent down to enter the short airlock tube into the tent. *I am tired,* Gretchen realized. *But there's no rest for the wicked. Just more work.*

Someone talking close by woke Anderssen from a sound sleep. She opened her eyes to find the tent dark and chill. The heating element on the roof spine was glowing faintly, but even with it working, the waste heat of their bodies and the heavy insulation could not keep the dreadful cold of the Ephesian night entirely at bay. Hummingbird was asleep beside her, his usual snore reduced to a gargling hum. Foggy with sleep, she peeled back the flap covering the transparent panel in the door. Nothing was moving outside. There was no wind rattling the tent or whining through the guylines holding down the ultralights. She frowned. *I heard something. Someone was speaking to me.*

Shaking her head, she pulled the edge of the sleepbag over her face and closed her eyes.

A hiss of static brought her entirely awake. Struggling out of the sack, Gretchen heard a voice—a *human* voice—trying to say something amid a wash and warble of heavy interference. Turning on her side, she groped for the comm on her z-suit and found the indicators glowing softly. A channel had come alive, the signal strength indicator fluctuating wildly. Lips tight, she twisted around to get the pickup bug in her right ear.

"Hatho . . . *sshhhsshh* . . ." The voice faded away, leaving only a buzzing hiss.

"Damn." Gretchen fiddled with the controls, but the voice did not return.

Hummingbird paused in the shadow of the Gagarin's wing, their tent repacked and slung over his shoulder. The sun was more than halfway above the eastern peaks. Gretchen was sitting in the cockpit, one booted foot lodged against the wing strut, head and torso under the control panel. Her comp was sitting on the seat, chirping to itself as it ran through a series of system tests.

"Is something broken?" The *nauallis* leaned in, brow furrowed.

"I don't know." Anderssen fiddled with a component module hidden under the bulk of the panel. "My comm has been picking up all kinds of strange interference. Started last night just after midnight. Sounded like someone was trying to raise us on the comm. But I can't find anything wrong."

"Ignore it," Hummingbird said in a flat voice. "The *Palenque* and *Cornuelle* are under strict transmission security. If something happens in orbit, we will not know." He paused, staring off into the distance. "There isn't anyone down here we want to talk to. Come, let's get airborne."

Gretchen lifted her head to stare at him. "Don't be so hasty, old crow. The atmosphere is already heating—if we want to make any altitude at the end of the day we want to time our arrival at the Escarpment for evening when the air starts to chill."

Hummingbird shook his head sharply. "There is no time to waste. We may not reach Mons Prion today in any case. And if we do not, then we must be there *tomorrow*."

"Fine." Gretchen shut down the diagnostic and began worming her way out from under the control panel. "I'll be ready to lift off in five."

The *nauallis* strode off without a word. Frowning and unsettled, Gretchen watched him open the cargo door beneath the *Midge* and begin stowing the camping gear. Her own compartment was filled with sheets of bonded hextile from the shuttle. Luckily, they were very light for their size. Getting the ultralights airborne in this thin air was going to be troublesome enough.

After stowing the last bits of gear, Gretchen strapped in and began a preflight check. Her panel showed green in all areas and the 3v of her kids was still tacked in place beside the airspeed dial. Russovsky had left her a whole set of little *santos*, which were plastered along the structural bar lining the bottom of the canopy window. She touched the icon of St. Paraskeva for luck, though the little picture had long ago lost power and did not flicker or move or give the blessing of the martyrs. While she was waiting for the wings to extend and stiffen, Gretchen glanced at the other *Midge*. Hummingbird was nowhere in sight. "Ah-huh. Hurry up and then wait," she said under her breath.

Peering around, she found no evidence of the *nauallis* and her hand drifted to the control pad for the comm. Feeling a little guilty, she tapped open a sub-audible channel to the *Palenque*. A moment later the buzz of shipboard comm locking onto her signal and negotiating security filled her ear. Then a sleepy-sounding Magdalena came on the channel.

Gretchen? Has something happened? We're not supposed to—

"I know," Anderssen said, lips almost closed, throat relaxed. "I'm on a sub-audible. Listen, can you do a remote diagnostic on my *Midge*? I'm getting funny sounds and voice traffic on my comm."

Sure. Magdalena said. *Just wait one . . . I have to download a diag package.*

The control panel flickered and a small new v-pane opened, showing a progress bar.

Gretchen continued with her preflight check, spinning up the engines and going through a pressure test on the wings. Despite all the time-in-flight the aircraft had endured, the pressure seals remained intact, without even appreciable leakage. "Now that," Gretchen said to her checklist with a grin, "is some fine Russo-Swedish engineering."

A beep announced the diagnostic download was complete.

Okay, Magdalena's thready voice echoed in her ear. *I'm starting a local systems check. It'll take about thirty-five—*

Gretchen jerked back in surprise as a gloved hand reached across her and slapped the system cutoff glyph on her comm panel. Hummingbird's muscular shoulder pressed her back into the seat and his eyes—barely centimeters from hers—were furious. The comm made a peculiar wailing sound as the system went into cold shutdown.

"Do you understand *anything* about being quiet?" The *nauallis* punched an override into the panel. Magdalena's voice vanished from Gretchen's earbug as the channel snapped off.

"What do you th— *umph!*" Anderssen tried to shove him away, but Hummingbird was much stronger than she was. His fingers tapped a series of commands, then he stepped back. Gretchen shivered, shaking off a clammy feeling. "I'm running a diagnostic." She said in a cold voice.

"I told you to ignore any strange sounds or readings." Hummingbird was furious. "There will be more auditory . . . phenomena. There may be visual events as well. You will ignore them. We will observe *complete* radio silence unless I initiate conversation."

Gretchen stared at him woodenly, trying to decide if she should speak her mind or not. Before she could say anything, he strode back to his ultralight and climbed aboard.

"Fine," Anderssen muttered, beginning to regret her impulsive decision to follow the Imperial judge. The other *Midge*'s engines coughed to life and the sand anchors released with a bang. Gretchen flipped a series of switches controlling her own startup. The wings stiffened and the microcontrol comps woke up, subtly altering control surfaces and airflow guides in preparation for flight.

Hummingbird's ultralight bounced across the sand, turning away from the wreck and into an intermittent, gusty wind. Gretchen followed, her hand light on the stick. "Stupid ass," she said under her breath. Then one eye squinted in concentration as she thought about what he'd said: "Hmm. So, what could be *listening* for us?"

Sunlight blazed through the canopy of the *Gagarin* as the ultralight buzzed past a towering pinnacle of slate-gray stone. Gretchen squinted, waiting for her goggles to polarize against the brilliant light. They did, but slowly. The two aircraft had reached an altitude where there was very little atmosphere to diffuse the glare of the solar furnace. She was sweating—the heat load inside the cockpit was tremendous—despite the freezing wind roaring past outside. Both engines were honking fuel warnings and the wing edges had extended to try and generate as much lift as possible.

Hummingbird's insistence on reaching the peak as quickly as possible had resulted in a very dangerous approach. The late afternoon heat robbed them of colder, heavier air and the morning thermals had faltered and failed, so there were no updrafts to push them higher. With so little lift under their wings, both ultralights were burning fuel at a prodigious rate. The *Gagarin* wallowed between two more knife blade–thin towers of stone and the upper slopes of the mountain came into view at last. Prion loomed above a wilderness of ravines, plunging canyons, skyscraping cliffs and long tongues of shattered tumulus. Gretchen could make out the shining silver wing of Hummingbird's ultralight above and ahead of her, though the *nauallis* was having just as much trouble gaining altitude.

Broken dark rock slid past beneath her feet, glittering with streaks of frost. Anderssen had seen gloomy sections of canyon hidden from the burning white disc of the sun. Fantastic shapes hid in the shadows, glittering with quartz and garnet and amethyst. There were caves—yawning black cavities flipping past with dizzying speed—and sometimes she could swear strange lights gleamed in the inky depths.

The portside engine honked angrily and Gretchen's free hand danced across the control panel, manually adjusting the flow of hydrogen to the engines. Trying to climb through such thin air was burning too much fuel. The comp was overrunning safety parameters on a second-by-second basis and kept resetting, destroying the smooth microcontrol necessary to keep the *Gagarin* aloft. Ridges of jagged stone blurred past, talons reaching out for the ultralight's fragile skin.

"We won't be able to get down," she muttered, sweat trickling down her nose. "We'll be trapped on some Sister-forsaken mountainside—if we don't crash first."

Unexpectedly, the comm warbled in response to her cursing and Hummingbird's flat, tense voice filled her ears. "I see the ledge and the antenna. Forward and right three hundred meters. Follow me."

The *nauallis*'s craft jerked up and away, out of her sight. Gretchen swore violently, then squeezed a last gasp of power from the laboring engines. The *Gagarin* lurched skyward and Gretchen swung the stick lightly to the right. The arc-shaped wing of the other *Midge* appeared again. Hummingbird's craft swung sideways and then went nose-up, bouncing down onto an impossibly narrow ledge beneath a massive black cliff.

Anderssen tried to stay calm and not jerk the stick wildly as bone-chilling fear flooded her body. The *Gagarin* swept across the ledge and she pulled up, skimming her landing gear only a meter from the roof of Hummingbird's canopy. There was a startled shout on the comm and Gretchen—teeth gritted tight—rolled left, the *Gagarin*'s outstretched wing jarring away from a wall of basalt jutting from the mountainside.

"Oh most gracious Virgin," Gretchen chanted, her entire world focused down upon the control stick and the wildly gyrating view of mountains and sky and cliff flashing before the nose of the *Midge*. "In thy celestial apparitions on Mount Tepeyac, thou didst promise to show thy compassion and pity toward all who, loving and trusting thee . . ."

Gagarin made a wide circle out into the rarefied air and came around on a second approach to the outcropping. Gretchen caught sight of the *nauallis* darting out from under the wing of his *Midge* and running toward the far end of the slanted, rocky ledge. There was just barely enough room to land one ultralight. Anderssen caught a glimpse of a tall silver and black pole rising up from a crevice in the rock.

Russovsky only had this one Midge *to land,* Gretchen realized, feeling her stomach crumple into a contorted, burning knot. *And she was a really, really skilled pilot. Oh, good little plane, remember how to do this!*

"Get out of the way," she screamed into the comm mike. "I'm coming in!"

The ultralight wallowed down—much too fast, she realized as the forward wheel bounced violently across shale—and she threw the engines into reverse. Grimly hanging onto the stick, Gretchen was slammed repeatedly into her restraint harness as the *Midge* jounced and slid across the ledge. Loose rock skittered away under wildly spinning wheels. The entire aircraft crabbed to the side, away from the cliff wall, and Gretchen was suddenly staring out the port window and into the abyss of a canyon with no visible bottom.

"Sister, guide me!" Anderssen goosed the starboard engine and the *Midge* spun away from the edge. The aft-starboard wheel slammed into a protruding rock and the *Gagarin* bounced up with a jolt. Gretchen's teeth cracked together like a hammer. She tasted blood. The stick wrenched itself out of her hand and *Gagarin* clattered through a complete circle. Anderssen grabbed wildly for the stick—overcorrected—and the *Midge* lurched over the lip of the cliff.

The ultralight dropped like a stone. Gretchen was flung back into the pilot's chair. Mumbling prayers in a constant, unwavering stream, she slammed the stick forward, trying to raise the nose and let the wings catch some air. The entire control panel flashed bright red and a honking noise from her earbug drowned out the distant sound of Hummingbird shouting in alarm.

Stone and sky rushed past.

Floating in unexpected freefall, Gretchen blinked her eyes clear and immediately became dizzy. For an instant it seemed she was rushing forward across a flat, rocky plain, with queer looking mountains rising in the distance. Then her eye registered thin veils of cloud standing vertically from the plain and she remembered the *Midge* was plunging down the side of an enormous peak. Anderssen's eyes snapped to the control panel.

Both engines had shut down and—without power—both wing comps had locked out surface adjustment control. The wheels skittered across basalt and suddenly *Gagarin* was drifting away from the cliff face. Even without comp control, the *Midge*'s curving wing could bite *some* air and get *some* lift. Gretchen closed her hand on the stick with infinite gentleness, feeling her stomach squirm with the unremitting sensation of falling. *But we're miles up*, she realized, *and that means I have whole seconds, even as much as a minute, to react.*

She pushed the stick forward, finding it terribly stiff without the comp providing powered support. The wings seemed to creak and the entire aircraft shuddered in reaction. Wind howled around the cockpit and Gretchen tried to bring the nose up slowly. "Inspired, we fly unto thee, Oh Mary, ever Virgin Mother of the True God!"

The wings shimmied into the right cross section and there was a heavy jolt. The *Midge* wallowed into a glide, slowing, and the altimeter stopped spinning so wildly. Gretchen dragged the stick to the right a point, then two. Her course angled away from the spires of a lesser peak and into clearer air. "Though grieving under the weight of our sins," she heard herself shout, as from a great distance.

Anderssen punched a shutdown glyph at the upper right of the main comp. The panel flickered, then died abruptly. All machine noise ceased. There was only a shriek of air roaring under the wing and whining through the landing gear. A heavy hand pressed on her shoulders. ". . . we come to prostrate ourselves in thy august presence; certain thou wilt deign to fulfill thy merciful promises . . ."

Gretchen started to count the beats of her heart, mouth filling with blood. The yawning chasm of the canyons below her grew larger. She could see rivers of crumbled rock and stone twisting between towers of stone. The wind had carved huge, shallow caves from the cliffs and pierced some ridges with winding tunnels. There was no sign of life—no green, no blue—only black and gray and ever-present rust-red.

"And . . . sixty!" Gretchen managed to gasp out, past bloody lips. Her thumb mashed down on the panel restart and she groped to switch her air supply to an oxygen pack. Chill air hissed across her face, drawing a cry of pain.

The comp flickered and woke up. The *Midge*'s flight control systems ran through a startup checklist, registered a dozen warning signs and flashed an amber alert on the panel. Gretchen overrode the query, hoping the engine failure hadn't fouled the fuel lines with ice. The mountains below had swollen into vast fields of brightly-lit boulders and gravel. She felt the stick quiver to life and the main panel rippled with light.

"Show me your mercy, blessed Sister!" She leaned right, swinging the stick over and the *Gagarin*'s engines kicked in with a thready hiss. Comp control reasserted on the wing surfaces and the entire aircraft suddenly came alive. Giddy with relief, Gretchen swung the little plane away from the onrushing mountainside and roared south along a steep-sided, V-shaped valley. Momentum bled away and she turned the ultralight into a wide, climbing turn.

Once more, the shape of Prion filled the sky, blotting out the horizon.

Hummingbird had winched his *Midge* to the far end of the ledge by the time Gretchen came around for her third landing attempt. This time she managed to drop her airspeed almost to a stall as the *Gagarin* drifted over the tilted slab. All three wheels set down with a gentle clatter and the ultralight rolled to a halt. Anderssen felt the aircraft leaning to one side and she adjusted herself in the pilot's seat to compensate. Moving carefully, she locked the wheel brakes and shut down the engines. *Gagarin* gave out a weary sigh of settling metal, plastic and composite. The comp panels dimmed down to standby.

Getting out of the cockpit proved a slow process. Gretchen was sore from head to toe—again—and had trouble standing. She wound up crawling away from the *Midge* with the winch line over one shoulder. Reaching the wall, she leaned back against dark, gray-streaked stone with relief. Grudgingly, the medband consented to dispense an antitoxin to break down the fatigue poisons in her weary limbs. Feeling the familiar, welcome chill flushing through her body, Anderssen was content to lie at the base of the cliff, the winch pad adhered to the nearest rock surface, and close her eyes.

The view from the mountaintop was stunning. The Escarpment slashed left and right to the rim of the world. She could make out the slowly advancing terminator of night to the east. Another vast desert lay there, though the feet of the mountain chain were deeply buried in blown sand. Tiny shining lights sparkled across the distant plains.

When Gretchen felt she could stand up without having both legs buckle under her, she stumbled back to the ultralight and released the wheel brakes by hand. Another trip back to the base of the cliff left her a little dizzy. *Too much altitude, too little oxygen for the rebreather,* she realized, checking the medband. The clever little device indicated a variety of oxygenating compounds were already flowing into her bloodstream. *Be fine in awhile.* Gretchen propped herself against the cliff again.

The nose winch on the *Gagarin* whined and complained, but managed to pull the ultralight up close to the cliff. Both wings had collapsed into their storage configuration. Squatting under the pitted canopy, Gretchen secured the wheel brakes again and managed to wedge the sand anchors into crevices in the crumbling stone.

"Hummingbird?" *Where is he?* There was no answer on the comm, though the indicator lights showed two responding units within range. *Hmm,* Gretchen worried, *he's left the* Midge *comm open. Shouldn't be wasting power like that.*

Gretchen surveyed the ledge—a hundred meters of tilted, corroded rock jutting from an equally decrepit-looking mountainside—with a frown. The *nauallis's Midge* was parked fifty meters away to her right, the whip antenna she'd seen while landing at the far end of the ledge to the left. For no particularly good reason, she set off to the right, clambering over rough-edged stone and slabs of tilted rock. She was halfway to the other ultralight when a cave mouth appeared in the cliff face.

The opening was tall, slanted and narrow. Anderssen peered at the floor, making a face when she saw the outline of boot prints in the gravel and dust.

"Old crow?" She whispered into the throat mike. Again, there was no answer, though some odd warbling static began to filter in around the edges of the comm band. Wary of the shadows—who knew what kind of life they sheltered?—Gretchen crept into the cave, her goggles dialed to light-intensification mode.

To her surprise, the cave seemed totally empty—there were no effusions of the spindle-and-cone flora which had overtaken the shuttle or even the tiny spikelike clusters she'd seen in the discarded pulque can. Instead the floor was a jumble of fallen stone, pebbles and dust. A blotchy series of tracks led off down the passage. Gretchen paused, digging a light out of her tool belt and adjusting the wand's radiance to the lowest possible setting. Her goggles would take care of the rest.

With the wand held out of her line of sight, Anderssen padded down the slot for another twenty meters or so. The ancient crevice ended, opening out into a larger chamber with a tilted roof of jammed-together boulders. Gretchen halted quietly and pressed herself against the wall, her thumb switching off the wand.

A queer blue radiance filled the chamber, reflecting from a ceiling covered with pendant crystalline fronds. The branches and whisker-thin needles seemed dead and lightless themselves, but the faceted surfaces gleamed with puddles of cobalt and ultramarine. Below them, the floor of the cavity was a bowl of crushed rock, surrounded by a thin circlet of something like blue moss. Gretchen resisted the urge to dial her goggles into magnification, though she supposed the "moss" was truly a forest of tremendously thin filaments, swarming with Ephesian life.

The unexpected presence of Doctor Russovsky captured her attention instead.

Anderssen froze, suddenly, simultaneously aware of the geologist lying on the floor of the cave, wrapped up in an old red-and-black checked blanket, and a muscular, gloved hand pressing against her stomach. Hummingbird was crouched at her feet, one arm out stiff to hold her back. A few centimeters from her boots, the circle of bluish filaments was crushed and broken, leaving a black gap in the carpet.

Gretchen backed up very slowly, unable to keep her eyes from Russovsky's recumbent form. Behind the sleeping figure was a camp table holding a big service lantern. A gear bag and an insulated foodbox sat next to the table. Humingbird rose, blocking out the scene, and together they moved carefully back down the tunnel.

Outside, the eastern sky had darkened further. Winds were playing among the spires of Prion, flinging a constant rain of sand to rattle against the *Midges*. Gretchen stopped just inside the mouth of the cave and dialed her comm to very short range. "That wasn't the real Russovsky?"

Hummingbird shook his head. Gretchen could see the corners of his eyes were tight with tension. "No," he said after adjusting his own wrist-mounted comm. "No respiration. No carbon dioxide residue in the air. It's some kind of copy—something like what you saw on the ship—but I don't think it moves or speaks."

"But she *was* here," Gretchen said, thinking of the whip antenna. "She must have slept in the cave at least one night, perhaps two, while she was installing the relay."

The *nauallis* nodded. "You saw the dead moss on the floor? I think she cleared most of the local microfauna out of the cave to make a safe place to sleep."

"Yes." Gretchen adjusted her breather mask. At this height, you needed to keep a tight seal to reduce oxygen loss. "Her lantern is a multispectrum one. If she left it tuned to UV all night, nothing would be able to get at her."

Hummingbird grunted noncommittaly. "But she didn't kill everything in the cave."

"Maybe she knew what was dangerous and what wasn't. Not everything in this ecosystem will want to consume us and our equipment." Gretchen smiled. "Just enough of them to kill us if we're not careful. So—what is this afterimage made of? Dust, like the other one? Something else?"

The *nauallis* shrugged slightly. "I'm not sure that is important, though an interesting question. She *looks* like the real thing. The table, the cloth—you can't tell a difference with the goggles dialed to hi-mag—but they aren't real."

"How can you tell?" Gretchen bit down on a follow-up question, seeing Hummingbird stiffen. "Ah, master crow, you don't have to keep secrets from me! We're all bundled up tight together, aren't we? Sharing the same piss-pot and cup." With a mighty effort, Anderssen kept a sarcastic tone from her voice, though she dearly wanted to twit him again. "Your secrets are safe with me. I swear I will never tell another soul—and if you doubt me, then when we're back on the ship, you can have me clapped in irons and sent off to the helium mines on Charon."

With the mask and breather and hood, Gretchen couldn't tell if Hummingbird smiled or not, though she was fairly certain at least the tiniest ghost of amusement might have creased his weathered old face. There was a distinctive *hiss-hiss* on the comm channel.

"The shape on the floor," he said at last, in a very careful tone. "Does not feel *out of place*."

"Oh." Gretchen licked her lips. "I see. But it should—if a human being were lying there, surrounded by human-made equipment—then you could tell there was a . . . dissonance . . . between the stone and dust and moss and Russovsky." She paused, a glimmer of thought brightening into realization. "This is one of your *tlamatinime* skills, isn't it? To tell when something *fits* properly or not? Like the debris from the shuttle—you moved those pieces of ceramic and hexsteel until they were properly aligned with the world around them—so they *fit* properly. And when they did—it's like they had been there forever—or at least, if they didn't fit right, you placed them on the ground as if a Mokuil had set them there."

Hummingbird shrugged. "Perhaps."

"Oh, Lamb of God bless and protect us!" Gretchen felt her temper fray. The man was obviously on edge, worried, even a little frightened. But could he admit such a thing? No. "Do you understand I don't *care* if you have some peculiar skill or hermetic training or secret universal decoder ring? I care about getting us both home, alive."

The *nauallis* pushed away from the wall and peered out at the *Midges* and the jagged peaks. The light in the sky was changing and there was an indefinable sense of gathering darkness.

"Well? Give over!" Gretchen didn't bother to disguise her irritation. "Just shoot me with your little gun later, if I threaten the Empire with such precious knowledge as you might dispense!"

Hummingbird turned slightly, face in shadow, backlit by the brilliant sky. "I would."

"I don't think so," Anderssen said in a tart voice, her nose wrinkling up. "You'd bluster and be all mysterious and withholding and I'd break your bald head open with a wrench before you bothered to put a hole in me."

"Hah!" Hummingbird laughed aloud, a breathy, thin sound. "You would try, too."

He shook his head, but the line of his shoulders had already relaxed. "Though everything seems to be *in order*, I am uneasy. We need to destroy the antenna and this afterimage of Russovsky. The 'ghost' first, I think."

"Do you know how?"

The *nauallis* shook his head. "You've already touched upon the problem. This apparition isn't out of place—most *ciuateteo* are disturbances of the natural order and their nature is to disperse once matters are set in their proper balance—but this one is already at rest."

"Hmm. I don't suppose we can leave it be? No? I thought not. Do you have any sense of what this ghost is made of? Is it dust, like the Russovsky on the ship?"

"No. The dead-seeming crystal fronds on the roof are a likely culprit, though."

Gretchen wrinkled her nose again. "So helpful. We need to experiment then."

The *nauallis* replied with a skeptical grunt. "With what?"

"With you, for a start." Gretchen tilted her head toward the hidden chamber. "You can tell the apparition is at rest and 'in order', right? Well, go see if you can divine anything more. I'm going to examine the radio antenna before the light fails completely."

Without waiting for a response—and heartily glad to be out of the cave—

Gretchen squeezed out the narrow entrance and set off for the relay. She heard a momentary *hiss-hiss* on the comm circuit and then nothing. Smiling slightly to herself and feeling entirely pleased to have bossed the *nauallis* around, Anderssen raised her head and began searching for the base of the antenna.

The bulk of the mountain had already cast the ledge into steadily-deepening shadow, so the onset of full dark caught Gretchen by surprise. The relay tower had been wedged into a flutelike wind-carved channel. Expansion bolts were driven into the rock on either side to pin the antenna in place. With some tricky climbing—more difficult for the heavy tools and gear slung on her harness—Gretchen had managed to get halfway up the relay. Now, with one boot braced against a lower bolt and a lightwand tight between her teeth, Gretchen was picking away at a thick cementlike layer coating the bottom half of the antenna.

"How did this get here?" Anderssen was puzzled by the encrustation covering the lower section of the relay. The material was suspiciously even in coverage and included both bolts and the pole. A hand tool splintered the surface, revealing shell-like layers. "This looks like lime concrete slurry."

Gretchen stopped and tucked the pick away. Wedging her shoulder into the space between the antenna and the rock, she wiggled a materials analysis pack out of her belt and—holding the cup in one hand—picked broken bits of cement from the antenna with the other. The stinging wind was beginning to die down but the relay was particularly exposed on the cliff, so Gretchen pressed herself into the rock and shivered while the cup woke up, detected a sample to compare against an internal database and went to work.

An hour later, Anderssen was sitting just inside the cave mouth, a comp on her knees and both feet centimeters from a circular heating element. The wind outside had died down to intermittent gusts, which rattled against a filament screen she'd tacked over the entrance. A second screen closed off the inner cave, leaving a five meter–long space where she'd stacked the camping gear. Among the things she'd dragged out of the *Gagarin* was a battered steel bucket filled with a cementlike crust. A brush was stuck in the long-solidified mire.

A noise drew her attention and Gretchen looked up in time to see the Náhuatl unseal the edge of the inner screen. His cloak and legs were streaked with pale white dust.

"There's food—" she started to say.

"What are you doing?" Hummingbird came over to her, face tense beneath his breather. "Put that away."

Gretchen frowned at him, still holding the comp in her hand. It was difficult to use in the thin pressurized gloves. On the surface of the pad, behind a protective covering, indicators were glowing softly as the machine talked to itself. "I'm checking to see if there's a gravity spike here or a strange field reading. Something to . . . hey!"

Hummingbird closed his hand over the device, shutting it off. Gretchen realized the *nauallis* was furious, his dark green eyes turned to smoke. "You rely too much on your cursed tools. Look around you, let yourself become quiet. This is a very dangerous place. I told you before, we must walk quietly here. Your sensor is noisy, it makes a racket like civets in a trash can! I could feel it down in the cave. *They* could feel it too."

Gretchen drew back, her throat tightening. She was tired, sore, and very close to complete exhaustion. His anger was a physical blow, making her start to shake. Oxygen hissed against her cheek as the suit reacted to her rising heartbeat. Grimly, she choked down a bleat of fear. "Step away, crow. We need our machines to survive down here. What happened in the cave?"

For a moment his gaze locked with hers and Gretchen could sense—dimly— the man's own weary exhaustion. She refused to blink and after a seemingly interminable period, he looked away. *Score one for the hard-eyed Swede,* Gretchen thought, though she remained impassive.

"You need to sit down and eat," she said, setting the now-quiet pad aside. Gretchen rose and pushed Hummingbird gently toward the opposite side of the heating element. His bags were already stacked there. "Just sit and be still—you're good at that, right?"

Anderssen was mildly surprised when the *nauallis* did as she said. She puttered about for a moment, then handed him a container of heated tea and a squeeze-tube filled with two kinds of threesquares mixed together. Hummingbird's eyebrows rose in surprise when he tasted the evil-looking brownish gel. "It's hot," he said around a mouthful of food.

Gretchen smiled and showed him a storage bottle with the word "tabasco" hand-written on the side with a black pen. "Very hot," she said, "from Chipotle district on Anáhuac. Smoked and dried, then rendered into liquid fire. Just like home cooking, huh?"

The Náhuatl nodded in appreciation and ate the entire rest of the tube. Then he closed his eyes and slumped back against the wall of the cave, the *djellaba* hanging loose around his shoulders. Gretchen sat back down herself, drinking slowly from her own tea. After a bit, the *nauallis* started to snore and she shook her head in amazement.

Well, she thought, putting the sensor-pad away. *I guess he thinks we're safe here. Or I'm supposed to stay up and watch all night. First I'm a porter, then I make him my special chile dinner and now I get to stand guard. Huh!*

Getting up again was painful—even with the medband's help, she was going to have serious bruises from the day's excitement—but Gretchen was very careful to take a worklight and sweep the entire camping space with high UV before settling down to sleep herself. *Tomorrow, if we're still here, I'll haul in all those damned tiles. . . .*

Gretchen opened one eye, saw the wall opposite her was lit by a pearlescent gray light, checked her chrono and closed her eyes again. *Too early,* she groaned, feeling like her brain had been ground fine and scattered in a toad circle for the gaunts to dance upon. *The sun should not be allowed to rise at this hour. Not at four in the morning!*

A particular sensation of grainy ash covering her skin made Anderssen twitch and shake her shoulders. Her fingertips found the medband, but stopped short of summoning up a wakeme injection. Grimacing, she opened her eyes to bare slits and then groaned aloud. Hummingbird was gone, his things neatly stacked, *djellaba* folded and laid atop a tool bag. She rolled up, rubbing grit from the corners of her eyes. "No showers. What an idiot I am . . . nearest shower is in orbit. Or at the base camp, if the water's still good."

Anderssen considered using water from the recycler reservoir to wash her face, but the thought of so many more days in this desolation weighed against such extravagance. Sipping from her mask tube, she ate another threesquare liberally mixed with hot sauce. The grainy, over-tired feeling persisted, hanging around like an unwanted morning-after bedtoy.

The *nauallis* returned while Gretchen was packing her things away, ducking in through the outer filament screen.

"Morning," Anderssen grunted at him, but did not look up.

"Something is attacking the relay antenna," Hummingbird said. He sounded almost as tired as Gretchen felt. "There's this crust all over the lower—"

Anderssen held up a sample cup with flakes of gray eggshell-like material. "Like this? I took some samples yesterday. My comp was analyzing them when you busted in last night and spoiled the party. It's not something attacking the pole, though." She hooked the battered old steel bucket over with the toe of her boot and upended the cup. The flakes matched the color of the dried goop in the bottom.

"This," Gretchen said, tilting the bucket toward the *nauallis*, "is more of Russovsky's work. Local dust mixed with water to make cheap, inert cement. She painted it all over the lower reaches of the relay, making a barrier against the microfauna."

"Oh." Hummingbird squatted beside his gear. "So there's nothing for them to eat."

"Exactly. In fact, I think most of this gray dust is waste exudate from the different kinds of microfauna." She grinned at the old man. "There is a *lot* of it around, isn't there?"

Hummingbird stared at her, impassive for a moment, then his lips twitched and a gleam shone in his eyes. Gretchen took this to be very close to hysterical laughter. The *nauallis*'s usually grim, composed demeanor returned within a heartbeat.

"Did you find anything in the cave last night?" Gretchen turned the bucket over and sat down. "Anything new about this copy of Russovsky?"

"Something." Hummingbird did not look particularly pleased. "I thought the shape moved a little bit, from time to time. In fact, I checked this morning to see if anything happened at dawn." He paused, scratching at a badly fitting edge of his mask. "She woke up."

Gretchen raised an eyebrow, but managed to keep from making a fool of herself by gaping.

"Or I should say, the *shape* woke up, threw back the blanket, checked its chrono . . ."

"And then?" Anderssen looked reflexively down the tunnel, as if Russovsky would appear momentarily and want breakfast.

"Then," Hummingbird's voice assumed a familiar toneless quality. "The shape folded up the blanket, gathered its equipment and walked out of the circle. Then . . . then it disappeared. Well, almost."

"How . . . almost?" Gretchen was trying to divide her attention between the *nauallis* and the recesses of the cave. The back of her neck was prickling in a very uneasy way.

"I saw something like a mist, or falling dust, as the shape left the chamber. I was in the tunnel, of course, and the 'disappearance' occurred only about a meter in front of me."

"And there's nothing there now? Just an empty cave?"

Hummingbird nodded. "Dust, stone and hanging crystal."

"Did you feel anything? See anything?"

Another grimace. "No. All is as it should be. Nothing out of place."

"So—what now?"

"We wait for night to fall," the *nauallis* said. "And see if the shape comes back. I distrust luck, but more observation may reveal something."

"I see." Gretchen started to sort through her tools. "How tired are you?"

Hummingbird blinked. "Why?"

"We still have a relay antenna to dispose of." She passed a wrench and a length of pipe across to him. For herself she hefted a multitool with a cutting attachment. "I'll climb up and cut it down in sections and then you can dispose of them in a suitable manner."

The sun was almost exactly at meridian when Hummingbird threw the last of the bolts over the edge of the cliff. Calcite-crusted metal spun in the air, then vanished into an abyss tenanted by shrieking winds. Presumably the bolt would make a ringing sound when it struck the ground, but Gretchen didn't think they would hear anything at all.

"You're sure this will get rid of them *properly?*" She asked in a sly tone, peering over the edge of the outcropping. "They won't leave traces behind?"

The sally gained her not so much as a grunt. Hummingbird climbed back toward the cave. Gretchen stared after him for a moment before shrugging and picking up the tools scattered at the foot of the crevice where the relay had been. As she did so, Anderssen made sure to tuck the comm core of the relay into a pocket of her harness. *What is an antenna,* she mused, stowing the wrenches and cutting blades, *but a long bight of metal? You can find one of those anywhere these days.*

Hands on her hips, Gretchen found her best glower rendered ineffective by the goggles, mask and rebreather hiding her face. "Two sets of eyes are better than one, crow. I *am* trained to observe, to find the hidden and sift patterns from chaos. Both of us can watch from the tunnel mouth."

"No." Hummingbird had removed his *djellaba* and *kaffiyeh*—they were of little use inside the cave—leaving him a short, stocky, thick-bodied tree stump of a man clad in scuffed black and gray. "You do not know how to be *quiet* and there is a presence—a hostile presence—in the cave which was only peripherally aware of *me.* We might as well throw a grenade in, as put you on watch."

He tried to step past into the tunnel, but Gretchen moved to block the opening. "I can be as quiet and as patient as you, master crow. Try me and see."

"Sitting quietly is not enough," he replied. "You were quick to see how I placed the debris from the crash—but can you do the same with yourself? Such things take training and time!"

Gretchen did not move and her mouth tightened fractionally. Hummingbird watched her with his flat green eyes, much as a snake might watch a plump bird.

"Show me," she retorted. "I learn quickly. Think of what a boon I'd prove, if I could keep my own presence from being felt on this world—then you wouldn't have to clean up after *me*."

His head jerked sharply and Hummingbird turned away from the filament screen. "Prove you can listen without interruption," he said, stepping into the outer doorway. The screen behind him glowed hot with the afternoon sun. "Stand there, in the middle of this space. Let yourself become at ease. Be silent. Put all noise and clamor from your mind."

Though taken aback by his changing mood, Gretchen did as he said. She stood silently, trying to dispel the tension in her back, shoulders and legs by will alone. After a hundred beats of her heart, she started to breathe heavily and her legs felt like iron bars, tight and unyielding. A tiny hiss of anger escaped her lips and she grimaced, fighting to relax. Her mind was astir with wild phantasms and urgent thoughts. *Be silent!* Berating herself did no good.

Hummingbird stepped away from the opening, brow furrowed. Without speaking, he moved to her side. Thick fingers touched the base of her spine, her elbow, the left knee. Grudgingly, she followed his lead and shifted her feet, settling her back, changing the line of her arm. The difference in her body was shockingly immediate. Exhaustion fell away and she coughed, feeling tension ebb from her chest. The tightness in her legs faded, leaving her with only a memory of soreness. Gretchen started to exclaim, but Hummingbird's fingertips were on her lips. The *nauallis* shook his head and she remained quiet.

"Now," he said softly, "you can feel the difference. This is a more natural stance for you, one in line with your body, with your mind. Now—for a moment—just be. If you cannot empty your mind—another skill to learn, as a child learns to walk—then begin to count in a simple mathematical sequence."

One, Gretchen thought to herself. *Two. Three. Four. . . .*

"Now sit," Hummingbird's voice was very faint, almost indistinct from her own thoughts. "Squat, let your body feel the pressure of gravity, let it fall, your feet will keep you up. Keep counting. Keep counting."

Slumped, breast pressed against her knees, Gretchen began to feel very tired. Her head wanted to drag to the floor, but somehow the interplay of muscles and bone kept her upright. Three or four hundred count passed and she shifted to one side. Despite the solidity of the posture, there was an itching sensation, a discomfort. Hummingbird stepped away, his boots whisper-quiet on the rocky, uneven floor.

"Good. Now move slowly until you feel at ease again. Bit by bit. Keep counting."

A full hour must have passed by the time Gretchen felt truly comfortable, her arms and legs limp but not heavy, her body curled into a ball, one shoulder against the same slab of stone she'd slept beside the night before.

Hummingbird's face loomed over hers, his goggles pushed back. Eyes like smoky jade stared curiously into hers. "How do you feel?"

"Fine," she mumbled and fell asleep before he could say anything more.

Anderssen woke to an odd tickling feeling. The sky beyond the filament door was entirely dark, so she guessed night had swung round again. Cautiously, she looked around the narrow, tilted chamber. Then Gretchen jerked upright, realizing Hummingbird had *tricked* her and—strangely—she did not feel sore. The persistent grainy feeling was gone. In fact, she felt remarkably rested, even *good*. Suspicious, Gretchen examined her medband, but the silver strip was happily asleep, all lights green, indicating no pharmaceutical intervention in progress at all.

"Crow?" Mindful of the situation deeper in the cave, she tried to shout quietly. As usual, there was no answer. Gretchen's peaceful mood dissipated immediately.

When Anderssen unsealed the filament screen leading to the deeper cave, however, she was careful to keep her mind suitably blank. A moment's effort turned off all of her electronics; the wrist chrono, goggles, her comps. Luckily, the rebreather and recycler were powered by the motion of her limbs. She couldn't make them any quieter without asphyxiating. Counting slowly seemed to do the trick and Gretchen let her feet find the way down into the cavern. In the darkness, she realized there was a distinct slope to the passage and her hands found steadily narrowing walls on either side. Though she didn't want to risk a light, after twenty meters a faint azure glow led her to the edge of the cavern where the Russovsky-shape had been sleeping.

This time she stopped and settled into the "heavy" squat Hummingbird had guided her into. Eyes closed, Gretchen waited, counting. Eventually, she felt itchy again and began to move from side to side, fingers outstretched to warn her of looming rocks. Strangely, after a few moments, she felt as if the room had grown larger and her questing fingers found nothing until the itching stopped. Gently, she settled to the ground, fingers finally coming to rest on stone as she opened her eyes.

The dusty floor was to her left and in the blue gleam she could see Hummingbird almost directly opposite her. Again, Russovsky was asleep under the red-and-black blanket. The table and lantern were—as far as Gretchen could tell—in the same position. Nothing seemed to have changed. The circle of faintly radiant ground cover was still interrupted by the dead, broken section. Crystalline fronds still hung from the jumbled ceiling.

What now? she wondered, turning her head slowly to look at Hummingbird.

He did not move, but his attention was fixed on the sleeper, not on her. Thinking of nothing else to do, Gretchen started to count again. Bored, she began a more complicated sequence.

More time passed and Anderssen suddenly became aware something had changed in the cavern. She stopped counting but managed to keep from stirring or opening her eyes. Without *seeing* Gretchen became uncomfortably certain the Russovsky-shape had woken up. She strained to listen but heard only a faint, dry rustling—no more than stone settling in the vault of the mountain. Her heart began to beat faster, but she did not leap up. A queer, electric tension began to build in the air. The prickling feeling on her neck returned, stronger than before. A terrible desire to leap up and shout in alarm came over her.

Gretchen resisted, resuming her count. *2579,* she thought, *2591, 2593, 2609 . . .* As she did a feeling of heat became apparent on her face, as if a torch or open flame were coming closer. The desire to open her eyes was very strong. Instead, she let her breathing slow and settled back, her limbs growing heavy again. The heat became very apparent, verging upon painful. Something brushed against her face, then withdrew. . . . *3217, 3221, 3229 . . .*

The warmth moved, shifting to her right, and then suddenly ceased. With its absence, Gretchen realized the intermittent sound had stopped as well. The cavern felt empty, though now—as if a veil of static or noise had been drawn back—she became distinctly aware of Hummingbird sitting opposite her. She could hear him breathing. Gretchen opened her eyes.

The blue circle was empty. Russovsky, or her copy, was gone. Hummingbird was right where she'd felt him. Gretchen felt a jolt, a bright flash behind her eyes, and wondered if the sick, queasy feeling in her stomach was supposed to be there. The *nauallis* slowly unfolded himself from where he'd been sitting cross-legged. As he did, Anderssen realized her skin was soaked with sweat and she felt clammy from head to toe. *Oh Sister, why do I feel so scared?*

"Well done." Hummingbird's voice was almost inaudible, tinny in the thin air. Gretchen moved to turn on her comm, but the *nauallis* shook his head. "You did well to remain still. But I do not think it is safe to move yet. Stay where you are."

"Why?" The word came out as a choked whisper. Her throat felt raw. "What happened?"

"The shape rose up," he replied after a moment's silence, "and became aware of you. She cleaned up the camp, as I related before, and turned toward you. For a moment, she seemed to reach out, but then returned to the pattern I saw before."

"Oh." Gretchen remembered heat on her face. "And vanished again."

Hummingbird nodded. "I fear," he said, in a very cautious tone, "the inhabitants of this world may sometimes express their curiosity through imitation.

Those here—and be assured, if you cannot feel them, *I can*—are not so adept as those who made the Russovsky which came aboard the ship. Perhaps . . ." He paused. "Perhaps these ones are immature."

Gretchen watched the *nauallis* puzzle over the matter, but soon found her attention drawn to the dusty circle where the shape had appeared. After a moment she frowned. "Crow? You're thinking the thing we see is the microfauna—grown enormous, assembled into something which can move, which wears the shape of a human? Why would it repeat these actions over and over again? Why vanish?"

The *nauallis* regarded her. Gretchen saw the corner of his jaw clench, then loosen.

"This cavern," Anderssen continued, "the fronds, the moss—it's like a recording mechanism. One that's broken, looping, showing the same 3v over and over again. We know Russovsky was here—she must have taken at least a full day to install the relay, maybe even two—and she killed off most of the blue stuff on the floor. Maybe this particular species is one of the imitators. But *this one* is injured."

Now she paused, still staring at the dusty floor. *There's something here.* "What does this stuff eat, anyway? It must take a lot of energy to make imitations of things."

"Does that matter?" Hummingbird sounded sour. "If you're correct, then destroying the rest of the microfauna here will remove the traces of Russovsky— What are you doing?"

Gretchen ignored the *nauallis*, stepping carefully into the dead circle. She went down on her hands and knees and began to examine the rumpled, dirty floor centimeter by centimeter.

"Anderssen!" Hummingbird's voice was noticeably strained. "Can't you feel it? We're being watched."

There was a queer tension in the air, an almost electric sensation. Gretchen paused, shutting out the sound of the old man's querulous voice. There was something—a presence—around her, but while there was a sense of sharpness, of intent focus, she did not feel threatened. Anderssen resumed her search, wishing she had brought some of the tools from her gear bag. The edge of her hand would have to suffice and she began to brush back the first layer of dust in short arcs.

Her fingertips moved across a lump of dirt and the feeling of tension in the cavern spiked. Gretchen stopped, hand frozen above the dust. Hummingbird made a gargling sound and she heard him moving—away, scuttling back up the passage. The faint blue glow brightened, throwing a steadily sharpening shadow beneath her.

Without looking up—a little afraid of what she might see—Gretchen plucked a smooth, round stone out of the dust. As she did, something flickered in the air— a shadow, a shifting light—and there was a glimpse of another hand—a gloved hand—reaching for the stone as well. Gretchen's fingers curled tight around the stone. The shadowy glove vanished. The light went out, leaving her wrapped in darkness.

"Hummingbird?" Her whisper fell on dead air. *Bastard!*

Anderssen eased back across the floor, wondering if the *tik-tik-tik* sound in her ears was the comm channel muttering to itself or something moving in the rubble. Now her heart was hammering, her throat tight. A heavy sense of oppression pressed down on her, inspiring a cold sweat. One of her boots touched stone and she scrambled back into the tunnel mouth. A moment later, Gretchen threw aside the filament screen, bounded across their hasty campsite and out into the midday Ephesian sunlight. Hummingbird's incoherent voice rang painfully loud in the enclosed space.

The horizon was a blue wall rising above the curving white dome of the eastern plains. Jagged mountains tumbled away to her left and right, leaving only empty air and the colossal plunge down the face of Prion before her. Gretchen set herself, swung back one arm and flung the stone out and away into the empty vastness.

Swaying a little, she started with surprise when Hummingbird caught her arm.

"What was that?" His fingers were tight on her bicep.

Gretchen wrenched her arm free of his grip. "Hands off, crow."

"Tell me what you found in there. Why did you throw it away?"

Smirking, Anderssen brushed dust from her hands and knees. "The cave really creeped you out, didn't it? You—the *tlamatinime*, the all-knowing one—you ran out of there pretty fast for such an old man."

Hummingbird drew back and the line of his head, the clenched fists and stiff shoulders, told Gretchen she'd scored a hit—*a palpable hit*, she thought smugly.

"You weren't kidding," she said after a moment of silent gloating, "about this male and female business, were you? I thought you were being difficult."

"No." The *nauallis* gave her an inscrutable look. "I was not."

"Hmm." Gretchen looked over the edge of the cliff. *Such a long way down. But you'd fly, part of the way at least.* "Russovsky forgot something in the cave, just a round stone she'd picked up somewhere. A native Ephesian stone. I doubt she even noticed she'd forgotten the little thing—there are plenty of wind-smoothed stones to pick up from the ground. But the cave didn't like it. Not at all."

AMONG THE BROKEN MOUNTAINS

The *Cornuelle* glided through an inky deep, a matte-black ghost among invisibly tumbling leviathans. Her main engines were at minimal thrust in an attempt to reduce her sensor profile. The sleek hull was in absorptive mode, darkness against darkness, yielding no hint of comm traffic or EM radiation. On her command deck, Hadeishi was keeping one eye on the ship's heat sump and one on the latest personnel reports when Hayes's terse voice drew his attention.

"Outrider Two has lost particle track," the weapons officer declared, staring intently at his panel.

"Outrider Two, engine full stop," Hadeishi barked, eyes swinging to the glowing depths of the threat-well. Drone Two was their lead dog at the moment, deployed nearly a thousand kilometers "inward" of the cruiser. Outrider One was accelerating back toward the cruiser, on the downside of its duty cycle. Three was outbound, snaking its way through the three-dimensional maze of the asteroid field to catch up with Two. The entire area within sensor range was quiet; the bridge displays showed only thousands of dots colored "navigational hazard" amber. The *Cornuelle* was a blue spark at the center of the well, with the three drones appearing as miniscule turquoise arrows.

"How long until Three reaches duty station?" The *chu-sa* leaned back in the shockchair, considering the situation. He wondered if Koshō had gone to sleep yet—she'd gone off-duty an hour ago—and decided not to call her back to the bridge. *She needs to sleep sometime.*

"Two hundred and thirty minutes, sir." Hayes turned questioningly to Hadeishi. "Shall I back Two out of there?"

"No," Hadeishi said. "Badger the drone with a nearby rock. Reduce outgoing transmissions to locational data. No broadcast, no highband emission. Switch everything else to record." Hayes was already at work on his panel, squirting a new set of commands to the drone. "When Three comes in range, establish a narrow-beam link to Two and relay back to us."

"Pinhole mode, aye," Hayes acknowledged absently, his mind entirely on reconfiguring the drone and dumping a new set of engagement and maneuver parameters to Outrider Three. A moment later he punched two glyphs and took a breath. "Commands away."

Hadeishi nodded, but *his* attention was now on the main panel, where ship's comp was replaying the particle trail data. *Curse my generosity,* he thought with a trace of bitterness. *I need Isoroku here to advise me, not stuck on a civilian pleasure barge—he knows engine patterns better than anyone.* The replay showed a wash of decaying, once-excited particle byproducts of the refinery's main drive meandering through the debris field. "Hayes, come look at this."

The weapons officer was at his side as fast as humanly possible.

"A *Tyr*-class refinery is almost ten times our size," Hadeishi remarked, contemplating the plot. "Her helmsman is following a path of least density, trying to keep incidental meteoroid impacts to a minimum as she moves through the field. But look, here the refinery suddenly shifts course into close proximity with this cloud of debris."

Hayes nodded. "They must have picked something up." A stylus in his blunt fingers sketched a new trajectory on the panel. "They're cutting through a 'hedge' into another area with less debris. A clear lane between the larger planetesimals."

"And we lose the trail at the edge of the 'lane.'" Hadeishi grimaced. "Could they have picked up the outrider?"

The weapons officer shook his head. "No, *Chu-sa.* The decay rates indicate we're still days behind them. They must have reacted to something on long-range scan."

Hadeishi settled deeper into his chair, stroking his beard. "Break down those decay rates and all the data we have on their engine plume. If they've badgered and know someone is looking for them, we need to get a solid estimate on how far they might have gone on minimum power."

"Not very far," Hayes said, tapping his stylus on the panel. "Think about how much mass they're moving. Even empty, a *Tyr* is a behemoth. I think they scooted into this 'lane' so they could coast and gain some distance. Somewhere out here—" the stylus sketched a box in the 'clear' area "—there's a pocket of engine exhaust."

"Because they corrected course," Hadeishi said, "either for distance or vector."

"I could send Outrider Two into the lane," Hayes offered dubiously.

"No." Hadeishi shook his head slightly. "There's no reason to try and hide a course change if you don't drop a sensor relay—or a proximity mine—behind to welcome a pursuer. The refinery captain is not a fool. His cartel wouldn't entrust so much expensive equipment to a novice. He'll pick a random vector, pile on velocity and coast again until he has to maneuver to avoid a collision."

The *chu-sa* paused, considering the cloud of amber dots for a moment. Then he nodded again, this time to himself. Hayes waited patiently, hands clasped behind his back, shoulders square.

"Hold drone Two on station until Three arrives." Hadeishi's voice had lost its contemplative tone. His mind was made up. "Recycle drone One as quickly as it can be refueled. The *Cornuelle* will proceed at one-third power to catch up. I want all three drones ready on point when we reach Two's current location. We will advance in a box formation, scanning the surrounding debris clouds for evidence of a third course change."

"*Hai, Chu-sa!*" Hayes's jaw tightened and a gleam lit in the young officer's eyes.

Hadeishi waved him away and slumped back in the shockchair, staring into the threat-well.

Now we close with the enemy, he thought, troubled. *Does he know we're here? Is he reckless? Is he wary?*

That was the question. A prudent, patient captain would simply wait for an opportunity to make hyperspace gradient out of the system when no one could see him. But an angry man, or a reckless commander . . . A ship that large could carry a great deal of mischief in secondary storage. A single proximity mine could cripple the *Cornuelle*. Two or three might kill her, if the cruiser happened to blunder into a flower-box detonation.

The ceiling lights in Hadeishi's cabin were dark, the only illumination cast from a small table lamp on his desk. Mitsuharu knelt on a cotton mat, facing the wall opposite his bed. Two framed pictures—not modern holos, but yellowed paper, cracking with age—sat within a small alcove. An empty incense burner lay before the photographs; an old man and a middle-aged woman in formal dress. Both seemed grim, their faces composed, though in his memory they were always smiling.

"At dusk, I often climb to the peak of Kugami." Mitsu bent his head, palms pressed together, fingertips against his brow. Stringy black hair fell in a cloud around his shoulders. He rarely let his ponytail go unbound, but certain devotions required an expression of sacrifice. He thought the loss of personal control an adequate offering. "Deer bellow, their voices soaked up by piles of maple leaves . . ."

The sharp, pungent smell of incense should fill the air around him, but the air recyclers worked overtime already. Mitsu accepted the absence of pine and rosewood as another sacrifice. His lips barely moved, offering the last of Ryukan's ancient poem to his mother and his father. ". . . lying undisturbed at the foot of the mountain."

What chant settled the racing hearts of my ancestors, Mitsu wondered, rising from his knees, *when they rode into the high grass to fight the Dakota and the Iroquois?* A deep bow followed and he closed the alcove with the tip of his finger. A metal plate sealed the little shrine, protecting the contents against a sudden loss of pressure or the g-shock of combat.

Hadeishi ran a hand across the spines of his books. His personal quarters should, by tradition, be spartan and bare. He was sure *Sho-sa* Koshō's cabin was a perfect example of approved Zen minimalism—all plain gray and white surfaces, perhaps small portraits of the Emperor and the Shogun, her *tatami*, the door to the closet always closed. Mitsu smoothed his beard, looking around at the terrible mess he'd made of this place. Every wall was covered with bookcases—well-built ones too, Isoroku was a dab hand for structural modifications—and every shelf was packed with storage crystals, audio-sticks, hand-drawn paintings in ink, paper-bound volumes, boxes of letters, Heshtic scrolls and paw-books, even things he'd found in the markets of Baldur, Marduk or New Malta. He was sure some of them held writing, but then again—who knew what they truly were? Laundry lists? Accounts of land disputes from some dead, forgotten world?

My whole life is here, he thought, aware of lingering sadness. *If the* Cornuelle *dies, all this will be gone.*

Hadeishi sat cross-legged on the *tatami*, picking up a hand-held comp. The pad came alive with his touch, displaying a set of ship schematics. Frowning, Mitsu considered the builder's diagrams for a standard-issue *Tyr* refinery. *What a monster*, he thought—and not for the first time—panning through screen after screen of floorplans. *We could almost fit the* Cornuelle *into the main boat bay.* The thought was amusing, but not helpful. He narrowed the view displayed on the pad to those sections housing the meteoroid defense system.

"Looks like an old *Koningsborg*-class battle cruiser point-defense array," he said wryly aloud after a half hour of examination. Finding the circuits had taken some effort—the sheer size of a *Tyr* made finding a single system difficult. "Hmm. But spread out over far more surface area."

He paused, brow furrowing in thought. *How big is the crew for this leviathan?*

Another hour passed before Mitsu found something like a crew-requirements list. Then he raised an eyebrow in cautious surprise.

Thai-i Huémac slid down a gangway ladder into first platoon's sleeping deck and found the narrow room unexpectedly crowded. A small, wiry man with prominent cheekbones and the coppery-bronze coloring typical of the Tlaxcallan highlands, the senior Marine lieutenant went unnoticed for a moment. A crowd of Marines in off-duty fatigues, all hulking backs and shoulders, filled the walkway between rows of bunks on either side. Smoke curled against the ceiling and bit the eyes of the men lying on the top, staring avidly down at something in the middle of the barracks.

Huémac stood quietly for a moment, cataloging the number of violations of shipside regulation visible to his experienced eye. He was impressed by the hushed, pregnant silence filling the room. The senior lieutenant *had* been wondering where all of second platoon had dissapeared too, but now he guessed the entire Marine contingent on the *Cornuelle* was packed into this one compartment.

A single voice, hoarse and pleading, rose above the quiet susurration of so many men and women breathing. "Oh great lord, oh gracious master, blessed Five Flowers. Look on these poor, pitiful subjects, see their smooth black bodies, their empty eyes, count the holes in their bellies. See them, see the four houses, see the black squares and the red. Please, master of flowers, giver of gifts, fickle one! Bless these five subjects, give them swift legs, strong hearts and every mercy!"

Huémac rolled his eyes—but only because not a single Marine could see his reaction—and swung nimbly up onto the nearest rack of bunks. Carefully bending low under the pipes and conduits and cable guides crowding the ceiling, he stepped over a half-dozen men to look down into the common area at the center of the deck. None of the Marines on the top bunks paid him any attention, save *Heicho* Tonuac, who was reading an illustrated *malinche* titled *The Tribulatory Life of Leda and her Swan* while chewing gum. The corporal stiffened to attention as the lieutenant stepped over him.

At the middle of the room there was an open space where two facing sets of bunks had been folded back into the walls. Huémac grasped hold of a return-air pipe and leaned out, looking down upon three men and one woman sitting on the floor below. Between them was a woven mat in the shape of a cross. Red and blue ceramic markers were scattered along a track of squares, filling each arm of the cross.

The woman was watching the man opposite her with a bored expression. In turn, he was rubbing both hands together, his voice now a mumble, a *click-click-click* sound rising up among the slowly curling trails of incense and tobacco smoke. Both men were staring sickly at the arrangement of the counters on the mat. Huémac squinted a little and pursed his lips in appreciation. Five solid red tokens had reached safety in the house of the Rising Sun, five blue in the house of the Moon. One red disc remained, sitting a very likely three squares from exiting the board in victory. One blue token lagged behind, an almost impossible *ten* squares from journey's end.

Huémac had played a little *patolli* in his time, but the pile of pay chits mounded up before the woman was of truly legendary size. The *thai-i* repressed a sigh. *I have got to convince the captain to sign off on promoting Felix to sergeant. . . .* Then the little burgundy-haired woman would be forced to limit her shipboard gambling income to the other sergeants and the officers. *Who might show a tiny shred of sense . . . and stay far away from her.*

Gambling—particularly on *patolli* or *tlachco* competitions—was an entirely legal expression of religious piety throughout the Empire, which pleased the Marines and sailors in Fleet to no end. Even the foreigners were only too happy to offer up incense, maize and pulque to Macuilxohitl Five-Flower on payday, hoping to gain the god's blessing in matters of chance.

Down on the floor, the man praying suddenly seized the five polished beans in his right hand and cast them onto the mat with a flick of his wrist. Huémac shook his head—throwing all five as 'spots' and doubling the roll to ten squares was entirely unlikely—no matter what promises the private made to Five-Flower. Throwing a one, two or three—any of which would help Felix, or even let her move the last token from the board and win—were far more likely.

The little black beans bounced, rattled and came to a stop. Private Martine was crouched on his hands and knees, muttering fervently. Three spots, two black.

"Face!" the private groaned. A hiss of indrawn breath filled the compartment as he advanced his blue token. Seven squares seemed an impossible distance. Felix reached out, nose twitching in amusement and scooped up the beans.

She did not pray or rub the beans. They left her hand with a simple flip and scattered across the mat. "Oh," she said in an aggrieved voice, "only eyes."

Her red token advanced two squares. One to go. Martine snatched up the beans and tried to match Felix's offhand toss. The beans scattered and rolled. Most turned up white. Four of them.

"Very good," Felix said, tucking wine-red hair back behind her ears. "Box is very good."

Martine gave her a sick look; blunt, chipped fingers sliding his blue token ahead. Three squares left. Felix gathered up the beans, smiled at the private and let them roll out in a lazy-seeming flip. They bounced on the mat, spinning, and four came up dark, one white. "Snake," Felix said, and removed her last piece from the board.

Martine stared hollow-eyed at the treacherous beans. His squadmates stared at him. Felix shoveled pay chits into an embroidered leather bag ornamented with a hand-stitched picture of a Scorpion ground-effect tank on the side. There was a tense silence. Perched above the tableau, Huémac schooled his face to impassivity and then—when the men behind Martine fully grasped they'd lost their last month's pay in a single game of *patolli*—he dropped lightly to the floor beside corporal Felix.

"Officer on deck!" someone bawled in fear and surprise. "Attention!"

Twenty-five men scrambled to adopt something approaching proper posture. Even Felix was on her feet, the embroidered bag already hidden inside her field jacket. Martine was looking rather pale, his squadmates pressing around him on either side.

"At ease," *Thai-i* Huémac announced, back straight as the vanadium core barrel on a squad shipgun. "Private Martine, whose mat and beans are these?"

"Mine, sir." The Marine swallowed and managed to stiffen to attention. More than one pair of surreptitious hands helped him. A squad had to stick together in the face of enemy fire.

Huémac looked consideringly at Felix, who was not smiling but was very, very attentive. "Do you even own a *patolli* mat, corporal?"

"Sir," Felix said in a very earnest voice, "I do not."

Huémac tried not to smile. *Sometimes you have to play these things out, as a public lesson.* "Do you like to play *patolli*, corporal? Are you a gambling woman?"

"No, sir," Felix said with an entirely straight face. "I never gamble."

The senior lieutenant looked around at the goggling faces of the Marines crowded into the barracks. Most of them were on the verge of apoplexy, though Huémac could make out one or two—including the relaxed *Heicho* Tonuac and his pamphlet—who were trying not to grin. *Squadmates*, the lieutenant recognized, *or men who'd bet on Felix rather than on poor Martine.* Huémac returned his attention to the sallow-looking private.

"Private Martine," he said very patiently. "Did you invite *Heicho* Felix to join your game of *patolli*? Is this your mat, token and beans?"

"Yes, sir." Martine's voice was very faint. He appeared to be having trouble focusing on the lieutenant's face.

"I see." Huémac raised his voice, so everyone in the compartment could hear. "I am sure *Heicho* Felix only joined your game to be polite. I understand she does not like to gamble. I suggest in the future, you scrupulously respect her wishes in this matter. Private, you should pick up your *patolli* board before someone steps on it."

Huémac stood there, stone-solid, until the crowd of Marines began to break up. They were glum, shamefaced and broke. Inwardly, he sighed in despair. *What was Martine thinking? He knows Fourth Squad lost all of their money last month!*

"Felix—you stay *right here*." The senior lieutenant did not turn, but he could feel the corporal freeze in her tracks and then resume a parade rest. Huémac waited, thumbs hooked into the back of his uniform belt, until the Marines had returned to their usual pursuits. Only *Heicho* Tonuac was still watching the senior lieutenant out of the corner of his eye while he pretended to read. Huémac turned, eyes narrowing to black slits, a hint of the steady anger he felt showing in his face. Felix stiffened, lips compressing into a bare rose-colored line. "The *chu-sa*," he said quietly, "in his infinite, godlike wisdom has tapped your squad, corporal, for some extracurricular activity. Normally, *Gunso* Fitzsimmons would be here to take on preparatory duties, but he is absent. So you will run every single man in your unit through a full workup on their combat z-armor, ship-to-ship assault gear and secure comm tech. Weapons is running up a simulator pack for you. I'd guess you'll have a couple days to run through the scenario."

Huémac almost smiled. "You'll be assault leader, Felix, so I will be watching you very closely. Your squad will have a 'hot' target and I dislike losing men. The *chu-sa* will be paying close attention to how you do in the sim."

"Yes, sir!" Felix was starting to look almost as pale as Martine, though the *thai-i* knew the young Marine was aware of what was coming, where the foolish private had been led blindfolded to the butcher's block. "May the corporal ask a question, sir?"

"Go on." Huémac tilted his head to one side, watching tiny beads of sweat begin to collect along the woman's hairline. He wondered how quickly a betting pool would start, wagering on the exercises in the sim. *Within the hour*, he supposed. *Maybe by the time I leave the compartment.*

"Who . . . who will be running opposition in the sim, sir?"

The senior lieutenant's smile widened, showing a full set of perfect white teeth. "*Sho-sa* Koshō has been assigned that role, corporal."

"Sir?!" Felix blurted, her face ashen. "The *Wind-knife*, sir? She'll—"

"She'll what?" Huémac asked curiously.

Felix seemed unable to speak and Huémac watched with interest while the Marine recovered her composure. Something like real dread had penetrated the corporal's usually unflappable demeanor.

"Nothing, sir." Felix stiffened to attention again. "Have mission guidelines been posted?"

"I have them," Huémac replied, his bronzed face once more composed. "You'll find them . . . challenging, I think. But *Chu-sa* Hadeishi has expressed great faith in your abilities, *Heicho* Felix. I hope you do not disappoint him."

"Thank you, sir." Felix started to look pale again. Her voice had strangled itself into a squeak. "Hadeishi-*tzin* asked for me?"

Huémac nodded gravely, a peculiar glitter in his dark eyes. "He did. He thinks you're *lucky.*"

"Still nothing . . ." Magdalena was curled up in a nest of Navy-issue blankets over-flowing the captain's chair on the bridge of the *Palenque*. Slitted yellow eyes watched another set of scan data unspool on a secondary v-pane. There was plenty of noise, static and ghostly warbling filling the comm bands down on the planetary surface. But there was a singular lack of recognizable traffic on Imperial and Company channels. "Parker, can you switch on the main array? Just for an hour or two?"

There was a grunt from behind her and the Hesht tilted her head back far enough to see one of the human's legs hanging out of a ceiling tile. Though the Navy engineer had managed to get the ship underway, the bridge systems of the *Palenque* were still mostly down. Coils of conduit, cable and guide-sheathing were exposed everywhere. Very few systems were working. There was no heat, no light. Other than the cold, the Hesht was very comfortable in the cavernlike space.

"Parker . . ." Magdalena began a harsh, throbbing growl at the back of her throat.

There was a scraping sound and the human pilot's face appeared in an open-ing between two of the tiles. Light from a glowbean shone around his balding head. "Miss Cat," he said, sounding wrung out, "the main comm array is shut down, turned off and locked out by order of our dear judge. If you want it active, you will have to persuade Stoneface down in Engineering."

"He eats moss," Magdalena replied, ears twitching. Finely napped black fur curled back from her fore-incisors and she let an inch of claw expose on her left hand—just for a moment. "*Rrrrrr* . . . they could be in trouble dirtside. Another pack might have them cornered. Her leg could be broken, she could be caught in the open, exposed!"

Parker sighed and crawled backward out of the overhead. His forearms were crisscrossed with scars and dried blood. Working in such an old ship was wearing on mind and body alike. He swung for a moment, feeling the gentle tug of the ship's acceleration, then dropped to the deck. *Palenque* was underway, engines barely lit, in a long corkscrew orbit out from the planet. In another five days, the pilot figured, she would be far enough away to switch to full power. Then—if Isoroku and his Marine helpers were really working down in Engineering, not drinking themselves insensible—the ship might be able to achieve gradient and enter hyperspace.

"Maggie . . ." Parker stumbled into the navigator's chair and wedged one thin shoulder into a space between two of the supports. The shockchair's heavy, plush seatback had been eaten, leaving nothing but a cage of metal strips. He reached for the pack of tabac in his shirt pocket and found only empty waxed paper., *Crap. No smoke.* "I know Gretchen's your packleader now and all—I know that's *important* to you—but she's gone off on her own . . . thing."

The Hesht did not look at him, once more encased in a suspicious number of blankets. Parker blinked, then stared at a blue sleepbag tucked in behind her. "Is that my sleepbag? It is. You stole my sleepbag! Give over!"

"*Rrr!* I'm cold, monkey! You're not. You're working. When you go to your den to sleep, I'll let you have it back."

"So—is all your fur for show or something?" Parker crushed waxed paper in his fist. "You're . . . plushy. But you're cold all the time. I don't understand."

"Heshukan," Magdalena said, baring the tips of her incisors, "was a warm, dry world."

"Oh." Parker started to hunt through his pockets for something else to smoke.

"You're out of bitter, smelly leaves," Magdalena said, staring moodily at the v-pane. Still nothing but static and garbage. She turned off the feed and began flipping through the various comm systems available to her. Most were dead and dark. "Maybe the hunters have some."

"Ask the Marines?" Parker rubbed his face wearily. "They were cadging from me yesterday. Stupid—why give them away? Have I lost my mind? I should have sold them, or kept them for myself!" The pilot pushed himself out the chair and gestured at Magdalena. "I'm crashing. Give me my bag."

Brow and nose wrinkled up in a grimace, the Hesht scooted to one side and let Parker recover his sleepbag.

"Agh. It smells like piss!" The pilot held his bag at arm's length, mouth pursed.

"You don't want it?" One of Magdalena's paws licked out and snagged the bottom of the bag with a curving white claw. "I made it smell *proper*, like a den-blanket should."

"I do want it!" Parker snatched the bag back. He shook his head, then made his way carefully off the bridge, bag trailing behind him like a fat blue tail.

Magdalena hissed at his retreating back and then rummaged around, adjusting her blankets. When she was done, the Hesht resumed paging through the comm channels. Her mood was even fouler than before.

Bandao arrived an hour later, two bulky packages under one arm, and found the bridge dark and cold, save for Magdalena in her nest, with four v-panes casting a chill gray light on her face. Maggie ignored him. She was busy keying commands into the system in one pane while the others were filled with closely spaced documentation or remote console feeds. Her moodiness had departed, replaced by a near-maniacal concentration on the work before her. Bandao took no notice of the slight and began hunting around under the command deck.

After a few moments, he found what he was looking for and plugged a field heater into a power socket under the navigator's station. Five seconds later, the olive-colored unit woke up and began to radiate a warm, dry heat into the area around the captain's chair.

"Two and four are stabilized," Magdalena muttered under her breath. Her claws made a constant, rattling *click-click-click* on the control panel. If she were a human, she would be sweating. If she were Parker, there would be a cloud of smoke like a forest fire around her.

Studiously ignoring the Hesht, Bandao paced around to the opposite side of her chair, installed a second unit and then disappeared back into the dark passageway leading into the main hab ring. Magdalena showed no sign of noticing his brief visit.

"Ah," she said in relief, rolling her shoulders. "That's better. Seven will do." Magdalena's nose twitched—there was a sort of hot metallic smell in the air—but the images on the panel drew her attention before she noticed the two heaters.

On her main v-pane, a video feed had appeared. The image was broken into seven sections arranged in an exploded hexagon, each showing a different view of the planet now receding behind the *Palenque*. The tip of her pink tongue showing, Magdalena watched the feeds very carefully. Seven matching remote console windows were live on another section of her panel.

"Synch one to seven," she muttered, tapping a series of glyphs with the little claw on her right paw. The upper left video shivered, then adjusted, conforming to the image mirrored in the center of the hexagon. "Good . . . synch two to seven."

Three-quarters of a million kilometers away, one of the peapod satellites still in orbit over the third planet made an adjustment, slewing to cover an equatorial region. The peapod's orbit had been degrading rapidly, but it was still in operation. The machine was aware—but uncaring—of a slight increase in the rate of collision with atmospheric particles. Almost imperceptibly, the satellite began to slow, dragged by an invisible fringe of the ocean of air surrounding the planet. Responding to the commands arriving over the telemetry link, the peapod made a series of minute adjustments to its orientation.

"Synch six to seven . . ." Maggie began to grin, foreteeth and sidemolars showing in a fierce display. ". . . and stabilize image." She tapped another patiently waiting glyph. The video displays from all seven peapods collapsed into one single image. *Palenque*-side comp picked up the dataflows and began to fuse them into one high-resolution feed. Magdalena waited anxiously, a fully extended striking claw clicking against the front of her cutting teeth.

The comp interped and interped again, trying to adjust for differences in the rate of flow caused by the angular distance between the ship and the peapods scattered around Ephesus. Hating the concession, Maggie stepped down the level of resulting detail an order of magnitude. *Palenque* comp chirped happily in response.

"Now," Magdalena growled happily, "let's look in on the crash site."

The multilensed eye in the sky shifted, concentrating on a barren valley near the northern ice cap. Magdalena was grudgingly satisfied with the resolution coming back out of the cribbed-together system, but the satellites were responding far too slowly to satisfy her impatient nature.

"Stupid tree-climbing machines . . ." When all seven peapods had focused on the crash area, Magdalena realized both Gretchen and the old crow had left the area. "Now where did they go?" She cleared the peapod documentation out of the secondary panes and brought up Russovsky's transmission logs and a plot of her flight path. "Hmm . . ."

The heaters continued to glow, surrounding the Hesht in a warm cocoon. Her face shimmered in the constantly changing light from the panels as she worked, long into shipsnight. By shipsdawn, the tired Hesht was staring at a grainy picture of a mountainside. The upper wings of two ultralights gleamed in late-afternoon sunlight and Maggie could make out the blurry shapes of Gretchen and the Méxica talking as they loaded gear into their *Midges*.

Hummingbird fiddled with his breather and goggles, trying to get them to lie comfortably over his nose and ears. Gretchen, passing by with the last of her personal gear, threw the comp and sensor pad into the front seat of the *Gagarin*.

"Hold still," she said over the comm, her own face mostly masked by the tail of her *kaffiyeh*. "There's a trick to it . . . there. How is that? Better?"

The *nauallis* nodded, finding the new arrangement suitable. For a moment, Gretchen thought he might actually thank her, but he did not. She was not surprised.

"So—you feel comfortable leaving this place now?"

"Yes." Hummingbird had spent the day sitting cross-legged in the cave, watching the passage down into the cavern. "We will follow the course of Russovsky's last flight."

"Sure." Gretchen peered at the *nauallis* curiously. "You haven't seen anything? *Felt* anything?"

Hummingbird shook his head. "We have a long way to go, Anderssen. We shouldn't waste any more time here."

"Really." Gretchen felt a cold, sharp anger boiling up in her stomach. With an almost physical effort, she forced her voice to remain level. "Aren't you going to ask me how I could find Russovsky's stone—when you couldn't? Or do you know already?" Her eyes narrowed. "You do know. You even know why these things are happening!"

Hummingbird laughed in relief, an abrupt, unexpected sound. "Know? I know many things, Anderssen, but I've not the slightest idea why the cave made a copy of Russovsky or kept repeating itself!"

Oddly, as the *nauallis* was speaking, Gretchen became aware of a queer flutter in his voice, as if two voices were speaking at once—different voices—and they were contradicting each other.

"You're lying." Hummingbird became very still. Gretchen looked around, entirely startled by her own statement and then she advanced on him. "You *are* lying and I . . . I can tell."

"Could you?" Hummingbird stirred, regarding her with a fierce, sudden intensity. "Very well—how did you find the stone in the dust?"

Faced with the question she'd wanted to hear all day, Gretchen felt entirely deflated. She was sure the *nauallis* already had some esoteric answer for her, and she realized she didn't care. "Never mind. Our real problem is what happened in the cave. There is *no reason* for an organism in this environment to waste energy making copies of things. At least—no reason I can think of." She drew back her hood, so the Náhuatl could see the fierce expression on her face. "Why don't you fill me in? Before we stumble into the next situation, and one of us is hurt, or killed, by my ignorance."

Hummingbird's lips had compressed to a tight line and his eyes grew dark and guarded. "There are secrets which cannot be revealed . . ."

Gretchen's face contorted into a snarl. A hand groped at her belt for a wrench, a hammer, a gun . . .

". . . so I will not tell you everything I know." Hummingbird said firmly. "But I will tell you enough. But first, think about what you did in the cavern. You've had a certain kind of training—from school, from university, from your parents, from the work of your hands—and you're skilled in a way of seeing." He paused, regarding her. "Did those skills show you the stone in the dust?"

Gretchen became aware her mouth was very dry. She licked her lips and took a drink from the recycler tube in her mask. Hummingbird's gaze did not waver or look away. Gretchen started to become nervous. "I . . . no, no I don't think they did. I didn't see the stone, not with my eyes. There was only an itch. Just . . . something was out of place."

The *nauallis* nodded minutely. He seemed to gather himself, jaw tightening, brow creasing. For a very long time, Hummingbird said nothing, staring at her with an unwavering expression. Just as Anderssen—tired of standing on a windy ledge while the day inexorably passed—was about to speak, he blinked and said:

"Think of a river, broad and running swift. The bottom is smooth sand, the banks thick with algae. There is nothing to disturb the current, the surface is placid. If you hover above the clear water, you can see into the depths, pick out details of patterns in the sand. Perhaps there is seagrass waving in the current. Put your hand in the water and you are surprised by the strength of the water—but now the surface is distorted, confused. A wake trails behind your hand and suddenly the water is no longer clear. Such an effect is obvious, even to the unwary.

"Consider a boulder, submerged and invisible to a man standing on the bank. The river may seem placid, but the current is distorted. A boat on the river may strike the rock before anyone notices anything amiss. The current may twist across the stone, eddying, rushing faster or slower. Now, in the constrained universe beneath the glassy surface, there may be places where the seagrass cannot hold, or places where an eddy falls, leaving a thick stand of growth."

Hummingbird made a motion with his hand, indicating the landscape around them.

"What you see here—the ruined surface, tortured mountains, desolate plains—is not the whole of this world. There are submerged currents. There is something here, something hidden. There is an influence, like my hidden boulder, which directs, confines, shapes all that happens on this poor, broken orb. We felt an echo in the cave—"

Gretchen felt her pulse trip a little faster. She blurted, "The First Sun people! Something interrupted their labors! They fled, didn't they? What . . . what did they leave behind?"

"Do not presume they fled," Hummingbird replied, raising his eyes to the sky. His goggles polarized into a shining mirror, reducing the sun to two blazing points. "Have you thought about the power of the First Sun people? They bestrode the stars as gods—we have seen the scraps and ruins they leave behind—and we are ants creeping across the floor of a deserted house. Our ships have visited six hundred worlds, only the tiniest fraction of the suns we can see with the unaided eye. Yet there are wonders which beggar our knowledge and skill even in such a tiny space. Have you thought what might lie beyond the rim of our domain?"

"Hasn't everyone? Every undergraduate class debates this in first-term xenoarcheology!" Gretchen began to feel the excitement of curiosity stir and tried to keep her voice level. "Where did they come from, the giants of the First Sun? Where did they go? Why aren't they here now?"

"They were destroyed." Hummingbird's statement was flat and cold. "There were—*there are*—powers which exceeded them in all ways. In age, though the First Sun races are impossibly ancient by our measure, in strength, though the least of the First Sun *valkar* could smash Earth to a cinder."

He tilted his head toward the vast sweep of mountains and canyons and plains. "One of the *valkar* was here, remaking this world into something pleasing—if such a term can be used. Then it fled to safety." Hummingbird fixed Gretchen with a piercing stare. "What made it run? What drove it away, what frightened a power capable of shattering an *entire planet?*"

"I . . ." Gretchen couldn't think of anything to say.

"Not man." The *nauallis* shook his head, laughing bitterly. "Not man! Not our tiny little empire! We are very small. Insignificant. But think about what happened in the cave—Russovsky left something behind, something equally small. What did you find?"

"A pebble." Gretchen squinted, trying to make out the man's expression. "Just a water stone, like the old-timers use on Mars. She'll have taken it out of her mouth at night and put it aside. Then she forgot in the morning and left. There are plenty of other smooth stones here."

"You saw what happened. The things which live in the cave reacted—their current was disturbed—I venture they were trying to eject the stone, like shrapnel from a wound. You saw what kind of distortion such a small, tiny object created."

Gretchen nodded. "But how—"

Hummingbird raised a hand, cutting her off. "This world is filled with echoes, Anderssen-*tzin*. Echoes of destruction and fear. Echoes of the dead. There are shades all around us, even now. You cannot see them—they are faint even to me—but enormous forces have been at play. The tread of the gods, if you wish to think of the First Sun people as deities. Your precious cylinder was in a fragment of stone—even I recognize the fossils in the ancient layers of sediment. The *valkar* consumed a living world and was then defeated in turn by something even more monstrous."

Pursing his lips, the *nauallis* stared off into the emptiness. "But I do not think it fled."

"What do you mean?" Gretchen moved into Hummingbird's line of sight.

"It is still here, somewhere. In hiding."

"Oh." Gretchen shook her head, trying not to laugh. His statement seemed preposterous. She wasn't quite sure if she was afraid or exasperated with the old México. "It's . . . hiding here? In a cave or something?"

"I don't know." Hummingbird looked entirely grim. "We see only echoes of its effects—ripples from a stone thrown a million years in the past. These crystalline entities, whatever consumed Russovsky and then vomited her up again, the corrosive dust, the fields of pipeflowers—they are reflections of a hidden power."

"Have you been taking some kind of psychotropic while I wasn't looking?" Gretchen failed to hide her complete disbelief. "How can you reach such a conclu-

sion after only being planetside for, what—three days? You don't have any data!"
She stopped, mouth open. A nagging thought had blossomed into certainty,
watching his inscrutable old face.

"You knew what was here before you came." Gretchen felt a little sick.
Russovsky. The crew on the ship. Doctor McCue . . . everyone who'd already died . . .
"Did the Company know?"

"No. No one knew." Hummingbird adjusted the hood of his *kaffiyeh* to shade
his goggles. "I have data—but not from this world. From another ruined planet. If
the proper authorities had known what was here, no civilian ship would have been
allowed in the system."

"Which authorities," Gretchen replied testily, "are the *proper* authorities for
dealing with *gods*?"

"I am," Hummingbird said quietly. "This is my responsibility."

"You? Just you by your lonesome or the whole of the *tlamatinime*?"

Hummingbird almost smiled. "Not all of the judges are privy to everything,
but as a whole we are entrusted—by both Emperors, by the Fleet—with keeping a
guard upon humanity."

"Do we need to be guarded?" Gretchen felt cold, even in the direct unfiltered
blaze of the Ephesian sun. "Are we sheep, who need a watchdog prowling? What
would you do if one of these . . . these *valkar* attacked a colony world or even
Anáhuac itself?"

"The world would die," Hummingbird said tonelessly. "But the *valkar*—the
gods of the First Sun—are scattered or dead." He paused. "Or sometimes they lie
hidden, trapped in a kind of sleep. This one must be dreaming, waiting for the
stars to change in their courses so it may wake again."

"What good can you do, then, if you cannot stop these powers?"

Hummingbird's eyes glinted angrily and Gretchen swallowed another acerbic
comment.

"We watch, Anderssen. We watch in the darkness at the edge of human space.
As a famous general once said, 'We stand guard so you may enjoy the untroubled
sleep of the innocent.' Your attitude, I realize, is a testament to a job well done by
my brothers and their predecessors. We are rarely idle. Many times men have
stumbled into danger. Colonies have been abandoned, stations lost. Ships disappear with dreadful frequency. In Tenochtitlán, in the district of the Weavers, there
is an unremarkable building which holds room after room filled with anthracite
tablets. The names of my brothers who have fallen in our quiet, unseen struggle
are inscribed therein. This is not a pleasant universe, Anderssen-*tzin*, where man
can roam without care."

The old Náhuatl scratched the back of his head. "We might be lucky here. The dust will help consume our tracks, our equipment, all traces of our visit. We just have to make sure there are no more 'memories' trapped along Russovsky's path."

"What about the cylinder on the *Palenque?*" Gretchen asked quietly. "You really think it is a trap? That it will have to be destroyed?"

Hummingbird nodded. "I know what the cylinder means to you. But such devices are far too dangerous to be deciphered or allowed into human space."

"I see." Gretchen felt ill. "Does your 'unseen struggle' include explaining these things to my Company? Maybe a receipt? Or am I expected to suffer quietly as well?"

"I will do what I can." The old México did not look away, but Gretchen didn't see the slightest hint he would help her, either. She sat down on the forward wheel of the *Gagarin.*

"What do you think will happen now?"

Hummingbird shrugged, squatting easily on the windy ledge. "All we can do is follow her trail and clean up what we can. There will be other . . . apparitions. We will have to break up their patterns, try and return things to their usual course. And quickly too, before we become part of the flow ourselves."

"Do your skills let you tell which boulders should be removed from the 'stream'?"

He nodded sharply. "The *tlamatinime* learns first to *see.* If the gods smile, what I cannot perceive, you will."

"Me?" Gretchen's nose twitched as she made a disbelieving face. "What do you mean *see?*"

"Perceive, then," Hummingbird said in a wry tone. "In the cavern, you felt something was out of place—this is the beginning of the *seeing.* I was surprised at your reaction. Most humans are nearly blind."

Gretchen felt insulted. "I'm a trained, experienced observer, Hummingbird-*tzin.* It's my job to see subtle differences in a substrate, in a dig layer, a field of loose stone and gravel."

"Trained by *science,*" he said, almost dismissively. "Trained with one set of tools at the expense of others. You're a specialist, Anderssen. A tool designed for a single task. Your personnel records are filled with praise, but this is not an archaeological excavation. This world is not depth-tagged or laser-gridded."

"The science you dismiss has built an entire civilization, crow." She tapped the breather mask covering the lower half of her face. "We're alive because of specialized tools. I wouldn't dismiss them as if they were toys!"

Hummingbird looked at his gloved hands, then at her. "Do you believe everything can be measured? Everything can be described?"

"What?" Gretchen was nonplussed. "Well . . . yes, I think so. Eventually. Our tools and techniques are constantly improving."

"I thought so once." Hummingbird turned his hands over, apparently interested in the pattern of the material covering his palms. "But I have learned—at cost, Anderssen, at cost!—this is not true. There are limits to human perception and human science—but those limits do not correspond to the limits of the universe. Not at all."

The old México looked up, gauging the progress of the sun against the dome of heaven.

"Time is passing, Anderssen. Consider this, while we are in flight: We—by we, I mean humans like you and I—exist within a bubble of the known. What we can see or hear or taste or feel. From this we have derived a description. This description is your science. Within the known, we build tools, live our lives, raise our children. Those tools let us manipulate the known, the material.

"But what of the unknown, Anderssen? What about the things we do not perceive? There is a universe of ghosts and shadows just beyond our living sight. Do you doubt the presence of the unseen?"

Gretchen shook her head. "No—I get your point. A human being doesn't even live in the same perceptual universe as a cat. Not without tools to extend vision, sight, smell, hearing. Are you saying your training lets you perceive the infrared or ultraviolet? See as a baleshrike sees? Smell as a truedog smells?"

"No." Hummingbird stood up and shook out his cloak. "I am bound by my physiology, just as you are. My nose—for example—does not have the physical receptors to capture the wealth of molecules a beagle may." He grasped the offending organ between thumb and forefinger. "Anatomy limits me. But laziness . . . laziness blinds men."

"Then what are you talking about?" Gretchen stood and swung open the *Gagarin*'s cabin door. "What do you mean?"

"Did your eyes physically change between the time you first walked out onto that soccer field and today?"

"No." Gretchen climbed into the cockpit of the *Midge* and squirmed into the lumpy seat. "They're probably worse. All right, so I know what to look for. I can recognize patterns—"

In the other aircraft, Hummingbird shook his head sharply. "Not so. The enemy of clear sight *is* accepting patterns in the world around us. To see clearly, you have to let your eyes take in what is truly before you, not allow a lazy mind to fit things into a familiar shape."

Anderssen closed the cabin door and began running through a preflight check. She started to speak and then looked closely at the control panel. Most of the *Gagarin*'s instrumentation was held in a v-pane, but there were certain systems served by archaic-looking dials and switches. *Everything you need to fly without the comp being live*, she realized. Gretchen ran a hand over the console, feeling smooth metal and rubber under her gloved fingertips. Most of the dials had cream-colored backgrounds with red needles or indicators. Flecks of rust were visible where the enamel covering the metal had worn away.

For the first time, she actually *saw* the console and all the minute, tiny details of wear and use. Not the sketchy, abstracted impression she'd had of the control panel before. Almost immediately, Gretchen felt her mind try to draw back—an almost physical sensation—and the sense of limitless clarity faded. She blinked and concentrated, trying to *see* the numbers on one of the dials. Now they were blurry and she started to squint.

"Focus is an enemy," Hummingbird said softly over the comm. "You're trying to limit your field of view in hopes of gaining clarity. Forcing sight won't work."

"How do you train, then?" Gretchen blinked furiously. Her eyes hurt. Her brain hurt! "How do you reach an objective without pursuing a goal?"

"You've already started—in the cavern—when I guided you to a natural posture. When you found a comfortable place to sit." The *nauallis* was starting to sound a little irritated. "We will talk of this again, later. Are your engines warmed up? We should lift off."

"Wait. Why are you showing me these things? Telling me these secrets?"

Hummingbird smiled, white teeth barely visible through the scarred canopy of his ultralight. "My other option is to kill you. But you are alive and a human being and your presence aids me. The universe is connected in odd ways and you might tip a balance in my favor. Besides, if things come to violence, you can get in the way of the enemy for a few seconds."

"Oh my," growled Gretchen, "that is nice. Very nice. Very Imperial sounding."

Hadeishi entered a briefing room sandwiched in between the bridge and the officers' mess. His senior officers stood to attention beside their chairs. Koshō turned sideways and nodded as the *chu-sa* reached the head of the table and set down a v-pad and some printouts.

"Good evening," he said, unsealing his collar. "Sit, gentlemen, sit. We are off duty."

Everyone sat down, though he couldn't say any of them were "at ease." *Sho-i Kohosei* Smith, at the end of the table, was sitting at parade attention, hands clasped tight on an engineer's workpad. Hayes and Engineer-second Yoyontzin were equally stiff. Just to his right, Koshō was watching him evenly, her face expressionless.

"This is not traditional," Hadeishi said, shrugging out of his uniform jacket. "But I think it is necessary." A little old man in a leaf-green-and-brown kimono appeared and took the jacket away. Hadeishi spread out the v-pad and several papers. He looked around the table and pursed his lips. "We have to find this refinery ship swiftly. I fear our current approach will take too long to yield results. So—we need to try something different. Do any of you have any ideas?"

The officers looked nervously at each other, then back at the *chu-sa*. No one spoke. Hadeishi hid an expression of dismay, but he understood their wary surprise. He had served in the Fleet for nearly twenty years, on a dozen ships. In all that time, he'd never attended a staff meeting where the agenda, problems *and* solutions presented had not been decided in advance. A commander might consult with his exec or with senior department heads about specific technical issues but he did not discuss problems in an open forum. Meetings were a venue for the command authority—be he a ship's captain or an admiral—to issue orders, perhaps make a small speech and show honor to the Emperor.

Koshō, in particular, looked as if she'd sat on a porcupine. Hayes was surprised and Yoyontzin was petrified. Only young Smith-*tzin*—who had finally worked through Hadeishi's reference to being "off duty"—had relaxed at all, allowing himself to sit back in the chair.

"Does anyone want tea?" Hadeishi turned away from the table and lifted his chin at the attendant. The little old man blinked in surprise and then scurried off down the corridor to the officers' mess galley. When the *chu-sa* turned back, Koshō and Hayes were staring at him in amazement. "I am having tea," Hadeishi said, emulating Smith and leaning back in his chair.

"Here is our problem," he said, spreading his hands. "We are hunting for a relatively small object in a huge volume filled with a great deal of obscuring debris. Our objective is to find the refinery ship quickly and quietly and remove it, by one means or another, from this system."

The attendant sidled up to the table, attempting to be unobtrusive, and Hadeishi paused. The little old man froze, staring at him in something like horror, as the *chu-sa* gathered up the porcelain cups from the tray and handed them around. Koshō took her cup reflexively, then stared icily at her own hand, which seemed to have betrayed her.

"I'll pour," Hadeishi said to the attendant and waved him away. Clutching the tray to his chest, the little old man backed out of the room, eyes wide in fear. "Patrick, you take a great deal of sugar, I believe?"

"*Hai*," Hayes said weakly, goggling at the *chu-sa*. Hadeishi filled his cup, then pushed a fat green bowl toward him.

"Help yourself." Hadeishi turned politely to Koshō, who had frozen into complete immobility. "This is a particularly good bancha," he said, guiding her cup—still clutched in a tight grip—to the tabletop. Hadeishi caught her eye. "Not the nasty stuff I drink in the morning."

Both of the *sho-sa*'s cheeks were suddenly suffused with two pale rose-colored spots. Hadeishi—though he felt tremendously cheerful—ignored her blush. He filled her cup halfway.

Neither Smith nor Yoyontzin wanted tea. The engineer was hunched down in his seat, trying to hide behind Koshō. The communications officer had finally realized there was a queer tone to the meeting, so he was trying to make himself as small as possible. Hayes had nearly emptied the sugar bowl into his cup before taking a long sip.

"How do we find the refinery quickly?" Hadeishi posed the question again and looked around at them expectantly.

"Not by poking around in the dark with a sharp stick," Hayes muttered, then froze. Koshō had turned her head to glare icily at him. The weapons officer became rather pale.

"I agree," Hadeishi said quietly. Koshō turned her head fractionally, her eyes narrowing.

"We are following Fleet doctrine," she said in a clipped, toneless voice. "Which is sound."

"It's too slow," Hadeishi said, leaning forward. "We don't have time to run down every particle trail and false reading our drones find. We do not have time to quarter this entire belt and peer in the radar shadow of every asteroid. We need to find the refinery *now*."

"Without going to active combat scanning," Koshō stated. Hadeishi nodded.

"What," the *sho-sa* said tentatively, "if we broadcast a message on the commercial comm channels, indicating a systemwide emergency. We could promise not to pursue or attack any ship immediately making gradient to hyperspace."

Hadeishi considered the proposal for a moment. Then he looked at the weapons officer. "Hayes-*tzin*, do you think the commander of the refinery ship would respond to such a message?"

Hayes blinked, stole a look at Koshō and then faced the *chu-sa* again. "Ah . . . probably not, sir. He'd think it was a trick."

"If the *Palenque* made transit immediately upon receiving the message," Koshō said, rather stiffly, "the wildcatters might become worried. The clumsiness of our message could be interpreted as honesty in a moment of crisis, rather than a ruse to draw them out."

"And then?" Hadeishi was almost smiling at his exec. "What happens if they appear on our sensors, engines hot?"

"If they are in weapons range," Koshō said, eyes glittering, "we disable their ship. Huémac's Marines storm the refinery and we bring these criminals before an Imperial court."

Hayes looked questioningly at Hadeishi.

"Unfortunately," the *chu-sa* said, "we must operate under a constraint of silence. A broadcast message is out of the question. We cannot draw attention to ourselves with any kind of broad-spectrum event." Hadeishi nodded to Koshō.

"So we cannot saturate the belt with mines, hoping to drive the refinery out of hiding."

"Very well." Koshō, to her credit, did not seem to have taken the rejection of her plan personally. "Then we will have to scan the entire belt very quickly, hoping to pick the refinery out of all this debris and rubble." The exec looked expectantly at young Smith-*tzin* at the end of the table. The *sho-i ko-hosei* swallowed nervously and nodded to both Hadeishi and Koshō.

"Leave to speak, sir?" Smith's voice was a little thin, but steady.

"Granted!" Hadeishi was impressed with the boy. Most midshipmen in the presence of command authority could barely stand up, much less speak. "You're sure you don't want some tea?"

"I'm fine, Hadeishi-*tzin*." Smith nodded in thanks. "I've been thinking about the same problem the last couple of watches. I mean—we can all see how slowly we're moving now—and I was wondering if there was a way to speed things up, search more of the volume at a time, you know, and I mentioned something to Koshō-*tzin* and she suggested I look at the specifications for the absorptive mesh on the skin of the ship and . . ." Smith had to stop and take a breath.

"*Sho-i Ko-hosei* Smith," Koshō said, smoothly interrupting the midshipman's rush of explanation, "has devised a means of improving the sensitivity of our gravitational field sensors."

"Go on." Hadeishi fought to keep from smiling broadly at his officers. In particular, at Koshō and Smith, who had obviously been trying to anticipate his wishes. *What a blessing is a good exec*, he thought, considering Susan Koshō fondly. *For all her cold demeanor, she is a fine officer.*

"Well, um, sir—you know we have a series of gravitational field sensors which let us track hyperspace transits, since they 'dimple' the g-field in the area where a ship made gradient. We also use them for navigational purposes, to avoid black holes and hyperspace eddies and so on. Well, a ship has mass so there is a faint distortion of the g-field around even the *Cornuelle*. I think . . ." Smith held up a v-pad showing a page of system circuit diagrams and equations. "I think we can tune the g-sensors on the *Cornuelle* to detect the mass displacement of a *Tyr*."

"Even if the refinery drive is shut down?" Hayes raised an eyebrow at the younger officer.

"Yes, Hayes-*tzin*, because we're going to be searching for the g-dimple caused by their antimatter pellet *storage*, not for an active A/M reactor." Smith started to grin, then composed himself.

"Storage? A/M doesn't mass more than any other particle—"

"True, true," Smith interrupted, "but antimatter is difficult to produce, so its packed super-densely in storage—I mean, positive particles are *easy* to find—and that makes a difference we can see. Well, I think we can see."

Hadeishi looked questioningly at Koshō. "Effective range?"

"Five or six light-minutes," she answered. "A very substantial volume."

The *chu-sa* nodded, fixing Smith with a considering stare. "Smith-*tzin*, why don't we use our gravity sensors this way as a matter of course? Why isn't this Fleet doctrine?"

"Speed, sir." Smith's face fell. "There's a lot of data to process. Normally, the system just watches for big differentials—a ship entering normal space throws a huge, easy to detect spike—but we need to reconfigure for a mass/density differential." He paged through his v-pad to another screen of equations and diagrams. "In this case, we're looking for an object making a sharper than expected g-dimple in local spacetime. So we've got to program the sensor comps to look for a specific, rather subtle scenario. And processing all this is going to take hours."

"How many?" Hadeishi was watching Koshō.

"Twenty to thirty hours to complete the first scan," the exec answered. Obviously, she'd already quizzed Smith to within an inch of his life about this proposal. "We need to extract all the gravitation and density readings from the navigation survey, then build a model of the area within range, then resample with the reconfigured g-sensor array. *Then* we can see if something falls out into our hands."

The *chu-sa* started to frown. "How extensively will sensor systems be degraded by this change?"

Smith swallowed nervously and looked hopefully at Koshō. The corner of the exec's wine-colored lips twitched. Hadeishi recognized the motion as the equivalent of a wry smile.

"While the array is in this mode, *Chu-sa*, we will be blind to gravitational events outside the immediate area of our detection sweep."

"So a ship could make gradient into, or out of, the system and we would be unaware."

Koshō inclined her head gracefully. "Yes. But inside the five to six light-minute range, we will have an excellent picture of the g-field and any related events."

"How long to switch the array between normal operation and this special mode?"

Smith shrank down in his chair, but Koshō merely gazed steadily at the *chu-sa*. "Five to six hours for the initial changeover, Hadeishi-*tzin*. Each skin array node will have to be reprogrammed and tuned by hand. We will, however, retain a comp image of the previous configuration for each node. Then, if we have to reset the nodes, we can do so very quickly."

Hadeishi gave her a look. He'd gone through more than one shipboard comp upgrade in his time. "Very quickly" meant one thing during normal operations and quite another in the heat of combat. He had a momentary vision of plunging into battle with the shipskin sensor array out of action. *That would be unfortunate.*

"Hayes-*tzin*, what do you think of this approach?"

The weapons officer's broad face was conflicted. "I'm worried, sir. If we take the g-array offline we'll be partially blind. I don't like that. On the other hand, we'll be able to search the belt far faster than we can now with the drones. And this way will be really, really quiet."

"What if we segment the shipskin nodes and only reconfigure half of them for this detailed search?" Hadeishi mused. "Leaving the other set for normal sensor work?"

The suggestion drew a slight frown from Koshō and hopeful looks from Hayes and Smith.

"Initial setup will be more complicated," the exec said. "We will have to divide the sensor feeds to the bridge into two discrete sets, which will require some work. The regular array will be reduced in capability, but we will not lose long-range g-spike detection."

"Combat effectiveness, Hayes-*tzin*?" Hadeishi raised an eyebrow at the weapons officer.

"Reduced, sir. Though truthfully there's a great deal of redundancy in the sensor array. We could probably lose half of the nodes and only be reduced ten to fifteen percent."

"Very well. *Sho-sa* Koshō, I entrust this project to you—with the able assistance of Smith-*tzin*, of course—and expect regular status reports. This has priority over other duties. *Thai-i* Hayes, pull in the Outriders for refueling and a maintenance check. Yoyontzin—" the engineer-second started with surprise and tentatively peered around the slim, stiff shape of the exec. "Master's Mate Helsdon and his section are reassigned to provide Koshō-*tzin* with the hands she needs to change out the sensor array. *You* will take charge of the Outrider refit when the drones are back in bay."

The engineer-second looked a little queasy. Hadeishi's eyes narrowed fractionally. *I'll have to discuss this one with Isoroku when he's back aboard. But not now.*

Hadeishi gave them all a stern look, saying "The Emperor expects you to do your duty!"

Then he stood up, forcing them to do the same. "Dismissed."

Koshō did not join the general stampede for the door, taking a moment to straighten her already perfectly arranged v-pad and notes on the table in front of her.

Hadeishi waited for the passageway door to close before he spoke. "Yes, Susan? Is something bothering you?"

"Will you be holding more of these meetings in the future?" The woman's face showed even less expression than usual. "Will you be soliciting comment and advice from junior officers?"

"If circumstances warrant," Hadeishi replied, wondering at her choice of words. They had a familiar ring to them. . . . *Ah yes*, he remembered, recalling an Academy first-year course, *circumstances of sedition and mutiny aboard ship.* "We will not," he continued, "be discussing opinions of command authority competence or operational concerns."

"I am very glad to hear that, *Chu-sa*." Koshō seemed to relax a fraction, though it was very difficult to tell. "Did you know Smith-*tzin* and I had been working on this g-array reconfig?"

Hadeishi nodded. "I did. Main comp informed me when the *sho-i ko-hosei* requsted data about systems outside of his security area. I saw you had approved the request."

"You said nothing."

"There was no reason to say anything, *Sho-sa*. Both of you are fine officers and understood the problem at hand. I saw no benefit to be gained from interfering in your work."

Now Koshō did relax and Hadeishi felt a sudden warm affection for her. *She worries about the boy*, he thought. "You did well to encourage him, Susan. He's very bright."

"*Hai*," she said, making a properly polite bow. "But he does not understand Fleet tradition."

"I know. He's still young and he's only served aboard the *Cornuelle*." Hadeishi sighed, stroking his beard. "I fear he will not do so well if transferred to another ship. We will have to help him if something like that happens."

As a general rule, Fleet did not like to shift crews around from ship to ship. The Great Clans, in particular, resisted attempts to reform the recruitment and staffing policies of Fleet. However, as men and women advanced in rank, they were often required to change posting to secure the proper duty slot. Within a clan-squadron, a junior officer would be taken care of by higher-ranking relatives. In such a case, Smith would be posted to a heavier-gauge ship—a battle cruiser or a dreadnought—where he could find clan-relatives to guide and protect him in the new environment.

The *Cornuelle*, unfortunately, was on detached duty—another result of

Hadeishi's low status in Fleet—and if Smith were promoted as he should be, then a posting to an entirely different squadron would be inevitable. Circumstances weighed against the bright young Englishman finding as understanding and lenient a commander as Hadeishi.

"We could keep him here, *Chu-sa*," Koshō offered.

Hadeishi shrugged. "We've a full allotment of junior lieutenants, unless someone dies or requests a transfer off-ship."

"What about Yoyontzin?"

Hadeishi's lips quirked into a half-smile. He looked sideways at Koshō. "You think he will suffer an accident in the coming action? A regrettable incident with a shorting panel or falling structural beam?"

Koshō drew herself up stiffly. "Of course not! I suspect *he* may request a transfer when this duty patrol is complete."

"Well," Hadeishi said, giving her a considering look. "I would certainly give such a request my full attention."

The exec nodded, gathered up her v-pad and notes and bowed.

"Dismissed." Hadeishi watched her stride out. *Poor Yoyontzin*, he thought in amusement. *Caught between Koshō and Isoroku . . . like a bug between granite and steel.*

Two *Midges* flew south, southeast—tiny silver specks against the dark immensity of the Escarpment. Sharp peaks towered thousands of meters above them, a sheer wall of basalt with sandstone feet. Deep canyons split the face of the range, spewing out kilometers of rubble to be swallowed by enormous dunes below. Gretchen fought to keep her eyes from straying to the horizon. When they did, her stomach twisted with a start of fear. The horizon tilted at a strange angle, one entirely at odds with her inner ear and the sensors on the *Gagarin*.

The mass of the mountain range to her right was so great that "down" had shifted, swinging off to an angle pointing at the base of the Escarpment. Hummingbird was suffering from the same problem—every so often his *Midge* would twitch over as he tried to correct an unexpected, unfelt bank.

Progress had been slow all day, but the navigation v-pane on Gretchen's console now showed they were very close to slot canyon number twelve. Russovsky's logbook had a note indicating the geologist had set down inside the canyon, where there was a sheltering cave. A second entry reported discovering a "cylinder."

Anderssen scowled at the tiny shape of the *nauallis's* ultralight. The México had remained silent all day despite her attempts to engage him in conversation. Hundreds of kilometers had rolled away under them as they flew past jagged peaks, steeply plunging canyons and endless bony ridges. Gretchen felt oppressed by the lack of human contact, but she'd held her tongue for the last six hours. In that time she'd thought a great deal about what the old crow had claimed in the cave. While Gretchen didn't doubt *something* had happened and had no doubt the *nauallis* held closely guarded secrets, she thought his out-of-hand dismissal of human-built technology was dangerously self-centered.

How could we survive down here? She grumbled to herself, *without spacecraft and ultralights and pressure masks and z-suits?* Millions of tools—an entire civilization—specialists by the planetfull . . . all of which were sustained, informed and generated by *human* science and technology.

Is he jealous? she wondered. *The* talamatinime *must be descendants of the priestly caste of ancient Azteca.* Curiosity stirred an eager head and she wondered just what kind of secret history—what hidden, almost-forgotten tales—had been handed down from priest to priest over the fifteen hundred years since the first Nisei merchant landed on the coast of Matlalzinca with a shipload of iron ingots, steel sword blanks and huge, long-legged riding "hornless deer." *A tale worth knowing,* Gretchen thought, biting her lip. *So much of the public record was lost in the Second Blow. . . .*

Despite an angry desire to shout at the thick-headed old man over the comm, Anderssen restrained herself. *We'll have to land eventually,* she thought grimly. Countless questions had come to mind since their last conversation on the slopes of Prion. *And then I'll sit on him if I have—*

"Hummingbird, look out!" Gretchen's voice rang thin and shrill in the cabin of the *Gagarin.*

The *nauallis*'s *Midge* had suddenly jerked sideways, toward the looming wall of the Escarpment. What at first seemed to be a black crevice in the mountainside was now visible as a huge canyon. Hummingbird's ultralight was sweeping toward the opening at tremendous speed. Gretchen immediately hauled right on the control stick and *Gagarin* swung round with gratifying speed. She stared out of the port side of the aircraft, searching for a telltale—*There!*

Far below, the sand was in constant motion, gusting thin streamers of reddish dust toward the face of the Escarpment. The dunes made sort of a nozzle where speeding clouds of grit rolled across the valley floor. Anderssen cursed, realizing they had come unawares upon the mouth of the canyon.

Static jammed the comm band and Hummingbird's *Midge* had disappeared from view. Gretchen stabbed a gloved finger at the control panel and the nav pane appeared. Keeping one eye on the controls and the other on the looming wall of basalt ahead, Gretchen saw the other ultralight had gone down near the mouth of the canyon. Winking amber lights indicated some kind of damage. Gritting her teeth, Andersen let the *Gagarin* spin into a precipitous spiral.

The little aircraft swept down out of the sky, skimming across the tops of the dunes. Sand and grit rattled against the windows and Gretchen angled away from the funnel-path centered on the entrance to the canyon. Her sensors now showed nearly a two hundred-k wind rushing into the slot. The *nauallis* had flown right into an invisible wall of air.

"Hummingbird, can you hear me?" Gretchen powered up the comm and began broadcasting on multiple channels. *Maybe microwave will work.* "It's Anderssen, I'm coming in to get you."

The *Gagarin* sideslipped low across the valley floor, droning up and down over dune after dune. The wall of the Escarpment rose to blot out the sky. Gretchen flew into shadow and the wind grew massively worse. The *Gagarin* shuddered in the twisting crosscurrents, wings rippling and flexing. The invisible river kept trying to suck her into the canyon mouth.

Waves of red and tan sand ended abruptly in a glassy, polished wall of black and gray stone. Gretchen pulled up, her stomach doing loop-de-loops, and circled. Peering out of the side door, she caught sight of a glittering rainbow flash very near the canyon entrance. Swallowing, mouth dry with fear, Anderssen rolled the stick right and *Gagarin* heeled over as gently as a turning shrike.

"Careful," she muttered, keeping an eye on the radar display. The entrance to the canyon flickered on the panel and the kilometers between her and the deadly opening spiraled down quickly. A kilometer short, she turned again, away from the cliffs of the Escarpment and touched down on the side of a sloping dune. *Gagarin* slid to a halt on a thirty-degree slope, though Gretchen's stomach told her the rippled sand was as level as a kitchen floor.

Engines growling, Gretchen retracted the wings and disengaged the brakes. Bouncing over the slope, sand spurting away from the wheels, she drove the aircraft up over the crest of the ridge. Three more dune ridges separated her from Hummingbird, but Anderssen took her time, letting the ultralight jounce along, all three fat wheels shimmying in the heavy sand.

The other *Midge* came into view, canted sideways, one wing crumpled into hard-packed gravel. Hummingbird rose as *Gagarin* approached, *djellaba* snapping around his legs. He waved. Gretchen waved back and let the ultralight *putt-putt* to a stop.

"Are you all right?" Local comm was awash with warbling static and queer shrieking echoes.

The *nauallis* nodded, tapping his earpiece, and began trudging across the sand toward her. Wind hissed past the door and whined across *Gagarin*'s wings. A con-

stant rattle of grit pattered against the canopy. Gretchen pulled a heavy lever set
into the floor and felt a sharp *thump-thump* as the sand anchors fired into the dune.

"... hear me?" Hummingbird's voice cut across the interference. "Anderssen?"

"I hear you." Gretchen swung the door open, feeling a buffet from the gusting
wind. Her right hand was already dragging a tool belt out from under the seat.
"How bad is the damage?"

"Manageable. Perhaps." Hummingbird ducked under the wing, his head
tightly wrapped in the folds of his *kaffiyeh*. Even at such short range his voice was
distorted by the comm cutting in and out. "Both pumps switched over, so not
much H_2 was lost, but the wing and landing gear are badly damaged."

Gretchen gave him a grim look, shook her head and began making her way in
the heavy wind toward the damaged ultralight. Hummingbird stared after her,
then followed, head bent against the blowing sand. Though she couldn't see his
face, the old México looked worried.

"Push!" Anderssen growled, putting her shoulder against the bent wing. Hummingbird was right by her side and together, straining and grunting with effort,
they managed to free the honeycombed length of composite and hexsteel from the
clinging sand. The entire *Midge* tipped over, rocking back on the port and forward
wheels. Wind gusted, threatening to tear the aircraft from their grasp. Gretchen
peered under the wing and her face screwed up into a grimace. The starboard
landing gear was twisted into something very much like a pretzel. She looked sideways at Hummingbird. "Can you hold this weight?"

He nodded, legs braced in the sand, broad shoulders against the underside of
the wing.

Anderssen scrambled around under the tail and threw open the cargo door.
Two heavy canvas duffels were squeezed inside. She grabbed both by their straps
and hauled them out. Slinging one over her shoulder, Gretchen staggered along the
length of the unbroken wing, the second duffel in her arms. Wheezing with effort,
she dumped the heavy bag on the ground beneath the wingtip and shrugged the
other into her hands. A recessed hook for a ground anchor flipped down from the
underside of the airfoil, giving her enough purchase to hang the duffel. The entire
Midge shivered and Gretchen heard Hummingbird cough in surprise as weight
lifted from his shoulders.

A moment later, the second duffel was adding its weight to the counterbalance
and Gretchen could nip around to starboard again. The *Midge* creaked into precarious balance on the two good wheels. Hummingbird was holding the wingtip
steady with both hands, a questioning look on his face.

"Keep hold," Gretchen said as she dug into her tools. She found a powered wrench, tested the tool—which responded with a high-pitched burring sound—and smiled. "Just for another thirty minutes or so."

Night came on suddenly in the shadow of the Escarpment. One moment Gretchen was working in a diffuse blue dimness, the next everything had plunged into complete darkness. She stopped, a welder sparking blue-white in her hand, and looked up. Hummingbird had found a cave, a deep overhang a kilometer and a half from the mouth of the slot, where they'd dragged the *Midge*s and their gear. Some shelter from the gusting wind was better than nothing.

"I need some light," Gretchen said into the gloom. There was a click on the comm circuit and the bright white glare of a camp lantern set on high flared around her. "Too bright . . . thanks."

The circle of illumination dimmed to a reasonable level. Hummingbird's feet appeared out of shadow, boots crunching on scattered, shalelike debris covering the floor of the overhang. The *nauallis* squatted, watching her work.

Gretchen had laid out an old blanket covered with the bits and pieces of the broken landing gear on top of one of the hextile pads. The main strut had snapped clean off when Hummingbird's *Midge* corkscrewed into the dunes, and the rest had been badly twisted by the impact. Gretchen was straightening each section of hexsteel with a set of wrenches and a jimmied-up guide. The little welder was on its last legs, but had lasted long enough to get most of the sections patched back together.

"You've done this before," Hummingbird said, fingers intertwined between his knees.

"All the time." Gretchen adjusted her goggles and flicked the welder to life. The burning white point hissed and spat, but there was very little smoke in such an anemic atmosphere. "Mechanical things are born to break in the field—no matter how new they are. Mostly the Company sends me places where there's no support—no handy machine shops, no supply dumps, no warranty service."

She grinned, thinking of the dig water filtration tower on Ugarit. Eighty-six light-years was a long way for a Poseidon SureClean Filtration Systems tech to travel to replace gunked filters or a bacteria separation unit which had failed to separate the more vigorous organisms living in the brown flood of the Hagit River. "You have to be handy with fixing things if you want to survive."

Gretchen set down the main strut, now repaired, and picked among the parts of the wheel housing. "Growing up in high timber on Aberdeen helped, though. Most students out of university don't know how to strip an engine or weld or . . . well, do any of the things we had to do at home."

"It's good you followed me." Hummingbird's voice had a funny tone and

Gretchen looked up, wondering if he were getting sick or something. Then she realized he was trying to be friendly.

"You're welcome," Anderssen said, after thinking about it for a moment. "You needed help, even if you didn't admit it. Like I said before, I can't stand by and let someone else carry all the load. Now—I don't mean to be nosy—but you're used to having an Imperial warship on call, aren't you? Filled with Marines in combat armor and assault shuttles, waiting for your signal."

The *nauallis* nodded, dipping his head. "Sometimes," he said, "an entire Fleet carrier battle group."

"We don't have one here," Gretchen said, looking up. Her voice was flat and tight. "We don't have spares and mechanics and a medbay an hour away. It's just the two of us. So be careful, old crow. You were stupidly lucky today."

"I know. . . . I was watching for the canyon mouth and didn't . . . I didn't notice the warning lights on the radar panel until about a second before I hit the edge of the wind."

Gretchen's mouth twitched and she held back a hoarse, mocking laugh. *Had trouble* seeing, *did we? Interesting . . .*

Hummingbird shifted, rolling back on his haunches. In the encompassing light, she could see his dark green eyes clearly, surrounded by a sea of fine wrinkles. "Tomorrow, if the weather permits, we'll need to go into the canyon. I went down to the edge of the funnel a little while ago—the wind has died down—so if we wait until full dark, we should be able to go in."

"Without being blown away." Gretchen nodded, lining up the repaired wheel housing bracket with the main strut. "Do you know what time the wind starts up?"

"Before dawn," he replied, rubbing the back of his head. "Doctor Smalls made a study of the wind patterns in the canyons—"

"He told me," Gretchen interjected. She slid the bracket firmly onto the strut and began repairing the broken weld line connecting the two. Sparks flared and hissed. "We'll only have a couple of hours to look around." Anderssen paused. "I'm coming with you into the canyon?"

"Yes." There was a *hiss-hiss* sound. "I think two would be better than one."

"Really?" Gretchen gave him a sharp glance. Not a glare, exactly, but enough to make him look away. "Will I need to be *quiet* again?"

"I don't know." Hummingbird looked out into the darkness. "There is a queer feeling here—something is close by, but I cannot feel more than a *pressure*. But everything here—rock, sand, cliffs, even the air—feels very, very old."

Gretchen suppressed an involuntary shiver. "The . . . dreaming power?"

Hummingbird did not answer, his attention fixed on the night. Beyond the mouth of the overhang, the curved ridges of endless dunes marched off toward a starry horizon. After a moment he twitched his shoulders and turned his attention back to her. "Sometimes, Anderssen-*tzin*, these . . . powers . . . have a subtle influence. A matter and degree of atoms. There are . . . I was once in a place where every action fell just a little foul. If you stepped, you came up just a millimeter short. If you reached, your target was always a fraction away." He shook his head from side to side. "A single misstep is nothing . . . but a million errors compounded?"

"You escaped." Gretchen held herself to have no *powers*, but she could feel an almost visible pain radiating from the man—from his tightly clenched fingers, his hunched shoulders—like a chill flame.

"Others—many others—did not." Hummingbird clicked his teeth together. "I was one of few. Anderssen . . ." The *nauallis* stopped, apparently unable to force his thought into words, then they came with a rush. "I . . . I need your help. I can teach you, show you, something of the world I see—quickly, too. Would you . . . do you want to *see?*"

Gretchen was nonplussed and carefully turned off the welder before setting her tools down on the blanket. Hummingbird had grown still, his green eyes shadowed.

"What do you mean by *see?*"

"As I do. You will be able to . . . apprehend the pattern of things, see that which is obscured by the overwhelming detail of the world, become aware of what is invisible to the lazy eye. I hope you will be able to become properly *still* as well."

Gretchen felt cold and hot at the same time. Her heart was racing. "How? Don't such things take years of training, meditation, effort?" *What will I see? What secrets will be revealed?*

Hummingbird reached into the folds of his cloak and drew out a small plain paper packet held between his fore- and middle fingers. The *nauallis* looked at the packet grimly. "Sometimes there are shorter paths than those trod by tradition."

The packet seemed to swell in Gretchen's sight, becoming enormous. She could hear the stiff paper scratching and rustling against something inside. *Grains of sand. A powder.*

"And in return? What do you expect of me for this gift?"

Hummingbird set the packet down at the edge of the blanket. "Go with me into the canyon. I want every advantage at my side, Anderssen, including you."

Gretchen shook her head. She felt clammy—and afraid—from head to toe. She licked her lips. "I have to finish fixing this landing gear. I'll think about it."

"Very well." Hummingbird rose and disappeared into the gloom outside the cone of light. The packet remained, glowing a soft cream, at the edge of the blanket. Gretchen turned the welder back on and resumed fitting the landing gear back together.

The stars had moved far in their slow, stately dance before Anderssen finished repairing the *Midge*. She carefully brushed herself down and limped stiffly back to the cave. Her right leg was cramping. The old México was at the mouth of the overhang, face to the night, legs crossed. Their camp lantern had been dialed down to a bare gleam against the rear wall. Gretchen sat down next to him and took a long drink from her water tube.

"Hummingbird," she said, "What does a judge—a *tlamatinime*—really do?"

"Those are two questions, Anderssen. You are making idle conversation."

"No, I want to know. Are all judges like you?"

Hummingbird laughed. "That is impossible. There is only one of me. Each judge is different as stones from stones or clouds from clouds."

"Do all judges know these secrets you've told me?"

"No." Hummingbird settled back against the wall of the overhang, staring out across the vast empty plain. "A judge has a duty, to see the people live a proper life, one pleasing the gods and benefiting all. The evil, the duplicitous, the amoral—the judge must take these influences away from the people, for they divert men and women from the right path. A judge must abide by the laws of the gods and of men; he must live a strong life. His example is worth a thousand punishments."

Anderssen began scratching lines in the sand between her boots. "You do not seem to be the usual sort of judge."

"No." Gretchen caught a faint impression of grief on Hummingbird's face. "My burden is heavier. I and others like me watch at the edge of human knowledge—in empty places like this—where our ignorance may lead to disaster. Individual human lives, in raw truth, mean nothing, but the race—our people—must live, and this requires vigilance and protection at all times."

Gretchen shook her head, dismayed. "Your universe seems filled with threat and horror. Is it worth it to live in such a place? Do I want to *see* such things? Do you really think humanity must be coddled in this way? Wouldn't—"

Hummingbird turned, eyes flashing. Gretchen felt his disapproval like a physical blow.

"You are very young, if you think men and women do not need protection. If you really believe this, you should take off your z-suit."

"Peace! Peace, old crow." Gretchen raised her hands. Her face grew still and Hummingbird—who had been about to speak sharply—waited instead.

"I have been thinking about my children," she said. "My mother and I—all the adults on our steading—watch after and protect *them*. Why am I angry if you watch over the Empire and all the sons and daughters of man?" Gretchen's mouth quirked into a wry smile, opening her palm toward him. "On the mountain, you expressed a low opinion of my science, of *tools*. But you are a societal tool your-self—a very, very specialized one—a soldier of the mind rather than guns or steel."

Even in the darkness, Gretchen could tell the *nauallis's* expression became sour.

"I am not making fun of you," she said, unsealing a pocket on her vest. The packet of paper unfolded under clumsy, gloved fingertips. Inside was a glittering powder. In the starlight, Gretchen thought the crystals burned a golden color. "You are aware of your purpose, which is far more than I could say. Do I take this dry or mix with water?"

The *nauallis* shifted, head turning towards her. Both goggle lenses caught the lantern light and shone brilliant silver. "Put it under your tongue. Let it dissolve."

Gretchen leaned her head back, fist cupped over her mouth. There was a sharp bitter taste.

"Now, you should lie down." Hummingbird was at her side, guiding her into the cave. His voice grew distant, then louder again, before fading away entirely. Darkness closed around her, a comfortable, heavy old blanket.

Indefinable time passed.

Gretchen became aware of a single voice echoing in a void. She tried to open her eyes, thinking dawn had come and Hummingbird was calling her to wake, but she found only limitless darkness, unbroken by any source of light. There was nothing to touch or smell, taste or feel. Only echoing sound, only the one voice—almost familiar—tense and irritable. Gretchen realized the sound was a man—a very old man speaking in a sonorous, trained way—arguing bitterly.

Immediately, the voice split into two. A young woman made a sharp, angry reply.

"Even the least organism must adapt to changing circumstance! Everyone in service to the Mirror knows you plead the poor mouth to the ruling council and the colonial office, saying the *naualli* are stretched too thin."

"We are!" The elderly man let his full voice boom in response. "The Empire is too large for us to protect—changes will have to be made—"

"Abandonment, you mean." Acid bitterness etched the woman's voice. "Reserving the *naualli* to watch over the 'important' worlds, the México colonies, the Fleet! What of the other settlements? You will leave millions of humans with-out even the slightest protection."

"We do not have enough men to watch every squatter's camp and unlicensed mining station." Gretchen could tell the elderly man was entirely sure of himself and his policy. Certainty throbbed in every perfectly enunciated syllable. "We hold a hundred worlds which *are not full!* Even on older colonies like Tlaxcallan and

Shinjuku there is room for millions. Those worlds are already watched, already guarded by the *tlamatinime*. Without more judges, we dare do nothing else."

"Then," the woman said, drawing a breath, "let us help."

"No." The man's voice was sharp and firm.

"Change the policy," the woman pleaded. "Let the *tititil* go out among the people. Let us watch in darkness, as the *naualli* do." Her tone changed, once more veering into anger. "Abandoning the frontier colonies will suffocate the Empire. You know as well as I what will happen to fresh populations sent to Tlaxcallan— or Shinjuku or Budokan—they will find only the lowest professions open to them. Doctors and scientists will toil in laundries or dig in the fields. They will be servants!"

"These are not matters for us to decide," the man said patronizingly. "Each man—and each woman—finds their own way in the world. Only the survival of the race is our concern."

The woman made an almost familiar hissing sound. "You don't care about the race. You only care about your *calmecac* friends and the hunger of the *pochteca* companies for cheap labor! What organism can thrive in an ever-shrinking niche? Nothing! If you cared about the race, you'd let us train alongside the men and stand watch as they do."

"Foolishness." A faint thread of irritation wove into the man's voice. "Women and men do *not* train together. The ancient traditions are wise to forbid such things. Like to like is the proper path. So it has been, so it will be." There was a creaking sound and Gretchen wondered in confusion where a wooden chair had come from. *There are no chairs in our cave.*

"You will return to your classes and duties, Papalotl. We will not speak of this again."

The elderly man's voice held a tone of complete finality. Gretchen strained to hear more, but the two voices dissolved into only one and Anderssen recognized the sound, at last, as Hummingbird muttering under his breath.

Without any kind of transition—no slow lightening, no sudden brilliance— Gretchen was staring at the roof of the overhang, her gaze fixed upon gray and black stone. The dark, striated rock was split with dozens of crevices and fissures. She could see the way each layer of clay had been compressed by the eons of terrible pressure into flat sheets with unexpected clarity. The violence of the mountain range's creation had tilted the ancient sediment, exposing the edges of the layers to the wind from the east. Now they eroded, millimeter by millimeter, and shaled away from the rooftop a finger's width at a time. Gretchen became uneasy, then almost frantic, realizing she could pick out the smallest detail of the eroding stone.

She could even see the faint, shining presence of minute Ephesian stoneflow-ers growing in cracks between the slabs. She could see them *moving* as the light of the sun began to gild the roof of the overhang. Though Gretchen was unaware of making a noise, there was suddenly a sharp gasp of pain echoing in her ears.

A shadow moved on the ceiling, almost lost among the crevices. She heard boots crunching on sand. Gretchen rolled her head to the side, feeling strangely empty, as though everything inside her body had been drawn out through a very small straw.

Hummingbird approached, silhouetted against the rising sun. Behind him, the wings of both *Midges* were shining with fabulous rainbow brilliance.

For an instant, as the shadow moved toward her, Gretchen saw something strange. A shifting cloud of Hummingbirds filled the mouth of the cave. Some wore their *djellaba* over one shoulder, some had none, the z-suits of some were dark, some light. Some of the figures had long hair, some short. One indistinct shape had pale skin. The sound of boots on gravel grew deafening, then subsided.

The old México leaned over her, smoky green eyes concerned. His mouth opened, one hand reaching down to touch her shoulder. Smoke billowed from between his teeth, curling around his goggles and lean, weathered face.

Gretchen closed her eyes, head thudding back on the blanket. She welcomed onrushing darkness with vast relief.

Magdalena leaned forward on one paw, yellow eyes intent on the main v-pane.

"What is he doing? Where's Doctor Anderssen?" Parker slouched against the control panel, his thin body enveloped in a big, bulky field jacket. He looked cold and a little ill, though the bridge was really very warm from the ring of heaters around the command station.

"She must be inside the cave," Maggie replied, adjusting the light levels of the feed. The dawn line had just passed over the eastern side of the Escarpment and everything was terribly washed-out. The figure of Hummingbird could be seen moving around the tied-down ultralights. The México knelt momentarily beside both of the *Midge*s. "He's checking the sand anchors."

Even in the jerky, disrupted image on the panel, Magdalena could tell there was a fierce wind lashing against the cliffs. Less than two kilometers away, a boiling cloud of yellow-red dust raged against the Escarpment. Sheets of sand roared across the valley floor and funneled down into a terrifying-looking standing cone at the mouth of the canyon.

Hummingbird turned and scuttled back beneath the overhang, the tail of his cloak snapping in the violent air.

"Looks rough," Parker said, chewing on his fingernails. "Those anchors had better hold. . . ."

"He's checked them twice already since the sun rose." Magdalena adjusted the camera view again, trying to get a low enough angle to look beneath the overhang. The image changed, but not enough. "*Ssssh!* Curse warband leader Hadeishi for trying to crash our satellites!"

Parker tapped on one of the secondary panels and grimaced at the resulting screen. "Almost no propellant left."

"No." Maggie let out a steam-kettle hiss of disgust. "I managed to stop them from degrading too much, but all I can do now is reorient their point of view. Some of the others are already deep in the atmosphere—they'll burn up soon. We'll go blind, eyes gouged out one at a time."

"Still no comm?" Parker started to chew on his other hand. Magdalena stared at him in disgust—his weak claws were already worn down to repulsive pink nubs.

"No—I was talking to Gretchen several days ago and we were cut off. I think the old crow is trying to impose comm silence. . . . Will you *stop doing that?*"

"What?" The pilot stared at her in surprise. Maggie's paw blurred in the air and seized his hand, turning over the ruined fingernails. "Oh . . . I just need a tabac, you know. Makes me nervous to . . . not have any." He grimaced.

Magdalena let go of his hand, then wiped her paw on one of the blankets surrounding her. "Bitter smoke means so much to you?"

"Yeah." Parker looked a little queasy and rubbed his wrist. "I'll stop." He put both hands in the pockets of his jacket. "So—hey—don't *Midge*-class ultralights act as a local comm relay? We could tap in and listen to what they're saying."

"Yes," Maggie growled, curling up in her nest again. "Which is all shut down. I suppose they have suit-to-suit comm working, but I've tried opening a long-range link through the peapods and there's no response. Feather-brain has everything locked up tight."

"What about accessing a backup system?" Parker looked painfully earnest. Both of his hands, flat-looking fingers and all, were out of the jacket pockets and being rubbed together as if he were cold. "You used the standard long-range high-band, right? Isn't there a secondary system on these aircraft?"

"Sometimes." Maggie gave the pilot an inscrutable look. "But the peapods do not mount microwave emitters. There's no way to punch an area transmission through the atmosphere."

"Really?" Parker started to smirk. He pointed at the main display. "How are you getting a transmission back from your satellites?"

Maggie showed him a full set of teeth, which did not properly impress the pilot. After a moment she relented, saying "To reduce emissions I am using a point-to-point laser link."

"You mean," Parker said, grinning, "to get around the main array lockout. And keep engineer stoneface from noticing your violation of the judge's orders."

"Maybe." Maggie stirred in her blankets and bone-white claws make a sharp, skittering *tik-tik-tik* on the panel as she queried the peapods. "A highband query failed to draw a response from the *Midge* onboard comm. So if we try a laser we'll have to drop a whisker right on the comm port, which seems very unlikely if we're firing from orbit and trying to hit a port which is probably underneath the wing."

"Not at all!" Parker seemed to have forgotten his tabac sticks and slid over the panel to stand beside Magdalena. "Look, let's bring up the mechanical schematic from the repair bay—not the standard manual, mind—but Pâtecatl's record of modifications she'd made herself."

The Hesht and the human both began looking through the dead engineer's records, searching for maintenance records concerning the expedition ultralights.

An hour later Magdalena coughed in delight and brought up a hand-annotated schematic on the command panel. Parker squinted at the diagram and smiled himself.

"That's it." The pilot ran a thin, tabac-stained finger over a layout of the *Midge* tail assembly, squinting to read a block of annotated text. "This is a military-surplus comm aperture bolted to the rear engine housing. Which is great." He frowned. "But why?"

"To communicate with the ship," Magdalena said, eyes bare sodium-yellow slits. "With the *Palenque*. Look at the other *Midge*." A claw stabbed at the image on the main display. Both ultralights were leaning hard against the cables holding them to the sand. Hummingbird's aircraft, despite the patched wing, was obviously newer and lacked the worn, battered appearance of Russovsky's aircraft. Seen from above, there were other differences—the extra comm aperture, larger air intakes, reinforced tail pylons. . . .

"Pâtecatl and Russovsky must have been busy." Parker fumbled in his pocket, but found nothing, not even a gum wrapper. "Crap. Stupid Marines. . . . Okay, see if you can get a lock with a peapod laser! If you can, we'll be set."

"Perhaps." Magdalena began sending a new set of codes to the satellites. She hummed as she worked, a deep rumbling sound in her chest. Parker became nervous after listening for a bit and sidled off the bridge.

By the time he returned, looking even more morose than before, the Hesht was watching as a targeting overlay wandered jerkily across the video feed from the surface. Hummingbird was nowhere to be seen and the wind had died down to intermittent gusts. Parker stared at the screen, then turned to Maggie with a perplexed expression. "What's going on?"

"Comp on a peapod is about as smart as a leaf-eater," she said, flashing both incisors. "It's having a hard time finding the comm aperture."

"Guide it to lock-on yourself," Parker said irritably. His right hand moved toward the control panel.

Magdalena raised a silver-frosted eyebrow at him. Long whiskers curving back around her face twitched in amusement. "How far away are we from the planet?"

"Oh. Yeah." Parker slumped against the console again. The *Palenque* was steadily accelerating away from the third planet. "How much lag is there?"

"Three light-minutes," she replied, turning her attention back to the screen. The targeting indicator was jumping from spot to spot, wildly painting the top of the *Midge*, the rocks, blowing sand, the left wheel as it groped to find the aperture receiver. "We'll just have to wait. Shouldn't take long."

Five minutes passed with Parker squirming like a kit who had to find some fresh dirt. Then the scatter-search pattern implemented by the peapod comp hopped into lock with the aperture. There was a cheerful chiming sound and a new v-pane opened on Maggie's panel as the peapod negotiated a channel with the *Midge*.

A sharp beep followed and Maggie frowned at the v-pane.

"I think we've got a lock," she announced in a dissapointed tone, "but the responder laser is not working properly." The Hesht scrolled through a log, whiskers flat against her head. "This model has a two-part system," she explained after a moment, indicating a sub-schematic. "The receptor itself can modulate a reflected signal along the path of the incoming beam, but only for basic comm etiquette. Real data return is handled by a second, separate laser. But we're not getting any response at all. I think this other laser is blocked out by Hummingbird's comm lockdown."

"So," Parker said, his brief excitement dampened. "We can only talk one way? How do we get any data back?"

"I don't know." Magdalena frowned at her displays. Luckily, Hummingbird had not emerged from the cave while the laser-whisker was gyrating across the landscape. The only motion visible below was the slow rocking of both ultralights in the wind. "I could send sets of command codes blindly, but . . ." She hissed, picking at her left upper incisor with the tip of a claw. "All we see are the ultralights and their immediate area. We need something to change visually in response to our signal. Ah!"

Her claw stabbed at the v-panel, running along the grainy, pixilated front edge of an ultralight wing. A curving strip of bright material gleamed in the Ephesian sun. "Here we are, blessed furry little kit." Her yellow eyes flickered back to the schematics on the other panel. "These lights are made of a phosphor material which can be controlled by onboard comp."

Parker laughed aloud. His thin fingers fluttered across the control console, bringing up the specifics of the LuxTerra illumination fabric. He ran a forefinger down a list of wavelengths. "We can pulse each phosphor in ultraviolet—that would cut through the clouds and atmospheric distortion—and the satellite cameras could pick up a datagram as large as the panel array will allow."

"Good." Maggie ran her claw down the middle of the command panel. Immediately, the workspace split in two. "Get to work on a receiver program to interp a multibyte array."

"Me?" Parker gave her a horrified look. "I'm not a comp-head! I fly shuttles, aircraft, pogo-sticks. . . ."

Magdalena smiled at him, showing a great number of teeth. "I'm busy, coding blind commands to reconfigure the *Midge*. So make yourself useful." She paused, nose twitching. "I want to know what the packleader is *doing*. Right *now*."

Parker swallowed nervously and dragged over an equipment box for a seat. "Sure. Sure. I'm working on it." He forced his fingers to the panel and cleared away everything but some editors. "Code—I wrote some code once. In school."

Maggie's lip curled. The smell of the human's fear-sweat made her nose twitch.

With the old México helping her stand, Gretchen stepped gingerly out of the over-hang. The sun had set and the wind had died down, leaving everything quiet and still. Anderssen was vastly relieved to have the world wrapped in darkness. Her head still felt altered, somehow, and she was sure the full light of day would be too much to take. Even the light of the stars—very clear, very bright, with a pellucid crystalline quality—hurt her eyes.

"Careful . . . there's a cable," Hummingbird pointed. Gretchen stopped, star-ing at the line of shadow stretching from the ground to the *Midge*. Something like a white flame winked at the edge of her vision, then brightened. After a moment's attention, she saw the cable itself outlined in pale fire. Gretchen swallowed and looked up.

The ultralight was glowing very softly. Every edge was lit by the same kind of faded, heatless brilliance. Each strut, window, airfoil—all were limned with light. Gretchen's heart skipped a beat, but a sense of delight filled her. There was no fear, only amazement at the glorious sight. She leaned on Hummingbird's shoulder and looked around. Both aircraft were spectral, incandescent ghosts standing out sharp against a limitless black background. The cables made sharp, tight lines to the ground—but the sand, the rock, the cliffs seemed to have disappeared. Only very faint lights winked in deep crevices in the stone.

"The . . . the *Gagarin* is glowing," she said softly.

Hummingbird's eyes crinkled up in response. "Yes. I imagine it is."

"What am I seeing?" Gretchen turned to look at the old México and found him equally illuminated, his *kaffiyeh* wicking with jewel-colored flames, face blazing with a pearlescent, gold-tinged light. She raised her own hand and saw her palm and fingers glowing in the same way.

"When first you begin to see," Hummingbird said, voice soft against the respirator's background hiss, "you will see too much. In this darkness, you are sensitive to even the least perturbation. By day, you would be almost blinded by the immense detail of the world. Right now, you are aware of the electromagnetic field around living things. The *Midge* is illuminated because our aircraft carry vibrations from their engines, from the motion of flight, from the powered systems onboard."

"I'm seeing an electromagnetic field?" Gretchen started to laugh. "That's impossible!"

"You see the light from a glowbean or a wand, don't you? This is the same, only much much fainter." Hummingbird took hold of her shoulders and turned her toward the open plain. "The 'helper' I gave you has broken down a barrier in your mind, a perceptual filter to which you've become accustomed since you were born. Look out there, into the emptiness. What do you see?"

"Nothing . . . wait, there's a faint radiance along the dune faces."

"Heat is radiating from the earth. Soon it will be gone and the sand and air will be the same temperature. Then there will be no difference for you to perceive."

Gretchen gave the old México a sick look. "Is this what you see? All the time?"

Hummingbird shook his head. "No. A student on the path must overcome many obstacles—this is the obstacle of *clarity*. I fear . . ." His voice changed timbre and Gretchen was aware of a change in the glow outlining his face. "The drug you took is one given to students who have been training and preparing themselves for months. But we have no time to guide your feet along the traditional path—"

"You're not supposed to be training me at all!" Gretchen interjected suddenly. Memories flooded back and she remembered the strange conversation in darkness. "I heard voices arguing as I slept—'only men may become *tlamatinime.*' Women must become . . ." She paused, trying to remember. The memories were fading, scattering like pine needles in a fall wind. "Skirt-of-knives said . . . she said . . . ah, it's gone."

Hummingbird had become quite still, his gaze fixed on Gretchen's face. "You heard a woman's voice? An old woman?"

"No—she was young—but there was an old man, he sounded like a stage actor."

The *nauallis* made a queer barking sound, which Gretchen remembered was what passed for laughter for the old man. "She was young long ago. But I was thinking of that day while you slept." He sighed, an honest sound of regret. Then he began to sing, but only for a moment. "We leave the flowers, the songs, the earth. Truly, we go, truly we part."

"You were there." Gretchen knew the truth of the matter even as she spoke. "You were in the room, a young man. The old actor was sitting in a wooden chair. He stood up to leave."

"Yes. And he was right—he *is* right—and I've broken an ancient law, speaking to you as I've done, giving you the 'helper', setting your feet on this path."

"I am in danger?"

"You've always been in danger," Hummingbird said in a sharp tone. "But now, today, you must learn to see again."

"I think," Gretchen said, "I see too much!"

Hummingbird nodded. "Yes—listen closely, there is not much night left. Your mind has been forced awake by the 'helper.' A veil of perception has been cast aside, letting you see as a human organism *naturally* perceives the world. Your mind is now exposed to a flood of data—a flood which in normal course is filtered, flattened, reduced to aggregates and symbols—but your consciousness is not ready to operate in such an environment.

"Now you must learn to concentrate on the important. You must learn to see selectively."

Gretchen felt itchy all over and shook her arms and hands. The z-suit felt strangely tight. "Didn't I see before? I mean—you're saying this sharpness, with everything seeming in focus all at once, even things far away—is what happens anyway?"

"Even so." Hummingbird raised his hand in front of her face. "But your mind was hiding the true world from your consciousness. Look at my hand tonight and you see every single bump and groove in my glove, you see the fire of my bodily electrical field, you see each pore in my skin. But yesterday? Yesterday you saw an *idea* of a gloved hand. An abstraction. A great part of human mental activity is devoted to reducing this raw flood of images and smells and sensations to remembered symbols. A hand. A man. A dog. An ultralight."

He swung his hand, indicating everything within sight. "Those symbols are not real, but they are very *convenient*. They let the lazy mind operate in such a confusing world." Gretchen could hear a grin in the man's voice. "Have you seen a baby watching the world? Their eyes are so wide! Their entire mentation is focused upon trying to understand *everything* all at once. A baby becomes a child and then an adult by replacing raw truth with layers of abstraction. By learning speech. By learning to read and to write. All those tools—the tools which build Imperial society and our science and our technology—hide the true world behind symbols."

"I . . . I understand." Gretchen felt faint and swayed. Clumsily, she sat down on the sand. The sensation of touching the earth, the sound of sand shifting under her hands, was nearly overwhelming. "What do I do . . . to be able to, say, move around?"

"Your body can handle everything," Hummingbird said wryly. "If you let it remember. Come, stand up. Let's go for a walk."

Nearly an hour later, Gretchen climbed gingerly across a slab of wind-polished stone and came to a halt, staring down into a wide bowl-shaped depression. To her right, a black lightless cliff rose up into the night. The bowl below her was strangely smooth.

"Where are we?" Anderssen slid down a splintered section of rock and came to a halt a handspan from the surface of the bowl. "This is hard-packed dust," she said, looking up at Hummingbird, who crouched atop the slab. "Not even sand."

The old México pointed to the cliff. Gretchen turned and saw—suddenly, as if the opening had materialized from the rock in her single moment of inattention— a door. She stiffened, feeling the freezing cold keenly through the insulated layers of her z-suit.

"This is where Russovsky found the cylinder." Hummingbird spoke very softly, though the trapezoidal opening in the cliff-face was entirely dark and still. "Do you see anything?"

Gretchen felt the cold settle into her bones and the pit of her stomach. Learning how to walk again had been easy—just a matter of keeping her mind occupied elsewhere. The body remembered how to breathe, how to walk, how to keep its balance—as long as the mind didn't try to interfere. Talking to Hummingbird about nothing of any importance had let her mind settle and regain its footing in simple physicality. The encompassing darkness restricted her vision to faint thready ghosts of heat and electricity. In time even they seemed to dim and fade as she got used to them. The *nauallis* claimed she could focus now, once her mind adapted, to bring clarity to bear on a single object.

"Go on," he said, remaining atop the slab. "Let yourself *see.*"

Gretchen sucked on her water tube, eyes closed, feeling her heartbeat speed up. Then she opened her eyes again and looked at the doorway.

"Nothing unusual," she said after a moment. "Worked stone. I don't see any lights inside. Should I?"

"I don't know." Hummingbird made his way down into the bowl. "I came here last night and watched for a time. There were no lights, no blue glow. But I feel uneasy. Everything here is so old . . . worn down by time. Such places are dangerous, being all of a single cloth. Differences," he said, "are easier to perceive."

"Are we going to go in?" Gretchen still felt cold and a nagging thought was beginning to curdle in the back of her thoughts.

"Yes." Hummingbird looked to her and then back to the doorway. "We have to see if Russovsky left anything behind in there."

Gretchen put a hand on his shoulder as the México moved to cross the bowl. "This is probably where she was replaced," she whispered, holding him back. "Her flight log shows she headed straight back to the observatory camp from here."

"I know." Hummingbird's hand clasped hers for a moment, fire mingling with fire. "This would mean her remains are within. And those we *must* destroy."

"Do you still have your little pistol?" Gretchen was digging in her tool belt.

Hummingbird nodded, patting his side. "It's not much use for eliminating evidence."

"Or for dealing with Ephesian lifeforms." Gretchen produced a compact lightwand. She adjusted a thumb control. "This is set to high UV," she said, handing over the lamp. "Everything else seems susceptible; maybe whatever is in there will be too."

The *nauallis* took the lamp with a shake of his head. "If there's something in there which can duplicate a human being almost to the cellular level, I fear it won't be affected by this."

"Then we need something bigger," Gretchen said, kneeling on the sand. Busy hands detached a variety of tools from her belt and began assembling them. Without looking up, she said: "Bandao-*tzin* felt he couldn't let me leave his company without proper equipment, so he sent this with me."

She held up a short-barreled, stockless gun with a hand grip and a fat magazine. Hummingbird grunted in appreciation and held out his hand.

"I don't think so," Gretchen said tartly, tucking the assault rifle under her arm. "You're going in first and I'll cover you."

"What does it shoot?" Hummingbird's appreciative smile vanished. He was eyeing the rifle warily now. "It looks like something the Marines would use."

Gretchen shook her head with a smirk. "No—it's Swedish. A Bofors Sif-52 shockgun. Throws explosive flechettes in a room-sized cloud." She locked the magazine back into place. A green light gleamed at the back of the weapon. "So I'll probably wait until you're out of the way."

"Of course." The *nauallis* did not seem convinced, but he turned away and glided across the hard-packed dust towards the door. Gretchen scuttled along behind him, keeping to his right, the gun leveled on the opening. When he'd reached the edge of the door, she stopped, steadying herself. The barrel of the weapon was a distraction—flickering with curlicues of orange flame—and she concentrated, remembering only smooth, dark solid metal.

Hey, she thought as Hummingbird stepped around the corner into the opening, *it works!*

The rifle was solid again, barrel heavy and entirely lacking in radiant light.

Gretchen scampered up to the door and peered inside. Hummingbird had tuned the lightwand down low, but the flare of ultraviolet made the chamber entirely visible once Anderssen's goggles kicked in. She saw a large, rocky space with a rumpled, irregular floor. The far wall was not that of a cave, however, but worked stone—much like the frame of the opening she was crouched against— holding a second trapezoidal door.

There was nothing in the chamber save Hummingbird, who was crouched only a meter or two away, the lightwand held out at a stiff angle. Gretchen scanned the rest of the room over the sights of her shockgun, then fixed her attention on the dark space within the second door. *There's something odd about all this . . .* she started to think and then her mind sort of froze up like a water pipe caught in the first chill snap of winter in the high timber. *Oh, blessed mother! O divine sister of Tepeyac!*

Unaware of the fear choking the words in Gretchen's throat, Hummingbird advanced into the chamber, keeping to the left-hand wall. He led with the wand, now burning purplish-blue in high UV setting, and crouched against the flat, smooth wall on the opposite side. Something had caught his eye and the *nauallis* leaned close to examine some kind of a spot on the wall.

"Hu–Hu–" Gretchen couldn't make her voice work, the word coming out a choked squeak. Though gripped by a terrible desire to flee, Anderssen crept inside, shoulder to the right-hand wall as she scuttled towards him. "*Hummingbird!*"

"Look at this," the *nauallis* said calmly, pointing with the wand at a smudge on the smooth stone. "Remains of a glowbean, I think. Russovsky must have . . . What is it?"

Gretchen was clutching his arm, the rasp of her breathing loud in her ears. "Look at the floor, at the doorways," she hissed, pointing with the barrel of the Sif. "They're *level.*"

Hummingbird nodded, though he tensed as well. "And so?"

"This is a First Sun building," Gretchen said in a tight, controlled voice. "This postdates the release of the eaters, the destruction of the surface, the rise of the Escarpment, everything. Your *valkar* made this place."

There was a *hiss-hiss* on the comm circuit. "I don't think so," Hummingbird said after a pause. "Look at this wall. This is not worked stone, not planed or cut or burned with a tunneller. The doorways are the same."

Gretchen peered at the wall, finding concentration and focus elusive amid the rampage of adrenaline coursing through her. "I . . . I suppose . . ." Then something odd about the surface caught her attention and she dialed up the magnification on her goggles. "Hmm. That's very strange—this surface is *solid*."

"Yes." Hummingbird moved along the wall to the inner doorway. Cautiously, he looked around the corner, then drew back. "Almost perfect, I would hazard."

Keeping the muzzle of the Sif pointed away from the México, Gretchen sidled up to join him. "Real stone isn't so smooth," she muttered under her breath, suspiciously checking the exit to the canyon. "It's usually porous, even a fine marble or granite. Filled with minute hollows, concavities . . ."

"True." Hummingbird looked around the corner again, leading with his light-wand. "But this is not stone as you think of stone. This is a wall assembled an atom at a time over a million years. Almost perfectly solid and more than a meter deep." He slipped into a corridor with walls slanting inward to a flat ceiling over a dusty floor.

Gretchen darted across the opening and swung the Sif to cover the passage. The tunnel reached back to end in an angled wall. Hummingbird moved carefully, one gloved hand pressed against the slanting wall.

"Watch out for this floor," he said, voice a low buzz in her earbug. "Like the walls, it is dangerously slick. There is very little traction."

Gretchen looked down at the dusty surface. A mirror image of her cloak, mask and rebreather stared back through a gray film. "Okay," she said, testing the surface with her boot. Sliding her foot from side to side elicited a queasy feeling like slipping on new ice. Pressing directly down seemed to gain some purchase. Ahead of her, Hummingbird was moving very slowly, taking his time and placing each foot with careful precision. Gretchen followed with equal care, keeping to the opposite wall.

The sloped passage turned to enter a second chamber at an angle. Hummingbird paused just outside the junction, risking a quick look inside before beckoning for Anderssen to join him. Gretchen moved gingerly to his side—her boots kept wanting to slip out from under her—hands grimly tight on the handle and stock of the Sif.

This room seemed to have no ceiling—or none she could see—and three smooth walls. The fourth, opposite them, was rough and unfinished. Gretchen's mouth tightened, making out irregular markings on the wall—inset spirals, whorls of raised, grooved rock—and she hissed in warning. At the base of the wall were scattered a number of cylinders.

"There." She pointed, indicating a section of bare stone which had been broken open. Hand-sized rocks lay in an untidy pile at the foot of the wall. Boot prints scuffed an ancient layer of dust. "Russovsky took the embedded cylinder away."

Without waiting for Hummingbird to respond, overcome by her own curiosity, Gretchen walked stiffly across the floor to the nearest cylinder. The artifact seemed much the same as the one Clarkson had cut open on the ship—a third of a meter long, four or five centimeters across—and the exterior was encrusted with the same kind of lime-scaling. Very gently, Anderssen nudged the device with the muzzle of the Sif, making the thing skitter across the impeccably smooth floor. The cylinder did not burst open.

She could feel Hummingbird's tension from the doorway, but Gretchen ignored him for the moment, moving to the cavity broken in the stone. Up close, she saw the wall was raw irregular rock, rising up through the floor at an angle and vanishing into impenetrable darkness overhead. The entire surface was crowded with fossils—more of the anemonelike structures, the fluted curl of something like a snail, serrated ridges indicating a swimmer with multiple spines. A flattened, bifurcated cone. Scorch-marks surrounded the ragged opening where small blasting charges had been used to split open the limestone.

"What made this place?" Gretchen whispered into her throat mike as she leaned close to examine the surface of the ancient sediment. She could see hundreds of specimens within arm's reach—a glorious view into a lost, dead world. "Did something survive after the *valkar* fled into hiding?"

"Ghosts." Hummingbird hesitated, remaining crouched in the entranceway. "You've seen what lived—the microflora—but they did not make this shrine. This is memory made solid."

"How?" Anderssen backed away from the wall, swinging the gun to cover the rest of the room. "You mean like Russovsky?"

Hummingbird waved for her to get behind him once she reached the archway. "I have not seen this before myself," he said in a low voice, "but the pyramid contains references to such things. The *valkar* is dreaming, but it is not powerless. A subtle influence extends throughout this world, power seeping from the hidden heart. Even when the crust was shattered and remade, not all memories of what lived here before died." He began to back up into the hallway. Nervous, Gretchen followed.

A white frost began to form on her breather mask, which was worrying. The night air of Ephesus was far below freezing, but the respirator should be trapping the water vapor in her breath. Only CO_2 should be escaping. "Crow, something's happening . . . it's getting very, very cold."

Hummingbird turned up the intensity of his wand and raised the light high. Shadows fled away down the passage.

"There's something here," the *nauallis* hissed in alarm, staring intently around at the glassy walls. Gretchen tried to hurry, but the glassy floor immediately betrayed her. One foot flew out and she crashed down hard on her right hip. A gasp of pain burst from her throat. The barrel of the Sif banged on the floor and the weapon flew from her fingers. The *nauallis* flinched, but kept up his steady, careful pace toward the outer room.

"Anderssen, quit playing about and get up," he hissed.

Gretchen tried to rise, but her hands slipped on the mirrored floor and she spun helplessly. One boot hit the wall and skittered away. Even as she groped for some kind of purchase, she saw a spreading reflection of grayish light spill across the slanted wall. The butt of the Sif hit her head. Gretchen twisted into a roll and flopped over onto her stomach. Grasping fingers closed around the weapon and her boot struck the wall square enough to stop abruptly. She looked up.

Hummingbird had backed past her in his flat-footed crouch. The little gun was pointing into the strange gray light, absurdly dwarfed by the bulk of his gloved hands. Gretchen twisted her head around and her eyes went wide. Reflex twitched the Sif into aiming position.

The passage was filling with a steady gray radiance. An indeterminate crepuscular color shone from the air. The doorway to the room of the sea had vanished in the endlessly repeating reflections of the mirrored walls, floor and ceiling. Where the gray existed, there was nothing else—no shadow, no stone, no edges or divisions. Gretchen realized, with a chill start, the light was moving rapidly toward her, spilling along the passage in a colorless tide.

"That's not light," she shouted into the comm, trying to scrabble backwards along the mirror-bright floor. The lead edge of the radiance was almost touching her flailing boots. Her finger twitched on the firing bead of the Sif. "It's something else!"

Hummingbird's answer was drowned out by a sharp blast. The shockgun rocked against her shoulder as a canister burst from the muzzle. Gretchen *oofed* and the recoil flung her down the hallway, legs and arms windmilling. She slammed into Hummingbird and they both flew back through the slanted doorway into the outer chamber. Behind them, a high-pitched *z-z-zing* ended in a blast of flame and light. Out of the corner of her eye Gretchen caught sight of the gray radiance rippling and twisting like a torn blanket in the strobe-light eruption of a hundred and sixteen individually packaged munitions.

In a cloud of dust, Anderssen untangled herself from the *nauallis*, hands working the reloading mechanism. Gretchen felt the heavy, solid *thunk* of a new canister levering into the firing chamber. Hummingbird scrambled up from the spreading dust as well, half-blinded by his disordered *kaffiyeh*.

"Clever," he barked sarcastically over a comm channel hissing with static and the same kind of high warbling wail Gretchen had heard in the cave on Mount Prion. "You must have done well in physics. . . . *Ai!* Run!"

Gretchen was still raising the shockgun to cover the tunnel entrance when the *nauallis* bolted for the archway leading into the canyon. A shout of dismay strangled in her throat as the radiance boiled out of the passage. She caught a brief, fragmentary glimpse of a cloud of rock chips, bits of metal and what seemed to be frozen flame suspended within the advancing gray.

"Crap!" Gretchen sprinted for the doorway and leaped through the opening, hands protecting her head. The roar of static in her earbug was deafening and she slapped the comm off. Both feet hit the dust, sending up twin plumes of heavy yellow. Staggering, Gretchen ran across the bowl and scrambled up the tilted slab on the far side.

In the darkness, she lost sight of Hummingbird among a jerking, disorienting blur of canyon walls and sandy cavities among glassy-smooth boulders. Damning his cowardly name, she slid across another slab and dropped down onto a wide, gravel-strewn moraine. Wheezing for breath, Gretchen jogged up the slope and at the top she turned, nervous hands checking her belt, the sling of the shockgun, her rebreather—all the tools she needed to survive. A cough died in her throat.

The radiance had spilled out into the canyon bottom. Now, from a distance, the *thing* looked nothing like any light or illumination she'd ever seen. Strikingly, there were no shadows or reflections cast by the color. Instead, the already dark canyon dimmed as the shape grew among the boulders and flooded from the doorway. Gretchen adjusted her goggles, but there was no change save in infrared, where she hissed in surprise to see the edges of the formless gray merging with the subzero night while bright points of heat blazed in the center of the mass. But even those sparks were dying as she watched.

"Oh, no," she whispered, backing up. The Sif was in her hands again, but Anderssen realized with a grim certainty the gun was useless. The fading heat sources were the still-exploding flechettes she'd fired into the color, being avidly consumed by this . . . this . . . "What is this thing? Hummingbird!"

There was no answer on the dead comm. Gretchen turned and ran as fast as she dared, scrambling past rounded anthracite boulders and slogging through deep drifts of sand and dust. A hundred heartbeats passed and suddenly, as she dodged between two menhirlike stones, a pair of powerful hands seized Gretchen and swung her aside, into a pocket of shadow in the greater darkness. She yelped, swinging the stock of the Sif around in a sharp blow to the unseen figure's head. The honeycombed plastic thudded into something solid. A glowbean flared to life and Gretchen found herself facing a wincing Hummingbird.

"Where . . ." Anderssen tried turning her comm back on. ". . . have you been? What is that thing in the canyon?"

"A hungry dream," Hummingbird said, though the staccato warble and keening in the background of the channel nearly drowned him out. "Or rather, what a current at the edge of the *valkar*'s dream made in this waking world."

"A dream?" Gretchen fought against a fierce desire to smash the butt of the shockgun repeatedly into the man's face until he made sense. "Dreams don't have form, idiot bird! They don't eat up explosive munitions like toasted maize and come looking for more!"

Hummingbird pushed the muzzle of the Sif away from his face with a fingertip. "Even dreaming, the *valkar* distorts the world with the weight of its presence. Even these dead stones retain some memory of a once-living world." He slapped a gloved hand against the glossy obsidian rising up above them. "Nothing survived the devastation intact. But you saw the effect Russovsky's stone had on the organism in the cave—even the pattern memory of an often-used artifact could stir the formless to take shape. This world is rife with parched, formless memories."

Hummingbird stopped, tensing. Gretchen turned, hefting the Sif onto her shoulder, muzzle down. *Gun useless*, she thought with very faint amusement. *Make a note for Bandao. Good for feeding colorless light.*

"I was very foolish to come here—*Hsst!* Something is coming."

Outside their tiny shelter, the gloom in the canyon—barely disturbed by the thin ribbon of brilliant, unwinking stars high above—deepened. Gretchen fought down a desire to bolt from their meager shelter. Hummingbird's fist closed on her shoulder in painful counterpoint to the static roaring in her earbug.

The color was there suddenly, gliding out from behind a house-sized boulder. Again the gray radiance did not extend beyond an indistinct, wavering shape. Gretchen's eyes widened, taking in a burning-hot point drifting within something like a bifurcated cone with a forest of tentacular legs moving restlessly beneath. She focused her goggles on the hot centerpoint and saw a flechette tumbling in place, hissing and spitting slow fire. The metallic sheathing was rapidly disintegrating. Apparently unaware of them, the color drifted past, a gray cutout against a flat velvet background.

Hummingbird's fingers clasped her wrist and the comm channel fell silent. He leaned close, pressing his mask against hers. "We have to get away from here or we'll be fuel too."

Nodding, Gretchen peered out around the corner, saw nothing—no wavering, indeterminate blotches of lightless color—and slipped out, weaving her way through the debris scattered at the mouth of the canyon. Hummingbird was right behind her.

Heedless of what might see them—if the color had eyes or something passing for an organ of sight—they ran up the broad, open slope flanking the entrance to the slot. Anderssen immediately started wheezing again. Her leg muscles sparked with pain and she nearly collapsed at the top of the ridge. Hummingbird caught her arm, dragging Gretchen to her feet.

"Run," he barked, voice a barely audible squeak in the thin air. "Don't—"

Gretchen looked back, trying to catch her breath.

Amorphous gray shapes were emerging from the mouth of the canyon. Not all were cone-shaped—some shifted and distorted in the brief moment of her glance—and others strode swiftly on long, stalklike legs. A sensation of hostile desire struck Gretchen like a physical blow, though at such a distance there should have been no way for her to ascertain expression or intent.

She turned and ran, head down, forcing cramping legs and thighs to bound across rocky, uneven ground. Hummingbird loped at her side, keeping pace, though Gretchen guessed the old man could easily leave her behind.

They were within sight of the cave—she could see both ultralights outlined by a soft glow against the night—when a gray shape raced past on dozens of insectile legs and spun to face them. Hummingbird drew up as Gretchen stumbled to a halt, surrounded by a drifting cloud of dust and gasping for air. She looked around only seconds later and the radiance was all around them in shimmering, pearlescent sheets. A trickle of cold pure fear in the back of her throat made Gretchen's teeth clench.

Hummingbird settled back on his heels, shifting his weight on the ground. Out of the corner of her eye, Gretchen was suddenly struck by a sense of his calm solidity. *Does anything disturb him?* she wondered wildly, fighting to keep from swinging the useless gun toward the enemy. The sight of the terrible gray hanging in the air made her feel weak and small and powerless. *Is he ever afraid?*

"*Tla xihualhuian,*" his voice echoed over the comm, woven into a rising and falling storm of static and queer shrieking wails. The *nauallis*'s hand extended, clenched tight into a fist. Grains of newly-crushed powder dribbled into the dark air. "*Tlazohpilli, Centeotl! Ticcehuiz cozauhqui yollohtli. Quizaz xoxouhqui tlahuelli, cozauhqui tlahuelli!*"

The México's voice grew stronger with each syllable. Gretchen's distracted comprehension slid away from the barely-understandable words. They were in a strange, archaic-sounding dialect—she recognized a few of the words—*yellow* and *green* and *wrath*.

"Do not move," Hummingbird said, the sound of the chant still ringing in his voice. "Become still."

Gretchen stared at him in horror. The *nauallis* was settling to his knees, back straight and shoulders square. Around them, the belt of the gray was advancing through the air like ink spilled into clear water. The bright points of heat were gone. In infrared the malicious cloud had faded almost to invisibility. Her heart hammering, Gretchen forced incredulous words between clenched teeth.

"Are you insane? They're going to drink us up like a sponge! Get up!"

"No." Hummingbird placed his hands on both knees, eyes invisible in shadow, his face a faintly gleaming mask of dim fire. "Let them come. . . ."

"Never," Gretchen snarled, swinging away from the old man. Before he could react, she sprinted away, aiming for a space where the drifting radiance seemed thinnest. At the same time, her finger squeezed the firing bead on the Sif and there was a tinny *crack* as another flechette cylinder accelerated down the fat barrel and soared away into the night sky.

Anderssen tried to leap the curdling indistinct color but failed, plowing through a thin drifting sheet. Immediately, she felt a chill, numbing shock. Gretchen staggered, nearly twisting her ankle on a hidden rock, then caught herself and fled. Gray clung to her legs and torso like the shredded remains of a gauze quilt or a thin paper banner. Against her black cloak and z-suit, the color shimmered pale and lifeless—fish scale without rainbows, a dead iridescence—but did not fall away as she ran. Cold blossomed in her side, cutting through the layers of insulation and radiation shielding built into the suit.

Off in the distance, the canister blew apart, filling the night with a bright, sharp blossom of red and orange. Hundreds of tiny explosions followed, the paltry air robbing their roar and clamor of its full-bodied rage. A twisting cloud of sand and grit billowed up into the black sky, lit from below by the fading reflection of the explosions.

Gretchen managed another twenty strides and then collapsed with a thin, despairing cry. A cloud of the omnipresent dust puffed up around her. Color dripped from her legs and stomach like fresh steam rising from a still-unfrozen lake in a high country winter. Muscles spasmed, clenching tight within her skin. Blinded by needlelike pain, Gretchen tried to force her legs and arms to move, but wave after wave of nervefire crushed her down into the sand and gravel again.

Hummingbird remained sitting amid the writhing circle of gray, eyes closed, his heartbeat steady as a temple bell calling the faithful to prayer. The color drew closer, puddling and seeping across the ground, still shadowless, emitting no light save the heatless glare of its own substance. Gray washed across his knees, his hands, up his arms. The *nauallis's* body shivered slightly, then grew still as the colorless tide mounted to cover his broad chest and then his face.

Choking, her mouth coppery with blood, Gretchen felt sweat freezing on her clammy skin beneath the tight grip of the z-suit. The dreadful color was pooling around her, covering her arms and torso, blotting out her sight of the sky. A single jewel-bright star gleamed for a moment amid the gray before being swallowed up.

Oh blessed sister, what do I do? Gretchen felt her body slow, leached of warmth, robbed by creeping, icy fingers. Her heart was still racing wildly and panic threatened to drown her mind as her body was being smothered by the color clouding around her. *Stupid old man! We shouldn't have gone down there. . . .*

Then, across a sputtering flood of near-comprehensible static and the tinny warbling of countless invisible birds, she heard the *nauallis* singing in his deep, slow voice.

"Nic-quix-tiz," the words came, somehow clear and distinct amid all the noise and fury rolling around her, *"nic-toh-tocaz nit-lama-caz-qui nina-hual-tecuti. Niquit-tiz tlama-caz-qui, pat-tecatl, tollo-cuepac-tzin."*

This time they did not sound so strange, so foreign to the Náhuatl Gretchen had spoken since she was a young girl, laboring over her alphabets and word lists in a low-slung white-painted school perched amid spruce and realfir on the ridge above Kinlochewe. The pacing and tone of the words were not the quick modern dialect, but something older and more resonant. A language which was complete unto itself, not crowded with Norman and Japanese loan words, where the sound of the old names was proper and correct. *Temachticauh* instead of *sensei* for teacher. *Totoltetl* instead of *tamago* for egg.

"I banish wrath," Hummigbird sang. "I pursue fear. I am the priest, the *nauallis*-lord. Let wrath, let fear consume me, the priest."

The suddenly understandable words tumbled through her consciousness and just as swiftly fled, but the clarity and conviction in the old México's voice settled into her bones like the warmth of a mulled draught. *He is not afraid, he is not afraid.* The thought spun around Gretchen and she fell still and quiet on the ground. *He is still alive.*

Though her heart was hammering hard enough to bring a spark of pain in her chest and cold sweat purled behind her ears, Gretchen surrendered, trusting to the steady voice ringing through the encompassing gray. Her fists relaxed and she let the gray enter her. *I am not afraid*, she thought as a rasping tumult of static swelled loud, roaring in her ears. *I am not afraid.*

There was a moment of wailing sound and a rush of prickling chill. Gretchen felt her body convulse, though she felt the sensation at an odd distance, and the gray radiance faded away. The sky was revealed once more, though the stars were now twinkling and shining, no longer hard, bright points. Hot wind brushed across her face, carrying a humid, decaying smell and the chattering angry cry of something crashing among the trees. Palmate fronds—serrated with slender triangular leaves—obscured most of the sky. Gretchen could hear the sea—surf booming against a shallow shore—not far away.

I am not afraid, she repeated to herself, sure that death was closing about her in a cold, implacable grip.

The sensation of lying in a muddy stream under a hot, tropical sky faded away by degrees. In some indefinable time, the vision became a memory—sharp and distinct, as if such a thing had happened to her only the day before—lodged among thoughts of Magdalena and remembrances of school and travel and her children throwing snowballs in the meadow behind the big barn. Gretchen realized her eyes were still open and the vault of stars above was cold and still again.

Tentatively, she tried to raise her head. Nothing happened. Slowly, the sky brightened and obscured. Gretchen tried to focus, to bring forth the *clarity* Hummingbird had promised her, but as she did the colorless gray returned, damping out the stars and the night sky. In the formless void, shapes and phantasms flickered—emerging from nothing, nearly reaching definable shapes or scenes—then vanishing again. Everything was so indistinct, so faint, her mind failed to grasp reason or purpose among the shifting gleams and tremors.

These are hungry memories, Gretchen heard Hummingbird say, his voice a weak thread amid the roiling nothingness. *They seek shape and purpose.*

I can be formless, Anderssen realized, *and I will not die.*

She let go, letting herself—sore muscles, bruised ribs and weary mind—fall into stillness.

Once more the gray faded away, leaving only crystalline night. Gretchen had a sensation of floating upon a limpid, dark lake without a visible shore. The water was heavy, holding her up, her body freed from the tyranny of gravity, in some balance where the rubbery tension of the lake surface could hold her weight. She could not see the lake—only the constant, unwinking stars—but was certain of its presence. All sense of frigid cold and weariness were absent. Even her thoughts—which had begun to feel attenuated, drained, parched by the relentless events of the day—were at peace. They did not hurry, but moved languidly, finding their own proper pace and rhythm.

I am finally still, she realized. *This is what Hummingbird meant.*

The nightmares and frantic memories of the gray seemed far away, reduced to insignificance. Gretchen perceived—as though she stood on a great height and stared down, finding a tiny dark speck in a field of gravel beneath a looming cliff of basalt—her body was alone in the darkness. There were no furious, malefic clouds of not-color swirling around her, no half-seen shapes drawn from the ruins of an ancient world, only stone and crumbled shale and dust.

Am I really alone? she wondered, though the thought had no urgency. *Was the gray merely hallucination? A phantom drawn up into a bewildered, confused mind?*

Something moved—a human shape—and entered her field of view. Gretchen felt the lake tremble and shift, unseen waves rolling her up and down. Gently, with no more than the sensation of sand and grit pressing into her back, she found herself on the shore of a vast, dry ocean. The figure—cloaked and hooded, z-suit half-visible in the pale starlight—leaned over her, one hand resting on a padded knee. The thin aerial of a comm pack arced up against the stars.

Was the gray only something I saw in a moment of clarity? The thought struck her hard, rousing a placid mind to hurried thought. Certainty gathered beneath her breastbone, solid and unmistakable. *Like the glow around the ultralights? Around the cable? The witch-fire of the dunes shedding their day-heat into the implacable night?*

"Hello." Gretchen's voice felt rusty, deep and scratchy, as though she'd woken from a long, deep sleep. "Give me a hand, huh?"

A glove clasped hers, drawing Gretchen to her feet. The motion roused to life all of her aches and hurts, drawing a hiss of pain and a wry grimace. The figure's *kaffiyeh* fell aside, revealing battered, scored goggles and a rust-etched rebreather. Anderssen squinted, surprised. *Hummingbird's equipment isn't so badly used. . . .* She stopped, frankly goggling, eyes widening in surprise.

A woman stared back at her from the depths of the hood, brushstroke-pale eyebrows narrowed over half-seen pale blue eyes. Gretchen felt calm flee, brushed aside by a shock of realization and confusion.

"Doctor Russovsky?" she managed to choke out.

Susan Koshō slid down a gangway ladder at speed, the instep of her boots straddling the rails on either side of the steps. She hopped off nimbly just before the end, letting her hands guide her to thump down on a nonskid deckplate. Straightening her uniform jacket and pants, the *sho-sa* turned in the tiny intersection and strode off down the right-hand hallway. A line of cargo staples ran down the center of the passage, offering a secure anchor for heavy straps holding cargo billets against the wall. Stenciled labels identified the pods as holding flash-frozen food supplies—potatoes, chiles, rice, onions, wasabi paste, buffalo meat, mutton, carrots, peas, mangoes—everything the kitchens would need to keep three hundred men and women from rioting over an unvarying diet of vanilla-flavored three-squares, recycled bodywater and vitamin supplements.

She reached a pressure door with a small sign reading JUNIOR OFFICERS' QUARTERS taped to the bulkhead. The crates stacked to the low overhead on either side of the hatch were labeled MEDICAL SUPPLIES. Stonefaced—though there was no one to see her—Koshō examined the seals on the cargo pods and found them intact. Pursing her lips slightly, she plugged her duty-officer's comp into the bottom crate's dataport and watched for a moment as the two systems conversed. The inventory request registered thirty-six full bottles of Usunomiya-city-brewed sake, in ceramic bottles.

Koshō considered opening the case, which had been placed in such perilous proximity to the JOQ by the ship's supply officer—a man widely regarded as being without pity or remorse or any human sense of mercy or decency by the crew—to see if the bottles were truly inside, or if they even retained any rice wine, but did not. The hour was deep into second watch and she had her own business to finish.

The pressure door yielded to her command insignia and levered up into the overhead with a hiss. Koshō schooled her face to perfect stillness and stepped through the hatchway into a thick miasma composed of human sweat, the acrid taste of metal oil, drying laundry and half-cooked food. A clamor of sound enveloped her as the hatch closed; music blaring from personal players, the clatter of two midshipmen fencing with rattan swords at the far end of the deck, people shouting encouragement to the duelists, an ensign arguing passionately with a bored-looking second lieutenant, the beep and whir of electronics, someone singing a Nōh ballad off-key. . . . The *sho-sa*'s nostrils flared slightly, then settled. Dark brown eyes surveyed the rows of bunks sitting over tiny desks and lockers with interest. Every square inch of the long, slightly curving room was covered with people, equipment, posters, 3v postcards or zenball schedules.

Forty-seven violations of shipboard regulations, she thought as her eyes returned to look down the long, crowded hallway. A very faint, calculating smile touched her lips. *Though none needful of real punishment. Not today, at least.*

A middle-grade lieutenant standing in front of the nearest desk, shirt off— revealing a jawless skull tattooed on a powerfully muscled cocoa-colored back— happened to turn at just that moment. He was dressing for third-watch duty, his tunic, uniform jacket and soft, kepi-style cap laid out on a neatly made bed. The Mixtec froze, seeing her, then his brain restarted with admirable speed and he stiffened to attention.

"Senior officer Koshō," he bawled in a voice worthy of a Jaguar Knight *gunso*, "on DECK!"

His voice echoed back from the far end of the JOQ in abrupt silence. The Nōh singer's caterwauling aria flew in counterpoint, but was immediately silenced. There was a commotion as men and women swarmed down off the bunks and leapt up from their chairs or the deck and formed two rows facing into the central walkway. Koshō nodded politely to the *thai-i*.

"You will be late for your duty station, Eight-Deer. Please continue."

The African bowed gracefully in response and resumed dressing.

Koshō took two steps into the room, politely removing herself from the lieutenant's way. "I require the assistance of *Sho-i Ko-hosei* Smith," she announced in an inflectionless voice. "The rest of you, as you were."

Everyone stared at her and not a few heads turned to look at the far end of the room. A murmur of noise carrying the midshipman's name flew down the walkway. The fencers were frozen en-pointe, the tips of their *boken* touching. Koshō saw Smith appear, hastily shoving a handful of pay chits into the hands of another midshipman, and hurry through the crowd toward her. As the baby-faced communications officer passed, the other junior officers relaxed and returned to very subdued, decorous activities. Koshō noticed, to her private amusement, two ensigns osculating on an upper bunk did not resume *their* extracurricular activities.

"Ma'am?" Smith made a futile effort to straighten his hair. "Is something wrong?"

"Come with me, *Sho-i.*" Koshō turned smartly on her heel and left the JOQ. Eight-Deer was gone, having fled quietly while her back was turned. The hatchway closed behind them with a *thud* and the hiss of pressurized air. "There's something you should see."

The ride in the core-transit car to the bridge ring was very quiet, which did not discomfit Koshō at all. She believed in the benefit of learning to wait silently and was not averse to helping others—particularly junior officers—improve their skills. Watching Smith-*tzin* fidget out of the corner of her eye, the *sho-sa* reminded herself she had learned these skills at a younger age, when sitting motionless, clad in the elaborate drapery of one of Hannobu's *juni-hitoe* for five hours while listening politely to scratchy, ill-executed music was a matter of course. *He does not have to wear four kilos of hair, golden pins and jeweled ornaments either. A good switching would improve his posture, though.*

A chime signaled the arrival of their transit car at the command ring and Koshō pushed away from her seat and kicked off to fly through the widening iris of the door leading to the bridge. Smith followed, entirely at ease in z-g.

The bridge was quiet and dim, the lights having switched into nightcycle. Koshō nodded to the officer of the watch and swung herself over to the communications station. Smith's usual configuration had been entirely changed, with the broad work panel split into three sets of v-panes. The *sho-i* dropped into his shockchair while Koshō took a newly added second seat. Out of habit, Smith strapped himself in and tested chair integrity. The sight brought a brief, warm glow to Koshō's breast. *Ah, but he does occasionally learn.*

"Reconfiguration of the shipskin is complete," the *sho-sa* said quietly, tapping her half of the divided panel alive. A new set of blank v-panes and controls appeared. Her console shone a light green, indicating a standby status. Curious,

Smith leaned over, checking the intermediate display, which was the fruit of *Thai-i* Helsdon's foregoing sleep for two days. While Smith's reduced primary panel showed the feed from the remaining, normally-configured sensor array, the intermediate display served as an amalgam of the two sets of data. At the moment, it showed the main battle plot from Smith's panel.

"Helsdon-*tzin* assures me," Koshō continued, "all of the new data feeds are online and the shipskin is properly reconfigured for g-wave detection."

Smith nodded, impressed, but he still looked a little puzzled.

"Your idea was a good one," Koshō continued in a low voice. Only a skeleton watch was on deck at the moment, so she felt safe enough to talk openly with this boy. The raven-wing of her left eyebrow curved up gracefully. "Did you feel slighted when *Chu-sa* Hadeishi tasked me to implement the concept, rather than you?"

"No!" Smith looked horrified—properly horrified—but Koshō could see a twinge of memory in the boy's pale eyes. "I'm only a junior officer," he said, almost stammering.

"You are correct," the *sho-sa* said quietly. "You are a junior officer. You've much to learn before Hadeishi-*tzin* is entirely comfortable with placing you in a lead role. But the day *will come* when he does, never fear." Avoiding the surprised look on his face, she activated the newly configured panel and handed him a v-pad already keyed to a set of security codes.

"Smith-*tzin*," Koshō said formally, "would you care to bring the new system online?"

The midshipman blinked once and then took the pad. Visibly gathering himself, Smith looked over the codes, then examined the g-scan panel. Koshō sat beside him quietly, keeping a very close eye on what he was doing. Taking a deep breath, Smith tapped open a comm channel.

"Bridge to Engineering."

There was an immediate, tired-sounding answer. "Helsdon here, Bridge."

"Are your crews clear of the outer hull?" Smith was searching frantically on the reconfigured display. Koshō continued to watch, an expression of mild interest on her face. "We are preparing to bring the g-scan array online."

"Wait one, Bridge." Helsdon's voice cut off with the squeak of a muted channel. A moment later, he came back on comm. "Bridge, we are clear. All crews are accounted inside the secondary hull. You are clear to activate the g-array."

Smith found the controls for the external point-defense system and toggled on a set of pattern cameras mounted on hard-points along the *Cornuelle*'s hull. Koshō's eyes narrowed in interest as he woke them up and fed in parameters for a close-hull scan. A moment later the comp chimed to announce the area immediately outside the ship was clear of people in z-suits.

"Hull clear," Smith announced. "Stand by for live power to g-array."

"Standing by," echoed back from both Engineering and the watch duty officer on the bridge.

"Power." Smith tapped a glyph of a running man bearing a twisting flame atop a brick on his stylized head. The third section of the communications station lit and data began to feed into the system. A preliminary plot began to appear seconds later. At the same moment, a string of amber lights flared on the panel. Smith jerked as if struck in the face and immediately punched a shutdown. "We have a partial systems failure," he barked into the comm. "Engineering, systems check!"

"Got it," Helsdon grumbled and Koshō could hear him scratching a stubbly beard. "Power conduits show green . . . hull skin feedback shows nominal . . . no pressure drops, no hull rupture."

Koshō watched Smith with interest. The boy was sweating, the back of his uniform shirt sticking to narrow shoulders, but he did not freeze or balk in the face of an unexpected situation.

"Are we radiating?" he snapped at both Engineering and the ensign riding the weapons panel. "Is there hull leakage?"

"No," came the answer a bare second later from Weapons.

Helsdon in Engineering was humming a little tune, but he chimed in a heart-beat later. "I'm seeing some queer readings from the reconfigured sensors in grid two-even. There must be some kind of data-formatting problem in the sensor feed." The engineer sighed audibly. "I'll take a crew and sort this. Engineering, out."

Smith let himself breathe out in relief, then stiffened, glancing sideways at the *sho-sa*. He seemed both exhilarated and near dead with fright.

"You will get your turn," Koshō said, taking back the v-pad. She was not smiling, being a proper officer, but her eyes glittered a little in amusement at his excitement. "There are always problems like this when we bring a new system online."

"Yes, Koshō-*tzin*." Smith made a sharp little bow, just as he had been taught in the Fleet officers' *calmecac*. Her eyes narrowed a little, considering him. The boy stiffened again, expecting a rebuke of some kind.

"A question—you did not believe Helsdon-*tzin*'s assertion that the outer hull was clear?"

"No—well, I believed *him*, ma'am—but . . . on my cadet cruise, ma'am, they had a punishment detail outside, repainting the hull numbers on the *Tizoc*. I was standing a duty watch on the bridge and Weapons decided to run a system test on the main sensor array. They checklisted with everyone they were supposed to—Engineering, the Marine detachment, Flight Operations—but they didn't ask the quartermaster. Number sixteen array went to full active scan and killed three cadets. Boiled them alive right inside their suits." Smith was looking a little white around the gills.

"Never pays to be hasty," he said in conclusion, avoiding her gaze. "Ma'am."

"Very wise," Koshō said, pushing herself up out of the chair. "Return to quarters. You must be alert and well-rested for the morning duty watch."

"*Hai!*" Smith bowed formally and then left the bridge, trying not to burst from unfettered pride.

Koshō watched him go, thinking about the past. *Dead men teach memorable lessons*, she thought with a certain grim humor. *Their sacrifice repaid a thousand times.*

The heavy carrier *Tizoc* was notorious in Fleet for the number of training accidents suffered by her ever-changing crews. Koshō had served on the ancient, outdated and frankly dangerous capital ship herself. Every officer did—*Tizoc* had born the brunt of cadet cruises for three generations—but most did not realize until they'd knocked around the Fleet for a tour or two that the 'curse' struck each and every cadet class with brutal, endlessly repeated efficiency.

Every officer in Fleet had been on watch, or on duty station, or even on the same work detail or in the same compartment, or at least in the same graduating class, as some poor unfortunate who died gruesomely as the result of careless procedure or sloppy handling or one of the millions of tiny errors which could doom a man, a ship, or a fleet. Cadets boarding the *Tizoc* for the first time were told the ship was named after an Emperor called 'He-who-bleeds-the-people.' Later, when they heard enough of stories from their shipmates and were sober enough to put two and two together to make four, the veteran officers called the venerable old carrier 'He-who-winnows-the-chaff' in tones of wary respect.

Koshō looked once around the bridge, saw everything was in order, and then kicked into the accessway. She felt tired and it was late. There would be a fullness of work in the morning, she was sure. Hadeishi did not allow an idle crew.

Pale rose and gold streaked the eastern rim of the world, heralding an ear-searing dawn.

A faint white illumination filled the sky, lighting scattered rocks, the tie-downs of the ultralights and then Hummingbird, still kneeling in the sand, palms on his knees. The stout figure of the México moved minutely and the man's eyes opened. His breather mask was caked with frost, the z-suit diagnostics on his wrist gleaming red. Stiffly, the man rose to his feet, ice flaking from the joints of his matte-black suit. Moving very slowly, Hummingbird made his way to the cargo door of his *Midge*.

Hummingbird rummaged through the cargo compartment and found a bag containing power cells. Fumbling with chilled, nearly nerveless fingers he managed to swap out the cells in his belt and let out a long, tired hiss as the suit heaters woke to life again.

"And in an hour," he husked, drawing on his *djellaba* and slinging the scarf-like *kaffiyeh* over his shoulder. "I'll be broiling."

The México looked around the campsite and was cautiously pleased to see everything still in place—the pressure tent inside the cave, the filament screen, the other *Midge*. He dug in the confusion of the cargo compartment again and dragged out some tubes of water and a package of threesquares. Holding them up to his suit light did not reveal any discolorations or other signs of infestation, so the *nauallis* stuffed them into the pockets of his cloak.

Prepared for a long walk, Hummingbird retraced his steps and then pressed on, following the scuffed, irregular tracks left by Anderssen's blind flight.

Gretchen was sitting on a low outcropping, her face washed in cool golden light, arms clasped around her knees, when Hummingbird finally caught up with her. The México came to a halt at the edge of a tilted slab of sandstone, looking up at her. Hot pink reflections of high-altitude ice clouds blazed from his goggles.

"Are you all right?" He sounded very tired on the comm, though the channel was perfectly clear at such close range.

"I am alive," Gretchen said. She did not look down at him, but raised her head to indicate the eastern sky. "Look."

The edge of a ruddy, golden sun would soon rise above the horizon. For a moment, Hummingbird saw nothing and then—a bright point stabbed down from the heavens, cutting across the spreading roseate glow before vanishing in a bright streak.

"A meteor," he said.

Gretchen turned her head, resting one cheek on her arm. "There have been three while I've watched. Doctor Smalls will be watching them too, from the *Palenque*, and he will be sad. They served him faithfully while they lived."

"His meteorology satellites," Hummingbird replied, climbing up onto the outcropping. "Hadeishi will have diverted them into decaying orbits—letting them burn up in the atmosphere."

"You shouldn't sit down," Gretchen said, unfolding herself as the *nauallis* approached. "Don't you see the color of the sky?"

The México frowned, forehead creasing, but then a faint dim line along the horizon caught his attention. "*Aiii* . . . it is dawn. The storm."

Together, they walked quickly back toward the cliff. Gretchen's feet were sore—she hoped she didn't have to run anywhere today—but she was more concerned with the odd way her sight was behaving. Suspicious, Gretchen changed the setting on her goggles to normal intensification. The shale and broken sandstone she was crossing remained sharp and distinct, despite the predawn darkness cloaking the land. *I can see in the dark?*

She stopped and bent down, running a hand across scattered chunks of eggshell-thin stone. A dissonant, queasy feeling roused, stirred by the motion of her fingers against something standing still. Gretchen slashed her hand back and forth, as fast as she could. *Odd and odder*, she thought, grappling with a perception of her hand moving very slowly, with sort of a staccato afterimage trailing along behind.

"Check the tie-downs." Hummingbird turned toward the overhang without looking back. "The filament screen needs to be repaired."

Gretchen looked up, catching a furtive glimpse of the *nauallis* stepping past the glistening sheet of monofilament. At the same time, she saw him both outside and inside the barrier. Anderssen blinked in surprise, lifted her goggles and rubbed her eyes. When she looked again, the tripartite vision was gone.

"Hurry," his voice echoed. "The wind will be rising soon."

The storm shrieked and wailed against the filament screen blocking the entrance to the cave. A rain of sand rattled endlessly against the magnetically-stiffened monofilament before slithering down into a steadily growing drift. A sustained high-pitched ringing—Gretchen thought it came from the cables holding down the ultralights—shivered in the air. She turned her face from the glowing, saffron-yellow light filtering down through the storm and the filament screen. Hummingbird was sitting with his back to a chunk of basalt, staring at nothing.

Gretchen scraped the last of a threesquare from the bottom of a battered steel cup. Today she was so hungry the sludge didn't need chile sauce to make it palatable. She waved the spoon in the air experimentally, but the blurred—or tripled—vision effect had faded. There was only a metal spoon in the dim light of the cave.

"Last night . . ." she started to describe what she'd seen, but then changed her mind. "I would feel stupid about running," Gretchen said, glaring at the old México-ica, "but you were running too. So what *did* come out of the cave? Were we ever in any danger?"

"We were," Hummingbird replied. He seemed tired, too. "Even at the end, when they had no more substance than a shadow, we were still in danger. I thought . . ." He stopped, considering his words. "When you ran, I feared things would go badly for you. I am glad they did not. We were lucky."

"We were idiots—*I* was an idiot," Gretchen said in a very sharp tone. "They *ate* the energy released by the Sif bullets, didn't they? If I hadn't done that, we'd have been able to walk right out."

"You did not know what would happen. I did not know either." Hummingbird made a dismissive gesture. "And I wonder if they *did* eat the bullets from your gun. I'm not sure they had the strength to do so. We might have seen only an echo of what the substance experienced. A living, moving memory."

"I saw a flechette in one, hanging in the air, as if the explosion *itself* had slowed down and was being consumed!"

"I wonder . . ." Hummingbird raised an eyebrow wryly. "If we go into the tunnel and examine the rear wall, it may be we find the impact marks of each and every flechette—if the entire passage has not collapsed as a result of the explosions."

Gretchen's face screwed up in a disbelieving grimace. "Does this happen a lot with your *sight?*"

"Sometimes." Hummingbird's expression turned grim. "Achieving clarity does not mean you have learned to discern truth from falsehood. The world around us is filled with too much data. Why else would our infant minds learn to hide so much from our consciousness? Some students are blinded by the clarity they achieve." He raised two fingers. "This is the second obstacle a student must overcome: control of sight."

"How long," Gretchen said, rather suspiciously, "does that take?"

"Years." Hummingbird's voice was flat. His right hand twitched. "The drug I gave you . . . is a shortcut. But one usually given only to students who have passed the first obstacle."

"Which is?" Gretchen's lips drew tight and a dangerous glitter entered her eyes. *What was in that packet? What did he do to me?*

"The first obstacle is fear, Anderssen-*tzin*. It is to achieve clarity of mind before you attain clarity of sight." The *nauallis* shrugged. "I admit giving you the *teonanacatl* was a throw of the beans. I was hasty."

Gretchen swallowed, her throat dry with a bitter aftertaste, and she drank deep from one of the water bottles. Even the stale, metallic taste was preferable to the flat, oily fluid from her recycler. "You seem to be a very reckless man, Hummingbird-*tzin*. Are you well regarded by your fellows?"

The *nauallis* did not reply, his eyes becoming guarded again. Gretchen stood up and put her cup and spoon away, stowing them in the little cook kit from her rucksack. Nervously, she paced the perimeter of their shelter, listening to the storm wailing outside and peering through the filament at the *Gagarin*. Both *Midge*s seemed to be intact, though they were straining against the sand anchors like hounds against the leash. Finally, when the unsettled, churning feeling in her stomach had leveled off to a dull burn, she examined her hands in the dim, sulfurous light from outside.

Gloves. Fingers. They seemed entirely ordinary. *Can I focus? How do I . . .*

She concentrated, trying to discern the superlatively sharp level of detail she'd perceived before, where every grain and pore and wrinkle in the gloves came into view. Nothing happened. Her head started to hurt. Scowling, she pushed up her goggles and rubbed both eyes wearily. *Stupid clarity . . . nevermind.*

"What are we going to do about the tunnel and chambers?" Gretchen hugged herself, feeling cold despite the suit heaters. "Don't you have to 'clean it up' somehow?"

Hummingbird nodded slowly. He pointed at the entrance to the overhang. "In my *Midge* there are explosives, somewhat more powerful than your shockgun. When the daystorm clears, I will go into the tunnel and place them."

Gretchen laughed, unaccountably relieved to hear something so mundane and practical from the old man. "You're going to blow the place up? Now that *does* sound like the Empire at work!"

"Each tool," he said stiffly, "to a purpose. Those structures serve as a focus for this 'color' we saw. They allow something to take a shape where it should have none. So, I will destroy the entire location and hope—hope, mind you—the memories clinging to the stones and rocks themselves are scattered into oblivion."

"And the cylinders we saw in the inner room?" Gretchen clenched her fists tight against her sides. "You'll bury them under a million tons of rock?"

Hummingbird nodded slowly, watching Gretchen's face intently. "I will."

"What about Russovsky? What do you think happened to her?"

"She stumbled into part of a dream, someplace where a fragment of this sleeping power seized and consumed her. In that moment, she was taken over, into its context, rather than our own. Something came back out—the shape you saw in the first cave—like a ghost, perhaps curious, perhaps a reflex of her own memory. Even a shape retains memory of its past."

"The version of her on the ship was only an echo?" Gretchen tried not to lick her lips nervously. "Do you think she might have survived the experience? Maybe she woke up later and found her ultralight gone, taken by the copy?"

Hummingbird was nonplussed. His eyes narrowed in suspicion. "Have you seen something to indicate she survived?"

"I . . . no, no I haven't seen anything I could swear was real."

"But you saw Russovsky, or something which looked like her." The *nauallis* gave her a sharp look. "Last night? When the gray was upon you?"

"Afterward," she admitted. "When the gray—the visions—had passed. She helped me up. I felt her hand—a physical hand—in mine!"

"And then?" The *nauallis* rose and came to her side. His green eyes were tense and sharp. Gretchen could feel him *looking* at her. The sensation made her skin crawl and she backed away.

"Then—nothing. I was distracted for a second and when I looked back, she was gone. I looked all 'round, but . . . nothing. Vanished."

"An illusion?" Hummingbird sounded as if he were questioning himself. "The radiance of the gray grew stronger when the flechettes exploded—and then it weakened very quickly, as if being so strong, so solid, exhausted the energy. By the time it surrounded us, there was barely anything left."

Gretchen spread her hands. "Maybe. I have no idea, really. You're the one with the secret knowledge. But tell me this—you stopped, you sat down, you let the 'gray' wash over you. Why? What had you guessed about them?"

"I risked." The corners of the México's eyes crinkled up. "Such ephemeral things as these, they exist on a very narrow margin. They are parasites. They need to 'eat' with as little cost to themselves as possible. If there is a rich source of what they need, they will flock to it like bacteria growing in the outwash of a factory power plant." One hand moved to indicate the mountain above them. "This is not a rich paradise. This is a desert. Here *we* are food, not just our bodies, but the exhalation of our breath, the leakage from our recyclers, radiation from our power-packs. The explosion of the bullets from your gun."

Gretchen pressed a thumb against her left eyebrow. A too-familiar tickling was starting to brew behind her eye. Swallowing a trace of nausea, she punched a code on her medband. "So—you're saying our fear and panic were enough to keep them alive."

"Fear," Hummingbird said, giving her a piercing look, "is always the enemy."

Gretchen turned away again, waiting for the chill rush of meds to blanket her rising migraine. Talking to Hummingbird made her very tired. She peered out through the filament, seeing the daystorm had settled into a reddish haze, reducing visibility to almost nothing. She did not feel at all well.

By mid-afternoon, the storm dwindled away into a herd of dusty whirlwinds dancing on the plains east of the Escarpment. A singular hour arrived, wherein the eastern sky was fully light and the air had fallen still. Gretchen and Hummingbird emerged from the overhang to find the ultralights partially buried in blown sand. The east steadily darkened as they worked, clearing a coating of dark cadmium-colored dust from the wings and making sure the air intakes and engines were free of microflora.

The sun passed behind the peaks of the Escarpment and shadow swallowed the camp. Hummingbird and Gretchen were both busy inside the overhang, packing the last of their gear into rucksacks or carrybags, so they did not notice the upper wing of the *Gagarin* suddenly glow with a soft, diffuse light. The forward edge grew dark for a moment, then pulsed once, then twice. A brief interval of darkness followed, before the phosphor array resumed flickering in a series of bright, sharp pulses.

After a moment, the light dimmed down to nothing, though close examination would show the phosphor array shifting state with dizzying speed. Inside the aircraft, the main panel flickered awake and a number of gauges and dials registered commands passing through the control system. The in-flight data recorder switched on and, after a flicker of conversation between the appropriate subsystems, went into "quiet" mode.

Then everything went dark again, save for the local comm relay, which was now awake and listening for suit traffic.

THE CORNUELLE

Mitsuharu sat in his office, overhead lights dimmed down to rows of faint orange glowworms. A single hooded lamp cast a circle of sharp white light on the papers, storage crystals and pens covering the top of his desk. A comp panel on the bulkhead was filled with a navigational plot—a bright dot for the ship and five hundred thousand kilometers of asteroid, meteor debris, interstellar ice and dust in all directions. The image had been building for hours, data flowing in slowly from the ship's skin fabric and the newly tuned g-array.

In the dim light, the captain's face was mostly in shadow, head against the back of his chair, eyes closed, thin-fingered hands clasped on his breast. The rest of the room, the stacks of books, the ancient pottery bowls and rice-paper paintings were entirely dark.

A sound recording was playing. Children were singing, their careless voices echoing from the walls of an unseen building.

> *Kaeru no uta ga*
> *Kikoete kuro yo*
> *Guwa . . . guwa . . . guwa . . . guwa*

In the background, the sound of trucks passing on a road mixed with the high, thin drone of a supersonic transport overhead. Dogs barked in the distance and a woman called out. The children splashed in water and sang another round, voices sweet in unconscious harmony.

> *Ge ge ge ge ge ge ge ge,*
> *Guwa guwa guwa*

In his memories, Mitsu knew the building had whitewashed wooden walls and a roof of green iron. Paper lanterns ornamented with pen drawings of birds and flowers hung from the eaves. Inside the house, the floors were glossy dark redwood, with *tatami* mats and rice-paper screens between the rooms. An old man would be sitting in his study, short white hair lying flat against a sun-bronzed scalp. He would be reading, a book turned into the cool light slanting down between the closely spaced buildings. The study smelled of mold and paper and dust and ink.

Guwa . . . guwa . . . guwa . . . guwa, sang the children in the yard. They were playing with frogs.

On the comp display, another level of detail slowly appeared, etching images of tumbling, shattered mountains of ice and stone and iron ever clearer.

In his memories, Mitsu knew the street in front of the little house was black macadam, potholed and crumbling at the edges. He heard a delivery truck putter past and saw an enameled red panel with the word ASAHI painted in black and yellow. Thick green grass sprouted from every crevice along the sidewalks. The walls of the houses were tinged with moss and tiny blue flowers.

On this day, as the children splashed in the mud, making frog pens of twigs and glass jars from the kitchen, the sun was shining through heavy gray clouds, making the air sparkle and shimmer. To the east, a line of mountains rose, white shoulders gleaming with ice and snow.

The recording ended. After a short pause, the scratchy, keening sound of a bow scraping across taunt gut string emerged from the quiet silence. The *shamisen* wailed up into the sound of falling leaves. A hand drum began to tap in counterpoint. Mitsu settled deeper into his chair, letting the warm fabric carry the weight of his head. The strings and the drum lifted into summer wind and a reedy bamboo flute joined them, carrying falling rain.

A man's voice—deep, hoarse, rich as the rivers and streams beneath the Golden Mountain, melancholy with longing for a homeland lost beyond the sea—began to sing. One of the musicians coughed, almost covering the sound with the hem of his kimono.

Kimi ga yo wa,
Chiyo ni yachiyo ni,
Sazare ishi no

Mitsu could see his father sitting on the edge of the porch surrounding the garden, face shining in the light of the lanterns and lamps. The *shamisen* across his leg was a dark walnut color, faced with amber-tinted pine. In memory, the hands were nimble on the strings, while the porch roof and the house walls gave his graceful voice a full, mellow echo.

Iwao to nari te,
Koke no musu made

On the comp display, the ship continued to move in endless night, skin taut against the fabric of space, straining to hear the slow lilting song of gravity humming in the void.

SLOT CANYON TWELVE

After hiding in a cave for two days, Gretchen felt relieved to be airborne and mobile again. The *Gagarin* hummed around her, engines chuckling, broad wings spread wide, canopy whistling with the familiar, proper sound of air rushing past. The night around her was blessedly still and the ultralight made a slow, tight turn in the narrow confines of the canyon. Sheer rock walls drifted past, shining glassily in the glare of the wing lights. Gretchen had turned off the collision alarm— though the canyon was hundreds of feet wide, the turning radius of the *Midge* brought the wingtips almost to brushing distance on each circuit.

Below, the phosphor-bright illumination cast by Hummingbird's ultralight made the canyon floor a sharp jumble of black and white, boulders and sand. Gretchen could see twin coils of water vapor rising from the idling engines. The *nauallis*, however, was nowhere to be seen. The tunnel entrance was a void of darkness against the matte nothingness of the cliff.

The momentary vision swept away as the *Gagarin* continued its turn. Gretchen tried to maintain focus on the aircraft and keep her slow, spiraling turn going, but she was worried. The México had been inside too long for comfort. *Feels like an hour,* she grumbled to herself. *How long,* she suddenly wondered, *would it take for the gray to make a copy of a single ragged crow?*

The *Gagarin* arced around again, now at least a hundred meters from the canyon floor, and she caught sight of something bright out of the corner of her eye. Gretchen looked down and to the side, trying not to reflexively swing the aircraft to follow her eye movement, and saw the trapezoidal door now lit from within by a cold, pale light.

"Hummingbird!" Gretchen's voice spiked in alarm. "Let's go!"

A figure bolted out of the opening, cloak flying out behind him. A too-familiar radiance filled the doorway and in the cold sepulchral glare she saw the man hurl himself into the cockpit of the *Midge* and slam the door shut. Cold oily light spilled out onto the dust, lapping around splintered sandstone and granite. Both engines flared bright with exhaust and the *Midge* leapt forward, sand spewing away from the wheels.

Gretchen pulled back gently on the control yoke and *Gagarin* soared up into the dark, constricted sky. The overhanging cliffs on either side rushed in, but she adjusted nimbly, sweat beading in the hollow of her neck, sending the ultralight dancing higher. Through the transparent panel under her feet, Anderssen saw the other *Midge* dart up the canyon, lifting off only meters ahead of the advancing radiant tide.

The cold light cut off—a shutter slammed on an empty window—and Gretchen felt the air in the canyon heave with a sudden, sharp blast. A cloud of black smoke jetted from the tunnel mouth, drowning the queer light, and Hummingbird's *Midge* wobbled in flight as a shockwave rolled past.

Gretchen wrenched her attention back to the business of flying, narrowly dodging the *Gagarin* around a jutting outcropping. The airframe groaned, complaining at such rough handling, but the *Midge* swept past the obstacle and soared on down the canyon. Below her, Gretchen was peripherally aware of Hummingbird's ultralight straining to catch up.

The canyon behind both aircraft filled with a black, turgid cloud of dust and ash. The cliff-face above the tunnel shuddered, still rocked by the violence of the explosion and then—with majestic, slow grace—splintered away from the core of the mountain and thundered down into the canyon. More dust, ash and grit roared up with a flat, massive *thump*.

Gretchen heard the blow, and grinned tightly, fingers light on the stick. This business of flying at night, even with goggles, radar and the strobe-white glare of the wing lights was tricky business. *I hope that's the end of the nasty dirty color,* she thought peripherally, some tiny corner of her mind pleased to see something which had threatened her destroyed.

The odometer on the control panel began to count the kilometers as they flew on into the night. There was a long way to go before dawn roused the slot canyon to near-supersonic violence.

———————

Behind the massive barrier of the Escarpment, dawn was much delayed. When the clear, hot light of the Ephesian primary finally pierced the canopy of the *Gagarin*, both ultralights were far out over the western desert. Hummingbird's *Midge* was only a hundred meters to starboard, easily keeping pace in the cool, thick morning air.

Gretchen clicked local comm open. "Shall we land?"

She hadn't heard a peep from the *nauallis* since they'd left the canyon. Watching the roseate glow of dawn creeping across the rumpled, barren landscape below them was interesting enough without his company. They had passed over a broad valley filled with pipeflowers in the predawn hours and Gretchen had been very glad the spindly, fluted organisms were quiescent after sunset. There had been places—deep ravines or defiles in the broken land—where jeweled lights had gleamed in the ebon blanket of night.

The palaces of the fairy queen, she thought, staring down at the traceries and cobwebs of trapped, frozen light passing below her. *And by day? Nothing, only desolation and lifeless stone. I wonder if Sinclair has dared see the desert by night, her veils drawn aside. . . .*

"Are you tired?" Hummingbird's voice sounded thick and muzzy.

"Have you been sleeping?" Gretchen frowned across the distance between the two aircraft. She couldn't make out more of the *nauallis* than the outline of his *kaffiyeh* in the close confines of the *Midge* cockpit. "We should set down before the air grows too thin—we need to conserve fuel after burning so much to reach the summit of Prion."

"Understood," he said, voice clearer. She could see him shift in his shockchair. "Pick a suitable location."

He was sleeping, she thought wryly, glancing at the autopilot display on her panel. *He slaved his* Midge *to* Gagarin *and tagged along like my little brother at a Twelfth Night party.*

Scratching a sore on her jaw where the rebreather strap was starting to wear, Gretchen began to scan the radar map of the land ahead, searching for a cave or ridge or anything which would let them escape the heat and brilliance of the sun. *I wonder what our trusty guide has to say.*

She punched up the travel maps in Russovsky's log and began going through the notes, wondering where the geologist had landed on her circumnavigation of the globe. After twenty minutes of keeping one eye on the horizon and one on the maps, she opened the local channel again.

"There's a place ahead," Gretchen said, squinting at the lumpish dun-colored landscape. "Russovsky calls it Camp Six—a canyon, an overhang big enough to pull a *Midge* into the shade—she'd stayed there two, three times. About an hour, hour and a half."

The *nauallis* responded with a grunt and Anderssen was disgusted to see him lean back in his shockchair, apparently asleep again.

The full weight of day was upon the land, flattening every color and detail to burnt brass. Russovsky's overhang stood in the curve of a long, S-shaped ravine where hundreds of tons of sandstone had crumbled away, leaving a fan-shaped talus slope. Gretchen climbed among the upper rocks, laboring to breathe as she pulled herself up onto a tilted, rectangular boulder. She stood up and the roof of the raw amphitheater was within arm's reach.

Curious, she scanned through a variety of wavelengths visible in her goggles. From below, where the two *Midge*s stood in partial shade and Hummingbird was puttering around the camp, setting up the tent and making a desultory attempt at breakfast, she'd seen a faint pattern on this rock, something like interlocking arcs or circles.

Close up she didn't see anything unusual, which Gretchen admitted to herself was par for the course. *Rock fractures or mineral deposits . . .* A little miffed at getting excited over nothing she looked around, taking in the barren, sun-blasted landscape. The ravine was very peculiar-looking to her eye—no water had run on the surface of Ephesus III for millions of years, so the bottom of the "canyon" was jagged and littered with fragile-looking debris. A similar canyon on Earth or Ugarit would have been washed clean, worn down, abraded by flash floods or even a running stream. But there was nothing like that here, only the evidence of constant wind.

No litter in the shade, she thought, *left by those who passed this way before. No broken bits of pottery, flaked stone tools, arrowheads. No detritus of bones from the kill, cast aside from where a fire burned against the stone, leaving soot buried deep in every crevice. Nothing but the spine of the world, open, exposed, left out to bleach in the sun. . . .* Gretchen thought she understood why Russovsky had spent so much time alone in the wasteland, drifting on the currents of the air, floating high in the sky in her *Midge.*

"Is there lunch yet?" Anderssen began picking her way down through the broken, eggshell-like slabs of sandstone.

"Yes," Hummingbird said in a grumpy voice.

Gretchen sighed, but said nothing, preparing herself for threesquares straight from the tube.

She was not disappointed, though the México had scrounged up some flavored tea. Still, protein paste was protein paste, even if the taste approximated the reddish dust covering every surface in all directions. Gretchen watched Hummingbird eat, making sure he finished his daily ration and drank all his tea. When the *nauallis* was done, she lifted her chin questioningly.

"Can you show me what to do? How to control this sight?"

Hummingbird looked up, green eyes clouded with distracted thoughts. "I can show you how to begin," he said slowly, as if each word were painful. "Small things. Simple things."

"Fine." Gretchen squared her shoulders, feeling a kink in her neck. *He's worried.* "Whatever you think is safe. Just being able to tell when I'm *seeing* or just seeing would be good."

The *nauallis* nodded, looking around him on the ground. "Take a moment," he said, voice subtly changing tone. "Close your eyes, let your mind empty, and feel around among these stones. Find one which feels right in your hands. Don't hurry. We're not going anywhere."

Gretchen did as he bid, though after finally sitting down to eat she felt very tired. Flying by night sort of implied sleeping by day, a little voice muttered in her head, not crawling about among broken shale. As before, when she closed her eyes a great commotion seemed to brew up in her thoughts. This time, the voices and memories and flashes of things she'd seen or done or heard were overlaid by a patina of exhaustion which made them distant and faded. Old sepia-tone images of her life. Despite a great desire to curl up in her sleepbag, Gretchen moved blindly around the camp, letting her fingers see the sand and grit and broken little stones.

Eventually, her hand touched something and she stopped. The bit of rock felt warm, almost hot, even through her gloves. Gretchen opened her eyes. She was at the edge of the rockfall, far from the brilliant demarcation of light and shade. The glassy, dark stone in her hand was curved and sharp along one edge. *Could make a tool from this,* she thought, turning the piece of flint over in her hands. *Without much work at all.*

"How does that feel?" Hummingbird said. He was lying down in the tent, his eyes closed.

"Good," Gretchen replied, becoming aware of the *rightness* of the stone in her hand. "It felt warm for a moment."

"Put it in your pocket," he said. "Now close your eyes again and feel about. But this time, find a stone which does *not* feel proper. One you do not wish to touch. Take your time."

Frowning a little at the *nauallis*, who had folded his arms over his chest and gone back to sleep, Gretchen tucked the flint into one of the cargo pockets built into her vest. Closing her eyes brought on a surging sense of drowsiness, but she soldiered on, letting her hands drift across the ground, letting her slow, crawling motion carry her wherever it would.

A little later, after cracking her head painfully against a boulder, Gretchen gave up the search as a bad job and crawled into the tent. Hummingbird was fast asleep, his partially detached breather mask serving as an echo chamber for a snuffling kind of snore. Gretchen made a disgusted face at him, then collapsed on her own sleepbag, utterly spent.

"This just isn't the same," Gretchen said, late in the afternoon, as she and Hummingbird were eating again, waiting for the sun to set and the air to chill enough to fly. "There's no campfire to sit around. No flickering light on the cave walls, no darkness beyond the firelight, filled with strange sounds . . . the gleam of eyes as hunting cats prowl by."

Hummingbird grunted, sucking the last of a puce-colored threesquare from its tube. Gretchen had not offered to share any of her tabasco, drawing an aggrieved look from the old man. "Our common ancestors," he said, wiping his lips, "would not have considered such a scene 'homey' or 'nostalgic'. The cough of a jaguar in the night was a cause for terror, not comfort."

"I suppose." Gretchen was kneeling in the knocked-down tent, rolling up her sleepbag. "So—I didn't find an improper stone this morning—should I look again?"

Hummingbird raised an eyebrow at her and then laid a finger on his temple. "Really?"

Gretchen rubbed her brow, then winced to feel the bump from running into the boulder. "Well, I guess . . . say, how long will it take me to learn the good stuff?" She started to grin. "Like flying or throwing lightning from my hands or changing into an animal, like in the old tales?"

"I do not teach such things!" Hummingbird snapped, suddenly angry. His face compressed into a tight frown and Gretchen moved back involuntarily. "The way of the *tlamatinime* is subtle, balanced. We follow the line of the earth, we do not break balance or distort what is."

"Oh." Anderssen eyed him warily, seeing an unexpected, fulminating anger shining in his lean, wrinkled old countenance. "Not a problem. I understand."

"I doubt that," the México growled, rising abruptly. "You've plighted troth to a *science* which barely acknowledges balance at all—much less attempts to move in accord with that which is."

"Wait a minute," Gretchen said, her own anger nettled by the fury in his voice. "Science seeks to understand, not to destroy. I was joking, old crow, joking." She paused, a flicker of doubt crossing her face. "Are there . . . there aren't judges who can fly, are there?"

Hummingbird looked away, attention fixed on the horizon, where the sun was sliding down toward night, a huge red-gold disk with wavering purple edges.

"No," he said after a moment. A hand waved negligently at the *Midges* parked in the shade. "Though we fly ourselves, with some help. But your science . . ." He sighed.

"I don't understand," Gretchen said, trying to keep from sounding antagonistic. "The more we learn, the fuller our understanding grows, the better mankind can exist in this universe. We learn, old crow, our *science* learns."

"No. No, it does not." Hummingbird rubbed the edge of his jaw, lips pursed, staring at her in an appraising way. "Your science . . . your science is about *control*, Anderssen-*tzin*, not about understanding. Now, listen to me before you raise your voice in defense of the beast which whelped you! I have met many of your colleagues; on Anáhuac, in the orbital colonies, on the frontier worlds. There are men and women among their number I admire. Many of them mean well. My quarrel is not with these people, but with the doctrine they serve."

"What?" Gretchen fell silent as Hummingbird raised a hand sharply, though her eyes narrowed in irritation.

"The basis—the seed, the root, the wellspring—of your science, Anderssen-*tzin*," he said, settling down to the ground, legs crossed, "is to make things happen the same way not just once, not twice, but a thousand times. It is to learn enough, discover enough, to allow a human being to *control* the processes of the universe. From sparking fire to forging a bronze knife to making a reliable breather mask." Hummingbird tilted his head a little to one side, amusement glinting in his dark eyes. "Isn't that the heart of your science? The evolution of a hypothesis into a theory? The definition of fact? Of scientific truth?"

"No," Gretchen said, feeling like she'd stumbled into a first-term philosophy class. "You're confusing the goal of engineering with the process of science. And not the first person to do so, either." She sniffed, tilting up her nose. "Engineering is about reliability and process control—but science . . . science is about learning why things work, not just how. Science . . ." She paused, failing to wrestle her words into something succinct and pithy. "Our science is just like your *seeing*, but born from the mind, from logic, not from an organic alkaloid."

Hummingbird grunted dismissively. "Logic is the construct of a human mind and prey to every failing thereof. The universe around us is not *logical*, not at its heart."

Gretchen's nose twitched, as at a foul smell. "There is always accident, chaos, uncertainty."

"Yes," Hummingbird said, starting to smile. "There is. The bane of your mechanistic technology—the enemy of order, the devil which must always be pursued, always driven out. Consider, Anderssen-*tzin*, if you turn in a dig report which is incomplete, which leaves data unaccounted for, analysis undone—is your supervisor pleased? Does he laud your efforts?"

"No." Grimacing, she made a *so-what* motion with her hand. "So we chase something unattainable—is that bad? Is that something to deride or disparage? You're pleased enough to ride in an aircraft which will work reliably! Disorder is no friend of humanity."

Hummingbird's head rose at her words and a calculating, weighing expression came into his lean old face. "Do you think so?"

Gretchen nodded, tapping her recycler. "Yes, I'd rather be able to see another sunset than choke to death on my own waste."

"There is a difference," Hummingbird said quietly, "between the individual and the race." He paused and the *hiss-hiss* of his air tube being idly bitten filled the comm circuit. "Are you familiar with the mortality rate among infants on planets newly colonized by the Empire? The so-called Lysenko effect?"

"Yes." Gretchen could not keep a dubious tone from her voice. Though the scientists on Novoya Rossiya were good Swedes, she did not agree with all of the work being done there. "Death rates among the first generation of colonists are high, but not unduly so for a new world being opened. First Settlement is dangerous work. But the second and third and fourth generations suffer from an incredibly high death rate among the young—sometimes as high as eighty percent. After the fifth generation, if the colony has managed to survive, the mortality rate begins to drop, eventually approaching, but never matching the Anáhuac baseline."

Hummingbird nodded. "This has been the focus of great debate. Many scientists have urged genetic modification of the colonists to better fit the parameters of their new worlds, so more children would survive."

"Yes, I have heard of this." Gretchen watched him carefully. As a rule, the Great Families did not colonize other worlds themselves, though they financed many settlements. The landless were sent out in their stead. There was great social and economic pressure on the *macehualli* to gain a landholding, even at great risk. She had reviewed the literature herself, in grad school. Millions had died. "The Empire has steadfastly refused."

Hummingbird smiled at the bitterness in her voice. The flat, golden light of the setting sun gleamed on his high cheekbones. "I will tell you a small secret, Anderssen-*tzin*. Nearly a hundred years ago, when this trend had repeated for the fourth time, the Emperor decreed that this thing, this genetic modification, would be attempted. A world called Tecumozin was selected and a generation of humans was pre-adapted for life thereupon."

"And?"

"They thrived for a time—two, three generations. Then a plague brewed up among them, something attacked the modifications which had been made to their core DNA. The entire colony was lost. The Emperor was perturbed and listened to us, the *naualli*, for a change." A brief flicker of irony colored his words. "A judge was sent and he went among the ruins, watching quietly and listening. What he found can—could—be best expressed as the planet being *angry* with the colony. No accord had been reached between the men who settled there and the fabric of the world around them. They had tried to gain power over it, recklessly. Very foolish."

"What do you mean?" Gretchen was disturbed. Every planet she had visited had held a particular, unique feeling or atmosphere. Ugarit was clearly different from Old Mars, but she had never thought of it as being "angry."

"What I mean is this; the race of man may come to thrive on an alien world, but he must reach a balance, he must pay a price for life within its shelter, and the price is blood. This is old, old knowledge among the México: All human life is sustained by the sacrifice of a few. In your terms, in the context of your science, the colonists needed to adapt in subtle ways to their new home. This is a delicate process and many die, unable to exist in the new environment. But a few live and prosper. And their children have found a balance with the new world. Your science is not subtle enough to rush the process, but we are a hardy race and *teoatl*, the fluid of life, is the opener of the way."

Hummingbird fell silent, watching her.

Gretchen stiffened, his words triggering a flowering of thought in her mind. Bits and pieces of studies she had read, personal experiences, stories heard around dig campfires, even the echoes of the old Church coalesced. "The Emperor sleeps soundly at night, does he, knowing the Empire is built on the bones of children?"

"This is the way it has always been. I hope it will always be so."

Gretchen felt sick, but there was a certain, cold sense to his viewpoint. To think progress could be gained free of cost, without struggle, was a child's daydream. She put down her tea, a sort of lost, distraught expression creeping into her face.

"You *would* let a station die—even if there were thousands of people aboard—to stop some kind of . . . infection . . . from entering the Empire. You'd just let them die. You'd let me die."

Hummingbird nodded. Gretchen felt his calm gaze like an iron band tightening around her heart.

"I would trade many lives to save our race," he said with a perfectly grim certainty. "A hand, any eye, a limb—as long as mankind survives, my work is done. An old man said this, long ago: 'It is not true we come to this earth to live. We come only to sleep, only to dream. Our body a flower, as grass becomes green in spring. Our hearts open, give forth buds, then wither.' So did Tochihuitzin say, and his words are as true today as they were then."

Gretchen's mouth twisted into an expression of complete disgust. "You're . . . you're not interested in justice at all. You're no more than an *antibody!*"

"Hah!" A sharp laugh escaped the old man. He grinned, teeth very white in the dim light beneath the overhang. "I am. A good word to describe what must be done for our tribe to survive. An antibody." He laid back down, chuckling to himself.

Parker ran his finger up a control gauge on the main pilot's panel and felt a subdued, distant roar shiver through the frame of the ship. "Commencing turnover,"
he announced on the public comm. "We are in z-g for sixty-five seconds."

The navigational display showed the *Temple*-class starship begin to tumble in
place, a constellation of maneuvering drives on the engineering ring blazing with
light. Parker watched silently, chewing on a rolled-up tube of plastic he'd scavenged
from Anderssen's kit. *Tastes better than the tabac,* he thought, feeling a twinge of
nervous urgency. His medband beeped sullenly, refusing to dispense more nicotine
into his system. The pilot scratched at a red abrasion along the edge of the silver
unit. *Freakin' company medical policy . . . it's my religious right. Goddamit.*

"Turnover complete," he said, sliding the maneuver drive control back to zero.
Another set of readouts was rapidly spiraling down to nothing as the ship completed the roll. The flare of exhaust guttered out, equalizing the ship's forward
momentum. Parker grunted in satisfaction. "Ship at . . . full stop. Main engines
zero thrust. Maneuvering drives zero thrust."

The view in the main display had shifted, following the rotation of the ship,
and a red spark glowed among black velvet and diamonds. Parker dialed up the

magnification, causing the half-disc of Ephesus Three to swim into closer view. "Better."

He turned, looking over his shoulder at the captain's station. Magdalena was barely visible, hunched down in her nest of blankets and quilts, only the thin yellow slits of her eyes visible. "Orders, *mon capitaine?*" Parker tried to look properly attentive, which was difficult given his unshaven face, sallow complexion and weary, fatigue-smudged eyes.

"I'm not the pack leader," she hissed in response. Her fur was getting matted too. "But we should stay."

"Okay," Parker said amiably. "I can nudge us into a long parking orbit, maybe spiral us back in a little bit at a time."

Commander's privy comm made an abrupt squeaking sound and Magdalena swung her chair around, scanning the feeds from various shipboard cameras. "Isoroku is coming topship," she said briskly, the tight fur around her nose wrinkling up. "With one of the Marines. Fitzsimmons."

"Starting delay one," Parker replied, as he tapped a series of glyphs on his panel, initiating a detailed diagnostic test of the ship's hyperspace generators. "That's four hours at least."

Magdalena was also in motion, keying a private channel to their Welshman, who appeared on camera in the mess area of habitat ring. Several of the scientists were also in the galley, trying to make an appetizing lunch from Fleet emergency rations and the remains of expedition supplies. "Bandao-*tzin*—Isoroku is heading to the bridge. He won't be happy we haven't left the system yet—see if you can locate *Heicho* Deckard. I can't find him on camera."

The gunner set down a cup of coffee and nodded, though he did not look up at the overhead. Instead, he said good-bye to Doctor Sinclair and wandered out into the main accessway, hands in the pockets of his jacket. Magdalena hoped he could run down the stray Marine quickly. She was a little on edge to be letting them run loose in the pack-ship.

The main door into the bridge cycled open, letting light from the access tube spill across a deck still showing gaping holes from their efforts to replace the damaged conduits. Magdalena wiped her hand across the surveillance v-panes and the entire panel went dark. She and Parker looked up with interest as *Thai-i* Isoroku pulled himself through the hatchway and kicked off to reach the edge of the command station. The Marine *gunso* followed, his hair a black, oily cloud behind his head, barely restrained by a snakeskin strap. Maggie thought Fitzsimmons looked a little worn down by the effort of restoring the engineering deck to service, though she supposed he might be worrying a little bit about Golden-hair. *As he should!*

"Repairs are complete." Isoroku's voice was gravelly and unused to conversation. He stared at Parker with narrow eyes, stonelike features showing nothing but incipient displeasure. "Transit status?"

"Running a preflight check right now," Parker said, concentrating on his control panel. "Should be finished in three, four hours."

"A waste of time," the engineer growled. "We've just finished tuning and adjusting every downside system—there's no reason to test them all again!"

"Procedure," Magdalena said, avoiding Fitzsimmons's searching gaze. The Marine was frowning a little and trying to get a good look at her control panel. "I'm sure everything will go smoothly with the test."

Isoroku turned his stone-hard expression on her and the Hesht felt a shiver of adrenaline. By conscious effort, she kept her ruff from stiffening, though facing a member of a strange pack without the restraining ritual of meeting-with-claws-sheathed made her queasy. "Our orders are to make transit from this system," the engineer said in a harsh voice, "for Ctesiphon Station as soon as possible. Both the main drive and the hyperspace gradient generator are now in working order. Pilot, have you plotted an entry vector and course?"

"He has not," Magdalena said, before Parker could reply. Her ears flattened back against her skull. She took care to speak slowly and carefully. "We are in no hurry, Isoroku-*tzin*. Nothing untoward has occurred on Ephesus Three or in the outer system. We are now at minimum safe distance for a transit, which means we can make gradient to hyperspace in minutes."

"We have our orders," the engineer said, a slight tic starting under one blood-shot eye. "The *tlamatinime* was very clear in his desire. This ship is to leave immediately. The *Cornuelle* will be following us with all speed."

"I understand your desire to rejoin your crew," Magdalena said, feeling her limbs tremble with the prickling rush of hunting-blood. "But I will not abandon my pack-leader in the midst of a desert with no hope of retrieval. The *Cornuelle*—"

"—will pick them up," Isoroku said in a sharp tone. He pulled himself sideways to the end of the command panel. Magdalena's chair turned smoothly, following him. Both of her hands—hidden under the blankets—flexed, claws sliding in and out of bony sheaths of cartilage. Deep grooves were already cut in the fabric.

"If they can," Magdalena said, black lips curling back from shining white teeth. "Yet the long-fang is far away, hunting among the flying mountains, farther than we from the planet. If something happens, then *chaguh* Hadeishi will have to race back at full acceleration to succor my pack-leader and your judge. The eldest-and-wisest wanted us to be *quiet*, Isoroku-*tzin*." She smiled, showing triple rows of curving white teeth. "Heshatun know something about being *quiet*. We will wait out here, for a few days, and see what happens."

"Our orders—" Isoroku's voice rose appreciably, twin spots of color appearing on his pockmarked cheeks.

"Are not valid aboard this ship," Magdalena hissed, body stiffening. "This is a civilian ship, not Fleet. Our salvage papers have been properly filed. You are our guests."

The peripheral vision of a Hesht happens to be particularly good, which let Magdalena keep an eye on both Parker—who had shrunk down behind his console with a waxy, distressed look on his face—and upon Fitzsimmons, who had anchored himself just inside the doorway, his back to the wall, fingertips on the grip of his sidearm.

"Our ship-den is in your debt, Isoroku-*san*," Maggie said, struggling to rein in her temper. "Your efforts to repair the engines are greatly appreciated, but we will *not* abandon our pack-leader."

The engineer looked to Fitzsimmons, who raised an eyebrow in response and shrugged. Isoroku's face screwed up in a bitter grimace. "What can you hope to do, if something happens to the judge and your 'pack-leader'?" Before she could reply, the engineer's nostrils flared minutely and he gave her a searching, sideways look. "How could you tell if they were in danger?"

"In just over a seven-day," Magdalena said, changing the subject, "Anderssen and the eldest-and-wisest will have returned to the observatory base camp. They will need to be picked up by a shuttle, yet we must be quiet in retrieving them." She looked curiously at Parker. "How far away is the *Cornuelle?*"

The pilot shrugged, spreading his hands. "No idea. They went 'dark' before reaching the asteroid field and we haven't seen a sign of them since. But if they are searching the belt, they must have moved further away from their point of arrival, which was two days at maximum acceleration from Three a week ago. I'd *guess* an intercept time of at least four days."

Magdalena shook out her shoulders, watching the engineer closely. She was sure the human male could estimate distance and speed as quickly as the pilot. There was just no reasonable or inconspicuous way for the *Cornuelle* to make the retrieval pickup. After a long moment, Isoroku's bitter expression grew worse, as though his face had been pickled in *yee* juice.

"Your 'pack-leader' has a plan?"

Magdalena nodded, swallowing a grin. "She does. We will pick her up—very quietly, very softly—in eight days."

"What if the *Cornuelle*—or one of her shuttles—arrives at the same time?"

The Hesht spread her hands, claws politely retracted. "Then we let long-spear-pack lift the wet cubs from the river and later, when we are all denned on Cte-siphon and fat with meat, we raise cups in their honor. *But if they do not come*, then *Palenque*-pride will be waiting and will snatch the drowning from the current and slip away, padding feet soft in the grass."

Isoroku's grimace did not waver, but the bull-headed man looked sideways at Fitzsimmons again. The Marine pursed his lips, tucked a wad of gum into his cheek and said: "Looks bad on the record, *Thai-i*, if you lose a judge by accident. There're not so many of them, you know."

The engineer's color deepened and he gave Parker and Magdalena a tight, angry stare. "I have no desire to see the *tlamatinime* or Anderssen-*tzin* die," he said, biting out each word with a click of his teeth. "Yet these orders were given for a reason. You are putting the lives of everyone on this ship at risk. You should consider what will happen if they die, if we die, or if something worse happens because of this course of action."

Magdalena stared back at him, a dangerous glitter in her eyes. "I will not be foresworn in my duty to the pack-leader, carver-of-stone."

Nodding sharply, Isoroku pushed away and sped off down the accessway. Fitzsimmons looked after him with a troubled expression, but then followed. He did not look back. Magdalena turned around in the circle of her nest once, then twice. Parker started to say something, but she hissed at him and he slunk off, avoiding her eyes.

Males, she grumbled to herself, feeling sulky. Her claws shredded the blanket. *Useless copper-stinking males. Bah!*

Later, when she had verified the locations of Isoroku, the Marines, Parker and Ban-dao on the surveillance cameras, Magdalena restored the v-panes showing the communications stream from Russovsky's *Midge*. Unfortunately, several of the peapod satellites had burned up in the atmosphere, reducing her 'eye' to a bare three orbital cameras. With such a reduced capacity to track and interpret the transmissions from the aircraft, she'd downgraded the feed to burst traffic, sending only compressed voice logs from the aircraft comm. She fretted about losing the video, but there was nothing to be done.

"In flight again," she muttered, watching a plot of the aircraft creeping across the vast curve of the planetary surface. A projected vector arced south-southwest. "Toward the observatory base. *Hrrrr*... three days at this rate, maybe four."

Checking again to make sure she wouldn't be disturbed, Maggie began listening to the latest set of voice recordings. After an hour, she gave up, rubbing sore ears. *Philosophy . . . kittens complaining about the food! They must be bored down there, just flying all night.*

The Hesht flipped quickly through some secondary data which had come up with the burst transmission, just making sure both aircraft were in good shape. As she did, a log section highlighted itself and chimed for attention. *What's this? A leak?*

"Parker," Maggie growled into her throat mike, "I need you to look at something."

"On my way," the pilot replied, sounding groggy and irritated. Maggie glanced over at the surveillance camera and her whiskers twitched to see the human male shuffling out of one of the cabins used by the scientists. His patterned shirt was on backwards. Turning her nose politely in the air, Maggie routed the log information to his navigation console and sat back, staring at the huge red disc of the planet filling the main v-pane.

A moment later, her head tilted to one side in confusion. "Where did that come from? What an odd color. Ah . . ." She opened another private channel to the crew's quarters. "Mister Smalls," she asked in a very polite voice. "Could you join us on the bridge?"

IN THE WASTELAND

A pair of glittering white contrails made two rule-straight lines against the velvety darkness of the Ephesian sky. Both *Midge*s hummed along, wing surfaces finely tuned to squeeze as much lift as possible from the thin atmosphere, ice crystals spiraling out behind them. In the *Gagarin*, Gretchen was letting the comp fly, her attention turned to the geologist's travel logs. Their flight path had carried them out over a truly vast desolation, leaving the uplands of the Escarpment far behind.

Gretchen looked over the maps one more time. Russovsky had marked them up with a variety of notes and scribbled amendments. Not all of them were in Náhuatl or even in Norman. Anderssen scowled, trying to make out a note marking an area they would fly over near dawn if they held their current course. *What is this? Old Russian, maybe.* She scratched her jaw thoughtfully, trying to remember how to read the blocky letters. Her grandmother had some books . . . thoughts of childhood yielded nothing but a memory of pine-smoke, nutmeg and pumpkin. Checking her comp found at least a phonetic alphabet.

"B-r-i-l-l-e-a-n-t," she spelled out, rather laboriously. Russovsky's handwriting was not the clearest in the world. "Or . . . brilliant. Hmm." *What does that mean? Well, something she saw from the air. Something very bright—perhaps even visible at night.* "Hummingbird? Are you awake?"

"Yes," came the answer—and the *nauallis*, for once, did not sound half-asleep.

"I'm looking at Russovsky's maps," Gretchen said, taking a moment to eyeball the horizon and the ground below. Sand. A barren flat covered with faint linear shadows. Anderssen grimaced, looking ahead. The field of pipeflowers disappeared rather abruptly into darkness. "And we've two options to reach the base camp. We can keep on this heading and enter an area she has marked 'brilliant' or swing north to follow a section of uplift."

"An odd thing to mark," Hummingbird replied. "Can I see the map?"

"It's on your comp . . . now," Gretchen said, tapping a glyph to send the file to his console.

There was momentary silence and then she heard the *nauallis* make a curious *hmm-hmm* sound. "This is in old script—Kievian Rus, I believe—and among those savages, the word 'brilliant' refers to 'almaz' or what we would term 'diamond in the rough.'"

"Diamond?" Gretchen shook her head. "So a geometric figure on the ground? That would explain why she could see it from the air."

"Not the shape," Hummingbird said, sounding a little puzzled himself. "Almaz is a cheap, colorless gemstone. There are Mixtec mining colonies on Anáhuac which mine the mineral for industrial purposes. It makes a particularly fine abrasive for certain processes."

"Hmm. If it's a mineral, perhaps Russovsky could see an open drift of the material as she flew overhead. Or . . . or her geodetic sensors revealed a vein of the stuff in the earth. She'd be sure to note something like that."

"Indeed." Hummingbird sounded satisfied. "So, do we swing north or not?"

"I think we should be careful," Gretchen said, checking her fuel gauges. "A day won't make an enormous difference one way or another and there's no sense risking—"

Out of the corner of her eye, Anderssen caught sight of Hummingbird's *Midge* suddenly lurch in the air and lose a hundred meters of altitude. At the same moment, her comp squawked in alarm and she heard the *nauallis* shout in surprise.

"I've lost an engine," he barked, the ultralight falling away toward the desert floor in an ungainly spiral. "Number one has shut down completely. I'm losing fuel on tanks four and five."

"Set down," Gretchen snapped, the *Gagarin* banking sharply to the right as she reacted. "I'm right behind you. Shut all your fuel feeds and go to an unpowered glide."

"Understood." Hummingbird's voice was calm and precise, though Anderssen immediately lost visual sight of the plunging aircraft. The contrail ended abruptly in a slowly falling cloud of ice. The *Gagarin* nosed over into a steep dive, wind shrieking under her wings, and Gretchen felt the pit of her stomach squeeze tight.

Her radar showed Hummingbird's *Midge* lose nearly a thousand meters of altitude before staggering into a kind of glide. By that time, Gretchen was swooping down out of the night sky, the falling ultralight in sight again. The upper wing of a *Midge* made a good reflector and by starlight her goggles could pick him out. Below them both, however, the land was dark and featureless, though Gretchen doubted the ground was soft as a pillow. *At least we're past the pipeflowers!*

"Switch your radar to ground-scan," she said tersely. "You'll need to find someplace flat—"

"Too late," Hummingbird snapped and his breath was harsh on the comm. Gretchen cursed—the altimeter jumped and radar suddenly revealed a broad, deep canyon rushing past below her—and pulled up, turning wide around Hummingbird, whose aircraft was skidding across the crown of a mesalike hill rising above the canyon floor. The *Gagarin* made a swooping, leisurely circle as the other ultralight bounced to a halt and Gretchen could make out rough, jagged cliffs on every side.

"Turn all your lights on," she said, hoping Hummingbird hadn't been knocked unconscious by the violence of his landing. "And put out your anchors."

Her breath puffing white in the chill air of the cockpit, Gretchen ignored everything but the radar image of the rock and stone and precipices below as she lined up to land. "Gently now," she whispered to the *Gagarin* as the ultralight drifted down out of the sky, airspeed dipping low, almost into a stall. "Easy . . . easy . . ."

The front wheel touched down, sending a shock through the airframe, and then the *Gagarin* was rolling to a halt a dozen meters from Hummingbird.

"The number four fuel pump is clogged up," Gretchen said, her voice muffled by the cowling around the engine. White fog billowed around her shoulders, oozing from the maintenance hatch in thin streamers. "Looks like a line cracked when you crashed and has been leaking hydrogen vapor into the casing. Everything's frozen solid." A little shaky from too much adrenaline and too little rest, she climbed down from the upper wing, holding tight to the wing struts to keep from slipping.

"Can it be fixed?" Hummingbird was unloading gear from the cargo compartment. He made a vague gesture at the dark, still night hiding the rugged mesa and canyon beyond. "Here?"

Gretchen gave him a sharpish look—completely lost on the man, given the lack of light—and ran her hands over the tools on her belt. "If we have a schematic of the engine and component details, I might be able to fabricate a new fuel line or fix the old one, but I don't know if the maintenance manuals are loaded into either comp." Gretchen tried to keep her voice light, but the prospect of doubling-up in one single remaining *Midge* made her feel sick. *We need both aircraft for the pickup,* she thought desperately. *The skyhook won't work with just one.*

"If they're not, we're in serious trouble." Anderssen cracked frost from her gloves, keeping her eyes away from the old man. "The weight ratio in one of these aircraft is marginal with one person and supplies. Two *can* fit, but not with much food, water or equipment. We could probably make base camp, but I don't know how long we'd last then."

"Don't worry." Hummingbird's tone was still perfectly even. "The *Cornuelle* will come looking for us soon and base camp is filled with Company supplies."

"It was," Gretchen said, picking her way across splintery, loose shale. There was a bitter edge to her voice. "You're thinking everything is still in place because we left so quickly. Maybe it is, but I've never seen an abandoned camp last—and with the microbiota here—well, I think we'll find bunkers filled with calcite flowers and beautiful stone cobwebs."

"Well . . ." The *nauallis* seemed to have lost track of what he was going to say. "What can I do to help, then?"

Gretchen pulled open the door of the *Gagarin* and slid into her seat. The lumpy confines were starting to fit properly, but she didn't know if that was because the chair had changed or she had. Biting her lip nervously, Anderssen started to punch up a document search.

"Anchor both aircraft," she said, fighting to keep a rising tide of despair from overwhelming her. "And . . . and set up the tent. Find someplace out of the wind— we're all exposed up here." Her voice trailed off in surprise.

Her search for "fuel line repair" had returned an immediate hit and the comp had helpfully opened a series of v-panes on the display, showing a complete schematic of the fuel pump, the circulatory system on Hummingbird's *Midge*, the specifics of the lines and tubes, and a checklist showing how to repair a broken one.

"What the?" Gretchen was entirely nonplussed. "There is no way," she said to herself, tabbing through the array of documents, "Russovsky shoehorned an AI into this comp. This is impossible. Just . . ." She blinked, staring at the checklist. The last entry read: *Buy your beautiful, smart pack-sister a drink, when we get back to the den. Paw Paw, Magdalena.*

"Maggie?" Gretchen stared around the deserted, windswept mesa top in amazement. Outside, vapor was still boiling out of the damaged *Midge* and she could make out the outline of Hummingbird as he stomped around, stitching the anchors into the rock. A creepy shiver ran up her back, making her switch her comm to a private channel. "Can you hear me?"

There was no answer, just the usual warble of tuneless static.

"Ok . . . maybe dear Magdalena is psychic." Gretchen read the checklist again.

Everything seemed straightforward enough, except one part about checking all of the fuel lines for microfine cracks. "How are we going to do that?"

The *Gagarin* rocked gently as Hummingbird unspooled an anchor line. Gretchen started to sort through her tools, reading each section of the instructions as she worked.

"All done." Hummingbird leaned against the *Midge*, one hand on the raised door. "I've put the tent in a crevice not too far away. Should be out of the wind." He stopped, watching her suspiciously. "What is it?"

Gretchen was regarding him appraisingly. "So, Hummingbird-*tzin*, an unbroken fuel line has a certain . . . wholeness . . . doesn't it? So someone with the *sight* should be able to see a crack or break or even a weakness—that would be a distortion of proper order, right?"

"Yes." The visible parts of Hummingbird's face became rather sour-looking. "They would."

"Good." Gretchen tapped the panel in front of her. "Here's a layout of the entire fuel system in your *Midge*. You need to check every centimeter for leaks or fissures. I'm going to fabricate a replacement for the broken line."

"Very well." Hummingbird stared stoically at the complicated spiderweb filling the v-pane. "Are these data on my comp?"

Gretchen nodded. "Make sure you have the hydrogen tanks locked off—we can't afford to lose any more fuel."

The old man nodded and turned away. Gretchen looked around the tiny cockpit and sighed. *Too small for this job.* She gathered up all her tools and plugged her hand comp into the main panel to make a copy of the instructions. "Maybe the tent is big enough."

A pale wash of violet was just beginning to tint the rim of the world when Gretchen climbed back up onto the *Midge* and unscrewed the engine housing. Hummingbird, wrapped in his cloak and a blanket, was squatting beside the main body of the aircraft, rubbing his hands together. Out in the open like this, without even the marginal shelter of an overhang or a cave, the night was ferociously cold.

"Pass me the other heater." Gretchen wedged the tube-shaped unit in above the pump and turned it on high-radiate. The unit was low on power, but she hoped there was just enough juice left to melt the ice and run the forced-air fan to disperse the resulting fog. While the heater hummed and glowed and blew blessedly hot air against her chest, Gretchen laid out her tools and parts on a technician's clingpad.

"You were able to make a replacement?" Hummingbird moved up next to her, angling himself into the warm draft from the heater.

"Yes," she said dryly, craning her head to peer inside the housing. "Modern science and technology triumph again. Did you check all the fuel lines?"

The *nauallis* nodded, arms wrapped tight around his chest. "Two show signs of damage. I marked them with colored tape. They've not cracked through."

"Yet." Gretchen brushed melting frost out of the way and began unscrewing the two valves holding the broken section of line. "We'll wrap them in steeltape later." She stifled a yawn. "This afternoon we'll press on and see if we can reach the camp in one long flight."

"Very well." Gretchen felt the old man shivering, even with his suit and the blankets and *djellaba*.

"Get in the tent," she said, giving him a concerned look. "You're losing too much body heat out here."

For a moment, Anderssen thought he would refuse and some sharp words about *pigheaded men* were on the tip of her tongue, but he nodded and climbed stiffly down. *He's had a big day*, she thought, watching him disappear in the direction of the tent. *Almost crashed twice. Very lucky, these judges, very lucky.*

The broken section of line came free in her hands and she put the part aside. A little can of compressed air blew out the usual gunk fouling the valves. "Huh. Should talk to Delores and Parker about maintenance on this bird . . . needs a tune-up."

Squinting, her goggles dialed up into a moderately high magnification, Gretchen eased the new line into the first valve. Her fingers were stiff from the cold, making fine work difficult. After the third failed attempt to line them up, she eased herself back and took a moment to warm her hands on the heater. Her eyes, back and shoulders were hurting from tension and cold and weariness. *Got to loosen up*, Gretchen thought, flexing her gloved fingers. *Maybe I should empty my mind and count*, she smiled a little at the memory of Hummingbird's pedantic, measured voice. Her brow furrowed, considering the situation. *Maybe I should . . . maybe I should try this with my eyes closed.*

The tube felt cold and round beneath her fingers, only a few centimeters long, ending in two delicate valve stems and a counter-rotating jacket to fix the connection tight. Gretchen let her shoulders and arms settle. She let herself count until the busy noise in her thoughts settled down and then faded away.

The warmth of the heater was almost hot on her left shoulder, but she shifted the tube gently until a familiar prickling heat suffused her fingertips. Trying not to lick her chapped lips nervously, Gretchen leaned forward slightly, letting the tube slide into proximity with the sleeve. Eyes still closed, working in complete, chill darkness, she slid the tube into the stem and finger-tightened the jacket, first on one side, then on the other. A moment later—it seemed like only seconds—she opened her eyes and smiled slightly to see the tube in place. *That was easy.*

The *Midge* tool kit had a specialized microdriver, which torqued down the two connections to the proper, factory-approved tightness. Gretchen sighed in relief when she was done and closed up the compartment with trembling fingers. A wave of complete exhaustion had crept up upon her and now dragged at every muscle in her body.

"Dawn soon," she muttered, climbing very stiffly down from the wing. The tools and the portable heater were slung over her shoulder, making what felt like an enormous, bone-crushing weight. "At least the tent will be nice and warm."

But the tent was too hot and the ground too hard. Hummingbird was snoring again, and she couldn't take the *heep-snort-heep* sound of his breathing. After laying in the sleepbag for an hour, too tired to remove her breather mask or even brush her teeth, Gretchen crawled out of the tent and into the mind-numbing cold again.

She climbed back up to the ultralights and made a desultory circuit, checking their tie-downs and anchors. The old México had done a fine job, each cable taut and balanced. Irritated, Gretchen walked to the edge of the mesa, stepping carefully among weathered, wind-blasted slabs and boulders.

The canyon below was entirely, impenetrably dark. Anderssen considered pitching a glowbean over the edge, just to see what might be revealed in the flickering blue-green light. The stars gleamed on her goggles, very bright and steady. The air had chilled to a supernal level of stillness, much as it did during the polar winter on Old Mars. *Good place for a telescope,* she thought, beginning to walk along the rim of the mesa, her back to the eastern sky. *But is there anything to see out here?*

Ephesus sat at the edge of one of the abyssal gulfs running through the spiral arm. There were few nearby suns, only clouds of dust, dark matter and interstellar gas. A lonely outpost on the verge of nothingness, hundreds of light years from another habitable world. Gretchen wondered, as she climbed a rough, rectangular outcropping, if the long-dead inhabitants had ever managed to pierce the envelope of air around their home world. Had satellites or orbital stations seen the *valkar* burst from the nothingness of hyperspace? Had anyone tried to escape? Or were the Ephesians still grubbing in the mud, trying to trap their dinner in woven nets or pit traps when the sky darkened with the killing cloud? *A million years . . . Earth was still a raw, primitive world. Only megafauna and protohominids fighting to survive in Pliocene swamps. Did we escape a similar fate by some quirk of chance?*

The thought made her feel despondent. Her heart did not easily agree with the prospect of a universe where man only lived and thrived by the fall of some random cosmic die. Gretchen realized Hummingbird's vision of a universe of frightful powers—of gods—offered a strange kind of comfort. *He believes men can alter the course of fate. He believes he can divert the engines of chance. Huh.*

Beyond the outcropping, a deep crevice split in the face of the mesa. *I should head back . . .* she started to remind herself, but then . . . *what's that? A light?*

Anderssen stopped and knelt down, peering over the edge into the darkness. There was a light. There were many lights, spreading in a delicate cobweb across the rock, making the ravine gleam and glitter like the stars above, a hidden galaxy of jeweled-colors and shining motes.

Like moss, a firemoss, she thought, lips quirking in a smile. *Life blooming from nothing. Even here, at the edge of annihilation.* Gretchen concentrated on the nearest filaments and was rewarded by a vision of delicate tendrils radiating out from a cone-shaped core. The surface seemed to glisten, though she doubted there was any kind of moisture in this system. *A superconducting energy trap, maybe? I wish Sinclair and Tukhachevsky were here. . . . They would love this. Ha! They'll be jealous when I tell them about all the things I've seen. God, I even miss that tub vodka of theirs.*

A sound interrupted her delight. Gretchen looked up, surprised. A cloaked figure knelt a few meters away, silhouetted by a wash of stars, *djellaba* and *kaffiyeh* wrapped expertly around narrow shoulders. An instant of surprise was replaced by a certain sense of recognition.

"What are you?" Gretchen stood up slowly, hoping to leave the firemoss undisturbed. Flakes of rock spilled away from her gloves, falling among the thready clusters. "You're not Russovsky, are you?"

"I am," answered the dark outline. The voice was hoarse, rusty, as if long unused. The shape stood as well, wiry blond hair hanging loose around her shoulders. "What are you?"

"A human being," Gretchen said, then stopped, horrified. Hummingbird wouldn't want her to give anything away. "A visitor."

"Am I a *human being?*" Russovsky came close and Gretchen could see her pale, lean face glowing with an inner light. Stunned, Gretchen realized she was seeing the pattern of a vibrant crystalline lattice seeping through the woman's skin. "My memories are strange. I was flying, high above the world. I was walking under the sea, among the bones of the dead."

"Yes, yes, you were. But you are not a human being now. You are an Ephesian, like the moss."

Russovsky looked down at the colony, her bare, unprotected face perfectly still. "No. I am not. The *hathol* are an incurious people, content with their long slow lives. I am restless. I need something I do not have."

"Everyone is restless," Gretchen laughed softly, breath puffing white around her breather mask. "Perhaps you *are* human."

"Are you content?" Russovsky moved closer and the light within her skin grew brighter. Her eyes shone like stars themselves. "Show me!"

Gretchen began to back away, feeling her way along the edge of the ravine. Something in the shape began to change and she felt the prickling of alarm. The voice continued to echo in her suit comm, but she realized there was no way Russovsky could make such a sound in the thin atmosphere, not without a comm link. She scrambled up and over the crest of the rocks. The figure stopped and was staring up at her. Without waiting for the shape to do something, Gretchen scrambled away as fast as she dared, heading for the tent and Hummingbird.

THE CORNUELLE

Mitsuharu was sitting cross-legged on the edge of his sleeping mat, a fall of snarled dark hair spread over his shoulders and chest when the comm lit up with an incoming message. An officious two-tone chime sounded, indicating a priority connection from the bridge.

"Hadeishi here," he said, putting down an ivory-handled brush. Guiltily pleased by the interruption—he did not enjoy the tedium of brushing—the *chu-sa* began plaiting his traditionally long hair up in a thick braid. "On screen."

Comm stabilized to reveal *Sho-sa* Koshō sitting on the bridge. To unfamiliar eyes the exec's stiff, controlled demeanor would have revealed very little beyond an impression of cool consideration. Mitsuharu saw a certain eager excitement in the tilt of the woman's eyes and the set of her mouth. There was also a brief, nearly undetectable, reaction of embarrassment to finding him almost naked, clad only in an undershirt, belt, trousers, boots, comm unit and medband.

"The g-sensor array has yielded up a match for the refinery ship," Koshō reported in a more-than-usually terse voice. "Distance is forty thousand k, by my estimate. Bearing two-six-three, elevation plus thirty-two."

"Right on top of us." Hadeishi allowed himself a quick, pleased smile. He botched the smaller over-and-under at the end of the plait and gave up, letting the shining dark hair, a little streaked with gray, lie loose against his back. "Deeper into the belt?"

Koshō shook her head, looking sideways at a hidden display. "Near the outsystem fringe. The bulk of the local drift is between us, so I've not been able to get a secondary detect with passive sensors."

"Clever." Hadeishi unfolded himself from the bed and found his uniform shirt. "Keeping close to the area they want to work, neh? And behind a shield of debris. What is their gravitational situation? Could they make gradient to hyperspace from their current location?"

The exec shook her head, an eager gleam of flickering in her eyes. "The local field is not smooth enough," she said. "They will have to bolt from cover if they wish to transit."

"A location fraught with compromise." Hadeishi sealed the shirt in a smooth motion with his thumb. "Their holds must be only half-full, but the takings are likely rich, enough to warrant the risk of remaining in-system. Have you laid in an intercept course?"

"*Hai, Chu-sa.*" Koshō stiffened fractionally. "Would you like to review the plot?"

"Not now." Hadeishi's thoughts were already leaping ahead to the next task. In any case, he had full confidence in Koshō's ability to maneuver the ship through this debris field. "I want to be in Outrider camera range as quickly as possible— while remaining hidden!" His tone turned serious. "If they bolt, we will have to catch them and we cannot risk a weapons exchange in open space."

Koshō frowned. Mitsu made a "go-ahead" motion with his hand.

"Hadeishi-*san*," she said, rather tentatively, "why not just spook them into making gradient? Then they'll be gone and the debris field will probably mask their departure from any . . . one who might be watching from Three."

"True." Hadeishi scratched at his beard in irritation. "I have considered this. Unfortunately, we know at least one shuttle from this refinery ship was operating in the atmosphere of Three—and what if they picked up someone or something? Though our *tlamatinime* is not currently aboard, I know he would be . . . ah . . . apoplectic if we allowed a gang of landless miners to make off with a First Sun artifact. Even a small one."

"I see." Koshō nodded. "I will arrange to approach under cover and in full stealth."

"Good." Mitsu cleared the comm channel and punched up *Thai-i* Huémac's quarters on the barracks deck. There was a brief delay and the v-pane cleared, revealing the bronzed face of the Marine commander.

"*Hai, Chu-sa?*" Half of the Zapotec's face was glistening with shaving gel.

"We have found our quarry," Hadeishi said, shrugging into his uniform jacket. "Are *Heicho* Felix and her squad ready to go?"

Huémac tensed, lips compressing into a tight line to admit anything less than perfect readiness to his commander. "Almost. They need some more time in the simulators—if we have time to spare, *kyo*."

Hadeishi nodded to himself and checked the navigational plot Koshō had seconded to his comp display. "Two, perhaps three ship-days, *Thai-i*. And then we will need to move quickly." He looked back to the Marine. "Is there a problem with the personnel assigned? Should *Heicho* Felix be replaced as team leader?"

Huémac shook his head slowly, though Mitsu thought he could see a tinge of concern behind the impassive, southern-highlands face. A near-open struggle flickered behind the flint-dark eyes. "No. Felix and her men have done very well. It's just . . ."

"What is it?" Hadeishi kept his voice conversational and polite. For the Marine to say anything less than "Can do, *kyo*. Done, *kyo*." indicated a serious problem. Not for the first time, Hadeishi wished his subordinates would not drink quite so deeply of Fleet tradition and doctrine.

"The simulations, *kyo*." Huémac actually glanced over his shoulder, though there was no one in his tiny cabin, before meeting Hadeishi's quizzical look. "They're monstrous—vicious—almost unbeatable. The assault team's been vaporized, holed, shot, incinerated, decompressed, blasted, and cut to bits every day. It's hard on the men to keep their heads up when they lose so often."

"And Felix?" Hadeishi cocked his head a little to the side. "How is she holding up?"

"She's still game," Huémac allowed, his expression brightening. "She gets knocked down, she gets back up . . . but she must be near worn out, too. The *shosa* has just been after her with a flint club, *kyo*. Relentless."

"I understand." In fact, Mitsu felt genuinely touched by Susan's efforts on his behalf. "Tell Felix to stand her men down for a day—all members of the assault team on shipside leave, no duties—and get some sleep. Tomorrow have them run through a full prep equipment check. They'll be on round-the-clock call starting in two days, so make sure they remember to eat. If anyone has trouble sleeping, override their medbands."

"*Hai!*" Huémac signed off, vastly relieved by the commander's temperate reaction. Hadeishi made a desultory effort at combing his beard and washing his face, but his thoughts were far away. His attendant fussed around, straightening up the cabin and brushing lint from his jacket. Mitsu let the old man go about his business, thinking of the future.

Now, I'll be the one having trouble sleeping, he thought as a tubecar whisked him toward the bridge. *And Susan will be nagging me.* The prospect of facing the massive cutting beam on a *Tyr*-class in a shooting fight did not calm his stomach. There would be little room to maneuver among the asteroids, which took away the *Cornuelle*'s advantages of speed and agility.

As the car slowed, Hadeishi felt an air of melancholy dropping away like leaves from the great oak in his father's courtyard, replaced by a surety of purpose he hadn't even realized was missing.

The *Cornuelle* held station in the radar shadow of a mountain-sized chunk of nickel-iron, skin mesh at full absorption, engines cold, every ship's system dialed down to minimal levels. On the bridge, where even normal lighting seemed unaccountably dimmed by standing to battle stations, Hadeishi leaned back into the embrace of his shockchair, entirely calm, and watched a v-feed from Outrider One.

Hayes was driving the drone from his Weapons station, broad shoulders hunched over the controls. Both Koshō and Smith were hanging on every flicker of data from their passive sensors and the point-defense network. On the v-pane, Hadeishi saw acres of jagged rock slide past as the Outrider inched its way around the nearer asteroid. The drone had been stripped down—*more work for the engineers,* he thought in amusement—to little more than a brace of cameras and a compressed air jet for maneuvering. Yoyontzin had claimed the modified skin-mesh on the Outrider would let it avoid detection on radar if the miniature ship did not betray itself with an exhaust signature.

So a machinist's crew—Hadeishi presumed that meant Master's Mate Helsdon and his wrench monkeys, who seemed to get all the tricky jobs—had dismounted the reactor core and plasma thrust drive and jimmied in a hand-built propulsion unit straight out of the "Firetower" era of space exploration on Anáhuac.

"Saw this on a 3v about the race to the moon," Helsdon confided to Smith, while Hadeishi happened to be in hearing. "Simple. Reliable. Not too fast—which is good. Don't want a missilelike velocity signature to pop up on someone's passive scan."

The Outrider crossed a range of spikelike peaks and emerged from shadow. The cameras adjusted to the faint sunlight, though Hayes did not make any course corrections. He was flying almost blind, letting the stream of telemetry returning from the drone via a laser-whisker guide him along a plot derived from the g-array scan data. Somewhere ahead, still out of sight, the refinery was lurking, hidden between the screening mass of two mammoth asteroids.

"Three minutes," Koshō announced, eyeing her navigation display. "You should have visual by now."

Hadeishi steepled his fingers and continued to watch quietly. Young Smith-*tzin* was sweating hard, eyes flickering back and forth between the confusing array of scan data. A problem with the software running the "consolidated" display had left him to reconcile the regular passive scan and the g-array by hand. The wild-catters did not seem to have deployed their own sentry drones, but . . .

The camera view changed again. The Outrider had passed into the shadow of the two asteroids. Now—dead ahead—there was a half-familiar outline floating in the ebon void. Points of light gleamed against a greater darkness, and they were not stars.

"Contact," Hayes announced in a whisper. "Stabilizing platform."

The Outrider slowed to a halt, hanging in the abyss, both cameras cycling through a variety of wave- and focal lengths. Shipside comp gobbled up the data and began building an enhanced image on the main display. Hadeishi sat up in his chair.

The keglike shapes of ore carrels became visible, the lights now revealed as EVA lamps strung along supports surrounding the massive containers. A cluster of circular exhausts came into view, the flaring nacelles blackened by plasma flux. A scale indicator appeared beside the screen. One of the *Cornuelle*'s shuttles would fit into the maw of a single thruster. The cruiser itself would fill only three of the dozens of ore carrels now visible.

"Drone hold position," Hadeishi said quietly, his eyes traveling along the bulky, mammoth lines of the refinery. Mazes of pipe filled the spaces between the ore containers. The actual ship itself was entirely hidden, save for the massive engines protruding from the globular mass. "Shift the Outrider so the asteroid backdrops the drone. We need a full scan workup of the refinery before we move to phase two. No sense risking a star or planet silhouette by accident."

He tapped a builder's schematic on a secondary v-pane. "Update the plans we have. I want to know about anything out of the ordinary, no matter how small. And see if you can get a registry number from a side-stencil or something."

Hayes and Koshō nodded before turning back to their panels. Mitsuharu opened a downship channel. "Engineering? This is Hadeishi. I would like hourly updates on refitting progress."

Engineer Second Yoyontzin hurried into the service bay at clockwise two on the engine ring. The high-vaulted space was crowded with machinery, men and the hiss of welding torches. A sharp, metallic tang of heated metal and plastic permeated the air. The atmosphere recyclers in Engineering had been operating over capacity since the *Cornuelle* had launched from the Teotihuacán Fleet contract yards sixteen years ago. A packet of schematics were crammed under his left arm, while his right fumbled for a fresh tabac. Spying Master's Mate Helsdon and his crew swarming over a box-shaped structure in the middle of the bay, the engineer turned their way, scowling furiously.

"Helsdon—come down here." Yoyontzin ignored the other machinists, most of whom were packing up their tool bags or doing fine finishing work on the sheets of hull fabric plated onto a big open framework of hexacarbon pipe. The Náhuatl lit the tabac and puffed furiously, feeling his nerves settle slightly, while the master's mate pushed up his work goggles and shut off a sealing torch.

"There's an addition to this platform," Yoyontzin said when Helsdon had climbed down, rubbing his face clean with a very dirty cloth. The engineer opened the packet on a nearby work table. Like every other square meter of the engineering ring, the metal surface was discolored, scored, chipped and pitted. It was also antiseptically clean. "*Chu-sa* Hadeishi just called down. He says to disable the broadband and laser comm on the platform. He wants a wire-spool instead."

Helsdon knuckled his chin, looking over the schematics. "How far from the ship to the refinery? Ah—six k—that's a bit of wire. Do we have that much comm wire?"

Yoyontzin nodded, his nervousness fading a little bit. "Of course—first thing he asked me. I've got a crew bringing it up from stores. So—you'll need to mount it underside, I think, keep the spool out of the way of the gas exhaust."

"And a patch to local comm. Wait—how is the assault team going to interface with a wire-based comm system?"

Yoyontzin grunted, exasperation plain on his face. "One of the Marines," he said in a rather disparaging tone, "is going to run a *second* wire roll from the platform into the refinery. We have . . ." He dug a glossy sheet covered with cutaway views and a picture of a combat trooper standing in a field out of the bottom of the stack. ". . . a field relay unit, Marine code 'Snorkel', which runs off the wire and handles short-range, scrambled comm. Backpack-sized unit."

"Sure." Helsdon shrugged. He didn't have the time or energy to worry about what the Marine assault squad was going to do once they were inside the refinery ship. His concern was refitting a maintenance platform to get them there and back again. "Do you have the unspool speed for the wire? Oh, good. Yeah, we can mount this—take a couple hours."

"Get on it." Yoyontzin's brief moment of good humor faded, remembering the rest of his discussion with the *chu-sa*. "There are some other . . . things."

Helsdon made a questioning motion with his hands. The engineer stubbed out his tabac on the edge of the table and then ground the rest out under his boot. The master's mate said nothing, but his mustache twitched in surprise.

"The platform needs to be ready to go at a moment's notice. We have the refinery ship on visual now, so as soon as the Marines are ready and command has double-checked their scan data, we'll be standing by for the order from Hadeishi-*tzin*."

"Right," nodded Helsdon, separating out the diagrams he would need for mounting the wire spool. "We're going to move the EVA platform up to boat bay two. The Marines usually assemble there and the lock doors are facing the right direction. What else?"

"Double-check everything." Yoyontzin's fingers were trembling and the look on his face made Helsdon stare in mounting concern. He'd never seen the engineer second in such a nervous state. "I mean it. The *chu-sa* is going in with the Marines."

"What?" Helsdon rubbed his ear, refusing to believe what he'd heard. "You're drunk."

"Wish I was." Yoyontzin tapped another tabac out of the pack and jammed it into his mouth. Pinching the lighting paper from the end and taking a deep drag seemed to steady him. His deep-set eyes narrowed in amusement. "I'll bet *Heicho* Felix is going to faint when she hears."

"I'll take that bet," Helsdon said, rather sharply.

Yoyontzin was surprised. "You're on—how does five quills sound?"

"Twenty." Helsdon crossed his arms, squinting at Yoyontzin. "If you're giving money away."

The pressure door to Hadeishi's office recessed with a hiss and then slid out of sight into the bulkhead. Susan Koshō stepped down into the comfortably-cluttered space. Her white duty uniform glowed in the dim light, sharply distinct from the dark-hued books and paintings covering the walls. Both of her hands were tightly clenched into fists.

"*Chu-sa?*" She looked around with a compressed, mostly-hidden expression of distaste. The untidiness of the commander's personal space always made her nervous, though the old man in charge of Hadeishi's quarters kept them scrupulously clean. There were just too many *things* here.

"Over here," Mitsuharu's voice came from a side compartment.

Susan trod gently across deep-piled rugs and paused in the inner doorway. Hadeishi had folded a table down from the wall of a narrow room lined with cupboards. The exec glanced around, puzzled, and then recognized the area as a servant's laundry station. The clever table was an ironing and mending board.

"What are you doing?" Susan stared at the combat suit laid out on the table with something like despair in her almond-shaped eyes. Hadeishi failed to suppress a small, polite smile. He was in an old, rather worn-looking short-sleeved kimono of dark blue silk. The back and shoulders were covered with a delicately stitched wading crane and cattails in golden thread. He turned his attention back to checking the suit seals with a microscanner.

"Prepping my suit," Hadeishi said. "*Heicho* Felix reports her squad has finished gear-check and is now ready to go, so I would be holding things up but Engineering is still mounting our hardline comm system."

Susan looked around for a seat, found nothing apparent—though she suspected some of the cupboards might slide out or fold down to make one: they had in her grandmother's house—and settled into parade rest instead. "You are determined to carry through with your . . . plan."

Hadeishi nodded, turning over one of the black, metallic sleeves of the suit. The surface was formed of overlapping, flexible ceramic plates. "Those skilled in war subdue the enemy without battle. If I go myself there is a chance of such success."

"Or you may be killed. This is a very risky maneuver."

Mitsuharu looked up, his narrow face grave. "I know. The art of maneuver is the most difficult—but in this tiny moment of opportunity, we *do* have some room to move. We hold a positional advantage. Given such an opening, I will risk myself for the best outcome. If we are killed or captured, you know what to do."

Susan nodded, staring at the combat suit with ill-disguised disgust. "You should not have loaned Fitzsimmons and Deckard to the civilians. They are our most experienced assault troopers."

"Water flows." Hadeishi replaced the sleeve and took up the other. "Felix will do."

Susan made a grunting sound and her pale, smooth forehead gained a sharp vertical crease. "Her performance in the combat sims has only been marginal. If there is resistance—"

Mitsu raised a hand and the *sho-sa* fell silent. "If you," he said quietly, trying to catch her eye, "are commanding the defense of the refinery with the vigor you showed in the sims, then I expect we will all die. But you are here, not there. Felix will be fine."

"Very well." Susan clasped both hands behind her back. Her gaze was fixed on a point somewhere over his head. "Navigation informs me our best-path return course to the planet will now take eleven days. I believe the *tlamatinime* Hummingbird requested we retrieve him from the surface in only ten days."

"We will not be returning to the third planet until our business here is concluded, *Sho-sa*. But I appreciate your diligence in bringing this matter to my attention."

"*Kyo*, the *tlamatinime* and the archaeologist could easily have encountered—"

"They are in some danger, true," Mitsuharu interrupted gently. "But they will be fine. Hummingbird will be fine. He always is. Our business is here, with the refinery. And it will be resolved very soon, one way or another."

"*Hai, Chu-sa.*" Susan's face settled into a cool, lifeless mask. "Do you require any assistance with your equipment?"

Mitsu put down the right-hand sleeve of the suit and rested his hands on his knees. He considered his exec for a long moment, then shook his head slightly. "I should do this myself, Susan. Such things are traditional. If you have a moment, please check with Engineering and make sure they've rigged something to keep the comm-wire from fouling."

Susan nodded sharply, turned and walked quickly out of the laundry room. Mitsu watched her go with a pensive expression. When the outer door hissed closed, he sighed and turned his attention back to the seals on the inner sheath of the armor. They always became stiff in storage, no matter what the armorer said. Sometimes they split, if not carefully looked after, reducing the wearer's flexibility.

THE PALENQUE

A subtle change in the background vibration of the ship brought Parker awake, his head throbbing from too much alcohol and too little nicotine. He threw back the hood of his sleepbag and squinted blearily at his chrono. *Three hours of wonderful sleep*, he thought, feeling the onset of a crushing dehydration headache. *I will never, ever, sit down for just one glass of Tukhachevsky's bathwater again. Ever. With or without herring.*

The pilot spread his fingers against the wall behind his bunk. With the *Palenque* under constant thrust, the habitat ring was locked in place, allowing him to feel some of the vibrations traveling through the spine of the ship. Something had changed; he was aware of a distinct flutter. A reading light above his head let him see well enough to punch up the comm code for Engineering.

"Parker to Isoroku-*san*. Are you awake?"

"Yes." The engineer's voice was terse and there was no video. "Maneuver drive three has started to stutter."

"Fuel feed?" Parker climbed out of bed and started to get dressed. "Fusion chamber flow control?"

"I don't know." Isoroku's face suddenly appeared on the comm screen. For a bald man in a Fleet engineer's coveralls, he seemed remarkably mussed. There were heavy bags under his eyes and a salt-and-pepper stubble darkened his chin. Parker assumed he'd been awakened from a sound sleep as well. "Fuel core pressure is constant, which may mean an intake line problem. As a precaution, I am shutting down all three drives."

Parker nodded, pulling a gray shirt on over his head. "I'll get to the bridge and balance the other two engines. And I'll tell our furry friend what is going on."

Isoroku nodded and the comm cleared to a default standby image.

By the time Parker pulled himself along the guide line into the bridge, Magdalena was awake and at her command station.

"What happened?" the Hesht female growled. "Engineering reports all three drives are offline?"

"Yes." Parker slid into the navigator's station and called up a drive schematic and the latest system alert logs and diagnostics. "Drive number three started to develop a thrust flutter sixteen minutes ago. Isoroku has shut down all three maneuvering drives as a precaution."

"How long will this take?" Magdalena was eyeing a chrono and flight plot on her display. "We have an intercept window to match if we're going to pick up the pack-leader."

Parker nodded, scanning through the diagnostic reports for drives one and two. They seemed to be running clean. The fuel system also seemed to be operating properly, which was troubling. *Problem's going to be in the fuel-flow system inside drive three, then.*

He punched codes for an engine restart on both drives, and then began working up a new thrust balancing configuration. "I'm going to bring one and two back online," he said to the hovering Maggie after a moment. "But we can't increase individual thrust without exceeding our 'quiet' threshold. So . . . it will be an extra twelve hours before we are inside the pickup window over Ephesus Three."

"What," Magdalena said, throttling back her temper, "if drive three comes back into operation?"

Parker made an equivocal motion with one hand. "Then we might be able to squeak back into the window, but probably not. We'll just have to see."

The *Gagarin* shuddered to a halt, wings creaking as they sagged, bereft of the lifting wind. Gretchen let go of the stick, grateful to be on the ground again, and tried to uncramp her right hand. Clouds of fine dust drifted past, gilded by the early morning light, obscuring scattered bunkerlike camp buildings. Groaning a little—all of her bruises were throbbing today—she reached up and toggled off the ultralight engines and power plant.

Outside, the camp had a familiar air of abandonment. The usual litter was missing—no discarded cans or forgotten clothing, no shutters banging in the wind, no stray half-feral dogs pacing stiff-legged in the streets—but Gretchen could feel the emptiness crawling between her shoulder blades.

I hate this kind of place. On edge, she swung out of the cockpit. Despite how things had gone in the slot canyon, the Sif-52 was slung forward under her left armpit, the pistol-grip only an instant from her hand. The weight of the gun was balanced by a bandolier of ammunition canisters. Gretchen turned on her heel, scanning the buildings for any sign of movement. Nothing caught her eye. The wind was gusting, smudging the sky white with dust, but nothing seemed out of place.

The camp felt dead, an abandoned toy cast aside by careless children.

Wrapping the *kaffiyeh* tight across her breather mask, Gretchen ducked under the wing and made short work of setting the sand anchors. Hummingbird approached, *djellaba* snapping around his legs in a dark, sand-mottled tail. He too was muffled tight, the glow of morning simmering in his goggles.

A hiss of static, then "Is there a hangar?"

Gretchen pointed. The largest aboveground building in the camp. "Tight fit for two aircraft, but we'll manage. Better get them inside quick—the wind is picking up."

Turning away from the wind, they both hurried across the quadrangle toward the maintenance sheds and the hangar building. Gretchen kept a wary eye out— her dislike of recently-abandoned places had not faded with age and time, only grown stronger.

If I have this sight, she realized, trying to suppress a chill of apprehension, *then I might see whatever is left behind.* The thought was not pleasant. Her curiosity only went so far.

"Locked," Hummingbird said, gruff voice nearly lost in the hiss of the wind.

Gretchen knelt, checking the mechanism. A bolt and bar assembly, sliding into a quickcrete footing and secured with a cheap padlock.

"Just like our barn at home," she said in amusement, rising and pulling a hexacarbon prybar from her belt. The tube extended with a snap of her wrist and a metallic *clank.* "Just a moment."

The lever slid in between the padlock and the vertical bar. Gretchen rotated the hexacarbon tube with a sharp, hand-over-hand motion and there was a groaning squeal as she put her shoulders into the turn. The soft steel of the padlock deformed like taffy and then parted with a ringing *ting!* "Help me with the door."

With both of them pushing against the articulated plating, the hanging door rattled up into the roof of the hangar, spitting sand and rust out of the tracks. Gretchen stepped inside, her lightwand raised high, and nodded in tight-lipped satisfaction to see the cavernous space empty.

"Good. Let's get yours inside first." Gretchen turned back into the wind. Both *Midges* were straining against their anchor lines, wings rippling like salmon skin under a heat lamp. "It's getting stronger. Hurry."

Heads down, they ran across the field, gossamer veils of dust rushing past. The still-rising sun was bloated half-again its usual size with rust.

"So." Gretchen pulled a pressure door closed behind her, shutting off the tunnel leading to the hangar building. Taking care to keep dust from spilling onto the recycler apparatus around her neck, she unwound the *kaffiyeh*. Hummingbird had done the same, leaving his cloak and scarf and other gear stacked up beside the door. "We're here at last, and better off than I expected."

Without a dozen people milling around and the smell of bacon frying and coffee perking, the base's common room was cold, echoing, and unsettlingly empty. Hummingbird sat on the nearest table, feet bare, running an electrostatic vacuum over his boots. Gretchen pulled up a chair—the plastic was badly discolored and the legs were streaked with a calcitelike crust—and sat down. She stared down at her own shoes, grimacing at the ragged edges of the soles and the general ruin of the uppers. *Even Fitz couldn't fix these.*

"I am going to go outside," Hummingbird said, banging his left boot against the edge of the table. Reddish grit rained down onto cracked quickcrete. "Before the weather gets any worse. I am . . . a little worried."

"Huh! Why? We've finally reached some shelter, where we can refuel and resupply and you're worried?" She pointed a finger at the roof. "We're even out of the wind. That tent was starting to smell."

"Yes." Hummingbird looked around, his expression becoming almost morose. "That is the problem. I had no idea the camp here was so extensive."

"Ah." Gretchen ran the edge of her thumb against the boot sole. The material was porous and spongy. Bits of glittering crystalline mica spilled out. She felt a little ill at the sight and dialed her lightwand into UV and stuffed it inside the boot. *My feet feel fine . . . sort of. I hope.*

"Well," she said, trying not to stare in sick fascination at her socks, "humans get kind of busy sometimes—I mean, they planned on being here for two, three years. A camp for a long-term expedition isn't just some tents or a carryall. It's a little town."

"I can see." Hummingbird fingered the goggles hanging around his neck. The glassite looked like it had been attacked with a power sander or a steel rasp. "I think—no, I am afraid we are too late. Man has been here too long, put too much of his mark on the land. Even our passage across the world has stirred up rumors, echoes. . . ."

"You mean the Russovsky-thing I spoke to." Gretchen swallowed, preparing herself for the worst, and tugged off one sock. The moisture-wicking, thermally insulated fabric disintegrated in her hand, leaving a blue ring of elastic material around her ankle. Suddenly, she felt light-headed. "Oh, oh sister . . ."

"You saw more than a rumor." Hummingbird was staring out the portholelike windows. Sodium-tinted shadows turned his face to graven brass. "I know it was gone when we went back—but such things are *real*. We're a stone, cast into a still pond. Though we sink and disappear, the wave from our entry propagates through this world. Some of the waves turn back upon themselves—well, you saw the effect—and the memory of our passing through this place is retained. Layers build on layers. . . ." His voice trailed off, wrinkled old face growing stiff in anger.

"Sure." Gretchen forced down a surge of nausea, bile tainting her throat. She felt faint, but gripped the edge of the table and waited for the sensation to pass. Hummingbird was saying something, but the words were far away and indistinct, unintelligible. Jerkily, she swung her leg up and put her foot across the opposite knee. In the muted yellow light from the windows, the sole of her foot was shiny and slick, almost glassy. "Uhhh . . ."

A trembling finger reached out to touch the discoloration—she felt a hard, smooth surface and jerked away again. "Oh blessed sister, deliver us from all the fears of the world, from evil, from want. . . ." *Is it deep? Why didn't I feel anything? Is it my whole foot? Oh, Sister, how deep does this go!*

"What happened to your foot?"

Gretchen looked up, sweating, and saw Hummingbird looming over her, eyes narrowed.

"I—it ate right through my boots."

The *nauallis* knelt beside her, firm hands grasping her ankle and toes, turning the sole into the light so he could see. Gretchen slumped back into the decaying chair, fist jammed into her mouth to keep from crying out.

But there was no pain. Hummingbird squinted, turning her foot this way and that. She could feel the strength in his fingers, immobilizing the offending limb better than a surgeon's vise. White-shot eyebrows gathered over dusky green eyes and then his face became still, wrinkles fading, a sense of release and settling peace washing over his countenance. After a moment, he reached into his vest and produced a small folding knife.

Gretchen's eyes widened and her leg tried to jerk violently away. Hummingbird's hand tightened and her movement was stillborn. "Hold still," he said, eyes focused on some unseen distance. The blade snapped out of the handle with a sharp click and he put a mirror-keen edge against the heel of her foot. Gretchen felt the world swim again, vertigo surging around her.

"You should start counting," he said, eyeing her with interest. "Or look away."

There was a scraping sound, but Gretchen felt nothing more than a tugging. She blinked, surprised. *Shouldn't it hurt?* The old man made a *hmm* sound and his fingers tightened. This time, Gretchen could feel more than a tugging; there was a sharp, piercing bolt of pain.

"Ayyy! Oh, sister . . . is that blood?"

"Sorry," Hummingbird said, cleaning the blade on his thigh pad. "Nicked you a little."

"How bad is it?" The pain parted a cloud of nausea. Her medband reacted, flooding her arm with a pleasantly cool sensation. Gretchen looked down and her teeth clenched. Hummingbird was carving away a slice of her heel; metallic, glistening skin peeling back from the edge of his knife. "Guuuhhh . . . why—why isn't that bleeding?"

"Dead skin," he said, lips pursed in concentration. "Whatever got into your boot doesn't seem to have done much more than eat up your calluses."

The *nauallis* finished with the heel and cleaned the blade again. Gretchen could feel her foot start to throb, but realized the sensation was more from the tight grip he had on her ankle than anything else.

"Now let's see . . ." He switched the blade around to hold as a scraper and began to work on the instep. Gretchen's leg jerked again and the chair gave out with a little groan as she moved. "Ticklish, I see."

"Just pay attention," she hissed, hoping his hand didn't slip again. Her fingernails squeaked on plastic. "I've only got the one left foot."

The view from the second floor windows was no better than from downstairs. The sun was gone, reduced to a muddy flare in the sky. A sickly yellow fog had swept across the camp, driven by wild, intermittent winds. Gretchen perched in a deep window embrasure, bandaged foot sticking out into the room, her eyes fixed on a narrow view of the quadrangle. Hummingbird had gone out into the storm— she'd seen him open one of the airlock doors and hunch out into the blowing dust—but he'd vanished from sight almost immediately. Grimly nervous, Gretchen kept one hand on the grip of the Sif at all times. Their gear was piled downstairs, but the echoing vacancy of the common room set her on edge.

Out in the blowing murk, the gritty fog parted for a moment. Anderssen stiffened, searching for the *nauallis*, and caught a glimpse of a dark-cloaked figure near the lab building. She frowned—the shape was moving strangely, a sort of duck-walked sideways shuffle. The head bobbed from side to side—and then the dust closed in again.

"What is he up to?" Gretchen spoke aloud, depressed by the leaden silence in the abandoned room. The echoes of her voice fell away, leaving another bad taste in her mouth. *It's almost worse to speak,* she thought in disgust. A frown followed. *He can't "align" an entire building, can he?*

A gust roared past outside the window, rattling the heavy pane. Even the bright patch of the sun had disappeared in a gathering darkness. There was an intermittent glow from the east, but the light was far too low in the sky to be the sun. Gretchen checked her chrono. Not quite midday. She put her hand against the wall, cheap plaster cracking away from the concrete backing at her touch. The entire building shivered in the storm. Snatching her hand away, Gretchen swung around on the window ledge and gingerly tested her bandages. Her left foot, which had suffered the most damage, was completely shrouded in healfast gauze, medicated antiseptic cream and a layer of spray-on dermaseal from Hummingbird's medical kit.

Her boots had been a complete loss, which left her slopping around in a spare pair of mulligans Hummingbird had found in a downstairs locker. *These would fit Tukhachevsky . . . okay, let's see about walking.*

"Ow. Ow. Ow. Dammit." Trying to walk very lightly, Anderssen limped down the stairs to the lower floor and began checking each of the rooms. She didn't think there were any ground-floor windows besides the portholes in the common room, but a queer prickling feeling urged her to check. The kitchen was entirely dark, as were the storage rooms behind the grill.

"We need to get the power working," she muttered after banging her knee on a chair. The circle of radiance from her lightwand seemed very small in the thick, heavy air. A handful of the precious glowbeans broke up the dimness, though they seemed very lonely once they were shining from the ceiling.

Moving carefully, she forced open a maintenance door on the far side of the ground floor. A sloping tunnel led down into close-smelling darkness. Gretchen paused—a low, extending rumbling sound penetrated the heavy walls—and she turned in time to see the portholes lit by the stabbing brilliance of a lightning strike. Almost instantly, the building shook and the *crack* was clearly audible. Dust sifted down from the ceiling of the tunnel.

"Okay. Time to stick close to home." Gretchen retreated to the pile of gear in the middle of the room and shoved two of the tables together to make an L-shaped work area. Putting down the Sif so she could unpack was a struggle, but her nerves settled a little after checking—and locking—all of the doors.

The intermittent rumble of thunder continued to grow, until the noise faded into the background of her consciousness as a constant rippling growl. The windows stuttered constantly with the flare of yellow-orange heat lightning. Squatting beside the little camp stove, watching a pale blue flame flicker in the heating unit, she was very glad the buildings were quickcrete rather than metal-framed.

The tea finally consented to boil, which reminded her far too much of a particular storm on Old Mars. She'd ridden that one out in an abandoned building too—a mining camp shaft-head in the barrier peaks around the Arcadia impact crater. *Too many tricky memories,* Gretchen thought, rather sullenly. "Why do all these places seem haunted?"

"Because they are," Hummingbird said, appearing out of the darkness, his step light as a cat. "Is there tea? Ah, good."

Gretchen lowered the Sif, though her heart was beating at trip-hammer speed. "Where . . ."

The door into the tunnel was still slightly open. She glared at the old man, who was stripping off his gloves, crouched over the tiny flame. "Well? What did you do?"

"I went here and there." Hummingbird dug out some tea, packets of sugar and a steel cup. "Seeing about the destruction of this place."

Gretchen's eyes narrowed. "You going to tell me *how?*"

"Doors." He said, stirring his tea. In the pale blue light of the glowbeans, his eyes were only pits of shadow, without even a jade sparkle to lighten his mood. There was a distinct air of concern about him, hanging on his shoulders like moldy laundry. "Opening and closing vents. In some places I moved those things which could be moved. Tidying up, as one of my teachers used to say."

"Opening . . . oh." Gretchen looked sharply at the partly-open door. Her stomach was threatening to churn again. *I'll have an ulcer out of this, if nothing else.* "Including the one at the other end of the tunnel?"

Hummingbird shook his head. "Nothing in this building. Not yet. We'll save that for last."

"What about the hangar?"

"No. I supposed we might need the ultralights again."

"That's very wise," Gretchen said with a sigh of pure relief. "Please don't destroy our means of transportation."

"Is there anything to eat?" The *nauallis* looked around hopefully.

Gretchen scowled. "Do I look like a cook to you?" She nudged one of the bags with her too-big boot. "Vanilla, chocolate, grilled *ixcuintla*, ham surprise, miso, all the usual flavors. And if you want any of my hot sauce," she said in a waspish tone, "you will have to ask very nicely."

Hours dragged by—measurable only by the tick of a chrono, for the storm-dimmed light in the windows did not seem to change—and Gretchen's feet began to itch terribly. Hummingbird had gone to sleep, leaving her to watch in the darkness. The afternoon dragged by and finally, when her stomach was starting to grumble about supper, Gretchen poked the *nauallis* with a long-handled spoon from the kitchen.

"Crow. Crow, wake up!"

One eye opened and the old México gave her an appraising look. "Yes?"

"How many teachers did you have?" Gretchen was curled up, leaning back against the baggage, two stolen blankets draped around her shoulders. "Is there a school for judges?"

"Not so much so." Hummingbird clasped both hands on his chest and looked up at the ceiling. "My father was a judge, so there were things I learned 'from the air' as he would say. When I graduated the clan-school, the *calmecac*, he took me aside." His face creased with a faint smile. "He was a strict man—much given to fairness and justice—but on that day he took the time to ask me if I wished to enter the service of the *tlamatinime* or not."

Hummingbird turned his head, giving Gretchen a frank look of consideration. "You should understand one does not become *tlamatinime* by intent. There are no civil exams, no waiting lists, no quotas. There is no one to 'talk to' about a promising son. The judges are always watching, listening, considering. We find *you*.

"So I was surprised when my father broached the subject. I think—looking back in memory—he was a little embarrassed to do so, because he was a judge, as his father, and his father's father, had been. Later, I learned the examiners found me suitable on their own and he'd learned of their decision from a friend." Hummingbird's smile remained only a faint curve of the lips, but Gretchen had watched him long enough to feel the depth of his emotion.

This is a precious jewel. Conviction grew, as Gretchen watched the old man speaking, that the crow's father had never shown him any special consideration beyond this one moment which was so clearly etched in his memory.

"He wanted me to consider the matter before they cornered me. To make my own choice. To escape the burden of family duty. To be free, if I wished."

Gretchen nodded, feeling a familiar weight of expectation pressing on her own shoulders. "But even so, you said yes?"

"Eventually." Hummingbird's smile vanished. "They were as patient as I was impatient."

"You?" Gretchen lifted her head in a sly smile. "You were the black sheep? The reckless, irresponsible child? Were you in a band?"

Hummingbird made a snorting sound and looked away.

When he did not turn back, Gretchen pursed her lips in speculation. *So sensitive!*

"What do I need to learn?" she asked, after some endless time had passed. "How do I learn—if there's no school—"

"There are no books," Hummingbird said in a stiff voice. "No tests. No sims. Only a teacher and a student, as it has been for millennia."

"Are you my teacher, then? Can I even *be* a student? I mean, you said women aren't accepted into the *tlamatinime*."

The *nauallis* sat up, jaw clenched tight. "There are women who learn to *see*," he said in a rather brusque voice. One hand made a sharp motion in the air. "But there are two . . . orders, you might say. One—the men—the *tlamatinime*, the other—the women—named the *tetonalti*. By tradition—more recently by law—the two are kept separate in all matters."

"So," Gretchen said, watching his face, "there are no female judges serving the Empire. They are . . . soul-doctors, is that what you said?"

Hummingbird's lips compressed into a tight, stiff line. "The *tetonalti* are not what they once were, in the time of the old kings. Though they too serve the Mirror, I prefer not to speak of their purpose." He made a pushing-away motion with both hands. "You are burden enough, just by yourself, without bringing *them* into the situation."

"How much trouble will you be in?" Gretchen tried to be nonchalant about the question, but Hummingbird's eyes narrowed at the light tone in her voice. "I mean, if women aren't supposed to learn these things—"

"Not enough trouble," he said, rather guardedly, "to see a certain cylinder back in your hands."

"So cynical," Gretchen said, hiding momentary disappointment. "I get the idea. I even understand," she made a face, "a little. It will hurt my children, that's all. That said—will *I* be in trouble if it's known I've started to gain this . . . sight?"

The *nauallis* nodded and rolled up to sit opposite her. "You will not be troubled by the Imperial authorities," he said. "I will not tell them what has happened. If you keep this to yourself, no one will trouble you."

"Will you show me more? Can you train me to control this clarity? You say some students have become 'lost-in-sight'. Will I become lost too?"

The old México hissed in annoyance. His fingers tapped on the crumbling floor for a moment, then fell still. "It might be best for you to forget all this, put these matters from your mind, turn your back on clarity and sight and all the rest."

"And how," Gretchen said, irritated, "do I do that? Right now I see double or triple most of the time—very disorienting. And then the hallucinations—I mean, I can almost perceive *things in this room*—people and voices—that aren't here!"

The old México looked around casually, then back at Anderssen. "Men talking? The smell of cooking? The half-heard chatter of music? The buzz of machinery?"

"Yes." Gretchen felt suddenly cold and turned abruptly, looking behind her. "Upstairs is better—it doesn't feel so crowded. But down here . . ."

"You're seeing," Hummingbird said quietly, "the shadows of man. The impression left on this room, this building, by the scientists who worked and lived here for the past year. We will leave shadows too, if I don't clean them up before we go. Right here." He made a circular motion with his finger. "Two indistinct shapes sitting on the floor, talking."

Gretchen felt a little sick again. "How long do these shadows last?"

"Usually," Hummingbird said, searching through his pockets, "they fade.

Someone else comes and sits in the same chair, eats at the same table. The shadows interfere with one another and dissipate. Have you ever entered a dwelling where only one person lived for a long time? Where they died? A house left empty afterwards?"

"No." Slow rolling creeps slithered across Gretchen's arms. She could feel every single hair on her arms and neck stand on end. "I don't like abandoned places."

"It is dangerous," Hummingbird said, finding what he was looking for, "for a person to live alone, in the same house or room, for more than a few months at a time. Shadows accumulate. A living person needs to move, to change, to see new things. Say a man lives in the same room, eats at one table, sleeps in the same bed in the same orientation for years on end. Shadows reinforce. The mind is affected by shadows—you're feeling the effects of this empty room right now—sometimes the shadows become more real than the living man."

"Oh." Gretchen managed to smile. "I'm pretty safe then—the Company moves us every year or so."

Hummingbird nodded, turning a square of folded paper over in his hands. "You don't believe me. But think about your children—how many times have they changed their room around? Put the beds under the window, away from the window, asked for bunk beds, didn't want bunk beds? Decided to sleep in the living room instead? Changed rooms, if they had the option? Didn't you do that when you were younger?"

The world seemed to gel to a sudden, glassy stop. Gretchen licked her lips.

"Now," he continued in the same implacable voice. "Do you have an elderly relative? Stiff, old, strangely frightening. A house filled with things you must not touch? Rooms filled with furniture no one uses and which must never be moved? Strict rituals of the home—dinner at the same time, always the same prayer beforehand, things done in just such a way? Do you remember how you felt, when you were a child in such a place?"

"I was afraid," Gretchen whispered, almost lost in memories of her great-grandfather's tall, dark house. "I couldn't breathe."

"It was dark, even when the shutters or drapes were open. Musty. It smelled of shadow."

Hummingbird's eyes were limpid green, sunlight falling through leaves into still water.

"Memory," he continued, "is a physical change in the human brain. So too are skills laid down by repetition. Perception is governed, interpreted by pathways created by experience. A child's mind is loose, chaotic, filled with a hundred, a thousand paths from source to conclusion. But as a man ages, as he grows old—"

"I know," Gretchen said abruptly. "I took some biochemistry at the university. Neural pathways in the brain become consolidated. Fixed. Memories are lost or discarded, replaced by different sets of connections. There are diseases which attack the pathways, trapping people in repeated time."

Hummingbird placed the packet of paper on the ground between them. "Lost in memory. Or they lose the ability to form new pathways, gain new skills, see the world afresh. Trapped in routine, bound in shadows. The mind becomes rigid. A quiet, unseen death—long before the body runs down to silence."

Gretchen roused herself, lifting her chin. "Don't the *tlamatinime* have homes? Families?"

"Of course." The corners of Hummingbird's eyes crinkled. "They are very lively and we rarely remain in the same physical building for more than a year or two. And in the course of our business, we are always in motion. We have restless feet."

"And this?" She pointed suspiciously at the paper packet. "This is like what you gave me before?"

"This is different." Hummingbird considered her with a weighing expression. "The first packet was a helper to 'open-the-way'. This . . . this is 'he-who-reveals'. For most students this substance will let you find a . . . a guide, would be the best description. A guide who can help you control the sight."

"What kind of a guide?" Gretchen's suspicion deepened. "Aren't *you* my guide or teacher in this business?"

The *nauallis* shook his head slightly. "He-who-reveals is already within you, but in most men and women he is sleeping. Sometimes, if a person is troubled or under stress, the guide will speak to their dreams, more rarely in waking life—a voice which seems to come from the air, offering guidance. The guide is outside yourself, yet privy to all you know, see and do."

"That is disturbing." Gretchen scratched the back of her neck. "A stranger inside my head? Will this . . . drug . . . let me communicate with 'he-who-reveals'?"

"This will wake him up." Hummingbird pushed the packet toward her with the tip of his finger. "For a little while. What bargain you strike with him is upon you to effect. No one else."

"And what does he give me in return?"

Hummingbird shrugged, an obstinate look growing in his lean old face. "Such things are none of my business."

"How can there be another . . . anything . . . in my mind?"

"You misunderstand. He-who-reveals is the self which looks upon self with clarity. You are one being."

"What?" Gretchen felt another chill. The *nauallis*'s words seemed slippery, their meaning darting away from her consciousness, silver fish vanishing into dim blue depths. "What is that supposed to mean?"

Hummingbird folded his hands. "He-who-reveals is the honest mirror. In your terms, he is the self without affect, without deception, without delusion. Have you ever tried to see yourself from outside? Perhaps, at the edge of sleep, you've seen yourself from above, as though your mind were separated from the body, able to look upon you with a stranger's eyes?"

"Yes." Gretchen rubbed her arms. "When I was a kid—I was scared to death I wouldn't be able to get back inside my own head. I'd be lost forever and I'd die."

"Fear," Hummingbird said, rather smugly, "is a barrier to sight."

"Fine." Gretchen gained a very distinct impression the old man was laughing at her. She picked up the packet. "I just put this on my tongue?"

Hummingbird reacted quickly, catching her hand before she could open the paper. "You should lie down first. There will be a physical reaction. And drink something. This is thirsty work."

The storm continued to rage outside. Violent yellow lightning flared among the roaring clouds and drifts of sand crept towards the windows. Visibility dropped to less than a meter. Hummingbird's chrono told him sunset had come, yet there was no apparent difference outside. The flare and crack of lightning stabbed through the murk. The building shivered with thunder.

Hummingbird waited, half asleep himself, while Anderssen lay on the floor, covered with blankets, a makeshift pillow under her head. The woman twitched and shuddered. Sometimes she spoke aloud, but even the *nauallis* could not understand the words.

Near midnight, with the wind howling unabated outside, Gretchen began to cough. Hummingbird rolled over and lifted her head. Her eyes opened wide, staring up at the blue-lit ceiling.

"Huhhh . . ." She doubled over, hacking violently. Hummingbird crouched down, supporting her arms. "Uhhh . . . it's too hot. Too hot."

Gretchen shoved the blankets aside, panting, her hair lank with sweat. Without thinking, she tugged the collar of her suit open, gasping for breath. Hummingbird scooted back warily and stood up, a worried frown on his old face.

"I can see," Gretchen said abruptly, her hands raised and trembling in the air. She stared at Hummingbird. "I can see your face, a sun hiding in clouds, your eyes brilliant jade, your face marked with red bands." Her expression twisted in horror, pupils dilating. Sweat flushed from her skin and ran in thin silver streams down her neck. "You're not a human being!"

"I am," Hummingbird said, remaining very still. "You are seeing the *nechichi-*

ualiztli—a mask of purpose and duty—not me! You must be careful or this kind of sight will blind you. Can you see your own flesh, your own hand?"

Gretchen looked down and her face contorted, the skin stretching back from her teeth. She began to shake, muscles leaping under the flesh like snakes squirming in a calfskin bag. "I can see I can see I can see."

Hummingbird moved carefully to the side, quietly, without disturbing the air. "What do you see?"

"Nothing! There is nothing there! Darkness!" Gretchen was shouting, though her whole body was frozen into trembling immobility.

"Where is your hand?" Hummingbird said, his face close to hers, watching the flickering *tic-tic-tic* of her eyelids from the side. "See your hands. Here they are. You can see them."

Gretchen's neck stiffened like a log, the tendons and veins standing out like wire. "My hand is gone. I am gone. There is nothing here. Nothing here." Her voice had the quality of a scream, though it was soft, not even a whisper.

"Remember your hand, remember what you saw when we were sitting in the desert? Do you remember how clear it was, your hand, so fine and distinct?"

"Yes. Yes. I remember." Gretchen slumped into his waiting arms, her body loose, each muscle exhausted. By the time he laid her down, she was sound asleep. Hummingbird breathed out, a long, slow, even breath, and a fine mist of smoke hissed from between his teeth, settling over the woman's body.

Sometime after midnight the sound of the wind changed. Hummingbird roused himself from meditation and padded to the window. The rattling hiss of sand against the porthole had tapered off. He could see the sullen flash of lightning far away.

"Hmm." The old man checked Anderssen, sleeping deeply under all the blankets he could find. Her skin was cold and clammy. Worried, he fished a stout wrist out of the covers and examined the medband with an experienced eye. Her body was suffering a toxic reaction, so he keyed a series of dispense codes into the metal bracelet and then tucked her hand away, out of the chill air.

The pressure doors on the main airlock had frozen shut, forcing the *nauallis* to detour around through the machine shop and out through a hatch jammed open by a chest-high drift of sand. Squirming out into the night, Hummingbird took care to adjust his goggles to the near-absence of light.

The smaller buildings—the lab bunker, the ice house, the sheds for the tractors and carryalls—had vanished under lumpy dunes. Hummingbird turned right and half-walked, half-slid down into a trough in front of the main building. He headed toward the hangar, peering out at the sky and horizon.

There were no stars. The storm had lifted for the moment, but it had not passed. Stray winds eddied between the buildings, throwing sand at his legs. Out on the plain, he made out vague twisting shapes. Lightning stabbed in the upper air, flickering from cloud to cloud. In the intermittent, brilliant light, Hummingbird made out roiling, swift-moving clouds rushing past. A white-hot spark flared in the middle distance and the *nauallis* saw, throat constricting in atavistic fear, a monstrous funnel cloud snake down from the boiling sky.

More heat lightning flared above and the bloated tornado danced across a range of dunes a half-dozen kilometers away. Millions of tons of sand sluiced up into the sky, the entire ridge vanishing. The air trembled, a shrieking sound rising above the constant wind, and Hummingbird began to run.

The main door of the hangar building was stuck again, the bottom of the articulated metal plating buried in a meter of sand. Hummingbird dodged around the side, feeling the ground shake, and found a service door that opened inward. The reflected glare of lightning threw the entrance into deep shadow, but Hummingbird did not hesitate. He threw his full weight against the locking bar and was rewarded with a deep-throated groan of complaining metal. Two hard jerks managed to unlock the mechanism and he stumbled inside.

Less than a kilometer away, the funnel raced past, shaking the air with a stunning *boom*. Sand rained down from the raging sky. Hummingbird shoved the door closed, fighting against dust spilling in between his feet. Luckily, the pressure door had a counter-rotating weight and once in motion the door closed itself.

The still, quiet darkness of the hangar was a bit of a shock. The heavy walls muted the roar and thunder of the storm to distant grumbling. Hummingbird switched on his lightwand and made a circuit of the big room. Both *Midges* were still in place, wings folded up, engines and systems on standby. The faint smell of idling fuel cells permeated the air. More out of habit than anything else, the *nauallis* shone his light inside the cockpits, into the cargo compartments, ran his hands across the engines and peered underneath.

And he stopped. His light shifted back, focusing on the forward landing gear of his *Midge*.

Most of the wheel was invisible, obscured by a dull gray coating—as if the quickcrete floor had grown up to engulf the landing gear. Hummingbird circled around to the front of the ultralight and found all three wheels encased in stone.

"Well," he said, jaw tightening. In the questing gleam of his lightwand, he saw Anderssen's *Midge* was similarly afflicted. He lowered the light, clicking his teeth together in thought. "I'd better check my boots again."

The funnel cloud broke apart far to the south of the camp, splintering into dozens of smaller vortices and then dissolving into a rush of sand and grit and sandstone fragments. The storm continued to move west, obscuring the plain with towering walls of dust. Clouds thinned, but did not part, over the camp. Stray winds gusted between the buildings, though in comparison to the violence which had just passed relative quiet reigned.

Russovsky stood on the crest of a dune, tangled blond hair whipping around her head, eyes fixed on the low, rounded shapes of the camp buildings. She wore neither mask nor goggles, though the apparatus of a rebreather and recycler clung to her back and chest. The once-glossy black skin of the suit was matted and dull, abraded by the constantly prying wind. Her boots had crumbled long ago, shredded by rocks or eaten away by the tiny, blind *maiket*.

At a distance, she could feel the presence of the human machine like the warmth of the sun-which-kills, hot and sharp, pressing against her face. The pattern of its movements, the residue of its passage, was clear in the air and upon the ground. There was familiar comfort in the humid smell humanity left behind, the traces of exhalation and sweat mixing in the cold sharp air. Far different from the clean, distinct impressions of the *hathol* or the furry blaze of the deep-dwelling *firten*.

A rumbling crack echoed from the north and Russovsky turned her head—a slow, methodical motion—to feel the twisting power in the storm building again. A vortex was building in the upper air, swirling currents rushing into a knot of power building from hundreds of kilometers in every direction. Soon the wave front would smash across the plain, pummeling everything in sight with unbounded rage.

Russovsky felt steadily building disquiet—not at the pending violence, for the pattern of the storm was as familiar to her as the shape of the camp buildings or the spreading stain of the *hathol* in the dune below her feet—but at a sense of disassociation creeping through ordered, clearly defined thoughts.

Black clouds staining a clear blue sky. Plunging ebon tendrils which flattened and distorted in the summer air, driven by winds at great heights.

Her memories of the-life-before were dying, fading, replaced by confused, diffracted images of things she was sure did not exist in her world, events she had never experienced herself.

A night sky so flushed with stars, night was barely different from day. A bloated, dim sun the color of rust. Obsidian mountains rising to unimaginable heights, rectangular black slabs shimmering against an ochre sky. Fields of silver flowers which constantly turned to face the sun. A sense of impossible age.

Did she see these things herself? Were they dreams? Russovsky examined memories of her life before this life and found them rife with the sensation of dreams and phantoms and half-seen images whelped from confusion or exhaustion. Yet there were no cyclopean towers, no vast cities dreaming under the cruel, brilliant sky of her human memories. These new memories felt strange, foreign.

They felt as things she'd seen with waking eyes.

Disturbed, she turned her attention away from such disorderly matters. The slow, comfortable song of the *hathol* permeating the dune slope drew her attention. Here was respite from the storm, from the bleak thoughts, from tormenting phantoms, from the nagging pressure of the distant machine. Russovsky knelt, hands flat on the unsteady slope. Her fingers sank into the muted glow of the sand-dwellers. A darker hue spread from her contact, spilling through the delicate threads and spongiform clusters forming the hive. Her own skin became tainted with the reddish radiance of the slow ones.

Russovsky became still, her body locked in position, and the red glow mounted through her arms, into her chest, flooding down into her torso. Even as her body began to crumble, flaking into translucent fragments, skinsuit hardening to stone and dissolving, the darker stain spread across the dune face, rushing through the fragile circulatory system of the hive.

The Russovsky-shape shuddered into a rain of dust, sand and stone fragments. Wind rippled across the debris, anointing the darkened hive with glowing red dust. A second wave of radiance flooded through the *hathol*, picking out the threads and tendrils in bright new colors.

At the base of the dune, where the dust gathered, where the heart-clusters of the hive dwelt under meters of hard-packed sand, the dark stain pooled, thickened, began to build toward the storm-tossed sky. An outline formed with visible speed, sand and dust and grit knitting into bone, sinew, flesh, blood, the triply-insulated rubbery layer of a skinsuit. In the fullness of time, long, ragged blond hair.

Russovsky flexed her arms, brushing husks of dead *hathol* away from her fingers. Bare feet broke free of an encasing shell and she turned toward the encampment. The suit was glossy and dark again, made new, refreshed.

The strobe-flare of distant lightning washed over her face. A muttered growl of thunder stirred the air, fanning her hair.

AMONG THE BROKEN MOUNTAINS

Hadeishi clung to a retaining bar, leaning in over the shoulder of the Fleet pilot at the controls of the work platform. *Heicho* Felix and her assault team were crowded in behind him, bulky dark shapes—combat armor and helmets matte-black to fade into the background, their tools, weapons and ammunition packs slung tightly against their bodies. Crates of hardware filled the rest of the very limited space. The platform slowly drifted forward, barely nudged by a set of four compressed gas jets. Hadeishi watched a passive plot updating on the tiny flight panel.

"Five hundred meters," the pilot's voice was steady. An EVA work platform was not the usual vehicle of choice for the shuttle jockeys, but this job required a steady hand and nerves. Though Master's Mate Helsdon had volunteered, the *chusa* had politely ignored his offer. The machinist was far too valuable to risk on a wild throw like this.

"Four hundred meters."

Hadeishi clicked his throat mike. Though the comm connection to the cruiser was on a hardline, he had no intention of making any more noise than absolutely necessary. A moment later, Koshō's voice was perfectly clear on his earbug.

No sign of activity. The exec sounded entirely at ease. *No sign of remotes or drones on picket. You are clear to continue.*

Hadeishi clicked twice, indicating he understood.

We have a match on the ship registration number from engine nacelle four. Koshō continued, sounding a little smug. Initial analysis had not found any identifying markings on the visible sections of the refinery. Everyone agreed the miners would probably have replaceable panels for use if they docked in port. The exec had not given up so easily, running all of the visual data through a variety of enhancement procedures. In time, a painted-over number had been found. *Ship registry out of Novaya Zemlya Station, Rho Triangulis system. The* Turan. *A Tyr-class mobile open-space refinery. Master of last record is unknown. Crew registry is unknown.*

"Understood." Hadeishi grimaced. He'd hoped to learn something of the man or woman he faced from the public shipping records in the *Cornuelle's* database. "We are at two hundred meters. Hold one."

The Fleet pilot looked up questioningly. Hadeishi keyed through a secondary comp panel bolted to the side of the carrel. Builder's blueprints and diagrams flashed past. After a moment, he pointed out a particular assembly.

"Left," he said carefully, "six hundred meters, then in about a hundred and full stop."

The pilot glanced out at the massive shape looming in front of them. Against the mountain-sized bulk of the *Turan*, the EVA platform was a fly buzzing against a temple column. The woman grinned, showing perfect white teeth in a cocoa-brown face, and gently swung the control stick over. The carrel tipped and scooted along the boundary of an enormous, round ore tank. Hadeishi gripped tighter on the bar, watching girders, panels, lading-ports, a ten-meter high "16" and intermittent singleton work lamps glowing against the darkness, drift past.

Hadeishi turned and caught Felix's eye. "Someone needs to watch the comm wire as we turn into the approach. We'll stop and untangle if we snag."

The *heicho* bared her teeth in a tense grin. One hand was clinging like a limpet to the overhead retaining bar, the other was steadying the blunt, wicked shape of a six-barreled Bofors Whipsaw squad support weapon. "Tonuac's on it."

"Good." Hadeishi swung round to watch the curving wall of ore tank sixteen drift past—then it ended abruptly, leaving a dark canyon framed by the looming bulk of tank fourteen. Despite an outwardly calm demeanor, Mitsu's hand clamped tight on the bar as the pilot swung the platform into the pitch-black space. "Steady as she goes, *Sho-i* Asale."

The Mixtec ignored him, her entire body concentrated on the delicate control required by the four maneuvering jets. Without even the faint gleam of the stars or the irregularly-spaced worklights, she was flying blind, guided solely by a carefully crippled radar unit whose power output could almost be measured in candles.

Hadeishi gained an impression of vast shapes rising on either side among a forest
of girders and pipes. Once the platform made a hard course correction to port,
then back again. The sound of his breathing was very loud in his helmet.

Asale was sweating too. He could see silvery beads slithering down her forehead, but the pilot's concentration never wavered. The platform glided to a stop,
then rose up, swimming past ill-defined structures. A single light suddenly
appeared—a recessed door with an illuminated faceplate and lock window—but
the pilot did not stop. The platform continued to rise, minutes ticking past. Then
she brought them to a stop, stabilizing the platform with two short bursts.

"We've got a problem." Asale looked up at Hadeishi, biting her lip in thought.
"We've got thirty meters to go, to reach the airlock you want. But the space ahead
is constricted—some kind of framework running crossways in front of the lock."
She fingered the blueprint, showing where they were.

Felix pressed in close, eyeballing the schematic, while Hadeishi was thinking.
"We could dismount here and go in on suit thrusters."

"No." Hadeishi wanted to rub his jaw, which was entirely impossible in the
suit. "We'd have to move the gear by hand—and we'll need it inside. What clearance do we need?"

Asale consulted the weak, scattered radar image. "Side to side we're fine, but
this platform is just a bit too high."

"Felix, cut off the roof." Hadeishi moved himself carefully into the space
directly behind the pilot. "We'll crouch down."

"*Hai, Chu-sa!*" Felix replied immediately, moving into the corner he'd
vacated. "Hand tools on cutting blade," she ordered the three Marines floating
behind her. "Cut the framework off at one meter. Then we'll push it clear—gently."

Hadeishi settled in to wait. He could feel a vibration in the platform through
his boots as the Marines began cutting through the framework of hexacarbon pipe
the engineers had taken such care to install. Losing the shroud of absorptive fabric
would reveal them to any active sensors in the vicinity, but he hoped the miners
had not decided to mount a targeting radar inside the ore-tank shield.

Felix's team worked with commendable speed, and only three minutes later
the encasing roof was pushed up and away, drifting back a few meters, hull-fabric
standing out stiff from the edges of the cut.

"Let's go." Hadeishi rapped gently on Asale's shoulder. The pilot nodded and
the platform began to edge forward. Far ahead, Mitsu thought he could make out
the oblong rectangle of an airlock door edged with tiny green lights.

Koshō turned away from the video feed transmitted by Felix's helmet.

"They are almost at the airlock," she announced to the bridge crew. There was a full complement at their consoles, though by shiptime this was early in third watch. Every hand aboard was awake and standing to battle stations. "Hayes-*tzin*, do you have a firing solution?"

"*Hai, Sho-sa.*" The weapons officer nodded sharply, his face mostly obscured by the helmet of his combat suit. The *sho-sa* was taking every precaution. At any moment, they could be engaged in a point-blank beam weapon shoot-out with a hostile ship sixty times their size. "One bird, sprint mode. Shall I load out?"

"Proceed." Koshō turned her attention to a camera view shot from one of the point-defense sensor clusters on the skin of the *Cornuelle*. Hayes tapped a series of commands on his panel. A section of the ship's hull retracted, revealing the mouth of a missile accelerator mount. Gleaming magnet rings shone brightly for a moment and then the snout of an Atlatl-IV antiship missile emerged with graceful speed. The missile exited the ringtrack and drifted free of the ship's hull.

Not the usual kind of launch, Susan thought, suppressing a snort of amusement.

On the screen, three z-suited figures drifted into view, guiding an EVA collar between them. Five minutes of careful work clamped the collar around the Atlatl. Two of the men jetted away, while the third accessed a control panel on the collar. Susan leaned slightly forward, watching for signs of trouble.

"Guidance test underway." Yoyontzin's voice burred on the intership channel. "Test is green."

Hayes tapped a glyph on his own panel. "Remote comm test is go." A v-pane appeared, displayed a variety of results, then vanished gain. "Test shows green. Remote control is live."

After acknowledging the results, the engineer jetted away from the missile and Susan waited patiently until all three men were processing in through number eight airlock. She looked to Hayes and nodded. Her own hand drifted above a pre-programmed point-defense weapons order.

"Sprint One is under secondary power," the weapons officer reported. "Maneuvering."

Susan watched the fully-armed Atlatl move away from her ship, accelerating slowly as the jets on the collar hissed thin streams of white vapor into the black abyss of space. Fifteen minutes later, the missile had vanished from sight, curving away around the mass of the asteroid screening the *Cornuelle* from the *Turan*.

"Sprint One has cleared self-destruct distance." Hayes consulted his panel. "Sprint One will be at launch station in sixteen minutes."

Susan nodded, allowing herself to savor an atom of relief. She had moderate faith in Yoyontzin's abilities, but the prospect of anything—much less an antimatter-charged shipkiller—colliding with the hull of the *Cornuelle* precipitated a cold sweat of tension. "Proceed with inertial guidance check and targeting comp test."

The weapons officer nodded, keying a new set of commands into his panel. There had been some problems with reconfiguring the Atlatl to acquire target, lock and ignite within the minute acceleration time frame required by their current situation. The manufacturers had not envisioned using the heavy-class shipkiller at knife distance. Susan wondered if the code modifications would hold up in a split second of reaction time. *As the gods will.*

She looked away from the view of the stars, returning her attention to the feed from Felix's helmet.

Hadeishi swung out of the platform, tucking in his legs to clear the ragged edge of the now-missing frame. Felix and her men had unloaded all of the gear, anchoring the crates to the refinery hull in a semicircle around the airlock door. Corporal Felix and Tonuac were crouched at the lock access panel, having removed the faceplate, with a cluster of cables snaking from the blocky comm relay into the opening. They were watching a hand-held spin through millions of control code combinations. At the far end of their hardwire, the *Cornuelle*'s main comp was prying at the commercial-grade control circuits in the lock mechanism.

"Almost through . . ." Felix motioned to the *chu-sa*. "Thirty-five seconds, *kyo*. Please stand out of the line of fire. Maratay and Clavigero will enter first."

Obediently, Hadeishi touched down beyond the ring of equipment, letting his boots adhere to the scarred, blackened hull. He found it wryly amusing that the EVA platform now seemed to be hanging in the air overhead. The two Marine privates shifted themselves to include him inside the immediate fire perimeter. Both men were crouched and braced against the hull, shipguns out and armed.

"*Sho-i* Asale," Hadeishi clicked open the comm. "You should back off, out of this confined space. Take station a hundred or so meters from the exterior ring of ore tanks and stand by."

The pilot frowned—Mitsu could see her worried expression through the glassite of her faceplate. "*Kyo*—what if you need extraction? I should stay close."

"We might not need pickup from this particular airlock," he replied, keeping an eye on the darkness among the gantries and space framing joining the ore tanks to the refinery hull. "Take your time and stay clear of the hardwire."

Asale nodded dubiously, but ran through her flight check and then—in a faint cloud of vapor—began to back the platform away from the airlock. At the same time, Felix stood and took up position to cover the airlock opening.

"We're in," she said, thumbing the safety on the Whipsaw to live fire, single-shot.

Hadeishi crouched down as the two privates swung round and took hold of the locking bars on the face of the lock. He did not bother to check his own sidearm. If things degenerated to a firefight, his own nominal skill with a pistol or assault rifle would not make much of a difference.

The airlock unbolting vibrated through the hull. Hadeishi could see the seal outgassing and then a brighter light flooded out as the heavy pressure door recessed and slid aside, leaving a half-moon–shaped section exposed. Maratay ducked inside, crabbing around the corner, gun first. Clavigero followed a heart-beat later and their voices—low and clipped—filled the comm channel.

"Clear. No hostiles."

"Clear. Inner door seal intact. No warning lights."

Felix signed for him to enter and Hadeishi swung 'round and inside in a single motion. He felt the tug of a differential gravity interface inside the white-painted chamber and oriented himself by the g-deck logo stenciled on the wall. Clavigero was already at the inner hatch, peering this way and that, watching for opposition.

"*Chu-sa?* We could use a hand here?" Felix was standing above him, boots still adhered to the outer hull, looking down impatiently. Tonuac was releasing the first of the equipment cases from its anchor.

"Of course," Hadeishi flashed a reassuring smile. Some officers would have been content to stand aside, but he did not believe in shirking and speed was of the essence. He braced himself and took hold of the lanyard attached to the first case. A blocky gray container marked with the ownership glyph of the Engineering department drifted solidly into his hands. Hadeishi swung it aside to the wall of the airlock and thumbed the adhesion patches 'live'. The case attached itself to the wall with a solid *thump*.

As Hadeishi hauled the equipment inside, Felix angled through their midst with the octopuslike assembly of the comp interface. There was a second access panel beside the inner door. She removed the faceplate with her hand tool in a series of crisp, flawless actions. Hadeishi, watching her out of the corner of his eye, was pleased to see the endless round of sims had imparted noticeable effects.

The *heicho* began clipping interface leads onto the exposed components. At the inner door, Clavigero was counting nervously, marking the seconds while the airlock was exposed to open space. The builder's blueprints indicated a two-minute safety interlock, past which an alarm might sound. Hadeishi hoped the miners had not wired a direct alarm system to the bridge.

"Stand by to pierce outer hatch." Tonuac swam inside with the last case. The bulky shape of a shipyard hexacarbon drill was strapped to his chest. As he did so, Maratay kicked himself out through the opening, catching the edge of the opened lock door. He swung round to face back inside. His motions had the same kind of con-trolled, endlessly-practiced grace shown by Felix in disassembling the access panel.

Hadeishi flattened himself against a wall now covered with gear. Felix ignored Tonuac as he powered up the drill and maneuvered the machine to sit flush with the airlock door. A series of lights on Felix's panel flashed amber in warning.

"Forty-five seconds," she announced in an offhand voice. Tonuac ignored her, checking the seals around the base of the drill. A pressure test showed green and he punched the GO button. Immediately, Hadeishi felt a thready, intermittent vibration through the wall at his back. The drill attacked the inner surface of the airlock door, ejecting a stream of sparking hexacarbon flakes through a side vent.

"Thirty seconds." Felix consulted her handheld and let the *Cornuelle* comp attack the access panel. This time, there was a barely noticeable flash of numbers and the inner door unlocked. "Door two unlocked."

Hadeishi clicked his circuit to the *Cornuelle*. "Comm will be dead in five seconds."

Koshō did not have time to reply. Felix rotated a locking ring and the hardline disconnected. The monofilament wire hung suspended for an instant before Maratay—his gloves protected by magnetically active pads—reeled the line out of the lock.

"Fifteen seconds." Felix glanced at Tonuac. The drill was still vibrating against the door.

"Twelve seconds." Maratay nodded sharply and moved out of sight.

"Door one pierced," Tonuac announced, disengaging the drill adhesion seals. He handed off the tool to Hadeishi, who stuffed it into the appropriate case. A cloud of drifting metallic curls floated around him. Outside, Maratay forced a pressure-sleeve into the fresh drill hole. The comm hardwire was tucked inside. Tonuac grabbed the connector as it eeled through the opening, slid a seal gasket around the device and handed off to Felix.

"Outer segment sealed." Maratay's harsh Gujari accent conveyed some of the tension Hadeishi felt. The Marine swung nimbly around the edge of the airlock door. He and Tonuac moved out of the door frame itself. "Inner segment sealed. Outer door cleared to close."

Hadeishi heard the comm channel chime open and saw Felix had reconnected the hardline to the relay. The system warbled happily to itself, signaling a clear connection back to the ship.

"Six seconds," she declared, one hand poised over the outer door control lever. She eyeballed Tonuac and Maratay to make sure they were behind the cross-hatched danger stripe and swung the control down. "Closing outer door."

A *thump* followed as the airlock engaged, rolled closed and slid into secure position. Tonuac kept an eye on the hardwire, guiding the monofilament with his hands. "Outer door secure. Pressurizing."

Two minutes later, the airlock was at positive, nominal pressure, the seals around the hardline were holding and the inner door rotated aside. Maratay and Clavigero sidled out into a dim, gray-walled passageway. Hadeishi waited until all four Marines had exited the lock and taken up positions on either side. He stepped out into shipside gravity and frowned.

The bulkhead opposite held a dark—apparently broken—map panel. Streaks of rust spilled down unpainted metal. He looked up and down the corridor—some of the overhead lights were missing, while everything had an unmistakable air of decay and long-overdue maintenance. The difference between the immaculate, shipshape *Cornuelle* and this *wreck* was striking. Hadeishi shook his head in dismay and consulted his handheld.

"Left-hand corridor," he said, trying to avoid staring at the deck, which had a thin sheet of some kind of oil shimmering underneath the waffle-grid flooring. "Three hundred meters straight on, then there's an internal pressure hatch."

Maratay moved out on point, gliding down the dingy passageway at a run. Hadeishi looked around again and clicked open the channel to the ship. "*Sho-sa,* what do you make of this?"

The crew is too small, Susan's voice came back, as clear as if she stood at his side. *And the ship is too large. According to the builder's plan, there are nearly a hundred and twenty k of corridor and pressurized space inside a* Tyr.

"Understood." Hadeishi closed the channel and bent to help Tonuac and Felix haul the rest of the equipment cases into the corridor.

One of the v-panes showing a peapod data-feed suddenly went dark. A warning light flared on Magdalena's control panel and the resolution of the composite image on the main display degraded markedly. Now there was only a flickering, indistinct image of a vast, sprawling storm seen from a great height. Barely better than looking out a window at the distant planet. And who knew what was happening under the mottled ochre clouds?

"Only one eye left. We see no better than a snake," the Hesht snarled helplessly. She wanted to pace or run or just crash through a stand of high grass, long legs blurring across hard-packed, dusty ground. Trapped on a tiny ship without proper exercise facilities, limping along at half-speed, a vast distance from the lost steppes of Heshukan, her options had been reduced to shredding the furniture . . . and now even the joy of exercising her claws palled. "Parker, engine status?"

A comm pane flickered and shifted as a hand in a work glove adjusted a camera lens. The blunt, broad, plant-eating face of Engineer First Isoroku glared out at her. "There has been no change since your last request for status. Maneuver drive three is *still* offline."

Magdalena showed her incisors in response, though she knew the challenge was lost on these humans. "Where is Parker-*tzin?*"

The engineer shifted and pointed with a tilted head. The pilot's work boots were partially visible, wedged inside some kind of maintenance accessway. A sort of muffled song was barely audible, leaking out from the opening. Maggie's ears twitched—Parker's idea of a pleasing tune did not coincide with hers. *Where are the yowls and shrieks?* "He, too, is still busy."

She could tell—feel, really, from the tense tilt of his head and the flare of his nostrils—that the engineer was getting rightfully upset by her constant badgering. Despite their standing difference of opinion over remaining in the system, the Fleet officer had set himself to work in an admirable way. Even a Hesht of her particular temper could see he was making an honest effort. Though every instinct screamed to rush ahead, to boost output on the remaining two maneuver drives— and emit a radiation signature visible throughout half the system—she forced her mouth closed, politely hiding her teeth.

"Isoroku-*tzin*," she said, forcing the words out in a strangled-sounding voice. "My apologies for interrupting your activities. Please carry on. When drive three is online, I would appreciate . . . *yrrrr* . . . being informed."

The engineer did not respond immediately. In fact, he squinted rather suspiciously at her. At length, lips pursed, he said, "Apology accepted," and signed off the channel, still frowning.

Magdalena ran half-extended claws through her fur, wondering what passed for thought in the heads of these tree-dwelling fruit-eaters. "*Rrrr* . . . what is going on down there?"

The storm-covered surface of the third planet mocked her, the single staring red eye of a monstrous serpent. Still on edge, she began experimenting with the different kinds of sensors mounted on the peapod. None of them proved immediately helpful.

"I think," a gruff human voice said from the entryway, "you've confused Isoroku-*tzin*."

Maggie turned and gave *Gunso* Fitzsimmons a level stare. In the daily routine of the ship, the Marines stayed off the bridge—Parker claimed they didn't like the smell, though of course *he* did—and contented themselves with gambling with the scientists, lending the engineer a hand and obsessively checking their equipment.

"I was rude," she said bluntly. "They are working hard and I am impatient."

Fitzsimmons nodded, drifting over to catch the railing circling the command station. "What does our interception window look like?"

"It shrinks." A claw tapped up a plot echoed from the navigational display. "This *Shhrast*-damned storm is making a mess of plotting pack-leader's pickup. Parker had hoped to make one pass around the planet. . . ." The v-pane showed the path of the *Palenque* shearing close to the Ephesian atmospheric envelope, then hooking away in a sharp return path for the outer system. ". . . and picking up speed like a slingstone out again. But now . . ." she sighed, ears limp with despair, "now we will have to decelerate into a parking orbit, losing precious velocity."

"Are you sure?" Fitzsimmons frowned, leaning over the console. He smelled strangely familiar—bitter, pungent, smoke and old wood—and Magdalena raised her head, plush nose sniffing the air. Then she grinned properly, ears canted forward.

"You've been avoiding Parker-*tzin*, haven't you?"

The Marine looked at her quizzically for a moment, then smiled in a very impolite way, showing stumpy yellowed teeth. "Use of tabac," he said in a conspiratorial way, "dulls the human sense of smell."

Magdalena shuddered, her fur twitching from head to tail. "A wretched weed," she hissed. "And this is enjoyed by your entire stunted, corrupt race?"

"Parker is a very religious man," the *gunso* said in a roundabout way. "But *Thai-i* Isoroku requested our assistance in keeping his engines—well, the Company's engines—free of tabac ash and other contaminants that might otherwise foul power junctions, mar the efficiency of computational cores and soil the sacred decks of the engineering compartments."

Magdalena hissed in delight. "You ate of his kill, pleading an empty belly," she said in mock horror, "while hiding your own in the river-pool! I saw you smoking his disgusting little sticks when we first came aboard."

"Sure." Fitzsimmons shrugged. The whole situation was water off his furless back. "Share and share alike, right? Though Marines are *never* caught short of supplies." He held up four pink wormlike fingers. "Air, ammo, booze and tabac. Don't need much else."

"He was generous," she started to say, but had to admit—as she had admitted Isoroku's efforts on their behalf—she did not miss the foul smell clinging to her fur and making her sneeze. "But I see the efficiency of the pack-ship is improved by this . . . deception."

"The Engineer First," Fitzsimmons said, scratching a jaw black with stubble, "is my superior officer. In the absence of other command authority, his operational requirements are my holy writ. But while it's fun to pick on Parker, we need to talk about getting Gretchen and the judge back."

"Yess . . ." Magdalena stared at the plot again. "If we still had the satellites we could see pack-leader and eldest-and-wisest take off from the ground, allowing us to adjust course properly. But with only one eye left—and that one losing more altitude each day—we are close to being blind."

"Well," Fitzsimmons said slowly, eyeing the display. "In drop school one of my instructors was always saying 'It's all about angular momentum,' which sort of applies here. There's a Marine assault-ship technique which could solve your problem, something Fleet pilots call the 'Pataya knot'. Parker's not the greatest shuttle pilot in the world, but he might be able to handle it."

Magdalena growled, giving him a suspicious look. She wasn't sure this hunter-from-another-den could be trusted. *But,* she reminded herself, *he was sniffing after the pack-leader, so he might soon be in her den as well.* "Show me this knot."

Unaccountably, Fitzsimmons turned a sort of russet color.

These blankets are real, Gretchen thought, awareness returning from unnaturally vivid dreams. *Real scratchy.*

For a moment she remained still, eyes closed, listening. The wind outside had died down to an intermittent moan. The camp stove was a soft hiss of burning gas. Hummingbird's spoon made a metallic sound stirring sugar into his cup. He was breathing as she was, momentarily free of the mechanical counter-rasp of the rebreather mask. Everything seemed very normal, even the sensations of chill air against her face and constant throbbing pain in her mutilated feet.

The darkness of her closed eyes was vastly comforting. There were no phantoms, no visions of impossible vistas, no cloudy indistinct body rippling with clouds of buzzing lights. She felt solid—terribly tired and wrung out like a dead towel—but having substance. *Okay, here we go.*

Gretchen opened her eyes, focused on a perfectly normal-looking roof formed of honeycombed prestressed concrete, crisscrossed by metallic tracks holding cheap lights, and was vastly relieved.

"There is tea," Hummingbird said. She turned her head. The effort of putting aside the heavy blankets could wait. The *nauallis* was watching her from the other side of the little stove, his face filled with open worry. Reaching over, he put a cup of steaming tea beside her. From close range, pitted and scratched metal revealed the foggy, indistinct image of a pale-faced woman with sweat-streaked hair. "How do you feel?"

Gretchen nodded, but was exhausted even by moving her head. After gathering her strength, she managed to say, "Tired."

Hummingbird nodded, the deep grooves and wrinkles in his face deeper and more distinct than she remembered. The faint reddish glow from the heaters lent him a sepulchral aspect. "How is your vision?"

"Only . . . one of you," she said, too tired to smile. "What . . . happened?"

His jaw clenched, then he visibly forced himself to relax. "The storm has mostly passed. I have tried to contact the *Cornuelle*, but there is no answer. Also, something has gotten into the hangar. Both aircraft have become one with the floor."

"Huh!" Laughing hurt, but the baffled look on the old man's face was priceless. Gretchen managed to worm one hand out of the blankets to take hold of the cup. The metal was only lukewarm, but the liquid inside burned her lips. She tasted more sugar than tea. "Told you so."

"Yes." Hummingbird tilted his head in acknowledgment. "You were right to be concerned. The rate of decay in the camp buildings is faster than I expected. But we should be able to clear out this set of rooms, get the generator started again and rig a positive-pressure environment. That will help."

Gretchen set the empty cup on her chest and stared at the ceiling again. "What day is it?"

"Plus fourteen from landing," the *nauallis* replied, taking the cup away to refill.

"Two days." Gretchen mumbled, feeling exhaustion overtake her. "The *Palenque* will be here. But we need both *Midges* in working order."

"How . . ." Hummingbird saw she was asleep again, a soft snore escaping her lips. "Working order? I thought we were done here, but . . ." He got up and began gathering up what tools he could find. "Must be a sledgehammer or rock chisel somewhere in these buildings."

Still limping, using a survey marker pole as a cane, Gretchen stopped beside the *Gagarin* and peered suspiciously at the undercarriage. The floor was remarkably clean for a base-camp hangar, which proved Hummingbird had been very, very busy while she was sleeping. For her part, Anderssen felt remarkably refreshed for a woman with two bad feet, a medband whining about alkaloid toxins in her blood and no immediate prospects of rescue from an increasingly hostile world entirely unfit for man.

"Kind of banged up," she said, biting her lip at the dents and chipping visible on the landing gear assembly. Curious, Gretchen put her weight against the wing and the wheel clunked over. The heavy rubberlike material was badly pitted. She looked over at Hummingbird, who was squatting beneath his own ultralight. "Good work to get this place cleaned out."

"Does it matter?" The *nauallis* spread his hands, looking at her expectantly.

"It does." Gretchen opened *Gagarin*'s cockpit door. "We need both ultralights to get off this rock. I was sure we were done for when your fuel pump froze up." She threw the comp restart switch and leaned back on the pole, watching the system spool up.

"We need only wait," Hummingbird said, eyes narrowing suspiciously. "The *Cornuelle* will return soon."

"The day after tomorrow," Gretchen said, shaking her head at his optimism, "one of the shuttles from the *Palenque* will make a skip-pass through the upper reaches of the planetary atmosphere. The approach will be entirely ballistic—no power, no radiation signature, no more evidence than a meteorite burning up in the mesosphere—and we will be waiting, both of us in a *Midge*, for a skyhook extraction."

"Impossible! A *Midge* can't fly that high and we'd asphyxiate or freeze before reaching an altitude where a shuttle could pick us up on an approach like that."

"If this were Anáhuac, you'd be right." The comm console beeped pleasantly and Gretchen felt her stomach sink. There were no system messages waiting for her. No mysterious notes from Magdalena. No word the *Palenque* was actually coming to fetch them. "But this is not Old Earth."

Anderssen shuffled out, the pole scratching on the floor. "Like Mars, this world's atmosphere is very thin. Maybe only half the depth of Anáhuac's ocean of air. Even the individual layers of the atmosphere are compressed or thinned. We only need to reach thirty k to escape. At such an altitude, in fact, we'll be worrying about broiling in solar radiation rather than freezing, but these *Midges* are pretty well equipped to protect us from the heat.

"Air is a problem, but we can secure these suits for a super-low-pressure environment. We won't have to stay at height long—in fact, we won't be able to loiter for more than about thirty minutes—but the shuttle will be there when we are."

Hummingbird was scowling, his face dark as a thunderhead above the Escarpment. "A skyhook can only intercept one *Midge* at a time—if your Mister Parker can keep his hands steady enough to catch us. And how do you expect one of these dragonflies to reach that altitude?"

"I'm not trying to get us killed," Gretchen said in a stiff voice. "But it is dangerous."

She ran her hand across the *Gagarin*'s wing, taking a long look at the battered, scratched, wind-worn surface. The ultralight had traveled thousands of k across this world, with two pilots of varying abilities, making at least one complete circumnavigation. Mountains, plains, all the diverse wastelands . . . all without complaint. A sturdy, battle-hardened plane with a brave heart. Gretchen blinked, trying to restrain a wellspring of emotion.

"We," she said, after clearing her throat, "are going to strip everything unnecessary out of this one. The fuel tanks on yours detach, so we'll stuff them into the cargo compartment, doubling our range." Gretchen tapped a pair of brackets on the underside of the airframe. "Beneath my seat are two chemical rocket boosters, which fit here."

She turned and gave the old man a weary smile. "This world does not enjoy an evenly distributed gravitational field. There are huge disparities of mass inside the crust and core. Near the Escarpment there are eddies where g spikes three or four times surface normal. West of here, out in the Great Eastern Basin, there is an area of very low g. Our escape velocity will be drastically lowered once we enter the zone. We'll use the rockets when the air becomes too thin to impart any lift at all."

Hummingbird blinked. "And if no one is waiting in high orbit?"

"We fly back down." Gretchen felt her stomach go cold. *No sense in lying. . . .* "I hope."

"Hmm." The *nauallis* clasped his hands and stared at the floor for a long time. When he looked up, a weight seemed to have lifted from him. "Even so, flying such a distance will take time. So we had best get started."

Gretchen nodded, then reached out her hand. The judge looked askance for a moment, then accepted her arm in rising. "Let me get my gear—you need a special socket wrench to unbolt the fuel tanks."

Three hours later, Hummingbird ducked through the door from the main building with the last of their baggage slung over his shoulder.

"I've good news," he said, dumping the duffel bags on the floor of the hangar. Gretchen looked up from the cockpit of the *Gagarin*, her face streaked with grime, oil and tiny flakes of shredded plastic. The shockchair had been dismounted and moved aside, an effort which required cutting away the armrests to make room for the second chair from the other *Midge*. The compartment seemed very bare with the side panels torn out and everything stripped down to bare metal. Only the 3v of her kids and Russovsky's icon remained, tacked to the overhead. The power cell worked into the paper had finally failed, leaving only a static, fixed image. "We needn't take more than one or two days' supply of food with us."

The *nauallis* unsealed one of the bags and dumped out four or five packs of threesquares onto the floor. They made an audible clanking sound, stone striking stone. Gretchen tried to grin, but she was very tired again. Even the effort of dismounting everything which could be removed from the *Midge* had left her shaking.

"Infected?" Gretchen took the opportunity to sit down.

"Some surface dust must have gotten into the bag." Hummingbird began separating the petrified bars from those still good. "And our water is down to maybe three liters, plus whatever is in our suit reservoirs."

"We can make more water," Gretchen said, rubbing her eyes. "The fuel cells generate waste H_2O as a byproduct. But they won't make food from nothing."

The old México clicked his teeth. "What progress?"

"Fuel tanks are moved and hooked up. I can't find any leaks, so I hope they're not there. If you help me lift in the second chair, I can bolt it in place. Then the rockets need to be mounted and control linkages tested."

"And then?"

"Then we'll be done and I can lie down." Her vision was getting hazy, but not from hallucinations. She started to slump over, then caught herself. "What?"

"Go lie down now," Hummingbird said. "I can do the rest."

"Okay." Gretchen wiped her hands on her thighs, which made absolutely no difference to the grime on her gloves or legs. "Think of anything else we can get rid of . . . I'm stumped. Weight is the enemy right now."

Hummingbird watched her limp into the tunnel, a pensive expression on his seamed old face. Then he stood up and went to the second shockchair, which was sitting beside the cockpit door. He braced himself and started to lift, grunting in surprise at the weight.

On the open plains surrounding the base camp, sunset ushered in a long dusk. There were no towering mountains to the west to swallow the sun, plunging the land into shadow. Instead, the sun settled amiably toward a brassy gold horizon. Heavily laden, Gretchen limped down a sandy gully between the half-buried headquarters building and the lab. In the soft gilded light the empty doorways and barren eyesocket windows no longer seemed so disturbing. She wondered if Hummingbird's efforts to align the camp had driven away the shadows he claimed inhabited abandoned places.

Beyond the lab building she paused at the edge of the crude shuttle field. The most recent storm had destroyed both of the vehicle sheds. The eight-wheeled Armadillo carryalls had disappeared. *Did we pack them up? Did Hummingbird do something with them?*

"Enough procrastination," Gretchen said to herself, sounding very much like her mother.

The Sif felt heavy in her hands. The gun carried a sense of solid menace, as though weapons obeyed some different order of density. Gretchen looked around, fretting at the thought of abandoning a perfectly good tool for almost no reason at all.

"But you're too heavy," Anderssen said, speaking crossly at the shockgun. "And useless."

Letting go proved difficult, though, and she wandered back and forth at the edge of the camp for nearly an hour before stumbling across a narrow fissure in the earth. Something about the unexpected opening convinced her this was a safe place to discard the gun.

The Sif clanked and rattled down into the shadows. Gretchen tossed the ammunition canisters in one at a time as she walked the length of the fissure. The bandolier was easier—the cheap old leather was cracked and ugly—and she just tossed it into the crumpled ruins of an equipment shed.

In the gathering darkness—more than half of the sun was now hidden behind the western horizon—Gretchen could make out familiar pale gleaming lights in the wreckage. Politely, she pressed her fingertips to her forehead before limping back toward the headquarters building. She hoped the microfauna in the sand enjoyed the meal.

"Sister . . . I should get rid of all this stuff." Gretchen fingered the tools on her belt and the work vest. There had to be at least six kilos of gear draped on her or tucked away in the thighpads on her suit or in the back of her equipment belt. She took out her trusty old multitool.

Grandpa Carl gave me this, she remembered, ratcheting the drill attachment in and out. *Middle School graduation. Long time ago. I can't throw these things away, they're my friends. I might need them.*

And, Gretchen realized with a sinking, sick feeling, she couldn't keep them either.

I'd better keep just this one, she resolved, limping back toward the main building, the multitool snug against her side. *Loyal service should be rewarded.*

Gretchen angled to her left, aiming to cut around the lab to the hangar entrance, when someone stepped around the corner of the low-slung building. She slowed, feet shuffling in knee-high drifts of freshly blown sand, and raised her hand to wave hello.

The figure—features obscured in a tightly wrapped *kaffiyeh* and respirator mask—paused, startled, one leg unusually stiff and something—she had no idea what—made her lurch to a halt. Gretchen's throat went dry and a familiar chill feeling stroked the back of her neck.

"Crow . . . ?" Gretchen backed up, realizing the bulk of the lab building hid her from view, should anyone look out the windows of the headquarters or even go outside the main airlock. "Stand away!"

The figure stopped, *kaffiyeh* coming loose, *djellaba* flapping dark around short legs. Gretchen squinted, trying to peer past the half-mirrored facemask. Startled pale blue eyes stared back through greasy blond hair. Gretchen felt the world come unglued again.

"Oh blessed sister . . ." Her voice sounded queer—strained and tight—almost lost in the gusty evening wind. The sun had vanished into the west, leaving behind a glorious sky glowing orange and red and dusky purple. Along the horizon, the vast sandstorm was still visible, burning golden with the last rays of day.

"I've been copied!" A double echo vibrated in her comm.

Gretchen flinched back, her stomach burning with a chill knot of fear. Unbidden, the *sight* crept up on her and the figure's arm blazed with a cool flame. She shook her head violently, trying to clear her untrustworthy vision.

Anderssen was suddenly only a pace away, reaching out to take her arm.

"Are you all right?" The face behind the mask was stiff with concern.

"Stay back!" Gretchen tried to scramble backward but her feet dragged in the sand and she fell. The woman stopped, a penetrating look on her face as Gretchen crawled away. She could feel—and almost see—a familiar cool fire in the watching eyes. A sense of heat flushed her face. Gretchen recognized the sensation and both eyes grew wide, casting from side to side.

Forcing her fingers to steadiness, Gretchen switched her comm live. "Hummingbird?"

Static, warbling, rising and falling in tuneless rhythm. *The voice of the wind.*

She shut down the comm. The sky was darkening steadily and down among the buildings night gathered around her. Anderssen did not move. She seemed to be watching her intently. Mouthing a prayer to the Sister to fill her limbs with strength and guide her to safety, Gretchen closed her eyes. Fear boiled behind her eyelids, clinging, cold, leaching thought of motion. Now, encompassed entirely in darkness, the night felt heavy, pressing against her from all sides. There was menace hiding in the darkness. *Why didn't I feel this before? None of this was here!*

"I need your help," her own voice said from the night. Her face warmed again, as though a bonfire roared and leapt only meters away. "Just come with me."

Gretchen gathered her legs under her, forcing the awareness of stabbing pain in her brutalized feet away, and drifted away from the sickly heat on her face. Her hands brushed across sand, gravel and slivers of rock, searching for just the right place to settle.

The voice followed her, not too far, not too close. "It's growing cold. We should go inside. Gretchen, I know this seems terribly strange to you. . . ."

Shuddering with relief, her outstretched hands found barren rock, exposed by the ceaseless wind and there, among chipped, splintered shale, was a sense of solidity, of rightness. Gretchen scurried onto the stones, halting when her left boot skidded out over unseen emptiness. Digging her hands into the loose rock, she exhaled slowly and opened her eyes.

A cloud of chilling mist wavered in the air. She could see a single, solitary light burning in one of the second-floor windows of the main building. Everything else in the camp was dark and deserted. The sense of menacing abandonment rushed back, stronger than ever. Even the stars seemed faint.

Anderssen approached, stepping over the ridges of sand. Her movement was odd—jerky, a half-motion slower than expected. The odd doubling and tripling of her vision returned, stronger than before, showing an Anderssen ablaze with the chill blue light or blocky dark or illuminated again. Nothing about her, no matter the wealth of detail in her face and suit and cloak, seemed even remotely human.

Hummingbird sang bravely when they came against him, she remembered, a sharp fragment of the dreadful night under the cliffs of the Escarpment. *Damn it, I can't think of any songs! I hate singing. Why would I have to sing?*

The shape paused and she saw it had reached the edge of the stone outcropping. Furling the *djellaba* aside with a deft motion, the shape settled into a crouch, puddled in shadow and darkness. Gretchen swallowed, closing her eyes in concentration. The warmth in the stone seeped up into her fingers, into her hands, filling her arms with strength.

"I am not afraid," she said aloud. The sickly heat returned, beating against her face. She started to sweat, feeling moisture bead on her neck and forehead—and then the dampness froze. Alarmed, Gretchen opened her eyes. The sky had grown fully dark, awash with pale emerald, topaz and carnelian stars, all trace of the blinding sun fled.

A faint blur of light tainted the sand around the crouching figure. As Gretchen watched, the blur thickened, brightened and spread. Slow radiant threads crept across gravel and scattered stone, winding their way onto the rocks. A fierce desire to flee gripped her, seeing the glassy illumination advance, but everything beyond the steady, solid warmth in the rock was cold and remote.

Wait, she wondered. *Is this something only visible to my sight, or is it real?*

The blur washed closer, now rippling in faint, ghostly waves across the stones.

What do I really see? Is anything really there? What if it's just an echo of myself?

Gretchen let her body become loose again. A stiffness in her arms and legs resisted, but slowly faded as she controlled her breathing. In the brilliant dreams, the turmoil of hallucinogenic visions and uncontrollable sight had been subsumed into a crystalline sense of order. In the perfectly etched world the bitter powder had shown her, there was sight and *sight*. There was the promise of focus and a diamond-bright perfection of intent.

She groped to recapture the sensation. Memory fled, vanishing in a chaos of confused images, in delirious phantasms. Heat burned suddenly in her fingers. Gretchen jerked back, forcing her eyes open.

The cold blur lapped around her feet and covered her gloves. Stunned, she saw clouds of tiny flickering particles swarming among the broken, dead stone. An effort to lift her hand failed—a steadily growing web of jeweled threads chained her to the ground. *Oh, shit!*

Gretchen dragged at her leaden arms, trying to wrench free of the spreading jewel-stain permeating the glossy black of her suit. Despite straining with both feet braced, she only succeeded in wrenching her shoulder. The sense of steady warmth vanished in the moment of effort, leaving the biting cold of the Ephesian night flooding in around her. A wild glance to either side revealed only darkness and some kind of pit or fissure in the earth. *Trapped! Both forelegs in the trap. I can't even gnaw free.*

Stomach churning with nausea, she looked across the outcropping, expecting to see the shape looming there in triumph. Instead, she gave a tiny, fierce shake of her head, stunned.

Anderssen rose, bloody feet bare on the gleaming sand. A queer emerald fire licked through her short blond hair, then faded away. The woman shifted her shoulders, letting the *djellaba* fall properly. Her face was bare to the thin, frigid air—the red welts of a breather mask worn too long were plain on her round cheeks, nose and neck—every tool and gadget was in place, comm and medband clasped around well-muscled wrists.

"Wha—" Gretchen rallied, violently collecting her thoughts. "You don't look like me."

The stance was all wrong, weight evenly distributed, not leaning to one side, favoring the wounded foot; even the face seemed distorted—lopsided—one eye fractionally higher than the other.

Hummingbird will be able to tell. Gretchen found the thought a frail comfort. *If he has time to see as she rushes out of the darkness or creeps up behind him.*

The chains of jewels dragging at her arms pulsed with delicate, subtle color. Gretchen felt something change and shift in her mind. Half-familiar memories stirred, clamoring for her attention. They felt strange—not soft and faded, burnished by the passage of time—but cold and clear, freshly struck from the die.

A sullen yellow sky filled with hundreds of bright pinpricks loomed overhead, a harsh, claustrophobic vault crushing the breath from her lungs. In every direction

endless ranks of vast obsidian towers soared in counterpoint to the sulfurous heavens.
She turned, images blurring past—more towers, some shattered and cracked with
age, some newly raised from the plain.

In the distance, heat haze shimmered in deserted avenues, yielding the sickly
black image of a vast, implacable lake. Somewhere, beyond the horizon, down just
such an avenue as this, ringed by the same colossal buildings, the lake was real; oily,
infinitely deep, stretching from horizon to horizon, a choking black band wrapped
around the wizened throat of an ancient, dying planet.

"No—I was never there!" Gretchen shouted aloud, filled with an all-encompassing fear for her own memories, her own thoughts. Voices roared in her ears, shouting and accusing her of monstrous deeds. "I'm not one of the things in the library! I'm not one of them!"

A cloud of brilliant stars spanned the arc of a blue-green world. Great whorls of
white cloud obscured most of the surface, but mottled green and brown continents
peeked through. Seas and oceans blazed blue, shining in the light of a dim yellow sun.

Across the face of the void, stars rippled and twisted, distorted by something vast.
Space boiled and tore, splitting aside. A shape forced its way through the burning gap,
something nearly dwarfing the world shining below. Tatters of space and time flew
past, the light of distant suns still reflected in long streamers of darkness. An ebon
shape swept across the world, blotting out any view of the green hills or shining seas.

In the passing wake, the fabric of space reknit, stars falling back into their accus-
tomed courses, the glare of the sun once more traveling as it had done for millennia.
Yet the spilling, fluid darkness already englobed the world, a tightening black web,
shutting out the sun, blocking the light of the stars.

"No . . ." Gretchen tried to concentrate, to hold back a titanic flood of images—not *her* thoughts, not things *she* had done—from overwhelming her mind. They crowded in, pushing aside memories of her friends at the university, time spent hiking in the tall pines behind the steading, the smell of coffee perking in her dorm room, the harsh taint of diesel in the fog as she hurried across the Quad to class. "Give them back!"

But her memories were dying. Wiped away. Replaced by images of a horizon boiling with black ink, of shining silver sparks raining down out of the sky, splashing into the sea, tangling in saw-leafed palmettos. *The single burning image of a four-fingered hand lifting a muddy cylinder from a stream.*

"Not mine. Not mine. Not mine!" Gretchen wailed, clutching desperately at carefully hoarded memories of two little girls and one little boy. The sound of Isabelle crying, swaddled in fluffy blankets. Duncan's face screwed up in a pout, thin little arms crossed over his chest, one of his grandfather's flannel shirts rolled up sixty times to fit. Tristan declaring she would be planetary president right after third form. Everything they had ever done or said or shouted. Bare feet pattering down wooden stairs into the kitchen.

A sharp sense of disassociation overtook her, a threshold breached by urgent need.

The sense of brilliant clarity from her dreams was suddenly there, around her, a perfect, frozen world of absolutes. Black stains upon her memory shone very clear in this incandescent vision. *Mine*, she raged, driving back the distorting clouds. Where the shimmering visions had lain entwined with her own imperfection, she summoned up every detail from faint traces, from ghosts, from the neural residue left in the rubble of invasion. *Mine!*

For a moment, she hung in a balance, staring into endless corridors of memory, where every lost day, every forgotten word, every kiss was still alive, poised for her to plunge into them again. Youth. Tiny wrinkled pink babies drawing breath for their first wailing cry. Tiny hands clasped in hers. Frost on the porch in the morning. Melting snow plunging from the steep, slate roofs of the university halls as spring sunlight shone through the last clouds of winter.

Freezing cold engulfed her hands and Gretchen hissed in pain. Her eyes were still open, staring at sand spun with a web of jewels, but the vision was very distant from her thought. A jolt of physicality shook her body, tearing her mind away from the swarm of memories and plunging her once more into the cold, bruised, bleeding, frightened body crouched on a bare stone outcropping amid desolation. "Ahhhh! Oh Sister . . . that hurts!"

Her work gloves and the z-suit covering her forearms had been eaten away, leaving nothing to protect her skin from the subzero Ephesian night. Her fingertips were turning black. Gretchen clutched both hands to her chest and cried out at a fresh burst of pain.

A rasping cough tore itself from her chest, then another. Tears froze at the corners of her eyes. Still afraid to move, she curled herself up on the bare stone, trying to protect her ruined hands with the bulk of her body. Cold closed in on her, heat seeping away through the damaged suit into the open sky.

In the darkness, Anderssen frowned, displeased. *There are no answers here.*

Tonuac, shipgun at high port, scuttled up to a pressure door at the end of the corridor. A dozen yards back, Hadeishi tensed, waiting for *Heicho* Felix—who was covering the Marine on point with her Whipsaw—to wave him forward. Tonuac crouched, keeping his head below the level of a glassite panel set into the door, and listened intently. A moment later he made a hand sign. Felix did not turn, but her hand slashed at the floor of the corridor. *Traffic ahead.*

Hadeishi settled in to wait. Maratay was right behind him, making sure the hardwire for the comm relay spooled out properly while keeping an eye on the *chu-sa*, who as an officer—a Fleet officer at that—needed constant supervision. Clavigero was ten meters behind, at the last bulkhead frame, watching the backtrail for unwanted visitors.

Nearly two hours had passed since they'd broken in through the airlock. The *Turan* had proved vaster than Hadeishi had expected. The schematics did *not* do justice to the endlessly snaking passages, countless levels, ramps, elevators, and gangways they had traversed to reach this point. From his handheld, Mitsu knew the corridor ahead was a main artery in the primary hab core of the refinery. Here, at last, they were reaching territory where they might encounter the crew.

"There's a galley and common area listed on the spec," he whispered to Felix. "Through the hatch and to the right about twenty meters."

"I know." The *heicho* grinned mischievously over her shoulder. "You know, in the sims, everything was very shipshape."

Hadeishi swallowed a guffaw. Nothing they'd seen so far had been clean. A thin layer of oily, pastelike grime covered every visible surface. Some of the gangways they'd climbed had left black stains on his gloves and boots. The *chu-sa* had neglected to pack an analysis comp with a sampler, but he suspected all this finely coated debris was residue from the refinery operations. He could feel the ship vibrating through his boots and shoulder—somewhere downship enormous machines were grinding raw asteroid rock down to a molecular grit for ore separation. Some process of the sort was leaking this slippery, invasive grime. *Civilians . . . is it like this on commercial, licensed miners, too?*

Shaking his head slightly, he nodded to Felix. "Is this a bad spot? In the sims, I mean."

"No." Felix adjusted her grip on the Whipsaw, dark brown eyes troubled. "So we're going to go careful."

Tonuac motioned, drawing her attention back to the door. The point-man keyed the pressure door open, revealing a brightly-lit corridor with rubberized carpet. Tonuac eased out, swinging his gun sharply from side to side, then signed all-clear. Felix was moving the instant Tonuac cleared the door, one hand guiding Hadeishi through the opening. Behind them, Maratay scuttled along, playing out hardwire from his spool. Clavigero sprinted up the passageway, running as quietly as he could to catch up.

Hadeishi caught a glimpse of a broad passage lined with working, reasonably clean overhead lights. There were even 3v posters of beaches and wooded mountainsides on the bulkheads. Tonuac punched the access plate of a door facing them as Felix and the *chu-sa* reached his side. The two Marine privates were crowding in behind, shipguns covering the hallway in either direction.

The door hissed opened and a man—a crewman with short, sandy hair and an armload of briefing binders in his arms—stepped through into their midst.

Hadeishi froze, startled. Felix smashed the butt of the Whipsaw into the man's face without so much as a heartbeat's hesitation. The miner jumped back with almost equal speed and the gunstock slammed into his binders. They flew everywhere in a spray of paper and diagrams.

"Intruder . . . *urk!*" The man's scream was cut off abruptly. Felix seized the throat of his braided jacket, lifted him bodily—an easy task for her suit—and flung him back through the hatch. Tonuac had already leapt ahead—the map showed a cross-passage leading to a maintenance shaft which rose to the bridge deck—and slewed to a halt, cursing.

Instead of a narrow, pipe-lined corridor, there was a ready room with an entertainment center, a wet bar and four very startled-looking miners. The clerk crashed past the Marine and took out a card table in a clatter of shattering plastic and plywood. The other men leapt up, shouting in alarm.

"Other way," Hadeishi and Felix shouted simultaneously. Tonuac short-stroked the trigger on his shipgun and jumped back through the doorway. A sharp *bang!* flung a room-suppression munition into the compartment. The miners scattered away from the bouncing black sphere.

"Portside," Felix shouted, shoving Hadeishi past her. Maratay darted ahead, still concentrating on the hardwire spooling out in a silvery ribbon behind him as he ran. The *heicho* cranked a round from the Whipsaw into the access panel for the compartment door. A violent, concussive *boom* followed and smoke billowed out of the wall. A second, muffled *whoomp* followed hard on its heels as the room suppression munition blew apart inside the ready room.

"Schematic is offset ten meters," Hadeishi commented into his throat mike as they charged down the corridor. "Reset and relay to my handheld."

Maratay skidded to a halt at another compartment door. "This one?"

"Knock it in," Felix shouted, waving Clavigero past. Tonuac had already dashed ahead of the *chu-sa* to take flank-point. The little Rajput Marine swung the comm relay onto his shoulder, hoisted up his gun and jammed the access keypad with the muzzle. The door cycled open.

An alarm began to blare, filling the corridor with eardrum-crushing noise.

Maratay sighed. The maintenance corridor was stacked floor to ceiling with crates. "No go!"

"Keep moving," Felix said, shoving her *chu-sa* ahead. "Go to access route plan three."

They jogged forward and suddenly a wide cross-passage opened to the right. Men in dark-blue uniforms were running toward them, overhead lights gleaming from steel-gray weapons. Hadeishi leapt aside and back—there'd been a compartment door—shouting "Sureshot! Sureshot!"

Tonuac and Felix had already spun to cover the new threat. Both froze as the *chu-sa*'s order registered. Maratay threw himself out of the line of fire, staying on task, but Clavigero skidded into the open and his shipgun twitched sideways automatically. His finger clenched tight and a burst ripped from the weapon, filling the side-corridor with a stuttering series of sun-bright flashes.

Hadeishi threw the wardroom door aside with his shoulder and rolled in. A man rose in surprise from a computer station, a still-smoking tabac dangling from his lip. Maratay rolled the other way, flipping the hardwire around the doorframe. Mitsu realized no one else could deal with the miner and sprang across the table separating them.

The man shouted, fell backward over his chair and Hadeishi jammed him to the deck with the point of his elbow. The suit-magnified blow slammed the man's head into the carpet, stunning him. Encapsulated in complete, unhurried calm, Hadeishi rolled the miner over and pinned him with a knee. "Maratay—restraints?"

The Marine tossed over a set of zipcuffs from a pouch at his belt.

Outside, the echo of Clavigero's shipgun had been swallowed in a roar of beam weapon fire. A lurid red glow flooded the hallway. Felix and Tonuac dropped through the door and swung to covering positions. A smoking, scarlet beam licked past, searing a three-meter scar on the opposite wall. The heat of the blast singed Hadeishi's combat suit, but his hands did not pause in securing their prisoner.

"*Chu-sa?*" Felix hissed, gesturing for Hadeishi's attention. "We've got to break out of here. Get ready!"

"Wait one," Hadeishi said, making a sharp quelling motion. "Clavigero?"

Here, kyo. The man's voice was harsh with adrenaline. *I'm in the main corridor, fell back to the last space-frame.*

"Hold position, Marine." The *chu-sa* clicked his throat mike. "Koshō, how many men in the cross-corridor?"

Six, two down. Susan's voice was refreshingly cool in his earbug. He had a very clear mental image of her in the command chair on the bridge of the *Cornuelle*, watching the combat v-feed with dispassionate, professional interest. *More will reinforce from the galley area.*

Hadeishi caught Felix's eye. The *heicho* was very tense and seemed ready to leap out into the corridor and take the miners on with her bare hands. "Sureshot, *Heicho*. No casualties."

"Two down now, *Chu-sa*," she replied, eyes flicking between his face and the angle of the corridor she could see. "Their blood will be up. N is high."

Hadeishi nodded. Fleet training assumed every operational plan would reach a point of failure at an indeterminate point of time offset from the 'go' moment. The possibility of failure was termed "n", which began accumulating even before operational kickoff. Some planning officers believed n accumulated for individuals as well—eventually your day came and there was nothing you could do to erase the failure-debt you'd accumulated. "Clavigero—suppress the backside corridor. Felix—exit options?"

The *heicho* dragged out her handheld, scanning through the level schematics. Outside, there was a sharp coughing sound as the Marine in the passageway fired two RSM rounds down the main corridor toward the galley. Hadeishi could hear men shouting in the distance, but their voices were drowned out by a heavy *whoomp-whoomp!*

"We're backed up against a bulkhead here, *kyo*." Felix pointed at the rear wall. "But both sides lead into other compartments. . . . What's he got?"

Hadeishi rolled the unconscious miner over. His name tag read GEMMILSKY and the tag for his ship department indicated he was a system tech. Eyes narrowing in consideration, Hadeishi rose, stepping to the miner's computer display.

"Ship's librarian," he said slowly. "Maratay—get the relay over here and jack in. Felix, we need some breathing room."

"*Hai, Chu-sa!*" Felix signed to Tonuac. The Zapotec craned his head to look outside, muttering under his breath to Clavigero. The Marine out in the hallway replied, but Hadeishi was concentrating on disassembling the desk. Maratay reached in, handing him a spare multitool and between the two of them they had the tabletop unscrewed as fast as humanly possible.

"Susan," he said, stripping a dust cover away from the comp unit hidden in the desk, "get Smith on this circuit. We need to break into their shipside comm."

Understood. A soft chime sounded as the midshipman came on channel. *Standing by.*

Hadeishi identified the comm interface and Maratay handed him a cluster of adhesive leads. *Been a long time since I had to do this*, Mitsu thought, his thoughts blurring into action as quickly as he could find the circuit ports and nudge the leads into place.

Under the watching snout of Felix's Whipsaw, Tonuac darted out from the door and across the passageway to the opposite bulkhead. Parts of the deck and junction facing were on fire, spilling a bitter, acidic smoke into the air. The intruder alert continued to blare, now joined by the honking of a fire alarm. The hallway leading toward the galley billowed with sleepgas from Clavigero's RSM rounds. Tonuac's visor adjusted automatically, shifting into multispectrum range. The resulting gray-tinted image showed him unconscious men scattered in the corridor. No one seemed to be moving that way.

"Mop up," he hissed at Clavigero, waving the Marine toward the ready room. "Sureshot, remember. Use tanglewire."

As the private loped off into the smoke, Tonuac glanced over at Felix, received the go-ahead and plucked a spare-eye from his belt. Sliding the hair-thin video camera around the corner, he watched the feed on a heads-up inside his visor. The enemy was gathering—the two men Clavigero had knocked down were gone, dragged away—and at least twenty miners were crouched along the walls. They had an amazing number of weapons to hand—but Tonuac didn't see a single man with a rocket launcher or in armor.

"Waited too long, my friends." Tonuac laid the eye down on the floor so it could continue to transmit. He checked to make sure his shipgun was set to fire RSM, caught Felix's eye—she nodded, the Whipsaw raised—and poked the muzzle around the corner.

Instantly, the air curdled with the *snap-snap-snap* of beam pistols. The wall beside his head blew apart as plastic and light metal atomized. Tonuac felt the shockwave slap his shoulder and neck, but the absorptive composite of his suit shrugged the blow aside. His shipgun coughed twice and he scuttled back before someone hit him with something big enough to punch through his armor. Felix waited for him to clear her line of sight, then overhanded a tanglewire grenade into the adjoining corridor.

The *whoomp-whoomp* of the RSM rounds detonating amid the miners was drowned by a chorus of exited yelling. More thick gray smoke flooded the passage, disguising the detonation of the tanglewire. The grenade bounced once and then shattered. Thousands of monofilament spools unwound at near-supersonic speed. Adhesive thread-ends blew in all directions and dug deep into the bulkheads, overhead and deck on impact. Within six seconds the corridor was blocked by a misty, half-seen web of magnetically active wire. Wherever the strands touched they adhered and fused solid.

The tone of the fire alarms changed, dropping in urgency. Flame suppression foam flooded from vents in the ceiling, smothering the fires licking along the walls.

Tonuac held position, waiting for Clavigero to return. On general principles, he fired an RSM round down the other branch of the main hallway. More sleepgas and smoke billowed up, making sight difficult for anyone not already in combat armor or using goggles tuned to the 'clear' wavelengths designed into the Imperial smoke.

"Four minutes at the most, *Chu-sa*," Felix reported, watching the v-feed from the spare-eye. The miners were milling about, confused by the smoke. Some of them had fallen down, overcome by the gas.

"Get me a directory." Hadeishi attached the last of the relay leads to the desk. Now the local network could be directly accessed by the *Cornuelle*. "And update our floorplans if you can."

Understood. Smith's voice was already distracted, concentrating on overwhelming the refinery ship's security systems. *Five minutes.*

"Maratay—we need a way out." Hadeishi consulted his handheld, then pointed at the upship-side bulkhead. "Through there."

The Marine nodded, slinging his shipgun. Between the two of them, they ripped away racks of data packs and printed books to get at the wall. Maratay dug into a thigh pouch and produced a reel of cutting gel. Hadeishi stood back, letting the private sketch the outline of a door.

"*Kyo*—they've seen the tanglewire." Felix was still watching the corridor. Her chrono was spinning, counting the seconds. "Someone's taken charge—they're falling back with a guard left behind. They'll flank us left, right, up, and down."

"Smith-*tzin?*" Hadeishi started to scan through the schematics of the level above and below their position. They were inside the main hab area, which meant the overhead—in particular—was the deck of the room above. Their own floor lay atop a maze of service ducts.

Working . . . the midshipman replied. *We have comm access. And registry information.*

"Master's name?" Hadeishi crouched down, turning away from the upshipside wall. Maratay knelt as well, then triggered the electrostatic charge in the gel. Felix, still covering the outside passage, didn't even flinch as the bulkhead ruptured with a rippling, strobe-bright *wham-wham-wham!*

Ketcham, Tristan, R. Born Chatham, Duchy of Kent, Lower Skawtland, forty-three years old. . . . Kyo, he's ex-Fleet! Discharged nine years ago.

"Clear," Felix barked and Maratay knocked the broken section of wall into the next compartment. Hadeishi waited for the Marine to sign the room was safe, then ducked through the opening. The new compartment was filled with racks of comp equipment. Some of it was on fire, ignited by the blast. "Tonuac, Clavigero—let's go!"

Hadeishi stood aside, away from the burning equipment, while Felix slid into the room, her Whipsaw drifting from side to side, a tireless shark. "Smith, pull his service record. I need reason for discharge. And get me those deck plans."

Working.

Tonuac bounced in, his armor spattered with smoking, still-molten plastic. Maratay and Felix were already at the far side of the room, trying to clear racks of equipment away to get at the wall. In the first room, Clavigero darted in and spun into cover. Stabbing bolts of beam weapon fire followed, setting the walls alight again. The Marine found a refractive grenade on his belt, pitched the stubby cylinder into the passage and rolled forward through the breach in the wall.

Another *crump!* followed and the main passageway filled with a cloud of metallic flakes.

Nozzles opened in the overhead of the equipment room and Hadeishi's environment sensor started to squeak about lethal levels of carbon monoxide outside his suit. Ignoring the alert, the *chu-sa* strode to the far end of the room. "We've got to go up," he snapped at Felix. "Schematic says there's a laundry on the other side of that wall on this level. We'll never get through."

Susan's voice interrupted his train of thought. *Kyo, we have a tap on their ship-side comm. Ketcham took a voluntary discharge after being denied promotion to command rank.* Hadeishi heard a pause in her voice, and guessed the rest even before she continued in a clipped, angry voice. *He filed a letter of protest with Fleet, claiming a México officer of lesser demonstrated ability received command of the heavy cruiser* Dundee *in his stead. Thai-sa Four-Mountain was named as the other officer.*

"Understood." Hadeishi understood perfectly. He'd even met the captain of the *Dundee* once. A fine example of the high-clan patronage endemic to Imperial capital ship squadrons. Four-Mountain wasn't a bad commander today, but he would have been very, very inexperienced nine years ago. Probably best suited for an exec's slot, not an actual Fleet command. For an aggressive commander, for a man wanting to make his life in the Fleet, being passed over in such an obvious way would have been hard to swallow. Ketcham was neither the first nor the last officer who'd left the service after being snubbed in favor of someone closer to the Seven Hundred Clans.

While he was thinking, Felix and Tonuac had made a hand-and-hand brace. Maratay climbed up, bracing one leg in their grasp and the other against a rack-array of data packs. The little Rajput drew a fresh circle of cutting gel on the ceiling.

"Wait one," Hadeishi said to Felix after Maratay dropped down to the deck again. "Stand by. Smith—patch me onto the shipside comm, direct channel to Ketcham if you can pick out his ident code."

There was a pause. Things seemed to have quieted down outside. Mitsu presumed this meant the miners were preparing to attack their position by some means. He unsealed his sidearm holster.

You are in-circuit, Susan said and a confused babble of voices flooded Hadeishi's earbug.

"Not here, Paulson," Ketcham barked, turning on the riggers crowding the hallway behind him in their z-suits, gloves clutching beam cutters and wrenches. "Go round to the 6-D gangway and up to level thirty-six. Secure the rooms above the 78-H junction and make sure they don't burn through the roof and move up a level."

Confused but spoiling for a fight, the riggers turned around and ran off down the passage.

The refinery captain swore to himself, peering around the corner into the H-port-side hallway. A round dozen crewmen were at his side, most armed with sidearms or beam cutters, though none of them were in armor. The passageway ahead was entirely choked with clinging black smoke. There was no sign of the tanglewire blocking crossway 78.

Ketcham grabbed the nearest shift leader. "Termovich, send a runner to get me a handheld. We need plans of this level and all the rooms. Leave two men forward here on watch and then fall back a frame—and send someone else to get pressure masks or even z-suits if they can find them."

Men melted away from the gang of miners, eager to make themselves useful and get away from the sound of the guns. Ketcham ran a hand through thick blond hair, thinking furiously. He figured they'd already exhausted the day's ration of luck by having him within shouting distance of the firefight when it started. Hardly anyone else aboard had any military experience, though you couldn't deny they were game for a fight.

"No heavy weapons inside," he muttered, "barely anything like combat armor. Miners, technicians, shuttle pilots. . . . Termovich, where's the nearest emergency engineering panel?"

"Back two frames, sir." The Novoya Rossiyan looked scared to death, which only mirrored Ketcham's own gut-twisting fear. Someone—Company mercenaries? Pirates?—had entered his ship undetected, in combat suits and armed to the teeth. Tanglewire and RSM rounds didn't come cheap. But what could they want? To steal the whole ship? Why sneak aboard?

"Get over there right now and drop the bulkheads all round this section and on the level above and below. We'll seal 'em off."

Captain Ketcham? An unknown, unfamiliar voice intruded. Ketcham started and stared around before realizing the voice was coming from his earbug. *There is no reason for further conflict.*

"Who the hell is this?" Ketcham's bellow caught Termovich by surprise, but the Rossiyan bolted away from the captain's volcanic glare. "Identify yourself!"

Chu-sa Mitsuharu Hadeishi, IMN Cornuelle, *at your service.*

"Fleet?" Ketcham's voice choked in astonishment. Then his brain—which seemed to have stumbled into tar—kicked into gear. He slapped his comm unit, scrambling the channel. "Override six-twenty-six," he shouted, desperate for even ten seconds of clear air. "Bridge, this is Ketcham. A Fleet Marine assault team has entered the ship. Lockdown all levels and accessways, seal the bridge and—"

None of this is necessary, Captain Ketcham. I need to speak with you directly, but I mean you, your ship and your men no harm. The quiet, reasonable voice had cooled slightly.

Ketcham found his sidearm in his hand—a silver-chased Webley 220 with an over-and-under magazine—and reflexively cycled a round into the firing chamber. The safety unlocked and the see-through-shoot-through sight activated. The board of directors had presented the pistol to him last year, a custom model from Toporosky and Sons gunsmiths. A small token of appreciation for four years of profitable service. A corner of his mind—a part long neglected, but not entirely atrophied from disuse—calculated he would need to be within fifteen meters for the depleted uranium rounds to penetrate a Fleet combat suit.

"You've killed three of my men already," he growled into the comm. "My ship is on fire. You're not making yourself welcome!"

If any of your men died, Captain, I apologize. My Marines have been firing solely RSM and knockdown rounds. I admit an eyesocket hit might kill a man, but that is not our intent.

"What do you want?" Ketcham stared down the back corridor, silently pleading for Termovich to hurry or the bridge to react to his override command. To his great relief, a distant banging sound echoed down the hallway and the lights flickered. The fire alarm cut off and was replaced by the shrill honking of a ship-wide red alert. "Finally!"

I am coming out into the hallway, the voice said, apparently unaware of the bulkheads sliding closed amid flashing lights and the drone of the alarms. *I will be unarmed. There is a matter we must discuss. Tell your men to hold fire.*

"What?" Ketcham turned, surprised. "What did you say?"

"This is necessary," Hadeishi said to Felix, gently moving the Marine aside. The *heicho* looked gut-shot, speechless, alarmed, and outraged all at once. The *chu-sa* drew his sidearm and spun the gun round so the barrel was firmly in hand. "Susan, status please?"

We're going to lose hardline, she replied, her voice sounding as tense as Felix looked. *The bulkhead doors are dropping all over the ship. The line might handle one kink, but not sixteen.*

"Alternate comm?" Hadeishi stepped to the door of the compartment and pressed the access plate. The door did not move. The *chu-sa* frowned, realizing the puncture alert had sealed all of the compartment doors even as the bulkheads in the pressure frames were coming down. He looked sideways at Maratay and raised an eyebrow. The Marine jumped as if struck across the face and rushed to swipe cutting gel around the doorframe.

Smith has a hunter loose in their system. I'll let you know when—sqqqwk!

"The hardline is down." Hadeishi turned away from the door, clasping his hands behind his head. Gel volatilized in a rippling streak of fire. Debris rained against Mitsu's suit and smoke coiled past. "*Heicho* Felix, deploy to hold this block of rooms. The *Cornuelle* will attempt to restore communications through alternate means. No one—*no one*—is to open fire without my express order, no matter what happens outside."

The woman nodded, nervously cycling the Whipsaw into firing position.

Hadeishi stepped through the opening into a hallway choked with smoke. The refraction grenade's payload had mostly settled from the air, leaving the floor covered with drifts of shiny metallic glitter. There was fire suppression foam everywhere, dripping from the walls and pooling on the ground. The smoke itself was separating out into oily layers as he walked out into the middle of the cross-corridor and emerged from the fog into sight of the miners.

One of the miners squeaked like a startled rat and his beam-pistol flared. Hadeishi was facing the weapon straight on, his hands wide, his sidearm extended on his middle finger. He saw a discharge corona blossom in the microsecond before his visor polarized and felt the beam glance from his left shoulder.

The *snap* of the ionizing beam rocked the hallway. Hadeishi staggered, nearly thrown down by the hit. A section of articulated armor plating on his shoulder glowed white hot for a moment, then the surface ablated away, shedding shell-like layers of composite destroyed by the beam. Suit chillers kicked in, bleeding away the heat, and the molten spot began to fade.

"I am unarmed," he announced, voice echoing from the suit's speaker, and tossed the sidearm to the floor. The gun made a clanking sound—very loud in the sudden, shocked silence—and fell over on its side. "I need to speak with Captain Ketcham urgently."

One of the men in the crowd—flattened against the wall, watching him over the muzzle of a massive handgun—twitched and Hadeishi turned slightly to face him. The man—the captain, Mitsu realized, spying rank decorations on a dark-blue uniform with red and gold piping—was tall and broad, easily a foot taller than the Nisei, with wavy blond hair and deep-set, narrowed blue eyes.

The very image of our ancient enemy, Hadeishi thought, continuing to walk forward.

"Stop right there!" Ketcham moved forward, the miners around him—most of them technicians and machine operators, if Mitsu was any judge of their work clothing and departmental insignia—shrinking back to make way. The gun centered on his breast did not waver. "I'll accept your surrender, Nisei, and we can discuss whatever you want once you're in the brig."

Mitsu shook his head. "Captain, the Imperial Navy does not surrender. You should remember the oath you swore at Academy—"

Ketcham's face twisted in a foul, ugly snarl of rage. His finger twitched on the trigger of the Webley and there was a deafening *crack* as the gun discharged in a gout of expelled gas. Hadeishi tried to throw himself aside, but the flechette round had already broken into a dozen supersonic splinters and at least four smashed into his chest, flinging him around like a broken doll.

Another bone-deep cough wracked Gretchen's body, coupled with a shiver running from head to foot. Vapor leaking from her mask formed a rime of ice across her collarbone and goggles.

I'm going to freeze to death. The raw thought managed to force itself past crippling pain. Gretchen lifted her head, staring around in the darkness. Through the fog on her lenses, the queer lights had faded away and the nighted shape of Anderssen was gone. Heartened, she rolled up, feeling bone and muscle creak. Though her hands were tucked into her armpits, they had lost all feeling.

The single light on the upper floor of the main building shone clear and distinct, a welcome beacon in the darkness. Gretchen forced herself to her feet, the twinge of her brutalized soles barely noticeable against the hacking cough torturing her upper body. She swayed, dizzy and short of breath, but managed to stumble forward.

Putting one foot in front of the other was torturous work, but she kept her eyes on the light in the window and kept walking. The drifts of sand now seemed to be monstrous ridges.

Near the corner of the lab building, she stumbled and fell. Lying on the ground felt good—for a moment—but then the cold seeped into her suit again. Gretchen staggered up, then slid along the building wall, leaning into the concrete for support. At the corner, she took a careful look around—saw nothing—and then limped stiffly across the quad to the hangar door.

The pressure door was locked. Bumping the access plate with her hip evoked no reaction.

"Shit." She lifted her wrists—eyes averted from the lacerated, discolored flesh— and clicked the comm band alive with her chin. "Hummingbird? Hummingbird?"

Anderssen? His response was immediate and surprised. *Where are you?*

"Outside, outside the hangar pressure door. I can't get in."

The side door has frozen up. Come around to the main airlock. It's clear now.

"Sure," she grunted, slumping forward against the wall. A wave of dizziness threatened to pitch her over onto the ground again but the cold ceramic of the hangar door caught her. She decided to take just a moment to regain her strength. "I'd love to. I'm hurt."

Gretchen jerked awake, barely cognizant of someone helping her stumble through the pressure doors on the main airlock. A little old man in a z-suit was holding her up, his wiry shoulder under her arm. Then they were in the common room and the air—the air was warm enough to breathe without a mask—and there were lights and a heater humming on the floor.

Hummingbird sat her down and bundled blankets around her shoulders. A minute later he was tipping a cup of warm—not hot—syrupy liquid into her mouth. Alcohol and sugar and something mediciny flooded her throat and then a matching warmth spread through her chest.

"Show me your hands." Hummingbird sounded concerned and his face tightened into a grim mask when he saw the blue-black sheen to her flesh and the ragged welts where the jeweled chains had bound her to the earth. His green eyes lifted to stare into hers. "What happened?"

"She was here—outside—she caught me on my way back from getting rid of the Sif."

"The Russovsky echo?"

"Yes," Gretchen mumbled, the frail burst of adrenaline ebbing away. "She looked . . . just like me."

Completely drained, Anderssen curled up and fell sideways into the blankets. Hummingbird rummaged around and found another blanket for a pillow. He put the heaters on either side of her and started to warm more of the rum/cough syrup/energy concentrate mixture on the camp stove.

He made her drink more of the nasty fluid. "The shape attacked you?"

"It tried. . . ." She frowned, trying to remember. Her head felt very strange inside, all jumbled and disordered. For some reason—and now she became cognizant of not knowing why—memories of her children and graduate school were very sharp and close at hand. Remembering what had happened earlier in the day was suddenly impossible. "Something happened," she said helplessly. "I saw her, but she was me. There were shining lights in the sand. I can't remember everything . . . properly."

"Were there two figures? Or just one, which changed?"

"One." She mumbled, feeling her wounded fingers throb. "I couldn't move—something had hold of me, of my hands . . . and you were there. There were—I had a vision! Yes, there were visions in my mind, someplace ancient, dead . . . under a foul yellow sky."

The *nauallis* squinted at her curiously, then carefully examined her hands. Clicking his teeth together in thought, the old man sprayed them with something cold and prickling from his kit, then carefully cleaned the welts. The pain of his touch lanced through her, drawing a whining cry, robbing the last breath from her lungs. At some point, she passed out.

"I'm really doing very well," Gretchen said, staring at her hands wrapped in more gauze and stinging from the dermaseal working away on the freeze damage. "Between my feet and hands I look like a cirq clown." She sighed, shaking her head, and gave Hummingbird an aggrieved look. "Aren't you the lucky one? You crash and walk away, while I fly halfway round the world and am fine, then I'm here at *base camp* for two days and I look like a tree-rigger on leave."

"You're lucky," he said, giving her a severe look. "Your medband was working the whole time and dispensed enough circulatory booster to keep you from losing any fingers or toes."

"Great—I could have suffered heart failure instead." Being flippant was making her tired, so she decided to stop.

"You're alive and will heal." Hummingbird squatted at her side, peeling back an eyelid with his thumb. "You might have more drug than blood in your system right now, but you don't seem to have become psychotic."

"Yet." Gretchen felt grainy and tired and wrung out. Again. "Is the *Gagarin* ready to go?"

The old man nodded. In the morning light streaming through the round windows, he seemed rather drawn and gray. "You'll want to check everything."

"I slept a day?" He nodded. "Then we need to get in the air. Where's my chrono?"

Hummingbird held up a mangled, pitted chunk of wire and metal. "No chrono."

"Fine. What time is it?"

"Six-thirty," Hummingbird said after rather ostentatiously checking his own bare wrist.

"Time to mount up." Gretchen lifted her gauze-muffled hands. "Help, please?"

The hangar door groaned, both track engines long since consumed by the microflora, as they dragged on the chains. Reticulated metal clanked and rattled and the door inched up. Gretchen found she could lend a hand by clinging limply to the chain and letting gravity and weight do the work.

As the door rose in fits and starts, the morning sun blazed on their faces, shining hot through unusually clear, steady air. Gretchen peered suspiciously at the lab building. There were no mysterious figures silhouetted against the skyline on the dune ridges, nothing lurking in the shadows of the recessed doorways.

"What did I see?" She let the chain fall from her fingers, turning toward the *Gagarin*. The ultralight looked rather strange with the rockets strapped underneath and its wings folded up in parking mode. The other *Midge* was gone—stripped of parts and then broken down and scattered in the desert. Hummingbird had been busy while she slept, going here and there, scattering their belongings to the four directions.

Gretchen hoped, with a rather sick, dreadful yearning, there would be a shuttle waiting for them at height, ready to take them away into a universe of hot showers and sprung beds and differently flavored threesquare bars. *I don't want to come back here. Not even if they offer me the dig director slot.*

"As I said before," the *nauallis* grumbled, "you saw an echo. A copy engendered by your presence on this world."

"With my memories—my speech patterns? What could make a copy like that?"

"Something," Hummingbird said, opening the door on his side of the *Gagarin*. "Descended from a race of machines designed to disassemble organic molecules into their component atomic parts. You saw the matrix of patterns in the cylinder."

"Maps." Gretchen opened her door and—wincing—slid into the seat. Hummingbird was not a large man, but the cabin of the ultralight was now very, very crowded. With the doors closed they were cheek by jowl. Anderssen reached across him and keyed up the preflight check. The sound of the fuel cells waking up and the engines turning over had never been so welcome. "Diagrams of what to destroy . . . the eater had to be able to differentiate between targets."

"Not an impossible step from such a mechanism to one which could recognize *and* replicate an equivalent molecular system." Hummingbird tried to strap himself in but found the spacing between the seats very tight. Gretchen rolled her hip to the side, jamming her face against the window so he could lock in. "At least in broad strokes. The thing on the ship could not sustain itself, not out of the magnetic field of the planet."

Thinking about what he'd said, Gretchen reached across and tested his restraints. "Solid. Okay, engines are up, fuel pressure is constant . . . controls are responding."

The *Gagarin* shivered as the wheel brakes released. Gretchen goosed the engines slightly and the aircraft clattered out onto the sandy ground. One eye watching the fuel line readings, she turned the ultralight and they bounced and rattled across uneven ground toward the landing strip. After clearing the buildings, the *Gagarin* shivered, struck crosswise by a heavy gust.

"But . . ." Anderssen turned the aircraft nose to the wind and felt the wings flex slightly, even retracted. She flipped a series of switches on the overhead panel. Both wings began to extend, micromotors whining with effort. "You're thinking creatures that can live down here can't survive beyond the influence of the, ah, the thing hiding in the world. They need its presence to live?"

Hummingbird nodded, trying to keep calm as the ultralight shimmied and swayed from side to side. The extending wings weren't providing any lift, not yet, but their cross section was providing the gusty, prying wind with plenty of surface area to press against. The *Gagarin* began to bounce backward across the field, raising clouds of fine, sticky dust with each hop.

"Even a nanomachine," he said, gritting his teeth and clinging to the support bar as they slammed up and down, "must be powered by some means. The safest way is a broadcast system, so they may be denied sustenance if they run wild. Hazarding a guess, I would say the sleeping *valkar* is leaking power on some wavelength the descendants of the planet-killers can absorb, can use. While they are within the beneficent aura of the entity, they can live, work, replicate themselves."

The aircraft jounced sideways, throwing Hummingbird against the door.

"Making a copy of something like a human must use a lot of power." A clanking sound signaled the wings reaching full extension. The sharp hops transformed into long, slow arcs. Gretchen settled her hands—still wrapped in bandages and feeling enormous—on the control stick and sideboard panel. "Hold on. Here we go."

Both engines flared to life as she ran up the power. The ultralight settled out of a bounce and Gretchen pushed to maximum thrust. The *Gagarin* began to move forward, wheels whirring across the gravel and sand. With the wings at full extension, the aircraft generated a tremendous amount of lift and they were airborne within seconds. The camp buildings rushed past under their wheels and Gretchen swung the ultralight around in a long, broad turn. They continued to climb.

The plains sprawled below them. The camp became a collection of matchboxes. Off to the east, the standing stones of the observatory and the jagged lines of the excavation trenches stood out against a dun-colored background.

"Comm check." Gretchen clicked her throat mike live. "Clear?"

"Loud and clear," Hummingbird answered. The roar of wind and the hiss of the engines filled the tiny, cramped cockpit. "It may be . . ." He paused and Gretchen wondered if he was at a loss for words. "Perhaps the Ephesian life-form you saw—whatever had taken Russovsky's shape, and yours—learns in this way, by consuming another entity, by taking its memories and thoughts, even its physicality into itself." The *nauallis*'s voice was almost tentative.

"Well," Gretchen said, filled with joy just to be airborne again, the nose of her ultralight pointed at the black vault of heaven. The *Gagarin* climbed steadily toward the southwest. Slowly, the dark sky swelled to fill the forward windows. The planet dropped behind, then bent away, the horizons receding into a white arc. "Then it tried to consume my memories. I can't remember much of what happened, but I know it was painful and unpleasant."

Hummingbird said nothing. Gretchen glanced aside at him and her eyebrows narrowed in concern. He looked ghastly. "What?"

"If that is true . . ." He turned to look at her. "How did it learn to make *your* shape?"

Gretchen blinked, then took a long swallow of water from her recycler tube. "Well," she said after thinking for a moment, "we'll know pretty soon if I'm a copy."

Ahead, the solid black bar of the sky was beginning to sparkle with the gleam of faint, diffuse stars. The hiss of the engines grew more strident as the air thinned.

Wind stirred in the empty hangar, scattering dust and *hathol* spores across the clean, smooth concrete. A rule-straight shadow delimited sun from shade, slowly edging toward the door frame as the sun moved in the sky. In the shadows, blowing sand and grit accumulated in a corner, gathered itself and began to exert an electrostatic field. More sand skittered across the floor. A nubbin of gravel compressed. The day continued to lengthen.

When the killing sun had passed zenith and the hangar was entirely in shadow, the collecting sand stirred, rose, sprouted long thin crystalline tubules. They knotted into the outline of two legs, a torso, a chest, arms, finally a head. The wind circled in the hangar, bringing a heavy cloud of dust and small stones.

Russovsky compressed out of the air, grit and debris rushing together with a sharp hiss. The shape's eyes opened and shook a dusty head. The husks and shells of the dead *hathol* and *firten* puffed away from a gleaming black skinsuit. Russovsky wiped her cheek, hand coming away covered with a glittering gray stain. She looked around the empty shell of a building.

Gone. He is gone. Russovsky considered her memories, finding them filled with moments of parting. In some of the vignettes there were tears, impassioned words, something she remembered as <*loss* | *sorrow* | *longing*>. She did not think these last two humans had lingered, delaying their departure, hoping to squeeze a few more seconds from the grasp of implacable time. They had moved with admirable efficiency. They had taken her *Gagarin* away.

Now there was something disorderly in her cold, perfect thoughts. The aircraft, the battered old *Midge*, held meaning—something tantalizing at the edge of comprehension. She wished the ultralight would return. Russovsky raised her hands, feeling the echo, the vibration of its presence. The machine had stood here, just so, wheels pressing against the concrete. Minute indentations had been left in the aggregate. Tiny flakes of rubberlike material from the wheels lay on the floor. Even the air itself, troubled by the wind as it was, had not yet forgotten the shapes of the wings, the body, the landing gear.

A shadow remained, still visible to her eyes in the chaos boiling behind the individual molecules of gas in the air. An absence where the *Gagarin* should stand. Something in her revolted at the void, pressed her to summon forth creation from nothingness, to fill an emptiness in the hangar which echoed dissonantly with her colorless memories.

Russovsky spread her hands and wind howled in the chamber. A dark yellow cloud roared in from outside, borne around her by billowing, violent zephyrs. Sand and gravel and dust flooded in, caught up in a standing tornado roaring and shrieking in the cavity. The roof groaned and shook, panels cracking away. All three walls shivered and the concrete floor splintered and cracked and crushed into more dust and grit.

The shape closed her hands. There was a thrumming *whoomp* and the air congealed.

When Russovsky dropped her hands, the *Gagarin* stood before her, wings retracted, metal struts gleaming with a newly manufactured shine. Even the wheels were glossy black. The shape paced around to the side and opened the pilot's door.

These memories, these motions seemed proper—they seemed right—and Russovsky wondered when a flush of pleasure would fill her heart, rising in her breast like the dawn wind. She settled into the seat. The display before her was cold and dark. Slender fingers flipped a series of switches on the ceiling panel. The right hand flexed the stick, checking the resistance and response of the control surfaces. She rolled her shoulders back and forth, memories flushing with strength.

The display did not change. The engines did not ignite. There was no familiar chuckling hiss of hydrogen filling the fuel lines. Russovsky moved her hand across the panel again. Nothing. The machine did not stir to life, did not shiver awake to answer her will.

Is this disappointment? The memories held many examples, though they were distant and cold, untouchable. Sealed away behind layers of glassite. *The machine does not work. There is no . . . fuel.*

Russovsky scrutinized the memories with more care. A universe of mechanical systems was revealed, awareness of thousands of substances and chemical processes was uncovered. And with them, the slow, growing conclusion the human had not known enough about the intricacies of their manufacture to allow Russovsky—as she now stood—to replicate them, even with a firm grasp of molecular control.

Again, an emptiness where memory suggested there would be <*fury | rage | despair*>.

There was something inside the human which was not in the *hathol*, a brilliant unique spark which could not be <*consumed | known | understood*>. Russovsky thought, considered and decided this was the emptiness she felt within. Something lacking which made even the carefully hoarded memories of the human Russovsky, as tightly held as Gretchen's children splashing in the pool, seem flat and lifeless. *I am like the* hathol *and the* firten, she thought sadly, *only a mechanical process of electrons and chemical reactions.*

Russovsky climbed out of the aircraft and walked to the hangar door. The sun was still high in the sky, but she turned and paced down to the edge of the landing field. Long blond hair luffed in the wind as she raised a seamed, weathered face to the sky. Far above, far away now, there was a shining bright speck. A gleam of metal and composite spiraling higher and higher into the black heavens.

Tendrils of hair began to break down, smashed by the radiation flooding from the blazing disk blazing in the west. Then the skinsuit turned gray and began to crack. The constant wind abraded Russovsky, chipping away at tools, *djellaba*, the threads of the *kaffiyeh*. Slowly, she eroded, eyes still raised to the slowly dimming spark high above.

Smoke curdled in the air, seeping back into the space blown clear by the Webley's concussive blast. Thrown flat on the deck, Hadeishi's combat armor sizzled with waste heat from the impact of the flechettes. Four hand-size blotches glowed cherry-red on his breast and side.

Alarms continued to honk in the distance. All three corridors had been sealed off by the pressure doors. A half-heard, half-felt vibration was absent from the usual run of background noise aboard ship. The air circulators had shut down when environmental override isolated the level.

Among the uneasy crowd of his men, Ketcham slowly lowered the pistol. The blowback mechanism had already reloaded the firing chamber. The riggers at his side started to inch forward, emboldened by the sight of the stricken black-armored figure.

"Wait." Ketcham's basso voice carried easily in the smoky, troubled air. "He might not—"

Hadeishi's head moved. The suit speaker, mostly destroyed by the impact, made a distorted growling sound, then the control fabric adapted to the damage. "*Uhhhh . . .* that hurts."

The *chu-sa* levered himself up from the ground, the mirrored faceplate of his visor reflecting the crewmen shrinking back from his movement. Ketcham raised and sighted the gun again, his face blank with surprise. The refinery captain seemed equally shocked at having shot Hadeishi and at the *chu-sa* surviving the blast.

"There is no quarrel between us, Captain Ketcham." Hadeishi's voice was slurred and tinged with a buzzing edge of feedback. He was having trouble breathing. He wondered how many ribs he'd broken. The Nisei braced himself with both hands and stood up, swaying slightly. "I know what Fleet did to you, but I am not the Admiralty or the promotions board. I'm just a ship captain, as you were. All I want to do is talk."

"About what?" Ketcham bit out the words, his blood pressure rising again at the very mention of the word "Fleet." He usually accounted himself a patient, reasonable man, but the very sight of the Nisei's black combat suit inspired stomach-churning hate. But the absolute, unflappable confidence of the man standing in the middle of the passageway gave him pause. Unless he was insane, no officer—much less a commander—was going to put himself in harm's way like this, not without an enormously good reason.

Hadeishi gingerly prodded the impact points on his armor. Hissing cherry-red slivers of metal poked from the outer layer. A heat haze trembled around them. He decided they were better left alone. "Captain, you should put on a breather mask."

Without the vents going, the smoke from the RSM rounds was beginning to percolate down the corridor. Most of the miners already looked a little green around the gills. Ketcham noticed the danger and backed up, waving his men back. They scrambled down the hallway in a confused mass, pushing and shoving each other.

The refinery captain ignored the dissipating gas, continuing to block the hallway, the Webley still centered on Hadeishi's chest. The *chu-sa* took two steps forward, then stopped. He reached up and unlocked his visor, letting the servomotors in the joint swing it up and away from his face. Ketcham's gimlet-eyed expression became even harder as he took in the classically Japanese features.

"A brave gesture," the captain said bitterly. "But you've proven yourself recklessly bold already. Say your piece."

Hadeishi thought he had the measure of his opponent. Seeing the man now, in person, and knowing he'd been a ship captain in Fleet had settled his mind about one thing. The sense of imminent death—a taut, blood-stirring tension vibrating in every muscle—had not slackened. Indeed, Hadeishi was very sure he was far, far closer to death now, staring down the muzzle of the pistol, than he'd been before stepping out into the corridor. He had, in fact, a very clear view of the inside of the pistol barrel from where he now stood.

"The third planet of this system is a First Sun artifact."

Ketcham did not blink or otherwise react. "I know, we saw the Company exploration ship in orbit when we . . . wait. The *entire* planet?"

Hadeishi nodded. "This system is now under interdict. An Imperial *nauallis* aboard my cruiser has issued a directive-six order encompassing the entire Ephesian system and everything within twenty-five light-years."

"Wha—" Ketcham shook his shaggy head from side to side in disbelief. "Interdict? The planet . . ." His eyes widened in astonishment. "A ship? The planet is a First Sun *ship? There's a planet-scale starship orbiting this sun?!*"

"It is necessary," Hadeishi continued in a firm, level voice, "for all human ships, yours and mine alike, to leave this system in the quietest possible manner. No comm transmissions, no hyperspace transit within detection range of the third planet. None of us will be allowed to return. In the fullness of time, a distant picket will be established to keep the unwary from stumbling into danger."

Ketcham gave him a pitying look. "Do you really think that will happen? The Empire will cordon off this sector and leave well enough alone?" He made a disgusted gesture. "If what you say is true, if that world is a *ship*, they will have survey teams and exploration drones and an entire bloody battle fleet here as fast as a reliable squadron commander can make transit from Earth."

"I know." Hadeishi nodded slightly, acknowledging the man's point. "I am not a well-connected man, Captain Ketcham. I am not *reliable*. My family is small and poor, though we have a noble name. I do not have any friends—" here he placed a sharp emphasis on his words "—among the great princes or the clan lords. But I do believe in duty and in honor."

Ketcham started to interrupt, his broad face twisting into a furious epithet, but Hadeishi made a sharp motion with his hand, cutting him short.

"I swore an *oath*, Captain Ketcham, to protect humanity." A finger stabbed at the refinery captain. "Including you and your crew. Now, what you do once you're out of this system is your business. But right now, today, I need your help before you leave."

Ketcham just stared at him. At the same moment, there was a soft chime in Hadeishi's earbug. He almost collapsed in relief and could not keep from swaying a little. The refinery captain did not lower his pistol, but a worried look flitted across his face.

"You're going to let us go."

Hadeishi nodded, realizing the pain in his chest was not all from bruised flesh and bone. "Yes—but I need your help first. I need you to help me restore this system to as close to its original state as possible."

"What? That's insane . . . there's no way you can disguise the base camp those scientists built on the planet!" He chuckled evilly. "Dropping a nuke or a c-boosted rock won't exactly remove the evidence without making a bigger mess."

"The planet is not my concern." Hadeishi keyed his medband to dump a higher level of painkillers and coagulant agents into his blood. A sensation of spreading dampness was creeping down his chest. Mitsu couldn't see the wound, but he guessed the impact had turned his left pectoral into a pulpy, shattered mass. He tried not to move suddenly or raise his arm. "The judge is taking care of business there. I need you and your ship to restore the mass you've extracted from the belt . . . *uhhh* . . . as near to the source planetesimals as possible."

"Dump my load?" Ketcham's gun rose again, though Hadeishi felt his legs give way. He crumpled slowly to the deck. On the nearly-muted combat channel, he heard Felix hiss an order.

"Hold your position, *Heicho!*" Hadeishi's exclamation caused Ketcham to stiffen in alarm. The miner had forgotten—in the brief space of time they'd been talking—there were Fleet Marines aboard as well. Now he eased back, squinting into the slowly-settling smoke. "Captain Ketcham, I'm offering you a trade. The ore you've taken aboard while in this system—all of it!—in exchange for your ship and your freedom." Hadeishi coughed abruptly and his head swam with pain.

A spray of reddish droplets glistened on the deck. *My lung is perforated.*

Ketcham was staring at the blood. His face was a little gray.

"You need to be in medical," he said, lowering the pistol.

"Will you . . . *uhh* . . . help me? Dump your load in predetermined points? Circulate quietly through the belt. We have a nav-track . . . *huh!*" Another cough racked him and Hadeishi covered his mouth. His hand was wet when the spasm passed. "My navigator has a plot of your path through the asteroid zone. You can retrace—"

"Medic!" Ketcham was at his side, fingers pressing on the release points around the collar of the combat suit. "Marines—your CO needs a medic right now!"

Hadeishi blinked rapidly, trying to clear his vision. All he could see was a swirling gray haze. "Susan? Can you hear me?" The refinery captain was still shouting and there were people running in the hallway.

Your signal is very faint on this tap, but I can hear you. What do you want me to do?

Mitsu blinked again. He felt a tight cold sensation in his chest and wondered what kind of drugs the suit was injecting. Was he still bleeding? Had one of the flechettes penetrated, piercing more than his lung, perhaps his heart?

Mitsuharu, you must remain focused and alert. There is still work to be done.
Susan sounded very angry. Hadeishi smiled, wondering who had made a mistake
on the bridge. Something must have gone wrong to make break her composure.
Smith. It must be the midshipman. Poor lad, she'd flay him alive.

*Mitsuharu! I'm sending in another assault team. Asale will dock and take you
off. Medical bay is standing by right now.*

"No, no." Hadeishi stirred, concerned. There was pressing business to con-
clude. His father would not approve, rushing matters in such an impolite way, but
he remembered there was really no time left. A big man was looming over him,
blue eyes very bright. The gray haze was thinning. Long rectangular lights were
shining through the mist behind his head. "Captain Ketcham, are you going to
help me?"

The big man's eyes narrowed. His thoughts seemed to burn so obviously in
the broad, high-cheeked face. Fear and avarice and worry struggled to capture his
attention.

"Captain," Hadeishi tried to speak clearly, though there was something wet in
his mouth. "If you will not help me, then my executive officer will be forced to disable your ship and imprison your crew. You will lose . . . everything."

Ketcham's face hardened, but at the same time, the spark of concern in his
eyes flared into open fear. Hadeishi coughed again and everything became very
hazy, very distant. *I'm shutting down,* he realized, thoughts moving very slowly.
The suit is knocking me out. . . .

"Susan." He whispered. "No shot. There is no . . . shot."

Both rockets sputtered, blew a thin trail of black smoke and died. The *Gagarin* hung in emptiness, a white-hot sun reflecting in the mirrored upper surface of the wing. The sweep of the horizon was filled with stars, with the darkness of the void. The rust-red disk of the planet below seemed very small and far away.

Gretchen stared anxiously over her shoulder, searching the black vault over-head for any sign of a shuttle. The *Midge*'s radar was scanning wildly, but nothing showed on the scope. Sweat streamed down her face, pooling in the suit, overload-ing the recyclers. They had passed through a region of intense heat, though now the windows were crackling with ice. Hummingbird was stiff as a board, clutching his restraints, knuckles white.

"Do you see anything?" Anderssen barked at him, craning her neck to try and see past the *nauallis*. Only stars and the wispy white arc of the planetary atmo-sphere were visible. Her medband began to chirp in alarm, but she ignored the alert. *Radiation*, she thought sickly. *Doesn't matter.*

She realized Hummingbird's eyes were closed and his lips were moving silently.

"Prayer might help," she laughed—only slightly hysterically. "But I need your eyes."

The altimeter began to fluctuate. Tumbling slowly, the *Midge* began to arc back toward the planet below. Low gravity or no, the mass of the world tugged at them, drawing them back into a hot, close embrace. She punched the old man in the leg as hard as she could.

Hummingbird's eyes flew open.

"Do you see anything?" Gretchen jerked her head sharply toward his side of the *Gagarin*.

The *nauallis* blinked, then turned, staring out at the ebon sky. "Nothing . . . there's only . . . wait—there's something shining!"

Gretchen rapped the radar display sharply and though the mechanism ignored her, a spark suddenly flared at the edge of the *Midge*'s detection range. Something was approaching at tremendous speed. "Oh thank the Sister, the Mother and the Son of God! Hang on!"

"I am . . ." Hummingbird's cry was drowned by a roaring hiss as Gretchen blew the last of their fuel and twisted the *Gagarin* away from the oncoming object. Surviving the next sixty seconds required reducing their intercept differential as much as possible. She slapped a control and the *Midge* trembled as the skyhook ratcheted out of the roof.

"Wings away!" Gretchen threw a lever and explosive bolts *banged* sharply. The cockpit shuddered as both broad, shining wings spurted away from the sides of the cabin. "Brace!"

For a moment, the *Gagarin* rushed forward, racing across the world below. The hissing stopped and the engines went dead. A light flared on the panel, indicating they'd switched to battery power with the loss of the solar panels and fuel cells. Gretchen felt cold pour into the cabin around her feet and did not look down. Instead, she forced her head back into the headrest of the seat and braced her arms.

Something flashed overhead, glowing red-hot and the entire world jerked away in a blinding jolt of pain. A flood of white sparks roared across her vision. A massive wave of sound slammed into her, battering her eardrums. Someone's scream was lost in a dragon-throated roar. Metal squealed, stressed beyond all expectation of design and manufacture. Gretchen caught a glimpse of the planet rolling past, then Hummingbird's face slack in unconsciousness.

The windows shattered as the airframe deformed, spraying glassite into the cabin. What little air remained was wicked away into a supersonic slipstream. Waves of heat boiled in, raging against her face. Blinded, Gretchen gritted her teeth and hung on. Somewhere above and behind her, there was a shrieking whine as cable spooled in at tremendous speed.

The blazing red shape—superheated air flaring around the *Komodo* in a brilliant corona—swelled over her head. For a single instant, a black maw gaped before her, limned with fire.

Everything slammed to a halt, flinging her violently against the seat restraints. She choked, feeling bone and muscle tear. The world outside went black, even the stars blotted out by a roaring, twisting storm of abused atmosphere. She was still bouncing back into the seat, a shattered retaining ring spinning free to fly out through the window, when the side door tore away.

A pair of hands reached in, seizing the centerline join on her suit. Something blazed blue-white at her back and shoulder, then she was free of the restraints and being dragged from the shattered wreck of the *Midge*. A combat-suited figure— broad, well-muscled—wrapped her in powerful arms and leapt back as a workline reeled in. They hit the wall of the shuttle's cargo bay together and his hand wrapped around a support brace.

"Clear to eject," shouted a tense male voice on the comm. Every other sound was overwhelmed by the shriek of air whipping around the hold doors.

Gretchen squirmed around—so slowly, time stretching like taffy—and saw, in a brief, perfect image: the crumpled cabin of the *Gagarin* sprawled on the deck of the cargo hold. The clamshell doors stood wide, Hummingbird in the arms of another man in a combat suit on the far wall of the hold, the launching pad rushing back, slamming into the broken, twisted metal of the *Midge*.

No!

The ultralight punched out into the darkness, spewing glassite and metal and bits of plastic. The *Gagarin* hit the shuttle's slipstream and blew apart, vanishing in the blink of an eye. Nothing remained, even the debris was already dozens of k behind, falling toward the planet in an expanding, jumbled cloud. The clamshell doors swung inexorably closed, blocking out even a momentary glimpse of the white arc of the planet.

Gretchen slumped into the man's arms, feeling their strength holding her up. *Poor little plane. After all you did for us, for me.*

"Pressure doors secure," Fitzsimmons shouted into his comm. "Kick it."

The shuttle engines lit momentarily, pitching the *Komodo* up into a higher angle of exit from the gravity of Ephesus Three. Somewhere ahead, the *Palenque* was waiting, swinging through its own wide orbit, gathering speed from the planet's gravitational pull. Glowing wings turned, catching a glint of the distant sun, and they sped on into the sea of night.

Gretchen became aware of a peculiar, antiseptic smell. Feeling strangely unencumbered, she opened her eyes and blinked in pain. Everything was so bright! A pale gray ceiling inset with soft white lights shone down on her. Walls of pale green. Chrome fixtures and subdued paintings in black, gray and brown on wrinkled rice paper. She looked down at her body and found a fuzzy cotton quilt laid across her.

"My suit . . ." Some kind of flannel pajamas had replaced her z-suit and Gretchen felt horribly, dangerously naked. Her arms clenched reflexively across her breasts. The sight of her hands was a surprise. The grungy, stained bandages were gone. Instead, patches of new skin shone pink in the clear white light. She flexed her fingers and found they moved without pain. The welts and ridges left by the jeweled chains were only faint reddish lines on her skin.

"No scars," said a tired male voice from her left side. Gretchen rolled her head sideways.

Captain Hadeishi was lying in an adjoining bed. He too was under a quilt decorated with oak leaves and cherry blossoms, wiry arms lying across his stomach. Seeing him without his uniform struck Anderssen as being particularly indecent, a feeling made more so by the sight of his muscular bare arms. Despite a lingering air of exhaustion, he struck Gretchen as being as clean, trim and at-attention as ever. Even on his back in a hospital bed.

"Our medical team does good work," he said, allowing her a small, warm smile. "Our esteemed judge is already up and about, though he did not suffer nearly so much damage as either of us."

"What . . ." Gretchen coughed, clearing her throat, and realized the crushing pain in her chest was gone as well. ". . . happened to you?"

Hadeishi turned back the quilts, revealing a huge patch of dermaseal covering his left chest, shoulder and arm. "Depleted uranium flechette burst at close range," he said, considering the repaired wound with a pensive, sad expression. "Very foolish. My death would have precipitated even more violence."

"Why . . ." Gretchen stopped, wondering if she were allowed to question a Fleet captain on his own ship—for this was most obviously the *Cornuelle*. Even before being gutted, the *Palenque* had never boasted such a clean, efficient, advanced medical bay as this.

"Did I put myself in front of a gun?" Hadeishi shook his head, amused with himself. "Because my father used to tell me stories about the samurai in their days of glory, before the Empire and the treaties of Unity and gunpowder. They would have ridden alone into the enemy fortress and challenged the rival lord to single combat. There could have been a great deal of *bushido* in what I did. As I said, very foolish."

"You lived." Gretchen wondered if she could ask for more blankets. Her bare skin felt cold and exposed without the snug, warm embrace of her z-suit. She tried to take a drink from the water tube, but found her mouth closing on empty air.

"There is water." Hadeishi pointed at a table beside her. There was a cup—plastic, half-full—and a little sick-shrine of offerings. Origami animals and paper flowers, Grandpa Carl's battered old multitool, a bar of "Ek Chuah"-brand chocolate and a fresh, shining 3v of three little children smiling up from a watery-green pool.

"Where did this come from?" Gretchen felt her heart lurch, knowing the original had been blasted away into nothingness with the *Gagarin*.

"Your exec sent the *xocoatl* and the picture over from the *Palenque*." Hadeishi's expression had become composed and polite again, but his eyes were shining. "The origami is from *Gunso* Fitzsimmons, though I did not know he had learned to make such fine examples himself. I suspect—" he visibly suppressed a merry grin "—he begged them from communications technician three Tiss-*tzin*, who is noted among the crew for her nimble fingers."

"That is very sweet." Gretchen ran her hand across the surface of the 3v. The electropaper was fresh and thick and carrying a full charge. Pressing her lips together and blinking back tears, she pressed the upper right corner of the picture.

Mom! Mom! We're mermaids! Mermaids!

Am not, I'm a merman!

She moved her finger away and the bouncing, splashing figures stilled. *I'll see you soon*, she promised them. *I'm coming home.*

"What about you?" Gretchen lifted her head, trying to see if the captain had anything on his side table. It was bare, save for a matching half-full glass of water. "Nothing?"

"I believe there were cupcakes," Hadeishi said, rather solemnly. "From Marine *Heicho* Felix, in apology for getting me shot while we were aboard the *Turan*. But I was asleep when she brought them by. I think," his eyebrows narrowed in suspicion, "Fitzsimmons ate them."

"Oh." Gretchen pressed the 3v against her breast. For a wonder, she didn't feel at all tired or sleepy. "That was rude. He's in the brig then?"

The passage leading into the number one boat bay was cold in comparison to the medical pod. Gretchen shivered a little, rubbing her arms. Fitzsimmons had tried to loan her a heavy leather pilot's jacket for the trip across to the *Palenque*, but she'd refused. The Marine spent enough time loitering around, all charming and friendly, without her borrowing his clothes. *I've been down that road before*, she thought, stepping over the sill into the cavernous, echoing space of the bay itself. *Next it's audiotracks and 3v recordings and before you know it, they're snoring in your ear late on Sunday mornings.*

One husband was enough, she thought, patting the sidebag filled with her paltry collection of personal effects. Most of the things in the bag had accumulated while she was recuperating in medical. Some photos, including a new one of the *Gagarin* and a dupe of the Rossiyan icon Russovsky had left behind, presents from the Company scientists: an ink-brush drawing of Magdalena on rice paper from *Sho-sa* Koshō: and instructions from the *Cornuelle*'s doctor.

The crewman guiding her through the maze of the ship turned. "This is your shuttle, ma'am. Have a safe flight."

"Thank you." Gretchen nodded and walked across the open expanse of the deck, following a painted walkway. The military shuttle loomed up before her, back-swept wings sleek and dark, the tail fins glossy and shining with the snake-eagle-arrow glyph of the Fleet. *A raptor where our Company shuttles are fat brown hens.*

"Anderssen-*tzin*."

Hummingbird stepped out from beneath the wing. Gretchen slowed to a halt, surprised and pleased to see him. "Hello, Crow! How are you doing? They said you'd been released from medical early."

The *nauallis* did not respond to her light tone, his face a chiseled mask.

Instead he looked from side to side as if making sure none of the crewmen work-ing in the bay were near enough to overhear. "You will have to file a report," he said in a stiff, rather cool tone. "I suggest you mention as few details about our foray to the surface as possible. Any scientific data you wish to relate is, of course, up to you. I would restrain any speculation about the life-forms on the planet to that which can be proven."

Gretchen felt her good humor—and living instead of dying usually made her very cheerful—fade in the face of this cold reception. Her eyes narrowed and she looked him up and down very slowly. He seemed larger in a cream-colored mantlelike shirt, pleated dark trousers and civilian shoes. In the z-suit he'd seemed small and wiry, lean enough to survive in the desert. *Now he looks like a Company lawyer,* she decided and the last of her cheerfulness disappeared.

"I guess I'm not a copy," she said in a dry tone. He nodded very slightly in answer.

Long absent from her thoughts, a memory of the cylinder-book surfaced. Considering the prize in retrospect, she weighed, judged and decided the secrets inside the ancient device would not be unlocked by her. The decision—made in an instant—left her oddly peaceful. *The kids will still have shoes, even if they're not imported leather.*

"The matter of your life aside, I understand," she said in an equally formal tone. "My report will reflect the professionalism and excellence of all Fleet and government personnel involved in the operation. I will take equal care with any conclusions which may affect the security of the Empire."

Hummingbird nodded, unfazed by the withering glare she'd turned on him.

"Is there anything else you wanted to know?"

He shook his head, hands clasped behind his back.

"I have one question for you, Huitziloxoctic-*tzin.*" Gretchen matched his for-mal posture, realizing with a tiny bite of delight she was noticeably taller than he was. She tilted her head a little to the side, pinning him with a considering expres-sion. "My medband has been taken away. When I get a new one on the *Palenque* or on Ctesiphon Station or at my next dig, will I find there is some kind of exotic drug in my system?"

The *nauallis's* expression did not change, but there was a dark flicker in his eyes.

"I've not experienced any unusual effects of *sight* since I woke up." Her lips parted slightly, showing white teeth. "Even when I settle my mind and let my thoughts become calm. Now, my memory has been damaged, but I haven't forgot-ten everything that happened down on the planet. Did you really think I was so untrustworthy you needed to drug me? Did you really think I would tell *anyone* you'd broken tradition to show me this tiny, paltry bit of your precious knowledge?"

Hummingbird did not respond, his face becoming even more still, more masklike. Disgusted, Gretchen turned away and climbed the steps into the shuttle. A crewman inside the door directed her forward and the pressure door levered up with a hiss to close with a solid, heavy *thud*.

Settling into her seat for the thirty-minute flight to the *Palenque*, Gretchen rolled her shoulders and let out a long, angry hiss. Against all expectation, she'd thought Hummingbird might trust her just a little. *Stupid old fool. Did he think I'd blab to everyone what I saw, what I did? I work for a bureaucracy too.*

And that thought crushed the rest of her lightheartedness. She rubbed her left eye, feeling an incipient twinge. *Reports. Oh, the reports I will have to file. Company property, loss of—one* Temple*-class starship gutted, one completely equipped base camp abandoned, two* Midge*-class ultralights destroyed, two* Komodo*-class shuttles severely damaged, ten Company staff dead in the line of duty—data recovered, minimal. Artifacts recovered—none. Opportunities for follow-up research—none, system sealed by Imperial interdict. Chances for staff to publish data and gain tenure, university position or even a publication byline—none, data sealed by order, Imperial Office of the* Tlachialoni*—the Mirror-Which-Reveals.*

Sullenly, she stared out the window, though the sight of the *Palenque* drawing closer did not lift the gloom weighing on her. *Maybe I should tell someone what happened . . . not the Company, maybe a 3v'zine like* Temple of Truth *or the* Xonocatl. *Then I'd have a few quills to shake in my hand.*

This time they had docked in the Fleet section of the docking ring of the enormous station. Everything was clean and shipshape, with deckhands and loading trucks to help them haul their gear from the *Palenque*. Even the air was quiet and cool, without the humid cattle mob of the commercial landing. Parker, Magdalena and Bandao were waiting at the end of the lock tunnel. The pilot was puffing on a tabac with a blissful expression on his face.

"Pack-leader! You look cheerful for a change." Magdalena grinned, showing only the tiniest points of sharp white teeth. The Hesht had a truly enormous travel bag slung over her shoulder. Anderssen had not asked what was inside, but suspected some equipment listed on the *Palenque* manifest as "destroyed" had actually survived. Her own tool belt and z-suit gear had been replaced in the same way. The Company was notoriously bad at honoring requests for replacing equipment lost on dig or survey—which resulted in endemic pilfering by all the dig crews.

"I'm off that tub, my initial reports are done," Gretchen said, waving a cloud of tabac smoke away from her face, "and we can go someplace on station where I can buy us all real food for dinner at a real restaurant."

"Damn." Parker stubbed out his tabac. "Do you think they have steaks here? Like, real ones? I mean—you know—Maggie's probably missing food that bleeds."

He ducked away, laughing, though the Hesht's claws were only half-extended in a cub's strike.

"Maybe." Gretchen put her arm around the man's shoulder and raised her eyes to the bulkhead arching overhead, stretching out her hand toward some glorious, unimaginable future. "Maybe we can even get mashed potatoes made from . . . potatoes!"

"Aw, boss, you're going to make me cry." Parker rubbed his eyes. Gretchen squeezed his shoulder in sympathy. "Next you'll say something crazy like they have real butter."

"Everyone have their gear?" Gretchen looked around out of habit, making sure no one had been left behind and everyone had their baggage and shoes and hats. As she did, Bandao caught her eye and pointed down the curving platform.

Anderssen turned and a smile lit her face. *Sho-sa* Koshō approached, sword blade straight in a spotless white Fleet uniform. Gretchen bowed very politely as she came up. "*Konnichi-wa*, Koshō-*sana*."

"Good morning, Doctor Anderssen." The officer returned her bow. "I am glad to see you and your team together again."

Everyone else bowed politely, and even Parker had the sense to remain silent while their *oyabun* spoke to the Imperial officer.

"Thanks to the generous hospitality of the Fleet, *Sho-sa*, we are all in excellent health and spirits."

"Good." Koshō nodded to the others, then stepped aside, hand on Gretchen's elbow. With a meter of polite space between them and her subordinates, the *Sho-sa*'s expression changed. "*Chu-sa* Hadeishi requests a favor," Koshō said, watching her intently. "A common acquaintance is waiting, a little ways away, and would like to speak to you again."

Gretchen frowned. "Need I guess who? Will he offer me an apology?"

"What passes for one from his mouth would not be acceptable in polite society." Koshō's calm face did not reflect the venom implied by her tone. "I will inform him you had already left when I arrived."

For a moment, Anderssen groped to speak, stunned into silence by the angry glitter exposed in the Nisei officer's eyes. After a moment, the *sho-sa* stepped back and settled into a pose of polite attention. The movement broke Gretchen out of her paralysis and she managed to squeak out a "No."

Clasping both hands in front of her body, Anderssen made a small bow. "I—we—are in your debt. I would be happy to speak with the *chu-sa*'s acquaintance."

Not very far away proved to be a conference room around the corner. Koshō ushered Gretchen into the rectangular room—cold gray walls, recessed lighting, tatami mats—and closed the hatch firmly behind her. Within, Hummingbird was kneeling beside a low teak-colored table. A leather jacket worked with subdued glyphs lay over his usual civilian attire. Gretchen's attention, however, was not fixed on details of his dress, but a massive gypsum panel covering the rear wall of the room. A low-cut bas-relief showed a pair of short-bodied lions leaping at a crowned man standing in a chariot. The king held a bow raised, one arrow already lodged in the throat of the first lion. Every line of the ancient carving gleamed with meticulous, superbly carved life.

How did that get here? Gretchen was nonplussed by the sight. Then she focused on the *nauallis* instead of the graven slab.

The old México inclined his head in greeting, but said nothing. As usual, his face was composed and expressionless. In this clear, directionless lighting, his eyes were flat chips of jadite. In comparison, Hadeishi's face—the *chu-sa* was standing a polite distance away—positively gleamed with welcome, though a 3v would not have captured the warmth in his eyes.

Gretchen set down her bag, removed her shoes and watched with mild curiosity as Hadeishi made a careful circuit of the room, and then placed a small black box on the table in front of the *nauallis*. The Fleet captain retired to the far corner of the room and knelt with his back politely turned.

"Anderssen-*tzin*." Hummingbird seemed to relax, though he remained as straight-backed as ever. His mouth was tight. "I must . . . apologize for speaking impolitely on the ship."

Gretchen did not bother to hide her surprise and she saw Hadeishi jerk minutely. "Apology accepted."

Hummingbird nodded and the grooves beside his mouth grew deeper. Gretchen stared at him in interest. Words were trying to come out, but the old man was having a hard time giving them breath. "Is there something else?"

"Yes." The old man shifted slightly. "I would like you to come with me. Though there is no precedent for a *nauallis* to take a female student, the situation—"

"No." Gretchen crossed her arms. "I have already thought about this. I have no desire to become a judge or *nauallis* or *brujo* or whatever you are. You showed me a glimpse of your world—and I'll admit the thought is seductive—but I don't want to spend even more time away from my family, from my children. So thank you for the thought, but I will not go with you."

Hummingbird became entirely still. He did not blink or otherwise show surprise, but the strength of his astonishment gave the air in the room an almost electric charge. Hadeishi had given up being polite and turned away from his careful examination of the Assyrian panel, watching both of them with open interest.

The old man's teeth clicked softly. "It is very dangerous for you to go on without training."

"I guessed." Gretchen reached for her shoes. "So I'm not going to go on. If I understand all of this properly, if I do not exercise the *sight* then my mind will forget what to do. Long-accustomed patterns will reassert themselves."

"You'd knowingly blind yourself?" Hummingbird's bronzed skin was turning a queer pale color.

"I choose to go down a different path, Crow." Gretchen's eyes narrowed in a glare. "Your way is fraught with danger and sacrifice. I have given up *enough* already. I'm not going to abandon my children or the profession I love." She pointed away from him with one hand. "Seeing past a shadow on a wall for an instant does not require me to step around the screen. You shouldn't presume others will follow your path simply because it is secret."

Hummingbird was frankly speechless. Clearing his throat softly to draw their attention, Hadeishi bowed to Gretchen. His expression was very composed, but Anderssen suspected he was fairly agog himself and wondered how quickly this story would circulate through the Fleet. *Perhaps never; the captain seems to be a very circumspect man.*

"Thank you for your time, Doctor Anderssen. Have a safe journey."

"Thank you, *Chu-sa* Hadeishi."

Gretchen turned to the old Mexica, who was staring at her with growing fury radiating from his weathered old face. "Don't worry," she said, bowing to him. "Though I nearly lost my life, I regret nothing that happened there." A grin flashed. "I certainly won't forget. Good day, gentlemen. Safe journey."

"You," Hummingbird bit out, "must not leave."

Gretchen paused, one shoe on. "I *am* leaving. And I really don't think you can force me to be your student."

"You could . . ." Hummingbird's expression became particularly sour ". . . be placed in protective custody."

"To protect me from myself? To assuage your conscience?"

"To learn control!" Hummingbird snapped. "To be properly trained."

Gretchen shook her head, feeling a thread of anger stir in response to his pigheadedness. "As I said, I do not wish to be trained. Now, I'd guess you're worried, but not about *my* health. No—you're worried about my pitiful salary, aren't you?"

The *nauallis*'s nose twitched as if a foul smell wafted on the room air.

"You think I will sell my little tale to a 3v for rude, raw gold, don't you?"

Gretchen shook her head slightly in disbelief. "I told you I wouldn't. You doubt my word?"

"What about young Duncan's tutoring?" Hummingbird made a jerky motion with his hand. "I know what he means to you. Your resolve may be strong today, but in a year? What about when the girls are old enough to apply to the *calmecac* schools?"

There is that. Gretchen hid a sigh, thinking of her bank account. *Nobility does not pay so well, but I will manage to make do. Somehow.*

"Fine," she said, forcing herself to let go of that particular worry. Her chin came up and her blue eyes snapped with irritation. "Then if you're so Sister-bless concerned, the Imperial government can make good the bonus I won't get from the Company. You stole my data, you can bloody well *pay for it!*"

Hummingbird drew back a fraction, as if she'd slapped him in the face. "Extorting the Mirror will not . . ." he began in a hot tone. Hadeishi, still sitting quietly and watching them both with a quizzical expression on his face, raised both hands slowly.

"If I may offer a suggestion," the *chu-sa* said in a calm, collected voice, "there is a middle way."

The hatchway hissed closed behind Doctor Anderssen. Hadeishi looked sideways at the México. Hummingbird seemed stunned and disgusted at the same time.

"This matter will have to be hidden," the *nauallis* said, the timbre of his voice indicating what the Nisei might call *fumeiyo*—disgraceful shame. "No one must know."

"I understand," Hadeishi said, thanking generations of stoic tradition for the ability to keep his face from breaking into a broad grin. "The blatant misuse of your station—of your honorable position—would cause disquiet among your peers."

Hummingbird turned slightly, favoring the slim *chu-sa* with a withering, furious glare.

Unabashed, Hadeishi continued: "Surely no other *nauallis*—or any member of the Mirror, for that matter—would ever use his familial connections to influence *calmecac* selection, or to sponsor likely candidates for entry into university."

"You," the old México growled, "are presuming upon our acquaintance, Nisei."

Hadeishi shook his head, lips pursed. "You have rewarded her honorably. She has rendered good service—no *goshi* ever did better, placing her life in the way of danger to her lord—"

"Enough!" Hummingbird turned away. "She is not my tenant. She is not of my clan, nor are her children! Once I will extend the advantage of my house to aid her. Once! And no one will know."

"I understand." Hadeishi clasped both hands behind his back. "Service for service." But silently, he added *So do all lords and vassals arrange their fates.*

After a moment of silence, Mitsu said: "You cannot make her accompany you."

Hummingbird seemed to wake, life returning to his sharp green eyes. He glowered at the Fleet officer, hands clasped stiffly behind his back.

"This is easy for you to say, Nisei. Your traditions hold that letting go of the world is the path to enlightenment. Mine are different. I have a responsibility to my student." His head tilted toward the hatch. "She has only passed through the first door. Her will, her intent, are weak and unfocused—at any moment she could be trapped by this new clarity, she will be lost, blinded by the simple ability to see. *Even if she tries to forget what happened!* What will happen to her then?"

Hadeishi nodded slightly, his elfin face serious. "Anything might happen to her. She might be killed or driven insane or turn away from her path. Hummingbird, you cannot save, or protect, every single human being. That is impossible. Men die."

"Yes, that is so." Hummingbird looked away, anger fading into bitterness, his weathered old face settling into its long-accustomed mask. "Men die."

Hadeishi pointed with his head, indicating the door. "Even your student will die."

"I know this!" Hummingbird's nostrils flared.

"Do you?" Hadeishi met his eyes with an unflinching stare. "I do not think so. Not yet."

GRETCHEN ANDERSSEN, MITSUHARU HADEISHI, AND SUSAN KOSHŌ WILL RETURN IN *HOUSE OF REEDS*.

COMING SOON FROM TOR BOOKS.

APPENDIX

The songs in Mitsu's memory of his father's house are:

The children are singing:

Kaeru no uta ga	*The frog's song*
Kikoete kuro yo	*we can hear it (the song)*
Guwa . . . guwa . . . guwa . . . *guwa*	*ribbit*
Ge ge ge ge ge ge ge	*ribbit*
Guwa guwa guwa	*ribbit*

The men are singing:

Kimi ga yo wa	*The thousands of years of happy*
Chiyo ni yachiyo ni	*reign be thine;*
Sazare ishi no	*Rule on, my Lord, till what are*
Iwao to narite	*pebbles now*
Koke no musu made	*By age united to mighty rocks shall grow*
	Whose venerable sides the moth doth line.